The

Coaching Rayna

Two-Book Series

Boxed Set

by Pebbles Lacasse

THE COACHING RAYNA TWO-BOOK SERIES

ISBN 978-1-989979-35-8

Cover photos and design © 2019 Pebbles Lacasse
First Edition June 28, 2019
Photographs by Sharon Seguin
Cover Model Chris LaPointe

Published by Pebbles Lacasse www.pebbleslacasse.com

Coaching Rayna

Book One

by Pebbles Lacasse

International Best Selling Author

Second Edition

COACHING RAYNA
by Pebbles Lacasse

Coaching Rayna Book One

ISBN 978-0-9920069-8-3

Cover photos and design © 2019 Pebbles Lacasse
First Edition June 28, 2019
Photographs by Sharon Seguin
Cover Model Chris LaPointe
Edited by Off The Shelf Editing

Published by Pebbles Lacasse www.pebbleslacasse.com

Acknowledgements

Special thanks to my cover model, Chris LaPointe, my photographer, Sharon Seguin, and all of my beta readers—there are too many to list, but you know who you are and how special you are to me.

I owe an extra big thank you to a special lady, my editor, Lisa Vincent. You are such an amazing woman, and I adore you. The smiles, comforting hugs and kind words you always have for me, mean more than you could ever know. I hold you in my heart, my dear friend.

Chapter One

Rayna

Doing the laundry isn't what I planned to do on my first Saturday off work in three weeks. Having lunch with my friends or taking the kids on an adventure would be so much more fun. But the chores have to get done. The kids are running out of clean clothes and all of my work scrubs are too dirty to wear again.

Shutting the door to the laundry room and pretending the piles of dirty clothes don't exist would be so much easier, but I can no longer avoid this mundane chore.

Would it kill the kids to throw in a load once in a while? I've taught them both how to do it, so I know their laziness isn't due to their lack of know-how. I'm a firm believer in teaching children how to do real-life tasks.

Instead of having a fun day with me, they're shut away in their rooms. To be honest, I'd rather that than have them follow me from room to room complaining that they're bored. Not like that's possible; their rooms are full of interesting distractions that should keep their imaginations alive and blooming.

I'm shaken from my thoughts. Is that a lawnmower I hear?

I immediately stop sorting colours from whites and pull the button to halt the gushing water filling the washing machine. I can't tell whether it's the dreamboat next door mowing his lawn or the neighbour directly behind my house...

My legs can't carry me up the stairs quick enough, even though I'm stepping two at a time. I nearly smack my head off the patio doors trying to look for *him*.

Yes! Damn, he's so fucking hot! I've been looking forward to this show all week.

I quickly pour a glass of wine three-quarters full of the nice pinot I opened last night. I must act aloof, as though I'm not outside to watch his sweaty, tanned skin as it stretches over his bloated muscles. My pussy tightens as I slide open the glass door and take a deep breath. Without glancing his way, I step out and close it behind me.

After setting my glass on the table, I squat my ass on the cushiony deckchair and rest my feet on the chair opposite. Being the smart cookie that I am, I always keep a book at the backdoor to make him think I'm reading and not ogling him while dreaming up a naughty fantasy.

Damn, it's hot today! I don't mind; the glistening sweat accentuates the ripples of muscle.

I always sit facing his yard. This way, I can drink him in without being too obvious. I open the book and pretend to read with my head tipped downward.

Nearly every Saturday for the past three years, I've lost myself in my imagination while staring at my hunky neighbour. His muscles flex as he pushes the mower around his enormous yard while wearing nothing but shoes and a pair of shorts that fit snug on his thick, muscular thighs.

His name is Simon Brenton, but everyone calls him Coach because he owns a gym and coaches people on how to reach their peak level of physical fitness. He's as strong as an ox; I can't stress that enough. The man's arms, chest, and thighs are massive, his waist tight and ripped. I imagine he can fuck like a machine. The power behind those thunderous thighs would have any woman screaming through multiple orgasms until she lost consciousness.

My fantasies have me in his arms, his thin lips on mine, pelvis rhythmically grinding against my needy vagina as he sinks himself deep into me.

Sigh...

I'm divorced, thankfully. I've had no intimate encounters in the four years since I gave the asshole the boot. My life is too busy working and raising my kids. I'm sure that's why I love to picture myself getting sexually mauled by my hot neighbour more often than what's probably healthy for anyone.

The best thing that happened out of the shitty marriage is two children. Kim is eleven, and Ken is thirteen. There's never enough time in a day for us to connect other than dinner time when we sit at the table together and discuss what's on their minds. There are days when I almost have to poke them with a stick to get them to talk.

My son is getting to the age where he thinks mom isn't cool enough to hang out with anymore. He used to be my little shadow, clung to me wherever I'd go, but things have changed. I miss that. My daughter still enjoys my company, but I'm sure she'll think I'm stupid soon enough, especially if she takes after me. I was rude to my mother too often during my teen years. Hopefully, she'll be wiser than I was.

Between my job, the kids, and the household, I'm exhausted when I flop into bed at night. Doing everything myself, without a partner or an accountable ex, is sometimes overwhelming.

Sex comprises me occasionally masturbating while using my helpful aides: my fat dildo and a vibrator. I'm usually so tired at the end of the day that I only want to sleep. Sometimes, when I've been unusually excited—like after watching Coach mow his lawn, for instance—I'll zip through masturbation just to ease my sexual tension enough that I can sleep.

I've gone weeks without having an orgasm. It's depressing, I know. I used to be extremely sexually expressive. What happened to me?

Coach probably knows exactly why I'm out here, but he's kind enough not to call me out. If he looks up and sees me, he'll wave. I'll lift my head and wave back, and he'll continue to mow while I quietly observe his sculpted body. I'm sure he gets an ego boost from women checking him out, and I imagine it happens a lot. I'm an out of shape older woman and not his type.

Sometimes we chat over the fence, but it's rare. We've had conversations over the years, ranging from politics to religion and even about our childhoods.

He's intelligent and well-spoken, which I find to be an alluring trait in a man. The sexiest thing about him is his ability to hold eye contact and not flinch, which intimidates the hell out of me. He's definitely an assertive man, and that excites me. He's far more alluring than my arrogant, cheating coward of an ex-husband who has no spine to speak of.

Coach occasionally has his friends from the gym over to his place. I love those days! They're all fit and muscular like he is. They sit outside shirtless under the heat of the sun, and I can't stop watching their brawny chests and backs as they carry on, boasting about their wild adventures with naughty women, or telling tales of their high school football highlights.

I wonder what it would feel like to have one of their thick bodies above me, using those powerful thighs and strong backs to fuck me hard. My pussy twinges at the thought. I couldn't pick their faces out in a line-up even if I had to, because I never stop staring at their bodies. I wish I could see what they have in their shorts that might please me.

The day after Coach moved in, three years ago, I went over to introduce myself and welcome him to the neighbourhood. I was captivated by his physical size, but his confidence attracted me most. I could barely speak. Everything I muttered sounded stupid, especially when I asked to meet his wife and kids.

There was a woman and a few children helping with the move, so I assumed they were his family. That's when he told me that he's never married and never plans to. The woman was his sister, and they were her children. Strangely, it pleased me to know that he was available but sad that my excuse to visit with him for arranged playdates with our kids was now void.

Coach has had many women come and go, but his present girlfriend doesn't talk to me even if we're both outside. Occasionally she'll wave, but we've never carried on a conversation. She doesn't seem shy. Judging by the occasional leers directed at me, she dislikes me. I don't recall saying or doing anything to her she could have taken offensively.

I'd rather not get to know her well, anyway. It would be too hard to fantasize about her bulked-up man tearing off my clothes and ravishing me if she complains about all his nasty habits. That might turn me off, and then I'd be right back to having nothing tantalizing to stare at on these scorching summer days. This is all I have to make me feel like a sexual woman, and I need it. I don't want to see him as an actual person with flaws. He's the perfect sex machine—at least, in my vivid imagination.

My tummy flutters just before he bends to pick up the metal table to move it out of his way, allowing him easier access to mow the grass beneath. When he lifts, his muscles flex and his skin strains to maintain them, but he moves the heavy table with barely a struggle.

That task would take the effort of my ex-husband plus his clone if he had one. Thankfully, there aren't two of that asshole. Just one of him is too many.

I've sucked back the entire glass of wine way too quickly and it's already going to my head. Maybe I should have eaten something today before I bled this glass dry.

Coach finishes and puts the table back and the mower in the shed before starting to pick weeds out of his vegetable garden. I've never seen his girlfriend lift a finger to maintain the yard, even if a weed stands tall right beside her foot. I see the way he looks at her, and I don't think she'll be around much longer.

He's down on his widely spread knees and bent over to reach for a well-rooted weed. He pulls, flexing his back muscles ever so slightly. The lumps on his arm shift and grow as he moves, stirring something primal inside of me. His flesh glistens under the vibrant sun.

I want to taste him. I imagine what it must feel like to lie beneath such a powerful man, my legs wrapped around him while he looks down at me, readying himself to penetrate my body with his swollen manhood.

My eyes close and I take in a deep breath, suddenly realizing that my book rests on my lap, covering my hand slid down between my thighs. I've been pressing on my excited clit.

I jolt back to reality, yanking my hand from my groin. My eyes shift here and there, looking to see if anyone has been watching me masturbate through my shorts while I stare at the sexy guy next door like the neighbourhood pervert. I'm relieved no one else is outside until my eyes meet Coach's accusing glare.

He's still on his knees, but the table has turned, so to speak. He's been watching me. I want to run away and hide, but it's too late. There's no denying he saw what I was doing. I'm so embarrassed and the heat flushing through my cheeks proves it.

A smile slowly grows on his face. I try to return the gesture, but my bottom lip quivers, distorting my mouth.

He probably can't see that detail from this distance. I feel the embarrassment continuing to fill my cheeks, proving my desire for him.

He lifts his thick arm to wave at me. I tip my head down while I wave, wishing I could go back in time to redo the last ten minutes. This time, I wouldn't have lost myself in the fantasy.

Coach tosses the weed he pulled before standing and brushing the dirt off his hands and knees. He looks up at me, still grinning like a man who has naughty intentions.

Oh shit! He's walking toward the fence separating our yards.

Should I go to the fence or tell him that I can't chat and then hide in the house? Damn it! I'm horribly embarrassed, but it would be rude to run away at this point. I grip the railing, fearing my trembling knees might give out, thus tumbling down the stairs in a most humiliating fashion. The way my luck is, it wouldn't surprise me.

As I approach the fence, his deep voice greets me. "Hi. Are you enjoying the day?"

The grin on his face boasts his sinful thoughts. His lips are thin, but the well-groomed beard and mustache frame them perfectly, as if they're a target for my lips to aim toward.

Snap out of it, damn it!

"Um, hi, Coach. It is a beautiful day." I swallow hard. "I see you mowed your lawn."

I sound like such an idiot. I'd have to be blind and deaf to not know he mowed it. Couldn't I have thought of something less ridiculous to say? Why can't I say anything brilliant to this man? I bite my lip again; I do that when I'm nervous or intimidated. At the moment, I'm both.

"So it would seem. You watched me mow my lawn." He accentuates the word "watched."

I can imagine what he wanted to say: "...while you were flicking your bean."

I'm so relieved that he's respectful enough not to comment on my masturbation, further humiliating me. I'm not even sure that's possible at this point.

I shrug, crossing my arms over my chest and trying to be aloof by looking anywhere other than at his seductive eyes. Even still, I feel their gaze burning into me. They stare right through me and into my soul, setting it on fire.

Fuck! Timidly, yet trying to seem nonchalant, I say, "Yeah, sorry. There's nothing else to look at that's remotely as exciting as you mowing your lawn."

Shit! I said he was exciting. Damn it!

"Watching me excites you?" He beams, resting his large, tattooed arms on the top of the slatted wood fence.

Each time we've talked in the past, he's been an absolute gentleman. He's insinuated nothing sexual could happen between us. Is it his intention to aim this conversation in that direction, or am I reading too much into his words?

"I don't know how to answer that. I mean, yes, you *are* nice to look at, obviously, and nobody else is outside, so there really is nothing…"

My words fall away. I swallow hard, suddenly realizing that my mouth is parched. I just might cough up the wad of cotton manifesting in my throat.

He must think I'm a sex-deprived, slightly older woman with ridiculous fantasies of being with a very fit younger man who has absolutely no reason to think of her as anything but a mother. He must laugh inside his head at my idiocy, but I'm relieved that he isn't blatantly obvious about it.

I'm not a perfectly thin or physically fit woman, but I'm not overweight. My stomach is still flat after having had two cesarean sections. I'm very proud of that. My legs are thick and strong, and my waist is small, but my butt is jigglier than I'd like and my arms are getting flabby. The best part of me is my breasts; they're large and still somewhat rest at the same altitude they originally grew at. Gravity hasn't had its demonic way with them yet, but I have noticed that they are not as solid as they were ten years ago.

I look up at him only to see his eyes staring at my breasts, which are barely hidden beneath my light pink halter top. I look down and discover my nipples have betrayed me. They're pointing straight out, directly at Coach, as if trying to torpedo me toward him.

He sighs and whispers, "You have beautiful breasts. I'd like to see them without the shirt."

Wait! What?

Shivers ripple up my spine, prickling my skin and forming tiny bumps from head to toe. Every strand of hair on my head feels like it's lifting. My bottom jaw once again quivers uncontrollably, so I bite my lip between my teeth but cannot hold it steady. I stare at his eyes a little too long and it feels very uncomfortable between us.

Say something!

"Thank you," I whisper with barely an audible voice. Damn it, that was a dumb thing to say! I could have said something more flirtatious than that, such as, "I would like that, too."

My eyes follow his Adam's apple as it slowly bobs in his throat when he swallows. I would love to wrap my lips around it while he fucks me deeply. I shake my head, hoping to clear the arousing thought, but it lingers.

"In fact, I'd like to see your entire nude body. You're a sexy woman. You know that, right?"

"Um..." I stutter, "I-I am?" Oh please, compliment me again.

He chuckles, replying, "Sweet thing, I know you watch me, but what you don't know is that I watch you, too. I can see straight into your kitchen from my office window."

He turns to point to the window facing my house. My eyes look back at his in time to see his tongue lick his top lip.

He confesses, "I positioned my desk so I can catch glances of you while I work. When you're in the kitchen at night, in that light blue nightgown, the really thin one," he pauses, "Well, it's my favourite. With the light behind you, I can see the silhouette of your amazing body. I fantasize about touching you over that nightgown."

My eyes are wide, face flushed a feverish red, and my mouth hangs open in surprise.

"Do you have any idea how often I jerk off while watching you make your kids' lunches at night?" he pauses again. "Almost every night."

Oh my God! Did I just hear that? He finds me sexy and masturbates while watching me perform a mundane task. Holy shit! No, he must be taunting me simply to see my reaction and then he'll let me down hard. A guy like him doesn't fantasize about a mother of two who's ten years older than him. He can have almost any young, fit woman he desires.

"You do?" I ask doubtfully. My mouth is painfully dry, and that glass of wine I guzzled is making me feel more uninhibited than my usual self. "I like watching you. I touch myself sometimes."

His sexy crooked smile is enough to make me swoon, but when his eyebrows bounce only once, my knees weaken. He radiates testosterone like an invisible aphrodisiac, making my thoughts cloudy. My pussy is so wet that I can feel its slickness. I wonder if other women experience his allure as intensely as I do. How could they not? He sure knows how to turn up the heat.

"Do you want to come over for another glass of wine?" he suggests with a deeper than usual voice.

He's sporting a very serious expression with salacious eyes that seem to pierce right through me. I can't prevent them from reading my deepest, darkest thoughts.

A bead of sweat trickles down the tanned skin on his well-formed bicep, and I nearly lean in to lick it simply to quench my ravenous thirst. My curiosity and desires are no longer my kept secret. I've opened a can of worms here, but I'm not sure I want to put the lid back on it yet. I've fantasized about this moment so many times.

In those dreams, he's always lived up to my expectations. What if he doesn't compare in reality? The fantasy will forever be tainted.

But what if he does?

"Yes, but I shouldn't," I reply, hating myself for turning down his offer. Whether or not his performance measures up to my high expectations, I'm sure we could have had an entire afternoon of steamy sex, had I accepted the offer, but I have priorities. "The kids are home and they'd eventually notice my absence."

He suggests, "Tell them you're going for a walk. I won't keep you more than an hour…unless you'd like me to. I'll gladly entertain you for the rest of the day."

I swallow hard while forcing myself to look anywhere but at his beckoning brown eyes. My body trembles and my skin craves his touch. His gigantic hands would feel so rough against my womanly flesh. Having two of his fingers inside of me, pleasuring me while he kisses and suckles my nipples, would drive me to cum within seconds.

My legs wobble, weak from the thought. I quickly grab the fence to steady myself. Surely, he knows the effect he's having on me.

His hand hovers over mine, middle finger delicately caressing my middle digit. The contact feels electric. A whimper escapes me. My eyes meet his once again. A smirk has grown on his thin lips and his eyes seem darker, so much more dangerous and enticing than I've ever witnessed. I'd be a fool to deny myself this opportunity. It'll likely never happen again.

"Okay, but I need a little time."

I have done no maintenance on myself for a very long time. Sex is absent from my life, so I don't bother. My stomach tightens like a vice when he wraps his massive hand around my wrist, slowly and assertively pulling me closer to the fence. We are face to face, looking at one another, our breath brushing over each other's faces. My entire body shakes, and I can't control it.

"Don't take too long, okay?" he whispers. His sweet breath is hotter than the summer breeze that caused his skin to glisten so perfectly. "When you're ready, walk in the front door and come down the stairs. I'll be waiting for you."

He releases my wrist but watches me as I slowly ascend the stairs, painfully aware that my weak legs could fail me at some point. I can feel the heat from his stare as it burns into my body.

The instant I'm inside the house and sure he can't see me, I slide down the wall, planting my ass on the cool hardwood floor. I rub my wrist, making sure he isn't still attached to me. My skin is super-heated from just one touch.

How will his touch to my more delicate regions affect me?

My endorphins are easing; panic sets in. Oh god, what have I done? I can't go to his place! If I walk into that house and he touches me, I know I won't be able to maintain control over my primal needs.

Do I want to hold back though? That's a good question. It's been too long since anyone has touched me. I hope I don't make a fool of myself.

Shit!

Even though I'm still unsure if I'm going to go see him, I hop in the shower and shave away all my stubble. I wash my hair and my skin with the prettiest scented products I own.

Yes, I think I'm going over there.

No, no, I can't!

But I really, *really* want to. I deserve this, don't I?

After quickly drying my hair and dusting some powder on my face to reduce the shine, I flip through my closet, looking for something to wear that might be appropriate, but everything I own is so damn boring. I've been a single, overworked mom for so long that my sexy attire has been stowed in boxes or given away. I figured someone should get use out of them.

Frustrated, I settle for a light summer dress and a pair of white silky panties.

I'm still shaking when I enter my daughter's doorway. She's sitting on her bed reading a book assigned to her for a school project. Knowing her as I do, I'm sure it's due soon. She puts everything off to the last minute. She's always looking for an excuse to avoid anything that doesn't completely captivate her attention.

"Hi, baby. I'm going for a walk."

"Can I come?" she asks while bookmarking her page and edging herself off the bed.

"No, you have to get that book read. When is the project due?"

"In two days," she confesses, pouting.

I sigh heavily and give her the GET IT DONE look. "Okay then, you'd better get busy reading. I'll be back in about an hour."

"That's a long walk. Where are you going?" she asks with her face crinkled up as she re-situates herself on her bed.

"Just walking. I need some exercise and the fresh air will help me clear my thoughts." I try to sound convincing. "Don't worry, you won't even miss me."

I blow her a kiss only to witness the infamous eye roll. She acts like she's too mature for silly love gestures.

I enter my son's doorway, even more nervous now. I take a deep breath to calm myself before poking my head in. "Hey, I'm going for a walk. You don't want to come with, do you?"

He turns his contorted face to ensure I see the over-exaggerated expression of his disinterest.

"Okay then, keep an eye on your sister and don't go anywhere."

Without a word, he turns back to his computer to continue with his online game. Maybe they won't miss me.

I make my way out of my house, locking the door behind me.

Chapter Two

Rayna

It's as if my feet have a mind of their own; no matter how hard I try to slow my pace, they move quicker than I'd like them to.

Before I know it, I'm inside his house and halfway down the seven steps, unsure of what I'm going to find once I get to the bottom. Will he still be wearing his shorts? What will I do if he's naked? I stop with two steps to go and take a calming deep breath, hoping to erase the terrified expression from my face.

He's wearing a clean pair of shorts and I smell the soft scent of cologne. He leans against the back of a black leather sofa, which sits in the middle of the room, and offers me a glass of wine. It wasn't all that long ago that I sat on it while we chatted. The girlfriend he had back then sneered at me the whole time, making me feel very unwelcomed.

I'm standing here braless, knowing that he will probably touch me in ways the woman he's dating now would definitely disapprove of. I'd love to record this moment and shove it in her bitchy face. What does he see in her?

He extends his arm further, expecting me to take it, but I can't get my planted feet to move. Strange how a moment ago I couldn't get them to halt. Betrayers, that's what they are!

Coach slowly stands and walks toward me, handing me the glass. I take it and take a gulp while his eyes burn into mine with volcanic heat. Although it's cold in his house, I'm boiling hot, and my womanhood is about to burst into flames.

I sip from the glass once more and then cast my gaze to his well-formed pectoral muscles. His tiny nipples jut out from the base of them. His chest cavity expands and contracts slowly as he breathes the air between us. I feel like I'm gasping, as if he's consuming all the oxygen in the room, leaving me breathless. I suck back another gulp of wine before he takes the glass from me, leaning toward me to set it on the table behind me. His steaming chest touches my arm, and I shiver.

Instead of him pulling away, his face hovers next to my neck. His lips almost touch my skin. His caressing breath raises tiny bumps that seem to spread throughout every cell in my body. I shake violently, eagerly waiting for a solid touch to confirm that this isn't just another daydream and I'm soon to awaken.

He whispers, "I want to taste your skin, kiss your sexy mouth and fuck you hard, the way you deserve to be fucked."

The instant his mouth presses under my ear, my legs waver. He wraps his powerful arms around my waist, taking my entire weight as if I were light as a feather. I nearly faint when his hand cups my ass cheek, pulling my groin against his concealed, erect penis.

Oh God, it's huge! I always imagined it would be, but figured reality would prove otherwise.

Coach lifts me and presses his lips hard to mine. His tongue digs deep into my mouth, exploring every inch. My mind whirls as our first kiss burns into my memory. I never want to forget how sweet his mouth tastes or how passionately he's kissing me.

I wrap my legs around his waist and my arms around his neck. My fingers weave into his thick black hair. I want to be as close to him as I can.

If this is a dream, don't let me wake from it.

He carries me to the sofa, his lips locked on mine. I remain wrapped tightly around him as he lowers us, pressing me into the cushions with some of his weight. He's so solid and heavy that I'm pinned and could not get out from beneath him if I wanted to; which I absolutely do not!

I'm enjoying that he has me under his control. I can pretend that I have no way of escaping his desires, thus not being responsible for my actions, but why deny the truth? I absolutely want him.

He takes both of my wrists in one of his massive hands and holds them together above my head, further restricting my movement and taking away whatever control I thought I still had.

A wave of panic tears through me. Will he let me go if someone walks in? Would he stop if I change my mind?

As if he can read my thoughts, his face pulls back and seems to soften. "If you want this to stop, say 'red' and it stops. Do you understand?"

I nod, not knowing why I can't simply tell him to stop.

He demands, "Tell me you understand."

"I understand, but why…" My whisper evaporates. I breathe heavily, knowing I'm about to give in to his sexual prowess.

He explains, "Red stops everything. If you tell me to stop, I won't. Do you understand?"

I nod, still not understanding why "stop" won't make him stop.

Our eyes remain holding one another's gaze while his hand glides up my thigh, lifting my dress up as it travels. When his hand is between my upper thighs, nearly touching my panties, he urges my legs further apart. Only my damp panties separate the most sensitive part of my body from his rough exterior.

The instant his thigh presses firmly against my damp panties, I gasp. He pulls at my other thigh until my legs spread wide, but he doesn't lean down against me. His body hovers just above mine.

Coach's deep growl seems to vibrate my chest as he kisses down my neck, his free hand squeezing my breast through the thin fabric of my dress. He pinches my nipple until I wince. I yank my wrist free and grab his bicep.

What the hell? That hurt.

In one swift movement, he's up on his knees, each of my wrists in his hands, and he sits me up. He tucks my arms behind my lower back and then pushes me back down, pinning them between me and the sofa. What is he doing? I try to pull them free because it feels awkward and confining. He stops moving and holds my shoulders still. His eyes burn into mine.

"Stay," he commands abruptly.

His voice is deep and threatening. My breath catches in my throat, fear ripples through me, but only for an instant. I decide to play along and remain in this position to see where he's going to take it. He removes his hands from my shoulders, giving me the choice to stay put or pull them free.

I don't move, not yet. I'm curious.

Coach's mouth covers the gusset of my damp, silky panties, instantly soothing away any concerns. His moans match mine as his teeth nip at my pussy lips through the thin fabric while biting and tugging on my panties with purpose. His fingers slip beneath the thin material, brushing against my excited clitoris and it twitches appreciatively. He tugs quickly, tearing the crotch of my panties in two, freeing my womanhood for his mouth to ravish.

I glance down to see why he's not kissing my pussy, only to see him staring at me.

"Do you want me to eat your cunt?" I simply nod excitedly. "Tell me."

"I want you to lick me," I reply in barely a whisper, my cheeks flushing at my uncharacteristic boldness. I've never been a verbal lover.

"Tell me you want me to eat your cunt," he insists and then blows cool air on my clit.

I can't say that word, it's absolutely too vulgar. His eyes remain focused on mine, but he isn't touching me. His mouth is an inch away, his breath now heating me to near volcanic temperatures.

I'm going to scream soon. I can't remember a time I have ever wanted anything this desperately.

He leans back on his knees, looking down at me, disappointed. "Tell me what you want, Rayna."

Nervously, I say, "I can't say that word." I feel awkward, like I'm being put on the spot.

"Cunt?" he asks with a grimace. I nod, biting my lips between my teeth. "Say it, Rayna. Say the fucking word. It's only four letters. I promise the world will not cave in around you."

"Please, I don't want to," I whisper, suddenly feeling insignificant.

He breathes in deeply. I watch as his eyebrows furrow and his eyes seem to soften. "If you can't say something as simple as 'cunt,' I don't think we are a suitable fit. I'm sure, as you've discovered, I'm not a gentle lover, and I want what I want."

He leans forward, uncharacteristically brushing a lock of hair from my cheek. Does he have a softer side?

"I'm sexually dominant; brutal at times. When I play, I play hard. I don't mess around with my pleasure. If you want to expand your mind, I'll be happy to take you into my world, but you have to want to do the things I tell you to, without questioning my motives. I'll expect you to do things that might be uncomfortable. All I'm asking right now is that you say the word 'cunt.' Do it now, or I'm going to ask you to leave and not come back until you are ready to do as I ask."

My mind is whirling, unable to decide. If I stay, he could do things to me that scare me. If I leave, I'll always wonder what he means by taking me into his world.

"Take a chance, Rayna. What do you have to lose?"

"You really are bossy," I sharply reply, not enjoying that I'm being given an ultimatum. "So, either I say that disgusting word or I go home, and you're done with me?"

"Yes." He hasn't moved, still kneeling and staring at me as if reading my chaotic thoughts. He's patiently waiting for me to decide. "It's only a word and nobody is within earshot to hear you say it other than me."

The best I can manage is to whisper. "Cunt." I feel my face flushing red; my shame becoming all too obvious.

"I'm sorry, I couldn't hear you. Try again, louder this time."

Even though he is calm and absolute, I watch the corners of his lips lift, alerting me to the pleasure he's getting from my mortification.

I nearly yell, "Cunt! Are you happy now?"

I swallow hard, trying to keep my emotions held back. I do not want to cry. I hate confrontation. My anxiety spikes and tears typically spill.

"You tell me," he replies as he grabs his erect cock through the fabric of his cotton shorts, proving the excitement my humiliation brings him.

His seductive smile makes my tummy flutter. I want him even more now, which confuses me. Why wouldn't I get up and leave, stomping my feet? Instead, my body proves its need for his touch. I think I'm more aroused than I have ever been. Could it be from saying that awful word, or because I did something I never do?

He lowers his face to my smouldering pussy, sucking my clit between his teeth and flicking it gingerly with the tip of his tongue.

Holy hell!

The world falls apart around me. I moan so loudly that it echoes throughout the room. His barely audible, devilish chuckle gently whispers into my ears. I'm spellbound. Take me, devil man!

He started off worshipping my swelling clitoris. But now, Coach teases me with his scarce flicking. He's enjoying how my body bucks in frustration.

"Your cunt tastes so sweet. Your juices are thick and slick, perfectly preparing you for my meaty cock. I want to drink you in." His lips press a full kiss onto my pussy. My hips lift in appreciation. With a deep, assertive voice, he demands, "Beg me to make you cum."

He wants me to talk nasty again. No, I can't do this. It's not in my nature. Besides, I'm not ready to cum yet.

Feeling ignored, he covers my clit with his open mouth, sucking hard while stroking his tongue up and down over my aching button. He pushes two of his fat fingers deep inside me with one quick thrust.

I cry out as his digits push completely in, his knuckles pressing firmly against my labia. Coach stays focused on one particularly sensitive spot inside of me. Each time his fingertips thrust, the sensations his tongue generously provides intensifies. He's not fucking at a steady pace but keeping it torturously sporadic and I never know when he's going to lick my clit or leave me craving it. He's making me come apart.

He lifts his mouth long enough to repeat his demand. "Ask me, Rayna."

I look down at his sexy, dangerous face as he mashes it against me. The world fades around me, my focus aimed at my pleasure button. I'm almost there. He lifts his face and I know he's going to ask again. I'll do just about anything to keep this going.

I scream, "Please, let me cum!"

"Cum, Rayna." His calm, deep voice sounds so far away.

He doesn't let up as my pussy clenches around his fingers. A violent orgasm erupts from deep inside of my soul. It is finally free to ripple throughout my body, setting fire to every cell of my being. I scream as my mind slowly falls into blackness, but his mouth and fingers don't let up for a second. My body bounces and jerks under the command of his tongue.

Coach kneels up quickly, unbuttoning his shorts and yanking them down his thighs and tucking them between his knees and the sofa cushion. His impressive, rock-hard prick juts straight out from his body.

It's glorious! He's so big! His is probably the most perfect erection I have ever seen. A tiny gleam of pre-cum glistens at the tip, catching my eye.

His teeth tear at a condom package, revealing the hidden sheath inside. He rolls it over his weapon with the skill of a man who's done it a million times. He leans forward, touching the fat tip against my slit.

He stops.

"Tell me you want me to fuck you," he demands, his excitement revealed in his voice. When I pause, he tilts his head and glares at me.

"Yes, please fuck me," I reply with aloud, quivering voice.

In one smooth movement, he's buried deep inside of my body. The shock of it ripples through me. I gasp, nearly coming from the sudden invasion. He's spreading my walls wider than any man ever has.

I open my eyes when he doesn't move. He's looking down at me. A dark, trance-like expression has enveloped his face. He looks like a testosterone-filled, emotionless machine, ready to fuck me harder than I've ever been before. And I want him.

He doesn't disappoint me when his hips lift, slamming back down onto me, shoving himself even deeper inside. The initial fullness shocks me and my hands spring free from behind my back, immediately slapping his ribs. He doesn't even flinch at my weak attempt to make him ease up. He continues to pound into me again and again.

The pain quickly becomes something entirely wonderful. Each time the tip of his prick pounds my cervix, my body weakens a little more. I want him even deeper if it's at all possible.

My fingernails dig into his arms, which brace his weight on either side of my chest. I slide up the cushion each time he crashes into me. His massive hands clutch my hips, lifting my lower half off the cushion and pulling me with him as he kneels back.

He flashes me a crooked grin that would signify a fistfight to another man with a quick temper. I'm quickly learning that he loves his dominance and the fear it creates in others.

He pushes his prick deep into me and holds me still. Only the rapid swelling and shrinking of his chest prevents him from looking like he's made of stone, a perfectly sculpted statue for my eyes to soak up and burn into my memory.

"Tell me to fuck you hard and fast. Tell me your hungry cunt wants to cum on my throbbing cock."

Coach isn't fucking around.

I now know that when he insists I say something, I'd better say it. Otherwise, the pleasure stops. I wonder if he's this persistent with his gym clients and if they appreciate it or hate him for it. I want to sample more of what he's offering, and I'll do almost anything to make that happen.

I yell, ensuring he'll hear every word, "Fuck me hard and fast until my starving cunt cums on your fucking cock!"

Wow! I sound like a loose-tongued whore.

An evilness burns from behind his eyes that fills me with a sudden unease. His expression softens as he studies my fearful eyes.

"When you cum, I want you to thank me. Do you understand? If you don't, I will stop." His gently spoken words ensure that he is not a vicious beast intending to hurt me, but a man with an intensive need to pleasure me. My anxious fear has me undeniably lusting for him.

"I understand," I say breathlessly, hoping he'll quit talking and get back to fucking me.

He nearly sings, "You're a good little slut and you deserve to cum."

The violent fucking ensues and doesn't let up. I don't even care that he called me a slut. This pounding is totally worth the humiliation of the insult. I know I'm not a slut, so it doesn't faze me.

He rams me like a wild man, pounding into me with impossible speed and force. The thudding against my body forces the air from my lungs in rapid succession. I can barely think.

My body is his toy to take as he will, my mind no longer able to make intelligent, responsible decisions. An orgasm locks every muscle in a seizure of painful pleasure I hope never to recover from. Screams pour out of me as wave after wave of heightened climax shreds through me, rendering me stiff and useless.

I open my eyes to make sure a man is fucking me and not the devil, but I can't be sure. Coach still fucks me hard while watching me with black pools surrounded by skin so red it's nearly purple. His eyebrows furrow. Soulless growls escape from deep in his massive chest as if the devil himself is tearing into me. Perhaps he is.

His eyes widen and glare, and that's when I remember his instruction. "Thank you!"

Coach stands quickly, grabbing me by my arms and yanking me to my feet. My weak knees give out and I nearly fall, but he scoops me up like I weigh nothing more than a bag of potatoes. He doesn't even grunt like I do when I pick up a grocery bag off the floor. He sprints to the back of the sofa, and then sets me down onto my feet, spinning me until I'm facing away from him.

His huge hand grabs the back of my neck firmly, bending me forward until I'm at a ninety-degree angle over the back of the sofa. He gently but assertively kicks my feet wide apart. His thick, powerful spread thighs press against my much smaller ones, pinning me to the back of the sofa and that throbbing prick buries deep into me again.

Oh, fuck! I didn't think it was possible, but he's reaching so much deeper inside of me in this position. I can't even cry out to beg him to go easier, but do I really want to if I could?

It hurt at first when he entered me on the couch, but my body quickly adjusted, and I will this time, too.

I've never been this full and overwhelmed by anyone in my entire life. I'm surprised to realize that I really like not having any say in what he does to me. I trust him in that he said he'll stop if I say "red" and that brings me comfort.

With one hand on my hip and the other on the back of my neck, he fucks me like it's the last time he will ever fuck a woman. The power behind his muscular body has me flopping around like a rag doll. If he wasn't holding my neck, I might get whiplash. The skin on my body feels like loose clothing as it ripples with each hard thud. Even the skin on my cheeks and lips bounce and I don't have a shred of decency left in me at this point to care what I look like.

I cum, hard. My wetness trickles down my parted inner thighs.

He releases my neck only to grab a wad of my hair, pulling me back until his mouth is next to my ear. My scalp hurts but I'm still coming so I don't give a shit what he's doing to me as long as he doesn't stop.

My pussy spasms around his thickness. He holds deep inside me. I relish the pause and gather my senses. His rapid, heated breath bounces off my ear. The only other sound is from my vigorously pounding heart rushing blood through my veins.

"Say 'thank you, sir,'" he whispers next to my ear as shivers continue to ripple through me.

"What?" My mind is still foggy from the violent fucking.

"Say 'thank you.' Since you forgot again, you will start calling me sir to acknowledge my sexual dominance over you."

"I don't like that." My voice sounds fragile and timid through panted breaths.

"Then you should have remembered to thank me," he whispers in a growl. "Now thank me properly, or we're done."

To get him to shut up and bring me back to that level of euphoria, I comply with his demands. "Thank you for the incredible orgasm, Sir! May I have another?"

Yes, I'm being a smartass, but what's he going to do about it? He won't throw me out. He hasn't cum yet and I'm sure he'll want to accomplish that before he tosses me aside.

His hand comes down on my ass with a thunderous clap. My ears ring and my eyes fly open. I wail! I pant as the heat from his hand singes my flesh, no doubt imprinting a giant hand-shaped welt on my flesh.

Before I can complain, he fucks me even quicker and harder than he had been, which is a tremendous feat. I didn't think he could be more intense, but I thought wrong.

Within seconds, I'm coming so hard that my body desperately wants to fuck back against him, but he's too powerful for me to compete with. He has all the control, and I am simply along for the ride. And what a ride it is!

Before I can finish thanking him, I'm coming again, and again.

A loud, beastly growl wrenches from Coach's throat, lasting longer than any breath I could manage right now. His prick swells, stretching my inner walls and forcing me into one final vicious orgasm. His muscles jerk, jolting his massive body.

A complete stillness overcomes him, and my hair slips from his grasp. A long, quiet exhale seeps from his very core as if he has satiated his devil.

I remain flopped over the back of the sofa, gasping for a full breath with his pelvis still pressed against me. I am limp, like an overcooked spaghetti noodle. He groans softly, leaning forward to kiss my back a dozen times before resting his forehead on it. His withering prick still lives inside of me.

He suddenly pulls away, his prick sliding out of my well-used vagina. I attempt to lift my chest, but I'm too tired. With more gentleness than I thought he had in him, he grips my shoulders, raising me up and turning me to face him. He pulls me against his sweaty chest and wraps his massive arms around my shoulders. Tenderly, he kisses the top of my head. It's a loving gesture that seems out of character from the man I knew a moment ago.

"You did well." His whisper compliments me while his body rocks me safely back and forth.

"What?" I ask, not sure why he thinks I did well when I did nothing to contribute, not even follow his simple verbal requests.

"You learned to appease my requests, even though you had an attitude. Also, you didn't beg for mercy." He seems proud of me.

I thoroughly enjoyed that, so why would I beg for mercy?

"I didn't know that was an option."

Coach scolds, "The option was always there. You accepted whatever I was doing to you. Do you remember when we first started, I told you to say 'red' if you wanted it to stop?" I nod against his solid chest. "You didn't use the word. You surprised me, is all."

"I should go. My kids will wonder where I walked off. The last thing I need is for them to report me as a missing person."

He chuckles as he releases me from his hold. He walks around the couch to get a tissue to wrap the condom in. His glistening muscles hypnotize me as he performs the simplest task of pulling his shorts back on. That man is a glorious mountain.

Now that I've seen him totally naked, I think he's even bigger than I had thought he was, or maybe that's the perception I have of him because of how he just overpowered me.

He fucks like an angry man with something to prove. I wonder what his reasoning is for needing to have that much control. Is he like this with everyone he's ever fucked or just the meek people such as myself?

"Can I ask you something?" I utter as he hands me a small towel. I watch him pat his forehead and chest with another towel while focusing his attention on me.

"You can ask me anything."

I clear my throat before beginning my interrogation. "Why were you so rough with me?"

Coach seems concerned. "Did I hurt you?"

"No," I reply quickly, easing the tension from his expression.

"I enjoy a good, hard fuck. As you can tell, I like control and dominance. The thought of making love bores me. And, before you ask, there is no deep-rooted reason behind this compulsion of mine. I simply prefer sex this way."

I cross my arms after handing him the towel. "Do you ever make love?"

Coach tilts his head, furrowing his eyebrows, and tells me an affirmative, "No." He tosses the towels through an open door.

"Why not?"

He sharply responds, "Why would I?"

I shrug, not really knowing how to answer that question. "I don't know. You love Alissa, right? So, do you two ever get romantic with each other? I mean, how do you show her that you love her?"

"She knows exactly how I feel about her."

I nod, waiting for him to elaborate, but he doesn't. "You do love her, right? If my calculations are correct, you've been dating her for nearly a year."

"I care about her wellbeing, sure. Making love is for people in love, and I am not in love with her."

He picks up the glasses of wine and hands one to me.

"You're not in love with her? That would explain why there's no ring on her finger," I say with a smile, hoping I'm not overstepping.

He stares at me, his expression beginning to look intense once again. He no longer has the calmness in his voice, taking me off guard.

"I will not marry her."

He's so sure of his statement. I can't say I've ever been that sure of anything in my entire life. When I married my ex-husband, I convinced myself that he was the best I could ever hope to have in a life partner, but I wasn't sure I loved him with all of my being. He turned out to be a son-of-a-bitch who spent his time chasing loose women and not caring for his wife and children like he should have been. The man only cared about one thing: his dick.

To this day, I sneer when I see him with his arm around his chosen tart of the month. When our kids had court-ordered sleepover visitations, which he rarely followed through on, I didn't know who would stay with them while he was out doing God-knows-what with God-knows-who. I think most of the girls enjoy playing housewife for a while, but when shit gets too real, they always leave him.

"If you've been with her for this long already, and you're sure you will not marry her, why not let her get on with her life so she can find someone who wants to marry her? I mean, if that's what she's looking for."

"Rayna, she knows I'm not the marrying kind. She is free to find another if she chooses to. I am not holding onto her. The two of us enjoy one another's company; we are plus-ones to special occasions, and we have a well-matched sexual rhythm between us. But that's it."

"Yeah, but…" I want to continue questioning him about this, but the look he gives me tells me to leave it for another time, if ever. "I should go."

"Thank you for coming over. We should do this again soon if you're still curious."

I clear my throat, ready to ask him what there is to still be curious about, but I decide not to. I gulp from the wineglass and set it on the table and then turn to walk toward the stairs. I don't even get to the first step before he grabs my arm, spinning me around to face him.

The warm palm of his hand cradles my cheek with shocking tenderness. His eyes look down into mine and for the first time, I notice the flecks of green in his eyes that break up the intensity of the brown. They don't seem so dark and intimidating at the moment.

How can these pretty eyes of his reveal that much petulance and yet still seem to have an overflow of kindness hidden within them?

Coach delicately touches his lips to mine, stirring the heat within me. Before the fire burns out of control, he sets me free and leads me by the hand up the stairs to the front door. He twists the handle and pulls it open, slapping me lightly on the ass as I take my first step outside.

I spin around and smile, blushing hotly as I recall the pain from the other slap he gave me while he fucked me, and how my body surprised me by reacting in an orgasmic explosion because of it.

The moment I walk through my front door, I immediately head to the bathroom to check my appearance. I can almost guarantee that I look like I've been repeatedly bounced off a fleshy brick wall. After burying my torn panties deep in the trash bin, I burst into a laughter that echoes off the bathroom walls. I immediately cover my mouth to muffle the sound. I don't need the kids asking me why I'm so happy.

Oh, what an interesting afternoon this has been!

Chapter Three

Coach

The hot water splashes against my back as I soap my chest and think about what just occurred with the woman I've been fantasizing about for three years. I always imagined that she'd be sexually uptight, and I wasn't wrong. However, she lets loose when her pleasure is at stake.

It might be possible to convince her to be submissive to me. I'll have to take my time breaking her in and teach her what that role entails. I can't rush anything with this woman. She'll likely run for the hills if I do.

I wasn't sure if I pushed her too hard today, but she didn't quit on me, which surprises me. I'm so thankful that she stuck it out. If she had left when I asked her to say "cunt," I would have been very disappointed at myself for being such a twisted fucking asshole.

I know I'm a dick when it comes to sex; I get that, but rough sex gets me off, always has. Rayna didn't seem to mind. Whether or not she returns to me will prove or disprove that theory.

If she'll let me, I'd like to bind her with rope, limiting her movements. Rope binding has always been something that I find to be very sensual. With her helpless and at my mercy, I'd caress and kiss every inch of her milky skin, occasionally nipping her with my teeth just to keep her on edge. I want to spank her ass until it's red hot and then fuck her so hard she screams and cums, drowning my cock in her wet pleasure while her pussy clamps down so hard I can no longer move inside of her.

All this thinking about Rayna being at my mercy has my prick standing at attention. I don't have a lot of time to jerk off, but it won't go away on its own, especially since Rayna is still vivid in my mind and probably will be all day.

I squirt a blob of body wash in my palm and turn my back to the running water. I grip my prick and stroke it quickly, squeezing its firmness while imagining Rayna's tight pussy wrapped around me, sucking me in deeper just before she cums and then bearing down on my hard-on as she reaches her climax. It isn't long before I blow my load, relieving my tension and the stiffness of my cock.

I've been secretly watching Rayna for three years. When I first moved into the house next to hers, she came knocking at my door to introduce herself. The moment I opened the door and saw those gorgeous green eyes, I immediately imagined how intoxicating it would be to look into them while I slid myself inside her body. The thought of it had me trying to hide the hard-on I was growing in my sweatpants.

Her voice was soft and sexy, which didn't give ease to my throbbing dick. Something about her held my attention, captivated me in an instant, unlike anyone ever had.

I watched her cheeks flush after she stammered through informing me that she was divorced. She must have thought what she said was inappropriate because she seemed to ramble nervously as she tried to shift the conversation away from her ex as quickly as possible. It was strangely titillating.

She said she had two kids. I wondered if she was lonely. She didn't seem the type of woman to sleep around randomly just to get the physical relief she likely needed.

Right then, I made a vow to myself that she was off-limits. Back then, I needed a woman hanging on my arm while dragging a shit-load of baggage with her like I needed a hole in the head. I had enough baggage of my own. No, I was sure I'd keep my distance, but I thought it would be interesting to tease the fuck out of her every chance I got.

When our eyes met at our first encounter, I held her gaze and didn't look away. She averted her eyes quickly and then ran her fingers through her hair, nervously tucking a loose strand behind her perfectly adorable ear. She liked me. It was obvious from the way her eyes kept dropping to my chest. I stirred something inside of her that had been dormant, but she didn't act upon her desires and I needed to leave her be.

Perhaps my intuition knew there would be a better time for us to be physical. Maybe I subconsciously feared she would run for her life, thinking that I'm a sadistic fucker. She wouldn't have been wrong. Or maybe I'm different now; not so angry and dangerous as I was then.

She never so much as said a single thing that led me to believe she physically wanted to be with me other than the way she ogled my body when she thought I wouldn't notice.

Over the years, I've gotten to know her two exceptional kids. I occasionally play with them, usually with water guns or cannons. I chase them outside our houses and it's a riot. They're sneaky when they want to be, especially the little girl, Kim. She is small and can hide just about anywhere, rendering her almost invisible, thus allowing her to sabotage my plans of attack. Ken is older, and he's not nearly as sly as his little sister, but he runs as quick as lightning when he wants to get away from me. I'm too big to run quick enough to catch him.

Every night, Rayna makes her kids' lunches wearing only a nightgown, which is usually thin enough to see her shape when the light shines perfectly behind her. Little did she know, her silhouette was being admired by my eyes from my office window.

I didn't lie to her when I told her that I usually jerk off while watching her. I can't help it, she's so fucking sexy and she doesn't even know it. Maybe that's what I find to be most attractive about her.

Little did I know back when I first met, but her life looks pretty good from where I stand now. Perhaps I've matured. Her kids are awesome, too. The only issue is her deadbeat ex-husband, but he rarely enters the picture enough to be a problem. I wanted to play with her back then, to sample her, but I knew I'd only hurt her, and she deserved better. She's a respectable woman and too good for the likes of me.

I have a fun girlfriend, of sorts. Alissa is more of a submissive than what I would define as being a girlfriend. Before we started playing, she and I agreed that love will never enter the picture and if one of us felt like we were getting too close, we'd end it. She's a toy that I play with when I need entertainment, and she gets off on doing anything I tell her to; submitting. As I said, she's a fun girl.

Alissa and I have been together for about a year now and I think it's about time to send her on her way. Even though we agreed that this relationship was only for convenience and sex, I think she allowed herself to develop deeper feelings for me. She tries to kiss me romantically and cuddle when we're finished having sex, and that isn't something she would ever consider doing in the beginning. I should really think about letting her go as soon as possible, as Rayna suggested.

I'm meeting my long-time friend, Brett, for a late lunch and if I don't get a move on, I won't be on time. I despise people who are always late. Sometimes, like today, for instance, things come up that need taking care of before other pre-scheduled plans. If Brett was given the opportunity to fuck his infatuation, I doubt I'd be upset that he was late or missed our appointment altogether, but he's a little different from me. He takes things too personally sometimes.

Brett is someone I tag-team women with. Most women have fantasies involving two men, and we are more than happy to help them live out that fantasy. It's a lot of fun, especially when we're both fucking her at the same time. First off, it feels amazing on my cock. Second, I get to rock a girl's world with my good buddy. The women we do this with are nothing more than a plaything that we send on her way because we have no heartfelt feelings for them.

I'd never share Rayna with him, not that she'd allow it, anyway. It's not that I have deep feelings for her, but she differs from all of those other women. She's better than them, more deserving of respect. No matter the reason, I'd never let Brett put his hands on her.

He's much rougher with women than I am, and that's not a simple task. He has no problem leaving ghastly bruises on them or choking a woman out until blood vessels around her eyes burst and she's nearly unconscious. He likes to fuck anally, but his dick is too huge for most women to handle in their ass. If I think she's too tight, he won't fuck her ass, at least not while I'm around. After she's schooled in how sadistic he is, if she's daring enough to go to him alone, it's on her.

When I pull up in front of Charley's bar, I see Brett sitting at one of the outside tables, drinking a beer. Damn, that beer looks cold and soothing. I think I'll order one, too.

"Hey! Sorry, man," I apologize as I approach Brett and grasp his hand, bumping our firm chests together while we pat each other on the back only once. It's a manly way to show our level of friendship without seeming too affectionate.

"No worries. There must have been a damn good reason since you're never late. What's your excuse? It had better be a detailed story about nailing a hot chick," he jests.

"Brett, do you remember me telling you about my neighbour?" I ask as I take a seat across from him.

He tilts his head and asks, "The one with the blonde hair and hot little body? You pointed her out last year when a bunch of us were over for a barbeque. Fuck, it was hot that day."

"Yeah," I nod, remembering how steamy it was. "Well, I finally got to play with her."

His eyebrows rise high on his forehead. "Fuck off! No way! Yeah? Damn, you're a lucky man," he exclaims and then sips his beer while smirking. "She's hot for an older woman. I can't wait to fuck that broad." He laughs sadistically.

I shake my head. "Not with this one, buddy. She's special. I don't know why, but she is. She's a classy woman, not just some fucking slut who'll do anything to ride a cock." I point directly at him and sternly say, "Hands off. I'm not fucking around. Sorry, man."

"Since when do we keep the hottest chicks to ourselves? We always share. Well, almost always. I wouldn't subject you to a boring starfish," Brett says, referring to lazy women who only lie on their backs and spread wide, waiting for us to do all the work. If we give her the opportunity to move about at her will and she refuses, she's a starfish. We always take the lead, but I don't like bitches who expect that.

He looks pissed off, so I assure him, "The next chick I fuck, I'll make sure she's one of those fiery bitches you like so much. She'll be a chick who wants her two-man rape fantasy played out by two vicious, well-built men. We can take her hard while she play-fights. Those chicks are a riot, am I right?" He looks at me, lost in thought. "Brett, is it a deal?"

"But I like your neighbour. She makes my dick hard," he pouts.

"Sorry, Brett, not this one. I mean it, stay away!" I demand, hoping he'll let her go. I chuckle. "You know what? Alissa is available now. On the way over, I called her and told her not to come around anymore. We're done."

"No, you didn't! Really?" He's shocked. He sips his beer, pondering taking her on as solely his. We've played with her together many times, so he knows how insanely wild she can be. He shakes his head. "Nah, I don't want to play with her without you. She was your chick and I don't want her to think she'll be dating me. There's something not right about that woman and I can't put my finger on it. She's fun to play with, but not to keep. It was about time you dropped her."

"I think she has the fucking warm and fuzzies for me, and that's why I sent her packing."

"Why the sudden change?" he asks, then swigs his beer.

I grumble, "Rayna suggested I let her go if I'll never commit to her. She's right."

"So, this Rayna chick is telling you what to do already, and you only fucked her once? She must be an impressive piece of ass," he teases, sucking back the last gulp of beer from his bottle. He hisses, "Now I really want her."

"Kindly keep the python in your pants. There are other people around," I remind him. I take a big gulp from my bottle but wave him off when he asks if I want another. "No thanks, I'm driving."

"Suit yourself," he says while tilting his bottle toward the watchful waiter.

"So, why don't you give Alissa a call? Like I said, she's available and you know she's a freak for vicious sex. She loves your cock in any hole. I'm sure she'll agree to play with you. That girl is perpetually horny, and as you know, she'll do anything you ask and love it."

"I know. Alissa is a fine piece of ass. I didn't think you'd ever let her go. That girl is a screamer, especially when we DP her." His attitude shifts and he leans in closer. "That always feels so fucking good, doesn't it? I'm not saying I'm gay or anything, but I can feel your cock fucking her ass when I'm deep in her pussy. It's like you're stroking my cock, good buddy."

"When you say it like that, it sounds a little gay." I look around to make sure nobody is listening in. "Can we change the subject before you get it in your ugly fucking head that you're going to rub your cock on mine before your next beer arrives?"

"Since you want to keep her to yourself for a while, you can at least tell me what she's like? Start with her body. Give me something to jerk off to. Does she have any weird moles, fish scales, four tits? Leave no detail untold," he begs.

I grimace and shake my head. "She's magnificent. That's all I'm saying."

He scratches his perfectly shaved chin. "She's a single mom, right?" He frowns as if that's a huge turnoff for him.

"Yeah, so?" I wonder what his issue is with fucking single mothers.

"Dude, if you date her, you'll have her fucking brats hanging around all the time. They'll start calling you Daddy. How will you get to use her body whenever you want if she has brats running around? Fuck that shit!"

I smile and reply, "Wow! Take a step back. We aren't dating. We only fucked once. It's not like we're in a committed relationship, for fuck's sake. If it turns into something bigger, I'll accept her kids, too. They come as a package and I think I'd be okay with that. Those kids are pretty cool!"

"Who the fuck are you and how do I get my crazy friend back?"

I laugh. "We all have to grow up sometime. You will, too, when it's time."

"So, you'd consider having a relationship with her? I thought your motto was to use them up and spit them out."

"Yeah, well..."

I stop talking to watch the couple sit at the table next to us. A tinge of panic sinks in my chest when I imagine them as being Rayna and me. I've held my heart behind a barrier for a long time. I wonder if I ever could truly love anyone.

"So, let's say you do date he and things are great at first, but soon she convinces you to buy a minivan—"

"No fucking minivan! I like my truck, thanks."

"We'll see," he teases, sips his beer and continues. "What happens if it doesn't end well? First off, now you're stuck with a minivan." I roll my eyes. "You two live next door to each other. That could get awkward. And the kids; what about them? They'd be knocking at your door, calling you Daddy and shit; crying because you hurt their mommy and now she's sad all the time. Did you think about that before you fucked her?"

"No, Brett, I didn't. My cock was hard, and she was there. As I said, we only fucked once. I probably scared her away with my sinister ways." I sip the water the waiter brings me. "So, just calm the fuck down and drink your beer. You know me; I live for today and don't fear tomorrow. I'll deal with shit if I need to."

He shakes his head and snickers. "I almost forgot! I met this chick today. She's a natural blonde; tall, thin, dangerous dark brown eyes, and pouty lips that could make a man beg for mercy. What do you say? I can set us up for tonight." He takes out his phone and taps the screen, searching for her number.

"No, I think I'll pass this time. You have fun with her and tell me about it tomorrow." I tease, "Are you asking because you know you can't completely satisfy her without my expert sexual talents?"

When he frowns and flings his coaster at me like it's a Frisbee, I burst out laughing.

"I'll do just fine, thank you. I know what I'm doing. I'm just saying that it's not as much fun without you. I mean, she'll fucking get off a lot more with two guys. I know how much you love to watch a slut lose her mind."

He looks at me with dreamy eyes while licking his lips.

"Stop looking at me like that. You're making me wonder if it's me you want to fuck. Cut it out!" I hiss, and he laughs.

There's something to be said about how great it feels when we both fuck a chick. Each man can feel the friction from the other man's cock through the thin skin separating the two canals. It's not a homosexual thing, I don't think. But, to have my dick stroked while I'm ass fucking a chick is mind-numbing. It's like having a tongue lick the underside of my cock, but while I'm fucking.

Brett is always the first to cum. He can never hold back. I often tease him about it, of course. That's what friends do.

"Are you heading to the gym today?" I ask, hoping to get away from this subject.

He shrugs, muttering, "I don't know. You?"

"Yeah, right after this. I have a new yoga instructor starting today. Carol will observe her, but I'd like to see how she does." My words seem to fall on deaf ears. "Hey, are you still with me or are you too busy concentrating on peeling your beer label?"

"What?" he asks, quickly shifting his eyes up to meet mine. "Yeah, yeah, I'm still here. Carol—new yoga chick—I heard you. Continue."

"What's going on?" I ask, but he simply shakes his head, not replying. Much louder than I should, I ask, "Is it the gnarly butt rash flaring up again?"

"Oh, come on!" He snickers while looking at the disgusted couple nearest us. "I got it from him." They look at me, then go back to eating.

"What's up?"

"Nothing. It's dumb," he says while shaking his head.

"Don't be a dick. Tell me."

"Am I losing you to a chick you barely know?" he asks. As if something gross dawns on him suddenly, he shivers. "Holy fuck! I sounded like a chick just there, didn't I?"

"I'm not going to lie; you kind of did."

"Damn!" He cups his pecs as if checking to see if they grew. "They have been sensitive lately."

"Are you getting your period?"

He debates. "If you're just finishing yours, then yes. Our men-sies are almost synced."

"Brett, you aren't losing me. We're friends first, chick-swappers second. I will always think of you as one of my closest friends. And I didn't *just* meet her!" I exclaim, tossing the coaster back at him, hitting him on the nose, and then throwing my arms up as if I just scored.

Brett glares at me as he touches the bridge of his nose. He smiles and replies, "I don't want it to end and I hate that you won't share her. I know that we'll always be friends, no matter what either of us does or won't let the other do. You're my brother from another, and I love you."

We grip hands like men do, but when the couple looks at us, he leans in and licks my hand. They roll their eyes.

"What? Are you against man-on-man love?" he asks them, to which they shake their heads. He's a scary-looking guy when he means to be.

"We're just messing with you," I tell them after seeing the fear in their eyes.

As if he didn't just terrify the people next to us, he casually looks back at me and asks, "Are you sure you don't want another beer?"

Sometimes the man worries me. He hasn't always struck me as a totally mentally sound person. But he means well, even though his ways of thinking aren't always what I would consider being of societal norms. Who am I to judge? I have my own fucked up issues.

"Yeah, all right. You talked me into it. I'll have one more, but I'm cutting myself off after that. I have to drive to the gym to do some paperwork and can't be sloshed while doing either task," I explain as he waves his hand at the waiter, pointing to his bottle and holding up two fingers.

Chapter Four

Rayna

I slept peacefully last night. I can't remember the last time I felt that relaxed. Perhaps I should have sex more often, and with an actual human, not with a hard plastic vibrator. Adult bedroom toys are great, but the satisfaction that comes from being physically touched by someone's hot skin, listening to their moans and feeling their weight pressing down on my body? Well, an inanimate object can't match it.

What am I going to do today?

Last night, I finished the chores I had planned on doing today. After I'd gotten home from Coach's, I had newfound energy which had me dancing around the house and cleaning every room lacking a good dusting and polishing. All the dirty clothes were laundered and put away. I even went to the grocery store before it closed so I could restock the kitchen for the coming week. My mind swayed between dreamland and reality, so I overlooked some items on my list.

I definitely should engage in this type of extreme sexual activity more often. I get more accomplished afterward.

With my second cup of coffee down, I make my way to the bathroom to take a shower. Right after I pull my nightgown off, the doorbell rings, of course.

After quickly pulling my nightie back over my head, I rush to the door, hoping to open it before the person pushes the bell again, possibly waking the children. It's Sunday and I have no plans for them today, so they can stay in bed all day if they choose.

When I get to the top of the stairs, I see my sister waving at me through the window in the door. I knew I should have bought curtains for it.

She holds up two large coffees, smiling and bobbing up and down like an idiot. I shake my head and then lift my wrist to look at an imaginary watch as if we're playing a game of charades. She stops bouncing long enough to roll her eyes like she always did when she was a kid. It used to make me instantly angry, but since she never outgrew it, I learned to let it go.

I pull open the heavy door to invite her in, taking the coffee from her hand before I let her pass the threshold. I'll think of it as a fee for the early intrusion. She kisses my cheek before flashing me another silly smile that's way too toothy to be legitimate.

"Please, come in," I say, sarcastically.

"Thanks, sis! I think I will. So, what are you up to?" She's way too happy and energetic. It's not even nine in the morning. I'm still groggy and I've been up for an hour.

"Why are you here this early? You never come over before noon. And on Sundays, it's never until around three in the afternoon." I follow her up the stairs and into the kitchen. "Did you shit the bed again? I keep telling you to pick up a bag of adult diapers. They rave about them on the television."

"Hardy-har-har! You're hilarious! And I didn't shit the bed. Gross!" She contorts her face for a quick moment before joking adding, "I haven't done that in a very long time." She pauses while her face lights up. "Funny story…"

Here we go! Every time she tells me something that starts with a "funny story," it usually means she was out drinking and had a life-altering sexual experience with some guy or girl.

She sets her coffee on the counter before reaching into the small paper bag she sat on the counter and pulls out a bagel. She peels the wrapper back and I see that it's smothered in cream cheese, exactly how I like it. I smile, so she hands one to me before lifting another from the bag. She picks up her coffee and makes her way toward the glass patio doors.

"Do you want to sit outside? The weather is perfect this morning, isn't it?" she asks, and I shrug since I have no idea. "So, I was out last night, met a girl at that old tiny diner down the street from where I work." She points north with her bagel. "She was hot, I mean *so* hot! We talked for about half an hour, and by that time, I'd already decided I would ask her to come home with me."

We sit at the table; me facing Coach's house and her facing me.

She continues with her arms flailing to embellish the story. "That's when she got a phone call. I tried not to listen in, but she made that impossible. She was talking, more like yelling, to the caller about some curtains that she wants back, and threatening that she's going to send her cousin to take them. So, I decided I wanted no part of the crazy bitch."

"Probably wise," I say.

"Right? So, I stood up, took my coffee and walked out the door, leaving her at the table, still yelling at her phone. I don't even think she knew I left until she hung up."

"That's quite a story," I say with exaggerated sarcasm because this story doesn't surprise me. Renee has this magnetism that attracts societal losers. "Are there any napkins in that bag?"

She looks in and replies, "No, lick your fingers. Germs are our friends." She licks her fingers as if showing me how. "So, back to my story. I went home, watched TV, and fell asleep on the sofa. That was around seven. I woke up at eight this morning!"

The sun reflects off her bright white teeth. I don't think she could smile bigger if I offered her money to do so.

"Are you telling me you slept for thirteen hours?" I stare at her in disbelief.

"Yup! Are you jealous?" She giggles while still smiling like a fool.

"Did rigour mortis set in?"

"You are so funny, but I can tell you're jealous. I'm more well-rested today than you are," she teases.

I snicker, no doubt blushing like a young schoolgirl recalling a kiss from a boy. Her statement has me picturing Coach fucking me from behind. I'm unable to wipe the smile off my face.

"No, I'm not jealous. I slept better than I have in a very long time."

Renee chews while looking at me with questions behind her gaze. I giggle, shrug, and then take a big bite, knowing she's trying to read my thoughts. She swallows after a sip of coffee.

"What's going on? You're being weird."

I cover my mouth so I won't spit on her. "What makes you think something's going on? Can't someone have a great night's sleep without there being a hidden cause?"

"Sure, they can, but you're blushing." She sips her coffee again.

We hear patio doors slide next door. We both turn our heads toward the sound. The amazingly well-built man, who fucked me so extensively yesterday, walks outside with a basket of wet clothes. He waves when he notices us. I lift my arm and wave back, trying to hide my growing grin.

"Coffee and breakfast? Did you bring me any?" Coach shouts.

Under her breath, Renee whispers, "Oh, yeah, beastman! I got something for you right here in my panties."

I shake my head and fight back laughter. "Sorry, my sister only brought enough for two, but I'll share some of my bagel if you're hungry."

He grins, waving his eyebrows. "Sweetheart, I would gladly eat whatever you'd like to share with me. All you need to do is ask."

My face is fiery hot. I quickly glance at my sister, who's staring at Coach with her lips slightly parted. She doesn't blink. Knowing my sister as well as I do, I can tell she's fantasizing about him.

"Maybe I'll bring something over later, after you finish your chores," I tease, surprising myself how flirtatious that sounded. I've never been good at flirting.

He licks his bottom lip while smiling, tilts his head to the side, and says nothing. We share an intimate look between us, a hot and steamy moment that makes my pussy twitch and my body temperature suddenly spike. I gasp and bite my lip. My sister slowly turns her head and looks at me with wide eyes.

She whispers, "Tell him you have something better for him to eat than a bagel. Go ahead, tell him. I dare you!"

I look from her to him. "I have something better than a lousy bagel for you to eat. It's hot and fresh, but no cream cheese."

Renee groans. "Why point out the cream cheese? Christ, woman!"

He shakes his head and crinkles his forehead. "You're really not all that good at the art of flirting, are you?"

I shake my head, cheeks flushing. "Apparently not. Sorry for having painted that image."

My sister whispers, "Way to be cool, Rayna!"

Coach snickers, and then turns to go down the stairs with his basket. Renee and I watch every movement he makes, both mesmerized by how his incredible muscles move as he performs such a mundane task. How does he make hanging laundry on a clothesline look so damn sexy?

"How the fuck do you live next door to that gorgeous creature and yet have never made it to his bed?" She moans. "What the hell are you waiting for? I would be all over that."

"He's with someone." I struggle to act like I don't have a dirty little secret.

Renee turns her face to me, and I know she thinks something's up.

She demands, "Spill it! Now, woman!"

I burst into belly laughter that I can't reign in while shrugging to suggest that I don't know what she's talking about, despite my hysterics and unconvincing, overdramatically, innocent expression.

Her eyes light up with surprise. Coach walks up his stairs with his attention on us. I don't doubt he's curious about what she's saying to me. I laugh even louder. He stops at the glass doors and watches us with a curious expression. Renee turns her head to look at him. He smiles at her and nods as a pleasant gesture since he's still unsure of where our conversation has taken us. I'm sure he assumes that I've said something about last night.

When she looks back at me, he slides his hand in his pants, smiling suggestively and pointing at himself, then me, and then giving me the come-hither, one-finger wave. My face lights up, eyes wide and mouth opening with a gasp.

What if the neighbours see him do that?

Renee quickly spins to look at him, but he's already in the house. She didn't see his rather lewd suggestion.

The look she gives me is priceless. Damn, I wish I had my camera handy. She's in total disbelief that her *innocent* older sister could ever be with a sexy beast like Coach. You'd think I'd just told her that I won an impressive award. Then again, I suppose in some ways,

I did. She shrugs her shoulders, urging me to spill the beans.

"Okay, yes." I pause. "Him."

"Holy shit! Seriously? When?"

"Yesterday, actually."

I smile like an idiot, mocking her typical silliness. She frowns in disapproval of the teasing. Renee leans into me with her elbows on the table.

"You've got to tell me; is he good?"

"Good, how? His body? Obviously, he has an impressive body; you can see that for yourself."

She's seen him many times before today, so she's familiar with his physique. I'm playing dumb purposely to drag this out and make her slightly crazy with anticipation. For once, I hold the crown as the woman with the best sex story. She rolls her eyes. *Annoying!*

"No, you ass! How is he in bed? Wait! No, don't tell me. Okay, it's okay, tell me. Damn it, no!"

Renee's torn, unsure if she wants to know. If he's a lousy lay, it'll ruin her infatuation with him. I snicker and wait for her to decide. She covers her eyes for a second and squeals before looking at me.

"Give it to me."

"He's very," I pause, "dominant. Coach needs to be in control. If you like that sort of thing, then yes, he's very good."

"And, did you like that sort of thing?" she asks with her eyes half shut as though she were in a trance-like state.

I giggle. "I really did. Several times, actually."

"Oh, nice! It's about fucking time you got laid." She sips her coffee. "How long has it been, anyway?"

"A long damn time. Too long," I confess.

She takes another sip of her coffee. "Are you getting together again soon? Oh, shit! What about his girlfriend? I mean, you said he's still with her. He's kind of an ass because he obviously doesn't give a shit about her. But on a better note, good for you, Rayna! Tame that wild beast. And fuck her. She's a bitch, anyway."

"He might have told her, I don't know. They have a strange relationship. He told me that she knows he will never marry her and that she's fine with it. He's obviously afraid of commitment."

"Uh-huh! But are you going to be hopping on that horse again soon? You need to be sampling more of that regularly." Her voice shifts to sound more jealous. "I can't believe that Adonis banged you yesterday. Are you full of bruises today?"

I sip my coffee, then nod. "The front of my thighs are a little bruised."

"Really?" She considers the unorthodox ways that could have happened. "What position were you in?"

"That's a smidge too personal, don't you think?" I exclaim.

"Don't be a bitch!" she hisses. "Tell me!"

"Probably when he had me over the back of his couch."

She moans. "Please give me more details. Let me have all the glorious details, you lucky slut. Leave nothing unsaid."

She leans back in her chair, holding her coffee with both hands, and resting it on her lower belly. She's quiet while I explain.

"He went down on me, and it was so good. He insisted I say 'thank you' after every orgasm he gave me, which I thought was weird. He swatted my ass when I copped an attitude after he reminded me that I had forgotten to thank him. It shocked me to realize that I quite enjoyed that swat." I look down at the table, embarrassed. "He pulled my hair, gripped my body, and then fucked me so damn hard; harder than I have ever been fucked."

She moans, again. "Damn!"

"When he looked at me, I'd swear he could read my thoughts. He's very intimidating."

She asks, "Will you do him again?"

"If he'll have me, I'll gladly visit him again. I could really use more of what he's offering."

Renee looks over my shoulder, most likely picturing him fucking her hard while pulling her hair. Having told her makes it so much more real. The entire thing seems like something I read in an adult magazine and not a genuine story I personally experienced.

"Sis, you'd better get your ass over there today and take off your clothes. Going by the picture you're painting, I'd say he could be exactly what you need to break you out of your abstinence. You're so busy being a mom that you forgot how to be a woman. You have needs; physical needs that vibrators can't fulfill." Her arms flail. "Go get him, babe! Just be sure to tell me every detail. Oh, if you can get pictures of his nakedness, that'd give me a better reference when you're telling me about him."

I'm about to tell her to fuck off when the backdoor slides open. My son's head appears. "Hi, Aunt Renee. What are you doing here so early?" He aggressively wipes the sleep from his eye.

"People, I get out of bed before noon, you know," she huffs. "Hi, big guy. How did you sleep?"

"Fine. Mom, where's the cereal?"

"Good morning to you, too," I tease, wishing he would have greeted us more politely.

He sighs. "Good morning, Mom. Where's the cereal?"

"I put it in the pantry. There wasn't enough room in the cupboard."

He shuts the door without saying thank you. I should be more like Coach and give his ass a little swat for being impolite.

A giggle quietly escapes me.

Chapter Five

Coach

I've been standing by the kitchen window, watching Rayna and her sister, Renee, ever since I walked back into my house. Both sisters are beautiful with their matching blonde hair and bodies that have every heterosexual man wishing they could have them.

Even though I find Renee incredibly sexually desirable, I've held an interest in Rayna for far longer and on a deeper level than what I'm used to. She's special; different in that she could easily steal my heart. What's worse is that I might actually want her to. It's unlike me to feel this way about any woman.

I don't know why I'm even considering it. She'll never let it happen. She's out of my league and I'd be wise to remember that.

Judging by how brightly Rayna's blushing, I believe she's telling her sister that I fucked her. I can't see her sister's face, but once in a while, Rayna bites her bottom lip and then smiles, tipping her head down shyly.

The main difference between Rayna and Renee is that Rayna is a lot more reserved than her sister. Renee seems to have no issue with expressing herself, no matter who's listening. She doesn't apologize if she offends anyone. Renee and I would get along great if we were to become strictly friends, which is not likely to happen, especially now that I'm fucking her sister. When Renee finds out I'm not into commitments, she'll hate me for leading her sister on.

Why am I even thinking Rayna would consider me as a romantic interest in the first place? Rayna is an incredible woman, but why would she be interested in an asshole like me as being anything more than a fuck-mate? She wouldn't.

She's a bit older than me and much more sophisticated and grounded. Maybe her being divorced and raising the kids, basically alone, has granted her a level of maturity that I know I can't match. I'm an asshole, and I know it.

I admire Rayna for her courage and strength. If it were me in her shoes, I would have shot the ex-husband; not because he was a cheater, but because he's a shitty father. The man has no idea how fantastic those kids are.

Ken is smart, no doubt smarter than I am, and he's only thirteen. He's going to grow up and be noticed for his intelligence.

Kim is younger; eleven, I think. She's smart, too, but has a shitty attitude, much like her Aunt Renee: carefree and happy to be herself and not strive for anything more. She might not become a household name for winning a Pulitzer, but she'll have a fun and interesting life to talk about in her old age. Who knows? Maybe she's smart as hell, but good at hiding it.

Rayna has done an amazing job raising those kids by herself. She's sacrificed her own happiness time and time again with no sign of appreciation from anyone. I'd have gone postal by now if I were in her situation.

I need to see her again.

My cock swells in my shorts. I ache to smell her hair, feel her soft, creamy skin, watch her sexy eyes as the lids slowly close when she's at the apex of her orgasm. That's when she forgets to breathe. I need to be inside of her, feel her heat around my cock, and the pressure when she's squeezing me so tightly as her juices begin to spill.

I slide my hand down my shorts and start to pump my fist around my erection. I focus on her innocently blushing cheeks. She's biting that same bottom lip I had pressed mine against not twenty-four hours ago.

My ass muscles flex as I push my pelvis forward, making my cock more accessible for the simulated fucking of Rayna's mouth. I can't be bothered to stop my shorts from falling to my ankles. I close my eyes to help me recall how shy and embarrassed she looked when I challenged her to say the word "cunt." That was a test to see if she would do whatever I demanded. If she had refused, we would have been over before we even got started. I needed to know she would be willing to try new things, no matter how ridiculous she thought the command was.

She should know that she can say and do unconventional things without the whole world falling apart around her. Her simply verbalizing that offensive word helped confirm my belief that she is brave and courageous.

I want her naked and under my control once again, and doing everything I demand of her. I want to awaken her to the possibilities of intense sexual fun and freedom. I know she's never allowed herself to be sexually liberated.

Rayna is standing when I open my eyes. I hadn't noticed that she's wearing my favourite nightgown. She walks to the glass doors, sliding it open. I watch for a full minute as she talks to someone inside the house. Her strong legs are bare and kissed by the bright morning sun.

With my knees slightly bent, my thighs flex until they hurt, which helps me cum. I jerk my cock so fast that my arm aches. My teeth clench and I tighten my abs, straining them as well. Sweat forms on my forehead and upper lip as I beat my meat at the sight of such a tasty woman.

I reach down with my free hand, cupping my balls and pulling them away from my body. Fuck! Rapid slapping sounds echo through my kitchen. I'm going to cum. I'm so close. Rayna steps into her house and out of my view.

No! Damn it!

Her sister is still sitting outside. I suppose I could picture my hand twisted in her hair, forcing her to suck my cock until she fucking gags on it. No, this hard-on is from Rayna and I'll keep it that way. I close my eyes again. I want to fuck Rayna's mouth until just before I cum, and then pull out and let go on her pretty face, temporarily marking her as mine.

Oh, fuck, yes!

My grunts are loud, but my windows are closed so I know Renee can't easily hear me despite the stillness of the early morning neighbourhood.

My eyelids open slowly. I'm elated to see Rayna coming out of the house in her nearly see-through nightie that does nothing to hide the fact that she isn't wearing a bra.

She plops down on her chair while looking directly at the window I'm watching her from. I'd swear she's watching me, and it thrills me. That woman's eyes seem to burn into mine, even if she can't see me through the tinted window. The instant she looks away, I close my eyes, remembering how hard I fucked her dripping wet cunt.

My climax shreds through me. I fuck my hand with every bit of reserved strength I have. A loud growl erupts from deep within my chest. My legs shake violently, urging my cock to let it go. Cum spits in short spurts onto the floor. My hand glides slowly, forcing wads of cum to collect on my fist as the few last wads dribble from the end of my dick. I squeeze the last remaining glob from my shrivelling shaft and raise my eyes to look at the woman who I know will somehow change me forever, and it scares me.

I flip on the water and begin washing the sticky cum from my hand and then wipe the floor with a damp paper towel. I get a pen and a small piece of paper from the drawer beside the fridge, jotting down my phone number, and slip it into my pocket.

Just as I'm about to step outside, it dawns on me that I should wipe the sweat from my face and make sure I'm not noticeably flushed. Rayna and her sister knowing that I recently jacked off is a hot thought, but I'd rather them not think I'm some kind of peeping Tom, pervertedly watching them while I choke my cock, even though I confessed to doing just that. Because her sister is there, I'd rather her not know. Rayna is probably freaked out enough after how rough I was with her yesterday.

I hate that I'm sadistic with a need to dominate, to watch women physically or morally suffer in order for sex to seem worthwhile to me.

The psychologist I saw years ago didn't really give me a straight answer as to why, so I stopped seeing her. Besides, she was really hot and I wanted to fuck her, but she let me know that was off the table. If I'd thought there was a chance I could bang her, I might have kept attending the sessions to see how far she was willing to go to understand me.

I pull open the door and step out, closing it behind me. After carefully walking down the stairs, because of my weakened leg muscles, I notice that she's gone in the house. Renee is still sitting at the table, drinking from a water bottle.

Instead of going back to the house, I walk to the fence to wait for her. Renee looks over as she's sucking back a rather large gulp of water that bloats out her cheeks. She nearly spits and has to take several swallows to get it all down.

After emptying her mouth, she shouts with sarcasm in her tone. "So, ah, what did *you* do yesterday?"

Rayna told her.

My lip twitches and my jaw clenches when I see her expression. The conniving little smirk she wears makes me want to grab her by her hair and slap her sassy fucking mouth before kissing her hard enough to hurt. I imagine myself fucking her mouth to shut her up if the slap doesn't do it.

I don't trust that broad to not make a move on me, even though she knows I fucked her sister. She might even do it simply because her sister sampled me. I can usually tell when a chick is a backstabber and I'm very sure Renee is exactly that. She wants to overshadow her sister; it's just her personality. Call it jealousy or low self-esteem. Either way, it's wrong.

"I mowed the lawn, did some cleaning and then I had a very heated workout with a new friend," I reply without a glimmer of emotion. My face is locked in a statuesque way, my eyes staring at her with intense intimidation. She will not control this conversation.

Renee laughs as she stands and hops down the stairs, quickly making her way to the fence. She reaches up and begins tracing a muscle on my forearm. She's making me want to throw her over my knee like she's a bad little bitch who needs to be taught boundaries.

If I ever had sex with her, which I won't, I'd love to punish this little cunt, but for my pleasure, not hers. I would get off on watching her plead with me to let her cum, and I'd consider denying her. It's not that I particularly want to fuck Renee. I'm simply annoyed at how she's so quick to flirt with me right after her sister told her that she and I were together. Bitches like this make my inner demon twitchy.

"From what I hear, you gave her one hell of a workout. You know, I've been known to enjoy a good workout now and then, but I've never sampled a musclebound fox like you. Maybe I should drop by after I leave here so you could fuck me the way—"

In a deep, fatherly tone, I hiss, "Stop talking right now. Just shut the fuck up and stop being a backstabbing cunt. She's your sister. Have some respect for her, if not for yourself."

She gripes, "You're a fucking asshole!"

My inner demon breathes fire at this point. I growl, "Bitch, you have no idea how much of a fucking asshole I am."

"Is that so?" she says while trying to sound cute and innocent.

I absolutely can't stand that immature, sassy female tone. My demon clenches his fists and trembles with a need to punish her. I'm going to fucking slap this twit if she doesn't fuck off. I know she's doing it to piss me off; I turned her down flat and insulted her pride in the process. But I haven't finished knocking her off her fucking pedestal quite yet.

My eyes burn into hers. After a few seconds of glaring, her cocky attitude is shaken, and I see her discomfort growing in her eyes, but she's stubborn.

In the deepest voice I can manage, I say, "Renee, get your fingers off me this instant. I know you feel insulted because I'm not caving into your immature act of betrayal toward the one person in your life that you should respect more than anyone. I will not fuck you, ever. Let's get that straight right now."

She snips, "Yeah, we'll see."

I look at her hand and she removes it from my arm.

"If you're stupid enough to ask me again, I'll be sure to tell Rayna about this little conversation. I still might, I haven't decided. You know what you're doing would hurt her, and I don't think you want that. So, why don't you get your sneaky self up those fucking stairs and get your hot sister back outside so I can talk to her."

She takes a step back from the fence. When she's far enough away that I can't reach her unless I jump over this fence, she tries to create a cover story.

"Well, good! You passed the test. I was checking to see if you'd agree to have me over with the promise of sex." She's back-peddling like a fucking coward. Her tone shifts. "I'm going to say outright that your eyes are fucking intense, dude! What the fuck is with that *I'm going to own your soul* stare? Fucking wild! No wonder my sister couldn't resist you. I knew there had to be something special about you to make her break her long-running marathon of celibacy."

I speak slow and deep. "I don't know if you're telling me the truth or if you're trying to cover your tracks. If it's the latter, I'd bet my house that you fucked her husband at least once. If that's the case, you'd better pray she never finds out. Now be a good girl, and go get your sister."

She laughs nervously as she walks away, swinging her tiny ass with every step. I'm usually great at reading people, but this broad has me second-guessing my intuition. What is it about these sisters that has me so off my game? I want to pleasure one while punishing the other.

Before Renee makes it all the way up the stairs, Rayna walks out the door. She looks at her sister and then glances past her and sees me. I shake my head, letting her know that I have no interest in the mouthy woman. She seems to sigh heavily, as if she had been holding her breath.

Renee says something that makes Rayna scowl at her. Her face slowly softens before she meets eyes with me. I pinch the small piece of paper between my forefinger and middle before holding it up. Renee sits down and watches as Rayna approaches me. The little bitch looks like something I said to her touched a nerve because her eyes look more sombre than usual.

Rayna walks down the steps and approaches the fence. She takes the piece of paper and sees that it's a phone number. "Yours, I take it?"

"Text me when your mouthy little sister fucks off. What's her problem, anyway?"

"Her problem?" she asks, unsure of what I'm referring to.

I tilt my head. "She was hitting on me. She said it was a test to see if I was a creep. But I didn't get that vibe. It just felt wrong. I'm all into sisters if that's your game. I doubt it is, and that woman doesn't interest me."

"She told me she tested you and you passed. Who knows with her? I think she's lonely. Hey, do you know someone who might be interested in entertaining my crazy little sister? Perhaps someone who looks like you and likes their women rather sexually wild?" She tilts her head and taps her lip with her finger. "Come to think of it, you'd be perfect for her."

"Like I said, she's not on my agenda." I try to frown even though I secretly wish I could humiliate that slut, enough to make her cry and call me an asshole again.

The thought makes me snicker.

I say, "I do know a guy that fits that description, but I don't want to set them up if she's only going to use him and spit him out. My friends are important to me. Tim is a really nice guy who wears his heart on his sleeve even though he has a bit of a wild streak. He's the bad boy with a good heart."

"So, just like you," she accuses.

"Nothing like me. I'm an asshole, through and through." If she only knew me better, she'd already know that to be true.

She rolls her eyes, not believing me. "I do understand the meaning of friendship and I can't promise she'll be on her best behaviour with him. You could ask him if he'd be interested in being with someone who loves a lot of sex? Tell him she's really cute; that'll help."

"Yeah, I could set her up with Tim. He's a good man who's good to women and does love a challenge. He's always been wild but has mentioned wanting to find someone special to settle down with. They might be perfect for each other. He's Black, is that a problem for her?"

She furrows her brow. "Why would it be? Love is love and it doesn't matter who you're giving it to or getting it from, as long as you're good for one another." She crosses her arms over her chest. "She won't care either way. If he's kind to her, that's all that matters. If he's not, I'll kick his ass, and I don't care how big he is."

I nod and snicker. "I have no doubt that you would. You're protective over family, and I admire that quality in a person. Let me think about it, and maybe I'll ask him tomorrow if I see him."

"Thanks," she says, looking back down at the folded paper.

"So, let's go back to the subject of you and me getting naked. I need your body and I think you want more of what I'm offering."

I purposely make my voice deep and speak slowly. Many people have told me that when I do that, I'm scary as fuck but its effects are like an aphrodisiac to most women. It seems to work well on Rayna, judging by how hard she just swallowed.

She refolds the paper and palms it as she steps closer to me and looks deep into my eyes and doesn't blink or look away, trying to get me to back down. She has no idea how doing exactly that makes my cock swell. Rayna easily intimidates me like no other woman ever could, other than my mother, of course.

My thoughts flash back to yesterday when I had her on her back and I was on top of her, fucking her. Her face flushed a cherry red when she was at the peak of her orgasm. She's so angelically beautiful when she cums.

"More of what you're offering," she repeats with an undertone of suspicion.

Her arms fold over her chest as she steps back, subconsciously letting me know that she's putting up her guard. Maybe I should have been a bit less obvious about my sexual intentions for this afternoon. Asking her to come over for a drink or something less devious might have been more appropriate, but I don't do romance.

I want Rayna to be my fuck toy; a hot body that I can entertain, pleasure and explore without worrying she'll become my love interest. It'll be hard to keep her out of my heart, but it's for the best if I do. This woman could seriously hurt me if I let my guard down. Besides, I'm no good for her.

I didn't fear falling in love with Alissa. But Rayna draws me in more than any woman I've ever met. Having secretly fantasized about her for several years, my need for her has almost overwhelmed me. I'll do almost anything to have her again. Just when I think I have her under my control, I want her to look at me exactly the way she is right now—with defiance.

"After yesterday, aren't you curious to see how far I can take you?" I ask with the same intimidating voice.

"Take me?" Now she's being obviously cynical. "And where is it you think you can take me?"

Good, I have her asking questions and not running away. Even though she seems doubtful of my ability, I know she's curious to find out how crazy things can get. I smile at her and then lick my bottom lip as my eyes intentionally scan down my favourite nightie.

"Rayna, I want to take you into my world, teach you how your body can receive pleasure in ways you haven't even thought of. Have you ever been bound and fucked?" She looks shocked but not scared. Good! "I want to do that with you today. If you're interested, text me. It's your choice completely, sweetheart."

That being said, I turn around and walk away from the fence without another word. As I make my way to the patio doors, I glance back at the fence where she remains. She's watching me with squinted eyes, as if trying to assess me. Maybe she's unsure of whether I really would tie her up. The paper I handed her is unfolded and pinched between her fingers, not crumpled up against her palm. That's a good sign.

With my hand on the door handle, I speak loud enough that she and her sister can hear. "Be more daring, Rayna. Satisfy your curiosity. You're allowed to do something for yourself once in a while."

With a crooked grin, I wink and then open the door and step inside, closing it behind me.

She'll text me. I know she will. Won't she?

Chapter Six

Rayna

My heart pounds as I watch him walk into his house and close the glass door behind him. He wants to tie me up. Why?

It's becoming more and more obvious that he's into some kinky shit. If tying me up to fuck me is the next step in this adventure, over time, how far will he take it? Will he want to beat me or hurt me for his own pleasure? I've heard of it, but I don't understand why anyone would want someone to hurt them. What pleasure can be derived from that? Then again, he spanked me once and I came very hard. Coincidence?

Do I even want to venture into the unknown? Better yet, do I have it in me to allow him to take my body however he wants? Is it even possible for someone as stubborn as me to give up control to that extreme; to become obedient?

I sit back at the table with Renee while silently reading his phone number repeatedly. She stares at me without saying a word. Am I trying to memorize his number in case I lose the paper? I don't know, but when I look up at my sister, she's grinning like an idiot. She contorts her face into the most overly dramatic expression I think she can manage without using her fingers to support it.

"What?" I ask rather harshly.

"What do you mean, *what*? Spill it, girl!" She leans toward me, putting her elbows on the table while hugging her water bottle close to her chest.

"It's his phone number. He wants to see me again," I say without trying to sound either too scared or too excited about the possibilities that lie in that statement. "So, what are your plans for the day?" I ask, needing to change the subject.

"Hmm, you're holding back. I think he said more than that. But if you would rather keep it to yourself, I totally understand. Just know that I'm pissed you feel the need to keep secrets from your one and only sister. Why won't you let me live vicariously through you?" she begs, wearing an exaggerated pouty face.

"Why? I've been living vicariously through you for years and it's not a fun place to be. Live your own life, Renee. Yours is much more interesting than mine, anyway."

"Not anymore," she huffs. "I haven't had an interesting person in my life in months. Sure, I've picked people up but as soon as I get to know them, they show their true colours and trust me, it isn't always pretty."

She leans back in her chair, looking more emotionally distraught than usual. She's always hidden her loneliness well. That must be a family trait because I can exude happiness even when I'm feeling emotionally desolate.

"Okay, what's really going on with you?" I ask.

She hesitates, then shakes her head. "Nothing you need to worry about. I'm fine. All is good. Let's talk more about your sex life."

"Bullshit, you're fine!" I accuse. "There's something going on and you need to tell me. I'm your big sister. You can tell me anything and it'll stay between us. You know that, right?"

She nods while looking down at her fidgeting hands. "I want to meet someone who is normal, or at least not fucking psychotic. Lately, I've been wanting someone to fall asleep with every night and wake up beside in the morning. I want something permanent, someone who won't fuck me over after I give them my heart. I wish I could find someone to grow old with."

"You're lonely," I tell her as if she doesn't already know.

"Yeah, I am, but I'll get over it. So, are you going to text hot-stuff next door?" she asks, suggestively waving her eyebrows at me while directing the subject away from herself, which is also a family trait.

I look down at the folded paper in my hand, trying to decide whether to continue this…this, what? Is it a relationship? Are we dating? I've never had a casual sex partner before. I've always committed to everyone I've been intimate with.

We are obviously not dating. This is just sex, right? Sex is exactly what I need, but can I separate my emotions from the physical? I've never had to. If I text him, I'll have to learn how to do exactly that. He wouldn't want to commit to me, anyway; I'm too old for him and my life is far too boring for a wild man like him.

"Probably, yes," I reply as my face flushes.

She's pleased with my response. "You need an untamed man to break you out of this lonely funk you've gotten comfortable being in ever since you kicked the asshole out."

"Tell me something and be honest," I suggest, waiting for her to agree. She nods, so I continue. "Were you really checking to see if he'd take you up on the offer to fuck you, or were you hoping to sample him for yourself?"

She looks down at her hands and confesses. "Honestly, if he would have said yes to me, I can't be sure. He's physically incredible, you have to admit that. His body is to die for and that sexy, deep voice of his vibrates my chest when he talks. I could melt under that man."

What a bitch!

"Thank you for being honest, but if I'm to be honest with you, I'm a little ticked off that you would do that to me. You're my sister. I would never do that to you."

She drops her head and swallows before nodding.

"I could ask him if he has any muscular friends who would be interested in being in a casual sexual relationship, or are you leaning more toward an emotionally committed relationship?"

I already asked him, but she need not know that.

"Um, sure you could ask him, but I'd like to have more than just a sexual thing. I don't want him to think I'm desperate for a man, so don't ask him outright. But if it comes up in conversation..." She cuts her sentence short and then shrugs.

I wonder if I should ask her about something that's been chewing at me for a long time. I'm a coward because I fear I already know the answer. Should I leave it in the past? People say that sometimes not knowing something is better than learning the painful truth, but I'm tired of carrying this question on my shoulders. Fuck it!

"Renee, can I ask you something else?"

"You just did," she replies with a chuckle. Her face falls serious when she sees that I'm not responsive.

"Did you proposition my husband?" I blurt out.

Her eyes tell me everything I need to know. For a moment, I wish I hadn't asked, but before I can stop her, she's quick to reply.

"Yes, sort of," she blurts out while tipping her face down. She slowly raises her eyes to better gauge my reaction.

I crinkle my forehead. "Sort of? What does that mean?"

I need to know everything. A painful fire burns inside my stomach and I'm not sure I can stifle it. Am I ready to hear the details? Judging by her reaction to the question, I'd better prepare myself for the worst.

"You will hate me."

I feel the heaviness of regret in her tone. I take a deep breath and let it out slowly. If she says what I think she's going to say, will I hate her for saying it? I suppose it depends on what she tells me.

With a coldness in my voice, I reply. "I could never hate you, you're my little sister. There's a chance I'll be furious, but you need to say it. I'm sure whatever you're about to tell me has been eating at your conscience for quite some time."

She swallows to prepare herself. "Shortly after you two got married, you had that party for New Year's Eve. Do you remember?" I nod, remembering it as best I can. I was very drunk that night. "Well, after everyone left and you passed out in bed, I was trying to help him clean up. I was drunk from all the tequila shots and beer chasers I had through the night."

I wear a pained expression from remembering the hangover that ensued. "We did drink a lot. It's hard to believe you were still standing when I was falling all over the place."

I smile when recalling that ridiculous moment we shared after I stumbled and slid down the wall onto my ass. I was sitting on the floor and she was helping me stand while we laughed so hard that I peed. I remember little after that. I have never been so drunk before that night, and never since. I don't care to experience that again.

"He grabbed me around my waist when I drunkenly stumbled into the kitchen and nearly fell. We were face to face. I tried to walk away, but he held me in place. I was so drunk. That's not an excuse for what happened next."

Renee shifts in her chair and looks at the patio doors to make sure the kids aren't listening. "Everything was whirling around me and I felt like I was in a dream. I thought he was trying to help me until he kissed me. I don't know why, but I kissed him back. To this day, I can't understand why I did that. We didn't stop there."

Angrily, I ask, "Did he fuck you?" I swallow hard, fearing her response.

Renee nods while tears stream down her cheeks. My mind swirls with so many images of the two of them fucking, and it turns my stomach. I can't believe she didn't tell me the very next morning after we had sobered up. I understand how things happen when you're drunk that you might regret in the morning. But she kept this a secret for far too long.

I feel so deeply betrayed by her, my sister. Betrayal by him became commonplace in our relationship. After a while, it no longer shocked me. But, not by my sister, whom I've never kept a single secret from.

"I'm so sorry," she sobs.

"I can see that you are. I am furious that you didn't tell me." I look down to see my hands shaking. "I always wondered if something happened that night because the two of you were different around each other. I suppose I should have asked. Knowing the truth at the time probably would have ruined me. But that doesn't excuse this. One more question; did you two get together again after that night, sober or not?"

She shakes her head rapidly. "No, absolutely not. I avoided him as best I could. He kept calling my phone and trying to flirt. I had to threaten him that I'd tell you everything if he didn't stop. He doubted I'd confess because of how much it would hurt you if I did. I wanted to tell you, but I didn't want you to hate me."

Sarcastically, I say, "Now your conscience is clear." I growl through gritted teeth, "He is such an asshole. I wish I had known that before I married him. Although, if we had never married, I wouldn't have my beautiful babies. If you had told me the next morning, they wouldn't be here because I would have left him."

"I'm so sorry. I know that doesn't solve anything. I should have told you, but you were so in love. I was selfish because I didn't want you to hate me. It was a stupid mistake. It only lasted a few seconds. I was so drunk that it almost seemed like a dream until he started calling me."

"I will eventually forgive you, but keep nothing this important from me again. If you even bat your eyelashes at any man I'm with, from this moment on, I will probably punch you square in the eye, hard!"

She sniffs and wipes the snot from below her nose with her napkin.

My hands aren't shaking as much, and I'm calming down. "It'll take some time for me to work through it, but you're still my sister and I love you. But you've got to give me some time."

I lean over and hug her while she bursts into a chest-heaving, blubbering mess. It should be me needing the consoling, but I expected this confession would come one day. I've already dealt with the anger, even though I wasn't positive. The worst part is, I will not cry because of what he did; I've cried from his betrayals too many times already. He isn't worth even one more spilled tear. The tears I spill will have Renee's betrayal written all over them.

I whisper, "He can be very convincing when he wants something. I swear, that man could talk an Inuit into buying a snow-cone maker."

After talking with Renee for a few hours, I think we've rebuilt our relationship, perhaps even stronger than it was before she confessed. I'm still hurt and will always harbour resentment, but maybe now we can be more like best friends than sisters. We love each other, there's no doubt about it, but now we're no longer holding anything back.

Renee left at around one o'clock with the kids. She said she would take them to the mall to catch some sales, maybe get them some new shoes. She has always loved buying them footwear. Her primary intention was to free me from my responsibility. She wants me to visit, and I quote her as saying, "the dominant fucking machine next door."

If I do, maybe he'll fuck the anger out of me, at least for a little while.

It's only quarter after one and she doesn't plan to bring them home until after dinner. I have plenty of time to visit with Coach. If I don't chicken out first, that is.

My heart thumps a little harder each time I picture his eyes staring into mine. I try to breathe slowly to ease the reminder that I'm a weak coward. After opening the folded paper, I can't help but think about how incredible his tongue felt on my pussy. It's been so long since anyone has touched me, let alone licked me. His tongue was so hot and wet, soft yet strong, gentle while still quite aggressive.

Yes, I desperately want that again.

I input his name and number into my phone, but instead of writing Coach as his name, I call him Sexy Muscleman. I type out a text with wildly shaking fingers.

Me: The kids are with my sister for a few hours. I am free. Do you still want me to visit?

He replies immediately.

Coach: Yes, I want you. Come now.

Me: I need to shower first. I'll be there in 15 minutes.

Coach: Sooner or I'll come over, drag you out of the shower and carry you over my shoulder to my house while you're still naked and dripping wet.

Me: Then you'd better stop texting me and let me get ready so the whole neighbourhood doesn't see my naked ass.

I wait, but no more messages come. I hope he isn't on his way over. The doors are locked, so his threat isn't a heavy concern. After a quick shower, I dry my hair while putting on a little make-up. I dress in a simple, light blue sundress and leave the undergarments in the drawer. I'll waste no time while waiting for him to take off my panties. Besides, I'd rather him not destroy another pair.

I slip my feet into my flip-flops and quickly make my way over to his house. For a moment, I debate whether to push his doorbell but decide to check first to see if he left it unlocked. He did. I push it open and walk in.

"Hello?" I call out.

"Up here," Coach yells.

I look toward where the voice came from. As I walk through his immaculately clean home, I notice he doesn't have any family pictures on the walls, only artistic paintings and drawings. I'm no expert, but they are impressive.

"Are you coming?" he asks loud enough for me to hear him from in the living room.

I follow a strange sound but can't figure out what it is, even as I get closer to the room. When I step through the doorway, I realize this must be his bedroom. I suddenly feel awkward.

The noises I was hearing were metal on metal. The buckles twang on the metal as he secures the leather-wrapped hand and ankle cuffs to the steel posts on each corner of his king-sized bed. The wall behind the headboard is jet-black but the other three are a soft creamy off-white. The bed dons a silky black fitted sheet but nothing else. A pile of bedding in the corner suggests he removed the other blankets and comforter, along with all the pillows.

His dressers look solid and heavy. The grain on the wood is not like anything I'm familiar with.

"What type of wood are your dressers made from?"

He looks at me oddly, as if wondering why I'm not questioning him about the situation he's about to put me in. He then glances at the dresser behind him before casting his eyes back to me. "It's Teak."

"Oh, I like it," I tell him as I stroke the top of the shorter dresser beside me.

I'm so nervous that it feels like I'm about to be de-virgin'd. I can't stop biting my bottom lip or cracking my knuckles. I don't know where to look or stand, and I don't know where to put my hands. My nerves are getting the better of me and I'm shaking, doubting I should be here at all. I have to remember to breathe.

Coach is wearing a pair of loose black shorts without a shirt. He's barefoot but has nicely manicured toenails, unlike most men. They typically have horrible, unmaintained feet and that turns me off.

"Do you need a drink, or can I get you to take your clothes off straight away? I want to watch you."

"I don't need a drink," I say, immediately doubting the legitimacy of my answer. A drink would help to calm me, but by the time it kicks in, we will have already started, and I likely will be too occupied to be nervous anymore.

"Would you like some help or do you know how to get naked all on your own?" he asks in his deep, seductive voice.

He leans his ass on the footboard of the bed, arms crossed over his chest, ankles crossed over one another, waiting impatiently for me to remove my dress so he can observe me—whatever that means.

"Why are you staring at me? It makes me uncomfortable," I whisper innocently, hoping he'll look away or something, but he doesn't.

"Are you ashamed of your body, Rayna? I sure hope not. You are beautiful, sexy, and I get hard from watching you." He licks his lips. "So please entertain me."

"I'm not twenty-one anymore," I say before giving in to his request and reluctantly pull my dress up and over my head, revealing my complete nudity.

His focus is on my eyes, not my body.

"I don't want twenty-one. Besides, you'd put most twenty-one-year-old little twats to shame. You are absolutely beautiful."

His eyes glide over my body, admiring every inch of my skin. My heart pounds quickly in my chest and I wonder if he can hear it as loudly as I can. I stand perfectly still, pretending I'm not being ogled by a man in his physical prime, while I'm aged, imperfect, and vulnerable.

"Turn around and bend over. Grab your ankles."

"What?" I ask, crossing my arms over my breasts as though I'm suddenly desperate to hide my nudity. I have never bent over and grabbed my ankles for anyone. Does he plan to just stand there and watch me?

"Put your arms down," he whispers assertively.

I keep them clenched. His eyes appear to soften, revealing a kinder side of him that rarely reveals. They remain focussed on mine and ease my anxiety.

"Come on, you can do it. Remember that you are beautiful to me. Now, drop your arms, turn around, and show me your ass. Entertain me, Rayna."

I slowly drop my arms down to my sides. I continue to look at him as he watches my face. He's patiently waiting to see what I will decide to do. It's my choice to play along or simply refuse. I can decide to be more sexually daring than I have ever been in my life by doing as he has requested.

Life is short, as the saying goes. I turn around, bending as far forward as I can before the back of my legs strain.

He speaks slowly and sensually. "You are so sexy."

I'd swear I can feel his gaze burning into my vagina. There's a sexual side to me that he seems to awaken so easily, like I'm under his spell.

"Stand up and turn around. Look at me with those gorgeous eyes of yours."

I do as he says, happy to feel less exposed.

Coach comes to his feet, rushing toward me with eyes that seem to read into my soul. He wraps one arm around the small of my back, hocking me against him. His other hand cradles the back of my head, holding me still while his brown eyes scan my face as if he's burning each feature to memory.

His mouth suddenly comes down on mine with so much passion he takes my breath away. My legs weaken, so I wrap my arms around his thick chest and hang on. I like how his calming words gave me positive strength, but I need the roughness of his body inside of me to pleasure me beyond my imagination.

He slowly drops to one knee, kissing and painfully nipping at my nipples before continuing further down until his fat tongue slips between my folds, finding my hidden gem, and then my eager wetness. I open my legs slightly, enough for him to get his face in a better position to lick my stiffening clit.

When I cast my eyes downward, I'm surprised to see that he's looking back. Our eyes meet and hold one another's gaze as his mouth tastes me. I moan when he sucks my clit between his teeth, holding it in place so he can flick his tongue over the most tender part of it.

My hands grab his head to keep it in place, as well as to help with my balance. My eyes close, and the world slowly spins around us.

If he continues, I will cum soon. My breath is heavy and erratic; my pussy twitches involuntarily. He must know I'm getting close. He is relentless, licking and sucking so perfectly that I'm nearly there in only a few moments.

"Oh, yeah! Don't stop!" I insist.

He continues working his magic, not altering the sensational rhythm of his licking and sucking. His mouth is ever so perfectly loving my pussy. The tension in my belly builds quickly.

I'm coming already.

Oh, fuck! My tummy muscles tighten, pulling my upper body forward. I'm still gripping his head, forcing it against my pulsing, fiery pussy. I jerk, gasp, and cry out. His tongue is still slurping until the hypersensitivity forces me to push his head away from my shuddering body.

Coach rises quickly, sucking my right nipple into his mouth, biting hard enough to make me yelp. He presses his mouth to mine, and I can taste myself on his lips and tongue. He explores my mouth, and all I can think is this beautiful tongue is my favourite muscle on his body.

His hands scoop my ass, lifting me off my feet. I wrap my legs around his firm waist and hang on tightly. My hands hold his head once again. My heart continues to pound wildly in my chest, having not yet escaped its confines despite its efforts.

Coach grips my waist, tearing me away from him and dropping me onto my back on the bed. He grabs my left ankle before I have even stopped bouncing. As he walks around the bed with my ankle in his grip, I laugh at how easily he can manipulate my body.

He rolls me onto my belly and pulls me so he can secure that ankle in a cuff. He doesn't waste any time fastening me down, spread wide like a starfish, face down, arms and legs tied to each corner post on the bedframe.

Fear of the unknown has me questioning my choices.

I'm so much more vulnerable than I was when I was simply bent over, grabbing my ankles. If he wants to hurt me, he could, easily. It's not like I can fight back in this position.

When I turn my head to see what he's doing, his shorts are sliding down his legs and dropping to the ground, revealing a very hard, fat prick.

I'm fearful of the unknown, but I desperately want him to fuck me like he did yesterday.

Chapter Seven

Coach

Fuck, she's so perfect. The sight of her spectacular ass takes my breath away. I want to fuck it today, that's why I want her in this position. For her, it'll be the most comfortable when I slide my dick inside her tight little rosebud. If she'll let me, that is.

My cock twitches at the thought of entering her backside. I really hope that isn't off-limits. If it is, I'll respect her wishes, but it will disappoint me.

She looks like she's getting more nervous than I'd like her to be, but watching her squirm against her bindings turns me on. Time to occupy her thoughts before she insists I set her free.

I step onto the mattress beside her and look down at the glorious creature with skin smooth as butter. She turns her head toward me, but the draping of hair conceals her expressive eyes.

I gently drop with my knees above her head and gather her hair in my palm. She's breathing heavily, nervously awaiting the unknown. She pulls her extremities to test their confinement in case she should want to escape. Using her gathered hair, I deliberately lift her head until she can see my face.

In a voice as composed as my excitement will allow, I tell her, "Red is the safe word. Use it if it gets too intense for you. If you can't speak, wave your hands and feet, and I will stop immediately. Do you understand?"

She nods. Her wide, inquisitive eyes have me wanting to kiss her to ease her worry. I don't want her to be afraid.

"It'll be okay. You'll like this, I promise." I smile to reassure her. "Verbally tell me that you understand using Red sets you free."

"I understand," she tells me, her voice quivering. She's nervous now, but won't be once I get started.

"Very good." I brush my hand down her cheek and cup her chin. "You will suck my cock now."

"Okay," she quickly replies, giving me permission.

I hadn't expected her to agree so easily. It's almost disappointing. I was hoping she'd put up a bit of an argument like she did when I asked her to say cunt and thank you. I wonder if she knows that I wasn't asking her to suck my cock; I was telling her what I was about to do. She has the option to say no, but I'm thrilled that she's copacetic about sucking my cock. I would never force Rayna to do anything she didn't want me to do. Talk her into it, yes, but I'd never force her.

"Open that pretty mouth as wide as you can. Let me see down your throat," I say, and then watch her do as I command.

She's eager to suck my cock. I rest only the tip between her lips. She tries to take more, but with her limited movement, she's forced to have patience. Is this a tease for her? Does she enjoy taking men in her mouth?

I want to jam my cock all the way down her throat, purposely, to watch her gag on it. To me, watching a beautiful woman choke on my cock while tears roll down her cheeks is fucking amazing, especially if she gets horny doing it. I've been dreaming of doing this exact thing for what seems like a lifetime; three years is a long time to hold a fantasy.

Now it's happening, and I have to maintain control. I take a deep breath to compose myself. She isn't used to hard sex, not that I know of, anyway. I doubt she's done anything nearly as rough as I am used to.

It's a struggle to stay in control; to harness my barbarous self. Terrifying Rayna isn't my goal. If I'm not careful, I could easily scare her away. However, not ramming her face against my belly while burying my prick into her throat until her body wretches, for me, is a hard lesson in self-control.

She looks up at me with the head of my prick between her straight, white teeth. She threatens to bite my cock, but her smile proves she never would. I pull my prick back and stroke it several times while I watch her study my hand movements.

With conviction, she asks, "Are you going to jerk off on my face or fuck my throat?"

What the fuck?

Is Rayna secretly a wild woman? Or is she acting the part to impress me? We will get along great!

"Oh, I'm going to fuck your throat."

I push my prick into her mouth so far that it's near the back of her throat. I hold still while watching her to see if she's going to protest. She's looking at my abdominal muscles, in particular, the V pointing toward my prick.

She hasn't gagged. Damn! Should I push further in, perhaps test the depth?

I pull out completely and wait for her eyes to meet mine again. When they do, I smile at her with wicked intention, letting her know that I'm pleased, but to prepare for more. She returns my grin and then opens her mouth wide, inviting me in while waving her eyebrows.

I slide in; all the way in. She holds true. I hold still and wait for her to gag. I'll stay like this until I think she needs air or she gags, whichever comes first. Nothing happens after five full seconds. I pull back a bit while she takes a few breaths from around the head of my cock, and then I push back in. This time, I don't hold still. I fuck her face, slow and steady, allowing her to breathe between penetrations.

What an incredible sight; my cock fucking deep into Rayna's throat. I've dreamed of this moment too many times. Am I dreaming now?

Holy shit, she is so fucking hot! If I keep fucking her mouth, I'm going to cum. All the times I've jerked off to the thought of doing this to Rayna are flooding back.

Instead of risking coming too soon, I pull out and lift my cock, pushing my balls against her lips. She sucks one into her mouth, gently pulling at it.

I can't hold back the loud moan that rewards her efforts. Fuck, this feels so good!

She releases that testicle, taking the other. Another moan escapes me. I have to stop. She's too good at this.

I want to own Rayna's body.

"Have you ever had a spanking that made your ass red hot?" She shakes her head after spitting out my testicle. "You're getting one today."

When I release my grip on her hair, she turns her head to the side, her cheek coming to rest on the silky sheet. Her eyes are wide and anxious, and she bites her bottom lip.

I step off the bed and pick up the firmest pillow from the pile of bedding in the corner. After sliding my left arm under her pelvis, I lift, allowing enough room to slip the pillow beneath. Her heart-shaped ass rests higher than her chest, giving me one hell of a view. I can't wait to fuck her, but I must stay in control of my needs.

My palm slaps on her right ass cheek with a crack, not hard, but she jolts, and an odd-sounding squeal fills the room. She holds her breath, waiting for the next hand-to-ass contact. I tease her by waiting until she exhales before slapping her left buttock. That cute yip doesn't fill the room this time and I find myself rather disappointed.

Between slaps, I delicately caress her reddening cheeks, occasionally pressing my lips to her heated flesh.

There's a fine line between pushing her limits and crossing them. I want her to realize that pain can be sexually stimulating.

She's panting and crying out with each slap. *Enough!* I pull her cheeks apart and dive in to tongue her asshole. I lap at it feverishly.

An exasperated groan escapes her, as if deflating every morsel of tension she's held onto for far too many years. I repeatedly let my mouth ride down her slippery slit, from asshole to clit and back, paying special attention to her swollen, stiff button.

I soak my finger with saliva and cautiously insert the tip on my middle finger into her ass, holding steady while I lap at her clit. Her body tenses, but she doesn't ask me to stop. I continue to slurp at her labia, hoping to distract her attention from the invasion. She quickly relaxes. I push deeper, inch by inch. I gingerly pull and twist to stretch her tiny hole until she can tolerate another spit-soaked finger. The gentle assault continues until my digits glide easily.

I'm not used to being this tender with a submissive, but Rayna is different. She isn't a submissive, she's more than merely a plaything I keep around to occupy my time and entertain my body. I want to please her so much more than I need to be pleasured by her.

My hands roam over her back, gliding down to feel the curve of her waist and the arch at the small of her back. She's a fucking goddess.

I kneel between her spread thighs and roll a condom over my cock before shoving it deep into her slippery pussy. She cries out and pushes back against me, eager to take me deeper.

My fingers find her asshole and glide in easily. She moans and bucks despite her restraints.

My pelvis presses forward, forcing my fingers deeper into her ass. She groans sharply. I don't hesitate for even a second. I pound into her, while my digits fuck her ass with the same rapid tempo. I pause only to pour some lube over my fingers. She doesn't even notice the third digit I slip into her ass.

"Yes, fuck me!" she yells as her arms pull forcefully at the restraints. Her legs battle just as ferociously.

I pull my fingers free, quickly punch my fists onto the bed on either side of her chest and lean forward to balance my weight. I fuck her sloppy wet pussy, slamming my hips against her rippling ass with so much force that her hips sink into the pillow. She springs up when I pull back, but I'm already coming back down on her.

The second time she cums, I quickly pull out of her. I can't get too carried away and cum too. Not yet! It takes me several breaths to regain enough control of my senses to speak.

"Has anyone fucked your ass before?" I ask her as I dribble lubricant on her pre-stretched hole.

She lifts her head, her voice soft and meek. "I've done it to myself but never with anyone." She pants, "I'm nervous."

Normally, those words wouldn't concern me, but with her, they do. I lean forward, pressing my body over her like a giant blanket, trying not to put too much weight on her. I must weigh twice what she does. I lovingly kiss her shoulder twice and wonder what the fuck I'm doing. I never show my gentler side.

"Would you rather I not?" I whisper behind her ear, knowing the heat of my breath will raise tiny bumps on her skin.

"Um," she hesitates. I feel her relax when I brush her hair off her neck and kiss the tender skin, ever so softly. "I want to try, but please be gentle."

"If it's too much, use the safe word. I'll go slowly at first, I promise. You will feel very full, like you have to take a shit. Sorry, there's not a more pleasant way to describe it. Try to relax and let your body accept me. If you want me to hold still, say 'still.' I won't move until you're ready."

"Okay, let's do this," she whispers.

My lips press to her neck once more.

I remain leaning over her, hoping she'll feel more at ease. Using great caution, I push the head of my prick in. I'm doing my best to relax my cock so that it isn't as thick as it usually is when I'm extremely aroused; like when I remember I'm with Rayna.

She tightens up and holds her breath, but says nothing. She's too tense to continue and likely too stubborn to tell me to stop, so I hold still.

"Breathe slowly," I whisper behind her ear. "Remember your safeword."

To occupy her thoughts, I continue tasting her neck with tender kisses. It isn't more than a few seconds before she relaxes. She nods, so I push forward, pausing when her muscles flex. Soon, every inch of my cock is buried into her backside.

With one arm slid under her upper chest, and the other hand weaved into her hair, I lift her head so I can kiss her parted lips.

She is so fucking luscious!

Our mouths mesh while the rest of our bodies wave against one another. I'm impressed she hasn't asked me to stop, or at the very least slow down. Instead, she's rocking her hips to meet my steady movements.

When I let her head rest back on the bed, I lift myself until I am up on my knees, looking down at my cock gliding in and out of Rayna's ass. The site is enough to make me want to let loose and ram her hard. I have to close my eyes for a moment to distance myself and regain my composure.

"Fuck, you're so beautiful!" I mumble as I caress my hands down her glistening, tanned skin as it catches the light just right, revealing the muscles on her arms and back.

Soft moans slip from her depths, ringing sweetly through my ears. She's enjoying this; I'm so pleased. My hips bump against her butt in a steady rhythm; it's hypnotic.

She's fucking back on me, welcoming me into the taboo.

God damn, she feels fucking amazing!

Get it together, otherwise, you'll cum before her and ruin it!

Beautiful Rayna...

I want her to cum a hundred times tonight.

"Coach, please rub my clit," she begs.

Using my free hand, I reach under her right thigh and slide my middle finger over her incredibly swollen, stiff clit. I dip my finger into her pussy to make it slick before caressing small circles over the bundle of highly sensitive nerves.

I slide my other arm up her chest, beneath her, resting my weight on my elbow, and then wrap my hand around her neck. My grip is firm, but I'm not applying enough pressure to restrict her breathing or blood flow.

She moans each time my cock glides in, breathing in as I pull back. My lips press behind her ear with the most tender pecks. I let my panting breath heat her skin.

"Oh, God... Yes!" she cries out.

Rayna's high-pitched whimpers grow louder with every exhale. Suddenly, she shrieks and falls silent, her arms and legs pull forcefully against her bindings as her body fights to fold in on itself.

Her hot cum drains from her spastic pussy, coating my fingers as they continue to roll circles over her very swollen, twitching clit. My cock is being strangled by the muscles inside her body.

That's it; I'm done!

My pace increases, as if my body has its own agenda. Five more thrusts and I'm holding steadfast. It's my body's turn to stiffen; frozen in the euphoria of a perfect orgasm.

My abs clench as I dump my seed into the condom.

Gradually, as if deflating, my weight presses down onto her. My lungs ache and burn, begging for me to breathe. A deep bellow rips from deep in my chest, followed by quick breaths in rapid succession. I'm dizzy. I can't recall the last time I'd cum that hard.

What the fuck is this chick doing to me?

"You're killing me, woman," I whisper as my prick slithers out of her ass. I gather my strength to lift my heavy chest off of her back.

Her cheek is flushed bright red, but it's her relaxed smile that captivates me. Her eyes are closed, so I carefully pick the scattered tresses of hair from her cheek and wait for her to open them.

She whispers under her breath, "Wow."

I remove the condom and toss it into the trash before freeing her wrists and ankles from the cuffs. I kiss and quickly massage each one. She doesn't move, remaining in the same position as if she's too exhausted to lift herself. I slide onto the bed on my back and pull her over until her head is resting on my bicep, her arm lying over my chest.

My gaze falls on her glistening face and I'm lost in the thought of what life would be like to wake next to this woman every morning. Could I love her enough to want to commit to her; to belong only to her? Could I ever be respectable enough for this remarkable woman?

I shake the thought clear, telling myself that it's simply an infatuation with my new human toy that's putting those thoughts in my head. I'm sure I'll tire of her soon and send her on her way, as she will do with me. She'll quickly realize how sick my inner demon can be when I finally set him free. Besides, she has a lot on her plate and I'm not sure I'm man enough to deal. The kids are pretty cool, but her ex-husband is a fucking dick.

Rayna pulls away from me. She gets off the bed and makes her way to the en suite bathroom, closing the door behind her without a word. I immediately hear water run and then the shower door close. I weave my fingers together behind my head and take a deep breath, releasing it slowly. I'll give her a few minutes before joini

Chapter Eight

Rayna

A smile grows on my face as the super-heated water rushes over my head. I just had a man's cock in my ass for the first time and I loved it!

My entire adult life and I've been too afraid to let someone touch my asshole, let alone stick their fingers and cock into it. I can't remember a time when I ever came that hard. I am utterly exhausted but feel amazing, kind of like I could run a marathon, even on my cooked spaghetti noodle legs.

Coach's hands slide around my waist, startling me. I didn't even hear him come into the bathroom. He guides me back against his chest, kissing my neck only. He exhales loudly before setting me free. I turn and look up at his handsome face. He looks down his nose at me. Even after what he just did, as gentle as he was, he still intimidates the hell out of me.

"Hi," I say, and then burst into a silly schoolgirl giggle, only stopping when I bite my lip.

"Hi," he replies. A sultry smile creeps on his face as he watches me acting oddly. "So, you enjoyed having anal sex with a real cock?"

Realizing that he will not be coy about what just happened, I decide not to play shy with him either. I nod a lot; too much.

"Yeah, so it would seem. If I had known that a long time ago, I would have done it a lot over the years."

"Can I ask you something?"

"Yes, of course," I reply.

He pulls several strands of hair off my face, tucking them behind my ear. "When was the last time you had sex, any sex, before me?"

"Honestly, I don't know. Aside from occasional masturbation, my best guess would be about six months before I kicked the asshole out of the house for the last time."

"So, the sex would have been with your husband, I assume?"

"Yes." I grimace.

My fingers glide along the muscles lining the center of his abs. His hands continue to pull wet hairs from my cheek.

"What was he like sexually?"

"Sexually?" I consider how to answer. "He wasn't anything like you, that's for sure. I mean, he was okay, but I rarely reached orgasm. I faked it a lot so he wouldn't pout. If he had gone down on me for over five minutes, I may have cum more often than I did. He was always in a rush to fuck me."

He smiles and shrugs. "I can't say I blame him. Fucking you is a pleasure. But you taste damn good. I'd be happy to lick you stem to stern for an hour if that's what it took to make you scream your way through an earth-shattering orgasm."

He waves his eyebrows. Coach's hand cups the back of my head, and his lips press to mine. Our tongues dance the tango as the water pours over our faces, rinsing away our sweat.

After we're clean, he steps out, gathering two towels from the closet. He tosses one on the floor just outside of the shower and then takes my hand, helping me step out. I try to grab the towel from him, but he refuses to hand it to me. Instead, he dries my body from top to bottom. When my toes are dry, he gets to his feet, flips the towel over my head and lets it flop around my neck to catch the water dripping from my wet hair.

I'd be wise to keep my heart and romantic ideals to myself. I should think of our visits as learning experiences only. We are not in a committed relationship!

He's not the type of man a single mother should give her heart to. He'll grow bored of me in no time, realizing that he craves the indecency of a sexually uninhibited woman. I am not her. I'm reserved, sexually uneducated, and painfully inexperienced. He'll quickly tire of my innocence.

He goes back to the closet to retrieve another towel to dry himself. I stay where I stand, eyeing every inch of his body as the towel skims along his muscles. He looks so strong. His thighs are thick and powerful. Perhaps one day, he'll let me measure them.

Coach hangs his towel on the back of the door and then turns toward me, placing his hands on his hips. He quietly stands in front of me, looking at me with a lost-in-thought, flat expression.

"Are you okay?" I ask, unsure of what's happening.

He smiles, "Yeah, I'm great! I'm contemplating what I should dare to do to you now."

I smile and shake my head in disbelief. "Are you kidding? I'm exhausted. How can you possibly still be horny?"

"Sweetheart, I'm perpetually horny. Even when my dick is soft, it'll only take a few seconds to be hard; if I think about sex, that is." He snickers and crosses his arms over his chest, making himself look even bigger. "I love sex. I thoroughly enjoy everything about it. The thought of exploring a woman's body is an incredible stimulant for me. And girl, your body has a lot of hidden secrets I want to uncover."

"So, what do you have in mind?" My face flushes, wondering what crazy position he'd like to put me in and if he plans to fuck my asshole again. Not that I'd mind.

His smile reveals his filthy thoughts. "My intentions? If you must know, my intention is to try something new with you every day until I know your body like the back of my hand. I'll learn all of your triggers so that I can fire you off with only a few touches. That's my goal, if it pleases you, Madam."

"Madam?" I crinkle my nose. "That makes me sound old, and I don't need reminding of that when I'm with you."

"Okay, I won't call you Madam."

"Why do you want to do this with me?" I ask, suddenly feeling self-conscious. "I need to know what you see in me. I'm so much older than you, and I'm not perfect. I have scars that only motherhood provides. So, what is it?"

Coach steps toward me, his eyes locked on mine. Strong in his conviction, he tells me, "I like you."

"Yeah, I can tell," I say, gesturing toward his stiffening prick.

He shrugs innocently as if his cock has a mind of its own.

My arms wave as I speak. "But why me? I mean, Carrie across the street is hot, and Lana two doors down is a long-distance runner so her body is strong. I just... I don't understand why you're with me and not them? Am I a joke or a pity fuck? Is that what it's called? I don't even know. See! I'm not up to date with the new terminology."

"No, never!"

Coach scoops me up by my ass. I squeal and wrap my arms around his head. He leans back so my chest presses to his. My feet lock together behind his back. He doesn't look away from my eyes for even a second as he carries me back to the bedroom. He lifts one leg to kneel on the bed and then lays me down, our bodies never separating.

As his lips press to mine, they open slightly to take my tongue into his mouth. His warm hand cradles my cheek and the other slips between my thighs. With his softest touch yet, his finger slips between my folds, tenderly stroking my clit up and down in a slow, rhythmic motion.

How does this man have so much knowledge about how a woman's body works? I wonder who taught him where to touch; how hard, how soft, when to do what, and when not to. He must have been an exemplary student because he has it down to a science.

I feel my clit stiffen under his expertise. His fingers slide effortlessly inside of me and a soft moan rides my exhale. I tighten my legs, pulling him into me. His fingers push deeper and fuck me faster while his palm presses down on my aching clit.

His heated breath caresses my neck, sending a powerful shudder throughout me, raising tiny bumps all over my flesh. He lifts himself onto his elbow so he can better study my face.

My only thoughts are of how much my body wants him; right now, and every single minute to follow. I've never had a lover this focused on granting me so much attention. He truly enjoys giving me pleasure, and that's something I've never known. Nobody has ever made sex all about me and my satisfaction.

My inner self screams at me to guard my heart.

To prevent my heart from wanting to feel for him, I close my eyes. If I can't see him, I can concentrate on how this delicious man is owning my body with incredible ease and not on how much I've missed the emotional closeness intimacy creates. What will sex be like when he knows my body's secrets, as he claims to be his goal? I'll be putty in his hands. Then again, I already am.

Leaving his fingers inside me, Coach slowly slides down my body, kissing and nipping at my tender flesh. In my thoughts, I beg him to lick my pussy. He takes extra time kissing above my clitoris, forcing me to lift my pelvis to trick him into slipping his fiery tongue over the most sensitive part on my body. That desperate bundle of nerves rules my every thought at this very moment. I yearn for his talented tongue.

The second his open mouth surrounds my clitoris, his delicious tongue presses flat. My arms spread wide across the bed, hands clutching the sheet to hold on as if I'm about to float off this mattress. I'm light as a feather, ready to blow away if he exhales too forcefully. The last thing I want is for the bond between his mouth and my eager body to sever, so I hold, unrelentingly.

Coach laps against my clit from the base and up over the tip, with quick repetition.

Oh, fuck!

I'm so close to losing control and completely giving myself, body and soul, to him to manipulate however he desires. I'll even risk him crushing my heart into a million pieces. I am his puppet. I am putty in his hands, permitting him to use me in ways I've never even dreamed of.

My head whips side to side in an ill-fated attempt to keep my mind clear, but I fail, and the delirium of orgasmic fog sweeps over me like the calm before the storm. I'm stuck at the peak of my climax.

An erotic scream fills the room. I'm sure it came from me, but it sounds so distant that I can't be sure. Blackness, like the darkest of night, envelops me. I hear nothing but the sound of my heart's vicious pounding until suddenly, nothing.

Ecstasy. Euphoria. Perfection.

Air rushes to my lungs as my consciousness revives, awakening a flood of racing thoughts. My lungs burn and my throat is as parched from voicing my approval.

He's going to make me love him.

My hands grasp his hair, holding his face to my twitching clit as the second wave of exhilaration tears through me, igniting every nerve in my body. Every muscle locks in a tight flex, and it's unrelenting.

My climax all too quickly rides to a close. His mouth lifts off my painfully sensitive clit, but his fingers continue exploring my pussy. He hasn't yet finished toying with me. He inserts another finger, waving and spinning his hand.

Oh, yes! Do what you will.

I am putty in his hands to mould however he desires me to be. He fills me more and more. My back arches, lifting my hips to take all he's offering, and quickly dropping to the sweat-soaked bed sheet.

I cannot get enough.

The stretch is exquisite. I want more; need more. My body opens itself up to devour him. I've lost all inhibition.

The pressure is immense, so much so that I fear he might split me in two. But I want him to do exactly that and worse; to shatter me into a million pieces, body and mind. I need my heart to feel again, to feel something, if even for a moment.

I'm jolted back to complete clarity. It feels like his entire body just popped into me. I screech, then instantly freeze. Pain and pleasure; both are overwhelming. Not a single muscle moves other than my pounding heart, which is desperate to burst from my chest. Tears seep from the outer corners of my eyes.

What the *fuck* just happened?

"Slow your breathing, Rayna," he whispers, with his face near to mine.

"It hurts, but..." My words fail me but my tears no longer flow.

My fingernails have dug into his shoulders, and he doesn't seem to care. He's so calm. Fuck, he's handsome! I'm baffled why this man desires me.

"Is the pain easing?" The deepness of his voice and the sedate manner in which he speaks has me eager to hear more.

"The female body is designed for childbirth. You will accommodate my fist if you can relax and slow your breathing," he explains with surety.

Fist? *What?*

With monumental effort not to freak out, I take several slow breaths to help ease my anxious muscles from their tensed state. I begin by pulling my nails from his flesh and dropping my hands back to the sheet beneath me. I take another calming deep breath, blowing it out as slowly as I can all while my eyes remain focused on his caring, brown eyes. My heart steadily pounds like a drum.

"Your whole fist is inside me?" I ask in disbelief.

He nods, wearing a tranquil smile. "Everything about you is beautiful, Rayna."

His free hand slides under my head, lifting enough that he can easily kiss my lips. The tenderness in his kiss is out of character for the badass lover I know him to be.

His buried hand spins gradually. I whimper against his lips. A strange sensation of coolness radiates from his fist outward. My thoughts fall away from our kiss. I break our connection as my head flops to the right.

I reach up, gripping a muscle on his back. My other hand strokes the powerful arm with the gingerly moving fist. This is becoming overwhelmingly magnificent.

This fullness is unconscionable. It fucking hurts, but brilliantly.

Coach cautiously moves his hand. From the deepest depths of my being, a phenomenal orgasm builds. If the world erupted into a molten lava hell around me, I wouldn't care as long as he continues doing exactly what he's doing.

I am calmly bursting at the seams, mute while screaming inside my mind without a hint of an audible sound. The fire within me rages while my very being remains motionless, wishing I could buck against the one thing that fills it so immensely.

My pussy spasms once, twice, three times.

A meek whisper has the effort of a thunderous scream. "Oh my God!"

My entire essence is floating. I've lost myself in a place that is blank, absent of everything except euphoria. I can't think or speak, nor move under my own power. My pelvis remains tilted upward, allowing his hand to invade me.

The room spins, darkening evermore. I think I'm dying and I'm grateful for the release.

He slides his hand out of me, and it's followed by a flood. I want to stay right here in this intoxicating moment. Nothing matters. Here. Now. Him. Me. Us.

My cheek stings, snapping the world into focus. I gasp. "You hit me!"

He snickers. "Rayna, you were blacking out, and I didn't hit you hard. Your senses are heightened."

I've never felt this relaxed in my entire life. My body feels like it weighs a ton. I can't even lift my arms off the bed. My legs have fallen open in a very unladylike manner, but I don't have the strength to regain some of my lost dignity. Judging by the sopping wet sheets beneath me, I think it's too late for that, anyway.

"How was that?" he teases with a smug grin.

"I never thought I could stretch." I take a breath. "How did you do that? I've never..." Inhale. "I mean, the kids were cesarean sections, so I've never been that open." Breathe. "Oh my God! How?"

Matter-of-fact, he says, "Constant pressure and patience."

"You must do this a lot. I mean, you're very good at," I listlessly wave my hand over my vagina, "at, you know...*that*."

With calm assurance, he replies, "I don't do it with everyone, but it's one of my favourite ways to bring a woman to a state of pure ecstasy. I love watching their faces when they slip away from reality and drown in their physical selves. Bringing a woman there is like a tremendous stroke to my ego, I suppose."

"Well, bravo." I clap with very little enthusiasm. "I'm so damn tired," I confess while shifting to snuggle up against him and burying my face on his warm neck.

He wraps his thick arm around my back, pulling me tighter against him. I feel safe, warm and much more comfortable with myself than I have been in a very long time. My emotions well up in my throat and despite my effort to hold back the tears, I fail and they spill.

Coach's arm holds me tighter still, without judgement, comforting me in my moment of weakness as though he were expecting this to happen. I sob for several minutes until I finally regain my composure.

"I'm sorry. I don't know why..." My words don't come.

"It's the adrenaline. No need to apologize. Just let it out."

His voice is deep but whispered with compassion. Even the vibration in his chest seems to comfort me.

The tears quickly ebb, followed by a deep yawn. I'm so sleepy.

Coach releases some tension from his hug so he can better look at my face. With a delicate touch that doesn't suit his dangerous exterior, he caresses away my tears. His eyes look into mine, failing to suppress a heartfelt emotion that a playboy like him should rarely allow. He's revealing a frailty that I hadn't expected from him.

As if he suddenly snaps out of a fog, he clears his throat while quickly sitting up. He picks up my towel from the floor to wipe the sweat from his forehead and chest. He then lays it over me, patting my covered tummy before making his way to the bathroom and closing the door without another word to me.

~

Coach

There she is, asleep on my bed in the same position she was in when I left to shower and regain control over my emotions. Christ, she's even more beautiful when she's asleep.

This incredible creature has me feeling things I'd convinced myself no longer existed. Over the years, I've fought so hard to suppress heartfelt emotions toward women. But here she is, unbeknownst to her, waking my heart from its cold, dark grave. I want her with me every day and all the time. I need to touch her, kiss her, hear her soft but stern voice, and drown in her orgasmic screams.

I bite down, close my eyes, and clench my fists. My inner demon is screaming at me.

Shake it off, Simon Brenton! Smarten the fuck up! She's just a broad, like any other. Rayna will not want you in her life forever. Get it together, dammit!

"Rayna," I bark.

She jolts awake, sitting up immediately, looking surprised and then embarrassed.

Goddamn, she's so fucking pretty. She winces when she shifts herself to the edge of the bed. Strangely, I feel sorry because it was my selfish doing that caused her to have this much discomfort.

She smiles apologetically, putting her hand out to accept the glass of water I hand her. She gulps some before giving it back to me. Her eyes never meet mine.

"Thank you," she says. Her sweet voice caresses my ears as well as my resistant heart. "I didn't mean to fall asleep. I should get going."

She stands, grimacing once again, and covering her breasts behind crossed arms. Her unnecessary self-consciousness reveals itself yet again.

I watch her sensuous body glide over to the small heap of clothing on the floor. She squats and shakes her dress as she picks it up, turning it this way and that until she finds the opening at the bottom. She pulls it over her head. Her small hands smooth it over her body while she looks down.

I'm overwhelmed with a flash of sadness, desperately wanting to grab her and rip that dress from her flesh. Now she's hidden from me, and no longer mine. Once again, she's my neighbour, Rayna, fully and completely.

Her eyes glance up. I nod, understanding that she doesn't belong to me. I must keep her at a distance. This woman is too much for me to handle. I'd probably beat her ex-husband to death if he came to pick up the kids, saying something vicious enough to stab at her confidence for the mere enjoyment of hurting her. He's like that.

I don't want her to leave without making her feel at ease and that we are still friends who can chat outside of sex.

"That guy I was telling you about said he'd be interested in meeting your sister. Text me her number when you get home and I'll forward it to him."

"That was quick," she says.

Another painful silence falls between us and lingers for a bit too long, making the situation seem unbearable once again.

"I have to get to the gym. I have a client coming soon."

Okay, that sounded like a bullshit line to get her out of here. I am; I don't have anyone scheduled until seven o'clock tonight, but I need to get away from her before she weakens me further. I can't shake the dreaded fear that if my heart opens for her, something bad will happen, possibly destroying both of us.

"Um, yeah, okay," she murmurs, nervously tucking her hair behind her ear. Her eyes have yet to meet mine.

As she tries to pass me, I put my arm up, preventing her from walking out of my life. I lean down and steal a kiss before dropping my arm, allowing her to continue on her way.

I stand, frozen in place, listening to her footsteps fade as she makes the distance between us seem vast.

Why do I suddenly feel so alone?

Christ, Coach, get your shit together!

Chapter Nine

Rayna

I've been soaking in a hot bath since I came home. Why was Coach so distant with me before I left? He did his best to make small talk, but it felt awkward. We went from being so connected to what felt like strangers in only a few minutes. Was he upset that I fell asleep in his bed? I can't see any other reason for his sudden frigidness.

Renee returns with Ken and Kim. The house goes from being so silent I could hear the distant sounds of laughter as people walk past my house to being as loud as a schoolyard playground seconds after the recess bell sounds. You'd swear I had five kids, not just two.

"Mom," Kim yells so loud that it echoes throughout the house. "Hey! Mom, are you home? Where are you? Aunt Renee bought me some new shoes. They're green and I love them."

Her voice grows louder as she runs up the stairs, down the hall, and into my bedroom. I think the new shoes have cement soles. As if I didn't already know that she's standing outside my door, she bangs on it loudly, making my ears ring. So much for having a quiet bath.

"I heard you, baby. I'm in the tub. I'll be out in a few minutes. Is Aunt Renee still here?" I ask, getting ready to unplug the drain and let my relaxation time disappear along with the lavender essence oil-infused water. Well, it was the perfect way to unwind from my exciting afternoon, even if it was fleeting.

"She's coming," Kim yells, louder than necessary to penetrate the flimsy door separating us. I hear them mumbling and then Kim's shoes stomp as she makes her way out of my bedroom.

The door pops open quickly, startling me. I cover my chest and crotch with my hands, sitting up so fast that the water splashes over the rim of the tub, forming a puddle on the ceramic-tiled floor.

She rolls her eyes in her carefree manner. "Calm down, it's not like I've never seen you naked before. Shit, we used to bathe together, remember?"

Renee plops her ass up on the counter, folding her legs like a child parked on the floor in front of the television to watch her favourite Saturday morning cartoon.

"Um, a little privacy, please," I spit.

"Get over yourself!" Renee smirks and looks as if she's about to learn the secret of youth. "So, tell me all about it."

"Before I forget to tell you, a guy from Coach's gym might or might not be calling you for a date. I asked Coach to set you up. So, expect a gentleman caller. It's not a sure thing; I'm letting you know that it could happen."

"You're setting me up on a date with one of Coach's friends?" she asks with irritation in her voice. She beams, "You're the best sister ever! Is he built like Coach? I hope so. Yay!"

"Don't thank me. I didn't set you up with anyone, Coach did. I'm not involved. After you meet the guy, you can either thank him or blame him, depending on how the date goes."

I look at her, then the door, and finally back at her as if asking her to leave.

She shakes her head. "We haven't finished this conversation yet."

I groan. "I would imagine he'll be fit, but I have no idea to what extent. I suppose you must meet him to find out."

"Now that *that's* out of the way, tell me all about your hot rendezvous with the smolderingly sexy stud next door," she pleads with a breathy voice. "Was he as aggressive as the last time?"

I nod and quickly explain, "I went over. And he was amazing. That's it. End of story. Now get the hell out of my bathroom!"

She laughs sarcastically. "Yeah, fat chance of that happening, bitch. Details, now!" I stare at her with wide eyes. She hisses, "That look only works on your kids and you didn't birth me, so spill it and don't leave out the tiniest detail." She throws her arms out to her sides. "I'm not leaving here until you tell me everything. Get out of the tub before you prune."

I mimic with a scrappy attitude. She will not leave. I stand quickly, not bothering to cover any part of my body. The bubble bath suds slowly glide their way down my skin in puffy patches, tickling my tiny hairs along the way.

Her eyes don't veer away from mine to look at my nudity. I don't care who you are; if you're naked in front of me, I'm going to look, even if I don't want to. It's an automatic reaction for most people, but not for my sister, strangely enough.

"If you're planning to sit there, could you not stare at me, please? If you look away, I'll start talking."

A fair ultimatum for my privacy. She rolls her eyes, smiles idiotically, and then covers her head with the hand towel she pulls off the towel rack beside her.

"Okay, I can't see your beautiful and no doubt well-used body. Spill your guts, you dirty little slut!"

I begin, "He used me very well."

While drying my body, I give her most of the glorious details, leaving out how I burst into tears when it was all said and done. She need not know that her sister is a big crybaby.

I'm sure she'd tease me, never letting me live it down. Even though she looks ridiculous with her head under that towel, I appreciate her giving me privacy. With my housecoat on, I pull the towel off her head. Her long hair scatters about her face as if she's just come in from a windstorm.

As she's finger-combing it back in order, she grins. She whispers, "You're a fucking slutty little MILF, aren't you?"

"Hey!" I groan.

"It's not an insult. I'm just saying that it's about damn time. Girl, you were so sexually repressed. I'm extremely happy you're getting your pussy pounded, finally! They say that after five years of abstinence, your virginity can grow back."

"That is so not true!"

"Yeah, I suppose it's not. If it were, you wouldn't have taken his fist." She taps her chin. "If I recall correctly, his hands are massive. How the hell did he get one inside of you? I mean, I have taken a fist now and then, but they were women's hands and much smaller. I'm impressed."

"He was gentle. It's obvious he's experienced," I reply as I run a brush through my hair.

"So, what do you think he'll do to you tomorrow?"

"Tomorrow? No, I have to go to work."

"So, blow it off!" she instructs while waving her hand in the air to add emphasis.

"You're a terrible influence," I exclaim as I hit a snag in my hair, gently tugging at it with the brush. "I'm a fool to trust you with my kids."

In her happy-go-lucky, cartoon-ish mannerism, she hops off the counter, laughing wildly while dancing herself out of the bathroom, leaving the door wide open behind her. I can still hear her laughing until she gets to the kitchen. I can't make out what she's saying to the kids, but laughter fills the air. She'd better not be telling them anything about Coach and me.

I dress quickly in a pair of shorts and halter top before making my way into the kitchen to see the new shoes Renee bought for them.

Renee looks at me and I mouth, "Thank you." She knows it's for more than just the shoes.

~

Coach

My appointment won't be here for another hour, so I decide to get in a quick workout before then. The hour speeds along as my thoughts of Rayna scramble around in my mind, making me lose count of my reps.

I stop to look at my watch and try to recall exactly what I've been doing for the past forty minutes. It all seems like a hazy dream. I'm sweaty and my arms ache.

Loreen is standing behind me with her hands clasped behind her back, quietly watching. She's donning a gentle smile. Her long hair is tied back in a tight ponytail that falls down in soft waves to her mid-back. The spandex she wears shows off the hard work and dedication she's put forth over the past six months. She's now thirty-two pounds lighter, only needing another twelve to meet her set goal-weight.

I'm very proud of her. Never has she given up, much less whined about the workouts I've assigned her. Even I complain sometimes, and I live for this shit.

"Sorry, have you been standing there long?"

She shakes her head. "Not too long. I called your name, but you were lost in thought and didn't hear me." She crosses her arms over her chest. "What's on our mind, Coach?"

"Nothing that you need to worry about, angel," I tell her while setting the weights down as gently as I can. "You should have slapped me."

"Uh, no! You're a powerful man, in deep thought. If I had slapped you, what do you think your instinctual reaction would have been?" She flexes her thin arms. "Besides, with these weapons, if I had, you would have never recovered."

"Hmm, you were probably wise not to hit me then. Okay, are you ready to crank it out?" I ask, clapping my hands together while smiling with cruel intentions.

"You bet! Make me beautiful, Coach!" she says, throwing her arms up in the air, gleefully.

I hold my hands out from my sides. "You are beautiful. You're gorgeous! Look in the mirror behind you." She does as I suggest. "Do you see that tight ass? You did that, not me. That's on you, babe!"

She admires her ass while rubbing her hands over her curves. A smile lifts the corners of her lips, but she quickly fights it off, pulling her lips tightly together.

"Enough of this shit. I don't want to get an ego. Besides, it's time to kick my ass."

I get her working hard. Sweat glistens, making her skin reflect the light, revealing more definition to her arms, which I find very sexy. As I watch her, my mind drifts to this afternoon spent with Rayna.

It wasn't so much the sex as the way she made me feel. That has me so distracted. I felt things I haven't allowed myself to in a long time. How is she so easily breaking through the iron-clad walls that surround my heart?

Loreen deserves my full attention, so I blink several times to bring my mind back into focus before she notices that I'm not watching her.

I'm introducing Loreen to a different machine when she rudely interrupts. "Enough about me. What has you so distracted tonight? Don't say 'nothing,' either. You owe me an explanation of why I'm not your one and only girl tonight." Her hands are on her hips and she's very intimidating for such a short woman. "Who is she, or is it he?"

"Oh, sweetie, I would court you if you were available and you know it," I tease with a sexy smile.

She laughs and waves the idea away. Loreen is happily married with six kids that drive her crazy most of the time. She once told me she would not wish it any other way.

"Oh, so it is another woman then, huh?" she teases. I shake my head, but she doesn't fall for my bullshit attempt at denying it. "Who is she? Don't play shy with me, kid."

I'd better tell her something, otherwise, she'll never let it go. "I've known her for some time now and we just started...something."

I don't say what exactly. I don't have to. She knows to what I'm referring: sex.

"You really like her and it's terrifying you. Am I right?" She doesn't give me time to reply. "Coach, you may have it in your head that you will never settle down with anyone, never marry, and never have children. But your heart seldom does what your brain tells it. It will do as it pleases. You can try, but you'll soon learn that you can't prevent it from wanting what it wants. You like her, I can tell. You like her a lot. So, what's the problem?"

"For starters, I was sort of with someone," I lie.

"Honey, if you're telling me that you're sort of with someone, you aren't really with them, and you need to let them go. Your heart is with someone or it isn't. If it's not, don't you think you should let her go on her way?" She talks to me like a mom to a son. "Maybe this woman, who has you all knotted up inside, is who you should be with. Obviously, she has a powerful effect on you. Maybe you should ask yourself why that is."

She makes sense, I suppose. I should listen to this woman. She's been married forever and seems wise about relationships. Deep down, I want Rayna, but taking on her issues? I don't know about that.

"Does she have a complicated history?" she asks. When I nod, Loreen looks at me with sad eyes. "You know, we all have some issues that follow us throughout life. If she didn't carry her history on her back, she wouldn't be the amazing woman that plagues your thoughts. It's our struggles that make us who we are. Try to keep that in mind."

I nod because she's right. I am who I am because of my life experiences. I lost my father at a young age. He battled cancer for a few years but eventually lost his fight. I watched him wither away while my mom did everything she could to keep everyone's spirits up and hopes high, even though she was screaming inside. We could all see it in her sullen eyes, but she let no one see her cry. She is the toughest lady I know.

My father's struggle taught me that one day I'll need to find an exceptional woman like my mother, and to care for her, knowing she will care for me, should the need arise. Also, not to take my health lightly, which is probably why I exercise so much. I try to live my life to the fullest, and I don't care what other people think about my choices. This is my life, and I'll live it how I want. If you don't like it, fuck off!

"All right, enough of this lazing around. Get back to work," I scoff.

She leers at me while taking another gulp of water. When I smile as if thanking her for her advice, she smiles. This lovely woman has nothing but honest friendship to offer me, and for that, I'm grateful. Loreen is a first-rate lady and I cherish the day she walked into my gym.

After she leaves, I shower quickly before swinging by the grocery store to pick up a few things.

Chapter Ten

Rayna

It's eight o'clock at night and the grocery store is nearly empty when the kids and I arrive. They want a different cereal than what I bought yesterday. I send them on their way to each choose a box that costs less than five dollars.

None of the fruit looks all that fresh, and the lettuce is limper than it was a day ago. I pick through the bananas for a bunch that don't already show the blackened scars from the abuse they endured before arriving on this shelf.

As I'm looking at the tomatoes, trying to find two that aren't as squishy as the majority, a hand presses against my lower back and I jolt, then freeze. Whoever it is, is standing very close. I can feel the body heat they're putting off. I turn my head and I'm met with smouldering eyes.

"Hello, sexy. Fancy meeting you here," he whispers, leaning in to place a fervent kiss on my neck.

I swiftly step away from him. "My kids are with me," I promptly announce as my eyes scan up and down the produce aisle.

He nods, seeming to understand why I don't want him to touch me. "How are you feeling?"

My face flushes. I look around to see if anyone is privy to my embarrassment, thus questioning why this super fit, younger man is kissing the neck of a less than perfect woman over the age of thirty.

"I feel great. If I could have soaked in my bathtub without my sister bursting in on me, I'm sure I would be less jumpy." My voice lowers more. "You have an efficient way of relaxing me, Mr. Brenton."

"You're so cute when you blush, Ms. Baxter." He scans the immediate area around us before adding, "I want to fuck your ass again." He licks his lips and I swallow hard, remembering how talented they are. "What are you doing later? I want to fuck your beautiful pussy, but I will taste you first. I get so fucking hot when you writhe on my tongue."

This man is a machine! I wonder how many times in a day he can ejaculate. Maybe one day, I'll ask him if he ever tried to set a personal best.

He's mesmerized by my body as his eyes drink me in. Most likely, he's running some wild fantasy through his mysterious mind. My pussy twitches at the possibilities. I shudder when an icy shiver runs up my spine.

"My eyes are up here, Coach," I tease.

His gaze meets mine. He takes a slight step forward, closing the distance between us. His deep, sexy voice whispers, "My beautiful little slut, I'll look anywhere I damn well want. If it were up to me, I'd spin you around and force you to bend over those tomatoes you seem so fond of groping." He takes another step toward me.

"I'd yank those shorts down and then bury my face in your ass, licking and tongue-fucking you. Then I'd stand up, free my stiff cock from its denim prison, grab your hair in my fist, and ram deep into your little snatch. I'd fuck you relentlessly. Everyone in the store would hear you screaming through your pleasure and they'll come to watch. What do you say; do you want to play a little game with me?"

I'm lost in the dangerous, erotic fantasy while noting that it's more thrilling than anything I could ever see myself doing. I shake my head as soon as I picture the very plausible scenario that would follow: either my kids would see Coach ramming me or the cops would put handcuffs on us. The thought of either horrifies me.

"It's okay if you don't want to play the public sex game. It's not for everyone. Come over to my house later. I'll be gentler this time since you're most likely still tender."

Coach tilts his head, looking even more enticing than usual, as if that were even possible. How the hell am I supposed to resist him? Damn those eyes!

"What about your girlfriend, Alissa? I mean, what will happen if she drops in when we're... You know; while we're doing something deviant?"

"Deviant?" he chuckles. "She can join in if everyone agrees."

"All joking aside, I'm serious."

Does this man trivialize everything that doesn't pertain to sex?

He replies, "She's not permitted to drop in on me unannounced. When we first started playing, we discussed boundaries. She knows better than to show up unannounced." Coach slowly licks his bottom lip while looking me up and down. "Come to my bed tonight."

Note to self: never show up unannounced.

I run my fingers through some errant locks of hair, tucking them behind my ear. "I don't know. If I decide to drop in, I'll text first. But don't hold your breath waiting."

His captivatingly white smile makes him even more desirable. How can I resist him?

My face doesn't flush, but the rest of my body heats quickly. When my clit gives me another shot of tingles, I cast my eyes back onto the tomatoes I've squeezed a little too hard. Its juice drips from where my thumb perforated its skin.

He looks at my hand and snickers. "You want me," he confidently teases.

"Hi, Coach," Ken says as he and Kim walk up, tossing their cereal boxes into the plastic shopping cart.

I was so taken by Coach's charms that I didn't even notice them approaching. My demeanour immediately switches from desirous sexpot to mama bear who needs to protect the children from the knowledge of my illicit affair with their friend and neighbour.

"Hey, little man! How are you?" Coach says while they do some weird handshake, fist-bumping routine. I wonder when they created that and why I didn't notice at the time? Whenever the kids were outside, I was never too far away. When Coach was playing with them, I was usually on the porch watching his sexy body, not so much the kids.

"Hi, Coach!" Kim says while admiring his giant arm as it waves around while greeting Ken. "Why are you here?"

He leans down and whispers, "Us big guys have to eat plenty of healthy food to keep us moving. We're like enormous trucks and use up a lot of gas to keep ourselves running. My tank runs out quickly. Why are you here and not at home doing your homework, little lady?"

She giggles while she high-fives him. "I already did my homework."

"Well, it's late. You should be in bed."

"It's not that late," she insists.

"Oh, I suppose you're right. It's almost past my bedtime." Coach feigns a yawn.

"We needed cereal for the morning and Mom bought yucky stuff. But she made us come with her even though Ken is old enough to babysit me. It's legal; my teacher said so. I don't know why Mom makes us come with her everywhere." She rolls her eyes just like her Aunt Renee and I shudder.

"I know why! Because she loves you and wants to keep you safe. In about ten years, you'll be wanting to spend lots of time with your mom, trust me. Moms are amazing and yours is the best mother of all time." He straightens and pats her shoulder while looking at me. He says, "I'd be honoured to spend lots of time with your mom."

His eyes don't leave mine until my son curiously asks, "Why? Do you have a crush on her?"

Coach raises his eyebrows and taunts Ken. "And what if I do?"

Ken looks up at him as if he's trying to decide if Coach is teasing him or if he really likes me. In my mind, I beg everyone to change the subject.

"You want to date my mom? Ew! Why?"

Nope, he will not let this conversation simply slip by. My eyes beg Coach not to answer him.

Luckily, Kim interrupts. "You can date my mom. You'd be good to have around for when we have to move the heavy furniture. I'd bet you could lift a car."

Ken turns his attention to his sister. He teases her in that annoying way kids have of harassing their siblings. "He can't lift a car, idiot!"

I hiss, "Hey! No name-calling."

"He could lift more than you can because you're a weakling," she hisses back at him.

Yes, the conversation has shifted, thankfully. Now's my chance to get away from him.

"Hey, Mom, can I go home with Coach in his car?" Ken asks.

Coach recently bought a sports car that's incredibly fast right out of the factory. Ken has been drooling over it ever since Coach drove it into his driveway.

The sizable man looks at me and puts his hands together as if he's praying. His eyes beckon me, much like a hungry man would beg for food. He hops from leg to leg like an energetic child, and in the same tone, begs. "Please, Ken's Mom, can he? Please, can he? Pretty please! With a big, red cherry on top."

I shake my head and whisper, "Never do that again."

He looks unfittingly uncool but also immeasurably adorable because of how well he's relating to Ken and Kim. They admire him and think he walks on water. He's the fun guy who gives them popsicles in the summer and runs around the house with a water-gun, sneaking up and soaking them on sweltering days. Ken never seems to manage a successful surprise attack, but Kim hides well, jumping out when he least expects her.

"As long as you're not a bother to Coach and you mind your manners," I tell Ken.

I look at the big goofy guy who's now holding his hand high in the air to taunt my son into giving him a very high five of which the boy can't possibly match, no matter how hard he tries to pull down Coach's arm.

"Are you sure? You don't have to."

"Nah, it'll be fun. Right, tough guy?" he replies, still holding his arm over his head. Ken finally gives up trying to reach.

Kim asks, "Can I go, too?"

Coach looks at Ken's smile drop from his face and sees the disappointment. He pats her on the head and sadly tells her, "Not this time, butterfly. This drive is for Ken. I'll take you to buy some ice cream on the weekend, but only if your mom says it's okay. If I take Ken now, you can use it as leverage to get her to agree to ice cream. I like ice cream. Rocky Road is my favourite. Do you have a favourite?"

"Yeah, strawberry. Okay, I'll wait to go for ice cream," she tells him, smiling oddly at him. Her cheeks flush. Holy crap, she's smitten!

I respond, "We'll see about ice cream."

"Kim's Mom," he begs, "come on, please?" Coach tilts his head and sticks out his bottom lip like a pouting three-year-old. I know he's doing it for their benefit. He adds, "We love ice cream so much!"

Standing before me is a troublemaking kid stuck in a seductive, full-sized man's body. I grimace and shake my head.

"You're an intolerable child."

"I'll never grow up! I'm like Peter Pan, Momma Bear. My green tights are at home, though." He winks at me.

I picture him in tights with his steely cock straining against the stretchy green material, my lips covering its thick girth as I try to kiss it through the tights. I bite my bottom lip, unsure of why picturing a muscleman in tights has me all flustered.

"I'd like to see those," I sass, shifting my weight to one hip with my arms defiantly crossed over my chest and a flirty expression on my face. Would he appease me as I do him?

He grins, winks and then heads off to finish his shopping without coming back at me with one of his witty wisecracks. My son is in the custody of someone who, not over three hours ago, took his mother's asshole virginity, if there were such a thing.

This is definitely weird.

"Come on, Kim, let's go get the toilet paper that's on sale and then hit up the ice cream aisle."

~

Coach

As Ken and I leave the store, I notice Rayna and Kim just getting into the long check-out line. The woman in front of her has a full cart so they'll be waiting there for a while.

Kim is gesturing purposely with her hands to help better relay the story she's telling her mom. Rayna bites her bottom lip, lost in thoughts that have nothing to do with what Kim is going on about. Every once in a while, she nods, making Kim believe she's listening to her.

Ken asks, "Can I drive?"

"I tell you what, when you're of age and have a license, you can drive it in a parking lot, an *empty* parking lot. Preferably one that doesn't have any poles, curbs or people. That's provided I still have this wicked girl."

"This car is badass," he says after he slides onto the leather seat and shuts the door.

I slide in behind the wheel after putting the groceries in the trunk. "Thanks, little man. Put your belt on?"

"Of course!" he replies, sounding very much like a thirteen-year-old kid who is coming up to the age when he thinks he knows everything and adults are stupid. "Fire this bad boy up!"

"No, no!" I take my hands away from the start button to teach the kid the lesson that every kid should learn from his father. But Ken's father is a dick, so I assume they haven't had this discussion. "This car, and every car, should be referred to as female. She's a wicked girl, with a bad boy behind the wheel. Get it?"

Here comes the question every kid asks: "Why are cars girls?"

"Let me teach you the similarities between cars and women. Never repeat what I'm telling you to a female because they freak the fu..." I rethink my wording. "Well, let's just say they won't like it. Okay, so the similarities between cars and women: both have a cool exterior, they're sleek and curvy, and they feel really nice when you're in them. You'll understand that when you're older."

"I understand it now," he says. I look at him strangely and he adds, "Phys. Ed."

I nod before continuing. "Some are loud and obnoxious, while some purr like a kitten. Some will run you right over if you aren't paying attention because some are fast, real fast—stay away from those, kid. Trust me. And that, young man, is why men refer to cars as being female. Oh, I almost forgot. Some are temperamental, so you need to give them a little extra care. And never, ever call them temperamental to their face unless you want to feel their wrath. Learn to duck; women like to slap."

"Oh. Okay," Ken says while nodding, absorbing the information.

I fire up the bitch and slow-roll out of the spot, eventually weaving my way around all the parking lot medians and onto the street. Instead of heading straight home, I stay on the main road for another five minutes before turning off. Ken looks out the window, noticing that I've passed by our turn off.

"Are you taking me to a secret location so you can kill me and hide my body?"

I look at him with an expression that screams 'you're-a-sicko.' "Nah, little man, too many people saw me leave with you."

I turn onto an empty road, barren of any other vehicles, and stop the car. She rumbles under our asses, anxiously waiting for the imaginary green light. I look at Ken, meeting his wide eyes. I smile and then look through the windshield. My foot slams down on the pedal and she launches, exactly as I knew she would. The tires grab the pavement and she's flying.

Ken laughs and squeals in the passenger's seat. He's a big kid so I figure he'll be safe from the airbag's velocity, but hopefully, my assumption won't be tested for factuality.

In seconds, we're zipping so fast that I'm nervous, not for my safety but his. If Rayna finds out that I took her only son on a dangerous ride, she'll likely flip out. I want to touch that woman again, soon. I let off the gas and coast, letting her gear down on her own.

"Hey, dude, don't tell your mom that we went this fast, all right? She'll kick my ass if she finds out."

He's still laughing when the car slows to an acceptable speed.

"I won't tell her we went this fast." He laughs. "Are you kidding? She'd kick my ass for not making you slow down. There's no way my mom could kick your ass, though."

"Should you be swearing?" I ask, not expecting an answer because I'm sure Rayna wouldn't allow it. "Another lesson about women: never doubt a woman's strength when she's protecting her young. Women will go psycho when their offspring are in danger. Enough talk about cars and your mom. Tell me what you really want to talk to me about."

Ken casts his gaze down at his fidgeting fingers, a trait he no doubt learned from his mother. He asks, "I tried to talk to my dad, and he said to ask Mom, but there's no way I'm talking to her about this."

"It's okay, little man, you can ask me anything. No judgements," I assure him.

He pauses momentarily before spilling his worries. "There's this girl, she's nice and I really like her. We've been hanging out together for about a month. Please don't tell my Mom about this." He pauses until I look over at him and nod. "Well, we've been kissing for a few weeks, but I want to, you know, touch her. How can you tell when a girl wants you to?"

Shit! It couldn't be something simple about jacking off, for instance.

"Well, I'm sure it's a little different with my women than yours because of the age difference. But when she's kissing you really nice, with tongue and passion behind those lips, she'll do this little exhale that has a subtle whimper in it. Usually, if you hear that, you can give it a shot. But, little man, be patient with her, okay? She'll let you know where she's going to draw the line. If you ever cross that line, you and I will have a problem. Do you understand me?"

I'm not sure he's falling for the bullshit tip about a whimper being a cue. But, if he does, and she doesn't do that whimper while he's waiting to hear it, he won't try to progress and therefore, there's no worry of accidental pregnancy. When he's a more mature age, he'll figure everything out for himself. For now, he's too young to fuck girls.

I remember being thirteen and terrified of the female gender. My dick would get hard whenever I looked at a hot little high school girl's ass or perky tits. I must have jerked myself raw a dozen times a day. Even back then I was a horny bastard. Not much has changed.

"Yeah, I would never make a girl do anything she didn't want to. I'm afraid to touch her so how can I cross any lines? I don't even know where the lines are."

Even though he's smirking, I know he's confused and needs more advice.

Why the fuck is the sperm donor that made him such a selfish asshole? His son needs his father's advice. I suppose I'll have to be a substitute for the loser. It's probably better this way, anyway. I'm sure the advice he'd give the kid would be to dip his wick whenever and with whoever would spread their legs for him.

I'm nobody to be teaching a young, impressionable guy what to do and not to do to a woman. I know very well that I'm not exactly the pillar representative of lovemaking. I'm rough; I know that. Sometimes I push harder than I should, but I'm never out to hurt a woman and I'd never make her do something she doesn't want to.

Hearing women scream excites me, but only if she's screaming because she's coming and not because I'm causing her serious physical or mental injury while doing something that she forbids. I won't cross any lines a woman has drawn. Never have, never will.

"Don't be afraid of sex. It can be a lot of fun, just be sure you're both mentally ready for it. If you're not prepared to take care of a screaming brat with a shit-filled diaper, keep your dick in your pants. There are a lot of things to consider before it gets to that point. All right?"

He nods, so I mess his hair.

"Do it for the right reasons, especially if it's your first time, or hers. Make it special for both of you, okay? It's something that the two of you will look back on for the rest of your lives. The question about how your first time went will come up in conversation more often through your life than you think it will. Make the true story a remarkable story."

"Thanks," he says, less uncomfortable with our conversation about sex.

"No problem, little man. Hey, if you ever want to talk—you know, guy to guy—and your dad isn't available, I live right next door. Come see me.

Chapter Eleven

Rayna

Kim and I have been home from the grocery store for almost fifteen minutes, but Ken and Coach are still missing. They should have been back long before we were. We would have taken the same route home since we're neighbours, so had he broken down or had an accident, I would have seen them.

I'm sure they're perfectly fine. Maybe they're doing guy things. It's not as if his father would ever take the time to play the dad role. How I married a man who turned out to be such a shitty husband and father will forever baffle me.

My phone rings so I quickly dig it out of my purse, thinking it'll be Coach calling to inform me that they stopped somewhere else.

Can my ex-husband read my hateful thoughts? His name is lit up on my phone. I roll my eyes and wonder if I should answer or let it go to voicemail. I just know he's calling to say he can't pick the kids up from school tomorrow. I wonder what ridiculous excuse he'll give this time.

I click the green square. "Hello, Rick."

"Hey," he replies sharply. "So, I'll pick the kids up at school tomorrow and bring them back to your place. I can't stay long so you have to go straight home from work, otherwise, I'll have to leave them there alone."

"What's so important that you can't spend a few hours with your children?" I ask, not too upset because at least he's putting forth an effort.

"Nothing you need to worry about," he spits. "So, will you be going right home or not?"

"I had plans, but I'll try to change them. Just don't leave them alone, okay? I'll go straight home, but you might have to stay for an hour until I can get there."

"Fuck," he whispers under his breath. "Fine, don't be any later!"

Rick hangs up without giving me a chance to say anything else, not that I care to acknowledge his little tantrum with a response. There isn't anything important that I had planned after work, but I didn't want him to know that. I'll take my time getting home tomorrow so he's forced to spend his slotted time with his kids.

It's nice when someone picks the kids up from school, that way I don't have to rush to get to the school on time. I close my eyes and take a deep breath, letting my resentment toward my ex-husband escape my thoughts.

The groceries are put away, and the fresh foods are washed and set in their appropriate spots. But still, no men walk through my door. Shit. Maybe they tried to call, but I didn't hear my phone ring. I left it in the living room.

I'm disappointed to see that they haven't tried to call. I look out the front window to see if his car is in his driveway. No sooner do I look out when I see Coach following behind Ken as they cut across my slightly overgrown front lawn. I make a mental note to mow that tomorrow.

Ken opens the door and walks in with Coach in tow. Both of them are laughing, easing my concerns. Seeing Ken having fun and relating to a man who's older than him makes my heart flutter. Coach does not understand how much this means to Ken, and to me.

"Hey, Mom, Coach let me drive the car!" he says with a lot of excitement.

My heart instantly feels like it dropped into my stomach. I literally push my hand against my tummy to get my heart back in my chest where it belongs.

"What the f…?" I ask, not finishing the swear word. My eyes immediately widen and scan Coach's face to determine whether I should scream at him or laugh at their joke. He's stoic and impossible to read.

"Was I not supposed to let the guy drive? He asked nicely, and he said please."

His lips aren't smiling but his eyes seem different, sort of wider than normal. He's going along with the joke, if it is a joke. It had better be a joke!

"If he drove your car and christened her with some scratches and dents, it's not on me. If you hurt my son, I will have to kill you," I say, not as much threatening as I am promising.

Coach leans in toward Ken and whispers, but I can hear him. "See, little man, your mom knows my car's a she, and did you see how she changed into a momma bear in the blink of an eye?"

Ken nods in agreement as he studies my face.

He tells me, "Coach said that cars are always female. I had no idea. I lied, Mom. I didn't drive his car, but he said I can when I'm sixteen and have my license."

Coach assures me, "Only in an empty parking lot. Ken, buddy, you can't leave that out. It's important to remember the detailed rules of said future endeavour and to ease your mom's concern."

"I look forward to driving her in a few years. Keep her polished for me, okay?" Ken teases.

"Anytime you want to come over to wash her, you let me know and I'll get you set up. Shit, I'll even help you start a fund for gas money."

Ken walks down the hall to his bedroom with an extra bounce in his step and shuts the door.

Coach and I are alone in the kitchen, and we make eye contact.

Instantly, the heat between us sparks, burning hotter than it should. The kids are only a few steps away. I clear my throat and shake my head to clear my naughty thoughts. I scoot over to the sink and begin washing the bowls from our ice cream.

Two huge hands slide around my waist, coming to rest on my belly. A set of sensuous lips press to the right side of my neck. I take in a sudden gasping breath as the tiny hairs all over my body stand on end. It's as though he's electrocuted me with his lips. His hard body presses against my back, and he pulls me into him. The bulge in his pants has my pussy clenching.

I stand with my wrists on the edge of the sink, a sudsy sponge in one hand, a half-washed bowl in the other. The water still flows. His touch has completely captivated me, recklessly taking over my sensibility. My eyelids sag shut when he lets out a heavy breath as if he'd been holding it for a long time.

I open my eyes when I feel his hand leave my body and reach for the tap's handle. He flips it down, shutting off the water before whirling me around and taking my mouth hostage with his.

Coach's hand is in my hair, cradling my head. His powerful tongue invades my mouth as I suck it gently. Our tongues dance a seductive tango. Coach's other hand is up my shirt and under my bra, squeezing my breast while pinching my stiffening nipple. Shockwaves ripple from the stiff little nub, shooting straight to my clitoris, plumping it as an insatiable hunger grows within me.

He has me pressed against the counter and under his control. I reach behind me and place the bowl and sponge in the sink.

His sexual aggression fires me up like no man ever has. If I want it to stop, I know he would. All I have to say is the safe word, and it's over just like that. I welcome his touch.

I try my best to keep my ears honed for the sound of the kids' bedroom doors opening.

Coach suddenly grabs me under my ass, lifting me, and setting me down on the edge of the sink. His hands have my shirt and bra lifted while his mouth sucks my left nipple with brutal harshness. I nearly cry out, instead imprisoning both of my lips between my teeth and bite down hard.

I really should put a stop to this. But, fuck if this isn't the hottest spontaneous sexual thing I've ever done!

He sucks, nibbles and squeezes my breasts, setting my vagina into a frenzied state of need. Coach lifts me off the sink by wrapping his arm around my waist, taking my weight like I weigh nearly nothing. His lips press to mine, exploring my mouth with a newfound yearning.

My legs wrap around his waist, and my arms fling around his neck, holding onto him. He couldn't shake me off if he wanted to. He takes me to where the two counters join and presses my ass against the corner, leaving me teetering on the edge of the counter.

I moan under my breath when he grinds his pelvis against mine, rocking like he's fucking me in an easy rhythm. Each time he presses his swollen bulge against my wanton pussy, I want to scream for him to get my shorts off and fuck me hard. For obvious reasons, I can't do that. As if he's reading my secret desires, I feel him pull at my waistband and the button on my shorts popping open.

"Red," I whisper when a moment of clarity breaks through. My legs release their ironclad grip. I shift so that I'm sitting more balanced on the counter's edge.

Coach stiffens. He groans softly, as if struggling to suppress his need to have me. His hands grip the counter so tightly that his fingers lose colour. He takes a step back, breaking all physical contact with me.

"Kids?" he asks, swallowing hard.

"Yeah, kids." I'm winded. "Sorry, I can't do this right now. Fuck, I want to!" If not for my flushed face, my quivering voice proves my need for his touch.

He lifts me off the counter and sets me onto my feet with one swift movement. He continues to look at me even though he's stepped away. He takes a few deep breaths and adjusts the bulge in his pants while I run my fingers through my hair. Hopefully, I don't look too dishevelled.

"Come over to my place," he instructs with a voice so seductive I nearly leap into his arms.

I hesitate momentarily, desperately wanting to take his hand and run to his house this very instant. I want him to fuck me like we're wild beasts in heat, but I have responsibilities.

"Kids. I can't." I cross my arms over my chest to keep from reaching for him. "The battle over showering should begin soon. It's getting late and if I have any hope of getting them to bed on time tonight, I'd better get things rolling. If they're tired, they're impossible to wake in the morning. It is a school night, and I have to work tomorrow, so I'll have to sleep, too." I'm rambling, so I bite my lip to stop myself.

"The shower battles? I don't follow," he questions, curiously.

I keep forgetting that he doesn't have kids. He wouldn't understand the struggle parents have to endure over their children's hygiene or lack thereof.

"I have to fight with Kim to get her in the shower, but I can't get Ken out until the water runs cold. They are opposites with personal hygiene."

Coach nods as if he understands. "He's jerking his meat." I stare at him, not sure I heard him correctly. "That's why he's in there for so long."

Oh, the horror! Not my baby boy!

"No way, he's just a kid," I hiss, doubting the truth to his statement.

"Come on, Rayna. Don't be naïve. When I was his age, I used to crack out two knee-shaking orgasms before the water ran cold. If you think I'm a horny fucker now, you should have known me back then."

"Um, no thank you! You were a child, and I was a grown woman. They would have sent me to jail, and I'd be deserving of the lengthy sentence."

"I would have wanted you back then, too. You're smoking hot." He stands with his hands on his hips, smirking at me. "I'd put money on it that Ken's friends have fantasized about seeing you naked."

I shake my head and roll my eyes. "Oh, come on! You're being ridiculous. No way! To them, I'm an old lady."

"Older than them, yes. Hot as fuck, definitely." He looks up at the clock on the wall above the kitchen table. "Well, I should let you get at it then."

I trail behind him as he makes his way down the stairs to the landing. Coach opens the door but turns and leans toward me, pressing his cheek to mine. He whispers in my ear. "Text me after the kids fall asleep."

I want to tell him not to wait up for a text in case they don't fall asleep until late, but he's sprinting across the lawn before I can. I'm not leaving the kids alone while they sleep just so I can get fucked the way every woman should be at least once in her lifetime.

"Kim, get your little butt in the shower," I yell while locking the door and shutting off the outside light. "Kim, *now*!"

Coach

It's ten o'clock and I'm sitting on my bed playing solitaire. I know this is a massive waste of my time. There are more productive things I could do, but I'm waiting for Rayna to text me.

I need to see her tonight, to touch her soft skin and taste her exquisite lips. I can't see any lights on at her place, so maybe she called it a night. I'll give her ten more minutes, and then I'll call it a night, too.

Fifteen minutes later, I'm lying naked in bed, about to doze off when my phone lights up and vibrates on the nightstand, jolting me from the weightlessness of consciousness escaping me.

Rayna: The kids are asleep.

Me: Come over right now.

Rayna: I can't. I'm not leaving the kids in the house alone at night while I'm busy getting some action from the guy next door. I can imagine the horrible headlines that would come from that.

Me: You think too much.

Rayna: I'm a mom. It comes with the job title.

Me: Meet me in your backyard.

Rayna: Why?

I don't respond to her last text. I'm too busy digging through my dresser for a pair of black fleece pajama pants and shifting my erection once they're on. After picking up a condom and my keys so I can lock the door, I make my way from my front door, through her gate, and into her backyard.

She's standing on her patio, looking toward my yard.

"There stands a sexy woman," I say in a low, deep voice, cutting through the silence of the night.

"Okay, you have me outside. I have to stay right here, so if you plan to coax me to go home with you, you might as well save your breath."

The cotton nightie she's wearing hangs halfway down her thighs. With great thanks to the light that's shining from the opposite neighbour's house, I can see clean through it. Her silhouette might be turning me on as much as seeing her naked does. Maybe it's the mystery of what's underneath that has me so aroused.

"I could throw you over my shoulder and take you home with me," I threaten.

She shakes her head. "If you do that, I'll scream, alerting the whole neighbourhood."

"And if they come, I'd lie you on the ground and fuck you hard while they watch."

"You wouldn't!" she suggests, proving that she doesn't know me very well. I simply raise my eyebrows as if to challenge her.

Not wasting another minute, I give her an order. "Get your sexy ass down here. I want you."

"What? Outside?" She whispers under her breath, "Oh my God!"

"Yes, outside."

"What if someone sees us?" She looks mortified as she glances around with her arms crossed over her chest.

"I could just fuck you on that lit up patio. The whole neighbourhood can watch. Although that sounds like a fun fantasy to play out one day, not tonight."

I know she would never allow me to fuck her where the neighbours could see us because she has kids that could suffer some backlash from our deviant behaviour.

"No, I'm not coming down there. I won't be able to resist you if I do," Rayna confesses through a quirky grin.

"Do you want to resist me?" I ask, knowing the answer. The kitchen make-out session had us both burning hot.

She hesitantly descends the stairs, looking at me with her seductive eyes. I could completely drown in them. She stands in front of me, nearly touching me but not quite. Her eyes have yet to leave mine as if she's daring me to make the next move.

She smells of sweet lavender. Fuck, I want this broad sucking my cock under my control. I'd really enjoy humping deep into her throat, again.

"Get on your knees," I demand.

"What if someone sees us?"

Her eyes jerk away to examine every backyard connected to hers. She takes a step away from me, showing me that she isn't as daring as she was trying to be a moment ago.

"Nobody's looking. People's lives are too busy to sit and stare out their windows at the empty yards. It's not entertaining." She's still looking around. "Now get on your fucking knees."

"I don't think so," she replies, making my blood boil.

If she were anyone else, I'd grab her by the hair and force her onto her knees, and then bury my prick in her mouth, stopping only if she spoke the safe word. I clench my fists, hoping to fight off my demon's urge to make her regret sassing me. I stand before her, my cock more rigid than ever. Rayna looks down, noticing that my fleece pants are no match for my obvious lust.

"Do you like it when I tell you that you can't have what you want?" she whispers in her alluring voice, making my cock twitch. "I think you do."

My nostrils flair and my jaw clenches.

Fuck, she drives me crazy!

"Take my cock out of my pants," I growl while glaring into her eyes as if threatening her.

Rayna doesn't look at all intimidated, and that turns my inner demon on even more. He loves a challenge.

She steps toward me while reaching for the waistband of my pants. Her eyes don't veer from mine. She slips both hands beneath the fleece material. She strokes the sensitive skin on either side of my prick but doesn't touch my erection. Her fingernails lightly scratch, tickling and teasing me. My upper lip twitches in defiance. She delicately caresses me, never touching my eager dick, and I let her do it.

She's driving me insane!

Chapter Twelve

Rayna

Coach is under the illusion that he holds all the control, but he's sadly mistaken. He's my subject and I'm feeling feisty. I know he won't stand here much longer and allow me to tease him. Soon, he will take back the control.

Giving myself to him is exciting. For once in my life, I don't have to be the responsible one who makes the world spin. It's a relief to give it all a rest and let someone else hold the reins for a while.

Sensing that he's about to lose his cool, I grab his cock with both hands and squeeze. His breath catches, releasing with a deep grunt. He approves.

"Pump my cock," he instructs. He lowers his pants until the waistband rests on his thighs, just below his balls. I don't immediately comply. At this moment, I determine what happens, not him.

Instead of jerking him, I squeeze the base until a small glob of pre-cum seeps from the slit at the end of his tense cock. Using my thumb, I rub circles on the tip, using the lubrication his prick was kind enough to spit out.

Coach stands tall, his entire body stiffer than usual. He looks so fucking vicious in the shadows of the night. I should shake in my boots, so to speak. But I don't fear him anymore.

"Why are you defying me?" he murmurs through clenched teeth.

I smile at him while biting my bottom lip, not answering his pointless question. My thumb is still rubbing the tip, but my other hand is slowly caressing up and down his shaft. Not pumping it, as he suggested.

Coach's jaw relaxes, just enough to suck in a deep breath. He's so massive. He towers over me, and he's probably twice my weight. Yet, here I am driving him wild. This is hot! So fucking intoxicating! I can see why Coach gets off on being in control.

"Because I want to. Why don't you get on your fucking knees and pleasure me?" I suggest with the same insisting undertones he so effortlessly uses with me. Any second now, he will have had enough of my entertainment, and the shift in position will change.

"Do you want me on my knees?"

"Maybe I do," I reply with a stern attitude.

"Tell me what you want, Rayna," he whispers.

His face tilts toward me while he licks his lips. He scans my body, taking in my curves. My knees weaken. Who is actually in control of the situation? I don't think it's me.

He's going to pretend to be my submissive, take orders and follow them through? What a role reversal this is turning out to be. I think I like it. In fact, I'm sure I do, even if it's only happening because he's allowing it.

Coach slowly sinks to his knees while looking into my eyes. His steamy hands caress down my body along my loose-fitting nightie. His fingers lightly tickle down my thighs by barely touching me. I fight off the urge to giggle by biting my bottom lip.

His fingers catch the hem of my nightie and lift, revealing my bare pussy to the whole neighbourhood. If they're looking. I know it's dark on this portion of the patio, but still, it's entrancingly dangerous. I could get used to being a naughty girl.

My eyes scan the yards, ensuring nobody is outside to witness my body being ravished by this brawny man. This is sexy as hell, like one of those stories people write in the erotic romance books I like to read.

Just the premise of getting caught is a thrill. Add in that a hulky, younger man is about to lick my pussy under the night's sky, is almost enough to make me cum before he even touches me. I can't wait for his tongue.

The air is chilly, so Coach's super-heated breath on my pussy sends shivers from head to toe.

I demand, "Eat my pussy."

He looks at me and grins devilishly. "Cunt."

I know what he wants. I had better say it even though I hate that word.

He's looking up at me, breathing hot on my anxious clit but refusing to taste me until I satiate his need to corrupt my moral values. I am definitely not the one in control.

"Coach, I'm demanding that you eat my cunt," I whisper to him with strong certainty in my voice. Embarrassment flushes my face. That was so vulgar!

"Good girl."

He smiles before grabbing my ass and pulling my womanhood against his mouth, allowing him to bury his tongue between my folds.

Oh, hell yes!

I am putty in his hands, willingly allowing my thoughts to slip away.

Anyone who's silently listening out their windows could hear my soft moans. My right leg shakes wildly. I open my eyes to the night and scan my neighbours' homes, making this much more spectacular.

Coach suddenly spins me around, positioning me so that my butt cheeks are directly in front of his face. His breath is fiery on my derriere.

"Bend over and put your hands on the railing," he insists.

Without question, I do as he says, no longer caring whether our neighbours are enjoying the show. His tongue is my best friend, and I want it on me again. After several hard ass-slaps that echo off the surrounding houses, my clit twitches wildly. I consider looking around to see if there's movement but prefer not to know if anyone has stepped outside.

Coach buries his mouth on my asshole, licking it softly and pushing at its puckered opening. My entire body shivers in delight. Before Coach, I had no idea a tongue on my asshole would feel so fucking wonderful.

My clit won't stop twitching.

"Bend over more and spread your legs wide," he demands.

I do as he says, bending and spreading until my feet are a little wider than my shoulders and my back is flat, putting me at a ninety-degree angle. The cool wind bites at my pussy.

His tongue licks from clit to asshole. I'm suppressing my moans, but still wonder if I'm too loud.

Oh my God! This is so fucking wrong!

Two fingers push into my pussy and flutter, twirling and fucking me so brutally that my entire body is bouncing off his hand, despite bracing myself with the railing. I hang on with all the strength in my hands.

He slows his punches, and then gently slides a finger into my asshole, burying it completely. Coach sucks my clit between his teeth, flicking wildly with his tongue. His hand pulls back, sliding all three fingers at the same time.

This is sensational!

He increases his tempo until he's fucking both holes in a quick and steady rhythm.

His tongue whips at my sensitive clit with impressive speed, nipping now and then.

He moans, and not quietly either. I shush him, but either he doesn't hear me or he's simply ignoring my plea. He opens his mouth wide, engulfing my swollen clit, swirling his powerful tongue as he sucks forcefully. The vibration from his moan has me hanging on the edge of orgasm. I fight to remain quiet, but he's louder than I am.

Mix his sexual talents with the fear of being caught, and I'm about to lose all control.

"Yes, oh, yes! I'm coming! I'm coming! I'm co…"

My voice fails. My breath burns in my chest. My heart ferociously pounds as my body stiffens. Anything else known to women, even chocolate, cannot match this momentary sublime euphoria.

～

Coach

I'm moaning, licking, sucking, and finger-fucking her two holes simultaneously. My arm tires, but I will not stop unless she's satisfied or my arm falls off. I'll do whatever it takes to get her to lose herself. She tightens around my fingers for the second time tonight. Another orgasm will soon sweep through her.

"Yes, Rayna, cum on my face."

Her pussy forces against my fingers while her asshole tries to pull my digit deeper. She clenches and my cock twitches. Her clitoris swells at the command of my tongue. Her orgasmic whimpers grow louder. At this rate, soon the sounds of her pleasure will echo off the surrounding houses.

It's fascinating how Rayna's sounds have me unable to think rationally. This woman has me wanting to give all of myself to her; my body, my heart and my soul. I know the neighbours can hear her and the thrill has my cock harder than ever. She deserves so much more from me than a quick fuck, but I won't last long tonight.

She cries out; lost in orgasmic ecstasy. I continue until I know she's completely finished. Before I stand, I slap her ass cheeks twice with both of my hands. She yelps while pulling her ass away from me.

As I'm getting to my feet, I wipe her cum off my chin and then lick my fingers to taste her once more. She tries to stand upright, but I grab the back of her neck and urge her back into position. She whimpers but plays along with my silent insistence.

I reach in the tiny pocket of my pajamas and find the condom. I rip it open with my teeth and then pull it out of the package with my one free hand and roll it over my aching prick with an incredible skill that only years of practice provide.

I aim my cock at her glistening slit and push all the way forward in one quick motion until I'm entombed deep inside of Rayna's remarkable body. She gasps and I grunt, neither of us caring in the slightest about the neighbours. Like me, she doesn't seem to give a shit what anyone thinks. We're lost in each other, and I will never have regret or apologize for it.

With both of my hands, I grab hold of her pelvis and pull her toward me as I buck forward. The lustful sounds of our panting mixed with the clapping of our bodies crashing together echoes off the houses with a sensuous beat that's music to my ears.

The moonlight casts a glow on her back, emphasizing the two shadowed dimples on either side of her tailbone. They wave to me after each thrust. I can't resist pushing her nightgown up to her neck, so I can watch her muscles move in the moon's light as she battles to maintain position.

My legs shake. I'll cum just before my legs ache so brutally that my mind will be too distracted to cum.

Rayna has orgasmed three times already, and she's building up for a fourth. She's so loud that I'm sure she's going to draw someone's attention. I see lights flicker on at the Jennings' household. I'd better shut her up or the cops will show up soon.

I reach forward, grabbing her hair and pulling her up so I can cover her mouth with my hand. I pin the back of her head against my chest so she can't pull away. She grabs my arm, trying to free her mouth, but I'm too strong. She squirms in my hold, trying to turn her face away.

That's right, sweetheart, make me work for it.

I muffle her cries under my grip, and the sounds stir my inner demon into a frenzy. It's hard to get enough oxygen when the mouth is covered, adding an element of fear.

I whisper, "If you need me to stop, tap my arm three times, but only if you absolutely have to."

She grips my forearm but doesn't tap. She doesn't know it yet, but when she cums, her mind will fog from lack of oxygen, heightening the euphoric intensity of her orgasm.

I place my other hand on her lower belly to keep her in place while I continue to fuck her with brutal force. My legs are really shaking now. I'm not only holding my weight but hers as well. I'm barely able to keep us upright.

My teeth clench, lips parting only when I suck in a quick breath. If I open my mouth to exhale, I'll grunt like a barbarian, and this is not the place for that.

She's still grabbing at my arm, trying to pry it from on her mouth, but she isn't tapping. I lift my palm long enough for her to take two deep breaths before replacing it. She wiggles in protest but realizes that there's no point in struggling. She cannot overpower me.

It's up to me to keep Rayna quiet. She has lost awareness of her surroundings. I very much like her this way.

A wave of newfound energy floods my body. I pound my cock into her, lifting her with each thrust. My legs have gone numb from the abuse. My body can't take much more. It won't be long now. I'm so close to giving in to my body's need to let it go.

No sooner do I consider letting my cum fly does her body stiffen, her pussy squeezing and forces so hard that I absolutely can't pull back, otherwise she'll push my cock out of her. Hot liquid seeps from around my prick and drips down my thigh. I need not move at all; the spasms her pussy inflicts on my shaft are enough to throw me over the edge. But I fight to resist.

My cock begs for release. I'm hanging on the edge, waiting for her to finish her orgasm before I allow myself the reward of a soul-trembling orgasm. Her muscles soften, and I know it's my turn to free my inner demon, but Mr. Jennings opens his backdoor and steps outside.

Bad fucking timing, dude!

He looks around, trying to see what woke him.

I don't fucking care anymore!

I slam her so hard that her arms and legs flop like a rag-doll. The sound of our bodies clapping together echo, revealing our not-so-secret fuck-fest.

There's no denying Mr. Jennings knows people are fucking somewhere nearby. I know he can't see me; the shadow I'm standing in casts a black hue over my body, blocking my presence from the full moon's bright rays. I believe Rayna remains hidden from his view by the large flower pot. He continues to search the shadows for the source of the sexual sounds.

I've spent all my energy pounding into her as if I were Satan himself. My inner demon is pleased. It's time to let myself go.

I clench my teeth, trying to contain the wails from my barbaric, growling demon. She holds as still as she can while I dump my super-heated cum into the condom. Her pussy twitches around my throbbing shaft, adding to the perfection of the moment. My muscles can barely keep us standing.

With an exasperated exhale, I have reached my goal of making her cum many times and then finally relieving myself.

Between breaths, I whisper in her ear, "Mr. Jennings has been outside for a few minutes. He's been listening to us while looking for the source." Rayna holds her breath. "Don't worry, he's been looking at my backyard. He's wise to think I'd be the sexual deviant performing such a daring act. What he doesn't know is that you are a bad little slut who likes to get drilled outdoors. Aren't you?"

I lift my hand from her mouth now that I'm sure she'll remain quiet.

She whispers as quietly as she can manage. "Can he see us?"

"No, we're hidden in a shadow. Just stay quiet for a minute. He'll give up and go back inside."

Rayna pushes my hands away and then spins to face me. "That was so exciting!" She looks exhausted and utterly dishevelled, but happy. Her hair is a mess, and her skin bears a thin layer of sweat. "Was I too loud?"

"Baby, you can never be too loud for me. You can scream if it makes you cum harder," I assure her with an exhaustive smile.

"Do you think he knows you're with me?"

She's beginning to let panic seep in, ruining this copacetic moment.

I pull her into a hug and kiss her head. "No, Rayna, he thinks it's me, not you. He does not know you're involved." I lean forward in time to see the man return to his house. "He's going back inside."

She pulls back from the hug and looks up at me, still wearing a freshly fucked and completely satisfied expression. "I'm going inside. You can't come with me. Go home. Oh," she takes a breath, "and thank you."

I pinch her cheeks between my thumb and forefinger, watching as her lips pucker to look like a fish. People rarely enjoy this. Judging by her frowning brows, she's irritated by it.

I kiss her fish-lips lovingly and then turn to leave without another word. She watches me open the gate and disappear through it, the gate latching behind me after it gradually swung shut.

This chick is really getting to me, and it's scaring me.

She's sexually inexperienced. She's not like any woman I've ever had the pleasure of seducing, but she's willing to learn.

Normally, I wouldn't give a woman like her a second glance. I would never take the time to train a woman from scratch before introducing her to my kinks like I'm doing with Rayna. She isn't ready for my level of kink.

Coaching her on how her body can be manipulated in ways that will take her to an incredible orgasmic state of being will be fun. I can't deny that. But I prefer a woman who has done all of this before and knows her role as a submissive.

What will she do when my inner demon sneaks out in full force, wanting to punish her with electric shocks or genital piercing for the simple pleasure of hearing her scream? Suppressing his need for torture will not be an effortless task.

Rayna may never be willing to go as far as I am accustomed.

This captivating woman differs from all the other women in my past. I don't know why I feel this way about her, I just do.

I want to take her into my world and teach her everything I know. But if I attempt to do that, she'll most definitely run away screaming. For that reason alone, thinking I can keep her as mine is off the table.

I can't let myself feel anything more than friendship and sexual desire.

It's better this way. Right?

Chapter Thirteen

Rayna

This day has been grueling. I cleaned the teeth of eight adults and two children.

One person came in with an abscess that stunk horribly. The youngest of the two children, while attempting to x-ray, bit me. Lucky for me, I was quick to pull my hand out of her mouth before she could chomp down hard enough to break the skin. She only made an impression but hadn't yet cut into me.

Her mother laughed through her embarrassment at how horribly behaved her child was while I sat there wanting to punch her in the face; the mother, not the child.

There's no way in hell I would have allowed my kids to behave so poorly. I wish I could yell at the idiotic woman about setting boundaries by demanding the kid show respect to people. That little girl will soon become a teenage nightmare who thinks the world owes her something and demands they pay up while she sits on her ass complaining about how awful society is.

I did the best I could with her teeth and suggested to our receptionist that she urge this family toward a pediatric dentist for the next time she needs a cleaning. Let her be someone else's problem.

By the time I pull in my driveway, I'm truly exhausted. Maybe that's because of the exhaustive pounding I received from Coach last night. I smile coyly at the thought of Mr. Jennings hearing me pant and moan through my heated orgasms.

Going into my house to face my ex-husband will be the absolute worst part of my day.

It's Friday, his day to pick up the kids from school. The courts assigned him only two days a month to do this, and he usually has an excuse for why he needs to cancel. A loving father would take this time to enjoy them and to go anywhere other than straight home. He's simply too self-absorbed to realize how great his kids really are.

As I stand in my entryway, I can see into each room he's allowed to be in. He knows he has to stay in the kitchen, living room, or TV room, but he's in none of those places. I'll bet that fucking asshole is in my bedroom again.

In the past, he's gone through my private things. I've never been able to catch him in the act. Today, I will. I bought this house for the kids and me with my money after Rick and I divorced. He has never lived here and never will.

As quietly as possible, I set my bag on the steps and slip off my shoes. I sneak down the hall without a sound. The kid's bedroom doors are closed, but I can hear their televisions. I would bet this house that Rick told them to go to their rooms and close their doors. He wouldn't have to deal with them then. At least I'm comforted in knowing they're home safely.

I come to my bedroom door and it's closed, instantly infuriating me. Rage flushes through my veins as my adrenaline spikes. I never leave my door closed when I'm not home. How blind was I when I walked down that church aisle and said *I do* to this dickhead?

I open my phone and start recording video before slowly opening the door. I can show it to the courts one day if it comes to that.

Careful not to make a sound, I push open the door. He's digging around in my t-shirt drawer. I don't know what he thinks he's going to find since there's nothing but shirts in there. I wait while he closes that drawer and opens the one directly below it.

"Rick, what the fuck are you doing in my room?" I yell.

He jolts and spins, suddenly looking like a dog who got caught taking food off the table. "Nothing! I'm just looking at your t-shirts." He looks at the drawer, then me, and back at the drawer before continuing. "I was hoping to buy you a shirt as a gift from the kids one day and needed to know the correct size."

"You're so full of shit, Rick." I look at my phone's screen to ensure I have him in the frame. "Get the hell out of my house. You will never step foot in my house again. Do you understand me?"

Fury rages through every cell in my body. I want to beat the bullshit right out of this fucking asshole!

The kids are standing in their doorways, their faces hanging in disappointment from their father's actions. Unfortunately, this isn't the first time they've witnessed their dad doing something sneaky. Nobody deserves to have their privacy invaded by anyone, especially by a person they've divorced.

Ken steps around me and begins a rant. "Why, Dad? What's wrong with you? Why do you always have to screw things up? Can't you just be a normal father for once? You need to leave. We'll be just fine if you leave and never come back. We don't need you. So, go! Get out! Leave us alone!"

By the time he's done his speech, he's screaming as loud as his cracking, teenage voice will allow. My heart breaks when his tears burst forth, pouring down his cheeks. I wonder how long Ken has been holding that anger inside, afraid to confront his father.

He's a soft-hearted kid who never wants to hurt anyone's feelings, other than Kim's, of course. She's his sister so she's fair game in the unwritten sibling rules of conduct.

I pull him into a hug to comfort him. He's gasping with sobs. Suddenly, he pulls away from me to pick up the small ceramic bowl off my dresser. He whips it at his father before I can stop him.

Rick tries to block it but fails. It hits him on the head and falls to the floor, shattering in tiny pieces. He looks at Ken and finally realizes that his son hates him, or at the very least despises him enough to want to hurt him.

Kim is crying loudly as well. She's still standing in her doorway, her little body frozen with fear. None of us have ever seen Ken this angry and it is heart-wrenching.

My poor little boy is hurting and has been for a long time. I failed him because I didn't see the anguish he's been carrying. I grab him and wrap my arm around his chest, pulling him against me. He's trembling.

Rick rushes past us, angry and embarrassed. Maybe he'll finally realize what a horrible father he's been to his kids. It's a slim chance, and I seriously doubt it. He's a hopelessly selfish human being. Somehow, he'll turn this around so that he's the victim and our son is the horrible attacker out to hurt him at my command. He blames me for everything that goes wrong in his life to this day, even though we divorced four years ago.

In the softest, calmest voice I can manage, I whisper to Ken. "Take Kim in your room and close the door. I'll be in to see you soon." My fingers brush through his hair. "Stay in there, okay?"

I hurry to follow Rick. He's standing in my foyer, furious, his face tense and flushed.

He points at me and I notice his hand shaking. "You turned those kids against me and I'll see you in court. Those are my kids, too. You made them hate me."

How dare he? My hands shake from the fireball raging in my gut. I pull open the door and point toward the road, urging him to leave. I don't dare speak because I'm too pissed off. I might cry which shows weakness, and he'll berate me for it. Besides, I know I'll say something I'll regret.

He stands before me with his arms folded across his chest, wearing a smug expression and looking down his nose at me. "I'm not fucking leaving until I talk to my son."

Probably louder than I should, I yell, "Were you not listening? He doesn't want to talk to you. Don't you get it? Did you even hear a word he said? Just go or I'll call the police."

He yells, "Call the fucking cops! I don't fucking care! This is my day with those kids and I'm not leaving until I talk to my son."

"I said get out! Ken doesn't want to talk to you and I will not force him. Just go! Get out of my house!"

I'm seeing red while dialling 9-1-1.

"Rayna, is everything okay here?"

Coach is standing a foot outside the door on the porch with his hands on his hips, filling the doorway. He must have been outside when he heard the yelling. I'm relieved to see him and yet worried that he won't be calm enough to deal with Rick's hot-temper.

"It's okay," I tell him while holding my hand up, urging him to keep his distance and not to get involved.

"Oh, and who the fuck is this asshole? Is he your knight in shining armour that's going to rescue you from the evil ex?" He looks Coach up and down. "Are you fucking this piece of shit?" Rick accuses while pointing at Coach.

"What?" I question. It takes exceptional restraint not to punch this asshole straight in his foul mouth. In a hushed tone, I spit back. "Are you kidding me? Who I sleep with is none of your damn business. You have no right—"

The operator picks up and I ask him to send the police because my ex-husband won't leave my house, he's scaring my children, and is becoming threatening to me and my neighbour. I give him my address before hanging up, even though the operator tells me not to. I want to record this interaction on my phone as proof of his defiance. Coach steps in the door, walking past me so he can stand between the two of us.

"The lady asked you to leave. You need to go now," he says in a very calm and deep voice.

If I were Rick, I'd be running out the door in fear of getting clobbered. But I know him, and he's too stubborn to reveal his cowardice. He'll try to pick a fight so that Coach will hit him, so he'll look like the victim when the police show up.

Coach looks huge standing beside my ex. Rick is not a big guy, by any means. He's tall but extremely thin. Ken takes after him with those traits.

"Are you going to make me leave? Try it! Put your hands on me. I'll fucking sue your ass!" Rick says while stepping toward Coach to taunt him. "This doesn't involve your stupid ass, so go pound more weight. You're looking a little flabby."

"Don't be an asshole in front of your kids. Leave."

How is Coach staying so calm?

"Or what? What are you going to do about it, huh? Do you want to punch me? Is that why you're here? Do you think it'll make you look like a tough guy in front of my wife?"

I cut in. "Ex-wife!"

Coach speaks slowly and clearly. "If you're challenging me to a fight, you must hit me first. But heed my warning; you will not come out of it well."

He has his fists clenched, and his jaw is tight. Rage is building inside of him. He's ready to pounce should Rick decide to initiate a physical fight. If Rick is dumb enough to swing, Coach will pummel him. I'm not sure I want that to happen; he is the father of my kids. Even though he's useless in almost every way, he's still their father and I don't want them to hear or see him getting a beat-down.

Rick slowly lifts his arm, putting one finger on Coach's chest to coax him into swinging first. Coach simply smiles at him. Holy fuck, he's scary!

I'd piss my pants if that look was aimed in my direction. Although, sometimes he glares at me with an expression much like this one, but it's not as intense. The difference is that he wants to fuck me hard, not fuck me up. I know how strong he is, and although I shouldn't care, I fear for Rick.

"Leave, Dad!" Kim stands at the top of the stairs, yelling at her father with a tear-soaked face. Her little body jerks from broken-hearted sobs. "Why are you trying to fight with Coach? He's a nice guy and wouldn't hurt anyone. And he's my friend, and you're not because you're mean!" She hiccups. "I wish you weren't my dad!"

Rick looks at Coach and then at me. An 'aha' expression erupts on his face. "You *are* fucking him! This muscle-head? This gets you off these days?"

He should never talk like that in front of the kids. I'm seeing red, on the verge of punching Rick myself.

Coach is ready to boil over but speaks in a soft voice to the tiny, weeping child. "Kim, please go to your room and shut the door. Wait there for your mother. I don't think your father wants to pick a fight with me. I won't hit him, Kim, I promise. He's leaving right now." Coach looks at Rick. "Isn't that right?"

Kim rushes off to her room, still crying and obviously angry, judging by how hard she stomps her heels. These kids will need a lot of hugs and time to talk it out. I want to make it all go away, give them a normal life, but their father defies me at every turn.

Rick glares at me. "You're a fucking whore and a shitty mother. Are you fucking this asshole while my kids are in the house? I'll see you in court, bitch!"

Coach growls through clenched teeth. "You'd better shut the fuck up right now. I will not tell you again. Not another word. I do not want to break my promise to Kim. Unlike you, I will always keep my promises to those kids."

"Don't you dare tell me what to do. You're nobody but a fuck toy for this whore. You don't have a say in what happens here, so fucking go home and shoot some steroids or drink some eggs."

Rick will not shut up. At no other time have I ever seen him reach this level of stupid while bearing no common sense.

For the benefit of the video recording, I announce, "Coach, I give you permission to remove this asshole from my house. I've asked him to leave countless times and he refuses. He has no right to be in my house. He's trespassing on private property."

Coach looks at me. "Are you sure?"

With my eyes wide and my head nodding, I reply, "Oh, I'm sure!"

Rick looks at the camera. "Make sure that thing's recording so I can sue him for assault."

Coach reaches out, grabbing the front of Rick's shirt. He spins him around with ease and then quickly shifts his hand to the back of the shirt's collar. He grasps the back of his belt with his other hand while Rick swings his arms, never hitting Coach hard enough to cause him any discomfort. He lifts Rick by the belt. He falls forward and hangs as if being held by a harness, like a dog, suspended by his shirt and belt with his feet and hands barely touching the floor.

Coach takes a few steps toward the door, but when he tries to get through, Rick grabs the frame and holds on. I swing the phone so it doesn't capture what I'm sure will happen next. Coach lifts his knee quickly, nailing Rick's fingers against the solid wooden doorframe. He screams and grabs his fingers with his other hand. I'm sure I heard bones break in at least one of his fingers. Judging by his pained expression, I'd bet money on it.

"You a fucking asshole! I'm going to sue your dumb ass! I'm going to take your fucking house! Let me go, cocksucker!"

I don't know when they showed up, but the police are walking up my driveway, watching what's happening with their hands on their pistols.

The female officer calls out. "Take your hands off that man and step away. Do it now."

Coach lets go, dropping Rick to the grass with a thud. He raises his hands to signify that he isn't a threat to the police. Rick jumps up and lands a punch to Coach's jaw. It barely moves him. Coach doesn't even drop his hands, but he's focussed squarely on Rick and I'd swear his eyes turn black.

Oh, shit!

The officer yells, "Get on the ground, now!"

While still glaring at Rick with evil eyes and flared nostrils, Coach obeys the officer's commands and slowly gets on his knees. He lays down, his eyes never leaving his assaulter. The asshole stands there, staring at Coach with hatred in his eyes and clenched fists. He wears a smirk that tells me he thinks he's won this battle.

"Get down now or I will Tase you," she yells as she steps closer to him with Taser in hand, pointing it directly at Rick. "Do it now, sir."

He looks at the cop and then nods, finally realizing that she's talking to him. He complies with her demands by dropping to his belly with his arms over his head. Damn, I was hoping she would blast him. He deserves it for everything he's put me and the kids through over the years.

I slowly walk toward Coach. "This guy is my neighbour and he was helping me. This is my asshole ex-husband who brought our kids home and then went through my belongings in my bedroom. I caught him on video, so he can't deny it. Coach came over when he heard Rick yelling at me. He only came to keep me safe." I pour it on, hoping they'll arrest him.

"He scared me. He wouldn't leave even after my kids and I begged him to go. He was very belligerent, so I asked Coach to get him out of the house for the sake of my children."

The officer nods at Coach. "You can get up now. Do you need medical attention?"

"No, thank you. I've been hit harder by frail women."

This has been quite an event, making this really shitty day even shittier.

Coach stands and joins me, wrapping his arm around my shoulder. He lets go of me almost right away so that nobody thinks we are a couple, especially the kids who are standing on the front porch, watching their father being handcuffed. They must have heard their father screaming or seen the flashing lights from the police car through Ken's bedroom window and were curious.

I race over to them and pull them both into a hug. "It's okay, don't be afraid. Dad simply got angry, that's all. I'm sure he'll feel terrible after he calms down, and then he'll apologize for being so mean to us today."

Kim whispers through her sobs. "Is he going to jail because he punched Coach?"

Damn, I was hoping they hadn't seen that.

"They will arrest him for assaulting Coach, but I'm sure they'll let him go later tonight." I look from one set of tear-soaked eyes to another. "Fighting is never okay. There are other ways to resolve issues. Can you two sit in the kitchen so I can talk to the nice policewoman? Will you do that for me?"

They both nod and then turn to walk into the house after taking one more look at their father, who is now being escorted to the police car. These wonderful, loving kids shouldn't be going through this.

Most of the neighbours are outside, watching as the worst moment of my life unfolds publicly; displayed for all to see. I'm a private person, so this is one of my greatest fears. People need not know my business. I approach Coach, who's talking to the policeman.

He asks, "Are they okay? They shouldn't have seen that. I'm sorry. Maybe I should go talk to them." He runs his hand through his hair, obviously upset. "If I wouldn't have come over, the situation may not have escalated."

"No, don't say that! I needed help, and you were there to give that to me. I can't thank you enough."

A lump is welling up in my throat. I smile and lean in to hug him, but the female officer calls to me before I can.

"I have to get your version of the events," she explains. "I'm sorry you had to go through this. How are the kids?"

"Shaken up. They're strong. They'll be okay."

"Can you tell me what happened here?" she asks.

I tell her the entire story, showing her the videos I took as evidence of what led up to him getting arrested. She asks me to send the videos to them. She tells me not to show them to anyone until the courts say it's all right to do so. It's not like I'm going to splash my business all over the internet, inviting strangers into my humiliating personal trauma. I hate it when people do that.

"Do you think he would have caused you physical injury had your neighbour not shown up when he did?"

"I don't know. Maybe. He is a very selfish, angry man."

She asks, "Has he caused you physical injury in the past?"

I look down at the grass and cross my arms. "Only one time. He slapped my face, and then pushed me backward. I fell onto the coffee table. My lip split and I was bruised, but that was years ago. Do I think he would have hurt me today?" I scrunch my face and tilt my head.

"Yeah, maybe. He was furious because our son yelled at him. I wouldn't put it past him to take his anger out on me. It enraged him when his daughter told him to leave. He thinks

I turned them against him, but he's a shitty father and the kids have had enough."

"You don't have to allow it, but is it okay if I talk to the kids to get their side of the story? You can be present, of course." She's a soft-spoken woman.

If the kids can tell their side, they might feel as though they hold some power in a situation that is so far out of their control. They probably feel helpless at the moment. Kids don't understand the mindset of adults, it's beyond their capability, thankfully.

"Um, yeah. I think they'd like to tell their side. You'll be kind and understanding, right?" I suggest.

"Definitely. Kids process things differently than adults do. I have three of my own." She shakes her head and shrugs. "So, I'll be considerate. I'll talk to them like I would my own kids, only nicer," she promises with a snicker.

"Come with me," I tell her, leading the way to my kitchen so she can talk to them.

She allows them the freedom to tell what they saw and felt, thus giving them back their strength. After she's finished, she gives them each a sucker. The officer heads back outside to join her partner and bring Rick to the jail for processing.

Chapter Fourteen

Coach

The cops just left with Rayna's asshole ex-husband handcuffed in the backseat of their car. I kind of hope they crash and he's pinned in the car while it goes up in flames. I'm sure Rayna wouldn't miss seeing his dumbass around.

I should keep in mind there was a time they were married, and she loved him. He's still the semen donor that created Rayna's two exceptional kids. They deserve so much better than him.

Rayna is in the kitchen talking to the kids to make sure they're not too freaked out while I wait just inside the front door. They seem calmer after talking to the officer. At least they aren't crying anymore. Seeing Ken and Kim upset like that broke my heart. Once again, father of the year!

I hear Ken say that he wants to get back to his video game. Rayna suggests that Kim take a nap. She promises to wake her for dinner. After the kids head to their rooms, she comes down the steps towards me. She looks at me with the most vacant expression and I can't read her.

I ask, "Are they okay?"

She takes a deep breath, releasing it slowly, and I see the anguish in her face. It's obvious she's emotionally drained. Instead of answering me, she wraps her arms around my chest, grabbing my shirt in her fists. I hold her as closely as I can and then I place a long kiss on the top of her golden hair. I gently rock her back and forth, soothing her the only way I know how; like my mother used to soothe me.

I keep my voice as calm as possible. She needs to hear that she did all right tonight. "You're an exceptional mother.

Those kids love you so much. Don't listen to what that asshole said. He was trying to hurt you. Babe, the kids; are they all right?"

She nods against my chest. "I think so. They seem to be better than I am."

"I can stay the night if you're worried he'll come back."

I hope she'll accept. Leaving them alone scares me. If he comes back, he won't be pleasant. What if that fucking asshole wants revenge?

I overheard her tell the cop that he hit her once before. She didn't know I was listening, and I won't ask her about it. But, after hearing that, it took every ounce of strength I had not to rip that car door off, drag him out by his neck, and beat him to a bloody pulp. I would have gladly served a jail sentence for it; it would have been worth it.

My parents raised me not to hurt women. Yes, it's ironic, and believe me when I say that it's a personal struggle within me not to hate myself for my kinky, sadistic ways.

I want to plead with Rayna to let me stay with her, in her bed so I can hold her all night. But I know I can't. The kids have enough to deal with.

As if she can read my mind, she says, "Sleeping the night with me, in my bed? I don't think so. The kids—"

"First off, I didn't say I'd sleep in your bed with you, although the thought crossed my mind. I'm suggesting I'd sleep on the couch. I think the kids would be perfectly fine with that."

"I don't know. I wouldn't want to put you out. You don't have to do that. You've done so much already. I'm sure we'll be fine with the doors locked."

I yell, jolting Rayna from this quiet moment between us. "Hey, kids!"

Rayna jumps away from me, ensuring they won't see us sharing physical contact. Their doors fly open, and they come rushing to find out why I yelled.

"Would you guys feel safer if I spent the night on the couch?"

They look at each other with concerned expressions before turning their gazes to their mother.

Ken asks, "Do you think Dad is coming back tonight? Would he hurt us?"

Rayna replies, "No, I don't think he's coming back tonight, and he would never hurt you. He loves you, even though he doesn't know how to show you that."

I add, "Look, little man, if he comes back tonight, it'll be to yell more, not to fight. If he sees me here, he might not try to cause any trouble, and if he does, it'll be directed at me, not you. Besides, wouldn't you sleep better knowing I'm here to keep you safe?"

I raise my arms and flex. Rayna's breath catches in her throat. She looks away, needing to collect herself before the kids notice her swooning. They both smile and nod.

Kim says, "Wow! You're the biggest man ever! I want you to sleep over."

Ken asks, "Mom, can he?"

"If Coach wants to stay, it's okay with me," Rayna replies, crossing her arms over her chest and clearing her throat after her voice cracks.

"Cool!" My arms drop to my sides while I smile at the kids as if I just won a grand prize. "Okay, I'll go get what I need and come right back." The kids smile as if they've won that same imaginary prize.

I slip out of the house, closing the door behind me. After grabbing my gym bag out of my truck and bringing it in the house, I quickly toss my pajama pants, a t-shirt, and a toothbrush in a small bag. Just as I'm about to head out, an idea pops into my head.

A few minutes later, I'm back at Rayna's. I take the baking ingredients out of the plastic bag, setting them out on the counter, away from where she's preparing dinner. She looks at me as if to ask why I've brought them.

I gloat. "I make the best oatmeal raisin cookies. Some have said they're better than what their grandma used to make."

"You don't have to go through the trouble. Really, this is too much."

I take her hand and kiss it. "Sweetheart, it was my choice to stay. I love baking cookies but rarely do because I'll eat them all. Here, I can make my *cake* and eat it, too, so to speak." I shake my head. "You know what I mean. It's a win/win situation."

"Thank you. Truly, thank you for everything," she whispers, looking at me with a loving kindness that turns me to mush. For a fleeting moment, I'd swear we can see into one another's souls. I like what I saw but fear that she'll discover the demon that lives inside of mine. I blink to hide him from her view.

"Think nothing of it." I'm quick to change the subject, averting my eyes, preventing her from seeing my evil side. "What are you cooking?"

"Chicken, mashed potatoes, corn, and steamed carrots."

"Damn, woman, that sounds delicious." I open the oven door enough to take a long sniff. "Mm-mmm! What can I do to help?"

She laughs and points to the table. "You can sit down and let me cook. You're too big for me to keep moving around you. Now get out of my way and park your rear."

Dinner goes well, as if nothing traumatizing happened a few hours ago. I had the kids laughing so hard at one point that Kim snorted. Even Rayna laughed to the point of wiping away tears. The kids think I'm hilarious.

Fear floods my thoughts when I realize my heart is waking up for Rayna and her kids. Fuck, don't do it! I'll only hurt them.

I stand quickly, take the plates, and set them in the sink. It's dangerous to sit around the table like a happy little family. It'll serve me well to remember that we're not.

Rayna will soon realize I'm a demonic fuck-monster, not a potential life partner. She'll be right to believe I'm not worthy of her and her kids, because I'm not. She doesn't understand the level of asshole I can be. She doesn't know I get my thrills from watching women scream.

While keeping my heart on ice, the kids and I hang out in the kitchen baking cookies and laughing while Rayna takes a soothing bath. I have to keep reminding Kim not to lick her fingers each time she balls up a wad of dough and then drops it onto the cookie sheet. It makes me laugh, but I secretly hope she isn't catching a cold or some weird childhood disease that she'll surely spread to the rest of us. But then, I wonder if the baking process is hot enough to kill off anything she might be carrying.

It isn't long before we've stuffed ourselves with cookies, having saved her only two. We're sprawled out on the U-shaped sofa, watching an animated movie. I jolt and see Rayna standing at the bottom of the stairs, looking at me. I must have dozed off. How long has she been standing there?

She tucks her hair behind her ear and then walks around the sofa, taking a seat next to her daughter. Kim crawls over to her, placing her head on her mom's thigh. Rayna brushes her fingers through Kim's hair, pulling some stray locks from her face and neck.

She looks up at me with a gentle smile so full of love that it reminds me of my mother's kindness. I can almost see how much love Rayna has for her daughter, and it makes my icy heart feel warm and full.

Ken stares at the television, lost in the excitement on the screen. I look back at Rayna, hoping to watch her with her daughter, but she's still looking at me. We don't smile; we simply hold each other's gaze.

What's she thinking?

My eyes slowly lower, noticing the nightie poking out from under her robe. I gently shake my head while biting my bottom lip. She's wearing that same light-blue nightie that makes my dick hard every time I watch her from my office window. My mood instantly changes from admiring her love to wanting to ravish her body.

I've told her how excited I get when I see her wearing that, so I'm sure she put it on to torture me. She knows I can't touch her tonight, not with the kids around. The wicked grin she's wearing while eyeballing my reaction proves her deviance.

Touché, Rayna! You win this time.

I shift, trying to hide my swelling prick, and she snickers.

At ten o'clock, Rayna finally tears the kids away from the television and gets them into bed. It's been a very long, trying day and I can see how it's taking its toll on all three of them. When Rayna returns, she's carrying two glasses of white wine, handing one of them to me. I sip it while watching her walk away from me and sit on the opposite side of the sofa. She folds her legs under her, letting her housecoat fall open, revealing more of the provocative nightie. She's not wearing a bra.

"Why are you teasing me?" I calmly ask with a deep voice. She drives me wild. She shrugs, smiling innocently, but says nothing. "How do you expect me to be on my best behaviour when you're this close to me, dressed in the nightie I fantasized about fucking you in?"

"Behave. Think of it as an incentive for when you can have me again," she teases in a sweet and sultry voice. She sips from her glass, keeping her sexy eyes set on me.

"You don't fight fair," I whisper, knowing I'm defeated.

"Are we fighting? Are we at war? If that's the case, is my strategy working? Am I winning?" She's being a brat; she's aggravating me, and I fucking love it.

"You're winning the prize of a spanking until your ass is red-hot," I say, sounding as if I'm joking when I'm really not.

Defiantly, she repeats, "Red-hot, huh? I'm not so sure that's a prize I want."

I snicker. "Oh, you'll like it. I'll reward you afterward."

Rayna teases. "It's too bad you can't take some of your frustrations out on me right now. I'd bet you could use my body as a stress reliever."

She knows me well.

I wish she'd open her legs and touch herself to further torment me, but I doubt she would. If she does, she'll be under me in a second, with my hard cock ramming into her, as I take what I want like the selfish man that I am.

"So, tell me about your sister. Why is she so…" I take a breath. "What's the word?" I ask, hoping to shift my thoughts. Talking about her sister will help simmer her sexual drive as well.

She quickly offers an appropriate word. "I think the word you're looking for is slutty."

"Okay, we'll go with that even though I appreciate sluts. Why are you saying it like it's a bad thing?"

Unless it's in the bedroom during sex, I don't think women's sexual proclivities should deem her a slut. That suggests a double standard between the sexes. If a man plays around, he's excused because it's considered sowing his oats or playing the field. If a woman does it, she's crucified and ostracized.

I like sluts. I am one; or at least, I was.

"I don't know why she hasn't settled down. She has always been a free spirit and tries to enjoy life to its fullest, which I admire. I think she's only had a few actual boyfriends, but they were fleeting. She had a girlfriend for a while that she really cared about. I'm not sure what happened, but it ended badly." She sips her wine. "She might be ready to settle down."

"Maybe Tim will call her soon," I inform her. "Now tell me, how is that delicious pussy of yours?"

She snickers. "My pussy?"

"I love hearing that word come out of your mouth. Would you like to ride my mouth?" I ask, hoping she'll say yes.

Her face flushes and I'm once again reminded of how naïve she is.

I can imagine the dilemma in her mind battling between her motherly instincts and her womanly desires. She shakes her head to turn me down. I know we can't start playing. But I want to make this woman cum hard on my face and then ride my cock, but we can't risk the kids hearing.

"Damn, you look delicious and smell like coconut. Strangely, I happen to be craving coconut."

"I'm sitting way over here. How do you know I smell like coconut?" she asks, doubting my nasal keenness.

I flash her my very best come-hither expression. She gulps down the last of the wine before standing to get some pillows from the chest. She then reaches behind the cushion on the sofa, grasping something and giving it a quick tug. The cushion flips over, immediately changing the sofa into a bed. The sheets are already on it. She tosses the blanket from the back of the sofa and a pillow onto the bed before turning to look at me.

"There you go; a nice, soft bed to lay your weary head."

"Lie with me," I whisper, not asking but telling her what I want.

"You know I can't," she whispers, filling us both with disappointment.

I want her to lie in my arms so I can hear her breathing and smell her coconut-scented skin. It's not about sex, although that would be the highest point of my day. I chug back the last of my wine and set the glass on the coffee table.

I wave her over. "Come here." She shakes her head so I place my hand on my heart. "I'll behave. I won't touch your body, I promise."

She hesitates before deciding to come to me. My eyes stay on hers. It's almost impossible not to look down at her nightie as it brushes against her thighs with each step. I lean forward and take her hand when she's close enough. I pull gently, leading her down until she's straddling my thighs, facing me.

"You are an exceptional mother. You're strong and kind. It's obvious that they are your universe. They're lucky to have you."

"Thank you, but I'm lucky to have them."

She leans in, pressing her lips to mine. I let her set the pace, gentle and patient, not rough and eager as it usually is when I kiss her. Her hands hold my face as our lips mesh, and our tongues calmly explore.

I'm not touching her, as I promised. My hands grip the edge of the cushion with tight fists. Keeping my hands to myself is like a punishment. I'm sure she can feel my appreciation of her attention swelling beneath her. I'm careful not to tilt my hips. I know it will push me beyond my ability to maintain myself.

Our lips separate, her sweet breath caresses my face. We're both eager to rip our clothes off and mould our bodies into one sweaty, erotic heap. She rests her forehead against mine. It's abundantly clear she's fighting the overwhelming urge to let me take her right here, right now.

She sighs heavily before sliding off my legs and taking a few steps back. I have yet to release the cushions from my vice-like grip.

My prick is uncomfortably entombed in my sweatpants. I am in such a heightened state of arousal that if I move even the slightest, I might grab hold of her, going against my vow not to touch her body. I want to give her what pleases me most: intense, orgasmic pleasure.

I see her swallow hard before whispering. "Sleep well. I'll see you in the morning."

I slowly nod, not saying anything. Instead, I watch her run up the stairs, waiting until she's out of view before flopping my head against the back of the sofa and taking a few deep breaths. My hands finally release the cushion. I open and close them several times to get the blood flowing through my white knuckles.

Remaining quietly seated for several minutes, I listen through the silence in the house for any cue that she may have changed her mind and is making her way back down to me. I don't know why I think she'll return, but I'm disappointed when she doesn't. I debate whether to jerk off before going to sleep. I'm deterred when I look around and remember the kids were sitting in here only an hour ago. That thought is enough to stifle my desire and soften my cock. I go to the bathroom and brush my teeth and then slide onto the sofa bed.

It's been an hour since Rayna went upstairs and I still can't fall asleep. I'm sexually frustrated. Knowing that she's upstairs lying alone in her room is enough to keep me awake. I keep fantasizing about sneaking upstairs, climbing into her bed and ravishing her body while looking into her seductive eyes.

I lift my head to listen to the hushed sounds coming from upstairs. Someone is tiptoeing down the steps. Even though it's dark, I can tell it's Rayna approaching the bed. She says nothing, which I find odd. She startles when I raise my hand toward her.

Perhaps she thought I was asleep, and she was hesitant to wake me. I wait for her to decide whether to take my hand and get in with me.

I'm relieved when her delicate fingertips glide along my palm. I lift the covers and roll onto my back. She slips off her panties and tosses them to the floor while I slide my sweatpants down to my mid-thighs.

She straddles my pelvis. Her lips quickly find mine. She will set the pace tonight.

I place one hand on her lower back while the other cradles her cheek. Rayna can use me tonight, taking what she needs. I'm ready to let her take her pleasure, but I hope I'm capable of having an emotional connection, should she desire it.

Our lips never part. In one swift motion, I am buried deep inside her. Our breathing is quiet but increasingly more impassioned, even though she hasn't moved.

This is fucking amazing; she is fucking amazing.

Rayna's curvaceous hips lazily rock, pulling me in and out of her as she glides her pussy against my belly, never once lifting her weight off my pelvis.

My heart is warming and becoming a part of her. It's abundantly clear that tonight means something more to both of us than did our previous raging sexual experiences. We are connecting on a deeper level, despite my efforts to keep my heart out of this.

Tonight, she's mine and I'm hers, completely. We are one. Tomorrow, things can go back the way they were. Right?

She makes love to me, letting her orgasm slowly build and easily take her over. I'm careful not to force my pelvis upward by remaining still so she can take me how she chooses.

This is easy for a control freak like me. My inner demon throws himself against the imaginary cage in which he's confined. I would much rather flip her over and take her hard and fast, but I sense that's not what she needs tonight. If I'm rough with her, it won't please her as much as being gentle.

Her orgasm rolls through her. She quietly rides the high, not moaning any louder than a whisper. Instead, her body trembles against mine. Her eyes meet mine, and that's when I see her tears welling up. Her emotions are so strong that she can't contain them.

For me, sexual intimacy has always been for sexual gratification or to gain a feeling of dominance, but for no other purpose. This is the most unbelievably loving moment I've ever experienced.

I couldn't possibly be more intoxicated by this woman.

My fingertips tenderly wipe the tears from her soft cheeks. We slowly roll, ending with me above her. I raise myself onto my elbows while kissing her forehead as her tears spill. I don't hump her; I stay inside her while kissing her cheeks and brushing away her tears with my thumbs. Never had I imagined wanting to be this gentle and loving while having sex. This is how I want to be for Rayna because she needs me to be.

"Please, don't stop," she whispers.

Following her request and make love to her, the same way she did to me. I kiss her lips, neck and cheeks, loving her with a newfound compassion that had been dormant. Her body slips into a silent orgasm.

I watch her in the silent calmness of the night. Her mouth opens as a quivering breath escapes her. Her eyelids remain tightly shut and her brows furrowed, lifting in the center just slightly.

I'm drowning in this moment. It's taking away any doubt I may have had that I care deeply for Rayna. At this very moment, I realize that I'm not afraid to love her, and willing to let her love me. I can't fear something I have no control over and I can't stop it.

My own euphoric, full-body and mind climax overtakes me. My body stiffens and then jerks above hers. A muffled grunt slips from my throat. As my lungs release a halted breath, my body suddenly becomes weightier on my elbows.

She looks at me and peacefulness graces her eyes. I stroke her cheek with my fingertips and hold her gaze for several minutes until my softening manhood slips from her, ruining the best moment of my life.

She lifts her face and kisses me lovingly once more. As quickly as she got into my bed, she wiggles out from beneath me and tiptoes back up the stairs, disappearing into the lonely darkness.

I feel warm and complete, something I have never felt.

It's only for tonight. Come the light of day, Rayna will remember that I am nothing worth loving and everything will go back to the way it was. She won't want to build a life with a man like me.

A fullness builds in my throat, but I harden my emotions, preventing my regret from spilling from my eyes. Instead, I close my lids, subconsciously waving goodbye to this incredible night. I felt the vastness of her love, if only for a fleeting moment.

I fear I will never recover.

Rayna

I make my way back to my bedroom, stopping only to peek into each child's room to ensure that they're in their beds asleep. When I shut my door, I lean against it, suddenly feeling alone in the darkness of this stillness of the night.

Although the air is cool, I can still feel the warmth from his kiss on my lips.

What happened between us? I can feel his love in my soul while his cologne graces my skin. I wrap my arms around myself, inhaling his scent and remembering how endearing his eyes were when he held my gaze. His patience stole my heart.

I will never be the same. *We* can never be the same.

My silky sheets caress my body with a delicate touch. They don't compare to how tender Coach's fingertips were as they brushed away my pain. He broke something in me.

I've been hiding behind the facade of a happy, single mother with few regrets. He let my heart reveal all of its wounds through the silence of my tears. Then he kissed them away without judgement or expectation of anything in return. He fixed what he broke.

Tonight, in Coach's arms, my wounds scarred over and I feel whole again. I will always treasure those moments in the darkness and how he loved me, even if it won't last.

How could I allow myself to love him? He told me that he will never marry. I cannot change him, nor should I fool myself into thinking I can. He's a playboy, and I'm too complicated.

The beautiful man, whose bed I crawled out of, will never be happy with me alone. I should stop fooling myself into believing that we could live happily ever after with the fairy tale ending people would envy long after we've passed. Actual life isn't like that. I, of all people, know this and should keep it in mind.

There was a time when I loved Rick and thought he was everything I could ever need a man to be. How wrong I was! Maybe I'm a terrible judge of character who will inevitably fall for the wrong man over and over...

Am I blinded by Coach's incredible ability to take my mind away from life's ugly realities, using only his sexual talents? My ex-husband's bullshit promises of having a happy ever after fooled me, so why should I think that Coach is any different?

I will not ask him to be with me and only me because he'll shoot it down.

Why do writers always taunt us with a forever after happiness when it doesn't exist? Books and movies should better reflect actual life, not spin tales of untruths that give us all false hope.

My eyes close. I recall how he looked in the darkness. His loving eyes stared at me as if begging me not to hurt him. His fragrant flesh was hot against mine; hot enough to thaw my frozen heart. He was everything I needed him to be, just then, and I will forever be grateful to him for that. My mind drifts off, holding his image.

I dream of his tender, loving touch. I welcome this sleep because I get to enjoy him more. We are one while the moon hangs overhead, but when the sun awakens, I will once again be boring Rayna and he will be Coach; eternally single and unavailable.

Chapter Fifteen

Coach

Something pulls me away from the sensuous dream I was having about Rayna, instantly annoying me. I dreamed that the beautiful goddess was sitting on a stool, her arms tied behind her back with rope in an elaborate design effective in both immobilizing her arms and creating a sensual image. I had her at my mercy. She was mine, body and soul.

Why do I hear kids talking in my house?

My eyes open. I'm blinded by the bright light beaming into the room. Damn, my eyes feel scratchy and ache painfully from the glare that's bleeding through my lids. I blink several times and rub them harshly. Where am I?

Oh, right! I'm in Rayna's basement. Her scent flashes through my mind, along with the sound of her hushed moans, the softness of her skin, and how lonesome her eyes looked when they were full of tears. She nearly broke me. Maybe she did, and I simply haven't realized it yet.

Something smells very appetizing. I'm starving. I would really enjoy a steaming cup of coffee to help chase the drowsiness away. I suppose I should get out of this bed and start the day.

With significant effort, I pull my legs to the edge of the foam bed. I step down onto a pair of silky white panties; Rayna's, I presume. I remember her taking them off last night. She must have forgotten to bring them with her. I scoop them up with one finger and hold them to my nose, breathing in her sweet scent. My cock instantly springs awake. Is it a pee-hard-on, or do I need a release? Perhaps it's both.

I slip my t-shirt on and stand, re-adjusting my sweatpants and the rock-hard sausage that's begging to take a piss. After flipping the bed back into the sofa, I stuff the pillow into the same chest I watched Rayna take it from. I visit the bathroom to relieve myself and jerk off as quickly as I can just to make my hard-on go away. Thankfully, it only takes a few minutes. I wash my hands, brush my teeth, and then head upstairs to see what all the giggling is about.

The kids and Rayna are busy in the kitchen and don't notice me make my way up the stairs. The sun beams through the patio doors, making it possible to see her silhouette through her nightie. I'm so thankful that I jerked my cock before I came up here, otherwise I'd be hard as steel from seeing how fucking sexy she looks right now. This woman does not understand how she affects me.

I fling myself from around the wall and yell, "Good morning!"

All three of them jolt and screech. I burst into hard laughter. Their faces are priceless!

"What the f… Fart?" Rayna yells, holding her chest, her eyes wide. "Dammit, Coach, that's not funny!"

"*Au contraire, mon ami.* From where I'm standing, it's hilarious."

"Coach, don't do that," Kim complains with a sour expression.

I pat her head on the way to the coffeemaker. "Sorry, little woman. I only meant to scare your mom."

"Nice," Rayna retorts, slapping me on the shoulder. I laugh even harder.

"Are you hungry?" Ken asks. "There's a lot to eat."

He isn't upset that I startled them. He thought it was as funny as I did. Scaring people to make them shriek must be a guy thing.

I stand next to Rayna as she holds a spatula, getting ready to flip a pancake. I want to wrap my arms around her, press my lips to her neck, and breathe in her scent. She carries her natural beautiful well, even though her eyes are still puffy from the lack of sleep, and her hair is unkempt. A light purple haze hangs under her eyes, reminding me of how late it was when she left my bed last night. If she would have stayed with me, maybe we could consider ourselves to a couple.

Nah, Rayna would never settle for a schmuck like me.

"Pancakes? Eggs?" She asks, stepping a little closer to me as she turns her back to the kids and adds teasingly, "Me?"

My voice isn't quiet. "The latter sounds tantalizing enough. I'll have some of that, please."

"Eggs it is." She smirks at me. "How many?"

"Hmm, how many do you have?"

"I only have three left. How do you want them?" she asks as she flips a pancake that's been swelling in the hot pan.

"Any way you want to give it to me," I suggest and she blushes.

I take a mug from the cupboard. I fill it with coffee and then sit at the table with the youngsters. "How did you two sleep?"

"I slept great," Kim replies.

"Okay, I guess," Ken tells me. "How about you?"

"Well, I fell asleep feeling very tranquil. I can't say I've ever experienced anything like that before. It was the best *sleep* I've ever had," I reply while looking at Rayna and trying to assess her thoughts.

She's looking at me, expressionless. I wish I could read her mind. Her face isn't giving me any clues whether she's happy with how things went last night or if she's regretting letting me glance at her heart.

Rayna looks away, scooping the pancake up and flopping it on a plate. She slips it in front of Kim and pours syrup on it, casting her eyes up to glance at me. She blinks several times, and walks back to the pan, still wearing no discernable expression.

Did I read too much into last night?

She breaks the eggs into the heated pan, sprinkles something over them and then covers it with a glass lid. I'm waiting for her to look at me, but she doesn't. She stares at the eggs, watching them cook while lost in her thoughts. What's she thinking? If the kids weren't here, I'd ask her what's taking her so far away.

After we finish eating, the kids head to the basement to watch cartoons. I hear the television blasting out strange noises, and the characters talking in annoying screeching voices similar to nails on a chalkboard. It's way too early in the morning for that. How does Rayna do this every morning and not go insane?

Rayna is putting the milk in the fridge when I slide up behind her and wrap my arms around her waist. She instantly stiffens and holds her breath. She doesn't have to hit me with a brick; it's obvious she doesn't want me to touch her. I immediately step back, putting some distance between us. She slowly closes the refrigerator as she exhales.

Without turning to look at me, she apologizes. "I'm sorry. It's just that I," She takes a breath, "I don't think we should read too much into last night. I was vulnerable. Not that you took advantage, obviously! It was my fault completely. I should never have been so…"

I interrupt her. "Rayna, it's okay."

She turns to look at me. Her face is flushed, and her eyes are glossy. "I shouldn't have put you in that position. It was cruel of me and I'm sorry. Please don't read more into it other than a pathetic moment of weakness on my part."

I look down at the floor, remembering how perfect she felt in my arms last night. "If that's what you want."

"I think it's best, don't you?" she asks.

"For who?" I ask, my heart suddenly thumping wildly in my chest.

"Please don't do this now. The kids are downstairs."

"Yes, they're downstairs and the TV is blaring. They can't possibly hear our conversation, Rayna. Do you really want to pretend last night meant nothing?"

It's as though she's trying to convince herself more than me. She clears her throat before explaining. "You know this can't happen. We are so different. You're young, single, and a bit of a playboy. No offence. I'm divorced, older, a mom, and definitely not as sexually experienced as someone should be in order to properly entertain you for the rest of your life. We both know I wouldn't be able to keep up with your needs. You'll tire of me and my boring, vanilla life, and then leave me and my kids broken, which is exactly as their father did. I can't put them through that again. So, yes, it is better for all of us if we don't read too much into last night."

Rayna is using her head, not her heart, and her face reveals that. She's being a protective mom. I can't blame her for that. It's one reason I respect her so much.

Maybe everything she says is right. I don't know. I can't see the future. All I know is that I'm drawn to her. From the moment we met, and after having been intimate with her only a few times, she's weaved her way into my heart. I want her and those kids in my life.

She crosses her arms over her chest. "Where has Alissa been these past few days? I haven't seen her car in your driveway."

"Alissa and I are over. I broke it off after you came to visit me on Saturday. It was time to let her go. You were right when you told me to send her on her way." I take a step toward her and stop. "At this moment, sweetheart, you couldn't be more wrong about us. I want you. I want those kids. Are you listening to me? Look at me!" I demand, but she refuses.

Rayna stares at the dishes in the sink with tear-filled eyes.

She says, "I'll bet you broke her heart. Understand, I don't want to be in her position in a year from now. I can't be a notch on your headboard, a conquest that you use for your own purpose and then toss away when some newer shinier toy comes along. I think we should stop before this gets out of hand."

"No, Rayna, I don't think we should stop. I want you because somehow you do something to me that nobody has ever done. You see me for me, for who I am. You always have. All those times we shot the shit about everything and nothing, I wanted more of you than you will allow." I step toward her again. "I can't see myself being apart from you, not anymore. The thought scares me. I don't know why, but it does. Rayna, I want to live with you, marry you, maybe give you more children, if that's what you want. You're such an incredible mother."

I inhale deeply, watching her examine my face to see if I'm weaving a web of lies or telling her the truth. That's when it happens. My heart speaks for itself.

"I love you, Rayna."

She struggles to take in a breath, as though all the air has been sucked out of the room. She puts her hand on her forehead, the other on her stomach. She whispers a heart-wrenching plea, "Simon, please don't hurt me."

I rush to close the distance between us, pulling her into my arms and kissing her passionately. It's something I've wanted to do since I woke up without her beside me. She kisses me back.

"You won't hurt me. Will you?" she whispers as she clings to me, her golden head pressing against my chest.

"I will try every day to do the exact opposite of that. I never want to hurt you. Date me. Date me like we're a proper couple. What do you have to lose, Rayna?" I ask while holding her to my chest with one arm draped around her shoulder. My fingers comb through her soft hair, brushing it away from her pale face.

"A lot if it doesn't work out," she utters, her hands gripping my back a little tighter.

"Mom? Coach?" Ken startles us and we leap apart, nervously. My heart is suddenly pounding in my chest, desperately trying to break free. "Are you two boyfriend and girlfriend?"

"Um, well," Rayna scratches her head, stalling. "It's complicated."

"Ken, I asked your mom to go on a date with me."

"Are you going to go?" he asks her, not frowning or smiling to give me a clue whether he approves. He's his mother's son, for sure.

"Um, I don't know," she replies while fiddling nervously with her fingers.

"Do you think she should say yes?" I ask him, thinking it'll give me bonus points with him. "Since you're the man of the house, I should ask your permission to take your mom on a date. So, what do you say about that idea, little man?"

"I think Mom should say yes," he quickly tells me.

We both look at Rayna. She looks scared as her eyes peer from him to me and back to him.

"You think I should go on a date with Coach?" she asks him, not sure she heard him correctly.

"Yeah, I do. He's a nice guy, Mom."

I yell, startling Rayna and Ken. "Hey, Kim! Come here, darling."

She runs up the stairs and into the kitchen. "What?"

"Tell me something. Do you think I should take your mom on a date?"

She looks at me for a few seconds before meeting eyes with her mom. "Yes, I do. I like you. You're nice to us and you're hilarious."

"Okay, fine! I'll go on a date with you," she blurts while rolling her eyes dramatically to make the kids laugh.

"Hey, kids, can I kiss your mom?"

Ken nods. Kim giggles, covering her mouth as shy girls do. My eyes meet Rayna's.

I spread my arms wide and announce, "I have their permission to kiss you."

As I'm slowly stepping closer to her, she puts her hand up to stop me, but she's smiling and laughing, confirming that she doesn't hate the idea.

"No! Stop walking! You don't want to kiss me," she says for the benefit of keeping things innocent in front of the kids. She's laughing as her face flushes bright pink.

The kids are watching and laughing. Ken cheers me on. "Kiss her, Coach!"

"What do you say?" I ask with a ridiculous toothy smile while she looks at me with wide eyes.

She playfully pushes me to make me stop advancing, but finally drops her hand when I'm standing only a foot away from her. She looks at me with delicate eyes. "Fine, kiss me then."

My lips touch hers and hold perfectly still. I tenderly slide my hand onto the back of her head. Our faces separate but hold near as our eyes meet. I press another tender kiss to her velvety lips while breathing her in. We don't open our mouths because the kids are watching us. It's hard to pretend they aren't; the laughter is a constant reminder that they're in the room.

When my face pulls back from hers, she playfully pushes me away, curling her lips into her mouth so she can taste me. Her face flushes brighter than I've ever witnessed, and I notice her hands are shaking when she tucks a tress of hair behind her ear.

"Okay, now that you've had your kiss, go home so I can get the kids ready for school. I have to go to work. Don't you have to go to work, too?"

I pout. "Yeah, I do. All right, I'll see you all later. Thanks for breakfast and saying yes to a date and a kiss."

"I can still change my mind on the date. You know that, right?" she teases.

"Nope, I have witnesses that will back me up. Right, guys?"

"I'll back you up, Coach," Ken assures me.

Kim corrects Rayna, throwing her words back at her in that spiteful way children love to do to their parents when the roles reverse. "You said you'd go, Mom. You always tell us not to make promises we have no intention of keeping."

I snicker and pat the kids on their heads as I pass by them. "See you kids later." I make my way across the lawn to my house but cringe when I look up to see a familiar car in my driveway. "Shit!"

I walk in the front door to find Alissa sitting on the sofa, staring at me with a furious expression. Her lousy attitude is not something I care to be privy to right after having the best night and morning of my life. The last thing I want to do is ruin this incredible high I'm on.

"We are no longer together. What are you doing in my house?" I ask as I walk past her.

She's not threatened by me. She's a true submissive so I'm taken back by her courage to confront me with so much attitude, but I won't let her know that it's pissing me off. I won't give her the satisfaction.

She crosses her arms while continuing to glare at me. "Just like that?"

I reply matter-of-factly. "Pretty much, yeah. What were you expecting; a sympathy card, a parting gift, what? Alissa, you knew we were only friends with benefits, nothing more. We did not have a deep spiritual connection. The arrangement was that we would spend time together, have sex, and go about our own business. And now it's done."

She scoffs at me while shaking her head. "Wow! I can't believe it's so easy for you to cast me aside. So, do you want to tell me who the new tart is?"

"New tart?" I repeat, snickering at her word choice. "What makes you think there's someone new?"

"This," she says, holding up a condom wrapper and a used condom that I had put in the trash bin. She must have sifted through my garbage and unwrapped wads of tissue to find it, which is absolutely disgusting. "And you didn't come home last night."

"Get the fuck out of my house and give me my damn key back. Better yet, keep it as a parting gift. I'll be changing the locks, anyway. If you ever come back here again, I'll have you arrested for trespassing. You need help. Digging through my trash is beneath you."

"Oh, I need help? No, mother fucker, *you* do! You should seek professional help. You beat the fuck out of women for sexual gratification. That is fucked up!"

"Is it? I don't recall you disagreeing when you were bound and coming while I was slapping your ass. But now, when I suddenly don't want you anymore, I'm a mother fucking abuser? Go fuck yourself! Get out of my house."

She stands and throws the used condom at me, pissing me off even more. If she'd have hit me with it, I can't say I wouldn't have thrown her over my shoulder and carried the bitch out of my house. My fists clench and my nostrils flare. If a man had done that, I'd beat him to a bloody pulp. But she's female and I will never put my hands on a woman when I'm angry.

Alissa stands right in my face, staring at me, but I refuse to look at her. I look to the right of her head, which I know irks her in ways that give me a slight satisfaction.

"Look at me!" she demands, but I don't. "Is she the bitch next door with the kids? You always had a thing for her. Didn't you? She seems to be way too vanilla for someone as messed up as you. But maybe she's a dirty hoe like the rest of the whores you fucked behind my back."

"I never hid anything from you."

I glare at her with obvious rage, and she flinches. She can't deny that I'm wickedly pissed off. My upper lip twitches and I know I'd better walk away before I do something I will absolutely regret. I take two steps back before turning around and rushing out the front door. I'm not giving her enough time to jump on me.

This psychotic bitch standing in my house is nothing like the woman I thought I knew. Now that I look back on our time together, I can see the tiny clues that should have tipped me off that she's a crazy, possessive bitch.

"Get out of my house or I'm calling the cops," I tell her as I make my way outside.

I stop when I reach the lawn, plenty far enough away from the door for her to walk through it without touching me. I don't need her telling the cops that I physically assaulted her. Because of how aggressive I look, and what happened last night with Rayna's ex, they'll likely believe her over me.

"I'm not leaving until I get my shit."

"Just go, I'll send your shit via courier."

"No, fuck you!" She turns and runs back up the stairs, disappearing down the hall toward the bedrooms.

Instead of dealing with her bullshit, I dial 9-1-1 and ask the cops to come so they can take an intruder out of my house. I let them know that I'm a big guy and I'm worried she'll try to say I hit her. I'd much rather they come and take her out of my house. It doesn't take more than a minute for them to arrive. They must have been close by.

Once again, the neighbours trickle out of their houses, curious why I'm being confronted by the police for the second time in less than twenty-four hours.

I have my hands up when they approach. These cops differ from the two last night and I'm grateful. If I'm involved in two incidents in such a close timeframe, I think they might develop some concerns.

"Sir, are you the one who called?" the first officer asks as he's stepping out of the car.

I nod. "Yes, I called. There's a woman in my house who will not leave even though I asked her several times to get out. She's my ex who never lived here, so she has no right to be inside. She says she isn't leaving until she gets her shit. Will you please get her out of my house?"

"Does she have any weapons on her or does she have access to anything inside that could harm us?"

"Does her evil glance and bitchy attitude count as a weapon?" I reply with a smirk, but they don't appreciate the humour.

"Does she have anything in the house that belongs to her? If so, what?" the second officer asks.

"She has two t-shirts, three panties, one pair of yoga pants, a pair of jeans, one or two pairs of socks, and a bra. Black, I think. I can give you a full description of each item if need be. Oh, don't forget her pink toothbrush and her hairbrush in the top drawer in the guest bathroom. She can take her shit and get the fuck out, but I want to make sure she isn't taking anything that belongs to me. She knows where I keep my money and my valuables. I do not put it past her to take everything she can get her fingers on. She wants to hurt me."

"You're very specific in the list of her belongings," he says, looking at me as if I've suddenly grown a second head.

"Well, I know the contents of my house. Will you check her to make sure she's taken only her belongings?"

The officer nods. "I'll call a female officer to pat her down and go through her purse."

Thankfully, they aren't simply going to let her walk off with anything she feels like. The officer puts out a call on his radio and then tells me to stay put while they go inside my house.

I wait for the cops to come back out while I yell at the nosy neighbours. "Mind their own fucking business! There's nothing happening here that concerns any of you."

Most of them go back in their houses, fearing my wrath, but a few nosy mother fuckers hang around to watch. They know I won't lay my hands on them because the cops are here.

I point to a house while looking at a smug man in his late fifties. "That's your house there. Isn't it?" I look at the house and back at him. My wicked grin and wide eyes have him uncrossing his arms and slinking home.

How Rayna hasn't noticed the commotion and come out to see if everything is all right baffles me. Truthfully, I'm pleased that she's oblivious. I know Alissa would scream at her or attack her if given the opportunity.

How Alissa hid her jealous streak also baffles me. Why would she want to be with me if she thinks I'm so fucked up? She once told me that I'm emotionally stunted with little chance of ever loving someone completely. She doesn't know me at all. Then again, I never let her see the real me.

A female officer drives into my driveway. After she's brought outside, I watch her frisk Alissa while she yells in protest. The officer finds a watch my grandfather gave me before he passed away, three of my rings, eight hundred and twenty dollars in cash, and all the photos I had ever taken of women in various positions and stages of undress. What was she planning on doing with them?

Those pictures are private and were secured in my safe, along with the money. I never showed her any of those photos, so how she even knew I had them has me curious. How she got into my safe without me telling her the code is also likely to haunt me.

I refuse to press charges but ask them how to put a restraining order on her to keep her at bay. After they give me the information, they send her on her way and follow her to make sure she doesn't go around the block and come right back to start trouble again. If she makes the mistake of coming back, I will absolutely press charges.

When I go inside, I put my stuff back where she took it from, and then check to make sure she didn't take anything that the cops didn't recover. After I'm certain everything is accounted for, I order a new and more secure safe. They'll deliver it tomorrow afternoon.

Chapter Sixteen

Rayna

After frantically rushing around to get everybody ready, somehow, I dropped the kids off at school on time. I start on the fifteen-minute drive to the dentist's office where I work while doing what I always do; I take this time to relax in silence.

Listening to music when I'm driving doesn't excite me like it does most people, especially in the morning. I can take it or leave it any other time of the day. This is my time to blank my mind as best I can before the busyness of the office consumes me.

Being a dentist is something I've always wanted to do, but I couldn't afford to pay for the continued education I needed to earn that degree. Instead, I had to settle as a dental assistant. It's not so bad. We do a lot of the same procedures, I just get paid less than they do.

No matter how much I try to concentrate on the drive, last night keeps flooding my thoughts. We made love. When I went downstairs to Coach's bed, I didn't intend to be romantic, but that's exactly what happened. I wanted it. I could even say that I needed it.

He was receptive to my tenderness and seemed to lose himself in my affection. It happened, and it was divine. I want to remember it as being one of those rare and perfect moments in my life that I will forever treasure. It may never happen like that again. I had a genuine connection to Coach, and it was perfect for both of us.

I click the phone button on my steering wheel to call my sister. She picks up on the first ring. "Hello, sister."

"Good morning! Are you at work?" I ask.

"Yeah, I just got here. I haven't gone inside yet. So, what happened?"

I wonder how she already heard about the commotion yesterday with my ex. "Oh, with Rick? Well, he really took it to a whole new level of idiocy this time. He got a bit out of control and then Coach came to my rescue. He punched Coach in front of the police and the kids, so they arrested him. They're charging him with assault and maybe trespassing because he wouldn't leave my house when I asked him to. But that charge might not stick because Ken initially invited him in the house. It was a giant shit-show. I'll probably have to hire another lawyer and go to court again." The silence is deafening. "Renee, are you still there?"

"Yeah, um." She takes a breath. "What the fuck? You rarely ever call me this early, so I was wondering what happened that was so crucially important you couldn't wait until later this afternoon to tell me about it. But, fuck! Holy shit, woman! Are you okay? The kids? How are the kids? Wait a minute! He punched Coach? That man has a death wish. Please tell me Coach beat that sardonic expression off his face?"

"Oh, no." I chuckle. "That wasn't why I was calling you. I suppose I should have called last night to tell you all of that. You asked me so many questions just now. I'll try to answer all of them. Well, the kids were shaken up and scared, but they seem to be okay now. I'm fine, too. And no, Coach didn't hit him back because the cops were watching. But he did physically toss him out of my house. So fun to watch."

"I'm sorry I missed it."

"It was great!" I snicker. "And, before you ask, Coach heard the yelling and came to see what was happening. He wasn't already in my house. He was at his place when it first started. Once everything calmed down, he offered to spend the night because he wanted us to feel safe. The kids pleaded with me to let him. So I did, and he stayed on the sofa-bed downstairs. Which brings me to why I was calling."

"Wow! So much action. I can't believe you didn't call me. You bitch! Okay, so continue the story and tell me the real reason you're calling me so early this morning," she urges.

"I couldn't sleep last night knowing Coach was in my house. So, I went downstairs and climbed into bed with him. He was awake, too. I made love to him."

"No, you did not!"

"Yes. Yes, I did," I confirm.

"Was he receptive?"

"Shockingly, yes. Very. I fucking cried," I confess, embarrassed at my feminine fragility, no doubt blushing even though I'm alone in my car.

Renee laughs as she talks. "You didn't? Oh my God, Rayna! How was he when you cried? Did he freak out?"

"He rolled me onto my back, wiped my tears away, and made slow, passionate love to me. It was heart-stirring. He was impressively tender and loving. Needless to say, this morning I was very nervous about how things would be between us over breakfast."

"And, was it horribly uncomfortable?" she asks.

I sigh and groan. "No, it was wonderful. He told me that he wants me and asked the kids if it was okay to take me out on a date. They surprised me; they want him to, so he asked me out in front of them. When I said I would go, he asked Ken if he could kiss me. You know, because Ken is the man of the house—Coach's words, not mine. Ken gave his permission and Coach laid one on me as the kids stood there watching and giggling. Strangely enough, it wasn't remotely uncomfortable. He was very respectful of me and the kids."

"So, you two are an item now, like, officially a couple?" She teases me the same way she used to as a child, with a silly song. "You and Coach, sitting in a tree, K-I-S-S-I-N-G."

"You are so immature!" I say, and she laughs. "In all seriousness, he's going to get bored with me. How can he not? I bore myself. I'll fall head over heels for him and he'll break my heart, leaving me more bitter than I already am. The kids will be hurt and think we failed because of something they did, even if I tell them otherwise. What have I gotten myself into? I must be crazy."

"You are not crazy. A little off the wall and over dramatic sometimes, but definitely nowhere near clinically insane. He's hot, and he seems to be really into you. Give him a shot, Rayna. You deserve to be happy. If it doesn't last, use your time together to make wonderful memories that you can look back on fondly while you masturbate. I'm joking, sort of. Seriously though, take a chance on him. Life is too short to be lonely because you fear rejection."

"Okay. I'll let this cowboy ride me until he finds a more interesting horse to run off with."

We both laugh, but I wonder whether I'm right to think he won't stick around.

"Before I forget to tell you, a friend of Coach's called me last night. We're meeting for coffee later this afternoon."

"You must let me know how it goes and send me a picture of him. I'm curious to see what he looks like."

"I'll text it to you. He already sent me one, so I sent him one, too. We agreed that there's nothing worse than spending time with someone you're not physically attracted to. It's awkward," she says.

The photo comes through and I'm instantly excited for her. This guy is as big as Coach, but his face seems to be much more placid than Coach's. He's extremely attractive, exactly how my sister prefers her partners.

"Very nice, sis! He's smoking hot. Enjoy your date and don't forget to tell me how it goes."

We say our goodbyes and hang up.

I pull into a parking space, shut the car off, and take a few deep breaths before getting out. Here's hoping it's a pleasant one and nobody tries to bite me today. I'm so tired that my reflexes probably won't be as quick as needed to avoid a child's chomp.

"Rayna!" A voice that is way too familiar pierces the surrounding air, stabbing at my ears like an ice pick. I don't have to turn around to realize that Rick is approaching me.

"Do not start trouble or I'll call the cops again," I tell him as I turn to look at him with rage in my eyes.

He's walking closer but stops about five feet away and doesn't take another step toward me. His eyes shout regret. Good, he should feel shitty about what he did to me and his kids yesterday. The stress he piled on Coach, who's innocent in all of this, was undeserved. Okay, maybe he's not innocent, but unworthy of Rick's spite.

"I'm not here to start trouble." He runs his hand through his hair the way he has for as far back as I can remember. He adds, "I'm sorry about yesterday. Are the kids okay?"

Did I hear him correctly? "Are you kidding me right now?"

He shakes his head. "I don't know what I was thinking. I'm so sorry. I can't believe I got so angry. I'll apologize the next time I see them."

"And when do you think that will be? You can't honestly believe that they want to see you. Do you? There's no way you can think yesterday wasn't terrifying for them." I take a few steps closer to him, finding a wave of newfound anger like a momma bear protecting her cubs from a predator. "You fucking terrified them."

He begins, "I shouldn't have—"

"They don't want to see you. Coach is their friend, and they witnessed their father punch him in the face. Do you have any idea how devastated they are about that? I sure hope for your sake that he doesn't decide to sue you." I take a breath to calm myself. "You will not see the kids until they say it's all right. If you want to fight me on this, I'll see you in court. I have video proof that you are a cursing, angry man who was violent with the kids present. If you don't think I will fight you on this, try me. I am so fucking sick of your shit. I've taken it again and again for far too long, and it stops now."

I'm so furious that I'm shaking, but I am determined not to cry.

"Are you sure he's only the neighbour and not your boyfriend? He seemed to be a little too protective of you to just be the guy who lives next door."

The man is pushing his luck with me. If he doesn't stop, I'm going to kick him in the groin to hurt his brain. He thinks with his cock.

"First, who I date or don't date is none of your damn business. You lost the right to know what I do with my body when you had your fifth affair, and I finally wised up and divorced you. Second, if I were dating him, don't you think the kids would have told you by now? Oh wait, you don't listen to them when they talk, so how would you know?"

He raises his voice loud enough that my co-worker, Kelly, stops to watch to make sure I'll be all right.

"Don't fucking start that shit, Rayna! I asked a simple question, that's all. Are you fucking him or not?"

I take a few more steps toward him until I'm a mere foot away from him and then smirk. Hushed, so she can't hear me, I whisper, "He fucks me raw and I love it. I cum harder than I ever did with you. He enjoys thoroughly pleasuring me with his mouth, unlike you. When he touches me, it's all about me and my satisfaction, also unlike you. So, to answer your question; yes, that man fucks me hard with his thick cock, after I've kissed and licked every inch of his muscular body. And the best part is that you can't do anything to stop it. So, choke on that, asshole."

For a second, I wonder if I've pushed too far, but I will not back down or show weakness of any kind. I learned this intimidating expression from Coach. I don't even blink. I won't show him an ounce of weakness. He means nothing to me other than that he was the sperm donor that produced my children.

"Did you have to choose the biggest goddamn asshole in the city to fuck?" He runs his hand through his hair again. He looks defeated, and I revel in it. Rick adds, "I fucking nailed him, hard, and he barely budged. He's a tank. How do I compete with that?"

"Compete?" I question. He shrugs as if he thought he might get me back one day. "Did you honestly think I'd ever go back to you? I fucking divorced you! You're a shitty father, a lousy lover, a cheating asshole, and I never should have married you in the first place. The only nice thing you ever did for me was give me those amazing kids. And you're such a self-centered dick that you don't even appreciate them. One day, you'll wake up alone, accompanied by your mounting guilt. You'll tell the drunk guy on the barstool next to you that you're a father but haven't seen your kids in many years and don't even know what they look like anymore. How pathetic will that be? You need to get your shit together and start being their father and not just their biological sperm donor."

"How can I do that if you won't let me see them?" he snidely asks, revealing that massive chip on his shoulder.

"Prove that you're not an asshole, and I'll consider it."

"And how can I do that?"

I roll my eyes. "First, don't harass me at my job. Next, get rid of whatever bimbo you're dating and find a respectable woman, and treat her right. No more strippers or college-aged women. You're an adult. Grow the fuck up.

That's all I'm asking. You aren't eighteen anymore, and you need to accept that. Now, I'm going inside and you're leaving. Call me when you get your shit together so we can discuss visitation, but you'd better give the kids some time to forgive you."

I walk inside to see all of my coworkers have been watching me through the giant plate glass window. They quickly pretend they were doing something other than listening in, but they aren't talented actors.

"Before anyone asks what's going on, I'll just say it now. He's being an asshole again and we'll leave it at that." I walk past them and head to the break room to put my purse in my locker.

Kelly slinks in behind me. "So, you're dating, huh?"

I look at her and shake my head. "Can we let this go, please?"

"All right, but if it morphs into something wonderful, will you let me stand in your wedding? Be sure to partner me with a hunky man. I'd prefer him to be single, please."

She walks as if she's a bride strutting down an aisle while humming the wedding march.

Chapter Seventeen

Coach

I've been at the gym, sitting at my desk for over an hour, and have gotten no work done. All I can think about is Rayna. Specifically, how she was with me last night. She made love to me, not just my body, but me: Simon. No woman has ever taken me down that rabbit hole. I wish I could go back.

Can we ever match that feeling again or will we forever try to get back there but never be able to? Was it simply a fluke? Why would she want to put herself in a position where she believes I'll only hurt her? I can't say that I blame her if she decides I'm not worth the risk and changes her mind.

I have to stop the what if's. Maybe I should get out from behind this desk and walk around, talk to some patrons. Few people are here this morning, but it's still early. Most people don't come to do their workouts until later in the day.

A beautiful redhead looks like she's about to stick her fingers where they might get pinched. What the fuck is she doing?

I jog over. "Don't put your fingers in there unless you'd like to get them broken."

She smiles shyly but doesn't say much other than a polite thank you. Her roaming eyes tell me all I need to know about her. She's a gym slut who works out for the sake of meeting men with muscles.

Best I leave her to her work out so she doesn't think I'm trying to hit on her. I'm definitely not interested. Normally, I would offer to stick around and help her, sort of feel her out. Then I'd bring her to my office to give her a more personal workout, but not on a morning like this after a night like that.

My cell phone vibrates in my pocket and I'm thrilled to have another distraction. I dig in and pull it out. My best friend, Tim, is calling.

"Hey, buddy. How's it going?"

He quickly replies in his typically smooth, deep voice, "Going good, Coach. You at the gym?"

"Of course I am, Tim. Where did you think I'd be?"

He chuckles. "I don't know, with your girlfriend maybe."

"Nah, she's at work and I'm here. So, did you call Renee?"

"Wow! She's fucking hot! Tell me why you aren't tapping that? Is there something wrong with her, like she has a tail or extra fingers? The picture she sent me only shows her face and shoulders, so I'm guessing the deformity is below the neckline. Seriously though, what's wrong with her?"

I'm amused by how excited he is. "You approve of her?"

"Yeah, but my question stands. Why don't you?"

As I make my way into the men's locker room to tidy up and make sure all is running smoothly, I answer. "Well, Tim, I've always liked her sister. A lot. I've been with sisters before, but this time it's different. I'm losing it, Tim! This woman has me all tied in knots and before you ask, I mean that metaphorically; I'd never let anyone bind me. I don't think I could ever submit to that degree." I chuckle. "Back to the subject at hand. I really like this woman."

Tim is silent. With the receiver next to my ear, I wait patiently for him to say something while I rearrange the dumbbells into their correct order, by weight. It irritates the shit out of me when people don't put things back in the proper spot.

He finally breaks the silence. "Sorry, I had to check the weather. I thought maybe Hell froze over and nobody told me. So, hard-ass Coach, who has ruined the hearts of many women—and their bodies, from time to time—is falling in love. How fucking romantic is that?" He laughs. "You know I'm only busting your balls. I'm happy that you've finally found a woman who'll put up with your shit and still want a somewhat healthy relationship with you."

"Thanks, but I've never ruined a woman's body, let's get that straight right now. I've used them until they're limp and bruised, but never ruined them beyond recovery." We both laugh. "So, when are you going out with her little sister?"

"This afternoon, actually. We're meeting for lunch, nothing special. Neither of us wanted to make it a big deal in case we don't click. We don't want to be stuck together for a whole evening of dinner and a promised stroll through the park or some bullshit like that, in case it doesn't feel right. We didn't want it to be too awkward if it's over before it starts. You know what I mean. Coffee and a sandwich are easy enough."

"She's really cute and kind of crazy, exactly how you like them. And she doesn't have extra fingers or a tail, that I know of, anyway. If I had met her before her sister, I'd probably have fucked her by now and tossed her aside, but I met Rayna first. I always thought of Renee as being off-limits to me. All this time I've lived next door, watching Renee strutting around, I couldn't understand why I never wanted to spin that little broad on my cock. Something kept telling me to leave her alone. Now I get it. Maybe she wasn't meant for me because Rayna was. Hey, can I ask you something and you'll keep it between us?"

"Yeah, unless it's really juicy, and then I'm putting it on a billboard." He laughs. "You know you can tell me anything and I wouldn't put it on a billboard. That's too expensive."

I scoff. "That's because you're a broke-ass mother fucker!" He protests. "Okay, last night, she made love to me and I absolutely loved it. Tell me the truth, am I turning into a pansy?" I ask, hoping he won't laugh hysterically at my soft-hearted query.

He takes a loud breath instead of teasing me about my insecurities in matters of the heart. "No, you're not a pansy. You're simply falling in love and that's outstanding, my friend. For the first time in your life, you found a woman who you consider being your equal."

"Nah, she's way better than I could ever hope to be. I don't know why she's so interested in a dick like me."

"It's got to be the sex. From what I keep hearing from the girls around the gym, and I quote, '*he's fucking amazing in the sack.*' Dude, the woman wants your pepperoni-sized pecker. Actually, I think she fell in love with your body before she got a glimpse of the wee fellow, but by then it was too late. I can't blame her for falling. It's a fine body you have, sir. Aside from the poor excuse for a cock, of course. I'm not into men but if I was…" He jokingly whistles a catcall. "Should I keep going with the tiny dick jokes, because I have plenty more where those came from."

"I'm so thankful you're not into men, but even if you were, a man's dick does nothing for me, even ones the size of elephant trunks, such as yours. I think I'll stick with Rayna for now, but I'll keep you in mind in case she smartens up and kicks me to the curb."

"Hey, I'll call you after the date to let you know how it went. I got to get going. My asshole fucking boss is glaring at me."

Tim's boss is his uncle and the two of them have a very close relationship. He raised Tim after his mother died when he was ten-years-old. His father was never in the picture because he died in a car wreck shortly after his mom became pregnant with him. His dad never even got to hold him. It's a sad story that Tim rarely talks about.

In a southern, teenage girl's voice, I reply, "Yeah, you'd better call me immediately after, girlfriend. I'll be waiting by the phone, crying into a tissue because you'll probably take too long to call me back and I can't wait to hear all the juicy details. Don't be surprised when I answer on the first ring."

He suggests, "Try the tissues with aloe, they are softer and won't scratch your pansy-like sensitive skin. Talk to you later, asshole!"

"Yeah, later."

After hanging up, I'm actually less confused about my feelings for Rayna. Tim's right. It's okay that I want her. Maybe I need her in my life.

As I'm exiting the men's locker room, I look over at the redhead who's bent at the waist with her legs together while she grabs her ankles. The chic is touching her forehead to her knees.

Damn!

Before Rayna, I would have been all over that tiny woman until I'd fucked her raw. I'd bet she's a pistol in the sack and a screamer. I like them loud.

She notices me walking up to her, watching her while she remains bent over. She waits until I'm within a few feet of her before quickly standing. She turns to look at me with a bullshit, disapproving expression.

I had better mind myself. I don't want to fall into her trap and play her game.

"Sorry, I didn't mean to stare. Can I give you a tip?" She nods cautiously while her eyes roam my chest, no doubt waiting for me to make a pass at her so that she can play the role of the innocent female being harassed by the big thug in a muscle shirt. "If you cross your feet, you'll get a better stretch. Try it."

She crosses her ankles and bends forward, not quite getting as close to her knee as she had been. When she stands, she's nodding.

"Thanks, I wouldn't have thought of that."

I'm sure she has and does it regularly.

"Yeah, no problem. We offer private coaching if you ever need any more tips. Whatever you're doing works well for you, but it's good to shake it up once in a while."

"Are you offering to coach me?" she asks in a high-pitched voice that would surely irritate me if she were screaming, even if she was coming on my dick at the time.

I'd bet it would be about as tolerable as nails on a chalkboard. I'm very turned off by her now. Something is seriously off with me.

"No, not by me. My schedule is already too full. Even if I could squeeze you in, I think you'll get a significant result if you talk to Carol or Lisa. They're very qualified." I glance around the room. "I think Lisa's already here, but Carol won't be in until this afternoon. I can go find Lisa and ask her to come and talk to you if you're interested. Otherwise, you're welcome to stop at the front desk before you leave to set up an appointment with either woman."

She's obviously disappointed. "I'll ask about it later at the desk. Thank you for the tip, though. I'm Reah." She puts her hand out to greet me, and I shake it politely.

"Call me Coach. It was nice to meet you, Reah."

She smiles flirtatiously as I walk away.

Through the mirror, I notice her watching me walk. She tilts her head and does a little dance like she's about to chase me, but she stops after only two steps, glancing around to make sure nobody saw her acting foolish. If Rayna wasn't in my life, I'd be all over that sexy little woman, but I'd have to put a piece of tape over her mouth just to get through it.

As soon as I set my cell phone on the desk, it vibrates. It's Rayna. The hairs stand up on the back of my neck. Something is very wrong. I can sense it.

I answer quickly. "Rayna? What's wrong?"

"Why do you assume something's wrong?" she asks.

"First off, you never call me. You text. Second, I got a terrible feeling when I saw your name. So, are you going to tell me what's wrong or will you make me guess?" I'm losing patience quickly.

"You are intuitive, I'll give you that," she says. Without meaning to, she nervously chuckles as though she's trying to lighten a tense situation. "Um, I don't want you to fly off the handle, but Rick was at my work when I got here this morning. I'm fairly sure I handled it, but it's Rick, so I can't be positive."

"That fucker has some balls!"

"Yeah, well, he's very jealous of you. I'm calling to give you a heads-up. He asked if I was fucking you. Initially, I refused to tell him, but he was getting out of control. The only way I could get him to shut up was to tell him that I was. It wasn't the right thing to do. I likely pissed him off even more. He's not acting right, and I don't know what's going on with him. I'm worried. If he confronts you, don't put your hands on him. He'll have you charged and then sue you. Try to have witnesses around you at all times."

"Don't worry about me. Do you think he'll confront the kids?" I ask, suddenly feeling like my chest is restricting as my rage builds. If he fucking hurts those kids, I swear I'll make that asshole suffer before I kill him. Nobody will ever find the body.

"I don't think so. Just to be safe, I called their school to let them know what's going on. They promised to keep them inside after school until I send someone to pick them up."

"Well, what good is that? He can send someone to get them, saying that you sent them," I say, getting a bit worried that she didn't think that through very well.

"Take a breath and calm down!" she hisses. "I'm not a fucking idiot! I have been raising these kids their entire lives and been dealing with their asshole father even longer. The school doesn't allow kids to leave with strangers who can't properly recite the secret sentence. Only she and I know it. If someone tries to pick the kids up, they will be sent to the office to talk to her before they even see the kids."

I crinkle my face and run my hand through my hair. "I'm sorry. I didn't mean to insinuate that you aren't capable of keeping them safe. That wasn't my intention. Those kids are very important to you. I want to protect them, and you. Try to give me a bit of a break, okay? I'm new to this."

"I get it." She takes a breath. "Rick gets jealous if he thinks there's someone in my life that isn't him. He's fine with having his tarts, but I can't have anyone." She sighs. "I just wanted to let you know that he might try to confront you. I don't think he knows where your gym is, or that you even own one, but I could be wrong. Just don't be alone. Promise me you won't put your hands on him."

"Rayna..." I hesitate because I don't want to promise that.

"Simon, promise me!"

She used my proper name. She must mean business.

"Fine, I promise I won't hit him. If he attacks me, I can't guarantee I won't break my promise to you. Rayna, don't worry about me. Keep yourself and those kids safe, okay? If you need me to pick them up at school, call me and I'll go. It's no problem. Besides, I like those little shits. They make me laugh."

"Thank you for the offer. If I get stuck at work and Renee won't be able to make it there on time, I'll call you. But I might call simply to hear your sexy voice in my ear."

"If you're alone, I can shut my office door and whisper in your ear while we touch ourselves."

She giggles. "Um, I'm not alone enough for that."

"Damn! Another time, then."

"Perhaps." I can tell she's smiling by her tone. "I have to get back to work. Maybe you can come over for dinner later, if you aren't busy."

"I'll have to get back to you on that, but it sounds good. Okay, call me if you need me for anything."

"I will. I'll talk to you after," she says before the line cuts out.

I'm furious at that bastard ex-husband of hers. That mother fucker confronted Rayna at her place of employment to ask her about me? Is he that much of a coward that he couldn't track me down to talk to me man to man? If I see that son-of-a-bitch, I hope I can keep my promise to Rayna. He'd better think twice before he hits me again. Before my phone hits the desk, it rings.

"Hello."

"Hey, asshole! How's it hanging?" It's Brett.

"Withered and to the left. I'm at work."

He laughs. "Yeah, I'm working, too."

Brett works as a programmer. I'm not sure what he does exactly, but he's a whiz on a computer. If mine fucks up, he's the guy I call.

After a lengthy silence, I ask, "So, what's up?"

"Um, not much. I was wondering how things are going with your neighbour. What's her name again?"

"Rayna. Good, I think."

"That's great. And the brats?"

I scoff. "They aren't brats. They're good kids."

"Have you given any thought to sharing her with your best friend?"

"No. Jeff didn't ask to share her, otherwise, maybe I would," I joke, using a fake name.

"And here I thought I was your best friend."

"Sorry, bud. And, ah…" I take a breath. "I think our days of sharing women are over."

"Fuck that! You'll come back to me. You always do. You'll play house for a while, get it out of your system. Then we'll fuck the hell out of her and be right back conquering bitches just like old times."

"No, we're done." I shake my head. "Even if I wanted to, Rayna would never go for it. She's not like that."

"You're fooling yourself. Give her the choice and she'll want to live out the dream of being with two hot guys at the same time, just like all the other broads."

"Not going to happen, bro." He groans. "I got to go. I'll call you next week and we'll have a beer. Okay?"

"If she gives you permission to go." He sucks air through his teeth. "All right, bye," he says and hangs up abruptly.

That fucking dude is weird, but I love him.

Chapter Eighteen

The chicken breasts have cooked and simmer in the Fettucine sauce. The pot of boiling water meant for noodles sits on the stove, waiting for Coach to arrive. He texted earlier to let me know that he would for sure be dining with us.

I got out of work early so I would have time to pick up a loaf of Italian garlic bread and still be on time to pick up the kids at the sitter's. The bread has been cut and laid out on the baking tray, ready for toasting. The crispy salad rests in the refrigerator with homemade dressing in a cup beside it.

Everything is ready to go, and all we need is Coach. I thought he'd be here by now.

I pick up my phone to check if Coach sent a text and I didn't hear it vibrate. Nothing shows up on my alerts. My phone rings, startling me. It falls from my hand, but I try to grab it as it continues to drop. It flips through the air as I try to catch it, but each time I touch it, it changes direction. I finally decide to let it hit the floor. It has a protective case on it, anyway.

"Hello!" I answer quickly without checking to see who the caller is.

"Hey, it's me."

Coach's deep voice rings through the line. I hear several people talking in the background.

"Hi! What's with all the commotion?"

He clears his throat. "I was on my way home, but someone hit my truck. I'll tell you all about it later."

"Oh, shit! Are you okay?"

He must be if he's able to call me.

Coach chuckles. "Yeah, I'm fine. I didn't take the car to work today, thankfully, but the truck's a write-off. If you need to get dinner served, eat. I won't be there for maybe half an hour."

"I'm so glad that you're okay. We don't mind waiting for you. The kids had an after-school snack, so nobody will starve to death."

"I might be a bit off on the half-hour estimate. You should feed the kids. I'll come over after I get done here, but only if the offer still stands, of course." I can hear someone talking near him. His voice is faint as if he's moved the phone away from his mouth, but I can still hear what he says. "Yes, of course. I'd bet my house on that."

Unsure if he still has the phone to his ear, I say, "I should let you go. It sounds like someone needs to talk to you."

"Rayna, I have to let you go. I'll be there as soon as I can."

He hangs up abruptly. I'm left wondering why he wouldn't tell me the details of the accident over the phone. I do my best to let my worry roll off my shoulders. I turn up the burner on the stove to get the water to a roaring boil before slipping the pasta in, and then I turn up the oven temperature to prepare it for the toasting of the bread.

"Kim, come and set the table, please," I yell from the kitchen. Less than a minute later, she comes hopping into the room.

"It smells yummy, Mom," she tells me as she tries to look in the pot on the stove, but she's a bit too short.

I take her by her shoulders and pull her away from the stove. "Thank you. Get your nose out of there before you burn it."

"Is Coach still coming? I'm starving! Do we have to wait for him?" she asks, pouting while she drops her shoulders and slouches her spine to appear that much more pathetic.

"He just called. He'll be here in about half an hour. He got into a car accident on his way here." Her eyes immediately light up with concern. "Don't worry, he's not injured. By the time the noodles cook, he might even be here. If not, we'll start eating and he can catch up when he arrives."

"I'm happy he's okay. I like him. He can probably eat a lot of spaghetti. Will this be enough?" she asks, revealing her serious concern that he'll go hungry.

I am so proud of her for being such a caring young lady. After kissing the top of her head, I assure her. "Yes, baby. I'm sure we'll all have plenty to eat. There's salad as well, so don't forget to put out bowls."

"Do I have to eat salad? I hate salad!" she whines, her posture drooping once again. There was a fleeting proud moment.

"Yes, you do, and what's with the sourpuss attitude tonight?" I ask while stirring the water as I drop the stiff noodles into the pot.

"I'm not a sourpuss! I'm starving!" She bends her body in the same pathetic posture while plucking forks from the silverware drawer.

I take a cookie from the jar and hand it to her. "Here, eat this. It'll hold you until dinner is ready."

Kim pops up straight with a gleaming smile. She eats the cookie as she hums and sets the table. At least while she's humming, she isn't whining.

It doesn't take long for the noodles and bread to be ready. After draining the water from the pasta, I scoop the sauce into the pot of strained noodles. When I look at the clock, it's been forty-five minutes since he called. I head to the bathroom to pee and make sure my mascara hasn't smeared under my eyes from the blast of steaming water that enveloped my face when draining the noodles.

"Kids, come and eat."

As I walk into the kitchen, I see Coach standing with his head leaning over the pot, with a noodle looped over his finger as its being lifted to his open mouth. He sees me and freezes. His guilty grin has me cracking up.

He quickly slurps the noodle between his lips, making the evidence disappear, leaving a glob of sauce on his chin. Instead of wiping it off, he grabs me, and presses his lips to mine while he chuckles from behind closed lips. We both cackle like school children with sauce smeared all around our mouths.

Ken walks into the kitchen, followed by Kim. They look at us like we're the weirdest people in the world. We use our hands to wipe away the sauce as nonchalantly as possible. They need not know we were kissing again. We try to stop laughing, but neither of us can for a full minute.

"What's so funny?" Ken asks.

"I caught him sniping a noodle," I say, omitting the kissing part.

They aren't laughing, which makes us crack up again.

The kids and Coach sit down at the table while Kim asks him about the accident. I listen as I serve each plate with Fettuccine piled high with the chicken placed on top. The bread and salad also go onto the table, but I fill the kids' bowls before sitting down to the right of Coach. He doesn't tell us much information, just that he's okay, but his truck is irreparable. He jokes with Ken that he will not replace it and therefore, he'll be driving the muscle car all the time, wearing her out before he's old enough to take her for a spin.

"Rayna, this smells delicious. Thank you for inviting me," Coach says while looking at me as if he's about to lean in and plant another kiss.

I nod, then glance at the kids, hinting that he needs to keep his lips to himself. He picks up his fork and swirls it in the pile of noodles.

Coach goes back to his house shortly after we finish dinner, mentioning nothing else about the accident. I think there's more to the story. I figure he didn't want the kids to overhear anything gory in case he fibbed to Kim and someone really was injured.

The kids understand that accidents happen and sometimes people get hurt or killed, but he might not know how much he should tell them. I'm curious about the details. Thankfully, he's not injured.

The dreaded battle with my offspring to get them either in or out of the shower ensues. I cringe at the thought of what Ken might do in there. Why did Coach tell me that my son's likely jerking off? Eww!

The moment they're in bed and the house is quiet, I slip on my nightie and open the book I've been trying to get to for over a week, but never seem to have the time to read. These past few days, Coach has been a bit of a distraction; a fortunate one, but a distraction, nonetheless.

Coach

The second I walk into my house, I lift my pant-leg to see why my shin is so damn sore. I discover a bruise starting at the middle of my shin that runs along the bone almost to my knee. I rarely bruise, so the sight shocks me.

When the truck's door crushed in on me, I didn't feel any pain in my leg, or anywhere for that fact. My first concern was if I was bleeding anywhere. My second was how to get out of my truck so I could check on the people in the vehicle that struck me.

There was no way I could open the driver's door because it was smashed inward. I slid my ass onto the passenger seat but had to fight to get my legs to follow. There was no pain, just adrenaline. I was angry at how difficult it was getting my legs free.

When I finally got out, one woman and two men were telling me to sit on the grass and not to move, that I may have an injury and didn't know it because of shock. I was more concerned for the other driver, a woman, who was still sitting in her vehicle.

The second that I walked up to the driver's door, I knew this was no accident. Alissa was sitting behind the wheel, not saying a word. Her face was bleeding from her nose and mouth, but she could still sneer at me with pure hatred as she followed me with her eyes.

She hit me on purpose!

The cunt really is a crazy bitch. The fire department was quick to arrive and cut her out of the car while a paramedic gave me a quick once over and the cops took my initial statement. Thankfully, the police that showed up were the same ones who dragged her out of my house. They immediately assumed that she hit me on purpose but said that they couldn't put it in their official report until the investigators finished with their assessment.

I will do everything I can to ensure she's locked up for as long as possible and given a thorough mental evaluation. That bitch needs to wake up and realize that I am not a man to fuck with. I would have thought she already knew that from the intensity of our sadist/masochist type relationship.

She liked it when I was extremely rough with her. I could let my inner demon take charge, satiating his desire to hear her scream in pain and pleasure before satisfying his own physical needs. Most days, she left here with bruises about her body. She enjoyed pain, and I got off on finding novel ways to torture her.

The accident enraged me, but keeping my temper in check while I was at Rayna's was the true test. It wasn't easy, but I think I pulled it off. Maybe I should have been an actor. I would have made an excellent one.

Since I've been home, however, I still haven't been able to calm my anxiety, even after pounding on my heavy bag for nearly an hour. Even though I had gloves on, my knuckles ache. I'm exhausted but still furious. I need to see Rayna. It baffles me how that woman can calm the beast within me when no one ever could.

It's quarter to eleven. Maybe I shouldn't call her. She's probably in bed asleep. Dammit, why did I wait until it was so late to realize that I need her? If I text her and she's asleep, maybe she won't wake up to it, but if she is up, she'll text me back.

I want to hold her in my arms, that's all. Angry sex would be great, but as pissed off as I am, I might get carried away and scare the hell out of her. I vowed to myself a long time ago that I would never get aggressive with a woman when I wasn't completely in control of my emotions. I never want to take it too far.

The debate about whether to text or call her gives me even more anxiety. I don't want to seem overly needy. Maybe I should deal with my rage on my own and leave her out of it. I've been doing it my whole life, so why do I feel such an urgency to see her? And why can't I calm down on my own? How can she have such a powerful hold on me when we only recently started an intimate relationship?

Rayna

I don't remember falling asleep, but I startle from chirping sounds, alerting me to a text message. The interruption of my sensual dream involving Coach is infuriating.

Coach was wearing black pants, unzipped, revealing the skin directly above the base of his beefy manhood. His hairless chest was bare, and his parted lips were lasciviously taunting me to taste them. My legs wrapped around his waist, and he carried me somewhere so he could ravish my body. My fingers weaved into his thick, inky hair. He was about to lay me down when my damn phone sang and woke me up.

I squint to help my bloodshot eyes focus on the small print. It's ten-thirty and my sister has texted me. She never texts this late. Something must be wrong.

Before reading the message, I dial her number and sit up with my heart pounding violently in my chest. It rings twice, each ring making my fear grow more and more dire.

"Hi, Rayna. Did I wake you when I sent that text?" she says with a spunkiness to her voice.

"What's wrong? You never text this late."

At least she isn't dead or in critical condition because it's not the cops or doctors calling.

She giggles. "Nothing, I'm fine! All is good, I promise." She snickers. "My date was this afternoon, remember? You asked me to call you to let you know how it went. So, I'm calling you now because he just left. I probably need not tell you that it went very, very well."

"He just left?" I roll over and read the time on the alarm clock, dropping the book onto the floor. It's barely past ten-thirty. "Did you take him to your apartment? Please tell me you didn't have sex with him on the first date."

"I did, indeed. And, let me tell you," she moans, "*dayum!*"

"How do you expect to have a long-lasting, loving relationship with someone when you have sex with them the very first time you meet? Come on, Renee. Why do you always do this?"

"Hey, you of all people have no right to give me shit about sex, dear sister. You were fucking your neighbour when you weren't dating. And you weren't having romantic sex either, so you can't criticize me."

"You aren't wrong. But, I've known Coach for three years, we've had many conversations, and gotten to know each other before we ever became intimate." I pause and then apologize. "Okay, I'm sorry for slut-shaming you."

I slide out of bed to pick up my book. I listen to her as I flip through the pages, trying to remember where I left off before I passed out, but quickly give up and toss it onto my nightstand.

She moans. "Oh, girl, he was so fucking good. It's not as if I've never had a man take complete control of a sexual situation before. I mean, I've been with dominant men, but not to the intensity of this guy. Tim was considerate but aggressive, if that makes any sense."

I have a wide, toothy grin because I completely understand what she means. Coach is rough and forceful while being caring and considerate. It's easy for me to lose myself in the sex we have. Being submissive has its advantages, but the harsher, more painful spankings are a bit too much sometimes. I'll happily take a burning ass if it gets him so excited that he pleasures me better than anyone ever has. It's a fair trade-off.

"It makes total sense. So, are you two going to keep seeing each other?"

"Oh, yeah! He's coming to pick me up tomorrow and take me to dinner. Who knows what will happen after that," she says with a seductive undertone.

"I'm happy to hear it. Maybe Coach is a good matchmaker."

She giggles. "Absolutely! I will have to give him a hug when I see him."

I scoff, wondering if she'll try to hump his leg when she hugs him. After shedding the image, I yawn.

"I'm happy for you, but I want to go back to sleep. Now that I know you aren't dead or dying, I can rest comfortably."

"Oh, shit, sorry! I didn't think you'd be asleep already," she says, apologetically.

"Normally, I'm not, but I started reading and then woke up to your text message. I didn't even know I was sleeping."

"Those are the best sleeps ever. That book must be boring; don't pass it on to me. Maybe the four of us can have dinner or something," she suggests.

I yawn again as I stretch, dropping my free arm to my lap as if someone paralyzed it. "That would be great. I'd like to meet him. Okay, I'm hanging up."

"Goodnight, sis. I love you!" she tells me.

"I love you, too," I say, hanging up and flopping over until my face is pressing into the duvet. I slowly turn my head and groan.

My bladder urges me to relieve it. With another groan, I drag myself to my feet and go to the bathroom. While I'm peeing, my mind drifts to how good it felt to have Coach's hot skin against mine. He brushed tears from my cheeks. I fell in love with him last night. How the hell can I already love him when we've only just recently become a couple?

Chapter Nineteen

Rayna

As soon as I'm snuggled under my cool sheets, my phone sings its tune once again. The brightness of the screen burns my tired eyes, even through my closed lids.

Dammit, Renee!

I spin the knob on my lamp, and the room comes to life. The message is from Coach. It says that he's standing at my patio doors. Why is he in my backyard? I text back to inform him that I don't want to have sex tonight.

His reply begs me to come to the door. I groan but decide to go to the kitchen to see what is so important that it can't wait until tomorrow.

I'm rewarded with a cool breeze in my face when I slide the glass door open. Coach is standing shirtless in the shadows cast from a cloud-covered moon. He looks mountainous and intimidating.

"Come in but be quiet; the kids are asleep." He looks distraught. "What's wrong?"

He says nothing. Instead, he wraps his enormous arms around me, pulling me against his hard body. The chill of the night wears heavy on his skin. He lifts me off my feet and holds me as I dangle in his arms. My slipper falls, landing to the floor with a soft thud. Coach sets me down while looking toward the hallway where one of my kids would stand had the noise come from that direction.

"My slipper fell off." I step back into it. "Are you okay?"

"It was no accident," he confesses, adding confusion to my sleep-deprived mind.

"The accident with your truck?" I ask, and he nods. "Why do you say that?"

"Alissa purposely drove into my truck. I would have told you earlier, but the kids were here, and I didn't want them to hear. This is a complicated adult problem."

"Holy shit!" I say louder than I should have. Coach shushes me while I cover my mouth with my hand after the fact. I whisper, "Come with me."

I take his hand and lead him down the hallway, sneaking him into my room. After closing my door and locking it, I walk to my bed and lift the covers, sliding under them. Coach stands at the end, silently looking at it.

"What's the matter?" I ask. "Get in, it's chilly."

He looks at me strangely. "This is your bed. You lay your body down and sleep here."

"So?" I thought he'd be excited to get into my bed and lay with me, maybe even make love to me again.

"Sorry, I never thought I'd be getting into your bed. This is your sanctuary and you're inviting me into it."

"You brought me to *your* bed, so why is my bed any different?" I ask, not understanding his train of thought. Has he been drinking? That would explain a lot.

"No, it's different. I wasn't taking you to my bed for any other purpose than to give you pleasure while getting my rocks off in the process. I wouldn't be getting into your bed for that purpose." He shakes his head while aggressively running his hand through his hair. "Never mind, I'm being stupid. Forget I said anything."

I pull the covers back on the other side of the bed and coax him in. "It's just a bed and it'll keep us warm while you tell me what's on your mind."

Coach slides in and lies on his back while looking around the room. He turns his face to me. His sunken eyes reveal how heavily his thoughts have been plaguing him. Something is going on, and I want to help him.

"Okay, talk to me," I whisper in the darkness.

He rolls his body to face me and his eyes scan my face. "You are so beautiful. Why do you want to be with me? Most women think I'm a fucking nightmare."

I smile. "You are not a nightmare. Yes, you have an aggressive side, but that's only one piece of your puzzle. There's more to you than that. I can see your marshmallow interior you fight so hard to suppress. You are caring, protective, gentle and you make me laugh."

"Last night, when you came downstairs, what we did..." He clears his throat; his eyes leave mine. "...that was new."

I hear the confusion behind his confession.

"We made love to each other," I whisper while brushing his cheek with my fingertips. "Have you never made love before?"

He presses my palm to his lips and then rests it on his cheek, covering it with his hand. "No, I don't do that. I can't stop thinking about it."

"Me either. It's been a very long time since I've felt close to anyone. For me, it was like we were joined and moving as one person. I could feel you; all of you. It terrified me and fulfilled me at the same time. That, I had never experienced before yesterday."

"Not even with that asshole when times were good?" he asks, referring to my ex-husband.

"Not even with him," I reply.

Coach closes his eyes for several seconds. "I think I love you, really love you."

I gasp and then swallow hard. "I think I love you, too. It isn't possible, is it? Can people fall in love this quickly?"

"We've known each other for three years. It's not like we were strangers before all of this." He looks confused, as if he's suffering with a moral dilemma. "I don't know what to do now. Tell me what I'm supposed to do. I never wanted to love anyone, but I did. I want you to be mine, and I want you to want me, too." His eyes squeeze shut as if he's riddled with anguish. "What happens if I let you in and you change your mind after I've given you everything that I am?" He rushes his words. "I might literally die."

"Feel it for what it is, I guess. I don't know if this will last or not because our worlds are so different. I can't have any more children so if that's what you need in your life," I shake my head, "I can't give that to you. Do you want to know my fears?"

He nods. "Of course."

"You're ten years younger than me and in a different stage of your life, so why would you even want to be with me? I fear that I'll give you my damaged heart and you'll soon tire of my boring life and then crush my heart into a million pieces. I won't survive it breaking again. So I'm just as terrified as you are."

Silence fills the room while we stare into one another's eyes, losing ourselves to the dimness of the room as it seems to darken around us. I see only his scared eyes as they reflect what little light exists around us.

I lean toward him and press my lips to his. I want him inside of me, not only physically but in my mind as well. I want his soul to dance with mine in the silence that surrounds us.

Coach rolls onto his back, pulling me with him. I straddle his waist. Our kiss is tender. Our bodies press together, parting for only a second so he can slide my nightie over my head, rendering me naked.

He sits up and his lips press to my nipple, suckling gently and rolling it between his thin lips. Every nerve in my breast awakens as the small nub stiffens just for him. My hands cradle his head to my bosom. A quiet moan slips away from him as he shifts to my other breast. His hands cup my butt, lowering me onto his erection.

He slips into me easily and completely, filling more than just my body. My heart feels as though it is swelling to twice its size. We gaze into one another's eyes and drown in each other's love.

His chest is warm against my breasts. With our lips pressed together, his tongue dances with mine. His firm grip pulls at my hips, directing me how to rock with patience. As he lies back, he takes me with him.

I'll revel in this moment forever.

Coach coddles my head in his palm as we kiss. Our bodies and souls have melted into one being. Oh, yes, he suits me like nobody ever has. Was he built for me and me for him? I'm losing control and I'm not afraid. I want him with me like this, always.

His body, my body, our body.

Our lips separate slowly, parting as we move together in a sensual, slow dance. His hips rock to meet my sway. My sensitive clit brushes along his smooth, heated skin. His grip urges me to ride him faster. His steamy mouth sucks at my nipple, shooting pulses of electricity straight to my clitoris, and pushing my mind and body toward orgasm.

I am consumed in the delirium of ecstasy.

My hips buck against him. I hold his face to my breast as his lips tug at my sensitive nipple with superb skill. I can't hold a thought as my mind clouds over.

The room disappears around us as I float into the glorious nothingness of ecstasy.

Euphoria.

He covers my mouth, preventing me from crying out as my body stiffens in his arms. My vagina pulses, pushes, and squeezes his swollen manhood as his hips hump with increasing intensity.

I jolt forward as a heavy breath bursts forth. My muscles ease, and I release his head to rest back on the pillow.

His eyes remain closed but they're weighted with genuine pain; not physical pain but emotional. I have to save him from this inner turmoil. This is too intimate for him.

He's falling too deep, and the fear of letting his heart go is excruciating. I have to pull him back.

"Take me as hard as you need to," I whisper.

His eyes widen and look into mine as if to thank me for seeing his struggle.

Coach immediately flips me off and onto my back beside him. He pops up onto his knees, quickly lifting and flipping me over so I'm on my hands and knees. He weaves his fingers in my hair, pulling my head back as he rams his throbbing prick deep inside my drenched pussy.

~

Coach

I fuck her hard, the way I like to, and don't let up. With all the strength I can muster, I hump into her, hoping to take myself away from the unfamiliar and overwhelming feeling in my chest. It's too much.

If she hadn't told me at that moment to take her how I need to, I might have died, or worse, I might have cried. What is this powerful feeling I'm having? Is this what love feels like? Why the fuck does it hurt so magnificently?

Her hair is silky in my hand, and I want to pull so hard that some will come out, like I usually do when I want to bury my emotions. But I can't do that to her, not to my Rayna. If she were anyone else, she'd be writhing in pain, and I'd be listening for the inevitable safe word to fill the room.

With my free hand, I hold her hip, pulling her back against me as I thrust forward, forcing my throbbing cock much deeper into her. I hammer her so ferociously that my legs spasm. Good, I welcome the pain. The severe bruise on my calf presses into the bed, and I revel in it. Physical strain makes my orgasms so much more sensational.

Rayna moans with each thrust and increasingly grows louder. Normally, I would enjoy her screams, but I have to think of the kids. I release her hair and reach around her face to cover her mouth. I pull her back until her head presses against my chest. I need to keep her cries muffled.

She grabs my thick forearm with a firm grip; her nails press against my skin. I continue to hold her face while she sucks in what little air she can through her nostrils. I know she's not getting all the air she desires, but I also know she'll cum harder this way. I have to keep her quiet, at all costs.

Her body stiffens, and her cunt squeezes my cock so forcefully I can't push into her. I muffle her scream under my hand, but it's still too loud. I pinch her nose with my thumb and forefinger, blocking any airflow and any sound from spilling into the silence of her bedroom.

She doesn't seem to care as her body rides the high of her climax, but quickly enough, she's frantically pulling at my hand. I hold for a few more seconds and then lift, but not completely. I can't let her face go in case she cries out and I need to shut her up quickly.

Rayna begins moaning so quietly it amazes me how well she's able to contain herself. She must have realized that I was only trying to keep her quiet, and she doesn't want me to muzzle her again.

I flip her onto her back and finally yank my pajama bottoms from around my ankles. I hurry to push my prick into her as quickly as I can; I don't want to be apart from her if I can at all help it.

My knees spread for better leverage. I lift Rayna's legs, folding her until her knees nearly touch her shoulders. I rest my fists into the mattress beside her. Her shins rest on either side of my neck.

There's nothing sexier than Rayna's orgasmic expressions, and I want to watch her lose herself.

I slam hard only once and hold steady, leaving my cock buried inside of her. Our eyes meet, and she smiles ever so slightly. I wink and then reveal my scary, aggressive expression. She bites her bottom lip and winks.

Excellent! She wants to feel my rage.

She's fucking *mine!*

I shift my weight forward, positioning her so my cock will hit her g-spot every time I pound into her. I pull back and ram, hard.

Her mouth opens, and her eyes close momentarily and then meet mine once again. She smiles.

I'm going to own her pleasure.

With my hand on her throat, I apply light pressure, not enough to hurt her, but it won't be comfortable. It's more of an intimidation than anything.

Without mercy, I fuck into her, straining every single muscle in my body.

Rayna's face is tense, but her bottom jaw is loosely ajar. I force each breath from her body with every merciless impact against her g-spot.

Holy fuck!

She's so goddamn beautiful.

Her legs force against me as her body stiffens and her delicious pussy pulsates around my prick, urging me closer to my own climax.

Her face shifts from a pained sexual expression to one of utter elation. But the calmness lasts for only a quick moment before the pained expression gradually returns and she's brought into another climax.

She cries out too loudly this time, before I can move my hand onto her mouth. She sucks her lips inward, between her teeth, biting down to force her lips closed, thus holding back the sounds of her ecstasy.

I'm relentless, not easing up for even one second. Not until I bury the pain in my heart. It doesn't ache anymore, other than from its rapid pounding.

If I can get her to cum one more time, I'll let myself go.

Fuck, I want to cum!

This is too fucking perfect and I can't take much more. My muscles burn from the incredible spasms. My back aches worse than from some of my toughest workouts. It won't stop me, and I refuse to ease up.

Rayna has to cum again.

Just one more, baby!

My inner demon wants me to set him free, but he'll be too rough with her. Tonight isn't about pain for pleasure, it's about both of us taking what we need to get us through the night. One day, she'll discover the demonic sadist inside me, but not tonight.

She slips her hand between her thighs. Her fingertips bump my cock as she masturbates her clitoris.

The touch has me clenching my teeth. I fucking want to cum, but not yet.

Her nails dig into my triceps, breaking the skin. I fucking love it!

"Hurt me, baby, I can take it. Cum for me."

Her eyes meet mine before rolling back as she loses herself in another powerful, cock-strangling orgasm.

That's it, I can't take any more. I let myself fall into the terrific absence of all mental focus. I give into the intensity of orgasm pleasure. I am lost in the darkness of my mind.

With a muffled grunt, my body jerks as hot seed shoots deep inside of her twitching body. My mind is in the distant abyss for what seems like an eternity. Oh, how glorious it all is. But it's only fleeting. I gasp and open my eyes to see Rayna admiring my face.

No longer able to contain my weight, I fall onto the bed beside her. My chest heaves and my lungs burn along with the rest of my body. With my arms at rest atop my forehead,

I continually roll my ankles, hoping to relieve the spasms in my calves that are so painfully irritating.

Rayna rolls over and rests her head on my heaving chest. Her arm drapes over my abdomen, fingertips brushing along my ribs. I hold each breath as I struggle to slow my heart rate so her head stops bouncing on top of my chest. I place my hand on her upper back and caress her soft skin, but my arm feels like it weighs a thousand pounds, so I rest it against her with my hand spanning her back.

We lay like this, in the darkness that only midnight carries. Neither one of us speaks.

Time passes, I'm not sure how much, but I should leave before we fall asleep. Waking up with the faces of two confused kids looking at my naked body as I lay next to their nude mother would be a nightmare to explain.

"Babe," I whisper, "I should go." I kiss the top of her head as I brush a few strands of hair from her sweat-stained face.

Rayna groans. "I know. Will I see you tomorrow?"

"Of course! I live right next door and you're welcome over any time."

I sit up and search for my pants, finding them jammed against the footboard. After slipping them back on, I find her nightie and hand it to her. She pulls it over her head, covering the most beautiful body I've ever had the pleasure of laying my hands on. I kneel on the bed, leaning over to kiss her lips so lightly that we barely touch. Even still, I feel the electricity between us. Our eyes meet and hold each other's gaze.

"Thank you for this. I needed to know it wasn't a fluke." My words cut through the silence.

"What did you think was a fluke?" she asks, her voice sounding angelic.

"How I felt the last time we were together. I wasn't sure if it was real or something I imagined."

"And?" she asks while tickling my beard hairs with her delicate fingertips.

I turn my face to kiss her palm. "It was no fluke. How I feel about you is real. I know that now."

Rayna smiles at me and then leans up to press her lips to mine. Our breath mixes as we taste each other one last time. I breathe her in.

Goddamn, I love this woman!

"I have to go before I don't," I whisper and then pull away from her with incredible regret. I cannot submit to it.

Be a considerate man and leave.

I can't stay the night in her arms no matter how much I want to.

Walk away, now.

I peek out the bedroom door before walking out, in case a child is roaming the hall. I hear the slapping of her barefooted steps on the hardwood floor as we quietly make our way down the hall. I turn around and take her in my arms, scooping her up as if I had just married her and I'm preparing to carry her over the threshold. I cannot resist kissing her passionately one more time before I leave.

I set her onto her pretty little feet and then walk out the front door, closing it behind me. I wait until I hear the lock click before my feet chill in the cool, damp grass in the dead of night.

I welcome my bed by flopping chest-down, pulling a pillow under my head and sliding my hands beneath it to plump it up. My wet feet hang off the side of the mattress. I'm simply too tired to bother with covers. It isn't long before I drift off into a pleasant dream that doesn't seem to last long enough, as it's interrupted by the screech of my alarm.

It's morning, already? Damn!

Chapter Twenty

Rayna

My alarm screams, piercing into one of the happiest dreams I've had in a very long time.

In it, I was much older than I am now. That part of the dream wasn't the best part, obviously. I was holding a beautiful newborn. What made it so fantastic was looking up from that perfect, sleeping baby to see Coach looking down at it with a wide, proud smile and a tear in his eye.

He referred to me as Grandma. The title shocked me and I looked toward the hospital bed. On it sat a beautiful woman, and she was smiling at me. I knew the woman was the grown-up version of Kim. She was a new mom.

I woke before I could find out the name of the baby or ask Kim how old she was. Was my dream a prediction for the future? I don't even know if it was a boy or girl. The blanket didn't give it away since it was the colour of burnt sienna. Most babies come wrapped in either pink or blue, but not in this dream.

Will Coach still be with me that far into the future? Is that what the point of the dream was, and not that Kim had a baby?

My thoughts drift to last night and how loving his eyes were in the beginning. They were all I could see. We had the best of both worlds last night; we made love, and then he took control of me, as he does so astonishingly well.

I could do that every day for the rest of my life. If he had spent the night with me, my body pressed against his, it would have been that much better.

All the kids know is that he just asked me to go on a first date. I can't suddenly spring it on them that he's spending the night. That wouldn't leave a very good impression. Throwing them straight into him sleeping in my bed might be a bit too hard to explain to their young, impressionable minds. I don't want them thinking their mom is easy, even if I am.

I jolt, realizing that I drifted off to sleep. Oh shit! Damn! After shooting out of bed, I knock on the kids' doors and yell that they have to get up and hurry because we overslept. I grab some quick sugar-filled breakfast treats and add them to the sandwich and fruit cup in their lunches, along with a juice box.

As I quickly make my way down the hall to my room, I remind them to hurry. Neither kid has opened their door and I doubt they're even out of bed, so I bang on their doors before flinging them open.

"Get up! Get up! Get *up*!"

I dress, put my hair in a ponytail and brush my teeth. They're whining that they hate it when I sleep in because they don't like rushing. Do they not realize how much harder it is for me to get everyone ready while they mope? I have to keep reminding them to do the things they would normally do in their unrushed routines.

Kim keeps asking if we can call in late so we don't have to rush, or better yet tell them we're all sick and aren't going in today. She wants to have a fun day. I remind her that I need to go to work so that we can eat, have electricity, and not spend the coming winter living in a cardboard box in an alley somewhere. She shuts up but sports an angry, pouty face.

Ken isn't voicing his frustration, but the angry stomping of every step is a constant reminder that I fucked up. I'm going to have to let Coach know that he shouldn't keep me up late anymore. It's obvious that I can't handle sleep deprivation.

We scoot out the door in record time, despite my slow-moving children. Verbally, I announce that I love them dearly. I considered driving off and leaving them to fend for themselves. Somehow, I get them to school before the bell rings and make it to work on time. Perhaps leaving later allows time for the congested traffic to clear.

I'm pleased with how well I pulled it all together and got us where we needed to be and on time. Now to get through the day without falling asleep or accidentally cracking someone's tooth because I'm too drowsy to pay attention.

When I get a break between patients, I text Coach to ask him if he slept in today like we did. He informs me that he woke at the right time, and so far, it's life as usual at the gym. How can he be so wide awake when I feel like I'm dragging a hundred pounds of sand in my ass cheeks? Seriously, I can't get myself in gear. I feel like I'm moving at a sloth's speed.

I also inform him that I forgot my lunch in the fridge because I was too worried about making sure the kids had something to eat in the car on the way to school. If I'd had something to eat in the car as well, I probably wouldn't be so nauseous now. He thinks it's funny and asks how long it will be before I get to sit down and eat. I tell him that I still have more than an hour to suffer through and that I've been munching on the sugar-free suckers we set out for the kids for after they've had their teeth looked at by the doctor.

This last half-hour before lunch seemed like it was four hours long, but I made it. I finish an older woman's cleaning and then make my notes. I inform the doctor about my concerns before heading to the break room to get some money from my locker. I'm going to hit up the sub shop across the street.

As I walk into the main lobby, I see Coach standing at the counter talking to Lara. I watch to see if they're flirting, but quickly realize that he isn't. However, the receptionist is biting her top lip and tucking her hair behind her ears. She's smitten. He keeps looking away from her, only meeting eyes with her now and then.

She stops talking. He glances at her, noticing that she's looking past him. He follows her line of sight and spots me walking toward them.

"What are you doing here?" I ask as he leans in to kiss my cheek.

"You said you forgot your lunch, so I'm here to feed you. Is it okay that I'm here?"

"Yes! How did you know it was time for my lunch break?"

"You told me in your text," he replies with a grin.

"Oh, that's right! So, you want to feed me? I was thinking about grabbing a sub. It's quick and somewhat healthy. Do you want to go there?" I ask, but he doesn't reply. He takes my hand in his and leads me through the glass doorway while my coworkers watch, some women sighing heavily.

"I had a better idea," he tells me as we walk through the parking lot, hand in hand. He takes me to a truck I don't recognize. "Welcome to my loaner truck. The insurance company is letting me use it until they can find a replacement for mine."

"Hmm, I like it. It looks bigger than yours was."

"Yeah, it's a full box. Mine was a short box."

Instead of bringing me to the passenger's side, he continues leading me toward the bed of the truck. He drops the tailgate. I see a few bags and two bottles of iced tea. He spreads out a red and black plaid blanket over the truck bed and part of the tailgate before lifting me up by my waist and sitting me on it.

"Scoot back a bit, babe."

I do as he suggests and watch him climb up and sit across from me as our backs rest against the wheel wells. He hands me one bag and nods, signalling for me to open it. Inside is a plastic container with slabs of baked chicken placed on top of a Cobb salad. I smile and thank him. He's so focused on opening his salad that he only winks at me and gets back to wrestling with his container.

We eat in the warmth of the early afternoon sun, enjoying the heat of the summer before the day wears on and it gets too steamy to sit outside. I tilt my face up toward the sun and close my eyes, loving how its rays feel on my skin. The coolness of fall will soon be upon us. The air is already crisp during the night, and the grass is cold and dewy in the early morning hours.

"You take my breath away," he whispers, interrupting the silence of my mind.

I tilt my face back down and then open my eyes to look at him. He's watching me while uncapping his bottle. I shake my head and snicker, lightly kicking his shin.

"Cut it out!"

His wince is strangely wimpier than it should be for such a big, tough guy. It's not like I booted him, it was only a tap with the toe of my shoe.

After clearing his throat, he asks, "Cut what out?"

"Flirting with me. You'll get me in trouble because I might decide to make out with you right here in the parking lot, in the back of this loaner pickup. I'm sure there's a country song about that." I take a breath. "Has anyone ever told you that you're a terrible influence?"

"Once or twice," he replies while rubbing his shin. He flashes me a sexy grin that makes my tummy flutter. "So, you want to make out with me in the back of the pickup truck? I'll have to take you to a deserted road so we can do that." He grins wickedly. "Sound like fun?"

I laugh and shake my head. "What am I going to do with you?"

"You can do anything you want with me."

"Anything?"

"Yes, anything. Tell me, Miss Baxter, what twisted fantasies roll around inside that exquisite head of yours?"

I think for a moment, but I'm not able to come up with a witty response. "I'll have to get back to you on that."

"Take your time, there's no rush. I plan to be around for a while," he assures me, and strangely enough, I believe him.

His phone rings. He looks at me while he answers it, putting it on speaker. "Hi, Brett. You're on speaker. What's up?"

"Speaker, huh? Who's listening in?"

"Rayna's with me."

I cut in to introduce myself. "Hi, Brett."

"So, you're the special one?" He groans.

"Um…" I mutter, not sure what to say in response.

Coach changes the subject. "Why did you call?"

Brett, sounding upset, says, "To ask if you want to go for lunch."

"Sorry, I'm having lunch with Rayna as we speak."

He grunts again. What is it with this guy?

Coach adds, "I thought we said we'd have a beer next week."

"Yeah, all right." He takes a breath, then sharply says, "Rayna, I'm sure I'll meet you one day. Can't wait to wrap my arms around you." He snickers. "Okay, I got to go."

He abruptly hangs up and Coach looks like he has something on his mind, but I can't read him.

"He's a strange guy."

He chuckles. "You don't know the half of it, and you don't want to. So, fantasies…" He takes a breath. "Where were we with that?"

My cheeks burn hot. "Okay, for instance, if I said I always dreamed of doing a man with a strap-on, would you let me do that to you?"

The expression he wears tells me that he isn't thrilled with that idea. "If it's one of your fantasies, I'll do it simply to please you."

"But, do you think it might be something you'd like to experiment with?"

"I don't follow," he replies, taking a gulp of his iced tea.

I blush. "Well, have you ever thought about how it would feel to have something in your butt? It feels better than you might think. Is it a fantasy you might have but are too dominant to admit?"

He shakes his head. "No, I've never wanted to do it. I don't think I'd care to be fucked in the ass, but if it's something you want to do, Rayna," he takes a breath, "I'll do it for you. You only have to ask."

"Hmm, I'll let you know," I tell him after taking a long drink from my bottle and emptying it.

Coach grimaces when he gazes off in the distance at the people walking across the far end of the parking lot. "Rayna, I want to take you out on our first date tonight, if you'd be so kind as to accept the invitation. Not only you, though. I want the kids to come, too. I'm not only going to be in your life, I'll be in theirs as well. I think it would be a fun way to assure them that they mean a lot to me, too. Does that sound weird? Am I stepping into territory that you'd like me to avoid?"

I lean forward and touch his cheek, meeting eyes with him. "I think it's wonderful, and they'll appreciate you including them." I scoot myself closer to him so I can tenderly kiss his slim lips.

His hand slides up my bare arm, heating my skin instantly. To keep things innocent, I sit back in my place before I lose myself and behave like a lovesick teenager, making out in my boyfriend's truck. I giggle at the thought, but he doesn't seem to notice.

"When do you have to go back to work?" he asks while putting our empty containers back in the bags.

After glancing at my watch, I pout. "Soon, like now."

He nods, shuffling himself out of the truck with no difficulty. I struggle to slide my butt along the blanket to reach the edge. He takes my hand as I slip off the tailgate onto my feet, and then he slams it closed.

I walk toward the front of the truck; him following closely behind. He grabs my hand and spins me around, planting his lips onto mine, his other hand weaves through my hair. I place my hands on his firm waist, remembering how solid he felt as his body slammed into mine last night, granting me so much pleasure. I never wanted it to end.

Oh, shit!

I pull my face away from his and look around quickly to see if anyone is watching us. I have to do my best to be professional. Kissing him is definitely not going to help me maintain my coworkers' perceptions of me as being prim and proper. If patients are watching, they could complain.

I put my finger up and purse my lips, silently telling him to keep his distance. He cracks up laughing. I smile at him before making my way back inside the office.

Lara looks at me and waves a come-hither finger, urging me to her. Reluctantly, I see what she wants, even though I know it's to discuss my relationship with Coach. I like Lara because she's hilarious and always seems happy with life.

"Who was that beautiful beast, and why is he with you and not me?" She rocks back and forth with her hands overlapping her heart. "I want one, too. Wherever did you find him, and can I place my order?" She rattles off questions while jokingly pouting.

I chuckle at her silliness. "He's actually my neighbour. I've known him for quite a while, but we only recently started seeing each other. Sorry, but I don't have any other available neighbours that look like him. If I did though…" I walk away with my hands raised and my shoulders shrugging.

During my thirty-minute lunch break, Lara told each person in the office that I left with a hulking gentleman caller. Everyone had questions about him and a few spat idle threats of physical injury should he break my heart. This is out of character for me; dating. Maybe they thought I'd go through life single.

Chapter Twenty-One

Coach

The gym is livening up with the regular afternoon crowd as well as a few newbies I don't recognize. As I walk through the free-weight section, I hear a tiny voice behind me call my name. I stop and turn, seeing that same flexible redhead that can put her forehead on her knees without much difficulty.

What's her name again? Shit! Rita, Reah, Renna… Dammit!

"Hi, how are you?" I ask, only to be polite. I have other things I need to get busy with, so I'm hoping she'll make this quick.

She stands with her arms clasped behind her back so that her overly enhanced breasts jut out, drawing my eyes. It's instinctual to look. I glance away, hoping she didn't notice, but I'm sure she did. It was her intention. She hasn't taken her eyes off me.

"I'm good, but I could use some help on that machine over there. Maybe you can show me how to work my Gluteus Maximus." She turns so I can see her perfectly round ass as she caresses it with her hands. "I think it's getting flabby. What do you think?"

"I think you look fine. How about I get Carol to help you?" I reply while purposely being passive with her.

"No!" she blurts out, spinning around while moving closer to me. With a flirty attitude, she adds, "I want you."

My body wants me to fuck this bitch like there's no tomorrow, but the constant interrupting thoughts of Rayna would likely make my cock go soft, anyway. Besides, risking losing Rayna for a slutty little tart would be the dumbest thing I ever did, and that would be quite an accomplishment. I've done a lot of stupid things in my life, but losing Rayna for a piece of ass would top it all.

"Look, lady, I'm in a relationship with someone so I'm not interested in your ass in the way you're hoping I am. A few months ago, I would have fucked you raw, but this is today, so I'll get Carol to help you if you need advise on your workout."

She crosses her arms over her chest and purses her lips. "Are you sure? I wouldn't tell anyone."

"Oh, I'm sure. Unless there's anything else, I really have to get back to work," I say as I stare at her with angry eyes.

I take advantage of her humiliation, making her squirm nervously under my gaze. This kind of shit makes my dick hard. Intimidating people like her and knocking them off their pedestal excites me every time. I should walk away before the swelling of my cock alerts people. She'll never leave me alone if she thinks she's the reason for my arousal. It's not her working me up; it's the control of the situation that's doing it for me.

After she huffs away, I turn and rush back to my office, shutting the door behind me. I reach in my pants and grab my swelling prick while still leaning against the door, preventing anybody from easily walking in. I squeeze firmly and stroke, slowly at first but working up to a more rapid pace. I pound my rock-hard meat while my pants slide down my legs. This isn't the first time I've jacked off in my office.

People walk past. The thought that they are mere inches away is a hell of a turn-on. With my free hand, I pull my balls down and away from my body until it hurts. I fist my cock as fast as my arm will jerk. Rayna's face pops into my mind. I see her lips slightly part, eyes squeezed shut, exactly how she looks as her orgasm sweeps through her body.

That's all I need to finish me. I cum quickly, cupping my hand to catch my jizz as my cock spits. After a few seconds, I bend to collect my pants and slide them up my legs. I use tissues to clean the mess off of my palm, and they stick to me and shred as I wipe. After a few calming breaths, I open my door and make my way to the men's room. I need to wash my hands before anyone greets me with a handshake.

Tim is drying his hands with a paper towel when I walk in. I quickly rush to the urinal and whip out my cock, not giving him enough time to put his hand up to shake mine. It's difficult to relax enough to pee right after I've spilled my seed. I want him to think that I had to empty my bladder so urgently that I couldn't take the time to greet him properly.

"Did you wait a little too long?" he asks while laughing. "I thought only children do that."

I chuckle. "So it would seem. Now I can't piss."

"Do you want me to run the water?" he teases.

"Would you mind?" I reply, looking at him over my shoulder.

The anticipation of the hypersensitivity from the initial urine flow might be why my body holds back. I groan when my urine flows and the tingles at the head of my prick tickle from the inside. Shit! I love and hate that sensation, but the soothing flow to follow is worth the initial discomfort. My sigh of relief has Tim laughing again.

He says, "Carol said you brought lunch to Rayna today. It sounds like you two are getting along very well."

Carol is one of our trainers.

"We are. Everything seems so much easier when I'm with her. She has this way of calming my inner demon like nobody ever has." I put my dick away and head to the sink to wash my hands. "I told her that I love her."

"Fuck, man! Wow!" He's shocked at my confession. "I never thought you'd say that to a woman. A man, sure; but not a woman. No way." He snickers, and I frown. "I'm proud of you, Coach. So, what did she say to that?"

I pull a paper towel from the dispenser. "She reciprocated." My smile is wide. "I'm happy, really fucking happy."

Tim launches at me, pulling me into a hearty hug and lifting me off the ground, which is quite the feat. Just then, a tall, thin man in his early forties struts through the door, stopping dead in his tracks. His eyes lock on the two muscular men hugging in the men's room. I know what's going through his mind.

We separate instantly. I quickly explain, "It's not what you think. I have a girlfriend."

Simultaneously, Tim says, "No, not what you think. He has a girlfriend, and he loves her. It was a congratulations hug."

I add, "Yeah, we're not gay. I mean, it's okay to be gay. We're just… We're not gay. Definitely not into men."

Tim adds, "Yeah, ah, no dicks for us. I mean, we have dicks, nice dicks, but we don't want other dicks. Gay is good, but, uh, not for us."

The guy snickers at our awkward overcompensation, which has us looking guilty. The thin man walks over to the urinal in a full-blown laugh. Not to seem like we're waiting to see his penis, we hurry out of the bathroom. That was an awkward situation.

"I'm happy for you, Coach," Tim says, patting me on the back as we walk toward my office.

I sit behind my desk and Tim parks his ass in the chair tucked in the corner opposite me. There's a pile of letters in front of me, so I sort through them.

"How did it go with Renee?" I ask.

His smile and waving eyebrow tell the complete story. I'll bet they had sex. If I know her as well as I think I do, she gave it up on their first meeting. Tim isn't a guy who would pass up a good fuck from a hot piece of ass like Renee.

"She is sexy, smart, funny and damn that woman is a flexible little thing."

"You fucked her?" I ask, my expression and shoulder shrug letting him know that I'm not surprised.

"No, it wasn't like that. I mean, we had sex, but she's not like the typical one-night stands I've had. I want to see her again. I like Renee. Okay, yeah, she's extremely sexual, but I like that in a woman." He pauses while I pop an eyebrow. "Dude, I took my clothes off, too, so you could say that I'm just as slutty. I have always wondered why it's okay for a man but not a woman. Shit, if I had a pussy and could cum as often as women do, I'd be naked and fucking everything that walked. And so would you. Don't deny it."

"I completely agree. I'd be fucking anything I could stuff inside myself. I don't think we men can handle coming that often, though. We'd probably drop from a heart attack after three in a row."

He smiles and jokes, "But what a way to go. Am I right?"

I agree wholeheartedly.

"I'm glad you two hit it off. If Renee makes you happy, go for it. She is definitely fine, and she is smart, I suppose. Even though we haven't had an in-depth conversation, I know that she doesn't drool on herself and her shoes are tied, so I assume she has some level of intelligence."

"You don't seem to like her very much," he concludes.

I shrug, wondering if I should tell him that she hit on me and then tried to cover it up with a lie. "I don't hate her. She's not for me, that's all."

"All right, enough about Renee and me." He leans on the desk. "Earlier, you said that Rayna calms your inner demon. Are you talking about your untameable, controlling, sexually sadistic inner demon?"

I chuckle. "Yes, that inner demon."

He furrows his brow. "But, you enjoy setting him free. If you're suppressing that desire, eventually it's going to show its ugly face. What are you going to do then?"

I look at him, knowing he's right. "Rayna is fine with what I've introduced her to so far. I haven't exposed her to the worst of my demon. I don't know how she'll respond. She's not as experienced as the women I'm usually with. I may have to keep that side of me secluded. I can't think about that right now."

"You need to talk to her. If you think you can go through life not expressing yourself sexually in the way you need to, it'll backfire on you one day. Find a way to let her know, Coach. You don't have to take my advice, but I highly recommend that you at least think about it."

Tim is right. No matter how much I try to tell myself I can keep my demon at bay, I know I'm only fooling myself. If she isn't accepting or willing to play, will she leave me? I would not expect her to stay if she's not into BDSM. I can be downright terrifying sometimes.

What if I end up cheating on her with a woman who accepts my freakiness? Fuck, I don't want to think about how much that would hurt Rayna.

"All right, you've said your piece, now get the fuck out of here. I have work to do, and you need to get your flabby ass working out. Hey, avoid that redheaded gym slut in the pink shorts."

Tim is definitely not flabby and knows I'm only joking. He's probably in better shape than I am. If he gets anywhere near the redhead, she'll likely pounce on him and start humping his leg. If I didn't have so much work to do, I'd lean out the door to watch her reaction to Tim as he struts past her. Rayna has a powerful hold on my heart, otherwise, I'd get freaky with that redheaded slut.

He leans out the door to see who I'm talking about. His whistle tells me that he sees her. "You walked away from that? I'm proud of you, man. You must really want to make it work with Rayna. All right, I'm out," he says, walking out and pulling the door shut behind him.

Chapter Twenty-Two

Rayna

The weekday is over, thankfully. I thought it would be a horrible day because of how rushed it started. Since my lunch break, things have been looking up. It was sweet of Coach to bring me food and eat with me. I wonder where he wants to take us on our first date?

All day, I haven't been able to get him out of my forethought. It doesn't help that my coworkers have seen the surveillance video from the lobby. Thanks to Lara, who was more than happy to show the video, they won't stop commenting on him. I've had several requests for Coach to set them up on dates with his gym buddies.

My workday is finally over. As I'm about to walk out, Dr. Jessik calls out to me. "Rayna, can I have a word?"

"Sure," I say, and spin around as he approaches. I was so close to being out the door.

"I heard that you're dating now."

I nod. "Yes, I suppose I am."

He shuffles his feet nervously. "I didn't think you wanted to date anyone. It's been so long since you've had a man in your life. I thought you weren't interested in dating. If I had known, I would have asked you out a few years ago."

His words shock me. I had no idea he was interested. To be honest, I thought he was gay. I've never seen him with a woman. Nobody has.

"Oh," I reply, not knowing what to say to the man. This is awkward. And why do I suddenly feel guilty? I shouldn't. "I wasn't looking. He's my neighbour and I've known him for several years. It just happened."

"Well, I thought you'd come around one day and let me know that you were ready."

What? "I didn't know you were interested in me."

He smiles while his cheeks flush. "I have been ever since you started working here. You didn't know?"

"Um, no. You never told me, so how would I know?" I shrug. "Please, tell me you haven't been waiting for me to come around. You have dated other women, right?"

He shakes his head. "I've been waiting for the right time to ask you out. When you started here, you were married, and then you were going through your divorce. After that, you seemed shut down and uninterested. I asked you to go to the theatre with me about a year ago. But you said that you couldn't because you wouldn't be able to find a sitter with such short notice. You mentioned that you never go out anymore and didn't really care to, anyway. I figured you weren't ready to date anyone."

I'm taken back by what he's saying. He hardly ever converses with me. He seems terribly shy.

"Um, oh, okay," I say while looking at him with wide eyes and a gaping mouth. I quickly close my jaw and look away. "I'm sorry, Dr. Jessik. I had no idea."

"That's okay. I want you to know that if it doesn't work out with this man, I'm here. I'm a nice guy, Rayna, and I love kids. I have money, a house, and a secure job, so I'm no shlump."

I smile, wishing this conversation would end. I have no interest in him. He's too old for me and way too shy.

"You are a gracious man, but—"

"Okay, enjoy the rest of your day."

He quickly scurries away with his head down, hands tucked into his lab coat pockets.

"You, too!" I say, probably louder than I should have.

As I open the second glass door, the heat of the day engulfs me. I instantly feel the heaviness of the humidity. Yuck!

The heat rising from the asphalt is scorching. I can feel it on the soles of my feet as it bleeds through my running shoes. The days are unbearably hot, but the nights are cooling down considerably, so I know summer is nearing its end.

The interior of the car is sweltering after baking in the sun all day. Even the cloth seats are hot, heating my skin through my pants. I turn the key and the car comes to life. Super-heated air blasts from the vents, slapping me in the face, and taking my breath away. I immediately turn it down and push the buttons to lower all four windows. It's so damn hot in here. I feel nauseous.

It wasn't nearly this steamy earlier when I ate lunch outside with Coach. If it had been, we wouldn't have sat in the sun very long. I put my hand in front of the vent and feel cool air seeping from behind the slats. I spin the knob to turn it on high. I'm hoping to relieve some of this nausea. Now I push all four buttons to raise the windows, shrouding myself behind the tinted glass, setting me apart from the noisy world around me.

Before I can slip the shifter into reverse, the backdoor whips open and someone hops in. I spin around but don't recognize the man, a pudgy, white man about fifty years old, with a clean-shaven face. He's wearing sunglasses, a baseball hat, a long-sleeved shirt and blue jeans. All I can think about in my panicked state is that it's way too hot for that shirt. It's strange how I'm wondering why he didn't pass out in this heat today, but I'm not fearing for my life.

I'm immediately stunned when he points a gun in my face and calmly says, "If you scream, I will shoot you. If you try to jump out or crash the car, I will shoot you. If you alert the cops, I will shoot you. Please don't doubt that I will. I don't know you, so I have no problem killing you. Drive, now."

My head is spinning, and I can't breathe. My face feels odd, like my nose and mouth have lost all feeling. Stars twinkle in my eyes and my hands and feet are numb.

Shit, I'm passing out! I try to take deep breaths but it's useless.

The world around me fades to black.

~

Coach

My phone rings and the caller ID tells me it's an unknown number. I answer with an angry tone, thinking it's likely a telemarketer. "Yeah?"

"Um, Coach?" The female voice sounds familiar. "It's me, Renee. Have you heard from Rayna today?"

Oh, I suppose I forgot to put her number in my phone when Rayna gave it to me. I never thought she'd call me. I passed it on to Tim and deleted that message from Rayna. Maybe I should add it to my contacts in case Rayna ever needs me to call her.

"Yeah, I had lunch with her. Why?"

She hesitates, spiking my curiosity. Finally, she replies, "The school called, asking me to pick up the kids because Rayna didn't show. When did you see her last and did she say she had to go shopping or something?"

The hairs all over my body stand on end. Something is very wrong. Rayna would never forget to pick the kids up from school. My heart pounds. I'm out of my chair with my keys in hand, ready to run out the door.

I have to find her.

"We ate lunch together, then I watched her walk back into the office at around one o'clock. I left and came back to the gym. She mentioned nothing about going anywhere after work, but I didn't ask if she had plans. I know she wouldn't be late for the kids because she's worried about the fucking asshole picking them up." I take a calming breath. "This isn't like her. Something's wrong. Did you get the kids?"

"I'm on my way to the school now. I don't know what to do," she says, sounding like she's about to go into full-on panic mode. Her sobs and snotty-nosed snorts begin.

As I'm rushing through the gym, alerting people who were minding their own business, I speak louder than I should. "First, calm the fuck down! Those kids need not know anything's wrong. You can't worry them about this. She probably went somewhere, lost track of the time, or her car broke down and her phone died. Who knows? I'm going to go look for her. Keep me posted."

I hang up and I'm out the door without a word to anyone. After pushing the auto dial number to Rayna's cell, I hear her voice asking me to leave a message. I'm instantly extremely worried and ready to kill someone if they hurt her. If that mother fucker ex-husband of hers has taken her, I swear on my life I'll kill that cocksucker slowly and painfully.

My truck is hot inside, but I don't care at the moment. I rev it up and drop the windows before taking off like a bat out of hell. I'll head to her place of work; it's the last place I saw her.

When I arrive, her car isn't in the lot and nothing looks out of place. I try the door, but it's locked. I bang on the glass, but nobody comes.

I get back in the truck and drive the most likely route she would have taken to the school, but her car is nowhere. Where the fuck is she? I call her phone again, getting the same voice message. Fuck! I search for Renee's number. She answers on the first ring, her voice soft like she's whispering.

"Did you find her?"

"No. I take it you didn't either."

"No, I'm at the grocery store she usually shops at, but I don't see her car in the lot. I was hoping she was here and stuck in a cash-out line."

I can hear the kids in the backseat of Renee's car. They're laughing and talking. It's a jovial sound. They have no idea that their mother could be going through hell right now. I'm thankful that Renee is keeping her concerns to herself.

"I'm going to call the cops. Something's wrong. I can feel it. I'd rather be overzealous than let this go on any longer."

She whispers, "Coach, I'm scared."

"Yeah, me, too." I swallow the lump in my throat. "Don't worry, we'll find her. You keep the kids oblivious for as long as possible. Hopefully, we find her before they know any different."

"I'm doing the best I can. We will find her." Her tone isn't convincing.

"Where does her stupid fucking ex live? I'm going to go talk to that asshole."

"No, don't! He'll only push you to hit him. You're too worked up. Call the cops and tell them about Rick and what he's been doing to cause trouble lately. Let them know that she has a recent restraining order against him. They'll question him. You stay away. Promise me," she hisses, sounding very much like her sister.

"Fine! I'm going to keep driving around. Did you ask the kids if she had something to do after work?"

"I already asked them. They said no," she reveals.

"Maybe you should go back to her place. I'll send the cops there to talk to you and the kids."

I can hear the tears welling up in her voice again. "I've driven the whole parking lot. She's not at the store. I'll take the kids home. Call me and let me know what the cops tell you."

"Renee, you need to tell the kids something. If the cops will show up, they might get freaked out. If you explain as calmly as possible, they'll be better off finding out from you."

"Good idea. I'll talk to them as soon as we get home," she whispers.

"Yeah, okay. If the cops tell me that they won't look into Rayna's disappearance, I'll call you. Otherwise, expect them soon. If I find her, I'll call you right away," I promise.

My rental truck zooms down side streets. If there was a lot of traffic or an accident, she would try to avoid it, but her car is nowhere. Where the fuck is she?

The lump in my throat finally bursts and a flood of tears spill. I wipe them away, but the dam has broken.

I scream as loud as I can, "RAYNA!"

Chapter Twenty-Three

Rayna

The light is blindingly bright, even through my eyelids. I struggle to open them, blinking several times to clear away the fog my brain is waking from.

What happened? Why can't I move?

Fear yanks me awake. I'm hogtied, lying on my belly in the backseat of my car. A wad of cloth is in my mouth with something tied around my head to keep me from spitting it out. I want to scream, yet worry that the person who did this to me might try to hurt me.

What the hell does he want with me? He can't ransom me. I'm living paycheck to paycheck and don't have rich relatives.

Tears stream down my cheeks and drip onto the seat where my daughter usually sits. They expected me to pick them up at school. What time is it? Did my sister pick them up? If the principal calls Renee, she'll know something's wrong. She'll call the police, I'm sure of it. I'm never unaccounted for.

Oh, please, let them find me before this man hurts or kills me.

The car comes to a complete stop inside a structure. The man shuts off the engine and gets out, slamming the driver's door harder than required to ensure it closes. I'm expecting him to open the door I'm facing so that he can pull me out and do whatever it is he's going to do with me.

Please don't rape me!

But he doesn't open the door. The anticipation tortures my mind.

I remain facedown inside the car for what seems like ten minutes or more. It is sweltering in here, making it difficult to breathe. My lungs don't want to inhale the scorching air, and my throat is so dry that I keep coughing.

He must not be coming back. I fight against my restraints, trying to figure out how to untie myself, but the knot isn't anywhere my fingers can reach. I'm so frustrated that I scream, not making much sound through the cloth. If he doesn't take me out of this car soon, I will die from the heat. But, do I really want him to take me out? What will happen if he does?

The door whips open. A welcoming blast of cooler air rushes over me, giving me an instant sense of relief, even though fear runs rampant through me. The man grabs my arms and pulls me toward him. I didn't get a clear view of him when he got in my car, but enough to know that I didn't recognize him.

Now he's wearing a mask. That's a good thing, right? If I can't see his facial features, I won't be able to identify him in court. That means he's likely to set me free after he's done doing whatever it is he has in mind.

Please don't rape me!

He pulls me out of the car, dropping me onto my face and chest. Pain explodes from my cheekbone outward, radiating through my entire face. It feels like my eye has popped out of its socket. I scream louder than I think I ever have in my life, but it's muffled.

White stars fill my vision. Am I going to pass out again? No, not now!

A sudden force to my chest knocks the wind out of me, bringing clarity front and center. I can't breathe. The overwhelming pain is nothing like I've ever felt before.

Oh, fuck! Someone, please, help me!

Stars circle my mind again. No! I don't want to pass out. I struggle with all of my strength to gasp for what little air my lungs can manage without moving my ribs. The stars are clearing. I continue to force myself to breathe even though it's excruciatingly painful.

He lifts me by the rope's knot that binds my hands and feet together. The strain on my wrists, ankles, shoulders, and back is unbearable. I hope he puts me down before my skin tears or my joints dislocate.

I'm screaming as loud as I can manage, begging for him to put me down.

He drops me again, but this time, I'm prepared and hold my head up as best I can and tightened my stomach muscle so the blow won't knock the air out of me or further injure my ribs. Pain stabs at my ribs, instantly burning the moment my chest touches the cement floor. The swelling in my cheek impedes my vision. The pressure on that side of my face is intense. That nostril will not stop leaking.

It fucking hurts so bad!

The man is talking on the phone, but I can't make out everything he's saying; only a few words here and there. I hear him say: he has me, nobody saw, and he'll wait; but nothing else.

The pavement is cooler than the sweltering air, so I rest my throbbing cheek against it. It's going to swell my eye completely shut if I don't get some ice on it. I highly doubt he'd be kind enough to get that for me. I'm almost positive my cheekbone is broken.

"Don't worry, pretty girl, it'll all be over soon enough."

The man speaks as he cuts the rope between my feet and hands. My legs flop down to the cement with a thud, and my hands remain tied but now rest against my lower back. It's not great, but better than being hogtied.

I try to talk but obviously can't with the gag in my mouth. He can hear me trying, though. Maybe he'll remove the cloth. I would like that very much. It's getting harder to breathe because the one nostril is swelling. Panic sets in, so

I scream, fearing that I'll suffocate, and the man won't even be aware of it.

The kidnapper flips me onto my back, pinning my arms underneath of me. He groans as he unties the mouth gag, removing the wad of cloth. I gasp but don't scream. The last thing I want is for him to put it back in. Besides, screaming would only make my throat and ribs hurt worse, as if that were even possible.

"Not a fucking word, bitch," he states while pressing on my swollen cheek with one of his sausage-like fingers. He's trying to get me to scream from the agony, but I fight hard not to give him that satisfaction. When he takes his finger off my face, he laughs. "Strong-willed, are you?"

The man tosses the mouth gag over my eyes and then walks away, leaving me lying on the cool cement. He's blocked me from looking around to see where I am, not that I recognized what little I've seen. I can hear him on the phone again but he's further away from me than before, so all I can hear are mumbles. I shake my head, hoping the makeshift blindfold will fall off, but I'm not that lucky.

Fortune seems to have left me today.

I silently plead to Renee and Coach to find me. I listen intently, hoping my subconscious hears one of them whispering to me, but I hear nothing except the kidnapper's mumbles. It's silly of me to think I could telepathically hear their responses. I'm desperate and holding onto whatever I think might get me through this ordeal.

I close my eyes and talk to my children, hoping somehow they will feel my love.

Kim, if this man kills me, please don't fear people. Not everyone is bad. Most people are honourable. Don't be angry.

Ken, don't seek revenge. Live your life to the fullest and be as happy as you can. Remember the pleasant times and don't focus on the last horrific moments of my life.

Kids, know that I love you with all of my being and I will be there to watch you pass through all the stages in your life.

Renee, raise my kids well, as I would have. I know you can do this; I have faith in you. That's why I put you as guardian in my will. I love you so much, little sister. I forgive you for hurting me. Find love and hang onto it.

Coach, find peace in your life. Don't be sad that you couldn't help me. This is beyond your abilities and it's okay not to be in control of everything. If I know you at all, you're driving around looking for me. I hope you'll be successful in your quest, but I don't think you'll find me here, wherever here is. If you can hear me, I'm inside some enclosure, like a garage or barn. I can't hear anything outside, like cars or people. Please find me before he kills me! In case you don't, you need to let this go. Don't hold the pain inside of you, it'll only weigh you down. I want you to find someone to love.

I pray that all of them can hear my thoughts or feel the warmth and love I'm sending them. If they can sense me thinking about them, it might bring them some comfort. I know they'll be searching for me and that gives me hope. It's unlikely they'll find me, but I can't think like that.

I shake my head back and forth, determined to knock the material from my eyes, but it only shifts, exposing my aching eye. It's not enough for me to see anything since it has swollen almost completely shut. The pain on that side of my face is outrageous, and the shaking only made it worse.

"Hey, bitch, I'm going to sit you in a chair. Can you behave?"

"I won't fight you." I speak with the softest, sweetest voice I can manage with my throat being so painfully dry. If he thinks I'm no threat, he might not further injure me.

He's much bigger than me; definitely not a bodybuilder, just big. He lifts me by my armpits and sits me on a solid steel chair. It squeaks on the floor when it slides against the concrete as my butt plops on it. He immediately unties my wrists but refastens them to the chair legs so my arms hang straight down by my sides. I'm relieved to have the blood flowing.

The mask is off, so I take this opportunity to look at the surroundings as he finishes tying me to the chair. It's an old wood barn. The mass amount of cobwebs on the ceiling and the level of rot on the unfinished walls give away its age. From what I can tell, the building is about large enough to fit three cars deep and three wide. It's a good-sized barn.

I take notice of all the huge toolboxes and how the tools are displayed neatly on the pegboard above the workbench. The floor is stained from the spills of oil and other automotive liquids. Some stains are fresh, but most have faded over time with newer stains overlapping them. A car is at the back of the garage directly in front of mine. It's covered with a light blue tarp, only revealing an extra-wide rear tire, like one that would be on a quarter-mile car.

The man says, "Don't say a fucking word and I won't have to shut you up. I'm sure you don't want a broken jaw to match that cheek. Do you understand?"

I nod and watch him as he shuffles his heavy boots to a workbench. His stride isn't as smooth as it should be. He has a limp from a possible wound on his left leg. He favours it. His ragged hair is black and hanging from the bottom of the baseball hat. I could use this information to help find him if he lets me go free after he's done doing whatever it is he has planned.

When he's close to me, I can smell his body odour, and it isn't pleasant. It's obvious he doesn't use deodorant, and if he does, he needs to change brands. I smell the oils and other chemicals in the barn as well.

There's no doubt in my mind that this is a mechanic's garage.

I try to focus on what I can hear, but there's only silence. I must be in the county where the traffic rarely comes. If I hadn't been unconscious, I might know how long we were in the car.

～

Coach

Where the fuck is she? I'm so goddamn enraged. My heart feels like it's breaking over and over. Every time I imagine someone hurting my beautiful Rayna, an overwhelming, eerie sense of dread rips me apart.

Why would someone take her? Why?

I pull into my driveway and park, quickly sprinting across the lawn to Rayna's house. Three cops are standing inside the doorway. All of them have their hands on their guns with their free hands held up, telling me to stop.

I plant my feet outside of the door. I'm shaking from the rage that's been flooding through my veins since I got Renee's first call. I hear her instruct them to let me in, so they step aside and nod apologetically as I pass. They're only doing their job, so I won't give them grief.

She's sitting at the kitchen table with Ken in a chair next to her. Kim is on her lap, curled up against her chest with tears streaming down pretty little face. She's trying to comfort the girl, but that's hard to do while she's just as upset.

"Renee, any word?" I ask, trying to keep my voice calm.

I don't want to frighten the kids any more than they already are. If they sense the violent rage that's eating me alive inside, it won't help to ease their worry. I know Rayna would want me to make the situation seem as light as possible for their benefit.

"Nothing," she replies. "The cops talked to Rick, and he has a solid alibi. I still think he has something to do with this, but they claim he doesn't."

I move closer to Ken and then rub his head like I always do. He gazes up at me with a sombre expression. Seeing the concern on his boyish face hurts me more than my own dread. I despise how desperate he looks right now.

The policeman looks up from his notepad, finally taking notice of me standing beside him. He immediately takes a step back while crinkling his brow and giving me the hairy-eye.

"Can you tell me where you were today?" he asks accusingly.

"Officer, I was working at my gym. I met Rayna at her workplace to bring her lunch because she mentioned that she had forgotten to bring one. I thought it'd be a pleasant surprise, and it was. We ate in the back of my rental truck in the parking lot of her workplace. I went straight back to the gym after she went back in the office. I was at the gym until Renee called to inform me that something was wrong."

"And where have you been for the past hour?" he asks while writing notes in his little pad.

"Driving all the routes she might have taken if she were going to the school to pick up the kids. I drove all over the place. Her car has vanished."

I stop talking because I have to fight off the urge to scream or burst into tears. That would not be helpful for the kids or Renee. Besides, if I throw a fit, that might get me arrested.

Renee and the kids look at me. They had faith I would find her. I tried but failed them.

Ken is still looking at me with desperation in his eyes. A child should never wear that expression. I have to turn away. I calmly walk to the bathroom and shut the door, barely making it inside before the tears burst forth. If those kids see me crying, they might fear that their mother is gone forever.

They have to believe that I'm staying positive. They see me as strong and dependable, so that's what I'm going to be for them. Rayna would expect that from me.

I pee while I'm in here and then wash my hands, and splash icy water on my pink cheeks and puffy, reddened eyes. After taking several deep breaths to gain strength, I slowly open the door with my shoulders back and my sorrow on the back burner.

Ken is standing in the hallway across from the bathroom, taking me off my guard completely.

"Is Mom going to be okay?" he whispers. His eyes plead for me to promise that she will.

I try to look stoic, not letting him see even a shred of fear. "The cops will find her. She'll be okay. Keep the faith, little man. We have to stay positive."

"How do you know? People kill other people all the time. The kidnapper could be killing her right now."

He erupts in tears. I see him as an inconsolable little boy, no longer like the pubescent teenager who seems older than his age. I take him in my arms and hug him tightly to my chest, running my fingers through his hair like I've seen Rayna do a hundred times before.

"Take a deep breath and keep telling yourself she's going to be okay. Your mom is smarter than anyone I've ever met, so if she can safely get away, she will. You know she'll do everything she can to get back to you and your sister."

"I know," he whispers, but sobbing gasps follow his gently spoken words.

I guide him into the bathroom and close the door. After looking in two different cabinets, I finally find a washcloth. I wet it with cool water and wring it out. I drop to one knee and wipe the tears from his cheeks. He takes the rag from me and finishes the job, holding the cool cloth to his eyes, hoping to reduce their heat.

"Can I ask you to do something that's going to be really hard?" I ask. He nods. "Your sister will look up to you for strength because you're her older brother. Little sisters do that. I need you to show her that you believe Mom's coming home, even if you have doubts. When Kim isn't around, you can cry like crazy to let it out." I lower my voice. "Don't tell anyone, but I cried, too; not because I think she's not coming home, but because I couldn't find her. I feel helpless, probably the same way you do. Just because I'm a grownup doesn't mean I have all the solutions. Can you be strong for your aunt and your little sister?"

He takes the washcloth from his eyes and swallows hard. "I think so." His little chest gasps again from his heavy sobs. He takes deep breaths, hoping to stop his tears. It helps.

"I know you're hurting. We are all in pain right now. Can I tell you something else?" Ken nods again. "I love your mom. I want to marry her one day. I told her that, too, and she said that she loves me back. I probably wasn't supposed to tell you that, come to think of it. Anyway, you know she has to come home so she can marry me. If you approve, of course."

He smiles through his sadness. "I'd like that. I won't tell her you told me."

"You should never keep secrets from your mom. They seem to know everything, anyway." We both nod. "Okay, take another deep breath and let it out slowly. Are you ready to go back into the kitchen?"

"Yes, I can do this. I'll try to be strong for them," he replies.

"I don't expect you to be a superhero, just do the best you can, okay?" I suggest, ruffling his hair until he swats my hand away with a quick chuckle. "Bud, nobody will fault you for crying, okay?"

We no sooner get to the kitchen when the detective is called out of the room by another officer. Whatever she's whispering to him looks important. The officer shows the detective something on her phone. I hear him ask her to send it to him but can't make out the next thing he says.

He enters the kitchen with his phone in his hand. After it vibrates, he holds it up in front of Renee's face and asks her if she recognizes the person on the screen. She looks closer, sliding her fingers along the screen to enlarge the image. She shakes her head. Kim and Ken also look, but neither knows who it is.

"Coach, is it?" the detective asks. I nod. "Do you recognize this man?"

He shows me the picture on the phone. It's not a clear picture so the guy could be anyone. I have no idea who he is. He's a big-framed man, built like someone who's been doing physical labour his whole life, but not a bodybuilder.

"Wait a minute; I saw him when Rayna and I were eating lunch. He was walking across the parking lot. It was strange that he didn't seem to be in any hurry to get anywhere and he was dressed too warmly to be taking a leisurely stroll. He kept looking back at us, but I thought nothing of it. I mean, how often do you see two people eating lunch in the bed of a pickup in a commercial parking lot? I thought he was curious." I whisper, "Is that him?"

If it is, I'll never forgive myself for not watching him more closely to see what he was up to.

The officer nudges me toward the cupboards so we can whisper without risking the kids listening in.

"It looks that way. The video shows him getting into the backseat of her car. He's there for about a minute, then gets out, opens the driver's door, pushes her over, and he gets behind the wheel. He drives away. Officers reviewed the traffic camera recordings to see if they could track where the car went. We could follow the car for three blocks, but that's where the city cameras end. We believe he was taking her out of the city. We have cars doing an area search for them, but..." His words break off.

"I'm going looking. Where was the last place her car was seen?"

"You can sit yourself down right here and let us do our job. We're looking for her, don't think we're not. You're too upset to be out driving around. Stay here and take care of her family."

I nod, but I'm angry as fuck. I don't want to be here, helplessly waiting, accomplishing nothing while something horrible could happen to Rayna. But, when I look around the table, the kids and Renee are all looking at me with so much fear on their faces that I know I have to stay for a little while and be strong for them.

Dammit! Fuck. Rayna, where are you?

Chapter Twenty-Four

Rayna

It feels like I've been sitting here for hours. My stomach rumbles from hunger, and my throat is so dry it feels like I'm breathing shards of glass. That's not the worst of it. I really have to pee.

"Sir," I call out, trying not to be too loud, which might anger him. I definitely don't want that.

He looks at me. "What do you want?"

"I have to use the bathroom," I reply, dreading that he will either let me go, watch me the entire time, and possibly rape me while my pants are down. Or, he won't let me go and I'll have to relieve myself in my pants. I'd much rather option two if option one will lead to rape.

"What do you want me to do about it?" he hisses.

"Do you have a toilet I can use? Please, it's becoming urgent."

"No, piss your pants if you have to go that badly."

I do not want to piss myself. It would be even more humiliating than I care to experience, especially if these will be my last moments alive. I'd rather not die wearing soiled pants.

"Please, sir?"

"I told you no. You aren't moving from that chair."

"I beg of you," I whisper, barely loud enough for him to hear me. Maybe he'll have a strand of compassion for me. I don't know how I can expect that of my abusive kidnapper. But he's a human being, so there has to be some shred of decency in him.

He stands and rushes toward me. Oh shit! I think I pissed him off. As he approaches, my fear is warranted when his foot lifts, slamming into my upper chest. The pain from my ribs is ghastly. Me and the chair flip backward, my head cracking on the pavement.

I can't breathe in, and my brain is spinning. Oh shit, I'm blacking out again!

Darkness takes over.

~

Coach

It's been about seven hours since someone took Rayna. Nobody can tell us anything new. My hope of finding her is fading and my faith in the detective's ability to come through has me itching to go find her myself. If I have to, I will bang on every door until she's found.

Why the fuck is this happening? Who took her? What for?

I stand up from the sofa, lifting a sleeping Kim off my lap and laying her down on the indented, warm spot my ass created. I toss the purple blanket from the back of the sofa over her tiny body and leave her to rest. She looks peaceful, as if she's dreaming of her mother being home and tucking her into bed like she should be doing tonight.

In the dining room, the police huddle around the table discussing information and potential leads. As I approach, the first officer sees me and stands between me and the table. I try to look around him to see what's so important that he doesn't want to share with me.

"What's going on?" I ask in a demanding voice.

"We haven't found any fresh leads. We tracked her cell phone and found it on the road two blocks from her work. We fingerprinted it, but he must have wiped it clean or wore gloves. We've talked to her coworkers and patients." He hesitates and scratches his head as if debating whether to tell me something. "Ah, there is one lead, but it's small. A witness saw the man get out of the backseat after she slumped onto the passenger's seat, as if she had passed out or," he takes a breath, "or if he drugged her. The witness can't be sure of what they saw. I haven't told Renee yet."

My rage has reignited, brewing deep inside me like lava. If I catch this guy, I will punish him until he begs me to kill him. I will bind that fucker and sadistically torture him and thoroughly enjoy doing it. My inner demon will rise and take over my body and mind, and I will welcome him.

The detective puts his hands up to calm me down. "Listen, you need to keep it together. If you go off, those kids will think she's dead. Why don't we go outside so you can get some fresh air?"

I turn with my fists clenched, nostrils flared, and my body stiff with rage. Once outside, I take a deep breath and purposely stretch my hands as I tilt my head side to side. This officer needs reassurance that I'm calm and not going to fly off the handle. As soon as he turns his attention elsewhere, I'll be in my truck and gone.

I will find her! These incompetent assholes couldn't find their dicks with a magnifying glass and a map. She needs me.

Rayna, please let me know where you are.

Before the detective goes back into the house, he tells another officer to monitor me. He must sense I'm about to run. I bide my time, waiting patiently for the cop to turn her back, forgetting that she's been appointed to babysit me. It isn't long before she chats with another officer. It's plainly obvious the two of them are having a sexual affair by how she's flipping her hair and he's puffing out his chest. I have to wait a few more minutes until they are deep in their conversation, and then I'm out of here.

I slowly pace back and forth across Rayna's driveway while the officer watches me. It isn't long before she turns her back to me. No doubt he's telling her what he wants to do to her when their shift is over. This is my opportunity.

As quickly as possible, I scurry across my lawn and hop into the truck, start it up, and pull out of the driveway before the officers realize I'm leaving. I watch in the rear-view mirror as the two of them run onto the road and throw their hands up, defeated.

I'd better get moving before they call in my plate and track me down. I have to find Rayna.

~

Rayna

The man's phone rings, startling me from a pleasant dream. I was sitting at the dinner table with the kids and Coach. We were laughing and holding hands. It was lovely.

My one functioning eye opens. I'm sitting upright in the chair again. He must have righted me while I was still unconscious. My head aches, and my mind spins when I turn my head too quickly. I hope the vertigo passes soon. I likely have a concussion.

My bladder is even more full now and I won't be able to hold it much longer. I strain to hear what he's saying into his phone, hoping I might hear him say a person's name. If I survive this, I will track the bastard down myself if I have to.

"You were supposed to be here already." He shakes his head. "Where the fuck are you?" he whispers, pausing between sentences, I assume so the caller can reply. "So, what you're saying is that I have to stay here and babysit this broad until you decide to come?" He paces back and forth. "When might that be?"

He turns to look at me and shakes his head. "That wasn't the deal. No! You've got two hours and then I'm letting her go. Then I guess you'd better get your ass here! Yeah, fuck you, too!"

He hangs up the phone and tosses it onto the workbench. His beady eyes glare at me from behind the mask. "Looks like we're stuck together for a few more hours."

"Who are you waiting for?" I ask softly, fearing he'll hit me because once again I broke his command of not talking.

"Shut up."

"What are they going to do to me?" I ask in the sweetest, most innocent way that I can manage without sounding pathetic.

He looks at me and tilts his head. "I don't care. My job will be done. When that car pulls up, I'm out. What happens after that, I don't want any part of."

"I see," I whisper, looking pathetic and vulnerable. I wish tears would spill, but I'm so angry that I can't bring them on. "I have to pee. Please, may I have some dignity?"

"Fuck! You can't wait?" he asks with obvious irritation.

I shake my head. "No, I'm desperate. It's been hours. Please?"

"Fine!" he yells as he rushes toward me. I cringe, half expecting him to kick me in the chest again. He unties my hands from the chair. "If you try to get away, I'll beat you within an inch of your life. Do you understand?"

"I understand completely," I assure him, but if an opportunity shows itself, I will jump on it and fight like my life depends on it because I think it does.

He grabs my hair and stands me up, then brings the ropes in front of me, binding my hands together. The ropes are tight and hurt my wrists. I complain in a whisper, "They're too tight."

"Good, then you won't escape. Go that way," he tells me, pointing in toward the hallway.

First, the smell hits me, but when he turns on the light, I nearly vomit. The toilet is filthy. The bowl is coated with orange and black mould, and on the floor surrounding it is stained with urine. I'll have to hover. I ponder letting it go in my pants instead of risking contracting an incurable disease from using his toilet.

"Are you fucking going or not?" he yells, pushing me into the disgusting room.

The stench is gut-wrenching. I wretch, but there isn't anything in my stomach, thankfully. I can imagine the beating that would ensue after that.

"Can you shut the door, please?" I ask, fearing how intense the smell will be once it closes.

"Fuck no! If you have to go, go." He's leaning on the wood-panelled wall across the hall with his arms crossed over his chest, watching me.

I unbutton my pants and let them slip halfway down my thighs while bending forward slightly to pull down my panties in a way that prevents him from seeing my vagina. I hover over the filthy seat and immediately pee. I don't think I could have held it for another minute had I tried. Shit, this feels good!

I look for a tissue, but I see none. What the hell does he use to wipe his ass after he shits? A shiver runs straight up my spine when I picture his shit-streaked underwear. Yuck! He smells horrid, so I know his hygiene isn't up to par.

"Do you have any tissue?" I ask while not looking at him.

"Nope. Drip dry," he mutters. "Just do it quickly."

I can feel his eyes on me, seducing me while I perform a basic human necessity. He's disgusting, and I pray that he's decent enough not to rape me. Even though he kicked my chest twice, making it painful to breathe, he hasn't touched me sexually. At least not while I was conscious.

I pull up my panties, trying to avoid letting him have a view of my bits, but it's a struggle because my hands are bound so tightly. They've gone numb so trying to refasten the button on my pants is impossible. I wrestle with the zipper until I have it pulled up, and then try the button again, but my numb fingers can't manage the simple task.

My captor suddenly grabs the top of my pants. I didn't even see him approach me.

Panic ensues! He's going to rape me!

I swing my arms frantically, screaming for him not to touch me. He's unaffected with the hits to his chest and face.

I don't see his fist come at my face until it's too late to duck. It lands, shooting the worst pain I have ever experienced in my life through my entire face. It felt like my skull broke in half. Did my nose flatten under his knuckles and every one of my teeth break, too?

Blackness is taking the pain away. I'm falling but have no motor function to stop myself from hitting the disgusting floor.

This time, I welcome the blackness.

Coach

I'm stopped at the streetlight where the last traffic camera saw Rayna's car. I turn the corner where the video showed it turn. I drive slowly, looking at all the driveways and garages that have their doors open or lights on inside. Maybe I'll see her or her car if I get lucky enough. The captor won't concern himself with random people in pickups driving slowly.

I cruise up and down each street in this insignificant town, searching for a clue, any clue, but I find nothing out of the ordinary. I should drive faster before someone calls the cops to report a strange man scoping out houses.

She's not in this town. If she were around here, she would have screamed by now and someone would have surely heard her. It's so quiet around here that the slightest odd noise would alert people to find the source. Besides, small-town people know everything that everyone is doing. This kidnapper would have to be very sly for them not to have noticed his misdeeds.

The county is where I would take a victim, like Rayna's ex-husband, for instance. I agree with Renee; Rick has something to do with this.

It's all my fault. If I would not have gotten involved and tossed him out of her house, none of this would be happening. That situation escalated his temper. I should have stayed out of it. He wasn't hitting her, only yelling cruel things. Maybe I jumped the gun. I wanted to protect her, keep her safe. I fear I've made a bad situation so much worse.

"RAYNA! I WILL FIND YOU, MY LOVE!"

People in the surrounding homes can surely hear my screamed promise, and I don't care.

Call the cops! I haven't seen one yet. How can they be looking for her if I haven't seen them and I've been all over this town, twice?

~

Rayna

The brightness of the overhead light burns harshly into my brain through my pupil. I can't even see a sliver of light through my other eye. It was swollen before he punched me.

Did he hit me so hard that he blinded me? Please don't let that be the case.

The world is spinning, and my face is in tremendous pain.

I look around as best I can. My guard has left me alone. My head spins with vertigo as I scan around the room. He really is gone. This is my chance.

I struggle with the ropes, pulling so hard that I feel my skin tear. My bones will soon break from the force. I don't care if I crush them, as long as I can get myself freed.

I'm unable to loosen them no matter how much I pull. Fresh blood flows down my fingers in streams; I can feel the warmth. Hopelessness consumes me, and that's when the tears fall. I'm devastated, not for my impending death, but for the sorrow the kids will surely feel. That is what's tearing at my heart. How will they grow up without a mother? Renee will raise them, but kids need their mom.

Someone will find me. I know they will, as long as I don't give up. I will survive this. For some unknown reason, I know this to be true.

I whisper it so the universe can hear, "I will not die today."

A warmth flows around me, easing my anguish like a loving hug, ensuring that I will survive. I smile softly and allow myself a moment to absorb the pleasantness of the air's loving caress. Snap out of it! Think Rayna, think!

I yell, "Hello?"

The smelly man comes out of the other little room by the bathroom, eating a sandwich. "You woke up. At least it was quiet when you were unconscious." I hear him smack his food around his mouth. "What the fuck do you want now?"

"I'm hungry," I tell him, unsure if I can chew anything with my face this badly beaten. He may have broken every bone on the left side of my face.

"You don't have time to eat. Sit tight, our company will be here soon enough," he says with a mouthful of food. A chunk of bread drops from his bottom lip after he mangled it in his mouth. "Why the fuck did you freak out? I was trying to button your pants since you obviously couldn't do it."

Dammit! "I thought you were going to rape me. Wouldn't you panic if you were in my position?"

"I suppose I should have told you what I was trying to do. Just sit there and shut up. It won't be much longer."

The man disappears back into that room again. I continue to struggle with my bindings, even though I know it's hopeless. Maybe the ropes will break free from the chair.

Our company will be here soon. Does that mean that I'll die shortly? I'm hoping they'll tell me why I'm about to die. Hopefully, the visitor cares to explain it to me. My present captor doesn't seem to want to answer that question. He might not even know.

Who is this mysterious person he's expecting? What will they do to me when they get here? Will the person torture me before they kill me or simply do it outright?

They don't have to kill me. They might keep me locked up somewhere. Neither option sounds very inviting.

Shit, Rayna, you have to get the hell out of here!

~

Coach

"Please, please let her be safe," I pray aloud.

I've been looking but can't find her car and the frustration has built to a breaking point. Where the fuck is she?

"Help me find her," I beg the universe to hear my pleas.

My emotions burst forth and I have to pull to the side of the road. I can't see through the waves of endless tears that flood my vision. I yell and pound on the steering wheel so viciously I fear the airbag might deploy, rewarding me with one hell of a punch to the face. I don't care. I need to let the rage out.

"RAYNA! Where the fuck are you? Dammit!" I scream at the tops of my lungs, collapsing against the steering wheel only after my rage turns into the pain of a broken soul and lost dreams.

Unable to yell anymore, I whisper, "Please. Rayna. I love you. Help me find you."

With my chin resting on the steering wheel, I breathe deeply and swallow hard, burying my emotions back inside where they belong. Outbursts like this will not help me find her.

What can I do now? Should I drive around more? I don't even know where to look; what town and how many towns? I could knock on the doors of every garage with its lights on. Is she being held hostage in a barn or a house? There are so many to search. Where would I even begin?

The evening sun hovers barely above the horizon and shines through the windshields of two cars as they pass by. It lights up the faces of the people as they go about their lives.

They don't know that my Rayna is lost and hurt, or worse, she may be dead.

I squint because the sun's reflection off the second car's windshield stings my bloodshot eyes. As it nears, I'm shocked that I recognize him. A cold heaviness floods my veins, making me feel weak with dread.

What the fuck is he doing in this town? My hands shake, making it nearly impossible to turn the key to start the truck. I have to follow that car!

As soon as he turns onto the next road and can no longer see me in his rearview mirror, I whip the truck around to follow him. He won't lead the way to Rayna if he thinks he's being followed, so I tail him from quite a distance. He must know a vehicle is behind him. It's not like I can hide in the county where the roads are long and straight.

"Take me to Rayna, you mother fucker!" I say between clenched teeth. "You wait until I get my hands on you."

My fists grip the wheel. I want to pound the accelerator and catch up to him, but I know if I do, he won't lead me to her.

Time drags, each second feels like a full minute. My inner demon is seething in anger, causing me to shake uncontrollably. The car turns into a long driveway that leads up to a small blue house that could benefit from some maintenance. Two large barns sit behind it, both have lights on inside. There's a spotlight illuminating the one car that sits beneath it. It isn't Rayna's but now I know where that fucker is holding her.

Why would he take her? What does he want with her?

I never thought he was psychotic, but he is a dangerous man who could cause her great suffering. I have to help her.

My heart beats like a powerful drum. I want so badly to follow his car into the driveway and beat that fucker to death, but I'm not positive he's alone and can't risk another person, or persons, hurting her while I exact my revenge on the fucking weasel by ripping his head off.

So as not to lead him to think I'm tailing him, I continue to drive past where he turned while keeping an eye to make sure he isn't retreating out of the driveway and heading back in the opposite direction. I hope like hell he didn't recognize me in this truck. He can't know that I'm coming for him.

As soon as I'm far enough away that he won't see the truck pulling off the road, I shut off my lights and park so close to the ditch that I'm surprised I didn't slide into it. I shut my door quietly and run down the street as fast as I can.

I'm coming, Rayna! Just hold on!

Chapter Twenty-Five

Rayna

A door squeals as it's jarred open. Someone else is here. I hold my breath, hoping to hear their voice. It's a man. I'm not familiar with his voice. I wait, staring at the doorway that leads to the hallway where the men are conversing just out of my line of sight.

I wish the room would stop spinning.

My captor is leading the way for the other man. When I finally see him, I'm confused because I don't know who he is.

He is very tall, extremely handsome, and stacked with muscles. His hair is black and styled perfectly, using a lot of products, I assume. His facial features are sharp and masculine, his skin shaved clean.

As he nears, he looks me up and down, as if assessing me.

Oh, no! Is he going to rape me? Is that why I'm captive; for sex? Why wouldn't this stranger opt for a younger woman whose body is better than mine? He's obviously younger than me. Does he have a MILF fetish?

He grabs my chin, lifting my face up so he can get a better look at me. His eyes are ice blue and gorgeous. Right now, they scare the hell out of me, but in better circumstances, I would be attracted to him.

"Tell me your name," he asks in a deep voice while wearing an impassioned expression.

"Rayna," I reply, my voice shaking. "What's yours?"

He looks at my eye. "This is bad. I'm going to get my ass beat for this."

What is he talking about? Who will beat his ass? Is someone else involved?

I show no fear. "Who are you, what are you going to do to me, and why am I here?"

"You ask a lot of questions for a woman in your position." He turns to look at my greasy captor. "Is that why she looks like this?"

"She fell out of the car on her face and then she tried to fight me, so I had to shut her down. I had no choice," he replies, obviously nervous enough that he takes a step away from the handsome stranger.

I yell, "You had a choice, asshole. I'm not a brawny woman, you could have easily restrained me without breaking my face!"

I'm more pissed off than scared. What do I have to lose from ratting him out? If they plan to kill me, at least my kidnapper will catch shit from the man who hired him to do his bidding. He's not pleased that I'm all bruised up.

"Tie her to the rafters so I can get a better look at her," he exclaims to the pungent man. His eyes still burn into mine. "I want to play with you. Trust me, gorgeous, you will love this."

My captor immediately begins freeing me from the chair but doesn't remove the ropes from my wrists. I try to fight him, so he carries me to where he wants me. He unties me.

This might be my only chance to either get away or go down swinging. If they're going to kill me, I won't make it easy for them.

The instant I am free, I spin around, twisting Smelly's wrist when he grips my arm. The second he lets go, I punt his balls and then turn to run toward the door faster than if a bomb is about to explode in my wake.

I only get a dozen steps away when I'm grabbed by my hair and yanked back, falling to my knees. My bloodcurdling screams should be heard a mile away. Perhaps someone will call for help.

He pulls me by my hair. My hands grab at the wrist of the sizable man. The man I kicked still crouches on the floor, gasping his breaths as he holds his aching genitals. He looks really pissed off.

My hair is set free, but only when his other hand grips my throat. He pulls my face close to his. His dangerous eyes blaze into mine. They're a beautiful blue but seem dark somehow. Perhaps his anger is changing his eye colour or my fear is clouding my vision.

His grip is getting tighter. He's choking me. I can't breathe.

My arms flail and punch at his wrist. My nails claw at his skin, hoping he'll let go, but he doesn't even wince. He seems to like that I'm fighting him. I kick at his shins, so he holds me at arm's length. I cannot reach his body with my arms or legs.

His words hiss at me through a clenched jaw. "Where do you think you're going? If I were you, I wouldn't try that again, you fucking little whore! Why don't you want to play with me? I'm not horrible to look at; at least, that's what I'm told."

He spins me around, loosening his grip on my throat but still rendering me captive. After pulling me back to his firm belly, he grabs my hair again and yanks my head back. I can't turn my head away from his full lips as they press onto mine.

His tongue burrows into my mouth. I try to bite down but the pain in my face is agonizing, especially in this position. Tiny bright stars fill my sight, so many that they're going black. I'm passing out again.

The bright lights once again bleed into my groggy mind, ruining a perfectly wonderful dream. It takes a few seconds for the fogginess to clear enough where I can think straight. He's tied my arms over my head with a hanging rope from the ceiling. My previously bruised and bloodied wrists ache.

My toes barely touch the ground. I can't relieve my wrists from bearing most of my weight.

The blue-eyed man stands in front of me with his arms crossed over his chest. He's watching me, expressionless. Maybe he's been waiting for me to wake. I think he prefers me aware when he tortures me.

"What do you want with me?" I question with a weak voice.

"You likely don't recognize me because we've never officially met," he tells me. "I'm friends with Coach, best friends to be exact. We have been close for a long time." He smirks, then slowly circles me. "Did you know that we are both aggressive with women? It's true. He told me all about you and how vanilla you were before he got his hands on you.

"He also told me that he cares for you and because of that, he won't share you with me. That really hurt my feelings. We've been sharing women since we met. All the women we get with, that are worthy," he leans in to whisper behind my ear, "we fuck them together. He's usually in her ass while I fuck her cunt. My cock is too big for most women's asses, but not all. There are the rare ones whose asses you can drive a fist into, and I have." He shows me his massive fist.

"Are you one of those capable women? I would imagine you are not. We'll see, won't we?"

"Are you going to rape me?" I ask, already knowing his intention.

"Don't be like that. You will like my cock, I promise," he replies arrogantly.

Fuck! My worst fears are coming true.

"And, what if I don't?"

"It doesn't matter, because I'm sure I'll have a marvellous time. The more you fight me, the more pleased I'll be." His matter-of-fact tone ends with a sadistic chuckle.

"You're into submissive and master play like Coach, right?" I ask.

He looks at me while standing so close that we're almost touching. I can feel his body heat. This man is enormous, bigger than Coach in height and girth.

"Isn't it obvious?" he teases with a shifty sneer.

I reply, hoping to strike a chord. "From what I've recently learned about sadism and masochism is that the submissive is the one with all the power. Isn't that right?"

"It is unless they willingly agree to a power exchange."

"You believe me to be the submissive in this situation, correct?"

He snickers, looking at the rope that binds my hands. "Another obvious point. What are you getting at?"

"Since you agree that I am submissive, let me say that I have not agreed to submit to you, therefore, if you touch me sexually, it's rape which is not acceptable with the BDSM community, unless I say it's okay. Am I right? Are you a rapist?"

I'm hoping to get through to him but doubt I'll be successful. Maybe my words will get him to respect me and he'll feel some compassion. I wonder if he has it in him.

"I am whatever I want to be. You don't seem to understand why you're here," he says as he yanks my pants down to my ankles.

No! Tears stream down my face. I've never been very successful at keeping my emotions intact when standing up to people who intimidate me. This massive man is about to rape me and there's nobody here to stop him. I can't get away on my own, I know this to be true. My initial kidnapper has vanished, just like he said he would.

Oh, please, someone help me!

"Please, enlighten me," I ask, hoping to prolong the inevitable. The longer I keep him talking, the more likely someone is to find me.

He pushes his groin against my pantie-covered womanhood and I wretch. His hands pull at my ass, humping me against his denim-covered bulge. He lets me go and I swing. I try to still myself using my tiptoes.

He circles me slowly as he explains. "I must say, I can see why Coach didn't want to share you. Your body is beautiful, exactly like he said it was. For a woman who's had kids, you look damn good."

"Why am I here?" I interrupt his speech with an angry attitude. "Get to the fucking point!"

"You want me to get to the point? Okay, here's why you're here. I want Coach. He's mine, not yours. If he has you, I have you; that's the agreement. We share our women, always. But not you." He lifts my chin so he can look in my eyes.

"He's keeping you for himself. If we stop sharing women, I won't get to have Coach anymore." He grimaces. "He's not gay, I get that, but I'll take him any way I can get him. If that means putting a whore between us, I can accept that. When he's in her ass and I'm in her sloppy cunt, I can feel his cock stroking mine. Do you have any idea how much that turns me on?" He steps back and takes a deep breath. His eyes stare off in the distance.

"It almost feels like he's fucking me. I can watch the expressions on his face change to reveal the agonizing glory of his impending orgasm. I know that if I push into the bitch all the way, putting pressure on his cock while he slams into her asshole, he can feel my cum wads pass through my twitching cock."

"So, you're gay? Is that what you're trying to say?" I keep my voice soft and understanding. "You love Coach and want him for yourself? I can understand that."

"No, bitch. I already had him, but you're trying to take him away. I had to see what was so fucking great about you that made it so easy for him to cast me aside.

Tell me, bitch, what the fuck makes you so goddamn special?" he inquires with his face so near to mine that I can feel his fiery breath on my lips.

I'm thankful his breath smells much better than the other guy's.

The hate in his eyes is sinister and burning terror into me like daggers. I cast my eyes down, trying to think of how to answer his question to calm him. He's breathing heavily, and his hands form into tight fists. He's going to hurt me now.

"I don't know why he likes me. I'm nothing special. I mean, I have kids and an ex-husband who's an asshole. I'm older than him and our fitness levels are inharmonious at best. He's a workout fanatic and I'm definitely not. If I can avoid exercise, I will. I get enough of a workout cleaning up after my two children; it's a full cardio workout some days. I don't know what you want me to say that will make you not want to hurt me. Do you want me to break up with him?" I exclaim while tears stream down my face.

He kisses my lips softly and then whispers, "Break up with him if you want to, but there isn't anything you can say that will stop me from taking what's rightfully mine. He promised to share his ladies, *all* his ladies, and I know he won't let you go. Our sharing days are over unless I take you now."

"How will that make a difference?"

"Well, if I've already had you, he won't have any reason not to share you with me."

"Was it a binding agreement that you and he share every woman that either of you has sex with? Was it a verbal agreement or simply assumed on your part?"

He doesn't answer. He's circling me again.

"He said the two of you have tag-teamed a few ladies, but never once did he say that you have an agreement to share every woman. If he had, I wouldn't be with him. I don't want to be shared by anyone. Please, let me go."

I'm no longer crying because I don't think I have any tears left in me to spill. I'm completely drained, mentally and physically.

I whisper, "Just get this over with."

"Not yet," he replies as he grabs my t-shirt by the collar and with a quick jerk, tears the material, exposing my bra.

"Do what you will, but please don't kill me. I have children and I'm a single mom. Their father isn't responsible enough to care for them properly. Please?" I beg. I have no other option at this point other than to plead with him.

"Kill you? Fuck, I won't kill you. I'm going to fuck you raw before giving you back to Coach. He needs to know that I'm still here and we share our bitches. He'll understand."

He stands a few feet from me, looking my body up and down but not yet touching me. So far, he hasn't assaulted me, other than rubbing his groin on mine, but there was no skin to skin contact.

"He won't be happy if you put your hands on me. Coach will not share me because he knows that I'm not some whore that lets anyone between her legs. I would never agree to it. If you touch me, he will hate you forever, if he doesn't kill you. You know that, right?" I calmly state, in a last-ditch effort to get him to back off. "He told you not to touch me, didn't he? If you really love him, you'll respect him enough not to do this because it will anger him."

"Bitch, I don't care if you're the sweetest, most innocent chick in the world. If you're fucking Coach, you're fucking me, too. He'll come around."

A loud crash coming from the direction of the hallway grabs our attention. The man quickly yells, "Hey, what's going on out there?"

There's no reply from the greasy man who must be in the other room. He walks toward the hallway, leaving me hanging by my wrists, defenceless and nearly naked. At least he isn't raping me.

I struggle to free myself, but my body weight pulls the ropes so tight that my hands have turned purple. At least they don't hurt anymore. Nonetheless, I keep struggling.

The man gets near the hall entrance and stops. "Hey, buddy, glad you could join us. I was hoping you'd show up. She's ready for us."

"Where's Rayna?" The familiar voice brings me newfound hope.

I yell, "Coach! I'm in here! Help me!"

Coach comes charging into the room, heading straight toward me.

Oh, thank God! He'll make this stop and set me free. When he's near enough to see how badly beaten my face is, he spins around, slamming his fist against the jaw of the bigger man, but the guy doesn't fall.

Coach

Brett stumbles but doesn't go down. I hit him so hard that I'm amazed he's still standing. My rage is at a level where I might rip his fucking head off his neck. If I charge him again, I will probably kill him. He isn't worth going to prison. All it will take is for him to swing at me and I will take him out.

"What the fuck, Coach? We share every girl," Brett says while gripping his jaw in his massive hand and moving it back and forth to check if it's broken.

"Not this one! I told you to back off! Rayna is not for sharing. What the fuck did you do to her face?"

I reach out and grab him by the throat with my fist pulled back, ready to blast him again. I want to kill him. He isn't a skillful fighter, and he's fully aware I could seriously injure him. He's seen me fight, so he knows I can be dangerous. He might be bigger than me, but I'm stronger and faster.

He struggles to reply. "I didn't do that to her face. I'd never ruin that pretty face of hers. She's gorgeous. Well, one side of her face is still pretty."

He chuckles, and my temper roars. My demon is begging for freedom to let loose. If he gets out, he'll kill Brett.

I punch him again, slamming my fist into his eye. He swings low, catching my abdomen, but he's slow and I was ready for it. An inch higher and he might have knocked the wind out of me. I pull my fist back again and let it fly. This time, he blocks it with his arm.

His fist cracks me hard on my cheek directly in front of my ear. It stuns me for a second. Just as my mind clears, I see his giant mitt coming toward my face again. I release his throat and block his swing, grasping his forearm in a vice-like grip.

Unexpectedly, he laughs. So, I hit him again, this time splitting the soft skin under his eyebrow. Blood spills into his eye.

"Okay, enough, enough! I get it, you won't share her. We'll get another girl to share. You can have this one for yourself since you're suddenly so fucking possessive!"

I want to hit him again and again, but I release him instead, fearing that if I don't, I won't be able to stop myself until he's dead. Both of us are out of breath but my rage still burns through my veins and my inner demon is pacing in his cage, begging me to set him free.

I take a few steps back, but my eyes remain focused on him, hoping to burn a hole through him.

"We're done! No more! Do you hear me? You are fucking done! I'm taking her out of here and you will not stop me. Do you understand?"

"Are you going to fuck me up if I say you can't have her?" Brett's tears spill, mixing with the blood that's still flowing from the gash over his swelling eye.

"What the fuck is wrong with you?"

He stands but doesn't come at me. He rants, spewing his thoughts in a rage. "Don't you get it? I want *you*, not her. You're mine. She doesn't deserve you, but I do. I've been here for you the whole time. We can be happy together. We'll even put a woman between us if you think it's too gay without one. It's time for you and me. Rayna can go back to her kids and her boring mom-life. She's no good for you. For years, I've been patiently waiting for you to come around, for you to realize that you love me and that we are perfect together." He looks pathetic and desperate as he spills his soul.

"What the fuck, man? We're done! You and me? Finished!" I hiss as I turn my back to him and rush toward Rayna.

He will not hit me anymore. Even if I hit him again, it won't hurt him as much as it will if I walk out of here and never talk to him again. When did he develop feelings for me? Was I oblivious to his advances? Could we have avoided this had I recognized his love for me?

Chapter Twenty-Six

Rayna

Defeated, the larger man drops to his knees and his tears stream down his cheeks. To make Coach understand, he professes his love through the desolate sobs of a broken man. "I fucking love you!"

"This isn't love, Brett," Coach says as he attempts to untie my hands, but the knot is proving difficult. "If you loved me, you would never do this. So shut the fuck up before I come over there and rip your fucking head off!"

Coach wraps his forearm under my butt and lifts me, enabling him to untie with the ropes that hold my wrists. As soon as the knot releases, my arms drop lifelessly between us. Pain erupts as my blood flows through my arms. I can't move them under my power, the agony is far too great.

Coach sets me onto my feet and gently touches the bruised side of my face. The pain in his eye hurts me worse than anything I've ever felt. He bends down, sliding my pants up my legs to grant me some dignity. He buttons them and then scoops me up, carrying my weak body past a shattered man weeping on his knees, watching the love of his life walk out with not another glance in his direction.

He holds me safely against his chest as he storms down the street. I'm not sure where he's taking me, but I don't care either. I'm with Coach and that means I'm safe. Coach doesn't put me down until he sits me in the driver's seat of his truck.

He kisses my forehead and asks, "Can you slide over?"

My hands aren't throbbing anymore, but my ribs stab at me when I shimmy from one seat to the other. I don't care.

I'm just grateful he didn't rape me. It could have been so much worse.

The second he's in the truck, I push the button to lock the doors in case either of the men follows us. He looks at me with a remorseful expression that makes my heart ache. I lunge at him, pressing the sore side of my face against his chest. I clutch onto his shirt with all my remaining strength. He puts his one arm over my back, holding me securely as he starts the engine and puts it into gear.

Each bump in the road is agony, but I will not voice my physical pain. I welcome the pain in my face as it bounces off his tummy; it's a reminder that I'm out of harm's way. My ribs ache in this position, but I don't feel any grinding, so maybe they aren't broken. His heavy arm resting over my side isn't making them hurt any less, but I won't ask him to move.

We've been driving for a few minutes when I finally break the silence. "What happened to the smelly man?"

"Don't worry about it," he sharply replies, lifting his arm off my ribs to brush a few loose tresses of hair from my face.

"I need to know."

He sighs. "I hit him with a pipe and he went down like a rag doll."

"Is he dead?" I hope he is.

"I didn't stick around to find out." He clears his throat. "I needed to get to you."

"I hope he's in horrible pain. He's the one who hurt me." There's so much anger behind my words.

"If he isn't dead, he's close to it," he assures me. "How is your face?"

"It hurts. I can't see out of my left eye. I hope I'm not blind. He dropped me on my face, on the cement, when he took me out of the car. Later, I fought him, and he hit me so hard that I blacked out."

My throbbing cheek presses against Coach's firm, warm chest. It aches, but the pressure makes it feel better, or maybe it's that Coach is with me and that gives me so much comfort. I'm safe. I didn't think I'd ever get to say that again.

"I love you, baby. I'm so sorry," he apologizes.

"Sorry for rescuing me?"

"No, of course not. If it weren't for my lifestyle previous to you, this never would have happened. If I wasn't around, the bullshit with your ex wouldn't have happened either." He takes a breath. "I'm bad for you, Rayna. I've done nothing but burden your life. Everything that's happened lately is my fault, all of it."

He sounds like he's crying. I hug him harder.

"Simon, don't leave me. I love you. None of this is your fault. You saved me from my off-the-wall ex and from those assholes. I still can't believe you kept your cool and didn't kill him."

"It wasn't easy. I wanted to beat him to death. I didn't know he was so fucked up in the head. We had lunch together the other day, and he seemed fine. He was my trusted friend, and I loved him."

The truck turns left, then right, coming to a full stop.

He shuts off the ignition. "I don't know what happened to him. I am so sorry, baby. Can you sit up? We're here."

I clutch my ribs as I right myself. He brought me to the hospital. I need a doctor to look at my eye and tell me that my vision is still intact. X-rays would be nice to know if I have fractured ribs or if they're just bruised.

Coach opens my door and helps me out of the truck. "Can you walk? I can carry you."

"I think I'm okay," I tell him as I gingerly take my first few steps.

He holds my arm for insurance. My chest hurts from that asshole's boot kicking me twice. I hold my torn shirt closed. My depth perception is off because I only have one eye to see from. It doesn't help that my balance is horrible because the world keeps spinning around me. I keep swaying to the left.

The bright lights in the hospital are like sharp daggers stabbing into my one good eye. Tears quickly blur my vision, making it even more difficult to maneuver myself around without looking like I'm drunk. Coach immediately brings me to the receptionist, who's eyes open wide when he glances up from his computer screen.

"Come right in," the man says as he stands and presses a button to unlock the door. He raises his voice to alert the staff. "I'm sending one in right now."

I hear the scuffling of shoes as the door swings open and several people quickly approach me.

"We got her from here, sir," the one nurse tells Coach as she takes my arm.

A male nurse gently takes my other arm to assist. He tells Coach, "Follow us. We'll need to get some information from you."

A security guard approaches, immediately setting his accusing eyes on Coach. Maybe he thinks he is the one who did this to me. Idiot! Why would he bring me to get fixed up if he's the one that smacked me around?

"Coach, stay with me, please," I yell back to him.

"I'm not going anywhere, Rayna," he replies, interrupting a man asking him questions.

"Can you tell me who did this to you?" asks the female nurse who's holding my arm.

"There were two men. Coach knows the one guy." They help me up onto a stretcher in an empty room. "Coach saved me."

A person in a white coat rushes in, and the nurses clear a path for her. She informs me that she's a doctor, and she's here to help. She asks me question after question, which I answer as best I can.

They cut my clothes from my body and I'm now lying here wearing only my panties, but I don't feel self-conscious; they aren't looking at me as though I'm a woman with sexual parts. To them, I am a human body in need of repair. The doctor waves them off, letting them know to leave my panties on me for now.

The doctor rattles off a list of tests she wants them to perform as she tries to shine a light in my swollen eye. Her fingers gently pry at the bloated lid and it bloody hurts! I tell her that I can't see any light.

The nurses scatter, following up on the doctor's orders. Coach stands at my feet. He can see all of my injuries now that I am nearly nude. When I was hanging from the rope with my shirt torn open, he must not have noticed the bruising on my chest and ribs. He most likely saw everything with the crimson hue of his own rage.

He groans with so much regret in his tone. "Oh, my sweet Rayna! What the fuck did he do to you?"

Pain shoots through my face when she presses on my cheek. I fight not to scream, knowing that opening my mouth will only increase the pain. I can feel scraping, like bone rubbing against bone.

My stomach violently churns and before I can warn anyone, I turn my head and vomit all over the male nurse's uniform. I'm surprised at how much fluid I puke up because I thought my stomach was empty. I hadn't eaten or drank anything in quite a while.

They feed a butterfly needle into my vein, but I barely acknowledge the pain it causes. Almost immediately, I feel lighter.

Drugs! "Thank you," I say with a slur.

The pain from them poking at my wounds was making it so hard to hold back my screams. With the drugs flowing into my vein, I couldn't care less if they poke. The pain is still there, I simply don't give a shit.

After several X-rays and a CT scan, I'm told that I'll need surgery to fix my shattered cheekbone, and my ribs are badly bruised, but not broken.

I sign the paperwork to approve the surgery as they're wheeling my gurney into an operating room. I ask if they called my sister to let her know that I'm okay.

A different woman with kind eyes tells me, "Don't worry, everyone knows you're here. The police have been searching for you. Did you know that?" I shake my head. "You're going to sleep now. Can you count backward from ten?"

I begin, "Ten, nine, eight, sev..."

Chapter Twenty-Seven

Coach

I tell the cops as much information as I can, giving them directions to the barn where I found Rayna. They want to know all about Brett, our history, how I came to find her. Basically, they wanted to know what role I played in this whole situation.

Their faces seem to soften once they understand I am the one who rescued her and wasn't present when she received those wounds.

After my interrogation, I'm walked to the X-ray room to get a picture of my hand. It's swollen, and now that my adrenaline has subsided, I can feel pain. I would turn down a painkiller if it's offered.

The doc tells me it's fractured in two spots, but that I don't require surgery; a splint will do nicely. She explains that Rayna gave the hospital permission to tell me details of her injuries and progress reports during the procedure. She is in surgery for a shattered cheek and to relieve the pressure on her eye. I need to hold her, make her feel safe, and prevent anyone from hurting her again.

The doctor leaves to get a splint for my hand. Renee and the kids peek into the room across the hall.

"Hey, in here," I say loud enough that she'll hear me, but not startle the two people on the gurneys beside me.

Ken runs in first and throws his arms around me. "Thank you for saving my mom. I knew you would."

I hug him back with my good arm, and kiss the top of his head, "I'm happy, too, little man."

Kim hugs my arm because she isn't big enough to reach me on this bed. "Thank you, Coach."

"How is she?" Renee looks tired, almost defeated.

I'm impressed she was able to keep up a strong appearance when she needed to. Now that Rayna's safe, her emotions let go. I put my arm out and wave her toward me. She leans in, pressing her head against my chest. She weeps, soaking my shirt. I don't mind. I pat her back to calm her.

The kids stand at the other side of the gurney while I explain what I know. "She's going to be okay. They have her in surgery for a shattered cheekbone. Her eye is swollen shut so they have to work on that, too. They don't think her vision is affected, but they won't know for sure until the swelling subsides." I take a breath and smile at the kids who look scared.

"She has bruised ribs and a bruise on her chest. She also has a concussion, which they will monitor. Don't worry, she'll be okay."

"Holy shit!" Renee pulls out of the hug, wearing the same expression of rage I must have had when I first saw Rayna suspended by the rope. "Who did this and did they catch him?"

The kids listen to every word we say. Now that they know what to expect when they see her, it won't be such a shock when they do. I don't want them to hear the awful details of how she got those injuries. That's something Rayna can explain to them, should she decide to, but it's not my place.

"They know where to find them; if they stuck around, that is. I don't know that I should say anything more," I say, tipping my head toward the kids.

She nods and digs through her purse, pulling out a twenty-dollar bill. "Do you remember where the cafeteria is? I pointed it out when we walked by it. Go there and get something to eat. I'll meet you there in a few minutes. Can you get me a small coffee? Don't go anywhere else and don't talk to anyone other than your servers. Stay together, no matter what!"

Ken takes the money and leads the way as Kim follows closely behind.

"Okay, tell me everything. Did they…" Her words catch in her voice as dread washes over her face.

"No, as far as I know, they didn't rape her. I believe I got there before they could."

"Who did this to her and do you know why?" Her hand shakes as she tucks a tuft of hair behind her ear the same way Rayna does.

"It was two guys. One I don't know, and the other is… He *was* a friend of mine. He was a very close friend and I can't understand his reasoning."

She quickly replies, "What was he going to do to her? Why Rayna? I mean, if he's your friend, he knows how much she means to you. So why hurt her? This makes no sense to me."

"He told me that he's in love with me and wanted me for himself. I had no idea he had those types of feelings for me." I tell her, rubbing my beard as if that'll help me make sense of it all.

"I don't understand this. How the fuck could you two be friends and you not know he was gay and in love with you?"

I look at her and debate whether to tell her our history. If she's as stubborn as Rayna, she won't stop asking until I tell her. Besides, it'll all come out in his trial later, anyway. Everyone will know about my deviant sexual practices. I'm not ashamed of my life choices, but I'd rather Rayna and her family not know the disturbing details of my sexual practices.

I decide to tell her. "We used to double up on women. Apparently, he was in love with me and got his thrills from being that close to me. When I wouldn't share Rayna with him, he was jealous." I shake my head and cross one ankle over the other.

"In his warped way of thinking, he figured that if he could just have sex with Rayna, that I would change my mind, and we could share her. That way, I would still be his. None of this is logical. It's all my fault."

Renee takes my unbroken hand in hers. "Yeah, it kind of is." I look at her face, and she's grinning. "Seriously though, you can't blame yourself for having a friend who's fucked up, especially if you didn't know he had this messed up way of thinking. It's not your fault."

I look away from her and swallow down my regretful sorrow. I'm grateful this conversation ends when the doctor comes back in the room carrying three braces, each a different size.

"I wasn't sure which size to get. We'll try them on and make adjustments to see which will fit you best."

Chapter Twenty-Eight

Rayna

Oh my God, my face hurts so much! What the hell?

I whimper, it's all I can do. My throat is so dry, and my arms feel heavy. Where am I? Am I still in the barn?

"Help me!" I yell but it sounds about as loud as a whisper.

I try to sit up by pushing my body up with my arms, but my limbs feel like semi-cooked spaghetti noodles trying to hold up an elephant. I cannot muster enough energy for a second attempt. I lie here feeling defeated and confused.

It's so bright in here. This doesn't smell or sound like the barn.

Why is my brain in such a fog? What's wrong with me?

A kind voice comforts me. "Rayna, you're safe. You just had surgery to repair your face. You need to rest. Are you having any pain?"

I'm able to open one eye. It's barely a slit, but enough to see a pretty nurse hunched over me, looking at my bandaged eye.

I attempt to swallow the imaginary cotton in my throat, but I'm unsuccessful. I mouth the word, "Dry."

"I'll get you some water. How's your pain?" she asks.

I shake my head. "Bad."

"Okay, I'll up your Morphine. You'll feel relief soon."

She fiddles with the machine and then locks it with a key. I welcome the drugs.

"I'll be right back," she says.

I watch her seem to float out of the room as if her feet barely brush the floor. I feel light, as if I'm floating as well.

I fall asleep before she returns, despite my determination not to.

Although I'm sure my dream was pleasant, I can't recall it. When I woke, I was instantly angry and wanted to retreat to the perfect dream. I hate everyone and everything right now. Time has no bearing on anything. Sometimes, I can't tell if I'm awake or asleep.

My face fucking hurts when I try to talk, and my stomach is viciously biting at my insides because I haven't eaten in…

What time is it? What day is it?

"Where am I?" I mutter with a hoarse voice.

I'm in an unfamiliar room. I like this one better than the recovery room; it's much darker. I'm a little less miserable. I roll my aching head to the side.

Coach is lounging in what looks like a very uncomfortable chair. His hand is in a splint. He's sound asleep and snoring, faintly. He looks so handsome with his head leaning on the wall, his face void of expression. I don't want to wake him, but I am so damn thirsty.

I reach for the jug of what I assume to be ice water, but my motor function is terrible and I can't grip it. If I try to lift it, it'll surely crash to the floor. Should I wake him?

When I swallow, my throat feels like it's sticking together and choking me. I try to cough but it's wimpy, like an exhale.

Coach startles and looks at me. He smiles as though he had assumed I was dead but came back to life.

"Hi, babe," he whispers as he stands up, taking my hand in his. "How do you feel?"

"My face fucking hurts," I tell him and then chuckle, but it causes horrific pain to my ribs so instead of laughing, I wince.

"Do you want me to get a nurse?"

314

Coach looks as if he's aged ten years, as if his guilt from feeling liable for his friend's actions is wearing on his soul. He looked so much younger when he was asleep.

"No, I only want you." My words sound frail but forced. He leans in to kiss my undamaged cheek and then my forehead. "What happened to me isn't your fault. I don't blame you. You didn't do this to me. Tell me you understand."

"I do. I know it's his fault, but I…" His words fail him. He swallows hard before lowering his head, burying it against my hip. He places my open hand on the top of his head and holds his over mine to keep it in place. I can hear the tears in his voice. "I should have protected you better."

"Oh, for crying out loud." Now my angry, drug-induced bitch is stepping in. "I told you it wasn't your fault. You could not have known he would go off his rock. How could you have protected me from him when you didn't know he was crazy? Do you think you should have been following me around everywhere I went, never leaving me alone? It's called stalking. Get that idea right out of that thick skull of yours," I say as I slap the top of his head, probably harder than I should, but my limbs are not yet fully functional.

He looks up at me with tears in his eyes. "I love you, Rayna. Get better and let me take you home. Marry me, my love."

"What?" I ask, unsure if he proposed to me or if I heard him wrong.

"I'm asking you to marry me," he repeats while smiling like a fool, eyes wide with anticipation.

I clear my throat and realize the imaginary cotton ball has wedged itself deeper into my esophagus. "Water," I say as clearly as I can manage.

He hands me the cup and helps hold it while I slurp its contents. I try to drink as much as possible, but my stomach protests. I'm only able to swallow two mouthfuls, but it feels wonderful as it slides down my parched throat.

"If you're serious about asking me to marry you, don't you think proposing while I'm lying in a hospital bed with my face broken is probably not the most romantic way to ask? Not like this, okay?" I smile with only half of my mouth. The opposite side of my face is horribly swollen.

"Okay, I'll go tell the nurse that you're awake. I'll be right back," he says and then sprints out of the room.

It doesn't seem like he's away very long, but I think I may have dozed off again. The nurse calls my name, and it irritates me. She says my name again and now I'm furious. I open my eye to seek her out and frown at her, maybe even cuss, I don't know. The drugs make everything seem like it isn't real; like I'm in a perpetual dream that keeps changing.

"There you are. How's your pain?" she asks with a voice I would normally see as pleasant, but I find it exceedingly annoying at the moment. I am so miserable, and she is simply way too peppy, but she has power over the drugs.

"It hurts, but I think I'm okay. My stomach is turning. I might vomit if I don't get some crackers and ginger ale," I say and then cough, grasping my ribs, hoping to make the pain halt. "Why does my throat hurt so much?"

"Sometimes when they sedate you, they insert a breathing tube, especially if they're working on your face. If your throat swells, they can still get oxygen into your lungs. It might hurt for a few days, but it will improve." She looks at Coach, who's been quietly listening. "If you go down to the cafeteria, you can ask them for some crackers and there's ginger ale in the machines by the elevators."

"Oh, I thought you might have some stashed in a room somewhere," he says with a shrug.

"Nope, we don't have stashes. You know, cut-backs." She shrugs.

"I'll go right now and be back in a flash." Coach disappears from the room again.

"I have to go pee," I whisper.

"Actually, you don't. You have a catheter. If you'd like, I can take it out, but you will have to page us every time you have to get up to go. We must assist you to walk to the bathroom, at least until you're off the Morphine drip. What do you want to do?"

"I'd better keep it in. I pee often, so I'll end up annoying you. When does the Morphine stop?"

"It's up to you and how you feel. If you don't want it, like it's making your stomach too nauseous, you can ask to stop the Morphine and take a different medicine in pill form or injection, something that might be more tolerable for you, but it won't work as well."

I shake my head and smile. "I'll keep the Morphine for now. I really hurt. Can you lift the head part of my bed? That might help."

"Sure! Tell me when to stop," she says as she raises the head of the bed.

My mind whirls for a quick second as my brain rights itself, making my stomach feel like it did a full somersault. Vomiting with sore ribs sounds like torture.

"Okay, that's perfect. Thank you. Do you know what they did in the surgery?"

She takes a tablet from her pocket and slides her finger across the screen. "Here you are." She pauses momentarily so she can read. "Basically, they had to put a plate in your cheekbone to hold it in place while it heals. Your eye socket has a minor fracture that will heal on its own, but your eyesight should be fine once the swelling subsides. You have some badly bruised ribs as well, which might also contribute to your nauseousness. In a matter of a few months, you'll look and feel as beautiful as you did before this happened."

I nod. "Thank you." I feel more at ease now that I know I'll heal up with no expected lingering issues.

She smiles and puts the tablet back in her pocket. "Ring the buzzer if you need me, okay?"

I nod as she rushes out of the room.

Coach walks in and gleams when he notices me sitting up. He teases, "Ah, look at you, sitting up like a big girl." He winks. "Is that better for you?"

"Yeah, I got dizzy during the ride, but I'm okay now. Thank you for going to get this stuff for me. Can you open the pop? I don't think my fingers are working all too well."

"Sure can, weakling," he teases with a smirk while cracking the bottle open. He hands it to me, never letting his hand get too far from it in case I drop it. I hand it back to him after only one small sip. The bubbles burn my sore throat. He sets it on the small table that hovers over my legs. He opens the bag of crackers and sets them down within my reach, besides the pop.

"Um, I need to thank you for saving me. I'm not sure if I did that yet. I don't know exactly what would have happened had you not shown up when you did. I'm sure it wouldn't have been good. He was about to rape me. He said he would send me back to you after he got his. Whether or not he would have let me go, I will never know."

Coach says nothing. He stares at my hand, which cradles perfectly in his sizable palm. I wait, but he remains silent. His jaw muscles flex now and then as he clenches his teeth. He's swallowing a lot. His face is flushed, and his eyes are glossed over. Is he going to cry again?

"Look at me," I demand with an assertive tone. He turns his face away from me, so I repeat myself. "I said, look at me, dammit!"

He slowly turns to face me, but when his teary eyes meet mine, I see an abundance of pain from a broken man. I lift my hand from his and cup his cheek, using my thumb to wipe a tear from his eye before it falls from his lashes. I smile at him, but the lump in my throat grows by the second. My tears erupt and spill down my cheeks.

Note to self: no crying until my swollen eye heals. This fucking hurts!

"Baby, I'm so sorry," he mutters between gasping breaths.

Coach stands and buries his face against my neck, pressing his forehead into my pillow. I try to hug him, but I can't get my arms around him, so I rub his thick arm instead, hoping it will suffice. I set my arm down when my IV needle wiggles in my vein, turning my stomach.

"I will only say this one more time and I need you to hear me. This isn't your fault. You saved me from a psychotic sadist who wanted to do horrible things to me. If you hadn't gotten there when you did…" I take a breath. "Tell me that you hear me."

"Okay, okay," he replies, his face remaining buried.

"I said, tell me you believe me."

He lifts his face until he can look into my one functioning eye. "It's so hard for me. A man should protect his woman, just as she should protect his heart. I didn't do my part."

I lift my hands and wipe the wetness from his rosy cheeks and then slap him hard enough that his head jolts. My smile is lame. His initial expression is surprise but soon, he grins and then nods, understanding that I'm trying to lighten the conversation.

"I love you." He kisses the healthy cheek with the gentleness of a butterfly's flutter. I'm grateful for his tenderness.

I whisper, "I love you, too."

"Do you want some crackers?" He stands and changes the subject.

"Maybe another sip of pop."

He opens the pop and helps me take a few gulps before putting the cap back on and setting it on the table. Dammit, that burns my throat, but my stomach is grateful.

"You look tired. Sleep," he whispers. "I'll be here when you wake."

"No. I will sleep if you promise you'll go home. Check on the kids and tell them that I am okay. They can come see me as soon as the doctor says it's all right. If they want you to spend the night, so they feel safer, it's okay with me. Just don't let my sister sneak down the stairs to make love to you, thinking she's me." I snicker when he tilts his head as if disappointed.

"If the kids want me to stay, I'll stay. No promises about your sister." He lifts his hand as is to slap an imaginary Renee. He grimaces. "That's not something you'll ever have to worry about with me. I'm not a cheater. Let me take a video of you so they can see that you're okay."

"Do I have any blood on me or anything yucky that might freak them out?"

Coach admires my face and then shakes his head. "You're beautiful." He aims his phone and says, "Okay, Mom, you're on!"

I look at the camera and try to smile, knowing I must look scary. "Hi, babies! I'm okay, but I may have to stay in the hospital for a while. Maybe tomorrow you two can visit me if the doctor approves. Aunt Renee and Coach will take care of you while I'm here. Be on your best behaviour. I love you both! I will see you soon."

He stops the recording and smiles. "All right, I'll go now. Promise me that you'll sleep. If you need anything, make a list and text it to me."

"I don't have my phone," I say, suddenly realizing that I don't know where my purse is. "My purse?"

"The cops found your phone near where you work; they pinged the signal off towers or something. They tracked it down, hoping you were with it. And I have your purse in the truck. The cops found it in your car and entrusted it to me. Your phone is probably in an evidence bag somewhere. I'm sure they'll give it back once it's processed if you ask them nicely. If not, I can get you another one."

"No, I'll talk to the investigators about it when I see them. They'll most likely be here soon to ask me a million questions. I'm suddenly very sleepy," I confess before a painful yawn erupts, bringing tears to my eyes.

He wipes away the tears from my uncovered eye and then kisses my forehead.

"Sleep, my love."

I plunge into the darkness of my mind. I don't even see him leave.

Chapter Twenty-Nine

Coach

Rayna has been home for a month now and she's healing nicely. Most of the swelling has subsided, but the yellow bruising seems to linger. Her face is still swollen. About a week after her rescue, the swelling to her eye eased and she could see again, which made her very happy.

She hasn't returned to work yet, nor has she left the house unless going to see a doctor and only if she has someone to drive her. I'm giving her plenty of time to regain her confidence and be independent again. She's nervous around men she doesn't know.

I expected her to have anxiety; I'd be worried if she didn't. The doctor that deals with the emotional aspect of her recovery said it will take time for the real Rayna to come back, if she ever does. He suggested we don't rush her or tease her about her fears, even if they seem irrational to us.

The kids have been amazing, helping her with everything from vacuuming to washing dishes. Renee has been picking the kids up at school most days and I do it on the days she can't. Rayna is working on Rayna and I'm absolutely fine with taking the backseat while she does.

Today marks the five-week anniversary to the day that changed our lives, hers more so than mine. It drastically changed our sexual dynamic as well. I wish she'd come back and be the Rayna that is fun and ready to try new sexual experiences. She only wants to make love tenderly in bed. I don't mind that so much anymore, but my inner demon is itching to burst forth. I feel selfish when I think about my needs. I know she isn't ready.

I've been working out at the gym extra hard, usually until my muscles are on fire. It helps to keep me in check. I've also been beating the hell out of my punching bag. It temporarily satiates my demon's urge for aggression.

Renee has taken the kids to her place for the night, so it's just me and my lady. When we're alone, we typically watch a movie and occasionally make love in her bed. I don't even expect that from her but she says she wants me, so who am I to deny her? Everything is moving at the pace Rayna is setting and I'm cool with it.

"Can we do something different tonight?" she asks before putting a piece of garlic bread in her mouth.

I look up from my plate, very interested in this conversation. "We can. What do you have in mind?" I'm thinking that she wants to go watch a movie in a theatre, perhaps.

Rayna clears her throat. "Well, you remember how he had me tied, right? I want you to tie me up the same way but with my feet firmly on the floor. I remember how horribly my wrists hurt from hanging by those ropes, and I never want that pain repeated. My feet have to be flat on the floor. Then I want you to—"

I cut her off. "What? I don't think that's a good idea, Rayna. You want to repeat the most terrifying moments of your life and make it into a sexual game?"

"Well, kind of." She sets the bread on her plate. She looks at me with desperate eyes. "Try to understand. I want you to make it fun and pleasurable for me. You'll have to be very loving with me, of course."

"Why, Rayna?" I ask, not understanding her logic.

"Because every time I fall asleep, I'm back in that barn. My wrists are aching, my toes can't support my weight, and the fear…" She shakes her head. "Well, it overwhelms me." She swallows hard. "I had no control in that situation. I need to feel like I'm in control. He took that from me, and I want it back. Will you do this for me?"

I search her face for a flicker of doubt, but she doesn't blink. She seems stronger from having asked me. Maybe she needs this. It might end up being a great turnaround for her, helping her to regain her strength. If not, it'll be the most awful thing I'll ever do to her and it'll change our dynamic permanently.

How can I say no to her? I can never deny Rayna.

"Okay, I'll do it. If for one second, I think it's too much for you, it's over. I will cut the rope and that'll be it."

"Yes, sir!" she says, smiling playfully. "Will you fuck me while I'm hanging there?"

My cock twitches and my inner demon wakes from his long slumber. While trying not to seem too anxious, I ask, "Do you want me to?"

She grins the same way the old Rayna did when she wanted me. She assures me that this is the right thing to do.

"Yes, but don't let your sadistic side join in."

"My demon." This is the first time I've given her a title for it.

She ponders the name. "Your demon? Hmm."

"I promise that I'll be gentle."

I watch her face and swear I can see her ashen skin tone brighten as a flush of pink once again livens the paleness of the remaining yellow bruises, making her look almost exactly like the Rayna I know.

"Thank you," she sighs as if a weight has lifted.

I nod. "We can go to my house. I'll use the eye-bolt in my ceiling. It'll hold the weight of two women. I made sure of it," I tell her with a wink.

She shakes her head and scoffs but knows I probably have tested it out exactly that way.

Instead of using rope, which I absolutely refuse to use on her wrists, because that's what he used, I secure soft leather cuffs on her. I string a rope through their cuff's loops, and pull her wrists together, knotting it in an easy release configuration. A clamp would take longer to free her from, so rope is best. While watching her face for any flicker of panic, I fish that rope through the large eyelet that's securely fastened to the eyebeam in the ceiling.

Before I pull the line and force her hands over my head, I ask, "Rayna, are you sure?" She nods. "What's your safe word?"

"It's red." She takes a deep breath while studying my face. Perhaps she sees the hesitation in my eyes. "Yes, I'm sure. I have to do this. I'll be stronger if I face it head-on. Just keep your *demon* on a leash or in his kennel."

I snicker because I adore the way she talks about my sadistic nature as if it were some type of devil dog. Somehow, she doesn't see my demon as being something bad, but something tameable. I like that very much, actually.

The beautiful woman standing before me is stronger than anyone I know. She's about to rewrite the most horrible event in her life, and I'm more hesitant than she is.

She mirrors me by taking a deep breath, then nods to signal that she's ready to begin.

I pull the slack from the rope, lifting her arms over her head until she stands straight with her feet firmly planted beneath her.

Fuck, she looks hot! My heart beats faster, and my cock swells in my jeans.

I assess her while silently reminding myself to keep my beast in check. This is about Rayna, not me. I watch her eyes until she looks up to meet mine. When I raise my eyebrows, she nods and smiles, proving to me that she wants to continue.

I move closer until I can feel the heat from her skin on mine. She smells so sweet, like a delicious dessert I want to taste and have melt in my mouth. My lips press to her neck and kiss gently. This is pure torture for me. I want to ravish her, spank her ass until it's hot pink, and then fuck her hard until she screams, and then fuck her more.

Her breathing has been calm and steady aside from the odd quiet moan escaping her lips. It's barely loud enough to hear. Slowly, I kiss down her body, ravishing her breasts, the tender skin on her tummy, and finally her sweetness. I'm careful to progress slowly, always touching her with a gentleness I'm not used to.

My tongue slithers between her labia, seeking the tiny button that fires her up.

She lifts one leg, resting it over my shoulder. I grasp her ass and push my tongue further back until I can slip inside her to taste her delicious nectar. My mouth sucks at her while she moans, her ass muscles tense and relax in my grip. Her whimpers shift to begging moans depending on where my tongue is.

I slip two fingers into her drenched canal. Rayna gasps, straining to push her wanting pussy toward me. My digits slide inside her with long, deep strokes. I think she wants me to pound her faster than I am. But she instructed me to tame my demon. So, for now, I'll be gentle, using sweet teasing torture. I have to remember to keep my demon in check.

She humps my face with increasing need. Her breathing is wild and loud. I want to make her cum, but not yet. She should enjoy this for a while. I'll get her to the edge, but ease off, only to bring her back to the edge of climax.

Before long, my fingers are filling her deeply and waving quickly while my tongue sucks and flicks at her swollen, stiff clit. She screams so loud that my ears ring. Her juices flow down my hand and chin.

Her body jerks feverishly, humping against my face, begging her climax to continue and never stop. I don't let up until her body softens. She's shaking from the adrenaline rush.

I unzip my jeans and pull out my throbbing cock and stand quickly. Lifting both of her thighs with a firm grip, I take all of her weight while wrapping her legs around the small of my back. At no point does she feel any strain on her wrists.

Her face flushes pink and glistens with sweat; exactly how I like to see her. I press my lips to hers and kiss her with passion but not aggressively. I will keep my demon on a leash until she permits me to set him free. Even then, she won't experience his idea of sadistic pleasures; not now and maybe never.

"Fuck me!" she yells.

She need not tell me twice.

I push into her, holding as soon as I'm buried completely. We meet eyes and hold each other's gaze. My hips wave back and forth. I fuck her slowly and rhythmically, keeping her calm but torturing myself worse than if I had a hot poker buried in my brain.

Fuck! I don't know if I can keep him contained. She's bound and under my control for the first time in over a month. I know I missed this but had no idea how much.

I grunt through my frustration. She looks so fucking hot! I desperately want to pull her head back by her hair while I ram her like there's no tomorrow. She knows this is hard for me. It's still fucking, but not the way I like it, the way I need it. I'm so close, but so far from what I crave.

She whispers, "Harder. Fuck me harder. Let him out." I shake my head in protest, but she begs. "Please?"

I squeeze her ass cheeks and pull back, thrusting into her with the force I so enjoy. Her head tips as I pump into her hard and fast. I let my demon out to satiate his needs but keep him under control. I growl like a barbarian, but keep my eyes on her to make sure she's okay.

I grasp a wad of her hair and pull back on her head, exposing her throat to my teeth.

"Fuck! Yes!" she pants.

I bite hard enough to dent her skin but not shred into it. I span my hand beneath her ass and push my middle finger into her tight hole. I pull up, lifting her body and bury my finger. Now I can fuck her with the fierceness I've kept buried for far too long.

Rayna stiffens. Her wail launches me into a carnal fit. I pound into her with the ferociousness of a sadist. My demon's hedonistic growls echo about the room, piercing our ears.

It happens so quickly, my orgasm tears through me suddenly and violently. I cry out and pull her groin against me so tightly that I might crush her. Fire erupts from my balls, scorching the inner walls of my dick as hot cum blasts from me, filling Rayna's twitching body.

I stand as still as I can, involuntarily jerking. My body refuses to release my cock from her. My legs are quivering under the strain of our weight, which seems magnified at this stage.

If I can keep my eyes closed, maybe this will never end.

"Coach," Rayna whispers.

My eyes meet hers. Hers are half shut, her damaged eyelid drooping slightly more than the other. She smiles at me with beads of sweat on her forehead. I snicker, and her laugh follows. We laugh until my limp prick slips out of her along with my sticky seed.

"Please let me down now," she asks, suddenly not looking so light-hearted.

I immediately yank the rope's quick-release knot I used in case she freaked out and I needed to free her immediately. As soon as I release the rope, she pulls at the cuffs in a panicked state. She quickly tears at the buckles with her teeth.

Her eyes are wide and unfocused. I grab her shoulders and pull her against me, pinning her arms between us. She's shaking but doesn't fight the hold I have on her.

"Breathe, Rayna! Breathe deeply. You're safe. I love you. I'll get the cuffs off. Just breathe."

After the cuffs are off, she lunges at me and wraps her arms around my chest. I hold her for several minutes and then walk her over to the sofa chair. I scoop her up and sit, cradling her on my lap in case her emotions overwhelm her and she wants to cry it out. She needs to feel safe with me; to know I love her and that I'll never let anyone hurt her again.

A long time ago, I had a submissive that needed this kind of attention after every playdate. She would cry for about ten minutes, and then she'd get ice cream from my freezer. We'd eat while she'd talk about anything and everything, usually shit that bored the fuck out of me. I wasn't listening to her half the time, but I don't think she noticed or cared if I was.

Sometimes I wanted her to get the fuck out, but she was a fantastic lay and would let me do anything I wanted to her. Besides, as her master, it was my responsibility to ensure her mental state was solid before she left. I never let my submissives leave feeling emotionally weak. One day, she decided she didn't want to play anymore, and I had to respect that. I wished her well before sending her on her way.

Rayna has fallen quiet, and she's breathing slowly and deeply. I'm fairly sure she fell asleep. I remain still for what seems like an hour, watching her angelic face and hearing her breathing is so much better than the sex was, or the dinner we ate, or anything that's ever happened between us.

I thought she was gone and never coming back. I have her right here in my arms and this is where we'll stay until she wakes on her own. She is safe with me, and I would die for her.

Rayna

"Coach?" I whisper, gently rousing him from a deep sleep. He opens his heavy eyelids and blinks several times to clear the fogginess from his brain.

"I must have fallen asleep," he says after clearing his throat. He teases, "You fell asleep first."

"Why didn't you wake me? We could have gone to bed and been comfortable." My fingertips brush through his bearded cheek.

"You weren't comfortable?" he questions.

I smile. "That's the best sleep I've had since before," she takes a breath, "you know."

"Hence the reason I didn't wake you."

After slipping off his legs, I lean in and kiss him. I reach out to take his hand to help him stand, but he slides his butt to the edge of the cushion and hesitates. I wait, but he doesn't take my hand. He's rubbing his legs and rolling his ankles.

"Did your legs go numb? Oh shit! I'm sorry," I apologize.

"Nope, not your fault." He slowly stands up as a complaint groans in his throat. Once he's upright, he smiles, while looking down his nose at me. He's very intimidating.

"See, no big deal. I'm good."

"Come to bed, rest your gigantic body."

I take his hand to lead the way up the stairs and into his bedroom. We curl up under the silky blue covers and notice that the sun is already rising. We only have a few more hours to sleep before I need to get home for when Renee returns the kids. They need not see their mom doing the walk of shame. The thought makes me shiver.

"Are you cold, babe?" he asks and pulls me closer to him.

"No, not at all, but you can spoon me anyway," I reply.

He kisses the back of my head as his big arm drapes over my waist and I feel safe. It isn't long before we're both lost in dreamland.

Chapter Thirty

Rayna

It's been five months since the kidnapping and my physical injuries have healed, but I'm still nervous around people I don't know. If they get too close to me, panic sets in, and I feel like I can't breathe.

I have returned to work and I'm not as worried to be out on my own, but I'm always aware of my surroundings. Maybe it's safer for me if I'm constantly on edge, ready to spring into combat if an assailant touches me. Although, I don't want to hurt an innocent man who's just walking past me and brushes my arm. It hasn't happened yet and I'm hoping it never does.

Coach's crazy ex, Alissa, made a deal with the court and ended up pleading guilty to reckless endangerment. It got her sentenced to six months in jail with a two-year probation. Coach was happy with that because he said that he hurt her emotionally and that's why she lost her shit and tried to hurt him.

He thinks it's fair, but I am furious that they didn't find her guilty of attempted murder. However, it didn't happen to me directly, so I'm working on letting go of my anger. Besides, I have my own problems.

The two men who attacked me face a whole slew of charges. The man who kidnapped me, who's name I learned to be Charley, spent a few weeks in the hospital and recovered completely. Except for the massive scar and the indent on his skull at the back of his head. He tried to have Coach charged for the assault, but the judge threw it out.

They sentenced him to six years in custody. With good behaviour, he'll be out in three.

Coach and I don't think he got what he deserved. The thought of him seeking revenge keeps me awake at night. I dread the man's release and fear I will lose Coach if his temper gets the best of him and he hunts him down.

As for Coach's friend, Brett, he only got two years because he didn't assault me physically. He threatened sexual violence but didn't go through with it, other than removing some of my clothing. They convicted him for holding me against my will and physically assaulting Coach. They sentenced him to one year in jail. But because of good behaviour and overcrowding, he was paroled a few weeks ago and has to check in once a week with a councillor.

The court wouldn't charge him with hiring Charley to kidnap me because there was no evidence to back it up. There is a Peace Bond against him that's supposed to keep him civil toward me if we should be in the same location. If he tries to talk to me, Coach, or my kids, they will send him back to jail to serve out the rest of his sentence. So far, he's kept his distance.

Coach rarely lets me out of his sight. If he has to, like when I go to work, he made me promise to have someone walk me to my car and make sure I'm locked inside before they leave me.

I appreciate that he's doing his best to keep me safe, but it's impossible to have a companion with me all the time. I have a life to live and can't always have someone to accompany me.

When I put groceries in the car, I always look around before lifting each bag and turning my back to set it inside. There will be no sneak attacks on this girl!

When I'm in my car alone, I crank up the tunes on the radio and sing as loud and off-key as anyone can, and then laugh at how ridiculous I must seem to other drivers.

I never used to enjoy the radio while driving, but it's my newest way of blowing off steam.

I can't yell or scream when I feel scared or overwhelmed. If I do, everyone will start walking on eggshells again, so to speak. I hated when everyone tiptoed around me, fearing I would break like a crystal goblet if they were to say or do the wrong thing. So, I take it to my car and yell through songs to maintain my sanity.

Coach's house has been on the market for two weeks, and the offers are pouring in. He said something about a bidding war, but I wasn't really paying attention to him. My mind was otherwise occupied, remembering when I was in the hospital and he asked me to marry him. I had told him it wasn't the right time to ask, and it wasn't. Well, it's been months, and he hasn't asked again. I wonder if he is nervous in case I shoot him down again.

I push open the front door and juggle the bags of groceries. I'm overloaded so I'll only have to make one trip, even though two trips would have been easier. It's almost as if it's a challenge to see if I can do it all at once.

After setting the bags on the floor, just inside in the entranceway, a sudden waft of deliciousness seems to slap my nose, awakening my senses and my hungry tummy.

"What is going on here?" I ask, as I walk up the stairs and watch them from the kitchen's archway.

Ken is stirring something in a pot on the stove. Kim is setting the silverware nicely on the table. Coach is nowhere to be seen.

"Did you two do all this?" They shrug. "Where's Coach?"

They say nothing, instead, smile at me. Kim gives it away by looking past me with a giggle. I spin around, expecting him to yell "boo!"

But he's down on one knee, wearing a perfectly fitted tuxedo.

Oh my God! This is it!

"Rayna, you have an incredible strength that amazes me every day. You are tough like a bull while having the gentleness of a ladybug's touch. You're wise when I am ignorant. You give me hope that even a schmuck like me can be loved by someone as perfect as you. I want to live out my days proving to you that I am forever yours, with every breath I take. I love you, Rayna. Please, marry me and make me the happiest idiot on Earth."

The kids stand beside Coach. Kim is giggling and jumping up and down while Ken video records the proposal on Coach's phone.

I stand here, not giving him any clues to what I'm going to say. I don't know why I'm making him wait. Each second ticks by, casting even more doubt on his face. How long should I make him sweat this out?

"Of course, I will marry you," I whisper.

A huge sigh of relief escapes him, as if he'd been holding his breath the entire time. He slips the most stunning, sparkling dix

amond ring on my finger. He pulls me onto his knee and kisses me lovingly, but PG-rated because of our young audience.

My tears fall as Kim leads me to my bedroom. She shows me a gorgeous red evening gown Coach spread out on the bed. She helps me put it on, and then brushes my hair and puts some lipstick on me. I slip on the heels that he bought to match the dress. I stand before the full-length mirror and admire how great I look. She smiles at me and tells me I'm pretty. I kiss her, then we head to the kitchen.

Coach admires my dress with a pleased grin before taking my hand and giving it a kiss as he guides me to the living room. Ken holds up Coach's phone as a beautiful melody fills the room. The kids watch as we dance closely to one another, except for the occasional spin requested by Kim. This is the most perfect proposal

I could ever have imagined. It's so much better than the first one and more intimate than if he were to take a knee at a fancy restaurant.

The whole time we eat dinner, the kids are talking about the proposal with every single detail overly exaggerated to near fairy tale proportions, but we don't mind. We are in our own little world. Our eyes meet after each bite of food. This amazing man will be my husband.

We helped each other through some awful things, and we came out of them with a powerful bond. We are unbreakable now; stronger than the diamond I wear on my finger. He is mine, and I am his.

I have asked him if his inner demon ever urges him to choose another woman so it can play out its worst sadistic desires. He always smiles at me and tells me that no woman will ever stroke the horns of his demon the way I do.

Our sex life burns at both ends of the candle, so to speak. Sometimes we enjoy the most tender and romantic lovemaking, where we seem to mould into one another and become one being.

Other times, he lets his demon loose, setting forth an evening of wild, vicious sex that takes its physical toll on us both. It eases his sexually aggressive nature while satiating my inner ravenous goddess. I am becoming a big fan of that side of me, thanks to Coach's demon. He says he's keeping his demon on a leash because I won't like him. If he's more intense than what I've seen so far, he might be right.

Soon we will marry, as we don't want to put it off any longer than necessary. It won't be a big, extravagant wedding; I've had one of those and it's not all it's cracked up to be. However, Renee will be my maid of honour. Her boyfriend, who happens to be Coach's long-standing best friend, will stand proudly beside him as his best man. So, it works out perfectly.

Renee has become someone I always hoped she'd be. She is no longer as scatterbrained, and she isn't hopping from one idea to the next, never finding something or someone to keep her entertained.

Tim holds her attention better than anyone ever has. She adores him, and he is head over heels in love with her. She's even been talking about having a baby or two. I never thought she'd love someone enough to commit to him and want to start a family.

As for my kids, they will grow up without their real dad in their lives. He moved across the country to live with some bimbo that he met online. He didn't even tell the kids he was leaving. When he was halfway across the country, he called me to ask if I'd do his dirty work for him. Like I had a choice. He's a coward and he'll never change. I'm glad he's gone, and I think they are, too.

The kids love Coach and he's so good to them. I wish he were their biological father, but he loves them so much that people assume he is.

They insist on calling him Dad, which seemed strange at first. It took a while before he could hear it and not smile like a proud fool.

I won't claim that our story is flawless from this point on because nobody's marriage ever is. We still have our trials, as does everyone, but I wouldn't change it for all the money in the world.

Who would have thought that two people, as different as we are, can come together and become an indestructible bonded force? I have calmed his bad boy ways, and he has saved me from my vanilla flavoured comfort zone.

I still sit on the patio with a chilled glass of wine and the book I've never read a single word of, and I watch the man who was once the mysterious, sexy, musclebound neighbour who turned me on by mowing his lawn every Saturday. Now, he mows *our* lawn while the twenty-something brunette, who's bought Coach's old house, sits on her patio with an open book of unread pages.

The End of Book One

If you enjoyed *Coaching Rayna, book one*, please take a moment to leave a review on the site you bought your book.
Great reviews and ratings help to earn
promotions and awards.

Keep flipping to read
Coaching Rayna: Bound Hearts, Book Two.

Coaching Rayna #2 – Bound Hearts

ISBN 978-0-9920069-8-3 print
ISBN 978-0-9920069-7-6 ebook

Cover photos and design © 2019 Pebbles Lacasse
First Edition June 28, 2019
Photographs by Sharon Seguin
Cover Model Chris LaPointe
Edited by Lisa Vincent & Nikki Brackett

Published by Pebbles Lacasse www.pebbleslacasse.com

Coaching Rayna

Bound Hearts
Book Two

by Pebbles Lacasse

Chapter One

Coach

I've been living with Rayna and her two awesome kids for eight months now and I couldn't be happier. I love what we've become; a loving family.

Ken and I are more friends than stepfather and stepson. I still call him my *little man,* but he's growing and will soon catch up to me in height. He's thirteen and has a lot of questions about sex that he's too embarrassed to ask his mom. I do my best to steer the kid in the right direction but it's not easy sometimes.

Kim, Rayna's daughter, is eleven years old. She likes to sit next to me while we're watching television so she can feel the muscles on my arm. She's a sweet girl and the spitting image of her mom. I love that little darling. I don't know how I'll be when she starts dating; an overprotective, threatening, chaperoning stepfather. Yeah, very likely. Nobody is going to hurt her!

I'm in to rough sex; BDSM to be more specific. My whole life before Rayna, the love of my life, I was a wild, vicious, sexual demon. Well, my demon still exists, I just keep him better contained these days. Little by little, she's setting him free, but I have to keep him leashed. I don't want to hurt Rayna.

I've always respected women when we aren't in the bedroom, unless they agree to be my submissive whenever they are with me. I'll admit I was an asshole to all of them. I treated them like shit; degraded them, chained them, fucked them hard and spit in their faces. Strangely, they must have enjoyed my abuse because those women kept coming back for more torture.

It satisfied the viciousness I carry within me, but my heart was frozen, locked inside an impenetrable vault. I kept everyone away from my heart. My friends were just that, friends. I do love them, but my lovers never felt even the slightest of heartfelt emotion from me. If they said they loved me, I forbid them to visit me again. Like I said, I was an asshole.

Until Rayna, that is. She woke up my heart with her eyes. Somehow, that woman looked at me when I was inside of her and it warmed my soul. From then on, she has been mine and I, hers. I will always love this woman.

Rayna was kidnapped, beat up and nearly raped, but I found her before he could hurt her in the worst way. I wanted to kill him. He used to be my friend, someone I used to share my submissive women with. Don't judge. Those women wanted to be with us. Taking two men at the same time can be an ultimate fantasy for some women. They thoroughly enjoyed it, trust me.

That guy, Brett, has always been a scary man. He is a true sadist. If a woman screamed in pain, something in him snapped. He's nearly choked a woman to unconsciousness. He liked to leave them battered and bruised. The women he hurt came back to him again and again, I don't know why. When he was with me, he would never injure a woman, he knew I'd beat the fuck out of him if he did. Sexual play, BDSM, was great but no dangerous play was allowed only visible bruises could be left on parts of their bodies that can easily be hidden from society.

It's been eight months since Rayna was kidnapped and she's doing well. She was quite skittish for a few months but she's a strong woman. She's overcome most of her anxieties and seems to be back to her old self, so to speak.

Rayna is coming out of the bathroom wearing a silky blue chemise that clings to her breasts as she walks. I'm hoping it will soon be on the floor. I never attack her. She lets me know when she's ready and how she wants me. Whether she wants it rough or gentle, she always gets her way and I never leave her unsatisfied.

"Master, would you like to use my body for your own pleasure?" she whispers in her sweet voice as she stands at the edge of the bed.

"I do. How hard would you like me to be?" I whisper back. I'm already getting off the bed and making my way toward her so I can make her my sexual plaything. I just need to know how far she wants to take it tonight.

"You can have my mouth and my pussy but not my ass. Breath control is okay and so is spanking, hair pulling, pinching and very hard fucking."

I walk up behind her and place my hands on her shoulders. She shudders as the heat of my palms radiates through her air-chilled skin. I hear her breath catch. Affecting her this way makes my dick swell.

"Take off your nightie," I whisper with my hot breath caressing her neck. Tiny bumps lift all over her body as if I've electrocuted her. She pulls her chemise slowly, teasingly up, exposing her ass, lower back and finally her shoulders. My dick stiffens even more when her hair falls to her shoulders and the nightie floats to the floor.

My fingers weave into her hair, grasping a wad and pulling her head around so I can kiss her mouth, hard. My tongue invades her while she opens wide. Her tongue, not knowing where to be, rests at the bottom of her mouth, occasionally waving when mine slides along its bumpy exterior.

My groan has her reaching up to cradle my cheek, which she knows she's not allowed to do, not during rough play. There are to be no tender moments after she requests me to

Master her. Those loving moments are for making love, which we are not doing.

I take her wrist and pull it behind her back, along with the other. There's always a two-metre rope in the nightstand. I pull open the drawer.

"Get the rope for me," I whisper in her ear.

She doesn't hesitate, leaning in with her face to clutch the rope in her jaws. She stands up, holding the rope tightly in her teeth with her head turned toward me, offering it to me. She's a good girl for not questioning my instructions.

After binding her hands behind her back, I turn her around to face me. "Get on your knees, slut."

She drops, her eyes still locked on mine, awaiting another instruction. I watch her lick her lips, waiting for me to drop my boxers, but she can wait until I'm ready.

On the dresser are a bunch of elastics she uses to tie her hair up. I take one and begin gently gathering her locks until I have a lovely ponytail high at the back of her head.

I drop my boxers and smile as my cock springs forth, solid and thick. Her eyes gaze at my prick. Her focus is to be on my face whenever possible, unless I tell her to look away. That is a rule I don't like her breaking. I don't touch my cock. I wait for her to look up at me, to acknowledge that she faltered.

"I'm sorry, Master," she says after her head tilts back and her eyes meet mine.

"Make it up to me, take my cock down your throat."

She licks her lips again, and with her eyes on mine, my cock slides into her mouth and down her throat with ease. I can't help but moan. It feels so fucking good; hot, wet, snug and deep.

I grasp her ponytail and hold her face against my belly with my prick still buried in her throat. I'm thankful that she's not a gagger. Instead, her body shifts, and her hands start to fidget with the end of rope within their reach, possibly giving her a sense of freedom, should she need it. I pull her head back quickly when I'm sure she's on the edge of panic.

Rayna takes a few quick breaths as her weeping eyes lock onto mine. "Thank you, Sir."

I tilt her head back down and aim my cock, guiding her by her ponytail, making sure she sucks me right.

"I'm going to fuck your throat again. Are you ready? I won't be kind," I warn her.

"I'm ready, Master," she whispers with a quivering voice. I can hear the concern behind her words.

She doesn't care for this, but I would never hurt her, and she knows that. I have asked her many times if she'd rather I don't do this to her, but she always tells me to do it because feeling like she's just an object for me to play with excites her. She enjoys not having any control, but she knows it will stop the second she wants it to.

"Open that beautiful fucking mouth of yours and don't move."

She opens wide. Her focus is on my lascivious grin. I press my hips forward, pushing half of my cock into her mouth and then pull back. She knows I'm getting ready to hump against her face, forcing her to swallow every inch of me.

I fuck her mouth gently for a full minute before gliding all the way in, pulling back until the tip of my cock rests on her lips, and repeating, over and over until she's out of breath and tears are streaming down her face. Since she can't say a safeword, if she wants me to stop while in this position, she's to lift and drop her lower leg on the floor quickly and repeatedly. I will immediately cease.

I grab her under the armpits and lift her to her feet. With the palms of my hands, I smear her tears all over her face and kiss her lips roughly. I suck her bottom lip into my mouth and bite and hold it until she whimpers. This is not a romantic moment.

I look down her body, "You are a beautiful woman."

"Stop it. I'm not," she replies, knowing that pisses me off when she denies her worth.

I pick her up and toss her onto the bed. She squeals as she bounces. I'm on her, straddling her knees, holding her legs together. She lifts her arms over her head, clasping them together, because she knows it's what I require her to do. I slap her right tit and watch the ripple flow. She doesn't yelp. Perhaps that didn't sting enough.

My palm slaps across her breast once again, and then the other hand matches the motion exactly on her opposite breast. They are bouncing, jiggling like gelatine each time my hand cracks down. Now she's whimpering. This pleases me. I stop when they are a lovely shade of pink and her nipples have stiffened up to being slightly larger than pencil erasers.

My mouth envelops her right nipple, sucking hard. I nip now and then just to hear her yip. Her other nipple is just as hard and entertaining to bite.

I slide my finger between her closed thighs, along her womanhood. She's so wet. With my finger drenched in her pussy juice, I lift my hand and shove two of my fingers in her mouth.

"Taste your dirty little pussy. Do you like it?"

"Yes, Sir," she replies even though my fingers are deep in her mouth.

I slide two saliva coated digits between her outer labia and pinch her clitoris between them. I pinch hard, watching her face tense and hear her breath hesitate. I ease off slightly now rubbing either side of it, alternating; one rubs up while the other glides down. I know she enjoys this. Her face says it all. Goddamn, she's fucking sexy!

Now that she's well lubricated, I push further between the clutches of her thighs, slipping those two fingers inside her, just the tips to tease her. Her pelvis tilts upward, giving me a bit more leeway to penetrate her deeper, but I won't, not yet.

As soon as she lets out the slightest moan, I rise up off of her legs just enough to lift and flip her body face down. Her ass is round and firm, not the ass of a thirty-eight-year old woman who's had two children. Most women my age, twenty-eight, don't have asses this perfect.

My finger traces her spine, leading down the crack of her ass. She lifts her pelvis as high as she can manage, which isn't much since I'm straddling her thighs. It's nice of her to offer herself to me. As a reward for her generosity, my palm cracks down on her butt cheek. She drops her hips back to the bed, burying her face in the comforter to muffle a cry. That doesn't stop me from doing it again.

Rayna's yelping into the comforter and trying to cover her ass with her hands, but it's no use. I just lift them using the rope binding her wrists. My hand cracks down three more times on her right cheek. I switch the rope to my right hand and punish her left cheek equally.

I slip two fingers between her ass cheeks and down to her wetness. They slip inside her easily. She's slick with arousal. I bet she tastes great. I sample her flavour, sucking my fingers loud enough for her to hear. She loves it when I do this. After releasing her wrists, I reach beneath her bound arms to grasp her ponytail, lifting her arms while pulling back her head.

"What are you?" I ask her.

"I'm your slut," she replies.

"You're my fucking little whore," I correct her.

"I'm your fucking little whore," she replies.

I slip my fingers back inside her cunt and start waving my strong fingers quickly and powerfully toward her tummy. I pull back on her head, lifting her arms higher in the process.

I know it's an uncomfortable position, but she isn't complaining, other than a few grunts.

Her moans are getting louder and starting to fill the room. Our bedroom isn't all that far away from the kids' bedrooms and we fear they might one day hear us playing rough. Rayna always makes sure they are fast asleep before initiating sex. I'd rather be safe than sorry, so I had better muffle her mouth.

I release her hair. I free my hand from between her legs and feed it down between her rope bound wrists, and pull them back with my arm, arching her spine in the process. It pleases me that she is so flexible. I stretch her until I can slip my fingers back into her pussy. This time, I slip my thumb over her clitoris and rub as I wave my fingers. I cover her mouth with my free hand to muffle her erotic sounds and lift her head just slightly, taking some of the strain off her arms.

She's going to cum, I can feel her pussy tightening around my fingers. Should I let her? Hmm, yes, I will. Now all I can hear is her low grunts and the sloshing sounds of my fingers in her sloppy cunt.

Her muscles flex, desperate for her body to straighten. My forearm is holding her bound wrists, but she's still pulling. Her hands are gripped into tight fists and her ass is rock hard. Her whole body holds stiff as the orgasm shreds through her. This is the moment I love the most; when I know she's at the height of the climactic euphoria I allowed her to experience. At this very second, I own her body, her mind, her pleasure. She's mine. At my mercy. I am her whole world.

Her body jerks several times, signifying that she's ridden through her orgasm and is not likely to scream. I free her mouth. She heaves out a long breath. Her groan, as I lower her to the bed and removing my hand from between her legs, is music to my ears.

I untie her hands and roll her onto her back, lying my body between her thighs. My prick is throbbing, aching to be inside her. I slip into her, one inch at a time until she has engulfed me completely. Our eyes meet, gentle smiles lift our lips just before I press mine to her. I wanted to make love to her tonight, as well as satisfy my dominant nature. The demon will stay locked away tonight.

Chapter Two

Rayna

It's early, six-thirty and I'm awake. After only five and a half hours of sleep, I'm exhausted. It's going to be a rough day. Don't get me wrong, I'm not complaining, it's totally worth it!

Last night, Coach took me as he craves; dominant and rough. I would never say that I don't enjoy it. I might not like some things he does, like rhythmically deep-fucking my throat or covering my mouth so I won't scream. For some reason, I cum really hard when he does. Maybe it's the oxygen restriction. Maybe the fearful idea that he could prevent any and all of my future breaths, I don't know. I just know that I don't like it, but my body sure does. And yes, I want him to keep doing it. Besides, by covering my mouth, I can relax knowing that I can't scream which would surely wake the kids. They don't need to wake up from hearing their mother screaming in ecstasy.

I have pancakes puffing up in the pan with a cup of strong coffee in my hand. My eyes feel scratchy and heavy lidded, and I can't stop my excessive yawning.

A pair of warm hands glide around my waist and pull my back against a strong, even warmer body. Tender kisses are placed lovingly just below my ear.

"Good morning love," I say.

"Good morning," he says. "Pancakes? You're up early. Is that because I didn't tire you out enough last night?"

I chuckle, "No, I just woke up and couldn't fall back to sleep. Do you want eggs too or just pancakes?"

"I'd love a few eggs," he says while heading to the fridge with me still in his arms. He releases only one, keeping me pressed firmly against him as he leans in the fridge, collecting two eggs. "Do you want any?"

I'm laughing at how puppet-like I feel. "No, thank you."

He walks me back to the stove, puts the eggs down on the counter and returns to placing delicate kisses on my neck. Fuck! I wonder if he knows that he makes my pussy twitch when he does that? If I tell him, he'll do it more often, which would mean that he would have his lips to my neck almost constantly. The man is so loving, but then sometimes, he's so detached that it doesn't seem like he is even in his body anymore.

"Do you want help?"

"Can you set the table and then wake the kids?" I ask.

"Absolutely!" he releases me, leaving my body feeling chilled, missing the warmth from his absent flesh.

"Orange juice for Ken and me. Apple juice for Kim and you, my love," he says each item as he takes them from the fridge, placing them on the table. "Butter, syrup, strawberries, blueberries, kiwi…"

After he has everything arranged to his satisfaction - *he's such a perfectionist* – he sings his wake-up song loud and way off key.

"Wake-up, wake-up!

Start your day with a smile. Your tummies are rumbling So, don't be grumbling.

Get your butts out of bed!"

The kids hate hearing that song because it represents waking up for school. Personally, I find it to be quite entertaining. To see the man I know in the bedroom to be raging with testosterone and dominant as fuck, as a happy-go-lucky, child-friendly comedian, just doesn't match up. But I love his dual personalities and the way he relates so well to my kids. He's a big kid himself, when he's not alone in the bedroom with me.

Ken is last to drag his tired, sagging body to the table. Kim is already starting to eat a strawberry when I plop a pancake onto her dish.

"Thank you, Mom," she mutters while yawning. Her wavy hair has wadded into a big knot that is going to hurt to brush through.

Ken's eyes are half shut but his yawn is wide and lasts a long time. I plop the other pancake onto his plate. He just sits there, hunched over, staring at the puffy slab.

"Hey you! Wake up over there," Coach teases Ken, tossing a slice of kiwi at him. Ken glares at him with an evil leer but Coach smiles at him and chuckles. Ken eventually smirks and picks up the syrup, pouring until he has a mote around his pancake.

They chatter amongst the three of them while I finish cooking. I'm the last to sit, just as the kids are finishing up. So much for having a conversation with them. They wander away, but Coach remains, still picking at the fruit and looking at me with questioning eyes. He seems to be sizing me up for some reason. Does he want to fuck before work? Sometimes, when the kids are in their rooms with their doors closed and getting dressed, we can close our bedroom door and go into the bathroom, close that door and have a quickie without them knowing. I'm up for that today!

"What?" I ask him after a full minute of him ogling me.

He smiles, "I'm going to take you somewhere tomorrow night. Don't worry about a sitter, Renee and Tim agreed to take them for the night. What do you say? Will you go out on a date with me?"

The way he speaks sounds like a teenager asking a girl out for the first time, he even made his voice crack. He's being silly, of course.

"That would depend on where you want to take me," I reply, with a sweet voice, complimenting his teenage roleplay. I even flip my hair and bat my eyelashes.

"Okay, that's hot! Can you do that later?"

"I can do it in our bathroom right now if you're interested," I suggest.

He sucks in a deep breath through flared nostrils, growling as it escapes him. "Fuck! I wish I could, love. I can't do it. Tim is meeting me early so we can work out before the crowd comes. We need our man time to discuss some things. Besides, I'm not a machine you know!"

As he stands to kiss my forehead, I ask, "What things?"

He snickers, "Just things. You know, guy things."

"Why do I think you're up to something no good? Oh, I know, because you usually are."

He places the dishes in the sink and then turns to kiss my forehead again. I stand up and look up into his eyes to judge his expression. I can't read him, and he isn't going to tell me anything. I could keep prying, but the man is like a vault when it comes to secrets. I respect that but wish it wasn't so easy for him to keep things from me. I'm sure it isn't anything I need to be concerned over.

"Fine! Don't tell me. I might have something in mind for later but if I'm left in the dark, I might not go through with my plan. And, that would be a pity," I tease. My hand brushes the front of his pajama pants, rubbing his prick as it does.

He groans, shaking his head with his eyes locked on mine. "If I tell you, it won't be a surprise. Do you trust me?"

I put the juice jugs in the fridge and then turn and look him in the eyes while crossing my arms. "I trust you with every breath I take, literally sometimes. Yes, of course I do. You saved my life once and I'm sure you'd do it again if I ever needed you to."

"Love, I would burn in hell for you," he whispers while sliding his hot hands up my arms until they are wrapped around my shoulders, pulling me in for a hug.

"Honey, you were likely scheduled to go to hell long before you met me." I laugh.

"There might be some truth to that," he replies, and I'm not sure if he believes that to be true or if he's just joking.

"Let me do the dishes and then I'll meet you in the bathroom. Give me ten minutes."

He kisses my forehead. "Sorry, love, I can't this morning. Like I said, I have to meet Tim at the gym."

"Fine! It's okay to say you don't want to fuck me. I get it. You're sick of me already," I say, teasingly.

He just chuckles but quickly, the entertained expression falls, and his eyes harden. "You are a being a little bitch and I'm going to put you in your place later.

My spine tingles and my pussy twitches. How is it that when he looks so vicious, it always arouses me to the point that my mouth suddenly goes dry and my body shudders? Fuck, he's so goddamn sexy!

"Thank you, Master. I will do what I can to piss you off continuously throughout the day, if it pleases you?" It's my turn to make his sex twitch.

His fingers weave in my hair, pulling my head back while he looks down at my face. "Be careful little girl."

"And, what if I whispered, fuck you?" I'm really taunting his demon to break free. I know Coach will keep him caged, the kids are home. I can tease all I want because I know he won't throw me over his knee, not right now anyway. Besides, I know he would never actually injure me, no matter how much I provoke him.

"Careful," he whispers slowly and with a very deep voice that makes my chest vibrate.

He frees my now matted hair, kisses my lips tenderly and then walks down the hall toward our bedroom. I do notice the raging hard-on he's shielding in case he runs into one of the kids in the hallway. I just giggle, loving the effect I have on that man.

Chapter Three

Coach

"Hey Tim! What's up Brother?" Tim grasps my hand, pulling me in for a two-pat-on-the-back man-hug.

"Not much, bro," he replies. "How's things with the fam-jam?"

He's always busting my balls about being an instant father to two young kids. Eventually he wants kids too, but it's his way of teasing me. He's happy for me, really he is, but fucking with your buddy is what guys do.

"Good," I reply. Together, we head to the locker room to dress for our workout.

"So, what's going on? You said you have something important you want to talk about?" he asks.

When I don't speak right away, he stops tying his shoes, realizing that I have something significant on my mind that requires his full attention. He shrugs, his way of telling me to spit it out.

"I'm taking her to Fallen tomorrow night. What do you think? Is it too soon?"

Fallen is a nightclub, of sorts. It's not just your everyday, run of the mill, nightclub. It looks a lot like a large house, but it's so much more. Not just anyone can attend. You must be invited by someone who has been regularly attending for more than a year and can't enter until you've had a thorough background check. The main door is always locked, with two very large men standing in front of it, holding the key, ready to rip you to shreds if you don't have the correct password, which is changed daily.

Tim introduced me to Fallen. He's also a dominant with sadistic tendencies. Renee, Tim's girlfriend and Rayna's sister, seems to love his dominant nature, but isn't so keen on playing the role of submissive, or receiving pain of any kind. Rayna is different. She endures suffering, using it to disappear into herself, thus heightening her orgasmic experiences.

Since Tim started dating Renee, he hasn't been to Fallen. I know he misses it, but he loves Renee. Hopefully he'll be able to return to what he loves, I just hope Rayna and I aren't there when that day comes. The last thing I want to see is Renee's smirking face when I'm playing with someone.

He nods, and I can see a bit of jealousy in his expression. "I hope she likes it there. Renee wouldn't. At least, I'm fairly sure she wouldn't. I don't know, maybe she would."

"Just don't bring her on a night when we're there." He shakes his head as if to say he won't take her anyway. "You can tell her that she wouldn't have to participate. Maybe you could just walk her around and show her what it's all about. It might sway her to give it a shot. Who knows, something might interest her."

"Yeah, I don't know. She's a fucking wild woman but she doesn't like dressing up in leathers or playing the whole dominant/submissive roles. She laughs all the way through it, which really irritates me to no end. We still have rough sex, but it doesn't go any further than that."

"Are you okay with that?" I ask, wondering if their relationship will continue for much longer if they aren't into the same sexual practices.

I'm no one to speak. Rayna was so vanilla when we first met. She wouldn't say the word *cunt*. Now, she's becoming a freak like me and I like it. So does she.

"I'm okay with it for now. I hold hope that she'll fall to her knees in front of me and beg me to punish her for being so fucking vanilla. I hope that day will come sooner than later."

"That day might not ever come. Renee can be a stubborn bitch when she is set on something. Will you stay with her if she refuses?" I ask, unsure if he's happy, or not.

"I love her, man. I really do. If that means I have to curb my sexual perversions, that's what I'll do. She isn't having sex with women anymore, trying to prove to me that she wants to be mine and only mine; her words, not mine. I don't want her to stop being with other chicks. I don't have a pussy and I know she craves it. I've told her to find a hot girl and have fun, but she won't. I suppose, if she's giving that up for me, not whipping her until she's welted simply for my own satisfaction, is the least I can do." He chuckles and shrugs.

He's right, I've also put my demon in a cage for the benefit of Rayna's limited past sexual experiences. The difference is that she's interested in taking things further, learning what it means to be my submissive. She also has masochistic tendencies, but nobody ever told her they were okay, so she hid them away. She thought she wasn't normal because she would become aroused at the thought of a man spanking or choking her during sex. The men she was with were never experimental, nor did they have an urge to bring her to incredible sexual heights. They never thought to show her the ropes, pardon the pun. Now she has me. I'm experienced enough to show her what she's been missing out on all this time. Little by little, I'm introducing her to new and exciting experiences.

Taking her to Fallen is a huge leap, but I want her to see the possibilities before her. If she witnesses other people enjoying the BDSM lifestyle, she might give herself permission to dive head first into these unknown pleasures. I want her to feel comfortable with what I would like her to do. I also want her to discover what kink turns her on. Rayna should be sexually, emotionally and mentally spoiled. I want to be the guy to do just that. I'll do anything to please her.

"You know you won't be happy if, for the rest of your life, you have to pretend to be something you're not. What if she never wants to play your way? Can you live with that?"

He shrugs, turning the question back on me. "What about you? If you take her to Fallen and she runs away screaming, what then? Would you leave her if she only ever wants vanilla sex for the rest of her life?"

"No way, man. She's my bitch and I'm her asshole. Her and I have been through too much to quit now. Will I miss it? Of course. So far, Rayna isn't afraid to let me be me... Well, she pretends she isn't afraid. I can tell she is, but she tries. I'll bury that side of me if I have to."

"You should reconsider taking her to Fallen. It might backfire on you," he warns.

I grumble, placing my gym bag in locker number one, my locker. I do own the place after all. Taking the locker of my choice is one of the benefits.

"Enough of this heartsy-fartsy shit! Are you ready for legs?" I ask with a wicked grin. He hates working his legs.

"Fuck! Let's get this shit-show over with!" He slams his locker with a sneer. "I'd rather do cardio and you know how much I hate cardio!"

Chapter Four

Rayna

I got off work early today. After zipping through the grocery store to pick up a few things for tonight's dinner, I fill the gas tank and then head home. I'm hosting a dinner with Renee and Tim at our house. It's always at our house. For once, it would be nice if we didn't have to do all the cooking and cleaning.

They are really hitting it off well. She claims the two of them are sexual dynamos so they're perfect for one another. She is always telling me how wild he is with her. I only tell her some things, leaving plenty out. She's on a need to know basis and she doesn't need to know.

She had sex with my ex-husband many years ago while I was still married to him, and I haven't forgotten. I forgave her, but I will never fully trust her again.

Renee made a pass at Coach before we were in an actual relationship, and she knew we had had sex. That's when I scrounged up the courage to ask her about her and my ex; it had been four years since I divorced him. There was always something in the back of my mind that had me wondering if they hooked up at some point. I always hoped I was reading too much into their chilled conversations. Deep down, I knew the truth long before I asked her.

She was drunk after a party at my house. I passed out. He took advantage of the situation. She didn't say no, in fact, she said she didn't protest at all. He was a cheating son-of-a-bitch all throughout our marriage but there's no excuse for fucking my sister.

Needless to say, I don't completely trust her and likely, never will. I love my sister. Don't ever think I don't. I would die for her in a heartbeat, but when it comes to men, she can't help herself. Coach turned her down flat and immediately told me about it. I think that's when I started believing he and I might be able to make a relationship work.

My ex-husband was a cheating, dirty, low-down asshole that still today, hasn't changed. The only difference is that he moved to the other side of the country with some whore of the week. It's unlikely he will ever call to talk to his kids or have anything to do with them. I hope he dies with many regrets about that. But I can't say I'm not happy to know he's gone. Sayonara, Jackass!

Coach has some crazies in his past. The playmate he was with when we started playing, was a real psycho. She served only five, of a six-month sentence she was handed, for attempting to maim Coach when she smashed his truck with her car. His leg was cut and bruised from his door shoving in on him, but otherwise he was unhurt. She had a broken nose from the airbag, a fractured wrist and bruised calves from the engine pushing in on her. They had to cut her out of the car. She got the worst of it, I'd say.

She was obsessed with him and wouldn't let him go. She's on probation now and forbidden to contact either one of us. So far, I haven't seen her around much. I'm happy about that. I don't trust that crazy bitch for a second.

He also had a friend who he used to tag-team with. That guy was something else! He kidnapped me and planned to rape me, but Coach found us, before he did. The guy was handed down a jail sentence and is still in custody, as far as I know. I try not to think about it because it makes me feel weak and vulnerable. I don't like that feeling.

It's strange how I enjoy it when Coach binds me with rope or handcuffs and takes me at his will. When he chokes me as I'm starting to cum, I fucking lose my mind. My orgasm crushes me! How I can enjoy these things with Coach after what his friend did to me, doesn't make any sense. You'd think I'd need to be the dominant one. I've come to realize that I, as his submissive, have more power than he does. Yes, he could hurt me if he so desired and I could do nothing to prevent it, but I trust him completely. If I say one word, it all stops, even if he is just about to orgasm. *That* is power.

The roast has been slow-cooking all day filling the house with a delicious aroma, making my mouth water the second I walked in the house. It only gets stronger as I near the kitchen carrying the bags of groceries.

The house is so quiet when nobody is home. I enjoy this time to myself, just listening to my thoughts about my relationship with Coach, the kids, my sister.

I toss two frozen apple pies into the oven to bake while I chop some potatoes, celery and carrots, tossing them into the slow-cooker, along with extra spices. After the pies are finished, I set them on the stove to cool, with a light towel covering them. I put the dishes in the dishwasher and make my way to the bathroom for a long, relaxing bath while the house is still peaceful and lonely.

Just as I'm getting in the tub, I hear someone walking through my bedroom. My heart thumps and a dizzying fear fills me. Who the fuck is in my house? The bathroom door slowly pushes open, furthering my agony.

Coach's face comes into view and I exhale an exasperated breath. "What the fuck? You scared me! I thought someone was in the house. Don't do that again!"

"I'm sorry, love. That was not my intention. The house smells awesome, by the way. I can't wait for dinner, but I could use a light snack to tie me over and you look delectable."

"I was just about to take a bath," I say as I step into the tub, much to his disappointment.

"You're really turning me down? I left work early because I can't wait until tonight to touch you. Are you going to make me beg?"

"I might." I smile as my body slowly lowers, disappearing beneath the bubbles, leaving just my head visible.

"Yeah, that's not going to happen. Get the fuck out of that tub," he says with a snicker.

I raise my arm, slowly dragging the sponge from my fingertips to my shoulder, along my collarbone and down between my breasts. I don't stop there, I continue to my pussy. My eyes never leave his.

His tongue is stroking his bottom lip before his face lifts, his Adam's apple bobbing, swallowing down his pride.

"Please, get out of the tub. I need you. I want to taste you. I want to make you cum on my face. I'm begging. Do you want me on my knees?"

I'm shocked that I have him under my control, and so easily. Maybe I should deny him more often.

"That might convince me that you're serious about needing to touch me," I tease, while squeezing my tits together. A puff of bubbles pushes between them, gradually gliding along. He's mesmerized, eyes admiring the bubble's journey.

He lowers himself to his knees and tilts his face toward the floor. My mind is whirling with so many questions. Why put his head down? Is that customary? One day I should ask him to explain the proper protocol.

I slowly rise from the tub and step out without drying my body. White puffs are slipping down my chest and legs, pooling at my feet. I walk over to him and take his hair in my hand.

"Come with me," I demand with a calm voice. I don't know who I've become at this very moment, but I think I like her. At any second, he will jump up, grab me and take me at his will. I'm good with that too.

He shuffles on his knees behind me, not standing, which surprised me. I lift my ass onto the counter, spreading my legs and leaning back, resting against the mirror. I wave my finger, ordering him to crawl to me. He does, without questioning. Before he can press his lips to my pussy, I stop him by pressing the palm of my hand to his forehead.

He looks up at my eyes just as I shake my head. His upper lip is twitching. His inner demon likely slapping his soul senseless for submitting his dominance to me. I can see the inner struggle through his eyes.

My fingers explore my pussy, opening my labia for him to admire but not touch. I circle my clitoris with the tip of my finger and make myself moan. He shifts, gritting his teeth and growling. How long can I make him wait? How long will he allow me to make him wait?

His eyes meet mine the instant I push my fingers inside myself. He looks angry, but I know it's only because he wants me and I'm not allowing it. Why he's permitting me to play this role in the first place, has me filled with questions, but this is not the time to ask them.

Has he been submissive at some point? I'm fairly sure he said he's always been dominant, but maybe he lied. I can't picture him as submissive to anyone, even me. What's happening right now has me on the verge of coming. Of course, my fingers have a big role in that.

I'm panting, moaning softly, while I watch his eyes study my hands, as they gently caress my clit. He's just biding his time, patiently waiting to ravish me. His cock must be raging hard, thick as ever and ready to fuck me violently. I can't wait.

My moans are riding each quick breath. I'm going to cum and he still only watches. This is so fucking hot! That's it, I'm coming. My body tenses, my fingers are barely able to continue their massage. My eyelids fall shut as my jaw falls open, no breath escaping my pleasure-filled mind and body. I'm floating in the nothingness that only orgasm can take me to.

It's ending and I'm disappointed. My body jerks. A heavy exhale bursts from my burning lungs along with a high-pitched whimper. My hands grab my breasts and squeeze. I open my eyes to see him still on his knees, his teeth clenched, nostrils flared and looking so fucking dangerous. Not touching me is torture for him, his shaking proves it.

"Fucking take me!" I demand with a quivering voice.

Coach leaps up onto his feet. He yanks my housecoat from the back of the bathroom door and pulls the belt from the loops. He rushes back to me, grabbing my ass to lift me and flip me on his shoulder. He carries me out of the bathroom and into the kitchen while tying one end of the housecoat to my right ankle, which I playfully kick to pretend I don't want to be his victim.

He sits me on the middle of the long island. "Turn and lie back." I do as he says, letting my ankles hang off the end of the counter while my body lies back against the cold countertop.

He pulls my right leg so it hangs at the knee off the side of the countertop. He loops the strap through the drawer's handle, under and around the end, through the handle of the opposite drawer and finally, pulling my free leg to match the other and wrapping it around my left ankle, binding it tightly.

I am left in a very vulnerable position with my legs spread wide and my calves hanging off the side edges of the counter. I lift my upper body so that I'm resting back on my elbows, looking down at myself. When I look up, he's standing at the end of the counter, examining my position with furrowed brows and pursed lips.

"You can still move. I don't like that. Stay there," he hisses and walks away.

"Like I have a choice?" I reply, snickering at my lack of freedom.

Coach returns carrying a blindfold, handcuffs, a dumbbell, and a bottle of something that might be a lubricant. It's not our usual brand, that I'm sure of. Our regular lube has a purple label, this one is yellow. I'm more curious about what he's planning to do with the weight as opposed to the switch in lubricant brands. He won't make me lift that, will he? It looks rather heavy, but he's toting it along like it's nothing.

"Lie back, put your hands over your head." I do as he instructs, anxious to continue what I started in the bathroom.

He sets the weight on the counter above my head and puts the handcuffs on my wrists one at a time. He slides one hand under the dumbbell and the other over, connecting the two together on the opposite side. If I want my hands free, I'll have to lift that heavy weight. I certainly won't be able to do that from this position.

Next, he puts the blindfold on me. Now all I can do is listen to what he's doing. Not being able to see his next move always leaves me a bit skittish, flinching with each of his random touches. I hear the fridge open and close and then hear a plastic bag rustling. What is he doing, having a snack?

I feel the chill from the lubricant, as he dribbles it over my clitoris, and it leaks down between my spread lips. It's cool but seems to heat up the longer it's on me. Oh no! Panic!

"Did you dump hot sauce on my pussy?" I shriek.

He chuckles, "Of course not."

"What the fuck?" I huff. "It's… it's hot!"

"No, it's warm. Calm down," he instructs in an overly calm voice. "What do you feel?"

"Oh… it's, it's tingling," I reply.

"Just enjoy the sensations."

Okay, wow! This is feeling magnificent all of a sudden – warm, tingling, arousing to no end. I think my clit is stiffening by the second.

Something extremely cold presses into me and I cry out. "What the fuck!"

I can't resist, nor escape its frigidity as it slips deeper and deeper into me. Whatever it is, it isn't large, but it isn't tiny either. Is it ever fucking cold! I'm panting and trying to pull my ankles free of the cuffs. My arms pull at the weight, trying to lift it off the counter.

"Hush!" he insists. "Enjoy the sensations."

"You said that already. Whatever you put inside me is ice cold," I complain.

His lips press to mine just as something pinches my left nipple. I gasp, trying to concentrate on his mouth and not anything else. His lips leave mine just as my right nipple receives the exact same pinch. Neither is letting up. It hurts but it's not game ending. He pulls them both simultaneously. The pain shoots down to my tingling clitoris and it's fucking breathtaking.

Whatever he slid inside of me is starting to warm up but it's taking a while to do so.

Something cool strokes and pulls at my clitoris and it's glorious. Wait, it's his fingers but why do they feel so cold? A clamp pinches onto my swelling button and pulls the hood up. It hurts but the urgent need for human contact has me whimpering and tilting my hips up toward the clamp, hoping to find a finger. Suddenly, my nipples are being pulled down toward my clit. He must have the three connected somehow.

Oh, fuck! I want him to lick my clitoris. I'm sure I'll cum almost immediately if he does.

Another cold hard object is slid into my pussy alongside the warmed one. What are they? Yet another is introduced, filling me as much as his cock does, but it isn't a cock, it's harder and colder.

My left outer labia is pinched once, and then again, and yet again. Neither pinch is letting up. Almost immediately, that punishment is subjected to my right outer labia. I'm afraid to move because the slightest flinch is painful. I have to give into it, let it have me.

Each clamp is tugged one by one, causing me to grunt when the pain of it shifting feels like it's digging into my skin, like a needle dragging on me.

Another hard, cold thing is pushed into me, spreading my pussy walls. A moan escapes me slowly as just one more icy object is slowly slid between the others, stretching my opening to its maximum.

Slim leather tassels gently slap my tummy, startling me from my trancelike state. He's going to do this now? Am I not hurting enough? The tassels come down on my thigh with a mediocre crack. The sting is pleasurable, not at all painful. I am starting to enjoy the flogger. When he first started using it on me, I didn't much prefer it, but wow, how that has changed.

He slaps at my thighs until I'm sure they're puffy and pink with small welts left in the wake from the leather tips. When his fingertips caress my hypersensitive skin, my clit twitches, alerting me to the pain the clamp is causing. A cry escapes me in a huff, which causes my breasts to jiggle and the clamps on my nipples to pull, tugging at my clitoris even more. I nearly cum.

He slides another cold thing into me, and I can't stop moaning, loving and hating everything he's doing to me. How defenseless I feel.

Sheer pain on my clit has my head jolting off the countertop, desperately pointing my blindfolded eyes at the source. From past experience, I know the cause is from removing the clamp, allowing the blood to freely flow. It won't last longer than a few seconds. A wail rips from my throat, shrieking the instant his scalding hot mouth presses onto my unbearably painful clit. He immediately sucks and rubs at the hypersensitive, swollen nub. I fucking love this, and hate this!

His mouth pulls and sucks me, driving me to scream through every breath. I can't stop screaming. It feels so fucking good and so fucking bad. My nipples are pulled by the clamps and I'm starting to lose my mind.

My pussy is filled with yet another cold object, stretched open further than I thought possible. I'm lost in the sensations in my body, not able to even moan anymore. All I can do is breathe and let myself fall into the absence of conscious thought; to let go of the earth's gravity and allow myself to float up to the stars.

I cannot feel pain anymore. Everything feels good. Each wiggle of my labia clamps shoots tender waves of pleasure directly at my clitoris He's playing my body like each key on a piano elicits a different sound with each stoke. My essence isn't here anymore. I don't know where I am, and I don't care if I ever return. I am lost. Lost within my body.

My pussy is stretched further, and I love it. Each piano key is pulling away, leaving a very sharp note in its wake. I'm drifting far, far away. I can feel my chest swelling with each breath and my back lifting off the countertop. I can't feel my skin, even though I feel like I'm on fire. It's a strange sensation that I welcome.

I hear someone moaning and I know it's me, but those are not sounds I have ever made. They are foreign and distant, as if from someone next door.

Slowly my mind is becoming clear and my soul is slipping back into my body. Light is easing into my right eye, alerting me to the brightness of earth. Soon it is very bright, too bright. My mask has slid off my one eye. I open that eye and recognize the ceiling light in my kitchen. Then I see Coach's shoulder bobbing up and down. He's fucking me, hard.

He's on top of me, his arms up along mine, his hands are firmly gripping my forearms near to my wrists. His body slams into mine, drilling his cock deep into me with a heavy thud. My vagina tenses as if it has a mind of its own, pulling me into another teeth clenching orgasm.

Coach growls so loud and deep beside my ear that I fear I may never hear right again. His body stiffens, jerking and flinching above me as his breath catches in his throat. His weight increases as if he's quickly deflating. Before it becomes unbearable, he lifts himself on to his elbows.

His heavily lidded eyes meet mine, but he doesn't smile. It's as if he's too tired, which is good because I doubt I could return the gesture, just yet. My body feels numb, tingly, full of life, but utterly exhausted.

Slowly, Coach slides down my spent body until he's standing on the floor. He does his best to quickly untie my ankles and unshackle my wrists. He lifts me, carrying me down the hallway, through the bedroom and into the bathroom. He sets me down on the edge of the tub and pulls the drain. Once the water has disappeared, he plugs the drain and turns on the faucet, filling the tub with hotter water.

He helps me slip in and then adds some lavender essential oil and some Epsom's salts. He kisses my lips and then sinks to his knees on the floor beside the tub, resting his head against his arm that lies on the edge.

"I love you, Rayna. I've never loved anyone as much as I love you. You have me, all of me, at your mercy. Please don't hurt me." I watch his expression turn to one of agony and see his eyes gloss over with wetness.

"Please don't hurt me. I can't take being hurt twice in my lifetime. But you, you could crush me worse than Rick ever could. I thought I'd never recover from him. I love you so very much."

He nods, sniffs and then clears his throat. "I want to take you somewhere tomorrow..." his voice fades away.

"I know, you already told me that. Renee and Tim are going to watch the kids," I remind him.

"Yes, but I didn't tell you where we are going. I want you to promise me that if it's too much for you, that you'll tell me, immediately. You won't crush me if you're too uncomfortable to stay. I just want you to promise that you'll give it a chance. I don't want you to judge too quickly. Can you promise me that?"

"Now you have me curious. I promise not to judge too harshly, too quickly. I'll stay as long as I can tolerate." I frown and add, "This would be a lot easier to promise if I knew what I was promising to."

He smiles and nods, raising his eyebrows. "Just tell me that you won't jump to a quick judgement. That's all I ask."

"Okay, I can promise that," I smile back while still squinting my eyes as if that will help me read his thoughts.

"All right then. You stay here and soak, you've earned it, and I will clean up the kitchen." He turns on his heels and starts out the door.

"Wait!" I shout. He pokes his head back in. "What were you putting inside of me? The cold things?"

He snickers and says, "Carrots," before retreating out the door.

"Throw them out!" I call out after him. I can feel the embarrassment flushing my cheeks to a hot pink. I wasn't freaked out at the time, in fact, I quite enjoyed the carrots. I'll never look at one the same way again.

Chapter Five

Rayna

Dinner is going really well. The meal is delicious, nothing burned or not cooked enough. Renee and Tim are laughing along with the kids as they talk about something silly that happened at school, this week. I've already heard the stories, but they seem to be slightly embellished on the repeat. That's okay, it adds to the humour.

My wrists and forearms are still a bit red from the cuffs and Coach's vicelike grip, so I decided to hide it with a long-sleeved blouse. I instinctively rub my wrist and then look up at Coach. His eyes meet mine then drop to my wrist. He frowns as he chews. He doesn't like it when he bruises me. His face suddenly lights up with a quirky grin.

"I almost forgot," he announces, standing up to retrieve something from the refrigerator. He returns to the table, setting a glass filled with chopped carrot sticks in front of Tim. "I almost forgot the carrots. Everyone likes carrots, right Rayna?"

He wouldn't! I stare at his face, trying to assess his expression to see if he is being a jerk and teasing me or if those carrots are the actual ones he fucked me with. I cannot read him.

"Go ahead, Tim. You'll like these carrots. I made them special, sort of marinated them." I watch Tim choose one and take a bite. My eyes couldn't get any wider. It takes everything I have to restrain myself and rip them off the table and toss them into the garbage, causing a scene.

Tim stops chewing and looks up at Coach, who is grinning like a fool. He says, "Hmm, yes, they do have a familiar flavour to them, but I just can't quite pin it down."

He hands it to Renee who rams the rest of his piece in her mouth and begins chewing. My arms feel like they're going numb. I can't even speak.

She says, "Yeah, what is that? It is familiar but..." She continues chewing, sampling the taste.

Tim adds, "Do you enjoy carrots, Rayna?" His face is very pointed. He knows what those carrots were used for. I have no doubt. "These carrots are coated in something delicious. Did you make the special coating yourself, Rayna?"

My words fail me. I want to scream at Coach but before I can, Renee very calmly says, "It's just a sweet glaze." She looks at me and says, "Corn syrup, maybe. It's nothing special. They aren't even that good."

I watch her shrug just as the guys crack up laughing. Renee and both kids are looking around the table, wondering what the hell is so fricking funny. I swallow hard, but I'm not laughing, just relieved.

Renee looks at me with a wide smile, oblivious to the joke. She asks, "Why are they laughing?" I simply shrug because I still can't form any words. I'm sure my face is red, proving my embarrassment. A look of horror swoons her expression. She adds, "Eww! Gross! Are you kidding me?"

Coach looks at her and says, "They're carrots I cut up from the bag, honestly!"

I take a deep breath and let it out slowly, glaring at him with eyes that just might melt that expression off his face. He shakes his head to assure me he was only joking. I look at the garbage and see a bunch of carrots tossed away. I simply shake my head.

Renee starts smiling and is soon joining in on the humour of the joke. The kids are looking from one person to the next asking us what's so funny. What am I supposed to tell them? It's not a joke I want to explain, and he will never tell them.

He says, "It's a joke from a long time ago. I dipped some carrots in dog food and fed it to Tim as a joke. Not these carrots though. I just thought I'd refresh the joke in his memory."

The kids are smiling to be polite and accepting the explanation, but not understanding why the others think dog food coated carrots are this hilarious. They shrug and go right back to eating.

Coach is going to pay for this later.

"So, you had a good afternoon, I gather?" Renee whispers.

I smile, feeling my face flush with heat once again. "Coach... he, he... um..."

"Yeah, I know what he *um*. I'm so happy that you're finally having a great sex life. It took a much younger, wilder man to get you to let your hair down. It's about damn time!"

"And, what about you?" I ask her while glancing at the kids to ensure they aren't trying to hone into our conversation.

"Things are great between us. He's a bit of a sexual freak, which is awesome. I wish he'd stop holding back though. There was this one time when he took it too far and I got scared. He was a bit rough with me. He was being very assertive and ordering me to do stuff, calling me a slut, or whatever. He even spanked me, over his knee like a naughty child! I couldn't stop laughing at him. I mean, I was a little high at the time, so it probably wasn't the best time to puff out his chest, if you know what I mean. I told him I didn't want to play rough and ever since that he's being very reserved, like he's afraid to get even the slightest bit wild. I mean, our life outside of the bedroom is absolutely incredible, but our sexual fire has been fizzling out. When we are intimate, he's so tender, but it's like he's acting and not really getting too into it. We used to get freaky, not anymore."

"Have you tried talking to him about it?"

"Yes, but he just tells me he loves me and doesn't want to push me into something I'm not ready for. He avoids that conversation, if he can."

"Maybe you should try again. Corner him. Take him out for dinner, somewhere he can't just get up and walk out without making a scene and casually lead the conversation in that direction."

She grins and whispers, "You just gave me an idea. I can't let him get away. I know exactly what to do and it isn't have dinner with him." I question her by frowning, and she just winks. She must have something naughty planned. "I'll tell you after I do it."

"So, where is Coach taking you tomorrow night?"

I shrug. "I have no idea. He won't tell me."

"Sounds questionable to me." Her eyes light up. "What if he's going to propose to you?"

My stomach drops out, and I suddenly feel very lightheaded and parched. I gulp a mouthful of wine while glancing over at Coach, who's listening to Tim. His eyes shift, catching my stare. We look at one another for several seconds. He smiles at me and then turns his attention back to Tim.

I look at Renee and reply, "No, that's definitely not it. I don't know what he's up to, but it isn't a romantic night out."

"Hmm, I'll dig a little deeper with Tim. I'm sure he must know something. Those two are like peas in a pod."

"I would appreciate a heads-up. He isn't telling me much," I admit.

"Does he usually?" she asks.

"Yes, always," I reply.

"So, to change the subject, how is work going?" she asks.

I roll my eyes, unsure of whether I should get into the topic or not. "I am supposed to go on my yearly convention with Dr. Jessik, but I don't know if I'm going to go this year. That's not true, I am going. I'm just not sure how I'm going to tell Coach about it. You know damn well he's not going to like it. So, I've been putting off the awkward conversation."

"It's been a year already? It feels like you just went." She takes a deep breath and lets it out slowly. "You are going to have to tell

him soon. When do you leave?"

"Well, I'm supposed to leave in a week."

"So, when did you think you were going to tell him? You are running out of time, sweetheart!"

She's right, I am running out of time. I'm an adult, for Christ's sake! I need to tell him. This is my job, my career! I go every year, so it's not as if I can just tell my boss that I'm not going to go because I have a jealous, control-freak as a boyfriend.

This is my life, my livelihood. I have worked for years to get to this point in my career where my boss might actually consider sending me back to school to further my education. If he thinks I am no longer taking my job seriously because there is a man in my life, he certainly will not give me the opportunities I have worked so hard for. My dream is to become a dentist and own my own practice one day.

"I will tell him, Renée. I'm just worried he will not accept the fact that I am going to Las Vegas with my boss, even if it is a work convention. What if he insists on coming with me? What do I do then? Do I tell him that he cannot come? I don't think that would go over well with him. It's not as if he doesn't trust me, it's just that his trust has never been tested by me."

"You had better bring it up soon or he's going to think something is planned with you and your boss, if you know what I mean." "Yes, I will. One day at a time. First, I need to find out where he's taking me tomorrow night and why he feels the need to be so secretive about it."

Renée nods her head, turning it to look at Coach. He and Tim are deep in a conversation, leaning in toward one another to speak in hushed tones.

I say, "Ken, if you're finished, please put your plate in the sink. You've got homework to finish, so please go get to it." He nods, picking up his plate and silverware.

"I'm finished to!" Kim says rather loudly. "Can I be excused?" I nod, much to her delight. She didn't eat much, rarely does. I usually make her eat more, but I'm not in the mood for that battle tonight.

Both kids scurry down the hallway and into their rooms, leaving us adults sitting at the table. The guys have stopped talking and are looking at us.

Coach asks, "So ladies, what's next?"

Renee replies, "Why don't we play a game of cards? That will keep us entertained. Maybe we could get into a game of truth or dare," she says, emphasizing the word truth. She looks at me raising and lowering her eyebrows several times.

Both Tim and Coach are frowning, questioning why Renee is acting so strangely. They look at each other and then at me, as if I'm going to confess.

"We can play a game of cards. What do you like to play, Tim?" I ask.

"I don't know," he replies. "I honestly don't remember any. I used to play Euchre when I was a teenager. I remember something about Trump, but not any of the rules."

Renee and I chuckle because we grew up playing cards with our parents. Every Friday night was game night with family and my parent's friends. Each week, a different house would host. It was fun, but once we became teenagers, we preferred to hang out with our friends. We pouted so much, they eventually begged us not to come. I regret it now. Some of those family members have passed away and the others are simply too old or too busy to continue the tradition. I think it died out with their generation. It's sad.

Coach confesses, "I haven't played a game of cards since I was about ten years old. I have never played Euchre and have no interest in learning it tonight. Why don't we retire to the backyard and have a fire?"

"Sounds great!" I reply. Coach and I cleared the table and stacked the dishes in the sink. After Renee and Tim head outside, Coach stops me from taking more things off the table. "Hey, what's going on?" he asks "What do you mean?" I play naïve.

"You were looking at me strangely and I'm just wondering why?"

"What's up?" I ask.

"Rayna, don't be like this. Tell me what's going on."

"Why don't we talk about it, later. Now is not the time, we have guests."

"They aren't guests. Tim is my best friend and Renee is your sister. They do not qualify as being guests. So, what's up?"

"Renée and I were just talking about sex. Her and I are having a bit of an issue and we were trying to work through it. When I looked up at you, you looked back at me. It was a coincidence, plain and simple." I smile, trying to be as convincing as possible. I don't want to discuss my work thing right now. "Why don't we head outside?"

Coach looks at me with squinted eyes, as if to assess whether or not I am being completely honest with him or if I'm holding something back. He leans in and kisses my lips with the utmost tenderness. I love him so much. I wonder why it took me so damn long to let him know how much I wanted him. He lived next door to me for three years while I dreamt about having his body. I could have been having him this whole time.

We spend the night chatting with Tim and Renée over the campfire, and we have a few drinks. We have a great time, likely better than we would have had we decided to play cards. I really like Tim and I think he is perfect for my sister. I just wish they could figure out what each other needs from their sex life and come to a compromise.

Renée has always been a wild child. She will be the first one to tell you that she is not strictly heterosexual. She enjoys penis as much as she does vagina. She loves the tenderness of the female personality, as much as she loves the masculinity of the male persona. With Tim, she cannot get much more masculine than him. He is tall, a bodybuilder and tough as nails, but he has tenderness and emotional softness that you wouldn't think a man with his rugged appearance would have. He looks mean all the time, even if he's smiling. He just has that face. Tim is a deep thinker with a tender heart. Renée can and does benefit greatly, by having this man in her life.

Coach and Tim have been best friends for many years. Coach set Renée up with Tim when I begged him to find her a man, as rough and dominant as he is. She was coming out of a relationship and finally realizing that she needed somebody who was going to be her life-mate, instead of just somebody she was spending time with and enjoying for the moment.

At the time, Coach and I were barely a couple. We had had sex once, but I didn't know that I wanted more than just sex from him. At the time, I also did not know that he wanted more than just physical relationship with me.

"Well, what do you think, Renée?" Tim asks after finishing the last gulp of whiskey from his glass. "I think it's time we take our leave."

"I agree," she says. "Rayna, I love you, woman! I am going to drive this big galoot home and tuck his ass into bed. I think he has had way too much to drink." She looks at Tim.

Tim stands up, wobbling slightly. "I am perfectly fine, thank you. There is nothing wrong with me, other than having a bit too much to drink. But, little woman," he points his finger at her, "you are still getting the fucking of a lifetime, when I get you naked."

I start laughing but she does not look all too impressed. "You know damn well your cock is not going to work, tonight. By the time I get you home and you take off your clothes, if you even make it to the bedroom, you will be passed out long before I get in beside you. Sex, my dear, is going to have to wait until tomorrow. I doubt you will feel much like having sex until at least tomorrow night. You are going to have one hell of a hangover in the morning."

Tim snickers, "Oh, yeah? You wait, little girl. When we get home, I am going to fuck you raw! I am going to hold your body hostage. I am going to pull your hair and spank your ass, until it is hot and you're screaming for me to stop. You are going to call me Master tonight. What do you think about that, Woman?"

The look on her face is disbelief. "So, now that you are drunk, you actually want to have crazy sex with me. How come when you're sober, you only want to make love to me?"

He looks at her and then at Coach. When his eyes return back to Renée, he smiles at her as if to announce that she is everything to him. "Lady, do you have any idea how much I love you?"

"Yes baby, I do. Can we talk about this in private, please?"

"I don't want to hurt you," he says. "You did not like it when I dominated you. I was afraid if I did it again, you would leave me."

"I am not going anywhere," she says, "I am so madly in love with you that I think I would die before I could ever walk away."

Tim launches for her, grabbing her around the waist and scooping her up in his arms, as he spins her around, kissing her lips, passionately. I look over at Coach and he is just watching them with a crooked smile. I wrap my arm around his and hold his hand, that's when he turns his attention to me while still carrying the same expression.

"I love him!"

"I know," I reply. "I love her."

"I know that too."

After Tim and Renée leave, Coach and I quickly clean the kitchen before looking in on the kids. They are both passed out, much to our happiness. It has been a long week and I want nothing more than to spend the rest of the evening with my man trying to figure out where he's planning on taking me tomorrow and why he is keeping it such a closely guarded secret.

Chapter Six

Coach

I know Rayna is going to harass me for information on where I plan on taking her tomorrow night. The best thing I can do is to keep her otherwise occupied, so she won't be able to ask me anything. I really enjoy the build-up, the suspense and the anxiety she gets from not knowing something. She's told me she doesn't like it, but I'm sure she does, in some small way.

As she walks into the bedroom, I grab her by her shoulders and spin her around, pressing my lips to hers, while weaving my fingers into her hair, holding her face to mine. My tongue works its way between her hot lips. I want to taste her. I've wanted to taste her all night. Rayna responds by wrapping her arms around my back, holding herself against me.

I wrap my arms around her and pull her into me as tightly as I can, without hurting her. Half carrying and half walking her to the bed. I kneel on it, carrying her along with me, as I slide her to the middle of the bed. My lips never leave hers. My tongue explores the depths of her mouth and the lingering sweetness from the last gulp of wine she swallowed only moments ago.

My hands work her shirt, pulling it up and lifting her bra, allowing her breasts to fall from below it. Goddamn, their warmth and softness in the palms of my hands. I adore the contrast between the creaminess of her warm skin and the stiffness of her nipples. Fuck, this woman is beautiful!

I kiss down her neck in between her breasts, pushing them against my cheeks, burying my face between them.

Tiny kisses are placed under her breasts, between them and on her nipples. Rayna weaves her fingers in my hair, holding my head, but not guiding me.

I pop the button on her jeans and slowly lower her zipper, kissing the tender hot skin beneath the denim as it's being exposed to the chill in the air. I pull her pants down over her hips and slide them off her legs, dropping them in a heap on the floor. She spreads her legs, urging me to bury my face between her thick thighs.

I hover my nose over her hotness, feeling the radiating heat on my skin and inhaling her seductive scent. My cock instantly stiffens. The tip of my tongue tenderly strokes between her folds, feeling they're smoothness and sampling her delicious tanginess.

Rayna's gentle moans add to my fire. I want to take her selfishly, but I don't deserve to, not yet. She is my queen and she has earned my restraint. I will not have my release until she is fully satiated.

I watch as her chest rises and falls quickly, anticipating the suction I am about to put upon her clitoris. I place my lips over her pussy and suck, dragging my tongue up and down her slit, hesitating just below her clitoris, not allowing her the pleasure. Rayna shifts her hips, desperate to redirect my attention. Not yet my love.

I wait until she's begging in faint whispers. "Please, please."

That is all I needed to hear. I shift my lips, closing them around her clitoris, sucking it between them and nibbling gently with my teeth. I let my tongue flick wildly, assaulting her stiffening pleasure nub. Rayna's hips lift to meet my mouth. Her legs squeeze my shoulders, trying to hold me to her, so I can't escape.

I slide two fingers inside her wanting pussy, resting my palm against my chin as my fingers wave, pounding against her G spot. She's so aroused, so wet! Her scent fills my nostrils, igniting a primal lust burning deep within me. Tonight however, I will not be rough. I will make love to Rayna. Tomorrow will present many new options for the rough play I yearn for.

She will see things that some would consider to be taboo, perhaps even vile. Maybe Rayna will see something that sparks her interest. She might not be ready just yet, but perhaps in the near future she will. If I continue to slowly introduce her to wilder and more intense pleasures, she will likely be more accepting of the play I seek. Tomorrow, I will enlighten her to the lifestyle that calms me and allows me to feel truly free.

Rayna is moaning, running her fingers through my hair and squeezing me with her legs. She's going to cum soon. I want her to erupt on my face, only then will I fuck her. I will be gentle and loving the way she seems to need me to be tonight. She always sets the mood to our romantic endeavors. How we play is up to her, not me, never me. If she wants to play rough, I am more than happy to oblige her and dominate her the way we both seek. We don't play hard, at least, not what I would consider to be hard.

Her body jerks and spasms, cries of passion hanging in the air, bringing sweet sounds to my ears. She exhales heavily, that's when I know she's finished. I don't even think she realizes how much I adore that. I slide up her body kissing her tender skin, loving how her chest rapidly rises and falls, lifting up, as if craving that touch. My lips find hers and adhere, lovingly kissing my Rayna.

I slide myself into her, burying my prick deep within her spasming pussy. She feels so good.

She cradles more than just my body. I have signed away my heart to her, much like selling my soul to her, in hopes she will not cast it aside. This woman owns me, completely. I will show her how much I love her with my body. If I could only stay in this woman, we would be together forever as one entity, existing for the sole purpose of keeping the other alive, for one without the other will cease to exist.

Her legs wrap around my ass, holding me deep inside her. Her arms stretch down my body and her hands pull at my lower back. Her eyes are closed, keeping her focus on the hurricane building within her, readying itself to explode, shredding her beneath me and ripping open her heart, so I can make love to that too. She taught me how to love, how to adore someone so much that you willingly give them every bit of you and trust them to keep you safe.

Even though her eyes are gazing into mine, she's not looking at me. She's looking at my soul, adoring my deepest core, and I welcome her in. This woman could crush me and take away my will to live, should she so choose.

My inner Demon is pacing while shaking his head, hating every moment of this. Deep down, where the Demon is imprisoned, I hold a shred of doubt. My mind will not allow her everything, not until she knows my truth. All of my truth.

Her lids weigh heavily over her eyes, slowly forcing them closed. Her head rolls to the side, her mouth opening wide, no words escape her. I watch her as long as I can, feeling the tight hold her entire body has on me. Goddamn I love this woman!

I can't do it anymore. I can't hold off. I'm exploding.

As my body twitches over her and my mind comes back into focus, I look down at her beautiful face, admiring her flushed cheeks

and puffy lips. Her hair is strewn about the pillow. Fuck me! She's sexy as hell.

I roll to my side and she curls up behind me. We fall asleep, her body pressed against mine, her chest against my back, her arm resting around my chest. Her forehead remains pressed against the nape of my neck. I can feel her breath heating my spine and I can't imagine anything being more perfect than this moment.

She did not ask me about tomorrow, but I didn't give her the chance either. I'm sure she'll be testing my ability to keep my plans to myself, but I will stay strong and not give in to her adorable ways, no matter how much she begs.

Chapter Seven

Rayna

The kids spent most of the day watching television and playing on their computers. Coach went to the gym because he had some client sessions scheduled. I have spent most of the day doing laundry, sweeping floors, dusting and repeatedly grimacing, while staring into my closet. I don't know what to wear tonight. Do I wear something very sexy like my red dress with the slit riding high up my left thigh? Do I wear something conservative like my pencil skirt, white blouse and blazer? Should I wear a sundress, casual, but still presentable and respectable?

"Gah!" I'm getting frustrated because he won't tell me anything about where we are going. How do I dress for the unknown? Why all the mystery? Is he afraid that if he tells me, I might decide not to go? Does he think I don't trust his judgment? I know he would never take me to a place that would cause me harm or somewhere I would absolutely hate to be.

"Fuck! I really wish you would just tell me, so I can plan my damn outfit! I hate not knowing." He's not home, so yelling at him is pointless, but it makes me feel a tinge better, nonetheless.

I take my phone out of my back pocket and sit on the floor just inside the closet. The season is changing, so my summer clothes are mixed in with my fall and winter clothing. I really need to organize this.

I dial Coach's cell phone and listen to it ring, wondering what I'm going to say to him that I haven't already said. Begging didn't help, it only made his dick harden. It clicks, but it's his voicemail instructing me to leave a message. As soon as it beeps, I simply say, "Would you just tell me what I am supposed to wear tonight!"

I hang up the phone and shake my head, wondering if I should just take a few outfits out and spread them on the bed, telling him to choose which one is proper for the occasion.

My phone rings almost immediately. I bet that's him. More angrily than I intended it to sound, I drill him, "Hi, did you get my message? I have been sitting here all day trying to figure out what the fuck you want me to wear tonight. Why the hell won't you tell me where we're going? Is it someplace I'm not going to want to be? Is it that bad?"

"Love, I would like you to wear something sexy, but you don't have to. You may dress in simply a skirt and bra, if you so choose. Anything goes at this place. I'm taking you to a place you have never been and probably didn't even know existed. Where we're going, you will not be judged by your appearance."

He sounds winded as if he was working out and stopped when I called. Maybe he ran to his phone. I'm not sure why he would, he can always call me back. Is he waiting for somebody else to call him? Why would he? Maybe it has something to do with tonight.

"Why won't you just tell me where we're going? I'm having so much anxiety that my belly is starting to hurt. I don't want to have intestinal issues, if you know what I mean."

"Rayna, okay, I will tell you where you're going when I get home. I should be done here in about an hour and a half. Can you wait that long?"

"And what if I say that I can't? Are you going to come home just so you can tell me? If you do, I promise to be very good to you," I say with a very sexy voice.

"I can't come home right now, love, I have a client coming in twenty minutes. I can't skip out on her."

"What if I were to come to you? I know you have a client and I wouldn't dream of interrupting your session. I could just come and watch you. I do love watching you sweat and grunt through the heavy workouts."

He chuckles and replies, "I'm not the one who's going to be working out. You are always welcome, you know that. I love having you here with me. If I could put you in my pocket and take you everywhere, just to keep you safe and be able to touch you whenever I want, that would be a dream come true. However, that is only in the world of make-believe."

"Well, maybe I'll come, just to see you. I'm only driving myself crazy here anyway."

"You should come then. I can introduce you to Loreen. I've been working with her for a long time and I'm sure she would love to meet you. She is the one that told me to go after my heart. I suppose you should thank her for that, if you are happy having me in your life, that is." he chuckles again.

"Okay, I will see you shortly," I say, hanging up the phone. I take another quick look at my closet and shake my head, deciding to leave the anxiety of choosing my outfit for later today.

"Hey kids!" I yell as I walk from my room and down the stairs towards the basement. Both of my kids are curled up watching TV, with their computers on their laps. Both turn their heads to look at me.

"Ken, are you willing to watch your sister for a while? I will only be gone for about an hour, if that. I'm just going to go to the gym, to see Coach. He has a client he wants to introduce me to." "I don't mind," he says while shrugging his shoulders.

"Kim, mind your brother," I insist. She rolls her eyes and shakes her head.

It's only a five-minute drive to Coach's gym. I feel awkward coming here because I'm not a member, not that I'd ever want to sign up. Working out at the gym just seems like unnecessary torture. He doesn't ever push me to join, not that I would need to officially join. He does own the place and I could come workout anytime I want. The only physical exertion I hope to be having on a daily basis, is sex, with Coach. That is a workout in itself.

I walk down the main path, trying not to stare at the muscular men, nor the super-sexy, fit women in their spandex pants and crop tops. My arms instinctively cross in front of me, trying to hide my aging physique. I'm not in denial. I really don't compare to these hot young things. Why is Coach with me and not these women? They could run circles around me, literally!

I see him on the lower level, watching a woman work her thigh muscles on one of the machines. She's sweating and puffing her cheeks when she exhales. Yeah, that seems like way too much work to me.

His back is to me, as I approach. The woman lifts her eyes, noticing me as I near. She nods at Coach, letting him know I'm behind him. He spins around and wraps his muscular arm around me, pulling me in for a soft kiss on my forehead.

"Hi love," he whispers.

"Hello to you," I reply. "You're busy, I can wait in your office." "No, no!" he quickly replies, pulling me over to meet the woman on the machine. She stands to greet me with her hand extended. "Loreen, this is my lovely Rayna."

"I'd hug you but I'm sweaty and gross. It is wonderful to meet you." She smiles as if she's proud of me for some reason. "He talks about you all the time. You must be one hell of a woman to have snagged this handsome hunk of meat. Many have tried, all have failed, except for you."

"Oh," I mutter, not sure of how to respond to that. "He is pretty great."

She looks him up and down with a smug look on her face. "He's a nice guy, but he's one hell of a tough-ass. He kicks my butt into gear three times a week. If he wasn't here to push me, I'd likely be sitting at home on the couch, eating chips and watching animal themed tv shows."

"Don't let her fool you, she's the tough-ass. This woman has six kids and still looks this hot. Can you believe it? Look at that ass!"

This is getting awkward. She turns around to show me her ass. Damn! It's round and firm, not the ass of an aging woman who birthed six kids. I've only had two and don't look that good and likely never will.

"You look fantastic! Six kids, huh?" I'm shaking my head in disbelief.

"Yeah, Coach has been whipping me into shape and I couldn't be more grateful to him. But you missy, you are absolutely gorgeous! He told me you were a stunner, but that didn't do you any justice."

"Thank you so much." I turn to Coach and ask, "So, you talk about me to your clients, do you?"

"Not all of them, just Loreen. She's the one who convinced me that I should grow up and stop being so damn afraid of having a relationship. And no, I didn't start the conversation. Loreen read me like an open book. She's very intuitive."

"I am. It's a curse sometimes. Like right now, you two need to talk about something important. Go on now, I'm fine on my own," she says, shooing us away from her.

"Did I mention how pushy the woman is?" Coach says, sure to speak loud enough for her to hear as we walk away. She simply laughs before sitting back on the machine to continue her leg workout.

"So, you want to ask me something?" he asks while opening the office door and escorting me inside.

I sit on the chair in front of his desk, while he takes a seat behind it. "You know what I want to know."

He takes a deep breath and lets it out slowly, looking somewhat disappointed that he has to reveal his well-planned secret outing.

"Okay, I'll tell you, but I don't want you to pass judgement and refuse to go. I'll explain the place as best I can. When you see if for yourself, it won't seem as bad as what your mind is going to build it up to be. But, then again, it might. It's been a while since I've gone." "Just tell me," I beg.

He takes a deep breath, looking unsure of how to start. "I'm taking you to an underground place that isn't listed in any directory. It's not somewhere just anyone can get into, you need to be a member or a member's guest."

"Are we guests or members?"

"I am a member, or at least, I was." He's assessing my face for a reaction but my expression hasn't changed. "It's been a few years since I've been. The owner and his submissive are very close friends of mine."

"Where are we going?"

"They call it Fallen, shortened from Fallen Angel. It's a place where like-minded people can get together, find partners, experience new things or just voyeur others as they do what comes natural to them - BDSM."

"So, it's like a bar?" I ask.

"Um, no, not exactly. There's never alcohol served. I'm not sure how to explain it. You'll just have to see it to understand."

"Will people be having sex?"

"Some, yes. Most won't be. There will be Masters with their submissives. Some will be bound, some won't. You'll likely see someone on an iron cross getting worked over. People will be doing whatever makes them happy. It's a place where just about anything goes, safety being the only concern."

I sit back in the chair and put my hand up to my mouth while I process the images of people getting whipped and beaten, fucking and being treated worse than a dog. I can't go in a place like that. What if I'm horrified and start crying?

"Please don't pass judgement until you've been there and talked to some of the people."

I'm terrified! "Talk to them?"

"Yes," he replies. "My friends want to meet you and show you around. Nobody will do anything to you that you don't ask them to. I want you to ask questions and so do they. They're very nice, I promise you."

"You talked to them about me?" I ask. He nods. "Do they know I'm not experienced with this?"

"Yes, and they know I've been slowly introducing you to this lifestyle."

"But, I'm not a submissive, at least, not in the traditional sense. By your own admission, your friend's woman is. How can I relate to her? I will never be a real submissive to you. In the bedroom is one thing but 24/7 is something else. Is she his constant slave?"

"She doesn't like being titled as a slave. She has submitted herself to him almost completely. When they visit her family, they act like a regular couple. They would never understand that it's her choice and that he didn't talk her into it. She came to the club with another couple as his secondary submissive. He made a deal with the other Master to borrow her for a weekend. She never went back to the other man. He treats her very well, you'll see."

"Are there any men submissives at this club or only women?"

"Both genders submit, but female submissives are more common." He stops talking long enough to assess my face. Fearing he may be losing me, he begs, "Please, just come with me and talk to people. Look around and see if something sparks an interest. If you hate it, I'll cancel my membership and we never go back."

"Okay, I'll give it a chance. To be completely honest, I think I'm more curious than afraid. You won't leave me alone, right?"

"Of course not. If you want to separate from me so you and Glitter can go to the ladies' room or wherever, just let me know that you're okay."

"Glitter? That's her name?" I cannot see myself spending time with someone called Glitter. "Isn't that a stripper's name."

"Gear started calling her Glitter because he said her personality shines like glitter. It stuck. She really is a lovely person. I think you'll like her. You two are both strong-minded women."

"Strong-minded? She's a submissive. They aren't strongminded," I snicker.

"It takes a very strong person to go through the things they do and still come back for more. Submissives are not weak people."

"I suppose I don't know enough about it to pass a fair judgement. All right, I'll go. I'm interested in learning more, talking to people and seeing what they do."

"I'm so pleased," he says, standing up and walking around the desk. He crouches down, taking my hands in his and kissing each of them. "I was afraid you'd refuse to go if you knew where I planned to take you."

"Now who's passing judgement?" I accuse with a smirk. I look down at the floor and shake my head, doing my best to seem distraught. "There's only one huge issue."

He frowns, his eyebrows nearly meeting in the middle. "It's okay, we can figure it out, whatever it is. Just tell me."

I tease, throwing my arms up, "What the fuck do I wear to a BDSM club?"

Coach's concern melts from his face, replaced by laughing eyes and a smile filled with gleaming white teeth. "How about that sexy red dress you have hanging in your closet? You'll look irresistible in that!"

"Are you sure it's enough? I mean, people are probably dressed in leather outfits. Am I wrong? I don't want to stick out and be seen as fresh meat."

He chuckles, "Love, you will be safe and admired. You'll fit in just fine. People wear all different types of clothing. Whatever makes you feel sexy, that's what you wear. You'll see."

"Okay then, I'll meet you at home, soon?" I question.

"Yup, I just have to check in on Loreen and deal with a few small things and I'll be out of here."

He kisses me tenderly, slowly prying his lips from mine. With a mere few inches between us, he whispers, "You are my dream come true. My heart beats for you and only you. You will always be safe with me. I love you."

My lips press to his, kissing him with love and passion, stirring an emptiness within me, an urge to have him fill me and make me feel complete. "Take me!"

Coach quickly wraps his arm around my back, pulling me against his hard body as his mouth works mine and his hand grips my ass, lifting me. My legs wrap around his hips and lock behind him, hanging on like a monkey to its mother.

He spins around setting my ass on the edge of his desk. His fingers work the button of my jeans and then the zipper. Our mouths continue to taste each other. He grabs my shirt and yanks it over my head and then his flies off. We are chest to bra-covered breast. He reaches down, ready to yank off my jeans.

The door flings open, startling us. Just as a rage builds on Coach's face, a sweet voice cuts in. "Hey, everyone is watching the show. Your blinds are open. I can close them if you don't want others to watch this hot scene unfold." Carol starts pulling down the blinds while giggling.

Coach stands up, taking my hand to help me rise up as he's handing me my t-shirt. I'm so embarrassed I want to climb under his desk and never come out. She wasn't lying, people are indeed watching us. I'm so humiliated, my glowing cheeks are proof.

"Thank you, Carol," he says. His face is also flushed a colour I thought I'd never see on his cheeks. Carol walks out, shutting the door behind her. I couldn't even look at her.

"I should go," I say with nervous laughter, while folding my arms over my chest. "Is there a back door I can escape through?"

He chuckles, "There is but you can go out the front. We didn't do anything everyone at this gym hasn't done, we just did it in front of witnesses. It's not a big deal. Half these women are probably jealous, and I know all of the men are. Well, aside from Larry, who's gay. I'm sure he enjoyed it anyway."

"You aren't helping," I comment.

Coach walks me out to my car, kisses me then heads back into the gym. Now for a little me time. A hot bath first, then I'll take an hour to put on my make-up and do my hair, slowly dress, while Coach watches on and then we will go. Somehow, I'll have to figure out a meal plan in there at some point. Maybe he can pick something up on his way home. That'll save me from having to cook anything.

Chapter Eight

Coach

I very much enjoyed watching Rayna put her make-up on and blow-dry her hair. I had to restrain myself from touching her, even though she wore nothing but a thin nightie. Oh, trust me, it was torture. I wanted to take her and fuck her so hard that I'd ruin her make-up and mess her hair, but she would likely have been pissed at me afterward.

First, she slipped on a pair of sheer black, stay-up stockings. Then she slid a lacy thong up her luscious legs, resting where I wanted to put my tongue; right between her ass cheeks. She continued to dress, slipping on a bra to match the black panties. She stayed like that while she put on her earrings, necklace and perfume. She slowly rubbed lotion on her arms, neck and cleavage. She knew she was driving me insane. Hell, she was doing it on purpose.

The moment she slipped her feet into her three-inch spiked heels, I couldn't resist. I rushed to her and spun her around so we could both look at her in the full-sized mirror. I stood behind her, admiring her while she watched me.

My fingers tickled down her waist, around to the front of her, and just under her bra. I grazed the tender skin all the way along the band below her breasts. She wrapped her hands around my wrists and slowly pushed them away from her. My initial thought was to grab her and take her, not giving a shit that I might ruin hair and make-up, but the look in her eyes had me fighting my instinctual urges.

She's been getting rather bossy with me lately. Any other woman would have been face down on the floor by now, my cock ramming deep into her cunt. But I don't want to do that to Rayna. I like that she's finding her sexual strength. She will learn her place. Either that, or she'll break me. I don't honestly know how this will end.

She continued what I was doing with her own fingertips, gradually cupping her lace covered breasts and pushing them together. Her left-hand slipped down her body and beneath her silky panties. I will remain in control of myself for now. She can be in control, but later, she's all mine. I will own that body before me and make her seize from orgasm after body-shredding orgasm, each taking her higher and higher until her mind floats in a dreamlike ecstasy.

Her fingers work beneath the silky fabric. Her eyes remain locked on mine, even when mine can't resist dropping to watch her masturbate herself. My cock was painfully hard beneath my zipper. I could have fucked her so violently right then, but I think that's what she wanted me to do. The look in her eyes told me that she was trying to get me to act on my urges. I wouldn't give her the satisfaction, not yet.

"Think of this as delayed gratification," I whispered in her ear before kissing her neck, while my eyes stared seductively into the mirror at hers. With every ounce of will-power I could muster, I walked into the bathroom, leaving her to wonder why I didn't take her as I usually do when she teases me.

Instead, I step out from under the steamy water and squirt some shampoo in my hand and grip my throbbing prick in a tight fist. I quickly stroke up and down my shaft. Her image rides through my memory, aiding the fantasy. In my mind, I'm forcing myself on her, ramming my cock in her pussy, so fucking hard that she begs me to ease up, but I don't, I fuck even harder. She'll beg and plead with me, enticing me to cum hard all over her made-up face, ruining her time-staking patience in applying it.

Now that I'm panting with my cum dripping from my fist, I'd better hurry up and get dressed. I don't want us to be late, not that there's any set time to go, I just like to be where I am supposed to be, when I said I would be there. Tardiness rots me, always has.

I can hear voices at the entrance by the front door. It's Rayna, Renee and the kids. Not wanting to be rude, I slip on a pair of grey sweatpants and make my way toward the noise.

"Oh, hey man," Tim says as I come around the corner.

"How's it going?" I ask.

"Good! We're going to take these little brats to the arcade on Tuscan Drive. From there, the theatre to see that new Claymation movie. It looks interesting."

I can't tell if he's just saying that to appease the kids' choice of movie or if he really does want to see it. "Sounds like a fun night. I'm jealous!"

Ken says, "Yeah, we compromised. Kim wanted a movie and I wanted the arcade."

"Then we're going to have ice cream before we go back to Aunt Renee's house."

"Hey, we should get out of here so you two can get going," Tim says with a wink in my direction. "Have fun."

Rayna looks at me as if asking me if he knows where we're going. She must know that I tell Tim almost everything. She tells her sister things she shouldn't tell her. I still don't completely trust Renee not to come onto me at some point. She did once and she always stares at me when she thinks I won't notice. What's to stop her from coming onto me again; the love of her sister? Nope, that didn't matter when she was fucking Rayna's husband. Why would it matter now? Tim keeps her level-headed, or at least he does for now. I just hope she doesn't get bored and crush his heart. He wears his heart on his sleeve, but most people don't know that about him.

They rush out the door, backpacks in hand, Kim skipping in front of Renee, as she mutters on about something cool that happened at school. Renee already looks tired. She's not the mothering type. I get a shot of humour whenever she offers to take them overnight. She always looks so ragged by morning.

The door closes. I look Rayna up and down, admiring the clingy red dress that does nothing to hide the stocking bands wrapping around her thighs. I'm sure Tim noticed. He'll likely tell me how hot she looks, the next time it's just him and I, alone. He would never be inappropriate with Rayna because he respects the boundaries of our friendship, always has.

"Are you ready for tonight, little lady?" I ask her.

She looks at my jogging pants and replies, "Well, at least one of us is."

"I'll be back in a few minutes, don't move."

I pull the locked chest from under the hanging shirts in my closet and dress, as quickly as I can. I put on something first, something I don't want her to see just yet. I finish with a black dress shirt, black leather pants and heavy work boots. I come down the hall and see that Rayna is still leaning against the door where I left her. I was expecting her to be sitting on the steps since her shoes can't be all that comfortable. I must be looking at her oddly because she smiles, shyly.

"You told me not to move, so I didn't. Isn't that what a good submissive is supposed to do; obey?" she asks. There's no hint of sarcasm in her voice and her face tells me that she's awaiting my approval. I step down the stairs slowly, looking her up and down as my prick stiffens at the thought of her giving herself to me completely and without hesitation. That would be a fantasy come true.

"Yes, that would be what a good submissive does. Are you my submissive, Rayna?" I ask, sliding my fingers through her hair until they cradle her head. I look down into her eyes while my cock continues to swell.

"When it's playtime, I can be your submissive. Be patient if I make a mistake, okay?" she begs.

"Of course," I whisper, kissing her bright red lips ever so tenderly. "You look stunning tonight. Everyone is going to want you... but you're *MINE*. You're *MY* submissive, *MY* little cougar. Yes, I like that nickname, Cougar."

"Cougar," she replies, looking a bit annoyed by my nickname. I knew the submissive role wouldn't last long. Oh well, I enjoyed it while I had it.

"What's the matter with cougar?"

"I don't think I like that. It insinuates I'm older than you."

"Well, you are older than I am and that is the nickname for a woman who has sex with younger men, isn't it?" She frowns even further. "Fine, what if I call you Cat?"

"C. A. T.?" She's still obviously, not impressed.

"Is that not how cat is spelled?"

"Yes, but it's still too close to cougar. What if we spell it K. A. T.?"

"I doubt we'll have to write it down, but I suppose K. A. T. will be just fine if it pleases you."

"I'm afraid to ask, but I suppose I should know ahead of time. What are you called? Look, I know you've been there before and people do know you as having a specific nickname, so to prepare myself, I'd like to know it, if you have one, that is."

"Yes, but I'm sure you can guess, if you think about it long enough."

She ponders for a moment while I usher her out the door, locking it behind me. I close her car door, after she's seated and make my way to the driver's seat. She has yet to guess my nickname.

"What are you wearing under your shirt?" she curiously asks as I sit. She reaches for my chest, feeling around.

"It's a harness," I tell her. She feels it through my shirt and bites her bottom lips. "Are you okay with me wearing it? I don't have to. I can take it off and leave it in the car."

"Do you normally wear this stuff when you go there?" she asks, I nod. "Then wear it. I think it's fucking hot! Why haven't I ever seen you in this before?"

"I didn't think you'd be receptive to it just yet. This atmosphere will make it seem more natural to you. If you'd like, I can dress for you one night. Of course, when I do, my caged freak wants to come out with a vengeance, so I'll have to be extra careful to keep him under wraps."

"Yeah, I'm not sure I can handle him quite yet. Little by little, the thought of meeting him doesn't seem so terrifying. Just how bad can it get anyway?"

I can't look at her, as we pull out of the driveway. "You aren't ready. That's all you need to know."

"Will I ever be?" she asks with the innocence that has me wanting to turn the car around and drive her back to the purity of her sheltered life. "I want to be ready."

What stops me is that I sense a tone of disappointment in her voice. Does she want me to free my demon? Should I even be considering it at this point? No, she isn't ready.

"Time will tell, but judging by the way things are progressing, I can't see why it won't happen eventually. You haven't shied away from anything I've proposed to you. You seem to like whatever we've done, which has surprised me, Miss Goodie-Two-Shoes." I snicker.

"I am not a Goodie-Two-Shoes! Well, not since you got your hands on me and corrupted me," she says with a loud laughter and a poke to my arm.

We arrive outside the house and I look to see Rayna's reaction. She's taking in the vast bricks that line the outer walls to the mansion-like building. The first time I was brought here, I'm sure I wore her exact expression.

My tummy is fluttering as I watch her reaction. I can't be sure if her expression is fear, meaning she'll run, or that she's thrilled, eager to expand her horizons. If she runs, that'll put a cap on the level of play we will ever engage in, but if she stays and enjoys it, my demon will very likely rear his ugly head, at some point. I expect that will make her fear me. I don't want her to fear me.

"Hey, Coach!" Rayna says, waving her hand in front of my face. "Hi! Where did your mind go?"

"Sorry, I was just thinking… it's not important. So, are you ready?"

She looks at the house again just as another car pulls in behind ours. The lights shut off and I hear two doors close. High heels are clicking on the cement as a woman walks past the driver's side of our car. She's a mistress, no doubt. She has on leather pants, highheels and a leather crop top. She crosses in front of our lights and takes the leash of a woman who walked past Rayna's window. Her submissive is dressed in nothing but fashionably wrapped ropes. Her wrists are unrestrained and hanging casually at her sides. She looks beautiful dressed only in rope. My mouth fills with saliva, hoping one day I will have the opportunity to bind Rayna in much the same fashion.

I look over at Rayna to see her staring at the two women. "Can you tie me like that one day?"

I don't think I heard her right, so I ask, "You want me to bind your body in ropes?"

"Yes, I do. She looks pretty. Don't you think?" "Let's go in," I tell her.

I step out of the car and walk around to her door, opening it for her. She steps out, leading with her stocking-clad leg. I'm becoming aware that I have a cock and it's loving the memory of her getting dressed.

She waits for me to shut the door, but I hold it open and begin unbuttoning my dress shirt. She's watching each button slip free. I want to taste the sweetness of her tongue, as it glides along the red lipstick decorating her top lip. When my shirt falls open, she reaches out, grabbing the straps that rest just under my pecs, with both hands, and pulls me toward her.

"You have to wear this for me later. Please!" she says with her bottom lip quivering. "Fuck! You look dangerous as hell. Fucking scary!"

I tilt my head down and give her my best threatening expression but she's too busy ogling my chest to notice. Her fingers are tracing the edges of the leather. A faint giggle warms my heart, easing my concern about my choice of attire for the evening. I was worried she might not approve.

"If you're finished, we can head in now," I tease. She nods, biting her bottom lip and flashing a shy smile.

I whisper into the ear of one of the very large, dangerous looking men guarding the main entrance. He nods, pulling a key from his shirt pocket and unlocking the huge, hand-carved wooden door behind him. He holds it open while the oversized lion doorknocker seems to size us up, as we walk over the threshold.

There is no music to be heard, not yet. The party is on the lower level. Up here is the social gathering where people remain dressed in proper street attire and abstain from play. People are sitting around chatting amongst themselves, as if they are guests at a fancy hotel and have no interest in the newest check-ins - us.

Rayna's eyes are wide. She looks scared but also intrigued. I think she was expecting to see leather-clad people in various stages of undress while others shriek from pain or moan from pleasurable touches. Not on this floor, that's one level down.

"Love, over here," I whisper in her ear while escorting her toward the elevator.

"I'm nervous," she says after the doors close, capturing us alone inside the small mirrored elevator.

"I am here. I will never leave you," I say after taking her arm in mine, to give her a stronger sense of security. "I will now call you

Kat."

"What shall I call you?" she asks.

The doors open and we step out, into a dim corridor lined with candle sconces. I stop and turn her to face me. "People here, call me Demon. You don't have to, but I would prefer you choose something other than my normal titles. Master or Sir would be suitable."

"Demon, really?" she asks. "When you would talk about your demon, I just figured it was a cute name you gave to your badass alter-ego. I didn't know it's the actual nickname that people call you."

"I'm not that person anymore, not with you."

"Would you be if I weren't around?"

"Very likely, yes," I answer her with the heavy dread of honesty.

"If I call you Demon, will you …"

"There you are!" his voice cuts into our conversation, as his arm slides around my shoulders.

I turn, wrapping my arms around his ribs and picking him up, just until his feet leave the ground, then set him back down.

"Hey, hey, don't bruise the merchandise," he teases. "How the hell are you? It's been too long."

"I'm doing well. How have you been?" I ask.

"Oh, you know, I can't complain," he replies wearing a wicked smirk, as his eyes shift toward the doors I've walked through many times. "Don't be rude, introduce this goddess in the red dress."

"Yes," I reply quickly, taking Rayna's hand in mine. "This is Kat, my…"

"Submissive," she finishes my sentence as she puts her hand out to shake his. Her non-restrained comment takes the man completely off guard. I look at her as if to let her know she spoke out of turn. She realizes her mistake, immediately dropping her hand and casting her eyes downward.

"Have you been a submissive for very long?" he asks her.

"No, Sir," she replies, keeping her eyes down.

"Is she living with you in a regular setting? Is there a mutually respected relationship between you?" he asks Coach.

"Yes, she is my girlfriend. We live together. She is new to the lifestyle and therefore still learning what is and isn't acceptable."

He puts his hand out to Rayna, so she puts hers in his. "My apologies, dear girl, I didn't know you are new. Forgive my reaction. Demon doesn't bring women who aren't trained. I suppose there's always room for fresh meat. Oh, I'm sorry, I should introduce myself. You can call me Gear, for now. This is my submissive, Glitter. She can show you around. I have some catching up to do with Demon."

Rayna looks up at me with fear in her eyes. "Actually, she's going to stick with me for the time being. Can we catch up later?"

He nods, taking her hand in his. "Kat, nobody will touch you here, unless you give them permission to do so. This is one of the safest places you will ever be. Think of this place as a church, only safer." He kisses her hand then walks away with Glitter's hand in his.

"May I speak?" she whispers.

"Of course," I tell her.

"It's just that Glitter didn't speak, so I wasn't sure."

"Our rules will be ours. We can set them up as we go along. If you don't agree with something, bring it to my attention immediately, so we can discuss it. You're here to learn. I would prefer you to remain quiet, unless asked to speak."

"Why Gear? It's an unusual name. And Glitter, what's her story?"

"He earned the name Gear because he can shift gears from playfully calm to sexually raging, quicker than anyone I've ever met. He would never hurt you, unless you gave him permission to do so. He's respectful, unless you tell him not to be. Glitter has a beautiful personality, she will captivate your attention when she's released from her submissive role." "Freed?" she asks.

"Yes, they live this lifestyle twenty-four hours a day, six days a week. They have been a couple for many years. They share this house. She has her own quarters set away from their joint living quarters so that she can have her one day a week as her own private time, separate from him. I think you'd really like her, if you got to know her. She'd be a great person to talk issues with, other than me, of course."

"Can we get started? I'm anxious and if I don't get moving, I might chicken out," she says. I watch her take a deep breath before leading her through the double doors, and into the lion's den.

Chapter Nine

Rayna

The heavy-based music is low enough that I can hear the sounds of people talking, moaning, begging and the occasional scream or moan from both men and women.

It's not as bright in this corridor, as was the last one. The further we walk, the louder the sounds become, and the more people we see. Bodies are clad in everything from designer suits to absolutely nothing. Coach was right, no matter what I had chosen to wear tonight, I'd fit in just fine.

One woman is wearing a leather hood with only eyeholes and nasal slots, to allow for airflow, otherwise she's completely nude. She is quietly sitting on a well-dressed man's lap while he talks to another equally dressed man. He has a woman at his feet, sitting on her heels with her head resting on his thigh as he strokes her hair as if she were his favourite dog.

Both women watch me walk by, with as much curiosity for me as I carry for them. Maybe they don't get many new people in here. The men look up to see Coach and I walking past and both of them nod at him before eyeing me from top to bottom. It's obvious they're talking about us by the way they don't turn their attention away. This happens with most people we pass by.

"Demon? Well, here's a sight for sore eyes! Where the hell have you been lately?" says a larger sized woman with short black hair and heavy make-up. She's dressed in a pair of denim shorts and a leather crop-top. Her black army boots are polished and shined. Behind her tails a very thin woman with scraggly blonde hair. She's wearing a white mini-skirt and red halter-top. She's balancing herself on a pair of red high-heels that would have most women begging to take off. She seems comfortable in them, or she's just putting up a good front.

"Trix, how the hell are you?" Coach replies with his hand out to shake hers.

"You know how it is; one day at a time." She looks me up and down, finally locking eyes with me and furrowing her brow. "And, who might this beauty be?"

I attempt to introduce myself, but hesitate, unsure if I'm supposed to speak or just let him do it. I wish he had told me all the rules of proper conduct for a submissive.

"This is KAT, my new submissive. She's new to the lifestyle." She looks shocked. "Since when do you train new submissives?" "She's... different," he replies.

Trix looks at him and nods, "Oh, I see. She's yours." "Just mine," he says.

"Welcome to our little slice of heaven. You couldn't have found a better Master, unless you had me teaching you the ropes. If you're ever seeking a dominatrix, keep me in mind. I'll treat you right. Besides, my cock is bigger than his," she laughs, and I smirk.

"But my hands are bigger and cover more ass with each swat," Coach jokes. She rolls her eyes. "How are you, Liv?"

The woman nods but doesn't say anything. In fact, her cheeks seem to be a bit puffed out.

"She's not able to speak at the moment. I told her not to wear panties tonight. She thought I wouldn't notice that she defied me, so she's being punished. Open your mouth and show Demon what colour they are."

Liv opens wide to show a pair of red lacy panties wadded up in her mouth. They must have been there for a while because they look very wet.

"I thought about shoving them up her twat, but this punishment suits me for the time being."

"Maybe next time she'll follow instructions better," he says while looking at the offender with steely eyes. She swallows hard but doesn't seem repenting. In fact, she appears to have worn them as a way to defy the woman and earn the attention of a punishment.

"I doubt it," Trix says. "I'll let you get settled; show her around this place. Oh, ah… Ranger's here. I thought I should warn you, so you can prepare yourself."

"Really?" he says with great interest. "I can't believe that fucker came back around."

"Well, you haven't been around for quite some time. He likely caught wind of your absence and thought he was safe to return," she says with a shoulder shrug.

"That motherfucker! I can't believe he has the balls to return." Coach turns to glare in the direction Trix's eyes lead him. "Good seeing you, Trix, Liv."

My hand is grabbed rather tightly, as he nearly drags me in the direction his furious eyes lead him. Who is this man she speaks of? What did he do that has Coach this upset?

I haven't seen this look on his face since he found me bound and beaten bloody, while his friend stood before me. I'm worried he's going to do something that will bring back all the memories of that incident to the forefront of my mind. I have been able to bury it and now I'm afraid of what he'll do.

We scurry past a lot of people doing things I really want to stop and watch. I hope we can come back after he deals with whoever he's racing toward. Through another doorway, I catch a glimpse of a man bound to a wooden cross. The only thing I really notice is that he's getting jerked off by another man. I've never actually seen a human on a cross before, nor have I witnessed anything else I saw happening in that room.

Coach stops so suddenly that I smack hard against his back. I can see his chest inflating with every deep breath. I look around his wide back and see three men and a woman sitting at a heavy wooden table. They are all listening to the man in the chest harness talking in a low voice. The woman looks up and smiles.

"Well, look who the cat dragged in." Is she talking about me? How did word spread so quickly that my name is Kat? She's not even looking at me, so the reference is merely the coincidence to the popular saying.

The guy in the harness stands up and walks toward Coach with his hand out. They shake hands and do that quick hug with a single back slap that men seem to always do. My guy isn't smiling.

"What the fuck is he doing here?"

The harnessed man puts his hands up as if to ask Coach to remain calm. "Now, you know nothing was ever proven. The ladies refused to tell their sides. We couldn't ban him without legitimate cause. You know the rules. Unless someone complains, there's nothing to investigate other than hearsay and accusation. As you know, there's always plenty of that going around."

"Get out of my way, Sprat!" Coach says slowly and clearly in a very deep and terrifying tone.

"Demon, you can't start a fight here. You know the rule."

"I don't give a fuck about that rule. Kick me the hell out if you want to, but that fucker is going down. I haven't been here in well over a year and I don't mind getting banned for life, as long as I get to kill that woman beating motherfucker!"

I swallow hard and pull my hand out of Coach's tight grip. My fingers were turning purple. He really hates one of the other two men and I'm not sure which one. The woman stands up and walks over to me, taking me by the hand.

"Come over here," she whispers. I follow her while keeping my eyes on Coach to see what he's going to do to the man, if anything. We stand against the wall a few feet away from the men in case a brawl ensues. "This could get very ugly and you'll be safer over here."

Coach turns to see where I am and that's when it becomes all too clear how he got the name Demon. His eyes have darkened as if they've sunken into his head and he looks bigger, much bigger. How can that be?

One of the seated men stands up and turns his back to Coach. He is wearing black latex pants and a sleeveless shirt. His hair is long and chestnut brown. He is very handsome.

He picks up a half empty bottle of water and turns around. He slowly starts walking towards the two men who are standing. He stops only a few feet in front of them. The man that was trying to calm Coach backs away with his hands up, as if to say he wants no more part of it.

The latex wearing man takes another step forward until he and Coach are face-to-face. "So, we meet again. It's really too bad we can't talk through our issues because I think we would get along, famously. If it weren't for the unproven rumors that were spread around by women who didn't want to face the fact that they falsely accused me of overstepping. I know they were yours. Afterthought has me wondering if I should have told them no, but you know how hot those chicks were. I think we should work at getting past this for the sake of the community. What do you say? Do you want to talk it through?"

"No, I don't. We did all the talking we ever needed to do. You are an abusive motherfucker and you should not be allowed back in this house. You and I both know those two girls were so threatened by you, they didn't want to say anything about what you did. As far as I'm concerned, someone should do exactly the same thing to you that you did to them. I would be more than happy to be that guy."

"So, what you're saying is you want to sexually satisfy me? I mean, I satisfied them and if you say you want to do to me what I did to them, that must mean you want to make me cum hard. Did you hop the fence during your absence? Not that there's anything wrong with it but I don't swing that way."

"You rope bound those women so they couldn't move and then you slowly hung them by their necks until they turned purple. They did not want that, but that's what you did. They told me they used their safeword, but you continued. Why the fuck won't you admit it? Are you ashamed? Just give me five minutes alone in a room with you and a length of rope and you will never fucking walk out of that room."

"Demon, I know damn well you could get the better of me in a physical altercation and I'm not challenging you to one. It's their word against mine. No proof has ever surfaced so I think we should just let this go. Why don't we just agree to disagree. When you're here, I will leave."

"I think you should leave and never come back. I don't ever want to see you again."

The man steps back with his hands raised in surrender. "Okay, I'm leaving. You can't stop me from coming here, but I'll do my damnedest not to be here when you are. That's the best I'm going to do. Do what you will."

The latex wearing man walks past Coach and disappears out the door. Everybody just stands there looking at a seething Coach, wondering if he's going to chase after the man or let him leave on his own, unharmed. He turns his head to seek me out. His eyes lock on mine with a sigh of relief, as if he's happy to see that I am still standing here and haven't run for the hills.

He puts his hand out for me to take it and weave my fingers in his. He kisses the back of my hand and thanks the woman who pulled me away from him.

"Kat, this is Mistress Kristi," he introduces us with anger still present in his voice. She smiles and nods and

I do the same, unsure whether I should thank her, myself or leave that up to Coach. I really wish I knew what my role was here. "Thank you, Kristi."

"For you Demon, you know I would walk through the gates of hell and back for you. So, why the fuck have you been gone for over a year? You just dropped off the face of the earth, without a single fucking phone call. I thought you loved me, man!"

He smiles and replies, "You know you're the only Mistress I love with all my heart. If only you were into dicks."

She burst out laughing and then puts her arm around me. "If you ever decide that his needle dick isn't enough for you, give me a call sweetheart and I will let you choose the size you want me to fuck you with."

Coach looks at me and says, "If ever I would allow you to be with a Mistress, Kristi is the one I would trust to keep you safe."

She points from him to me and back to him. "If you allow her to be with a Mistress? Since when have you forbidden you're submissives from choosing another person to entertain them when you're not around?"

"I never forbid it. If they went with another dominant, they didn't come back to me. This one is special to me. This woman is mine."

"No shit?" she says, crossing her arms over her chest and taking a step back. "Kat, I don't know what makes you so unique, but I can't wait to find out. Congratulations!"

I suppose Coach wasn't lying when he said he has never been in a committed relationship before me. I had thought that maybe at least once throughout his life, there will have been somebody who may have come close. I think I was wrong in assuming that.

"I'm going to show Kat around. She's new to our lifestyle, so I'm going to show her the possibilities. If you will excuse us, we will get back to exploring. I'm sure I will see you all soon."

They wave us on, and we leave the room. I'm rather impressed how I have managed to stay quiet for so long. I think this is the longest I have gone without saying anything, especially when I've had so much I wanted to say.

Coach pulls me off to the side and puts his hands on my shoulders. "Are you alright? I'm sorry you had to see that. Do you still want to be here, or should I take you home?"

"If you take me home right now, I will be angry at you. I am not exactly clear about what that guy did to those women and I'm not sure that I want to, but we came here for the purpose of opening my eyes to your lifestyle and dammit, that is what we are going to do. Enlighten me, Demon," I say rather tauntingly.

He smiles wide, showing me his beautiful white teeth. I don't know where the angry demon disappeared to but the guy standing in front of me doesn't look like he has a mean bone in his body. He's so young and cute. His face appears lighter, with a tiny glint of deviousness in his eyes.

"I should also mention how proud I am of you for not speaking when not asked to. It's not a rule I remembered to mention to you and I'm proud of you for playing the role of submissive, so well. You will be rewarded."

"You're not going to do anything to me here in front of people, are you?" Apprehension is swelling up in the pit of my stomach. The thought of being spanked or sexually pleasured while others watch does seem like an arousing idea, but also extremely terrifying. I don't know these people. I don't know anything about this house. Perhaps one day I will feel comfortable enough to let him do something like that, but today is not that day.

"My love, you are here today to learn, not to entertain the other members. Come with me to see what my world consists of."

I follow him as he walks me from room to room, giving me a few moments to watch whatever is happening, before moving on to the next. My pussy is so wet that I can feel my lips slipping against one another as I walk, further heightening my level of arousal.

I want to try a lot of these things, but not all. One of the rooms has me queasy. I cannot fathom why, but a man is sticking hypodermic needles through a woman's labia while she sits bound and shaking, tears streaming down her cheeks. It was horrifying, something nightmares are made from.

Chapter Ten

Coach

The scene in this room has Rayna gripping my arm tightly. I can feel her shaking.

"Why is he doing that to her?" she whispers.

"She enjoys it," I reply, knowing she isn't going to understand. Rayna enjoys some pain, but she's never been introduced to anything like this and I doubt she'll ever be interested in taking it to this level.

"That has to hurt like hell," she says while wincing when he slides a needle through the hood of her clitoris. The woman cries out, but takes the pain like a warrior. My dick is throbbing in my pants, not at the needles, but at the woman's reaction to them. If Rayna was any other woman I'd brought here tonight, she'd be on her knees sucking my cock down her throat, until I filled her belly with my jizz.

"Watch her reactions, her facial expressions, her breathing. Trust me, she's not even here anymore. He's taken her to a whole new platform. The man taking her there is very skilled in the placement of needles, allowing her the most pain and heightened pleasure imaginable." I can barely control my breathing, to keep it at a slow and steady rhythm.

Rayna watches for a moment as he begins attaching wires to one of the needles penetrating through her clitoris.

"Have you ever done this to a woman?" she asks the one question I was hoping she wouldn't. I don't want to lie to her, but I don't want her to run away, believing I'm a sadistic fuck.

"Once, but it isn't my thing. Perhaps I'll tell you about it another time," I reply. "Now quiet down."

She looks at me and then down my chest to the swollen lump in my pants. She places her hand on my cock and squeezes. My eyes are burning with desire as I glare into hers. She has to know when I say something here, she's to heed it.

"Why are you touching me?"

"I needed to know if you enjoy watching this woman suffer," her expression is filled with concern.

"I'll never do anything to you that you don't approve of, you know that." The last thing I would ever want is for her to legitimately fear me.

"That's not it, I know you won't. You're very aroused from watching a woman in agony. How can I compete with that? Would you like to hurt me, make me suffer like she is?"

"I just told you, I would not do anything to you that you didn't approve of. Now stop talking."

"That's not what I'm asking," she hisses a bit louder than she should.

Mic looks at Rayna with an angry leer, and then at me as if to tell me to control my submissive. I nod, grasping her bicep and pulling her away from the doorway to rush her down the hall. I push her into the bathroom and shut the door, locking it behind me.

"You must remain quiet when in the open viewing rooms. Nobody is to speak louder than a whisper. If you were anyone else…"

"What? What would you do if I were anyone else?" she questions with a challenging attitude, lifting her eyebrows tauntingly, while pursing her lips.

"Do you really want to know? Should I show you?" Fuck! My dick is so goddamn hard.

She replies, "Do you want to punish me because I caught you in a lie?"

"I did not lie. I said we would talk about it later."

"So, you don't enjoy needles? Well, your cock tells a different story."

"Later, I won't say it again."

"Oh, you won't say it again, huh?"

"I am going to punish you because of the disrespectful attitude you have right now. You seem to have forgotten that you are my submissive. You told me you were when we first arrived. Do you remember? So, tell me Kat, are you my submissive, or not?"

"Yes, I am," she replies, still giving me the same shitty leer, further taunting my level of patience.

As quick as I can manage, I grab her hair and pull her face to mine, kissing her harder than I ever have. My other hand grabs the neckline of her dress and yanks, tearing it to expose her bra. Rayna tries to grab my arm to stop me from ruining her dress but I'm stronger than she is. I grab her bra and jerk it down, forcing her tits to pop out from the top of it.

I squeeze her left breast hard and then pinch her nipple until she screams in my mouth. She knows she can yell the safeword and she will be freed instantly. She won't say it though. I know she won't. She's way too stubborn to let me have that satisfaction. Good!

I slap her tit and then pinch the other nipple equally hard, while she struggles to stop me. Again, she screams against my invading tongue. I grab her neck and apply pressure, not enough to stunt her breathing. My fingers and thumb are pressing against her carotid arteries to slow the flow of blood to her brain. She needs to learn that when we are here, I am in control.

Her lips are going still, and her body is becoming heavier. She's weakening. Good! With my hands still weaved into her hair, I release her throat and push her onto her knees.

"Take out my cock and suck it!" I demand.

Rayna reaches for the waistband of my leather pants, using it to steady her on her knees. She quickly pulls my zipper down. My cock springs forth, hard and thick. She opens her mouth, so I pull her head until her mouth is over the head of my cock and I hold her there. She wraps her lips around the head and sucks, rolling her tongue over my piss hole. She could make me cum in seconds, if I were to let her.

She looks up at me with defiant eyes. Fuck she's sexy! I love that she challenges me, but I'll never tell her that. I pull her face toward my belly, burying my cock down her throat. She wretches, but I don't immediately set her free. Her hands grab my thighs, but I hold her head, sternly. The second time she gags, I yank her head back. Tears are filling her eyes, but are not yet falling.

"I fucking own you!" I hiss.

"No, you don't," she hisses back. She's really pushing her boundaries and I'm so madly in love with her because of it. This woman owns me, not the other way around, and she knows it.

"We'll see," I growl through clenched teeth. My inner Demon is shadowboxing.

I pull her head forward, sliding my prick into her throat again, this time, she doesn't gag, which I find to be disappointing. I hold her in place, humping my prick down her throat, again and again. I won't stop until her tears are running down her cheeks taking her mascara with them. I will mess her make-up and not allow her to make herself presentable before we leave this room. She, along with everyone here, will know she is under my control.

When I pull her face back, the evidence of my punishment is evident with black tears dripping from her chin. She isn't crying, it's just a reaction from gagging. She can make me stop with just one word, Red.

If I keep making her suck my cock, I'll definitely cum. I want to fuck her good and hard. I make her stand using the grip I have in her tangled hair. I spin her, so that my arm is at her waist and she's bent over facing behind me, her waist held tightly against my hip. The grip I have on her waist is vicious. She cannot get away.

With her unable to stand straight up, I yank the hem of her dress up, exposing her lacy thong. I start swinging my arm, spanking her ass until she's crying out and fighting to get away. Her ass is hot and red, swollen with my handprints covering both cheeks.

I grasp the thin material that runs between her ass cheeks and yank, lifting her feet off the ground, but the lace won't give. I pull it to the side, that'll do. My fingers reach between her folds, slipping in her wetness. Fuck, yes!

I shove two of my fingers into her drenched cunt and wave, rubbing her g-spot with a roughness that has her moaning within seconds. She isn't fighting to get away anymore. Now she's squirming and trying to hump my fingers, but my grip on her body is extensive.

Her pussy is tightening around my fingers. She's going to cum. No, she won't! I pull my fingers out just before she reaches orgasm. I resume cracking her ass, alternating from one hot cheek to the other. She's fighting to get away again, panting and wailing, but not saying the word to make it stop.

I jam my fingers into her again, and fuck her hard, not giving her any mercy. It isn't more than ten seconds before she's ready to cum again. Just before she does, I stop again, removing my fingers and continuing with the punishing slaps. She's fighting me and yelling.

"Fuck you! Let me go! Fucking stop!"

"Say the word if you want it to end," I reply in a calm voice.

I ram my fingers back into her and bring her close, again. I repeat this action eight-more times, getting her so near to climax that her body begins to tighten and then stopping, to inflict more pain. She isn't screaming from the pain anymore. Her moans are loud and deep, like a growl.

She's learning what it is to lose herself on that fine line between pleasure and pain, blurring it to the point where you can't tell the difference between the two. This is where I wanted to take her. She needs to experience this for herself, so she can fully understand why that woman would challenge her body in that way.

This time, I don't pull my hand away. My fingers flail wildly inside her as her muscles tighten and cease to ease, holding her in a violent full-body spasm. Her cunt is gripping and pulling and pushing at my hand. A flood of hot cum sprays from her depths, coating my hand and splashing to the marble floor.

I am relentless, not stopping even when the grip she has on my fingers is so tight that I can hardly move them. Her body is quivering, twitching and jerking to get free, but I don't allow it. My fingers don't quit, continuing to invade her body with force until she erupts into a second raging orgasm that has her knees shaking to the point that they give out. I'm holding her up now, keeping the momentum going until she rides completely through her climax.

I stand her up and scoop her into my arms, dropping to one knee and sitting her on the other. Her head rests on my shoulder, her arms hang limply around my neck. She's so weak and I know she's trying to get the fogginess of the euphoria to fade away.

"I'm sorry I had to punish you, but you needed to know your place. I wanted to prove to you that the threshold of pain can be pushed until the person can't decipher between something hurting and something giving them absolute pleasure."

"Yes, I understand," is all she manages to say.

"I love you, Rayna," I whisper, kissing her forehead tenderly.

"I know you do. Thank you," she replies.

"Are you okay now?" She nods, rising to her feet. I hold her elbow knowing her knees are still going to be weak. She wobbles, but quickly regains her control.

"Stand against the wall while I clean the floor." Using paper towels, I clean her cum from the black and white marble.

"I have to pee," she informs me.

"Go ahead," I reply.

"You're going to stay in here when I do?"

"Yes," I tell her. "I don't want you to make yourself look presentable."

"What? Why not? I'm not going out there like this," she tells me.

"Yes, you are. They need to know that you have been punished for your bad behaviour."

"Why? What business is it of theirs?"

I smile at her and tell her, "Just go pee, or don't. You can hold it all night if you choose."

Her eyes are shifty. I can tell she's uncomfortable. Rayna has never used the toilet in front of me. She's way too proper for that.

"So, in your mind, it's okay to gush cum on me, but I can't watch you urinate?"

"It's just…" she shakes her head. "It's a private thing."

"Are you going to go or not?"

"No, I'm not peeing in front of you," she informs me.

"Last chance." She shakes her head. "Okay! This is going to be a fun night," I chuckle, guiding her out of the bathroom while she fusses with her torn neckline to keep her bra covered breasts hidden from inquisitive eyes. It's no use, I purposely tore it wide open. She gives up, leaving herself exposed. The dress is garbage now. I'll gladly buy her a dozen more.

I walk her straight back to that same room. The woman is sitting on a chair wiping her vagina with a cloth. There is blood on it, but not much. I see Mic standing by the chair she was bound to. He's spraying it down and cleaning it with a white rag.

"Mic, my sub has something to say to you," I say as I approach him, putting Rayna between the two of us. He looks down at her, but she doesn't look at his face.

"Sir, I'm sorry for interrupting you. It'll never happen again." Her voice is soft and apologetic.

Mic grins and replies, "Did you not realize that you needed to be quiet?"

"Yes, Sir. I had questions about what you were doing to her."

"What questions? Ask me," he says while putting his finger under her chin, lifting her face so he can admire her smeared makeup.

"I didn't understand why she would let you do that to her. And, Coach, I mean Demon, was very aroused from watching her suffer.

I wanted to know if he'd ever done this to a woman."

"Was it explained to you?"

"Demon punished me for interrupting you. He didn't tell me directly, if he's done this before. I do better understand how pain can urge on pleasure. I just can't fathom getting needles stuck through my clit."

"The woman's name is Em. I suggest you talk to her. She can answer your questions better than I can."

"Thank you, Sir," she says. She looks at me and I nod, releasing her arm. I watch Rayna walk over to the woman who is now pulling a black dress over her head.

"So, how the hell have you been Mic?"

"I'm good Brother. What's happening with you?"

I look over at Rayna and smile. "She happened."

He glances at Rayna and then puts his hand out to shake mine. "Congratulations, man. I never thought either one of us would ever let ourselves get shackled."

"Oh, I had no choice in it. I fought it, but she won."

"I had no idea you preferred the chicks with a few years on them."

"It's not her age that caught my attention. It's everything about her." I change the subject before he asks me how we met. "How about you? Anyone special?"

He nods toward the woman talking to Rayna. "That one. She is the one for me. I don't know if I can say I'm shackled, but I sure like her a whole lot. She's fun to play with, but also a great conversationalist. She's university educated, not like my usual prey."

"You're still calling women prey," I chuckle.

"Are you going to tell her everything she wants to know about all of your past subs, and the stories that still haunt you?"

"Yeah, I will. I won't lie to Kat, but I won't elaborate too much either."

"And about the last girl you were here with? Does she know?"

"I'll tell her about Sara, when the time is right."

"It's in the past," he replies, as if that'll soften the painful memories.

"It'll change things," I say with a sigh. "All right Mic, I have to get her home. Hopefully she'll want to come back."

He puts his hand out, so we grip and do the two-pat-hug. "All right man. I'll see you soon, right? You better not stay away so long this time. Oh, by the way, she's fucking hot!"

"You don't have to tell me," I say as I'm walking away to collect Rayna.

Rayna's laughing with the woman, as if they're old friends. Now that I'm closer to them, I can see just how beautiful the woman is. Her skin is smooth and flawless, eyes wide and deer-like, and her lips are full and inviting. Her hair is pulled back in a high ponytail, but the black tresses still hang with a slight wave all the way down to her butt.

"We should go." I don't give her an option to stay.

"If you wish," she replies. "Em, this is Demon."

We shake hands and greet one another with casual pleasantries, ending with my apology for interrupting their conversation and stealing her away. I take Rayna's hand and lead her down the corridor, nodding at the people I used to know and claimed to be good friends with. I no longer know them, unable to even remember their names.

I open the car door and close it once she's settled. After putting my dress shirt back on and buttoning it. I slip in behind the wheel.

Rayna looks at me, while I look at her.

"So, what did you think of the place?" I ask her.

She smiles and takes a deep breath, raising her eyebrows and holding them high, as her breath seeps from her lungs. "It was different. I can honestly say you've taken me to a place that I've never been. It's crazy in there. I mean, it was so interesting; wild, but in a non-chaotic manner. Everyone seemed happy, as if all their

daily life's stress was left at the door as they came in."

"And, what did you hate about it?"

"I didn't like how angry you were with that man. What did he do to make you hate him so much?"

Here we go! "He was one of my good friends. He was enjoying my submissive behind my back. If I was playing with more than one woman at a time, I always told them about each other. I expected the same respect from my playmates. However, I was to be their only Master. It was a hard rule."

"Surely there's more to it than that."

"Yes, there is." I don't want to tell her any more than that, but I know she won't let it go. "Lisa was her name. She was the ultimate submissive, everyone wanted her. We were together for almost two years. One day, that asshole convinced her to let him Master her. She

434

wouldn't tell me, or anyone, what happened except that he hurt her. She left our community without an explanation to me or anyone else. She was found a month later floating in the river after having been tortured to death. Her killer was never caught. I doubt it was him who killed her, but I blame him for her death. If he hadn't hurt her, she never would have sought a sadist outside of the safety of our community. She tangled with a psychopathic sadist, who fucking used her like a piece of meat."

"Fuck! That's horrible. I'm so sorry. Why didn't she stay with you after he did what he did? If you two were so close, why would she leave you because of him?"

"This is where my guilt lies. I pushed her away for getting involved with him in the first place. She was supposed to be with me or ask permission to be with another. She didn't."

"She betrayed you. It's understandable that you were hurt by that. You obviously cared for her a great deal."

"No, it isn't like that. I didn't love her. I enjoyed her company.

She was my friend, just my friend."

"Are you sure?"

"Yes, I'm sure. I know the difference between a physical friendship and love. I didn't forgive her and now she's dead. I blame him. I will always blame him. He shouldn't be allowed in Fallen anymore. I don't know exactly what he did to her, but I have a good idea."

"You said there were two women that he hurt. What happened to the other one?"

"She moved away. People said her job took her to a different city but I'm not so sure. She called me to tell me what he did to her and probably did to Lisa. She hung up before I could tell her to come back. I wanted to tell her that he would be dealt with. She never reached out to anyone from our community again."

"So, why didn't the women go to the police and tell them about the assault?"

"What cop is going to believe a masochist was assaulted by her chosen sadist? They would have laughed them out of the station with a *you got what you asked for* comment to worsen the blow. The chosen house representatives handle the complaints and decide whether someone should be banned, or not. The women wouldn't talk about it, so nothing could be done. He wasn't banned. I threatened to kill him if he returned, but I stopped attending, so he was free to come and go."

"I will be sure to avoid him," she promises.

"I will never put you in a position where you need to defend yourself. I fucked up once and it nearly cost you, dearly. It'll never happen again."

She sighs, recalling that horrible night. "Let's go home."

Chapter Eleven

Rayna

It's been three days since we went to the house. I've been ravishing Coach, as often as I can. He's been unusually quiet though. I'm giving him his space to work through whatever emotions were brought forth from seeing that guy. I think Lisa meant more to him than he wants to admit.

Some days, being a dental hygienist feels like the worst career choice I could have ever made for myself. I originally wanted to be a dentist, but getting married and having kids, stood in the forefront. I had to settle for a lighter education. Do I regret having my kids – never! Do I regret my ex – absolutely! He's out of the picture now and I couldn't be happier to have watched him leave. The kids haven't heard from him in over a month. He'll never win Father of the Year Award.

I'm between patient cleanings and taking a quick break before my two-o'clock arrives. I drag my weary body to the lunchroom and drink my coffee as quickly as I can, without burning my mouth. I really need the caffeine, after the late-night romp Coach threw into me. We didn't get to sleep until well after one in the morning. Five hours of sleep just isn't enough for me.

I pull my phone out of my locker and text Coach.

Me: How's your day going?

Coach: I'm busy as fuck. How about you? *Me:* Good, but I'm tired. Well worth it though ;) *Coach:* I agree. I'm with a client.

Me: I just wanted to check in with you.

Coach: Later tonight, I'm going to fuck you hard.

Me: Looking forward to it!

Kelly pokes her head in the lunchroom. "Hey doll, your two o'clock is here."

I drop my head and groan. "Fine, I'll collect him in a minute." "Okay," she replies. "Why are your eyes lugging around all that purple baggage beneath them? Did your hunky man keep you up late again last night?"

I snicker, "Yes, he did."

"I can't say I wouldn't do the same. If he were my man, I'd never get any sleep. How do you keep your hands off that hot body of his?"

"Who said I can keep my hands off him?" I wink.

"He is so fine! You really have to set me up with one of his strongman friends. I could go for a barbarian-style, beast of a man." She dances a hip-humping cha-cha. "I need a thick-thighed man to give me a good hard fucking with some power behind it!"

I start laughing when Dr. Jessik walks around the corner and stops dead in his tracks. He's watching her hump the air, grunting and groaning, as if she's getting fucked. She spins around and jolts backward like she received an electric zap. Her high-pitched yelp has me in hysterics. Poor Dr. Jessik is so embarrassed that he isn't sure if he should continue forward, or turn around and come back later.

"Sorry, I was joking around with..." she clears her throat while blushing a raging red. "Excuse me," she mutters while walking past him.

"She was just joking about..." I stop talking, not wanting to get into what got her started.

Dr. Jessik once told me that he had been waiting for me to be ready to date, so that he could ask me out. I had no idea he even liked me. It wouldn't have worked out, him and I, we're just too much alike. Two people who are boring, will be extra boring together. I need a bit of fire in my relationships and Coach is exactly the spark I need to keep me from wasting my life away.

"She's a very excitable woman," he replies with an awkward smile. He plugs in the kettle.

"That's an understatement," I say with a smile.

After taking his mug from the cupboard and tossing in a tea bag, he asks, "Would you like me to pick you up so we can travel to the airport in one car? Don't worry, we won't be alone together. I'll be picking up Dr. Myri and Jennifer along the way."

"I'm not worried about being alone with you." I had forgotten about the convention. "I'll have to let you know about that. I haven't made any arrangements yet."

His eyes fill with concern. "You haven't told your boyfriend about the convention, have you?"

"It just kept slipping my mind." I'm not lying, it did. "I'll talk to him tonight. What time is the flight?"

"Kelly has your flight and hotel information in a packet at the front desk. I believe our flight leaves at ten-twenty in the morning. I could be at your house at eight-forty-five, after I've picked up Dr. Myri. Jennifer's apartment is closest to the airport, so we'll collect her last."

"I'll have to let you know later in the week."

"You are coming, right? You go every year."

I nod with a smile, "Of course. I wouldn't miss it."

"How are things going with, ah… what's his name again?"

"Coach."

"Right! Yes, Coach, because he's a bodybuilder; a very large, muscular young man." His jealousy is sadly, obvious, despite his efforts to suppress it.

"We're doing very well together. He really is a good man and he treats me like a queen."

His smile is faulty, not quite reaching his eyes. "As he should be. Seeing you so happy is a consolation. You deserve the very best of everything. Of course, you should insist he allow you to get more sleep. You're looking quite tired these days."

"The kids weren't feeling well last night, so I was up late," I lie because I don't want to hurt him. He's a wonderful man, just not my type.

"Well, I hope they're feeling better this morning." He turns to pour the boiling water into his mug.

"Yes, they are."

As he's walking out of the lunchroom, he pauses, "You don't have to lie to me about your sex life. He's a young man and you're a beautiful woman. I'm sure he's very capable of having a voracious sexual appetite. I wouldn't want to take my hands off you, either."

I don't reply to his confession. First of all, I'm not sure anything I could say would make him feel any better. Second, I'd rather just leave the conversation to die.

It would have been better had he not said anything about his feelings for me. At least we wouldn't be so awkward toward each other. Is he trying to make me feel guilty for not giving him a chance with me? How was I to know he had a thing for me? Besides, he didn't say anything to me until he saw me on Coach's arm. If he liked me so much, he should have told me earlier. He said he didn't think I was up for dating after my divorce, but I hadn't been with my husband for four years, at the time he announced his feelings. How was I to know?

I get up and walk to the sink to reluctantly dump the remainder of my coffee. I rinse my cup and set it in the tray. As I turn to leave, I bump face-first into his chest.

"Oh, I'm sorry," he says as he backs up, waving his hand for me to pass.

"My fault completely," I reply as I shuffle around him.

I'm happy to be away from him. I wish things could go back to before I knew his feelings for me. He was always oddly behaved when alone with me, but at least it wasn't weird, for me anyway.

* * * * *

I finished with my last patient, finally ending my work day. Arriving home at three-twenty, dog tired, I just flop my body face down on my bed, burying my face in the fluffy pillow. I have been dreaming of this moment all day.

The kids are doing their homework quietly, at the kitchen table, while they eat a snack. The house is still and drifting further and further from my thoughts.

"Love, wake up."

"No," I reply, angry that I'm being interrupted from a pleasant dream about Coach, the kids and I having a nice barbeque at the local beach. I don't know why I was dreaming that, but it was wonderful, nonetheless.

"Rayna, it's six-thirty. I made dinner. Come eat something," he replies, as he gently brushes stray locks of hair from my face.

I groan, "Do I have to get up? It's really six-thirty?"

"Yes, love, and you do."

"Fine!" That complaint comes out louder and more vicious than I had intended, but he just laughs.

He jumps on top of me, straddling my ass. His hand weaves in my hair and pulls just enough to let me know he's being his dominant self.

"If you don't get up, I'll punish you, whether the kids are home and awake, or not. But, if you come and eat something, I just might make you scream from pleasure tonight. What do you choose to do,

Rayna?"

I giggle, "What if I want both?"

He lifts his left leg off me and then grabs my hips, spinning me onto my back. Damn, he's so fucking fast and strong! His mouth comes down on mine while his hand slides up my shirt, cupping my breast tenderly. Our mouths mesh in a heated contest to see whose tongue will take the lead in the tango they've started.

His fingers tease my nipple, not pinching hard, but just enough to send tiny zaps of lust to my heating pussy. I want him now, not later. A moan escapes me, taunting his manly desire to continue, momentarily forgetting the small humans roaming about the house.

Coach suddenly pulls his face back from mine and removes his hand from under my shirt. He speaks as if he's trying to convince himself to back away from me. "Food, we need nourishment.

Children… children are within earshot. Must feed the little people."

I laugh at how hard it is for him to reason with his testosterone riddled mind. He hops off me and onto his feet, holding his hand out for me to accept. With a final groaning complaint, I allow him my hand so he can pull me onto my feet. He doesn't stop there. He flips me onto his shoulder and slaps my ass cheek, hard.

"Let me help you get to the table, lazy woman." He cracks my ass again, this time I yelp. "Do you remember what happened the last time I carried you to the kitchen?"

"Yes, and it has forever changed the way I perceive carrots." I'm not lying, I get wet when I see them. His laughter fills the room.

Coach carries me into the kitchen while I laugh and cackle, slapping his butt. We come around the corner and the kids start laughing. They think him carrying me is hilarious. My face feels like it's going to explode from the blood build-up. He sets me down on the chair I normally sit on and then kisses my lips just once.

I am laughing because the kids are in stitches. Kim snorts, which has us all busting up. Tears are streaming down my face by the time Coach hands me a plate with lemon chicken and asparagus with a side of herbed rice. It smells delicious. My mouth waters. I love that he enjoys cooking and excels at it! He's much more creative in the kitchen than I am.

Halfway through our meal, Coach asks me, "Love, would you like to go on a date with me, this Saturday?"

I look up at him and stop chewing, pushing the food into my cheek. I cover my mouth with my hand and ask, "A date?"

"Yes! You know, when two people go someplace together and have a great time."

"Um, not this weekend."

He furrows his brow, and asks, "Are you tired of me already?" I smile and shake my head. He knows I can't get enough of him. "No, um... I have to go away to a convention... for work... to Las Vegas... with some of my coworkers."

He sets his fork down on his plate and wipes his beard with his napkin. "You're mentioning this, now?"

I suddenly feel very small and young, like a teenager asking her parents if she can go to a place knowing they won't approve. I simply shrug, unsure of what to say.

"Rayna, I'm not going to stop you from doing something that will benefit your career. I just wish you would have told me sooner, before I made plans for us."

"I'm sorry, and you're right, I should have talked to you about it long before now. I would invite you to come, but you would be so bored. The only fun thing we do is go to the pub on Friday night, for drinks. After that, it's one lecture after another, product sampling, ego stroking... It'll bore you to tears."

Ken announces, "I can babysit Kim so Coach can go!" I shake my head, and reply, "Not for an entire weekend." "Your mom's right, little man. Maybe next year," Coach says.

Ken pouts, stabbing an asparagus and watching it flop on the end of his fork. Kim has been sitting quietly, eating her chicken, not caring to participate in the conversation.

He chuckles, "Love, you don't have to invite me to come with you. I want you to go, have fun, party and schmooze with the people who can boost your career. If I'm there, I would only be a distraction to you, anyway."

"It's just... I don't want you to think I don't want you there."

He reaches for my hand, lifting it to his lips and kisses it, as if my skin is as fragile as the wings of a butterfly and if he presses too firmly, he'll tear me.

"I don't think that. Next weekend, you are mine to do with as I please," he replies before taking his glass to the sink to refill it. Before he sits, he leans his mouth just behind my ear and very quietly, whispers, "Every chance I have to take you, I will, so be ready for me. I'm going to fuck you raw and eat you until you scream."

My pussy tightens and my clit twitches. I can feel the heat radiating from between my legs, which are squeezed together. He sits and continues eating dinner while I bite my bottom lip. I want him now. If the kids weren't here, I'd do or say something sassy, just to provoke him to pull me over his knee and spank me. Of course, he would pleasure me afterward. He never leaves me wanting for anything.

"Do you need me to drive you to the airport?" he asks, as if what he just whispered to me isn't affecting him in any way. I admire his self-control. He can be furious about something, or be thrilled, but he has this uncanny ability to prevent his face from revealing what's going on in his thoughts. I can't do that, never could. Everyone knows exactly what I'm thinking.

"Um," I clear my throat, "no. Dr. Jessik offered to pick me up. We're carpooling with two other people from the office. He's coming at eight-forty-five, Friday morning."

"If you change your mind, I'd be happy to drive you," he assures me with a smile.

Chapter Twelve

Rayna

Coach has licked, fucked and dominated me so much this week, my whole body is tired and sore. Not so much that I have to turn him down, of course. I want him, over and over again. Not once has he made love to me, though. It's been hard, rough and I'm usually bound. It's great, but I'd love it if he would be gentle tonight. I leave in the morning and want to hang onto the loving closeness I feel after lovemaking. He likes it rough, I know that. The man is a goddamn machine!

I come out of the bathroom after my shower to find Coach standing in the middle of the room wearing his leather pants, heavy black boots and his harness. This is how he dresses when we go to Fallen. It's so fucking exciting! I know what he's capable of doing while he wears that outfit. Of course, I understand that he doesn't need the leathers to be his dominant self, but they add to the allure.

The way he's looking at me has me swallowing, despite my suddenly dry throat. I stop a few feet from him and stand with my arms hanging down at my sides, eyes on his, as he likes them to be.

"Tonight, I am going to make you mine. You'll remember this night, all weekend." His voice is deep, and his words are spoken slowly.

"Yes Sir." I will be his obedient submissive tonight, as I have all week. He must have something extra special planned for me.

"I need to ask if there's any reason anyone will be seeing you naked. Will you be using the pool and changing room? I will be marking you and I wouldn't want to leave marks on your skin where they could be seen. Too many questions erupt from that. They might think I'm abusing you."

"But you are abusive," I reply as a joke. The look on his face has me wishing I hadn't said that.

"Is that how you feel?"

I shake my head and approach him quickly, placing my hands on his thick and solid biceps. "No! It was a joke. A poorly timed joke, but a joke nonetheless."

"I am going to be marking you tonight."

"What? You want to mark me? Like, how?" Is he planning on cattle prodding me? I hope it's a payback for my poorly timed joke. "Bruising," he replies as if he's asking to braid my hair.

"You want to leave bruises on me? But you said you don't like to do that."

"I said I don't like to leave marks that can't be covered and that I would never permanently scar a woman. Bruises in places nobody can see, pleases me."

"I don't plan on using a pool or changing in front of anyone." I wonder if I would have been better off not to tell the truth. He is going to mark me, whatever that entails, I'm sure I won't like it.

He nods and says, "You remember your safewords?" I nod, dropping my hands to my sides once again. "And if you can't talk?" "I am to shake my head, hands or feet to get your attention."

"Very good."

He takes my left forearm in his hand and walks with me to the end of the bed. I am guided to stand with my butt leaning against the footboard. He cuffs both of my wrists and ankles, and binds them to the frame, leaving them spread wide like a starfish. My feet stand far apart and it's already becoming uncomfortable for my legs.

"Open your slutty mouth." His voice rumbles my chest. Dirty talk. I like it.

I do as he says. A rather large ball is shoved between my jaws. The band is fastened behind my head so I can't spit it out. He stands with his body flush against mine. The heat of his chest warms my neck. He pulls my hair until my head tilts back and he can easily lick my lips. His other hand wraps around my throat, applying enough pressure to quickly change the shade of my face to a deeper red. When he releases me, I pull a deep breath in, through my nose.

I watch as he lifts a towel. I hadn't even noticed it when I left the bathroom. I walked right past it. It was spread across the nearby dresser, covering something. He picks up a few of the objects and walks back to me. He squats down, fiddling with my pussy lips. A harsh pain inside of me, fiercely shoots from my clit up to my bellybutton. It's a clamp, a very tight one. My protest is muffled. I'm sure he planned the ball in my mouth to prevent me from screaming, which would alert the kids to our play. They are asleep and our bedroom door is locked, of course.

He applies weight to the clamp and it fucking hurts! It's a pain that will ease into pleasure once my brain can shut out the world around me, but I'm not even close to that point. He will take me there, I'm sure of it. I welcome it. I crave it.

"Open your eyes," he insists.

As I do, the pleasant sting from the tips of the flogger slap at my tits. I jolt and yelp. The leather tassels lick my skin, quickly turn it pink. I love it and hate it, at the same time.

"Lift your chin," he instructs.

I do as he says, tilting my face toward the ceiling. I try to stay focused, but when the tips of the tassels slap at my breasts and nipples, I cry out, the sound escaping through my nostrils. When he thinks I've had enough, he tosses the flogger onto the bed. His fingers grasp my nipples and pull. I love this. I know that I shouldn't, but I do. The pain shoots straight down to my clit, but by that time, it's as stimulating as if he were caressing it with his fingertips.

He squats and rubs some lube on my asshole before working something into my butt. He slides it in and out a few times and then holds it in. I hear a whooshing sound and feel the object growing inside me. It's getting bigger and bigger. Fuck! My clit is burning, begging to be freed from the clamp or for even the slightest touch. As he stands, his fingers glide on either side of my clit, torturing it sweetly. It hurts like hell when the clamp moves but the tenderness of his touch counteracts my hatred of the ache. He stops touching me, all too soon.

Coach walks to the dresser to collect a stick that's about as long as my arm. It's thin, like a switch one would pluck from a tree, but firmer. He cuts it through the air so quickly, it whistles. My eyes open wide when I realize that he might want to hit me with it. I'm rocking my head back and forth, not enough where he'll think I'm tapping out, but it gets his attention. I need him to explain this new stick he's carrying before he touches me with it.

"This is a rattan cane. It can be very painful, but it can also feel very good. This will likely leave bruises on your skin, if I want it to." I'm still protesting. "If after you've tried it, it's too much and you don't want me to use it anymore, wave your right hand. Do you understand?" I try to say *yes* but I merely manage a mumble.

He glides the cane along my right nipple and then lightly taps it. Strangely, I like it. He taps it again, harder this time. Yes, I enjoy that. Once more, the cane contacts my stiff nipple, harder still. No, I didn't like it, but I can bear it. I lift my right hand but don't wave it, letting him know that I've reached my threshold.

He strokes my right nipple with the cane and then *twap, twap, twap*. Three harsh taps in a row. I'm grunting and gasping. Ouch! Fuck! My hands clench into fists and I try to curl my body, so he won't be able to access my nipple, but it's no use. My range of motion is quite limited. I look at him with anger in my eyes. It's not directed toward him, so much as the cane. He enjoys when I protest.

"You don't like that?" he teases. I grunt, knowing I can't form words. I wouldn't tell him I hate it because I don't. It's strangely arousing.

He reaches between my legs and around the clamp, which hurts like hell when he touches it. His fingers stroke between my labia. He retreats, stuffing his glistening fingers in his mouth and sucking them.

"You have a very wet little cunt," he whispers.

I watch as he picks up some more clamps and weights. He stands in front of me and says, "Take a deep breath."

I do as he says. He pinches my nostrils, preventing me from breathing except for the minute amount of air I can suck around the ball.

He reaches down, taking the painful clamp from my clit ever so slowly. The pain rushes through my whole body, desperate to escape me with a scream, but I can't manage more than a muffled wail. He drops the weighted clamp before slapping my clit with three of his fingers. Holy fuck! My knees buckle, putting strain on my shoulders. I fight to regain my legs beneath me, but he slaps it again before I can. This time, the sensation is a mixture of pain with unbelievable, rock my world, roll my eyes back in my head, kind of thrill.

He taps my clit repeatedly and I'm right on the verge of coming, but I need air. I'm not getting enough from around this ball. His fingers release my nostrils and I immediately exhale the full breath that was burning my lungs. I'm quick to take in more and more air, panting feverishly. I'm there, right there, holding on the edge of a mind-blowing orgasm, but it isn't happening.

It's like when you're on the verge of a sneeze but it just won't come. It's the same sense of urgency, the horrendously wonderful tickle, that mind-numbing need. But, there's no relief, no relief at all. Holy fuck, this is awesome!

My legs are locked straight with my hips shoved forward until my wrists are straining against their bindings. I'm holding perfectly still, breathing and waiting for my body to let go. He taps, over and over, never touching my clit for more than a second. Never letting me have my reward.

Suddenly it stops and he's no longer tapping or touching me in any way. My orgasmic urge is subsiding, and I want it back. I need his touch. I'm begging, pleading with him, with the universe, with every cell in my body.

Something cool slides along my clit. I open my eyes and look down, seeing the cane pushed up between my pussy lips. It feels great; firm and smooth - but there's overwhelming fear that he's going to strike it with the that piece of wood. If it hurts as much as it did on my nipples, I will be waving my hand for him to ease off.

He pulls my labia apart with his free hand and lightly taps the side of my swollen button. It doesn't hurt nearly as much as I thought it would, but then again, his goal isn't to cause me pain. He's stimulating me, bringing more blood to the area to heighten my sensitivity, not that I really need more of that. Again, he taps. I watch the concentration in his expression as he aims his rod on either side of my throbbing clit; one side, then the other, back and forth.

I try to say, "Just touch my clit, please," but the words don't form into anything understandable. A long line of saliva oozes from my bottom lip, barely missing his forearm on its descent to the floor.

"Do you want me to touch you... here?" he asks, pressing the cane on top of my clitoris, moving it back and forth slowly. "Like this? Is this what you want?"

I don't know how long I've been staring into his eyes. The green flecks floating in the brown begin to dance. Maybe I'm simply losing my focus. My mind is definitely whirling from my body's heightened state of arousal. Time is irrelevant to me at this point.

He won't let me cum. This is another session of edging; teasing aimed to take me to the edge of climax, but not allowing me to throw myself into the light, airy, pillowy softness of orgasm. There will be no release, not yet. I would be disappointed if he allowed it so soon.

I want to enjoy this for a little while longer.

Coach smiles wickedly as he rises to his feet. I'm begging, which is what he likes me to do. He once told me that to hear a woman beg for her orgasm, is the most enticing way to stroke his ego. He loves the ownership that those pleas bring. I didn't understand at the time, but I get it now. He wants to know he owns my orgasm, my pleasure - me. If only for just that moment, he is my everything. It's a moment he can drag on and on, until he gets his fill.

My thoughts are fleeting, and my body is bound and shaking, but I feel free. Freer than I have in a very long time. Nothing matters except his touch and since I have no control over that, I am nothingness. I am simply here, detached from reality, time, even sound has vanished. My screams leave me but never reach my ears. Can he hear them? Am I indeed screaming?

My muscles jerk hard and I'm snapped back to reality. It's overwhelming to have all of my senses and thoughts slam back into focus, so quickly. I'm shaking so violently. I have to allow myself to hang from my wrists and clear my thoughts, giving my body a moment of stillness.

He returns from the dresser with something in his hand, but I couldn't care less what it is. I just want to go back to the nothingness. But I want to cum too, repeatedly. He straps a vibrating wand to my right upper thigh using a leather belt.

He spreads my labia, placing the bulbous end against my clitoris.

With this ball in my mouth, my *thank you Sir* sounds more like *ga-goo-er,* but Coach's smile tells me that he was able to understand. The vibration slowly revs up. Oh. Fuck. Yes.

"You may cum whenever you want, as many times as you want. If you become too loud, I'll shut it off and then it's over. Do you understand?" he whispers with his mouth next to my ear. I'm confused; have I not been incredibly loud already? I was screaming with deafening tones, in my head anyway.

I can only nod my head. My deep chested groans sound more like the purrs from a wilderness cat than from a woman. My asshole suddenly feels even more full. He pumps the balloon again. I had actually forgotten it was still in there. One more pump and I'm so goddamn full! Too full! I wave my hand and try to talk. Instant relief when the balloon deflates quite a bit.

I'm hurdled into the most beautiful euphoria. I'm finally coming. Yes, it's happening! I'm floating, lifting off my feet, slipping out of the bindings that imprison me to the bed frame, and rising up, up, up to the ceiling.

This one doesn't ease as quickly as most orgasms do. This one lingers at the high point, holding me in its clutches. I never want it to end.

Twap! What the fuck? *Twap, twap*. No! Why? Why is Coach drawing my attention to my breasts, away from the glory of my climax? *Twap*! It lands directly on my nipple. I want to scream, not because it hurts, but I'm fucking livid that he stole me away from my well-deserved orgasm.

My clit is painfully sensitive to the vibration. I try to tilt forward and back, left and then right, but neither direction shifts it off my hypersensitive little button. Saliva trails from my chin all the way down my belly, as

I continue this battle I cannot win. He made sure I couldn't wiggle away from the wand. He knew I would try.

More punishment from the cane, this time his aim is directed to my left inner thigh. Fuck! I think the sharpness of the sting is worse than it was on my breasts. It's not a sting that stops right away, it tends to linger and burn in strips along my tender flesh.

My clit feels hot, swollen and aching but it's fully aroused yet again. He increases the intensity of the vibration and I'm losing myself to it.

Chapter Thirteen

Coach

Rayna is coming again, so much harder and more intensely than she usually does. The muscles in her abdomen have been flexed for fifteen minutes now, with no sign of letting up. Her legs and arms are shaking vigorously. Tomorrow, she will feel this night. With every little movement, she'll think of me. She'll curse me, and yet want more of me because of it.

The cane stings her skin with every contact. I love canes. Not as much as the close contact from using my hand, but the lingering effect from the cane, is more dramatic. I've caned women until their skin let go. I won't do that to Rayna. It's not that I wouldn't get off on it; I am a sick fucker. I know Rayna well enough to know she wouldn't appreciate it. Never would I do anything to make her angry at me.

I set the cane on the floor, so I can walk my fingertips along the welted stripes that dance on her breasts as her chest rises and falls. Her creamy globes jiggle from her shakiness, and I can't help myself. I lean in and bite her flesh, not hard, just enough to make her yelp.

I squat in front of her to admire my handiwork on her inner thigh. Five perfectly spaced lines trail down to her mid-thigh. Christ, that's a work of art. I can't say I've ever spaced my cane this consistently. My fingers trail from one line to the next, loving the way the pads of my fingers sense their heat.

My cock is thick and craving to be inside her. I don't even care what orifice I slide into, as long as it's wet and hot.

Her body tenses again, jerking in a spastic manner that seems more alien than human. Her cum is spurting onto the floor each time her pussy spasms. Saliva dribbles down her chin, between her breasts and drains in a slick line toward her clit. A moment after her orgasm ebbs, another wave rolls through her. And then another. And another.

To stop her from holding her breath and losing consciousness completely, I unstrap the belt and pull the cord from the wall plug. I untie her ankles, leaving the cuffs on and then do the same for her wrists. She is so weak that I do not trust her legs to hold her weight. I scoop her up and carry her limp body to the bed and lie her on her back.

She's so weak that her legs fall open, inviting me in. I unzip my pants and pull them down just enough to free my cock and balls. I slam into her pussy and hold still, until she opens her eyes. I want her to know she's with me. The thought that she might be imagining another man makes my jaw clench.

She opens her eyes when I start to unfasten the buckle holding the ballgag in place. Her lids are heavy. She seems to be having a tough time regaining her focus, but she soon manages to meet my gaze.

"Just love me," she whispers with tears streaming from the corners of her eyes.

Her words punch at my heart with a tender cruelty that makes it feel like it's bleeding. How was I to know all she really wanted from me was for me to make love to her? What I just did to her was my way of showing her how much she means to me. Does she not see that? I'm with her now, in her bed, between her legs, and my heart beats only for her. Does she not know that I love her more than I've ever loved anything or anyone, in my entire existence?

"I will love you every second, of every minute, of every day, with every heartbeat my body can manage, until I take my very last breath." I whisper, vowing to be hers for the rest of my days and I can't be any surer that it's what I want. She's what I need.

My lips meet hers. I hold her thigh in one hand while I swoop her other leg between my knees. I slowly fuck her, while pulling her thigh up as close to her chest, as possible. Our mouths taste each other as if it's this one thing that will keep this very moment alive, forever.

My hips lift and lower, rhythmically waving between her split legs. I can feel her pussy tighten around my prick and I doubt I can hold off much longer. I pause to regain my control, but my orgasm is already beginning to erupt into a mind-numbing climax. I ram Rayna into the mattress, hardcore. I own her! No, she owns me!

Coming feels like such a relief, but it hasn't satisfied the tightness inside of me. My cock has yet to soften, in fact, it's painfully hard. I reach down, cupping her welted breast, and caress the hot, lifted skin. Another urge builds quickly. I continue my relentless pounding, fucking her, as fast as I can.

A second rush of hot semen releases, and a wail erupts from the deepest reservoirs in my soul, most likely coming from my inner Demon. He's frustrated that I refuse to let him roam freely during playtime. One day, I'll set him free, but if Rayna can't accept him, it's back in his cage he goes. I had never thought I'd see the day that a woman would mean more to me than my Demon ever could.

I whimper and coo, "I love you! I fucking love you! Oh my god, I fucking love you!"

I collapse onto the right side of Rayna, while still holding my painfully sensitive cock inside of her. Soon it will shrivel and slip free from her. It'll be a sad moment for sure. Being inside of her is the best feeling, ever. I wish we never had to be apart.

A few seconds after it slips free, I roll completely off her and fling my arms up onto the pillow above my head. I grab it and slide it under my heavy head. Rayna curls into me. Her slackened movements prove to me just how tired she is.

"I love you, Coach," she whispers.

I kiss her forehead. "I really do love you, Rayna." I kiss her again, placing my hand on her back to help hold her against me. "If you wanted me to make love to you tonight, why didn't you say so when you came out of the bathroom?"

She does her best attempt to shrug. "You were all dressed. You know I can't turn you down when you look so good."

"Next time, just tell me you would rather make love."

"But this was great, too."

"Just promise."

"Okay, I promise." She pauses for a few moments before breaking the silence that fills the dimly lit room. "Coach, why did you use a cane on me?"

"Because I'm a sick son-of-a-bitch," I laugh, trying to make light of my sadistic, inner asshole, and hope she'll be satisfied with that answer.

"No, I mean, why? Is there a reason why you would want to pick up a cane and use it on someone? I guess I'm asking if the cane has a special significance in your life?"

I pause for a moment before replying, trying to decipher if there is a significance or not. "Nobody has ever asked me that. I don't really know. Canes leave straight lines, welts and sometimes bruises. They can also break skin with just the right swing. It's painful and the cries that follow the high-pitched snapping sound, almost mimics it. Maybe it's all of those reasons or just that I love the feel of the cane in my hand. I really couldn't specify."

Rayna yawns, "It's going to be a long day tomorrow."

"Sleep, my love," I kiss her head and sigh, my eyelids weighing heavily.

She slides off me, under my protest. She laughs, "Let me go, I have to pee."

"Let me pour you a hot bath with some Epsom Salts and lavender oil." I begin to pull my back off the bed, but she puts her hand against my chest and pushes me back. "Are you sure?"

"Yes, I'm fine. My butt cheeks don't hurt anymore. My nipples are still stinging, but they'll be fine. Besides, I'm too tired to sit in a tub. I have a very busy day tomorrow, so I'd rather just sleep."

"Well, if you're sure."

"I'm sure. I'll be right back."

"Don't be long or I'll be asleep," I call out as the soft slaps of her bare feet draw distance between us.

"OH MY GOD!" she nearly yells loud enough for the kids to startle awake.

I leap up and run to the bathroom, nearly falling over the stool at the end of the bed. I hop while limping to ease the ache from a scraped shin. I push open the bathroom door. My eyelids slam shut, protecting my eyes from the brightest light I've ever seen – or so it seems, at this very second.

"What? What's wrong?" I ask while fighting to open my watering eyes.

"This!" she says, pointing to her breasts and thighs. "You fucking bruised me! I have welts. Like, a lot of welts! What if someone sees them?"

"You said you weren't going to be changing in front of anyone and you said you wouldn't be putting on a bathing suit, so you'll be all right." I don't see what the problem is.

She turns her whole body to face me. The look on her face carries anger. "Why? Why would you do this to me?"

461

I lean against the doorframe, feeling the exhaustion wain on me. "I told you I was going to mark you. You are marked, as I said I would do. What's the problem?"

"What's the problem?" she hisses before turning back to look at herself in the mirror. "This! This is a problem! What if the kids see it?"

"How are the kids going to see it? You're leaving in the morning for the entire weekend. By the time you return, they'll be faded, considerably. I don't understand why you're getting so upset. It's not like I locked a collar on your neck and kept the key hidden from you or bruised your arms so everyone would see. I didn't brand you. Your marks are minimal and will disappear; no harm, no foul."

"No harm, no foul..." her words fall away. She stares at herself, shaking her head. She whispers, "Never again."

Her eyes have yet to meet mine. I think I really fucked up. "So, no more cane. Got it! You're going to be okay. If you could have seen yourself coming when I was creating those lovely welts, you would beg me to do it every day."

Now she turns, staring angrily into my eyes, without blinking. So, this is how the kids feel when Rayna is about to punish them.

No wonder they don't like it.

Her finger points at me and shakes. "No! No!"

She pushes past me and into bed without another word. I shut off the light after looking down at my calf to see if it's bleeding. It's not. Slipping under the covers, I look over at Rayna. Her back is to me and she's curled into a ball. I roll, attempting to pull her against me, to comfort her, but she swings her hand back, nearly hitting my balls. So, I can't touch her? This won't do. I grab her shoulder and yank her onto her back.

"Don't touch me!" she hisses.

I flip off the covers and hop on top of her legs, pinning her in place. "We need to talk about this."

"No, we don't. Let me work through it."

"Please, talk to me. You're obviously angry. My question is whether you're angry at me for putting those marks on you or for showing you that you enjoyed receiving them? Are you angry that you agreed to be marked and that you were somewhat excited by the thought of it? But now, seeing your body with the physical reminders of your twisted sexual desires, has you unsure of how to express your emotions? Does being angry at me help with all of that?"

"How do you know how I'm feeling?"

"You are not the only one to experience this. Whatever you tell me, whatever you want to talk about with me… you need to know that I've heard it all before. What you're feeling is normal. You cannot shut me out. If we are going to be in a relationship, I need to know how you feel, where your limits and fears lie. Shutting me out when you are hurting or confused, will not help you. Do you trust me?"

"You know I do."

"Then trust me enough to tell me what is going on in here," I say while tapping her head with my finger.

"You pretty much hit everything on the nail. I don't know how I feel. I mean, feeling it – the cane – was painful and awful, but my body used that to create something so wonderful and powerful. To

actually see the horror that got me off, is…" "Is shocking," I whisper.

"Yes, I suppose that's a good word for it."

I flop down behind her and toss the covers back over me. Hugging her to my body would be exactly what she needs, what I need, but I'm afraid to push her. She might bolt to the sofa downstairs. Rayna likes to keep things in her head, mulling them over and over, until she's come to a conclusion as to whether something is good or bad, healthy or destructive.

"Can I hold you?" I whisper.

"Not tonight," she replies.

I roll onto my back and stare up at the ceiling. The painful beating of my breaking heart is more than I can bear. Fuck! Why am I such an asshole? Whatever possessed me to think it would be okay to mark her? She said it was okay. Maybe I took advantage. I don't know. I can't take the damn silence. She'll be leaving tomorrow morning, likely before we have time to talk about this. Fuck! She can't get on the plane while she's angry with me. What if she decides to leave me forever? No! Oh god no!

The covers pull as I slide off the bed. My feet quickly take me around the bed. I drop to my knees and lay my forehead on the comforter inches from her chest. I feel her lift her head, and then her hand touches the top of my head and I grasp it, holding it in my hair. "Please, please don't leave me. I won't survive. I need you. I love you. I am yours, always." I can't hide the rawness in my voice. "I'm sorry, Rayna. I'm so sorry. Please, don't leave me."

She leans up on one elbow, wrapping her other arm over my head and down my back. Her cheek rests against mine, pinning my other cheek into the mattress. No words leave her mouth but she's speaking volumes. Rayna isn't leaving me for overstepping her limits. She doesn't hate me.

"I'm not leaving you. I will never leave you. The marks startled me. I wasn't expecting them. They barely even hurt anymore. You'll have to give me some time to decide where I want to set the limit on marking me. Give me time, that's all I'm asking."

"Okay, I can give you all the time you need. If you don't hate me, why won't you let me hold you? As a dominant, it's my job to ensure my submissive is physically, mentally and emotionally secure. You refused me that. I thought you hated me."

She shakes her head slightly, "I don't hate you. I could never hate you. Now, get into bed and hold me, so we can sleep. I need to sleep, so I'm not too tired for the flight tomorrow morning."

I nod and stand up, quickly making my way back into bed. My nerves are settling, but my head is all over the place. I shouldn't be questioning my actions, especially since she didn't call out her safeword. She shouldn't be angry at me after the fact, but she is angry, and that worries me. What the fuck is this woman doing to me?

* * * * *

I happen to catch the concerned expression on Rayna's face when I open the bedroom door. She turns away from the mirror, pretending she wasn't just staring at her brownish-purple, cylindrical bruises. The fake smile she wears is aimed to deter me away from what I just saw, it does not reach her eyes.

"Are you almost ready to go?" I ask her.

"Ah, yeah, I think so," she says while scratching her forearm, still sporting the makeshift happy expression.

"Do you want to talk about it?" I ask her.

She shakes her head and turns away from me. I know she wants to get dressed, but that means she would have to remove her nightgown. I'll see her body when she does. Instead of giving her privacy, I wait silently.

"Can I get dressed?" she asks.

"Of course," I reply. "Do you need any assistance?"

"Of course not!" she shrugs. "Maybe the kids need you?"

"Rayna," I whisper, as I slowly approach her. "It's okay to take off your nightgown. I've already seen the marks. Just now, when I opened the door, you were looking at them. Show me, love."

She grimaces, "Well, I suppose since you were the one who marked me, you should be entitled to savour the moment."

Her nightie falls to the floor in a heap. Her eyes are locked on mine, I can feel them. She's waiting to see if I lick my lips or show any sign of arousal. It's important that I don't. My eyes meet hers and I just look at them.

Stoically, I ask, "So, what do you think of them?"

She shrugs, "I don't know. They're bruises that you inflicted upon me, so I'm supposed to be upset about that. But I can admire the skill it takes to apply the cane as uniformly as you did, to create the perfect spacing between the stripes. I also remember how incredibly painful it was and how I used that pain to heighten my senses, bringing forth one of the most powerful orgasmic experiences of my life. So, to be completely honest, I'm not sure how I want to feel. Choosing one emotion over the other, is impossible."

"I can understand that. Are you angry with me?"

"No, because I know how much it would hurt you if I was and how unfair that would be of me. I said you could mark me, I can't deny that. If I told you to never do that again, I know you wouldn't. That's how I know how much you love me. If I asked you to, I believe you would give up all of it, for me."

"I would," my words follow a harsh swallow. I don't have to tell her that I'd be miserable because of it. We both know the truth.

"But you'd be very unhappy, in turn, making me unhappy. I don't want you to stop introducing me to new things. Just promise me that you will never bruise my skin again, not like this anyway. Accidents happen, but this is purposefully done to mark me, and I don't like it."

I take her in my arms and hold her cool skin against me. "I promise to never mark your body on purpose, ever again. I will not cane you or do anything else that might taint your skin. This, I vow to you."

She pulls back and meets my eyes. "I didn't say I didn't enjoy the cane and the pain it produced. I just don't want the bruises. Maybe you shouldn't do it so hard next time."

"Next time? You liked it enough for me to do it again? But you just said…" I step away, scratching my head. "You don't want me to mark you, but you enjoyed the pain you received when being marked. Okay, I think I understand. I will have to think of alternative ways to create the same effect. Challenge accepted."

She smiles shyly before beginning to get dressed, not once looking back into the mirror until she's fully clothed. I have been watching her. I've tried not to, but I'll admit that I'm a sick fuck and I want to touch the marks, lick them and then drop her to the floor and fuck her hard to relieve my deep-rooted ache for release. I won't do all of that, because I don't know how she'd react; badly, I'd bet.

"Did you enjoy looking at them?" she asks.

I reply, "I'd rather you not ask me that question. I'm sure you already know the answer." I watch Rayna's eyes drop to my crotch.

I'd be lying to her if I tried to deny my arousal.

"Do you want to hit me again?"

I furrow my brow. "No, I want to lick them, touch them and then fuck you hard. Is that what you want to hear?"

"I just want to know what you're thinking, that's all," she whispers.

"I'm remembering how the cane felt in my hand. The way you flinched from the contact. The pain behind your muffled screams. The way you became quiet as you bravely absorbed the pain. How hard you came and how often. How wet you were. The way your limp body felt heavy in my arms afterward." I look up at her and take a deep breath.

Rayna walks over to me and takes my hand, leading me to the bathroom. She locks the door behind us and pulls down my sweatpants. My prick springs forth, hard and dripping with precum. She rolls the end of her finger over the slit, lubricating the end of my cock with my own slickness.

She pulls down her pants, yanking them off one foot. After sliding her butt onto the counter, she spreads her legs, leaning her back against the mirror. "Fuck me. Admire your handiwork."

Is she serious? I don't care! I want her, she's offering, I'm taking!

I push forward, burying my prick deep into her pussy. It's surprisingly wet. My eyes watch the marks on her inner thighs dance each time I hump into her. I want to cum and it's only been a few seconds.

Rayna lifts her blouse and bra, revealing the bruised stripes on her breasts. I fuck into her three more times, it's all I can do to bear it. My orgasm overwhelms me, forcing my eyes closed while I spill my seed deep inside of her. I'm still jerking when my eyelids slowly open.

She's looking at me with a curious expression. "You really got excited when you saw the bruises, didn't you?"

"Yes, I did." I feel slightly humiliated. Was that her objective; to make me feel like shit? "I'm sorry that I'm such a sick fuck."

"You aren't a sick fuck. You are a bit strange and not what I'm used to, but you can't help being who you are, and you certainly can't prevent what turns you on. We'll work around it, okay?"

I nod and smile. My shrivelling prick slips from her semen drenched pussy, making me shutter. She finds it to be humorous. I snicker and then rinse off using the washcloth I left in the sink earlier. She points her finger toward the door, impatiently waiting for me to leave before she sits on the toilet to let my seed drain from her.

I stand outside the closed bathroom door. "Really? You still won't pee in front of me? I have licked and loved every inch of your body, but this makes you uncomfortable?"

"No, I won't. If you have a fetish for urination, don't ever tell me. That's a deal breaker for me. Now, go away!"

"I'll keep that in mind. Okay, you'd better hurry, your ride will be here in fifteen minutes."

"I would have been ready if you hadn't distracted me. Now leave me alone."

I walk through the bedroom and into the hallway. The idea of being without Rayna for two whole nights, already has me feeling lonely and she hasn't even left yet. I'll have to keep myself busy with the kids. Maybe I'll show up in Las Vegas and surprise her.

Hmm, I'll have to give that some thought.

"Hey kids! If you get ready for school and don't miss the bus, we'll have pizza and beer tonight!" I yell out as I make my way toward the kitchen to see if the kids are eating their breakfast

I hear Rayna yell something about *no beer*, but the kids are talking and laughing too loud for me to hear what she said. I got their attention, and that's a good thing.

"Don't get your panties in a bunch. I'm referring to root beer! What do you take me for? Huh?" I yell back to tease her. She mumbles something else, but I'm walking into the kitchen now, so I don't even try to strain my ears. I roll my eyes dramatically and say, "Moms! Right?" They laugh even harder.

* * * * *

Rayna slips into the passenger's seat while Dr. Jessik tucks her suitcase in the trunk. He waves and I nod. Something about that guy has me not trusting him.

It's obvious to me that he has a thing for Rayna. I wonder if she has a clue. She might think he's a shy man and is awkward around everyone. Maybe it's just that I don't know him all that well, or maybe he's especially timid around me for a reason. He's not Rayna's type, at least, I don't think he is. She doesn't like men who are quiet and reserved, like this guy is. Still, I wonder what his intentions are.

The kids hop on the bus shortly after Rayna leaves with Dr. Suspicious. As I'm getting in my truck, I call Renee, not that I like talking to her.

"Hello," she answers on the first ring.

"Hey, Rayna just left."

"So, you're calling me because?" she questions.

"What would you say about watching the kids while I surprise Rayna in Vegas? I can leave after dinner tonight."

She's quiet for a moment. "Yeah, I don't think that's a good idea."

"Why not?"

She scoffs, "Why do you think? Think about it for half a second. What do you think she's going to say when you suddenly show up at her work convention?"

"Hello, is a good start."

"You're such a dumbass!" she says, irritating the hell out of me.

"She's going to think you don't trust her."

"That's not it at all. I want to surprise her, in a good way. She'll be thrilled to see me."

She laughs purposefully because she knows how much I hate her smartass attitude. "She'll send you back home. Why don't you just let her be? Seriously, can your dick not manage to have one fucking night without shoving it into her? Why can't you just jerk off, like most men do?"

That's all I can handle of her shitty attitude. I hang up, thoroughly pissed off. She's such a bitch, especially with me. I have been nothing but respectful of her since she started living with my best buddy, Tim. She's been a total bitch to me ever since I turned her down when she made a pass at me, and then made light of it so Rayna wouldn't be angry at her. She's nice as pie when somebody is within earshot.

If I threw her over a table and fucked her hard, I'm sure she'd soften up to me, but that'll never happen. She irritates me so much that I'd tease the hell out of her after beating her ass red hot, and then I'd fuck her backside until she wet herself. I won't, because I respect Rayna and Tim too much. But, fuck, I want to teach that cunt some fucking respect.

My workouts today are going to be rough. I hope my clients are ready for me. I'll make sure to workout heavy so I can let off some steam before the first person shows up.

Chapter Fourteen

Rayna

My seat on the plane is next to Dr. Jessik. I wonder if he conveniently arranged for me to be beside him, crammed against the window. I cannot easily escape to the bathroom unless I slide over him with my ass inches from his face. Why we are sitting together, has me scratching my head. Wouldn't it make more sense to have Jennifer and I sitting together, leaving the doctors to talk shop? This new seating arrangement isn't typical. Jennifer gazes my way with a frown and I wonder if her seatmate will take offense. I take notice of the pout I'm wearing and do my best not to look so disappointed.

Most of my time on the flight is spent reading. Renee gave me a book about a woman having an affair with her boss. I sure hope Dr. Jessik hasn't read it. He might think I'm giving him a hint. He is busy reading too, but I've noticed that he hasn't flipped the page in about ten minutes. He must be lost in thought.

"Rayna, would you like a drink?"

"Yes, actually. White wine would be perfect."

He leaves, returning a few moments later with two drinks. After handing me a plastic cup half filled with wine, he takes his seat.

"Thank you, Dr. Jessik."

"Rayna, please call me Ray. You're always so formal with me."

"Oh, I didn't know you preferred to have me call you by your first name. It's strange that I never thought to ask you." He seems a bit put off by my comment. I should say something else. "I suppose I just respect you too much to call you anything other than Dr. Jessik."

He smiles, "Thank you, Rayna. It's nice of you to say that. I want you to think of me as a friend, not just your boss. We are friends, aren't we?" he asks with a nervous tick in his left eye.

"Yes, we are." We hardly speak for the rest of the flight, other than a few common pleasantries.

When we get to the hotel, the four of us have rooms next to or across the hall from each other. It's convenient for when we are expected to attend a function together. This way we can arrive as a group.

The first thing I do is text Coach to let him know I arrived safely and my room number. He doesn't respond, so I unpack and take a quick shower to liven myself up. The flight was torturously boring, to say the least. The book wasn't very interesting and the few short conversations between Ray and I, fell flat. I slip on my jeans and red blouse, fix my make-up and brush out my hair. After checking my phone again and not seeing a response from Coach, I make my way to Jennifer's room. She is talking to her mom on the phone, when she opens the door for me.

I flop on her bed, propping a pillow behind my back so I can sit up comfortably. She rolls her eyes and waves her hand, as if to urge her mother to finish talking. I can picture the future, when my kids are talking to me and doing the same thing, and it irks me.

She hangs up and drops her phone on her bed. "So, what's new with you?"

"Not much. I wish we could have sat together on the plane."

"No kidding! Dr. Myri is so uninteresting that I drifted off to sleep a dozen times while he was talking. Golf! Fucking golf! The man has nothing better to do in life than chase a tiny white ball around a field? Really?

The man needs to find a woman, or another man, no judgement! He needs to get laid! Seriously, his life is so dull."

"He must like the monotony," I laugh, because she's right. I've been stuck talking to him and it's always about golf. Dr. Myri has never been married nor seems all too interested in being with anyone. Nobody knows his sexual orientation, but everyone has their opinion. He's a nice enough person, just dull as fuck.

"So, you left that hot, young thing alone for an entire weekend just so you can come to Vegas for a boring dental convention? What's wrong with you?" she says while I shrug. "You could have at least brought him, so I'd have something interesting to stare at while I'm here."

"He's staying with the kids," I tell her. I'm pretty sure I'm blushing.

She looks at me and then rolls her eyes. "Get a sitter! Dammit woman! This is Las Vegas, home of sin. Then again, maybe you want to sin all on your own this weekend. As the saying goes, *what happens in Vegas...*" she waves her eyebrows.

I laugh, "No, I'm not here to misbehave. I'm here to schmooze with the big-wigs of the dental community."

"Tell me honestly, is he as good in bed as I would imagine any fit, strong, sexy, younger man should be?"

I slap her arm and blush even more, "Yes, he's incredible, and that's all I'm saying about that topic. What about you? Are there any hot men in your life?"

She shrugs, "No, not anyone special. Maybe I'm just afraid to settle down with anyone in case something better comes along."

"Well, just remember, age is catching up with you. Soon you'll be my age and finding a good man gets harder as we get older. More of them are taken, the good ones anyway, and the rest want younger women. Find a man that you can love and not want to smother in his sleep. There are no such thing as real-life fairy tales. Relationships can be hard sometimes, but very rewarding too."

"Okay, enough dragging me down the depression hole for one evening. I brought this!" she announces, holding up a bottle of Tequila.

Before I can protest, she's pouring us each a shot in the disposable plastic cups stacked up by the coffee maker. She hands one to me and then taps my cup with hers. We slug it back and wince. She immediately refills them. We chug that one too. I hold my hand over the rim of the flimsy cup, refusing to allow her to pour me another shot.

By the time the doctors rap on her door, I'm already feeling a bit lightheaded. This is going to be a short night if I don't get some food in me soon.

The four of us eat at the restaurant we always eat at when we first arrive. It's only a ten-minute walk. Before returning back to the hotel, Jennifer and I decide to do a little shopping at some of the local stores, while the doctors attend a meeting meant just for dentists. Later, we meet up with some of the other convention attendees in the pub on the main floor of our hotel. The drinks start off light and go down slowly, but as the evening wears on, the drinks start to take their toll.

At eleven-thirty, I decide that I've had enough. Jennifer wants to party on, so I start to make my way down the corridor to the elevators alone. I stumble and reach for the wall, surprised when my hand doesn't touch it. Someone has their arm around my waist. I turn to see a swaying Dr. Jessik.

"Hey, Dr. J, I mean Dr. Ray. Wait, no, it's just Ray, right?" I'm giggling like a drunken fool. Who am I kidding? I am a drunk fool.

"Are you all right Rayna?"

"Oh yeah! I'm great! How are you… Ray?"

"I'm just fine. I'm going to walk you to you room."

"Don't be ridiclll... ridiclll... silly. I'm fine! Go... party on dude! Life is short. You need to get laid! We all need to get laid more often. I mean, shit! I shouldn't talk like that in front of you. You're my boss!" I start laughing, but I don't know why. I'm more intoxicated than I should be when talking about such a private topic, especially in the presence of my boss.

He escorts me into the elevator and pushes the button to our floor. I try to focus on the numbers above the doors, but they are just a bright green blur. When the elevator stops, my knees waiver but I grasp the railing to steady myself. I am so fucked up! I should know better than to try to keep up to Jennifer. She's a seasoned drinker who loves hanging out at the local bars in search of the perfect man.

I stumble down the hall while laughing and dancing, or at least, my drunken attempt to dance elegantly. I'm sure it's anything but.

"Do you want to come in?" I ask when we arrive at my room. I'm not sure why I'm inviting him in. I probably shouldn't.

"Rayna, as much as I would love nothing more, I think I should not enter your room. You are quite drunk, and therefore, might do something you'll regret in the morning."

"Okay, problem solved," I say when I push my door all the way open and flip the doorstop down to prevent the door from closing. "See, you'll be safe now."

He reluctantly follows me in and sits on the sofa chair. "Whisky, vodka, rum... what do you like?" I ask while searching through the minibar for the small bottle of white wine I had my eye on earlier.

"I'm fine, thank you."

"Nope, you have to pick one." "Whisky," he replies.

After tossing it to him, I crack the bottle of wine and take a swig, directly from the bottle. I flop in the other sofa chair and smile at him. He's still blurry.

"Ray, are you happy?" I ask him.

He clears his throat and then opens his tiny bottle. "Not especially. I'd like to be happier, but we don't always get what we think we deserve."

"And what do you think you deserve?"

He smiles, but it fades quickly. "I like you Rayna. I wish you were mine, but I understand that you're with him and I wish you the best."

"Thank you," I reply, not entirely sure what I'm thanking him for.

"I just hope he's good to you."

I start giggling when I think about what he did to me last night. "Oh, he treats me good. I mean, it's bad sometimes, but I like it. I like him. I really like him. We're getting married... eventually. I don't know why I haven't picked a day yet. He stopped asking me about it. Maybe I'm just gun-shy about getting hitched again. I don't know. It didn't work out so well for me the first time. Why am I telling you all of this?"

"What do you mean by it's bad sometimes?"

"Well, he's... he's kind of... he's rough around the edges."

"Does he hurt you?"

"No, no, it's not like that. I mean, yeah, sometimes, but it's not what you think. Why can't I stop talking? I shouldn't be telling you this stuff. It's private between him and I."

"I don't mean to pry. I just need to know if he's hurting you."

I smile at him and lick my lips. "Listen, he hurts me in ways that I like. He would never do anything I didn't want him to do. He asks and I either condone or dismiss. I have the final say. I hold all the power in our sexual relationship. He might be the aggressor, but it's about me. It's all about me."

"I would never hurt you. Nobody should ever hurt you."

"That would get very boring. Don't you think? I'm sorry, I'm not trying to insult you. I'm not normally a bitch. I'm not, I promise."

"You're one of the most intelligent, caring, thoughtful people I have ever met. Bitch isn't a title you could carry very well." He takes a deep breath, letting it out slowly. "Rayna, don't let him hurt you."

I had better explain before he calls the cops to tell them Coach has been beating me. "Ray, he's a dominant and I'm his submissive. I hold all the power. I used to think a woman who let a man do what he wanted to her, no matter what it was, was stupid and powerless.

It's quite the opposite. I allow him to do the things he does. If I say no, it's a no. He taught me that I am incredibly strong. I will forever be grateful to him for that. You don't have to worry about me. I am going to be just fine, whether he's in my life or not. He loves me and will always protect me from harm."

"Just because he saved your life, doesn't mean you owe him anything."

"Dr. Jessik, Ray, I know that. I love him. I really do. He's good for me."

He swallows down the last sip of whiskey from the small bottle and slowly puts the cap back on. "Well, I'm always here for you. If you ever need to talk or need protection, I'll do what I can." "Protection?" I ask.

"From him," he whispers. "Judging by what you're telling me, he's going to really hurt you one day. I just hope he doesn't hurt your kids."

"You haven't listened to me at all, have you? He loves my kids and I trust him with their safety. I trust him with my life and the lives of my children. Don't you dare, even for a minute, think he will ever hurt them."

"I'm sorry, Rayna, I just don't understand," he says as he stands and makes his way toward the open door.

"Do something for me?"

"Anything."

"Do some research on BDSM before you pass judgement on my lifestyle. You can't make an informed opinion if you aren't first informed."

"Get some sleep. We have a long day tomorrow," he says before gently kicking the doorstop to dislodge it, as he walks out. The door swings shut with a slam, locking automatically.

Why the fuck did I tell him all of that? I'm not a great secret keeper when I've been drinking. Maybe that's why my ex-husband used to get me drunk and then ask me a hundred questions; questions he knew I would never answer if I were sober.

I pick up my phone. I had forgotten to take it with me to the bar, after having tossed it on the bed with all the new clothes I bought. I squint to read the text message lighting up the screen. It's a message from Coach saying that he's sorry he didn't get my text earlier. I video call him. It rings twice before he answers.

"Hi love. What time is it?" He sounds groggy and it's dark on the screen.

"Oh shit! Sorry! It's around midnight here so that would make it about three AM there. I shouldn't have woken you. I wasn't... I didn't even think about the time." My words are very slurred, and my eyelids feel heavy.

"Rayna, are you drunk?"

"Yeah, a little bit. Are you mad at me?"

"Why would I be mad at you? Are you in your room with the door locked?"

"Yeah, Ray locked it when he left. Well, he kicked that door thingy thing and it shut, so it's locked now."

"You had a man in your room, and you're drunk?"

"Yeah, no... it's just Ray. Dr. Jessik is a nice man. He's nice. Like, he likes me so he's, you know, nice to me. He walked me back to my room to make sure I got back safely. See, he's nice!"

"But he was in your room, alone, while you're drunk," he says with an angry tone.

"Yeah, but he's a nice guy, like I just explained to you. Are you mad at me? Why?" I'm beginning to get upset.

"I don't want men in your room when you're drunk, Rayna."

"What are you, my father?"

"Rayna, don't push me."

"Don't push me," I mock him. "He was a perfect gentleman. We had a drink, chatted and he left. And now I'm calling you but you're kind of being a jealous dick and I don't like it."

"A jealous dick?" he asks. "Rayna, you need to go to bed now. This conversation isn't going in a good direction and you're about to say something that pisses me off."

"Yeah?" I say with a smirk. "Would you like to throw me over your knee and spank my ass like you did at the mansion? That fucking hurt! It was okay, I guess."

He's quiet, other than his breathing. "Yes, I want to punish you for getting drunk and bringing a man into your hotel room with you. Yes, I am jealous, but I am more concerned for your safety than my emotions. Do you not understand how badly your decision could have played out?"

"Well, I guess it worked out just fine, didn't it? I'm safe, talking to you and not in his arms. You're going to have to realize that I can take care of myself. I don't always need you to swoop in and rescue me."

"I did need to rescue you, or did you forget?"

Now I'm fucking angry. "That asshole took me and hurt me because of you, not because of anything I did. He was your friend, whom I had never even met. He never would have even known who I was if you hadn't told him. So, you can blame yourself for that, not me."

"I do, Rayna, every day." I can hear the sadness in his voice and instantly regret saying what I said.

"I'm sorry. I know you do and it's not your fault. I don't blame you. Look, I'm going to let you go because I'm drunk and I'm talking just to hear myself talk. I don't mean to be cruel or to pick a fight. I love you, and I miss you."

"I was going to hop on a plane and surprise you, but your sister suggested I don't."

I snicker, "She's a wise woman. I would have accused you of not trusting me."

"That's what she said," he replies. I'm sure he hates to admit that she was right. "All right, love, sleep it off. Call me tomorrow, okay?"

"I will. I love you!"

"I love you, too!"

After hanging up, I flop back on the bed. That's when my stomach wretches. I make it to the toilet just in time for the first wave of vomit. I spend the next few hours hanging onto the toilet seat for dear life. At one point, I contemplate my sudden death as being an easier way out of this situation. I will survive this night.

Chapter Fifteen

Rayna

The rest of the weekend was uneventful in comparison to the first night. Ray was still sociable with me, but I could feel the tension between us. He hadn't said anything else about our chat until we were getting back on the plane to come home.

As we lined up to wait for our turn to enter the plane, he whispered in my ear, "I did some research, as you suggested. I have a better understanding but it's not for me."

"I appreciate that. Thank you," I told him.

He added, "Just know that I'm here for you if you ever want to talk."

When I turned to look at him, it was the first time I had noticed just how green his eyes are. They were quite stunning. "Thank you."

"I won't tell anyone anything you told me, so you don't have to worry about that."

"I appreciate that," I replied as I stepped into the plane.

* * * * *

The flight home seemed quick, probably because I drifted off to sleep, shortly after takeoff. The drive to my house seems to drag on twice as long as it should. I need to see my kids. It sounds strange, but I miss the smell of their hair. I wonder if other mother's miss that when they're apart from their offspring. I miss Coach too, but for different, more adult reasons. I also miss his hugs and how I disappear in them. There is no place on Earth where I feel safer, than in his arms.

* * * * *

It's been three days since I returned home, and life is back to normal. Coach has ravished me every night. He even gave me oral sex this morning before we got out of bed. He feels guilty for coming down on me, while I was away, but I don't mind. I'm reaping the rewards of his ample apologies. I've had a hop in my step all day because of this morning.

We sit down at the dinner table and begin dishing food onto our plates. Kim tells us all about her day at school. I finally have to tell her to start eating because her food is getting cold and the rest of us are mostly finished. Ken doesn't say much except that he has an algebra test in the morning that he's worried about. He turned down my offer to help him because he knows I suck at algebra. Coach admits that he hated algebra and wouldn't be of much help to him, in fact, likely hindering him.

"Rayna, go on a date with me Saturday night," Coach insists more than asks.

"A date? Where would you like to go?"

"How about the same place I took you last time we had a date?"

My eyes shoot to the kids to gauge their reactions, as if they somehow know about Fallen, but they aren't paying us much attention. I look back at him and nod, raising my eyebrows excitedly. A wide smile erupts on his face that overcomes his eyes, pinching them closed almost completely.

"Say, eight o'clock?" he poses.

"That sounds great. I can ask Renee if she'll babysit."

"I can babysit Kim," Ken interrupts. So, they were listening in on our conversation after all.

"I don't know about that," I reply.

Coach adds, "Yeah, I think it might be too much."

"I'm almost fourteen!" he hisses. "None of my friends have babysitters anymore."

Coach is looking at me, waiting for me to decide. They aren't his children. He won't tell me what to do when it involves them, unless he thinks I'm making the wrong choice, and then he'll still pull me aside to say his peace.

"Fine," I finally reply, after making them wait until I can sift through all the possible things that could go wrong. "I'll make sure Aunt Renee will have her phone readily available, in case you need her. Promise me you won't hesitate to call her if you get scared or something doesn't feel right."

"We promise," they both say simultaneously, and a lot more excitedly than I would like them to be. I still have a tickly sensation at the pit of my belly. I think that's normal for parents who are about to leave their children home alone at night, for the first time.

Coach is looking at me with no expression at all. I can't read what's on his mind. I widen my eyes slightly as if to ask him what's on his mind. He quietly watches me for another full minute without so much as a facial tick, making me rather anxious.

He finally whispers, "I'll work it out."

Oh, shit! I hadn't even thought about the fact that they'll be home when we come back from a highly sexualized night of voyeurism, aroused to the point of wanting to ravish one another in a loud, moaning, screaming, growling physical attack, like two uncivilized beasts. If the kids are home, we'll need to remain very quiet, which I hate doing when we're that aroused. I can't go back on my decision now.

What does he mean he'll work it out? Is he going to gag me with the ball again, so that I can't scream? I don't like it when he covers my mouth and nose, preventing me from making any noises, because I can't breathe. I cum very powerfully when he restricts my breathing, but I still don't like the sensation of fire in my lungs.

We climb into bed after what feels like a really long day. The kids are asleep with their doors closed and we are snuggled up under the lightweight comforter, warming our cool skin against one another. My hand glides down his washboard abs in search of his cock. I want him inside me, whether that means in my mouth, pussy or ass, I don't care.

Coach grabs my wrist before I can grasp his manhood. He pulls it up to his mouth and places tender kisses on its palm.

"Love, I want us to wait for satisfaction until Saturday night." "What?" I ask, not sure I'm hearing him correctly. He snickers, "I want you to wait until we go to Fallen." "Why?" I ask while pouting.

"Trust me, it'll be more fun when you're desperate for release."

"I don't like it but, fine, I'll go along with your little experiment." I snicker, knowing I can use my showerhead when he isn't around.

"No masturbation either," he announces, as if he were reading my thoughts.

I groan with disappointment, but nod anyway. "Fine, no masturbation either. Why do you want me to wait?"

"You'll see. Now get some sleep," he whispers, after kissing my forehead.

Chapter Sixteen

Coach

I plan to introduce Rayna to something new this Saturday, but I don't want to make her uncomfortable in the process. An easy introduction is what I'm hoping for. Would I love to tie her up to an iron cross, flog her after weighting her pussy lips, fuck her with my hand and make her cum in gushing waves, all while a crowd of people watch on, speaking in hushed tones? Yes, I would! But Rayna isn't ready for such an adventure, just yet. She may never be.

To help me with this, I secretly met with Gear, yesterday. We hashed out a scenario that will both entice Rayna and satisfy her, without throwing her into the deep end, so to speak. The last thing I want to do is scare her off.

It's finally Saturday afternoon and we've just finished the weekly house cleaning, laundry and grocery shopping. Now we'll relax before getting ourselves ready to attend Fallen. I've already snuck my leathers into the car, along with the outfit I bought for Rayna. She has no idea that I went shopping without her, for her. Every time I think about her wearing what I bought, my cock stiffens. Of course, not having any release for the past three days hasn't made it easy to keep my cock from springing forth when I see a hot chick bent over at the gym, with her firm, round ass jutting into the air, begging to be spanked. Needless to say, I've been hiding out in my office a lot more than usual.

I'm sitting on the sofa downstairs watching a show about racing cars, when Rayna straddles my lap. She wraps her arms around my neck and starts kissing me with a heated passion that she's avoided since I asked her not to orgasm. I slide my hands around her hips and grip her ass firmly. She starts grinding her pussy against my swelling cock, as if she's actually fucking me.

She lets out a soft moan and I can't resist her. I grab her under the arms and toss her onto her back on the cushion, quickly slamming my hips between her thighs. She lets out another moan as my mouth presses to her. I grasp her wrists and yank them over her head, joining them in my right hand, pinning them. With my free hand, I quickly reach up her shirt and yank her breasts free from her bra. I pinch her nipple with enough force that she winces and tries to wiggle away. My mouth relentlessly abuses hers, forcibly tongue raping her.

I slide my hand beneath the waistband of her yoga pants and make haste toward her pussy. I surpass her clit completely, not giving her the satisfaction of even a graze. Instead, I slide two fingers into her drenched hole and bury them deep. She softly moans, lifting her hips to allow me easier access. I fuck her while stretching my fingers apart each time I pull back. I'm straining her opening and she's becoming very aroused by it. I'm getting to know Rayna's body very well; what urges her closer to orgasm and what turns her off. I love watching her expressions and the clues that provides.

I pull my hand from her pants and shove my fingers into her mouth, forcing her to taste her own juices. She stares up at me as she sucks my digits deep into her mouth, lapping at them until all of her flavour is gone. I release her wrists and stand up without so much as another touch.

"You should call your sister to make sure she's going to answer her phone if the kids call tonight." I reach into my sweatpants and shift my throbbing cock to a less straining position. Her eyes are shifty.

"What the fuck?" she says.

"What the fuck, what?" I reply, playing dumb.

"Um, why did you stop?"

I chuckle as I'm walking away. "I asked you not to enjoy yourself until tonight, or did you forget?"

"Oh, come on! That's not fair!" she says as she chases after me.

"You started it, woman!" I laugh as I run up the stairs taking two at a time.

"You're an ass!" she laughs as she runs to keep up. She almost has me by the time we're almost at our bedroom.

Ken steps out of his room, nearly getting himself lambasted by me. Ken squeals and ducks back into his room, but it's too late. Fearful that I'm going to take him out, I leap to the side, slamming myself into the doorframe of the bathroom. I just barely avoided him. Fuck, that hurt!

Rayna runs around me to make sure Ken is all right. I'm happy to know he's fine but my face really fucking hurts. She turns to check on me and that's when Kim whips open her door with eyes wide, fearing that the house might be falling down outside of her bedroom.

I touch my face when I feel the warmth of blood running from my nose and upper lip. Yup, that's blood all right! Kim is just standing in her doorway, unsure of what's happening.

Ken keeps saying, "I'm sorry. I didn't know you were coming this way. Why were you running?"

Rayna pushes me into the bathroom and wets a washcloth with cold water and applies it to my lip. "Wow, you really hit that wall hard!"

I turn and look at Ken to reassure him. "Little man, it wasn't your fault. Let this be a lesson to you kids not to run in the house."

Kim adds, "We already know that lesson. Why were *you* running?"

Seems right to retort to her sassy comment in a childish way. I reply, "Because your mom was chasing me, of course!"

Rayna and I are laughing but the kids are too concerned over the blood to find the humour in my immaturity. Oh well, I tried to break the tension.

I look in the mirror and notice a split in my lip and a red mark on my nose, but it isn't so bad. I've had much worse than this, from fighting when I was young and stupid.

"I think you're going to be okay." Rayna has stopped examining my cut and is now pinching my nose, which has me grimacing at her. "Oh, don't be such a big baby!"

"Big baby? Is that a hit at my age or a simple coincidence?" I'm joking, of course. She simply rolls her eyes and shakes her head.

"Hey, little man, you okay?"

"Yeah, I'm fine! Are you?"

"Oh sure, I'm good! If your mom gives my boo-boo a kiss it'll heal right up." When I pucker my lips, I can feel it swelling. It hurts. I don't like pain. I love giving it, but not having it myself. It's rather sadistic to say, but that's how it is.

She puts her hand on my chest and shakes her head. "Um, no! You're still bleeding. Hold that cloth to your lip. Kim, can you get the ice bag from the freezer, please?"

"The blue one?" she asks. I nod so she heads to the kitchen.

Rayna insists, "Sit on the toilet and let me get a better look at it."

I take a seat just as Kim returns with the squishy ice pack and hands it to me. "Thank you, angel."

Rayna is examining the cut on my lip and I can't help but think about how much I love her and these kids. Had I smashed into him, he would have some serious injuries; broken bones or some internal bleeding. He's getting taller but he's so thin and well, I definitely am not. I'm a tank! So, I'm relieved, so very relieved, Ken is unharmed.

"Yup, you're going to live! Of course, I can go get my needle and thread and stitch it up for you if you'd like. Maybe we should heat up a scalpel and cauterize it. Or, I could just punch you on the other side of your lip to even out the swelling." I know she's joking around. I've heard her say similar things to the kids when they are wounded.

"I think the ice will be enough but thanks." I stand up and give her a quick hug but reach out and grab Ken, pulling him into a hug. "I'm so glad you're not hurt!"

He wraps one arm around me and says, "Nah, I'm good. Sorry you got hurt. You can really move fast for a big guy. I thought for sure I was a gone-er!"

We both chuckle but it's more of a relieved reaction than anything. Rayna scoots the kids back to what they were doing but Ken doesn't head back to his room.

"I have to use the bathroom. That's why I was walking into the hallway in the first place. I can't believe I didn't pee my pants when I saw you coming at me."

"Wow! That's a strong bladder you have, little man. I'm not so sure I would have held my waters if I saw something my size coming at me." He nods and closes the door after we've left the room.

In the bedroom, Rayna sits on the bed and takes a deep sigh of relief. I sit beside her and take her hand in mine, the other still holding the ice pack to my face. We just sit here for several minutes, silently contemplating a thank you to the universe for me not being half a second faster. Had I been one step ahead, I would have crushed him, and we wouldn't be sitting here right now, grateful for his safety.

"I'm going to take a bath. Funny how quickly a mood can change, isn't it?"

I nod and reply, "Fuck me! I saw him and…" I stop to swallow the lump in my throat. "That scared the hell out of me!"

"Me too!" she says and then pats my hand before letting it go. I watch as she makes her way to the bathroom and starts the water pouring. As the door closes, I lie back and rest the ice pack on my mouth and nose and close my eyes.

"Hey big man." The sweetest voice pulls me from the silence of sleep.

For a moment, I had forgotten about the ice pack until it starts to slide off. I toss it aside and grab Rayna, yanking her towel off and tossing her to the bed. She lands on her back and I'm on her before she can resist.

I bury my mouth on her pussy and quickly begin lapping and sucking at her clit. I know she's been aching for this for a few days now. She thinks I'm going to let her cum, but I'm not going to be that kind.

She's moaning in less than a minute. Her hips are rocking against my face as I work her clit into a stiff, swollen nub. Her breathing is becoming more rapid. I make sure to pay attention. She's close, very close. Just as her breaths start to shorten, I stop.

I stand up and pull off my shirt and pants, revealing a very hard cock. Her eyebrows are furrowed and her lips are parted. She doesn't want me to stop but she's eyeing up the pipe that sprung from my pants.

When I turn to walk away, she slams her fists onto the bed and groans angrily. "That's not fair!"

I know it's not. It's downright cruel. She doesn't realize that this is a punishment for me, as well. I would love to make her cum on my mouth and then fuck her until she can't cum anymore, but I made a request and I have to stick with it. She doesn't know why I'm holding her off, but she will, soon enough.

While I'm in the shower, she slips in and flushes the toilet. The scalding water pours over my back for a split second. I wail a highpitched screech, sounding like a little girl, to which she laughs hysterically.

"How does that saying go? Revenge is a dish best served *cold*? I disagree, don't you?"

"Yes, I absolutely disagree," I sink back under the lukewarm water, to cool my superheated flesh. "That was unfair." "I beg to differ," she replies as matter-of-factly.

"You'll pay for that later," I assure her.

"Trust me, I've been paying for it for three days already. I owed you!" She ducks out of the bathroom before I can reply to that statement. Oh, she will definitely pay for that.

* * * * *

We pull up in front of Fallen and shut off the car. I reach into the backseat to collect the bag I hid earlier. Rayna is watching me, curious to know what I have.

"I bought something for you to wear tonight, but before I show it to you, I'd like your word that you'll wear it, no matter what it is."

"You want me to promise to wear something even if I don't know what it is. Um, that's scary! It could be anything. Besides, I am already dressed in the little black dress you bought me to replace the one you tore."

"Yes, and you do look sexy as hell in it, too. But, as you know, you can wear anything at Fallen without judgement, so why not throw caution to the wind and promise to change into what I have picked out in this bag, for you."

Rayna hesitates, but eventually agrees. I open the duffle bag and hand her the plastic bag from inside. "When I put this on, whatever is in here, will you refer to me as Kat, until I take it off?"

"If you prefer me to I will, as long as you call me Demon while we're here."

"I did last time, didn't I?" she suggests. I know she's right. I grin and shift my eyes to the bag she's holding.

She opens it and digs her hand inside and takes out a red latex skirt. She smiles and then reaches back in the bag, pulling out a latex bra, and a pair of silky black panties with lace trim. She looks back in the bag but doesn't find anything else.

"What, no shoes?" she teases.

"The heels you're already wearing are perfect."

She nods, "Is that why you asked me to wear these particular ones?"

"Yes, now let's get out of the car and change our clothes."

"What?" She looks at me, startled. "You want me to change my clothes right here in their driveway?"

"Yes, I do. Where else do you plan on changing?"

"I just thought we could change in the house, in a bathroom or somewhere more private." She's looking all around for people who might be waiting to catch a glimpse.

"Listen, nobody here cares if we're outside naked. There aren't any neighbours who are close enough to see us, not with all these trees lining the property. I'm going to be here beside you. Trust me, nobody will care either way."

I open my door and bring the duffel with me. I round the car and open her door. She's reluctant to get out.

"You can wait in the car until I come back out, but it won't be for a few hours. You choose," I challenge her.

I pull off my shirt and unbutton my pants. She's still looking around but at least she's out of the car. She slips off the panties she's wearing and steps into the new ones. Then she pulls on the skirt, lifting her dress as she does. I catch a glimpse of the lacy panties and immediately, know I made the right choice. They fit her perfectly and they look sexy as hell.

I pull on a pair of black leather pants, heavy black work boots, but no shirt. I slip on leather forearm bands that lace up like a corset starting at the wrist and end halfway up my forearm. I like these bands because they look mean, at least I think they do.

Rayna has slipped off the black dress and is preparing to remove her bra. She's looking around with the clasp in her hands, ready to take it off as long as nobody is watching her. She moves quickly, flipping off her bra and pulling the new one on in record time. She seems relieved that no one saw her.

I can't stop scanning her body. Fuck, she looks hot! I want to bend her over the hood and fill her with my cock. It was difficult to get her to strip outside, I likely won't get her relaxed to the point of letting me fuck her out here. What a pity that will be. Maybe after I'm finished with her in the house, she'll be so calm from the endorphin rushes I plan to give her, she'll let me do anything I want to her.

"Do I look okay? I feel silly," she says, pulling at her skirt and top. "I think the outfit is too small. I would never buy this for myself."

"I know. I want you out of your comfort zone. Kat," Her eyes dart up when I say that name. "you look fucking perfect."

"I do?"

"I wouldn't say you did if I thought you didn't. Now, fold your dress and leave it on your seat so it doesn't wrinkle. That'll be hard to explain to the kids when we get home, if they happen to still be awake."

"Oh, right!" she says as she folds her dress.

I stuff the duffel back in the car and place my shirt and pants on the front seat. She slips her hand in mine and smiles at me. I pull her against me and kiss her lips, smacking her on the ass at the same time.

"Don't tease me," she whispers.

"Don't tell me what to do, Kat. You speak when I tell you to.

You know the rules," I reply, giving her my most devilish smirk. "Oh, we're starting the role play already?"

"You asked me to call you Kat after you changed, so I assumed we'd be assuming our roles. And you're breaking the no talking rule," he reminds me.

"Well, I actually don't know all the rules," she replies while returning the devilish smirk.

I whisper in her ear, "Careful, little girl. I'll take away your skirt if you misbehave."

Rayna doesn't say anything else, heeding my warning. She knows I'll follow thru with my threat. I turn and lead her to the main entrance. After passing the guards, taking the elevator and walking down the corridor, we enter the main hall where the majority of house visitors are sitting while some stand in small gatherings. All are chatting and watching others discipline their submissives. Some people are even fucking. Some are either giving or receiving oral sex. I allow Rayna time to watch the activity, so that she'll know it's okay to do these things with me, in front of people, when I ask her to.

I take her down the hallway, past old friends and acquaintances who nod at me or say a quick greeting. Just as we near the room I've arranged for us, I see *HER* coming toward me. I debate whether I should tell Rayna the history between this woman and me before she gets too close, but she's too quick in her approach.

"Sir," she says, bowing her head as a sign of respect to me.

"Sara, how have you been?" I ask her after putting my fingers under her chin to lift her face. She's so fucking cute! I enjoyed those pouty lips of hers, especially when they were wrapped around my cock. I release her chin now that she's looking up at me.

"I am doing very well, thank you for asking. How have you been, Sir?" she asks while shifting her eyes toward Rayna. She quickly focuses her attention back on me, so I don't scold her for looking away, as I used to do.

"I'm doing very well. This is Kat, my submissive partner. Kat, this is Sara. She's a past submissive of mine." Honesty is best.

Rayna looks a bit shocked, but politely smiles to greet her. She looks at me as if to ask if she can speak. I nod. She says, "It's lovely to meet you. Perhaps one day we can have a chat."

"I'd love that! Would Sir approve?" she asks me. She's knowledgeable about how the relationships between Master and Submissive can be very restrictive. I simply nod. She asks, "Master Demon, if you would be so kind as to give Kat my phone number, I'd be extremely grateful."

"I can do that," I reply with my eyes burning into hers. I'm picturing all the past pleasures we shared; the roughest and most aggressive standing out first and foremost. I would love to make her scream again. She has the softest feminine voice when speaking, but her screams had my Demon sighing happily.

"Thank you, Sir." She looks at Rayna and whispers, "You're a very lucky woman. He's a wonderful Master, but he sure was cruel when I misbehaved. I'm sure you already know that all too well."

"That'll be enough, Sara. Where is your Master?" I hiss disapprovingly.

She bows her head. "I don't have a steady Master, Demon." Her eyes look up with her head still slightly bowed in an apologetic manner. "Nobody is as good a Master as you, Sir."

"It was good to see you again, Sara. I'm happy to know you are well."

"Thank you, Sir. Very nice to meet you, Kat," she replies sweetly, but the lingering mutual stare has me a little nervous. What will they talk about, if I do indeed share her number with Rayna? Will Sara tell her everything? Will she also describe just how vicious my Demon can be?

I can't tell if she's jealous of my new submissive or if she's genuinely happy that I have one. Knowing her the way I do, I'm sure she's happy to meet Kat and is somewhat jealous, but she would never do anything to interfere with the union between my submissive and me. She knows better than to defy me.

There were times I was a bit cruel with her, but she never complained. I treated her like she was a piece of meat that I could toy with. She kept coming back for more. She and Rayna have more in common than either of them knows. I'm sure Rayna will ask her what happened to end our playing and Sara will tell her about Brett; the asshole who also hurt my Rayna.

"I'll call you," Rayna tells her as I lead her away from the woman wearing leather shorts and a black bra with army boots on her feet. She always wore those boots.

Sara was in the armed forces for several years and did a few tours overseas. She fought in many battles. Getting shot in her right heel ended her military career and forever impeded the smoothness in her steps. I used to wonder what she was like before war forever tarnished her soul; before the smell of gunpowder mixed with blood burned too deeply into her that she could never fully recover.

Wearing high-heels is out of the question for her because her ankle won't hold her balance. She was released from the army with a medal for saving two men whose injuries were much worse than hers. Not only does she have physical scars, her mental woes were so much worse. She once told me that ever since she became a submissive, she's slept better than she had in a long time. Letting herself work through that pain via physical restriction and pain/pleasure, she's overcome quite a bit. It's her way of escaping her mind, even if it doesn't always last very long.

When I enter the room near the end of the hallway, it's all set up for us, just as I had asked Gear to do for me. Rayna is looking around the room while her feet remain in one position, as if she's too nervous to continue walking.

"Do you have any questions?" I ask her.

She looks at me with wide eyes. "Why are we in this room?"

I smile and say, "You said you wanted to be bound like the woman walking in the drive way with her domme. Well, I'm going to make sure that happens today. The only issue is that I am not all that skilled at elaborate rope binding and I'd like your first time to be done by someone very skilled."

"Not you? I'd rather you do it. I don't want anyone else to see me naked." She says, eyes so wide that she looks nearly terrified, to the point of wanting to run in the opposite direction.

"You will not be naked," I assure her. She seems to take a bit of solace in that.

"Demon, my man!" Gear walks through the door and shuts it behind him. "How the hell are you?" He puts out his hand to shake it.

"I'm very well, and you?" I say, shaking his hand and patting him on the back twice after a quick hug.

His eyebrows furrow while he looks at Rayna's body, not her face. I know this isn't going to be sexual for him. He's admiring her skin so he can decide on the perfect colour of rope to use that will compliment her colouring. His arousal isn't from the bodies themselves but the way they look bound and incapacitated. To him, the person bound is just flesh and bone, soulless and without their own thoughts. They are empty vessels that are his to use for his own artistic and possible sexual satisfaction, but it's not promised. He won't be fucking Rayna, just binding her for me to toy with.

"Very well, actually. Glitter just returned from an unscheduled trip. Her sister in Vancouver had a baby boy. She visited her own while I stayed here. Babies aren't my thing." He approaches Rayna, finally acknowledging that she's a real person. "So, what are we looking to do with you today, Kat?"

Chapter Seventeen

Rayna

He's asking me what I want him to do. How would I know? My eyes dart to Coach.

"I'm picturing her in a web," he tells the tall man.

He smiles and asks me, "Can you put your arms behind your back and cross them, grasping either forearm with the opposite hand?"

I put my arms around my back and cross my forearms over one another. It's not exactly a comfortable position but it doesn't hurt me either.

"I'm going to be touching your body while I bind you. Don't worry, it won't be sexual for me," he warns before he gently repositions my arms until they aren't pulling so tightly behind me. It's less uncomfortable. "I think black would stand out wonderfully against your pale skin. "You can relax your arms for a few moments."

I drop my arms and look over at Coach, who is now leaning against a high stool with his hands on his hips and admiring my body. Glitter is standing next to him and whispers, "She looks good in the latex, doesn't she?"

Gear cuts in, "Hell yes, she does! Good enough to throw over my knee and spank her ass through that skirt."

"Maybe one day, but not today, Gear," Coach tells him. "She isn't trained well enough just yet to be sharing her."

He tilts his head when I look at him with questioning eyes. Would he really allow another man to spank my bottom? I don't believe he would, he's way too jealous and protective of me, to allow that. I'd rather not have another man spank me.

He agrees, "Mhmm, she is rather unseasoned. If you ever change your mind, I'd love to see her grovelling at my feet."

I can't help but shudder at the thought of being on the floor at his feet and begging for whatever it is he thinks I need. At the same time as the cold shiver runs up my spine, my thoughts are pulled to the yearning that my vagina seems to have. Do I really want to grovel at this man's feet? My brain says no, but my body disagrees.

His voice is soft, and he has a smoothness about him that makes me think his touches would be tender, even if they hurt. I think he'd whisper degrading things in my ear, but his mannerisms would make his words sound sexy. I imagine he is very sexually experienced and could teach me everything I need to know to be an excellent sexual partner for Coach. Why am I even sizing up this man? There's no way in hell Coach would allow him, or any man, to touch me sexually. If someone ever hit me, I think Coach would lose his shit. He nearly killed the guy who had me kidnapped, beaten and then, nearly raped. I have to get my thoughts back on what's happening here and now. Those thoughts will only drag me down into the dark hole of depression that I fought hard to escape from.

"Take off the skirt, Kat," he orders with little concern that I won't.

I take a deep breath and let it out slowly. Coach nods, so I follow the instructions given to me. My thumbs slip under the waistband and slowly begin to push my skirt down past my hips. It falls to the floor. I stand before two men in heels, a black lacy bra and matching panties. Never, in my wildest dreams had I pictured myself in this situation.

Gear takes my hand and asks me to lift each foot as he pulls the latex material from around my ankles. He gently folds my skirt and hands it to Coach. I'm starting to feel like I'm not myself, not really.

I take a breath and let myself slip into sub-mode.

"The bra as well," he insists.

I look at Coach to see him nodding at me. When I hesitate, he quickly warns me, "Take it off or I will take it off for you."

His voice is deep and threatening, but his expression has my pussy twitching. I can't believe how horny I've been these past few days. The slightest touch to my clit will likely have me humping whatever it is that touched me. Maybe that's why he wanted me to wait; he wants me desperate and needy.

He isn't giving me a choice. Do I want the other man to see my breasts? Well, they are still quite perky, given I am thirty-eight years old and having had two children. I quickly remove it and place it in the man's outstretched hand. He doesn't even glance down at my erect nipples. After handing the top to Coach, he starts wrapping the rope around my wrists, over my shoulder and around my body. He walks around me, placing knots here and there.

My pussy is getting moist and hot. I am consciously aware of my quickening breaths. This is extremely arousing for me. I love the feel of the rope pressing against my skin and holding me in place. The way his fingers graze my hypersensitive flesh when applying a knot has me whimpering.

"Beautiful," Coach says after walking around me to examine the incredible weave. "You have a spider's web design on your back that is absolutely breathtaking."

His fingers slide down my back and under the ropes by my shoulder blades, gripping them firmly. He yanks me back until his chest thuds against the knotted web that spans my back, startling me.

The other man stands in front of me, admiring his artistic work and tracing the ropes with his fingers. Every now and then he touches my super-sensitive skin with his cool digits, sending shocks straight to my pussy, igniting the fire between my folds into a raging, desperate inferno.

Coach's hands reach around my chest and pinch my nipples. I nearly come apart. My knees weaken and my breath catches in my throat, escaping only when he releases them.

When I open my eyes, the man has left us and is now sitting where Coach was while I was being decorated in the black rope. Coach walks me over to the full-length mirror and stands behind me as I see the fancy design on my chest for the first time. He said there was an intricate design on my back, but the front is quite beautiful as well. I turn to look at the back and I'm captivated by its beauty.

"Please, Demon, will you take a picture?" I know I'm speaking out of turn, but I really want to capture this image.

"Sit on this stool," he tells me.

I sit, but he rearranges me until I'm sitting sideways, and then he pushes my legs wide apart. He ties a blindfold over my eyes and tells me to hold still. I'm not too keen on being blinded, but I trust Coach. I hear the click of the photo being captured on his phone and then feel something metallic squeeze my left nipple. I yelp louder than I should have in comparison to the moderate level of discomfort. The shock of him touching me when I can't see that he's about to, has me on edge. During other play sessions, he put much tighter and heavier ones on my nipples, and I was able to bear through it just fine. After the second nipple is decorated, I hear another click from a camera.

I screech when someone, I'm assuming it's Coach, grabs the web at my shoulder blades and pulls me back until I'm leaning against his hand. I'm nervous that he's going to drop me. My abs are straining to hold myself up, just in case he does let go, not that he would hurt me on purpose.

Coach pulls up on the left nipple clamp. Just before I'm about to scream, he lets it go. His hand slaps down on my pussy lips, shocking me more so than it causes me pain. Again, he slaps, but this time it stings. My automatic reaction is to pull my legs together.

He slaps my right thigh. "Open your legs." Reluctantly, I do as he instructs. "Good girl. I'm going to slap your clit five times and I want you to count them out."

"Thank you, Demon," I whisper, not meaning what I'm saying.

His fingers slap my clit and I yelp. My body jolts up and my back arches. "Fuck!"

"Count," he whispers.

"One," I reply. A second slap to my clit, harder than the first. "Ah! Two! Fuck!"

"I'm going to increase the intensity each time. What number comes next?"

I hesitate to reply, too afraid to speak because I know he'll slap when I do. He pinches my tender clitoris between two fingers and rolls it slowly and tenderly. It's more sensitive than what I'm used to.

I moan softly, "Three."

He slaps again, and I clamp my jaw shut, sucking air from between my teeth. If I open my mouth, a wail will fill this room. His fingers stroke up and down my pussy several times coating his fingertips with my slippery wetness.

"Does that feel good, Kat?"

I moan, "Yes, Sir."

He slaps and it hurts so much, it's dizzying. My body lurches upward, stopping only because he's holding onto the ropes. The wetness increases the sting.

"Was that number three?" he asks.

"No!" I pause, "Four! That was four. Please, no more. Please?"

"I love it when you beg," he whispers as his fingers continue to massage my pussy. "I'll save the fifth one for another time, but I won't tell you when I'm going to do it. Don't forget to count it when it happens, or you'll get another."

Coach lays me back so that his thigh is holding up my lower back and my head is hanging toward the ground, my ass still planted on the stool. This feels awkward and scary, like I'm going to topple over at any second. I love it and hate it. The support his hand was giving to my upper back falls away, furthering my insecurity. A vibrator presses onto my hot, swollen clitoris.

"Yes! Thank you, Coach... Demon!" I correct myself, hoping he won't stop the pleasure because of my faux pas. Luckily, he doesn't, not yet anyway.

Two of his thick fingers slip into my drenched pussy and push deeply into me. He waves them, stopping only to fuck me with them several times before pausing to wave once again. I no longer care if I fall over as long as he doesn't stop what he's doing.

The cycle repeats, over and over. I let myself fall into it, giving myself completely to the sensations from the vibrator and focus on relaxing my pussy, so his fingers can fuck me hard without resistance. He takes that as an opportunity to penetrate me with another digit, stretching me wider and further fueling the fire in my belly.

The sheer agony of the nipple clips being released has me screaming through my moans. That's all I needed to start the whirlwind of agonizing pleasure.

A toe-curling orgasm shreds through me like a tsunami, overcoming my conscious thought. The room around me has fallen away and I'm floating off his knee, suspended only by his fingers and balanced by the vibrator.

My body stiffens. My breath holds, burning hot in my lungs. His hand is met with a flood of hot cum as my mind falls still. An involuntary jerk from my aching abs jolts my mind from the euphoric emptiness that only an orgasm can suck you into.

He sits me up and holds me in place while I catch my breath. As he's pulling off the blindfold, the brightness of the lights has me squinting, but through those slits, I see people standing against the walls. Panic sets in.

"No! How could you do this to me? I'm so embarrassed! Why?" My words are louder than I'd planned, but I'm so angry and scared and humiliated.

The room suddenly echoes with applause. My eyes dart from person to person. They all seem pleased, which eases that insecurity telling me I'm not good enough for these people.

My sights rest on Coach. He looks in my eyes and whispers, "Love, they really enjoyed you. You are the star of the evening. How excited did you get from knowing Gear was watching? How thrilling was it? You had no idea the rest of them were watching you, so you were relaxed enough to get lost in the moment. If I'd told you there was a crowd, you wouldn't have let yourself go. Do you hate me?"

Tears start to stream down my face, and I can't wipe them away to hide my emotions from the lingering onlookers. Most have started to wander out of the room. Coach stands me up and pulls me into his arms, resting my cheek against his hard-pectoral muscle, to hide my face from roaming eyes.

"Can you untie me?"

Gear walks up behind me and begins unknotting the rope, walking around me in the process while Coach stands back and watches. My legs are weak, and Gear somehow knows when to help balance me, letting me go when he believes I'm in full control.

He stops in front of me after most of the web has been removed. "You are a lovely woman and I would be honoured to bind you again. You are a pleasure to watch when you've let down your guard and you're lost in a mix of pleasure and pain. Truly, you are. Demon is a lucky man." Having said that, he finishes untying my hands.

I rub my sore wrists and roll my shoulders to ease their stiffness. "Thank you for tying such a lovely knot on me. I really enjoyed myself. I would be honoured to be your subject again soon, should Demon approve."

With that, he nods and walks away, taking the rope with him. We're alone in the room, finally. I look over at Coach who has been leaning against the wall with his arms crossed over his chest, looking like a badass. I don't say anything and neither does he, we just stare at one another.

Coach suddenly rushes toward me. His fingers weave into my hair and his other arm around my back, pulling me firmly against him. His mouth presses to mine with so much neediness. He's been waiting for three days for relief and for him, that might as well be an eternity.

His lips work mine with a fiery passion. He grabs my ass and lifts me up. I wrap my legs around his waist and lock my feet behind his back. Oh, yes! I want him to take me hard, right here, right now and I no longer care if anyone watches.

He carries me over to the wall and leans my back against the cool paint. I can feel him fussing with his zipper and then his cock rubs against my wet panties. His finger pulls them aside. In a flash, his stiff, fat prick is filling me, thrusting hard and deep with an eagerness that I thoroughly enjoy. His carnal grunts rattle my very core.

He fucks me hard, rough and with hedonistic cruelty, but I love it and want more. He leans back just enough so I can watch his bestial expressions. His nose is flared, teeth clenched, lips pulled back and his eyes seem dark, like a predatory animal. The kind man I know Coach to be, isn't this man. This fuck does not revolve around love. He's fucking me for a purpose; to own me and make me his, just his.

The second his hand wraps around my throat and squeezes, I grasp his forearm with both hands and try to pull it away. When his eyes meet mine, I don't recognize him.

"You're mine, you little bitch! I fucking own you! Tell me!" he growls and spits.

I don't know how he expects me to tell him when I can barely breathe. His eyes glare into mine with a dark hollowness that I fear. I find him to be dangerous, but also sinfully exciting!

I mouth the words, *I'm yours*, just as an orgasm seems to explode my insides, shattering me into a million pieces. His cock swells as my pussy tries to strangle it with its rippling spasms. He releases my throat to slam his palm against the wall beside my head, as if he's trying to stop it from falling over and crushing us.

His body pounds me several more times until it seizes, stiffening painfully, as his prick empties its jizz deep inside my spent cunt. He exhales with a long primal howl that echoes from wall to wall. Each breath he expels sounds more like a canine's growl than a human's groan.

With his head hanging down, his eyes shift up at me from under his brows, slowly lifting his face while his eyes remain locked on my sights. He's still breathing through a clenched jaw. He seems to be battling with his Demon.

"Put him back in his cage," I whisper.

"Don't look at me!" he hisses through clenched teeth.

I cast my eyes down, but out of the corner of my eye, I can see his are closed tightly. He hasn't moved his hands from holding up the wall. My legs are still wrapped around his waist. I reach up and place my hands on his cheeks hoping it will help him to calm down. Instead, he glares at me and grabs my hips, pulling my legs from around him. He nearly drops me onto my feet and walks away as he tucks his withering cock back in his pants. I watch him pace back and forth. Moving toward him will be a bad idea, so would talking. It didn't work well the last time. Strangely enough, I'm not afraid of him or his craziness.

He stops pacing and looks at me with an expression I recognize.

"Coach, welcome back."

"Did I hurt you? I don't think I hurt you."

"No, definitely not! That was fucking hot!"

"Good," he replies, as he retrieves a few paper towels for me to wipe myself off with.

"Are you okay?"

"Yeah, I'm good. I kept him under control."

"That was under control? Christ, I hope you never completely lose control and beat me," I joke, to lighten the mood, followed by a snicker.

"It's not funny. I don't want to hurt you. You are not ready for Demon. I can be cruel and hurtful... you aren't ready."

I stroke his cheek and smile softly, "You don't scare me. I thought I'd be afraid of your Demon, but now that I've seen him behind your eyes, I'm not afraid. You have more control than you think you do."

He kisses me softly and whispers, "You aren't ready."

"Maybe you aren't ready because you love me. You didn't love those other women, so their feelings didn't matter to you. There's more to lose if I fear you, isn't there?"

He nods, "That's it exactly. I'm not ready, but neither are you." He takes the paper towel from me and hands me my skirt.

"My panties are soaked. Can I just take them off?"

"I would prefer you to be panty-free anyway. Give them to me," he says with a grin.

I slip them off and hand them to him. He doesn't toss them out, which strikes me as odd. Instead, he tucks them into his back pocket. I take his hand in mine and follow him out of the room. People in the hallway smile at me as we walk past them. I smile back while my cheeks flush red hot. Will I ever get used to this?

Chapter Eighteen

Rayna

"Now that you've discovered your fetish, I want to show you something," he whispers to me.

"My fetish?" Since I'm still supposed to be in submissive mode, I'm careful not to let anyone hear me speak, especially when I'm not being asked to speak.

"Ropes, rope bondage," he replies.

"Oh, I thought you meant public sex," I snicker.

"I'm hoping that excites you, as well," Coach whispers with a sexy grin. He holds his finger up to his lips to inform me that I need to be very quiet now.

He takes me into a large room. My breath is taken from me by the beauty before me. Suspended in rope are three women, each is bound to the other forming a small circle. Their necks are tied to hold their mouths against the vagina of another. Each woman is seductively licking and kissing the pussy before them. Their arms are bound behind their backs, each woman's position identical to the others. Their legs are spread wide and bound. If it weren't for the ropes, they'd look as if they are floating on their sides, weightless in the air. I am in awe of their beauty.

I don't know how long we stand here while we watch each woman come to orgasm. Their moans and jerking bodies draw me, captivating my heart and mind in a fantasy-like dream. I wish I were one of them, even though I've never imagined I would desire to taste another woman's sex. Maybe one day I will.

A man much shorter than Gear approaches the woman with the light brown hair. He quickly unties a rope setting her face free from the other woman's pussy. He grasps a wad of her hair in his hand and proceeds to slap her in the face several times, hard. She gasps and cries out. He grabs her by the neck and lifts her slowly, holding her up to use her own body's weight as a means to put pressure on her throat. Her face is reddening quickly. He spits on her cheek before letting her go. She's gasping quick breaths while still reeling from the constant lapping torture on her sensitive clit by the woman still bound to her pussy.

Him and Gear begin unbinding the women one at a time, gently lowering them onto their feet and holding them until they are steady and completely unbound. Each woman gets a long hug and a kiss on their head.

The crowd of onlookers has dwindled but a few remain. I can feel Coach watching me, as I watch them. His eyes have been on me throughout most of the show.

"Beautiful, isn't it?" he asks.

"Yes, very much so. They were floating. Orgasms make me feel like I'm weightless and floating. They actually were floating, well, sort of. I wonder how incredible that must have been for them."

"Do you want to try it some time?"

"Lesbianism?" I ask with a fearful expression.

"Sure," he replies.

I shrug my shoulders. "I don't know. I've never desired another woman, I'm not sure I'd like it. If they went through the trouble of binding me like that and I hated it, that would be a pity. Besides, I don't know how to lick a pussy."

"I would imagine that you would do to them what you want done to you."

I shrug, "I don't know if I could."

"Maybe one day I will order you to do it," he teases.

"Can I refuse that order without punishment?" I tease.

"Not without punishment," he replies, kissing my forehead after he does. I wonder what that punishment would entail.

The last woman is set free. She's the one who Coach introduced me to shortly after we arrived. What was her name again? Sara! Yes, that's it. The man who struck her is holding her in his arms and rocking her lovingly. I can't hear what he's saying to her, but she's smiling and nodding. Her eyes remain closed. He continues to carry her for another minute before setting her down on her feet. He cradles her face in his hands and whispers something else. She smiles and nods before thanking him.

Gear walks up to her and takes her hand in his, kissing the back of it. He also talks to her for a moment before she thanks him and moves toward the bench where the other two women are dressing.

She slips into her black leather shorts and crop top, and then steps into her black boots. She sits and ties them up while I watch her. Coach is talking to the shorter man who was assisting Gear, while he skillfully folds the ropes into beautiful braids and tosses them into a plastic bin. The two seem to be old friends.

I let go of Coach's hand which immediately draws his attention. When he looks at me, I glance over at Sara and then back at him. He nods so I make my way toward the woman, admiring the indented red marks from where the ropes sat. I sit on the bench beside Sara while she pulls her shoelace to tighten her boot.

She looks at me and with surprise in her voice, says, "Oh, hi! Nice to see you again."

"You too. I saw you up there. That was beautiful. Can I ask you some questions?"

"Of course," she says as she sits up to give me her full attention. "Are you bisexual?"

She smiles, "Um, not really. Well, I don't know. I suppose you could say that I am. I don't like to put a title on

515

my sexuality. I prefer a thick, hard cock, but I'll have sex with a woman if my master asks me to. I don't hate it, by any means. It is pleasurable to watch a woman come to orgasm because of something I did. I gather you haven't had that experience?" "No," I reply.

"Are you opposed to it?"

"Um, I don't think so. If Demon asks me to, I will. This is going to sound silly. How do you know if you're doing it right?" I can feel my cheeks flushing.

"Kat, just do what you have always hoped your oral sex partner would do to you. Women love clitoral attention, but we have very sensitive nerve endings on our labia too. If you are only manipulating the clitoris, it could easily lose sensation. Move your tongue around now and then to stimulate the surrounding area as well, and you'll make her cum. Some women are much harder than

others, but stay at it and don't get frustrated."

"That's true and men don't always get it right."

"Demon is really great at oral sex, but I'd say more than half the male population don't have a clue," she says with a giggle.

"So, have you been with Demon many times?" I tried not to sound jealous, but I think I did.

"Oh!" she looks worried. "Did you not want to know that?"

"No, I understand he has a past; a rather extensive past. For some reason, I just didn't picture you and him having sex. I know you did. I just want to know…" I say as my words drift off.

She nods, understanding what I'm asking. "He fucked me and punished me, ate my pussy and had me suck his cock. It was rough to the point of being brutal, at times. I liked it very much. My favourite part of the pain is the initiation of it, when that first blast of pain riddles through my body like an electric shock. At first,

I think I won't be able to adjust to it, but after a few seconds, my mind overruns it, allowing me to accept the pain for what it is; a reminder that I'm still alive. As for Demon, I enjoyed him. Trust me sweetie, there was absolutely no love connection between us. Besides, I doubt that rock on your hand is from another man who is kind enough to let you spend an occasional evening with a guy like Demon. No man is that generous unless he's involved in this lifestyle. Don't take this the wrong way, but you aren't experienced, and the only women Demon plays with are. Going by those clues, that ring came from Demon. By watching how gentle he is with you, it's brutally obvious that he is madly in love with you."

"You didn't just watch him fuck me in the other room then," I tell her, not realizing that it came out sounding resentful, which wasn't my intention.

"Did Demon hurt you? He can be cruel sometimes, but most of his subs are into that."

"He didn't hurt me, but my fiancée wasn't behind his eyes, something else was."

She nods, fully understanding what I mean. "Yes, that would be his Demon. He's an angry beast, a take it hard and rough type personality. I desire that in a Master. Nobody does that level of bad, as good as he does. He is the best without ever crossing the psychopathically sadistic line!"

"Do many women agree with you? I haven't met any of his submissives that aren't seriously disturbed. I mean, I've only met one and she was insane."

"I heard about his ex-submissive and how she tried to kill him with her car." Sara chuckles and bends down to finish tying her boot. "There are some obsessive, crazy bitches out there."

"Yeah, I don't like that woman very much. Did you know her?" I ask.

"No, she isn't from our group. I don't recognize her name."

"She's a crazy one. Anyway, thanks for answering some questions for me."

"Kat, anytime! Hey, if you'd like to be entwined in with us next time, just let your Master know. I'm sure he wouldn't mind lending you to them. It's really a great way to escape your mind if you allow yourself to feel the pain of the ropes and the weightlessness of the air beneath you."

"I might be willing to do that," I reply. "Thanks for tolerating my naivety."

"Don't be silly. Anytime you have questions, just ask me." She smiles and then continues tying the laces on her boot.

I walk back to Coach's side and take his hand in mine. He's talking to two women, one is obviously a dominatrix, the other I'm not sure of. He leads me out of the room and back down the hall. Instead of walking straight toward the exit, he turns down another hall and starts looking around, as if he's searching for someone.

He pulls me along and then stops in front of an average sized man who has another man's wrist handcuffed to his. He hands him my panties, which seems to elate the man. He looks at me and then stuffs them under his nose, taking a long sniff while his eyes stay locked with mine. I would never imagine Coach would have given the man my panties to arouse himself with. My eyes must be huge, as I watch him enjoy my scent.

"This is Kat," Coach tells the man.

"Kat with the lacy black panties. They're still damp from your excitement. Thank you, Demon," he says before taking another long snort. His handcuffed friend seems to be irritated by his master's actions. He seems disgusted that the man is adoring the scent of a woman.

"Enjoy," Coach says with a pat on the man's back.

I follow him out of the house and back to the car. Once we're outside in the cool night's air, a shiver has me holding my arms over my chest.

"Are you cold?" he asks.

"It is quite cool out here for this time of year. Don't you think?"

"It is. Let me warm you," he says just as he spins me around by my shoulders.

He bends me over the front quarter-panel of my car, holding me in place by pinning my leg with his thick thigh. He yanks up my skirt, exposing my naked backside. I can feel him fussing with his zipper and then this hand sliding along my ass cheek as he strokes his cock.

"Don't move," he instructs.

I rest my head against the hood and wait for him to penetrate me, but he doesn't. Is he just going to jack off on me? I patiently wait, hoping he'll fuck me.

"Suddenly you're not so shy to be naked outside," he says. He pulls at the eyelets holding my top together. It springs open. He yanks it out from under my chest. My tits are resting against the cold metal of the hood. My nipples are so hard they're aching. He temporarily moves his thigh so he can quickly yank down my skirt.

"Do you like being naked outside?"

"Yes, Sir," I reply even though I'm not completely sure I do. After having people watching me cum like Niagara Falls all over Coach's hand, this isn't nearly as embarrassing.

I feel his wet fingers slide between my ass cheeks to moisten my asshole. His finger slips inside and starts pulling at the opening to stretch it. I hear him spit and feel the spatter slap on my asshole. He has good aim. I'll give him that. I breathe slowly and relax my ass enough that he can slip in two and then work in a third.

"Stand up," he says while moving his leg and grabbing both my biceps. He spins me around and leans his ass against the car. He spreads his legs, backing me in between them. He releases one arm but keeps hold of the other.

"You're going to fuck my ass out here?" "Yes, shut up," he instructs.

His prick lines up to the opening of my butt and gently enters my ass. To my surprise, he slides all the way in with little discomfort. He's so tall that he has to spread his legs wider so I can keep my balance and not have to rise up on my tip toes in my heels.

He wraps his hands around my pelvis and slowly lifts and lowers me. My asshole glides up and down his rock-hard cock, swallowing deep into me. He fucks me slowly and gradually as the odd person or two walks past. Nobody gives us much attention, which seems odd.

A beautiful, lone woman, the one who stops to watch, asks, "Can

I be of assistance, Demon?"

Coach looks at her and says, "Yes."

I'm not only shocked by his reply, but when he grips my hips tightly and lifts me, I squeal like a mouse in a trap.

"Open your legs," he tells me.

"What are you doing?" I ask while complying to his request.

"No talking!"

My legs hang over his while his prick remains buried deep in my ass. The cool air chills my clit instantly. He spreads his legs and asks her, "Would you be so kind?"

She looks at me and says, "Hi, I'm Candy. What's your name?" "I... I'm Kat," I stutter.

"It's nice to meet you."

She bends forward and starts licking my clitoris. Her lips form a seal around it as her tongue dances around my swelling nub in a well-choreographed ballet. With his cock slowly gliding in my ass and her tongue talentedly swirling my most sensitive flesh, my head tips back as a gasp of cool night air inflates my lungs. My hands reach back and grasp his huge biceps for balance. I am going to lose myself.

I look down to see her shoulder length, light brown hair and can't believe a woman has her mouth on my pussy. Holy fuck! She is really good at this! Her mouth is so soft and small, but skilled, like no other I've experienced, even Coach, who I thought was the very best at orally manipulating my pussy.

Her mouth sucks my clit like she's sucking on an ice cream cone which is driving me wild. All of a sudden, her mouth is absent. The cool air feels frigid as the wind glides along my super-heated pussy. I look down when I hear Coach moan and he stops fucking me. Her head is lower and I'm quite sure she's mouthing his balls.

He starts fucking me again when her mouth lands back on my clit. A few of her delicate fingers slip inside of my pussy with ease. I nearly cum right then but she's stopped slurping at my clit.

I open my eyes to see her standing up, leaning in toward me. Without another thought, I lean forward and take her cheeks in my hands, pulling her mouth to mine. Our lips press together as our tongues explore one another's mouths. Her lips are small but so soft. Her face is warm and smooth, like mine. I can smell my pussy on her skin and it's turning me on.

Her fingers are working my pussy, pushing into me and pulling back slowly. All of a sudden, I feel her knuckles enter me and I know her entire tiny hand is buried within me while Coach's raging hardon pumps in and out of my asshole. I flop back against his body and cry out. The pain and pleasure are in a battle to see which will take over. Pleasure quickly wins.

She fucks me slowly while spinning her wrist. I'm so fucking full! I have a woman's hand inside of me! She's fucking me! He's fucking me! I wail through a body-rocking orgasm while she rams me with her fist, and he slides his prick in my ass. I can't believe I'm doing this! And in public!

My body is coming back down from the climax just as her lips encircle my unbelievably aroused clitoris! My hands are gripping my tits so tightly that I know I'm going to bruise, but I like it. She's sucking and rolling my clit while spinning her wrist, all while Coach's cock fills my ass.

The air feels hot and humid as I float out of my body and away from reality. I am not screaming or moaning, just silently still in what feels like the weightlessness of death. The closer I come to orgasm, my body feels like it's swelling bigger and bigger, about to explode.

In my mind, I'm begging them not to stop, pleading for mercy and yet urging this agony to continue. I want to throw myself over the edge to end the incredible yearning ache my body is suffering, but I know that once I do, the orgasm is complete, and it will all end. It's torture, sweet torture.

My body jerks hard as I'm ripped from the pleasures of ecstasy and into the painful burning that comes with post orgasmic clitoral stimulation. She rises up, but continues to fuck me with her hand.

I'm immediately whirled into another climax the instant the fingers on her free hand begin rubbing circles over the sensitive nub that is likely ten times the size it normally is.

My panting screams are floating off into the trees as if disappearing further than my body can float away to. A final wail and I collapse against his chest, barely able to breathe, never mind holding up my own bodyweight.

Her hand pulls from my pussy at the same time his cock is taken from the depths of my ass. I can feel Coach's breathing become raged and intense. His groans are loud and with purpose. It takes all the strength I have to look down to see what she's doing. She's looking down and I think she's watching her hands jerk his cock, if that's what she is indeed doing.

He growls viciously just as his torso tightens, ending with sharp jerking that has me being tossed around on his lap. If he weren't holding my arms, I would have likely slipped off of him. He's still catching his breath when he sits me up and then grips my hips to lift me off and set me on my feet.

I'm surprised to see how short and tiny this woman is. I knew she was small, but she is quite a bit shorter than me. Coach is still lying back on the hood while I hand her my skirt to wipe her hands on.

"Thank you," she says.

"Sorry, I don't know how absorbent that will be, but it's something to clean up with."

"It's great, thank you. This isn't the first time I've had pussy and cock juice on me. Thanks for letting me play with you two," she says with a wide smile.

"That's the first time she's had a woman on her pussy," Coach tells her as he's sitting up.

"Really?" she looks so happy about that fact. "I'm honoured to be your first, Kat."

I smile, sure that I'm blushing, but happy the dimness of the evening might hide it. "Thank you. Sorry, I'm not sure what to say."

She leans in and gives me a quick kiss and then curtseys for Coach. "Thank you, is perfect. Have a great night you two." I watch her skip the rest of the way to the house like a little girl. I haven't had a sexual liaison anywhere nearly as strange as I have tonight, in my entire life.

Coach stands up and kicks off his shoes. He drops his pants, stepping out of them as he starts untying his leather wrist wraps. He's completely naked, outside, in plain view of anyone who happens to pull up and he isn't concerned about that in the slightest.

After what just happened, why would he be?

"Are you all right with me having asked her to join us?"

"Oh, yes," I assure him. "That was incredible!"

"Then why are you just standing there and not getting dressed?" His smirk seems almost childlike.

"Yeah, I suppose I could do that. Why are you looking at me so strangely?"

"I was sure you would protest by saying red. You surprised me tonight, is all."

"Is that why you allowed her to join in, as a way to test me?"

"No love, it wasn't a test. This was just a lucky opportunity that you didn't skip on."

"I'm glad I didn't. Eating a pussy though, I'm not sure I'm up to that just yet."

I duck into the car to retrieve the clothes we will be going home in, the same ones we arrived wearing. As we get dressed, I catch him checking me out.

"Stop that!" I joke.

"What?"

"Looking at me. We're done for the night. There's no way I can fuck again."

"Who said anything about fucking?" he teases.

In the stereotypical dumb blonde voice, I reply, "You have exhausted me, Master Demon." I flutter my eyelashes at him.

"Keep that up and I will fuck you, again."

I shove the other clothes back into the duffel bag and then hand it to him. He walks around the car and opens his door, shoving the bag behind the driver's seat to hide it away.

He drives us home while I tell him everything I loved about tonight, and how having the ropes tied elegantly against my flesh, restricting my movements, would excite me. Sara had suggested I express to Coach how willing I am to become a piece of Gear's beautiful artwork, that way he might be more inclined to allow me to participate in the future.

Coach smirks and nods. It excites me to imagine being bound and suspended, and secretly hope he might set that up for our next visit. Would he even be willing to allow another man to put his hands on me, even if it's for a non-sexual purpose, as it would be if he decorates me in rope? I want to experience pleasure while beautifully dangling, but I don't want Gear to be the one bringing it to me. I don't even know the man.

Chapter Nineteen

Coach

This week has been grueling, and incredibly stressful for me. Normally, a visit to Fallen with a pain-slut would help me work through that frustration. Rayna isn't a pain-slut. I highly doubt she would allow my Demon out of his cage, so he can play with another woman.

The tension at the gym have been high. Some much-needed construction started on Monday. It's been loud and inconvenient, bringing on plenty of complaints from some of my patrons. I've had to partition off the men's locker room with a temporary wall, which some of the dickheads hate because they have to walk further to get to the free-weights room. My reply was simply, *'Dude, you can use the cardio'*. That didn't always go over very well but fuck them and their laziness.

It's the women's locker room that's shut down for repairs. They need to share the men's locker room, without fear of ogling eyes from those horny motherfuckers, me included. A quick, but sturdy wall, solved the issue. Unfortunately, it blocked that particular entrance to the men's free-weights room. They're a bunch of big fucking babies and I'm sure they'll get the fuck over it. If they can't make slight accommodations for the lovely women who come here in spandex to work out, they can fuck off and not come back.

I want more women at the gym. To allow for that, they need more lockers, showers and toilets. When the gym first opened, there wasn't much need for a large women's change room, because the ratio was fifteen men to one woman.

Yeah, they were stared at, a lot. Now the ratio is more like five to one. Needless to say, I think the men can make small, temporary sacrifices for the women. It'll only be a few weeks until the wall comes down. A few weeks of nagging, headache inducing, annoyances.

There are two construction workers that I had to ban from the premises because they wouldn't stop watching the female patrons working out. As if it wasn't bad enough that they were watching them but the comments that were being whispered were seriously offensive. Five women complained on the first day and they were only at the setting up stage. Their behaviour would only get worse and I knew it, besides, they weren't getting their work done in a timely manner and I need that room finished as soon as possible. Those fuckers tried to deny it, but I showed their supervisor the video of how they were standing around, pointing and staring. He sent them to another work site but docked their pay for that day. They called me every name in the book on their way out of the building, escorted by myself and three other very large men. I love those guys! They always have my back, and I'll always have theirs.

It's only Thursday and I already can't wait for this construction to be finished, even though it's going to be a few more weeks still. But the women's locker room was small and needed to be expanded. It was time. More women have joined the gym in the past six years since I've owned it, than I thought would; tenfold, at least. We decided that by bumping into the gymnasium, we could create a big enough locker room to comfortably hold enough lockers and space for their growing numbers. Not a lot of people were using the gym for anything other than aerobics and they almost never used that side of the court. That void space will not be missed but the new design will be appreciated by the ladies.

Rayna set up a dinner tonight with her sister and my best buddy, Tim. The two of them have been living together for a few months now. Tim wants to propose to her, but I don't think it's a good idea, just yet. Shit, they haven't been together all that long. Rayna and I have been engaged for seven months and she hasn't even brought up the conversation of actually getting married. I think she's a bit gun-shy because of the shitty asshole she married the first time. I fucking hate that bastard, not only for how he treats Rayna but because of how shitty he is, as a father.

Anyway, I haven't been able to chat time with Tim in almost a month. His shift at work changed. Now he works steady days and spends his evenings with Renee. He's so pussy whipped it makes me gag. The man has no social life that doesn't revolve around her.

I used to see him at the gym during the day. I miss my friend.

I'm going to be here at the gym, until five tonight. My last appointment is at four, with a new client. Her name is Barbie. Stranger still, it's her birth name and she looks so much like an actual Barbie doll; her face, I mean. Anyway, she's a competitive bodybuilder, who's about to start hard training for a competition. Her last coach was badly injured in an awful car accident caused by a forty-year old stoned driver. You'd think someone that age would know better.

Her training with me will be temporary, just until her coach is back on his feet. I know Barbie from seeing her at other competitions. She's fucking built like an amazon bitch! I'd love to fuck her hard and make her scream. She's solid as fuck, ripped and beautiful. Rayna would never give me permission to have this woman, and I wouldn't do anything that might cause me to lose her. The thought of that makes my chest hurt.

I've had strong women, and let me tell you, there's definitely a difference in how hard I fucked them. They're solid, stronger and sometimes more sexually aggressive than an average woman. They like to fuck back, even when I'm hammering their ass with everything I've got. Like I said, strong as fuck!

Lisa, the yoga coach, slips into my doorway and says, "Your four o'clock is here." She's working the desk until her class starts in about an hour.

"Oh, four o'clock already? Dammit, I'm in the middle of something. Okay, I'll be there in a few minutes."

"She's in the changing room, so take your time," Lisa says as she walks away.

I pick up the phone and dial Gear. It rings three times before I'm asked to leave a message. I do, asking him to call me tomorrow at the gym and tell him my phone number in case he's misplaced it and doesn't have Caller ID. It has been a while since he's called me here.

I want Rayna to experience the suspension. I'd love to play with her while she's suspended. Her first time should be calm and relaxed, so she can fully appreciate the feeling of floating. That's how it has been described to me. Personally, the idea of being immobilized while hanging from ropes, makes my inner Demon twitchy and ready to pounce. It's not something I've ever wanted to experience.

I gather my papers and tuck them in my drawer. Locking the door to my office, I head toward the change room. My timing is perfect to intercept Barbie, who is just coming out of the room.

"Hi Barbie?" I ask with my hand out to welcome her.

She shakes my hand and smiles. "Yes, that's me. You're Coach. So, do people just call you Coach all the time? Do you have a real name or were your parents both psychics who could foresee your future lifestyle choice?"

We both chuckle. "My real name is Simon, but yes, people just call me Coach."

"All right, Coach it is. If you piss me off, I'm going to call you Simon, like your wife likely does when you fuck up."

I can't tell if she's joking or not. If she does call me Simon, I'm going to have a sudden vicious desire to pin her down and fuck the hell out of her, until she apologizes and calls me Master instead of Simon or Coach. I really hope she doesn't use my real name. Nobody calls me Simon anymore, not even Rayna. If Barbie wants to taunt me and play games, I'll put her in her place faster than she can beg me rip her clothes off and fuck her hard.

"Do not call me Simon," I say in a very demanding voice.

She scoffs, "Why not? What are going to do about it?"

Her taunting has my cock twitching and my inner Demon shadow boxing in his cage.

"Just don't do it," I reply with a leer that would make most men back down.

She stands right in front of me with her face a foot away from mine, as she pulls her hair up into a messy bun. Her smirk has my palms burning, wanting to spank her ass, just to wipe the challenging grin off her face. Her hands drop to her sides, and her eyes scan up and down my body.

"Fine, I won't. I will admit that I'm curious, what would you do if I did call you Simon?" Again, her gaze follows my frame to my feet and then back up to meet my eyes. "It might be fun to tussle with you. I know you're married, so I'll back off. She's a lucky woman. You look like one of those guys who's angry enough to fuck like a raging beast."

I want to grab her throat and slap that sexy mouth of hers. I'd force her onto her knees and fuck her mouth while her split lip bleeds all over my cock. My teeth clench and I swallow hard. Why am I letting this hot, mouthy woman spark me up? I'd better calm down before my cock stands up to show her that she's right.

"If you'd like, I can always find you another trainer."

"Why the fuck would you do that? I want you. You're one of the best, so I hear. I left my nice home and moved into a shady motel, so I can train with you, in this city. So, are we going to train or what?"

"Fucking right, I am the best," I said with a boastful grin. "Okay, I went over your file, all is good. Today, you're doing legs. I think your calves could use some work."

"Fuck you, my calves are awesome!" she jokes while sticking out her leg and pointing her toes. "Okay, let's get at it then!"

I watch her work through the routine her coach has set up for her. There are a few tips I give, that make her quite happy. I think we'll work out well, if I can just manage to keep my cock in my pants. She's so fucking hot, and her confrontational personality would make a great jousting partner for my Demon.

At five o'clock I leave her to handle her cardio workout on her own. The construction workers are still hard at work when I leave. They seem to be right on schedule. If I'm lucky, maybe they'll finish earlier than expected. The other trainers; Carol, Lisa and my new guy, Joe - will keep an eye on things. Carol is the shift supervisor, so she'll be here until ten-thirty when we close the doors. Lisa is leaving at seven, but Joe will stay on to help Carol clean the equipment after everyone has left. They've been giving each other sexy eyes for about a week now, so they'll likely be fucking after they lock up tonight. I don't care what they do, as long as they clean up their mess before they leave, and I do not want drama into the workplace.

I have fucked plenty of women at the gym, so telling them not to, would be hypocritical. Some of the equipment here allows for great fucking positions. I think the smell of sweat in the gym, the atmosphere, the equipment and having a hot woman, bent over a bench with her bare ass in the air is one of the most common sexual fantasies for gym rats like me.

* * * * *

After dinner, I spark up a campfire in the backyard and give the kids each a poker to roast their marshmallows. Last week I promised them they could make s'mores but there hasn't been time to make good on it. Kim has been reminding me relentlessly, every day, since I made that promise. She's cute and I love her, but she is a determined little girl. When she wants something, she won't stop until she gets it. It's a great quality to have. If I didn't know better, I'd swear she had my DNA. She's just like me, only better. Way better.

Rayna, Renee, Tim and I are drinking the wine while the kids hold marshmallows over the crackling fire. It's a great night for this; the breeze is light and cool, but not cold. Although it's very dark, the sky if painted with very bright stars.

"So, when's the big day? Have you set a date yet?" Renee asks both Rayna and I.

Rayna clears her throat and runs her fingers through her hair, tucking an errant strand behind her ear. "Um, no, not yet. There's no rush."

"I would love to make you my wife tonight if you'd just say the word. But, like I said, I'll wait until you're ready." I take her hand and kiss the back of it. "What about you two? Any plans for making it legit?"

Tim smiles while looking at Renee. He's rubbing her back while she looks at him. She says, "We've joked about it, but no, not really."

The kids are completely ignoring us while they stuff their faces and gape their full mouths to gross each other out. Siblings are great at being disgusting to one another.

"I was thinking of taking Rayna out Saturday night. Will you two be available for phone calls from these young'uns, should one come?" I ask.

"Saturday night?" Renee's phone wakes up as she clicks on her calendar to see if she's available. Thank God it's dark, so no one can see when I roll my eyes. I know she doesn't have any plans. Tim confirmed it when I called him Monday to set this up. "Yeah, I'm free. Tim?"

"Just like I said earlier this week when you asked, we have no plans," he assures and then grins like an asshole. "Where are you going?"

I clear my throat and lie for the benefit of Renee and the kids, "Just out to dinner, maybe some live theatre." I look at Tim with an expression that screams *asshole*! He already knows where I'm taking Rayna. We discussed it on the phone on Monday.

Renee doesn't know about Fallen and I'd like to keep it that way. Even though she's not into BDSM, she acts like she's the shit when it comes to sexual deviance, which really annoys me. She really knows how to get under my skin and make me itch. I'd swear she does it on purpose.

Rayna quickly changes the subject, "So, back to you two and talk of marriage."

Tim shifts in his chair, but says nothing. Renee turns to look at him, expecting him to respond. When he doesn't, she shakes her head, disappointedly. He's told me that he wants to follow tradition, to get down on one knee to ask her, but he has his concerns. He's worried that she's still in the honeymoon phase of their relationship and will eventually tire of him. I wonder about that too, but haven't told him. I know he'll ask her when he thinks the time is right.

"How is the construction going?" Tim asks me. Now he is trying to change the subject.

"The last thing I want to do right now is talk about the one main thing that's stressing me out. It's a beautiful night, the stars are bright above us, we are warming our feet by a campfire with family and friends. Talking about work will not be part of tonight's discussion."

"Understood! Cheers to a quick completion, my friend," Tim says while holding his glass toward me. We lean in and clink them together, with a nod of our heads.

Rayna adds, "It's been chaotic, but it is coming along quite well. Everything is on schedule and the workers aren't bothering the patrons anymore. It is going to look great when it's finished. The women really needed a bigger room."

"I will have to come by when it's finished to take a look," Renée says, while watching me. When I glance her way, she quickly looks back at her sister. Yet another perfect moment in life, is ruined by Renee, as I know exactly what her intentions are. She doesn't care about the construction at my gym. She's made a pass at me before, and I wouldn't doubt she would try it again.

Tim is my best buddy and if she's willing to cheat on him with me, I know damn well she already has, or soon will be, fucking someone else. I am just going to have to make sure that Rayna is at the gym when Renee visits. Then again, I would like to know what she has in mind before she accepts a marriage proposal from Tim. I want to know if she loves him enough not to cheat on him.

* * * * *

Tim and Renee left around ten o'clock. The kids were already sound asleep by then. Rayna is just getting out of the shower and I'm lying in bed. In a few minutes, when she climbs into bed, her lavender scented skin will be warm and soft. I wonder what nightie she's going to put on. She knows how much I love the blue one.

My mind flips back to before we lived together. I owned the house next door. For three years, I watched her, secretly admiring her. My favourite time was at night, when she would be standing in her kitchen making the kid's lunches. The way the light behind her would cast her silhouette against the light blue fabric. It never failed to make my cock hard. I used to jerk off while I watched her, and she had no idea I was doing it. I wanted her something fierce, but always thought she was too good for me. I still do.

I hear the unmistakable thump of the loose rack, as she hangs her towel behind the door. I could screw that thing in better, but if I do, I won't get the little flutter in my chest knowing she'll be opening that door and walking out to me, at any second. I always wonder what she'll be wearing, if anything. The light turns off as the door opens. She walks out, completely naked. This is even better than that damn blue nightie! The look on her face tells me everything I need to know. She wants me.

As she approaches the bed, she asks, "So, where are you planning on taking me?"

"You know damn well where I'm taking you," I tell her with a devilish smile.

"And, just what do you plan on doing while we're there?" Rayna slowly sways back and forth with her hands on her waist.

I lick my lips, looking up and down her impeccable body. "One thing I plan to do is fuck the hell out of you, in front of everybody. What do you think about that?"

She suddenly looks very nervous, clasping her fingers together in front of her, as if to hide her body. So many thoughts riddle my brain. Should I not have said that? Maybe I'm pushing her too far, too fast. Should I slow it down? What would be the point of slowing it down? I plan on doing that and more, with her eventually, so why sugar-coat it? She has been introduced to Fallen and didn't run away screaming. Maybe she will be fine with whatever I do to her. Maybe not.

"You want to fuck me in front of everybody? It's one thing to fuck me in front of one stranger but to do it in front of thirty of them... or more... I don't know if I'm ready for that." She's overthinking herself into a state of panic. I had better say something to ease her concern, before she outright refuses to return to Fallen.

"You have watched people getting fucked, sucked off, whipped, choked. You even watched somebody get stuck with needles. Trust me on this, nobody is going to judge you for letting me fuck you."

"It's not that I'm worried about people judging me. Being fucked is a personal thing. I was raised to believe allowing a man into your body is supposed to be a sacred thing. Forgive me if I'm having trouble letting that go. This life is all new to me, but I'm trying. I think I've been very receptive to everything you're introducing me to, so far. Even after you fucked me in front of that woman, and then invited her to play. She ate my pussy and fucked me with her whole hand. I was okay afterward. It surprised me that I was so all right with it, actually. Coach, sometimes I just need a minute to catch my breath."

"Come to bed," I say as I flip the covers making it easier for her to slide in beside me. As she's climbing in, I say, "Love, I will give you all the time you need, if you really need it. From what I have witnessed so far, you start off being afraid, but as soon as I give you no choice, like when you were bound in the web of rope, you gave yourself up to it. You have yet to use your safeword even though the option is always there. That tells me you've been enjoying everything you've been experiencing."

"I suppose you're right, but this is different. When you fucked me at Fallen, nobody was watching us. Well, that one girl outside, but it was only one person. It'll be a whole different ballgame when many people are watching. What if I do something stupid?"

"Such as?" I question with a snicker because I have a pretty good idea what she's going to say.

She shrugs, "What if I fart or something?"

I start laughing, but quickly fight to contain myself when I see the look on her face. "Love, farting is a natural act that can't be helped sometimes. When something is plunging in and out of your body, the force of that can make all kinds of weird things happen to you. Sometimes, people fart! Nobody judges anyone for that. We have all experienced it."

"Not me! It would be humiliating," she replies, rolling toward me and sliding her arm over my belly, so she can rest her head on my chest.

"Do you want to know what I think your problem is?" I feel her nod. "I don't think you're afraid. I think you are intimidated because you are inexperienced and those around you at Fallen are not. Let me just remind you that everyone there was vanilla at some point. Well, maybe not exactly vanilla when they arrived at Fallen, but we were all new to this lifestyle, at one point in time. People there are very understanding. They know you're new. They will not judge you harshly if you make a mistake. Even the most experienced sub will err sometimes. Of course, they typically do it on purpose because they want the attention of a punishment."

"They want to get punished? Why?"

"One day, you will understand the answer to that question. For now, how about I just introduce you to different scenarios, and let you decide what you favor and what you don't. We can go from there. I am going to fuck you in front of everybody on Saturday, so prepare yourself for that. If in fact you hate it and never want to do it again, so be it. But I want you to keep an open mind. Promise me you will try."

"Fine, I promise to keep an open mind. If I make a fool of myself, I will make your life miserable for weeks. Got it?"

I start laughing, "Yes, Love, you will make my life miserable for weeks."

I roll towards her, coaxing her onto her back. She instinctively opens her legs, allowing me between them. I kiss her lips lovingly, until she moans under her breath. My lips brush her neck, kissing her clavicle as I make my way down to her breasts. Her skin is still drenched with the sweet scent of lavender oil. She's soft as silk, the way only a woman can feel.

Her nipples stiffen between my thin lips when my tongue rolls over them. Her breathy moan is like music in my ears, swelling my prick. Tonight, I will make love to Rayna. I will mold my body into hers until we become one person, one entity, moving in perfect sync with the universe. How did she weave herself into my heart so easily? I need her. Goddamn, I love this woman!

Sliding down her body, I glide my hands beneath her thighs to lift and spread them wider. Her womanly scent fills my nostrils as I place a loving kiss to the most tender part of her body. My tongue gently laps at her excitement, tasting her sweet tanginess. My lips form a seal around her clit, pressing firmly against her while sucking hard and teasing her swelling nub with a viciousness that I know will push her over the edge. Should I allow her to fall so easily?

I've been patiently waiting all day to have Rayna's fingers weaved through my short hair and to feel her moans on my mouth. I've wanted to taste her, smell her, feel her heat. I won't let her cum, not yet. I want to be deep in her core when she does. I need to savour the way her muscles squeeze my cock in the most delirious of ways, as if desperate to strangle it with pulsing spasms.

I flip her onto her belly, holding her legs together tightly, with my straddling thighs. I grip her hips and lift her ass just enough that I can slide my cock into her wet pussy. While leaning forward on one elbow, I slip my other hand beneath her before using my weight to press her hips into the bed. My ring and forefinger glide on either side of her clit while the middle digit taunts and teases the nub with tender touches and light strokes.

My hips lift and lower, using purposeful thrusts to sink deeply into her. I shift my arm until it's under her chest, enabling my hand to reach her throat. I'll wait to apply pressure until she's almost there, ready to float off into the void existence she craves to escape to. Those precious few seconds are euphoric.

Her breath is forced from her body, sounding more like heavy grunts, as my hips thrust against her ass. I won't rest my full weight on her, fearing I will crush her tiny frame.

She's going to cum soon. Her clit is stiffening between my digits. I tease her by holding my fingers still for a few seconds, stroking a few times and pausing once again, only to repeat. I'm driving her wild. Her moans are desperate. Her pelvis is pressing down onto my hand. It's harder to fuck her, but her thighs squeezing around my cock, is one hell of a firm grip. I slip in and out from between her cheeks with only a portion of my prick still inside her. Fuck, she feels so goddamn tight like this!

I won't last much longer. This feels so good. I'm so fucking close! My hand grips her throat enough to make it harder for her to breathe and to get blood to her brain. I know this is heightening her pleasure.

My finger is quick to manipulate her clit, stroking and rubbing it until her body stiffens. Her pussy clamps down around my cock in the most mind-numbing way. She's coming! I let myself slip into the delirium of those few seconds where nothing in this life matters except the supreme elation that engulfs me. I've craved this all day.

My hand eases off her throat and she cries out, burying her face in the mattress. My fog clears slowly as our bodies twitch and our muscles ease. I roll off her covering my forehead and eyes with my arms. I hold each breath hoping to quickly, slow the pounding of my heart to a normal pace.

Rayna slides her body up against mine, resting her ear on my shoulder. I turn my face to look at her, as I lower my arm onto her back, snugging her panting frame against mine. My kisses to her lips are soft and effortless, perfect for the moment.

She rests her head back down and whispers, "You are an amazing lover. Sara was right."

She takes me off guard. I wasn't expecting a comment like that. "Where did that come from?"

"It just popped into my head," she replies as her finger swirls around my nipple.

"Are you jealous that I used to fuck her?"

"No, I'm not. You're mine now. I know you have a past, but," she pauses, but doesn't continue her thought.

"But?"

"Is it strange that I wish I had been a fly on that wall, just so I could see what you used to do to her? I mean, she said you can be cruel. I'm curious to know what she meant by that."

"You want to know what I used to do to her that's so different from what I do to you. Is that right?"

She debates with a long *hmmm.* "Yes, I think I do. Am I weird for wanting to know?"

"No, nothing you do is weird, other than how you look when you tweeze your eyebrows. That goofy way you contort your face, isn't normal." She laughs and pinches my nipple. I jolt and slap her hand away, rubbing the little nip while I chuckle. "Hey, stop that!"

"Seriously though, is it weird?"

"No love, it's not weird to want to know what your partner used to do with a past lover. I think it's human nature to need confirmation that you're better than they were."

"Yeah, but in this case, I know she was better than me," she comments.

I kiss her forehead and vow, "I promise that making love to you is one hundred percent more satisfying than what I used to do with her."

"If I asked to watch you do to her what you used to do, would you show me?"

I'm stunned. "You want me to play with her while you watch? Did I hear that correctly?"

"Yes. If I asked you to do that for me and she's willing, would you do it?"

"Is this one of those trust tests women give men to see if they'll cheat on them?"

She laughs, "No, you paranoid freak! I'm asking if you want to punish her how you used to?"

"Have I thought about it? Of course, I have. Do I dream about playing with her again? No, I don't. I have you in my life now and that's more important to me."

"Okay, let me put this in layman's terms so you can understand what I'm asking," she says while lifting herself up. She straddles my hips and looks down at me, forcing me to give her my full attention. "I want to watch you in action, the way you used to be, before me. I'm curious to know how you earned the nickname Demon. I want to see, but don't want to be on the receiving end of his wrath when I find out just how cruel he can be. Does that make sense?"

"Can I think about it?" I ask, still not believing that she wants me to play with Sara. "You realize that I'll likely fuck her, hard. I want you to picture that, really see it in your mind, and understand that you won't be able to forget seeing it afterward. I want you to fully understand the complications that could develop, as a result of that action."

"I have pictured it, a thousand times. At first, I was a bit jealous. Now, it really turns me on. Just now, I was imagining that I was her and you were on her, entering her, pleasuring her, making her cum. It was hot and I wish I could have watched it."

I look up at her to assess her expression. Her crooked smile with pursed lips and sexy eyes says it all. She absolutely is excited by the image in her mind.

"I was making love to you just now, mostly. With her, it's completely different and will never be soft and gentle or loving in any way. With her, it was always rough and angry, vicious sometimes. She enjoys being ruled with an iron fist. It will always be like that with her. Under no circumstances will you be allowed to interfere once I get started with her. Do you understand? Nothing; no talking, no touching."

With a hint of contained excitement in her voice, she swears, "I completely understand. I will be very quiet. You won't even know I'm there."

"If you do interrupt, I'll punish you for it. I'll be rough with you, as well. When I'm in that state of mind, it's difficult to pull myself back. I can, but why would I? If you want to be a part of it, you'll be treated just as she is."

"I understand. I like Sara. Her and I could become great friends."

"Friends?" My eyes open wide to question that. First, she wants me to fuck the woman, and then says they could become friends, afterward. "You're a strange bird, Rayna."

"Yes, I am. I think you knew that and that's why you sought me out in the first place. You somehow knew I was a freak, even before I did."

"I had an inkling. But, all this talk about watching me while I let my Demon take over another woman's body, has my cock growing hard and thick. What are you going to do about it?"

"I'm going to suck you off until you cum down my throat," she replies while gliding down my body. She's giggling like a preppy, high school cheerleader with a sexy secret and I'm not so sure I like it. I never did like girls like that, but I'll gladly take Rayna's mouth, annoying laugh or not.

Chapter Twenty

Rayna

I have one patient left. A set of x-rays and a cleaning, and then I'm free for the rest of the day. By three o'clock, I will be out of here. Both kids will be staying after school today. They signed up for programs that require them to stay late on Tuesdays and Fridays. I like it because I get some free time to myself and they have something to do that interests them, other than computer games.

Ken joined an archery program. He said it makes him feel like Robin Hood. Robin Hood was a thief with good intensions, so I'm torn between liking the reference, or not. Either way, he's happy, so I'm happy.

Kim joined a group that studies astronomy. She's always enjoyed looking at the stars and the moon. I bought her a telescope last year for her birthday, and she's used it quite often. Her and I had a shooting stars night, last summer. We camped out in a tent in our backyard. She used the telescope for a while, but she wasn't quick enough to catch them before they shot away, so she packed it up. We zipped ourselves into our sleeping bags and laid with our heads sticking out the flap of the tent so we could watch the streaks in the sky, the old-fashioned way – with our eyes. It was a memorable night for sure.

Before my patient arrives, I think I'll go to the stockroom for privacy, and call Sara. I'd like to see if she does want to meet up or if she was just being kind in saying that she'd like us to be friends. Coach gave me her number, but I've been too nervous to call her. After my pillow talk with Coach last night about watching him be with her, I'm more excited than nervous at this point. My hands are still shaking and my stomach feels tight.

It rings twice before her soft voice answers. "Hello?"

"Hi, Sara. This is Kat calling. Do you remember me? I was with Demon."

"Oh! Hi Kat! Of course, I remember you. How are you?"

"I'm doing well. And, you?"

"Things are great for me. So, Demon gave you my number, I gather. Hmm, I wasn't sure he would."

"Yes, on Sunday morning. He was very happy to give it to me. To be honest, he was trying not to seem too enthusiastic about me calling you. But he knows I could learn a lot from you."

"Maybe, yeah. I've been in this lifestyle for almost eleven years now, so I've experienced a lot; some good, some not so good. I'd be more than happy to answer any questions you have. I'm so glad you called! So, what's up with you today?"

"I was wondering, if you aren't busy, maybe we could meet for coffee somewhere. I'll be finished here at work in about a half hour and then I'm free for a few hours. I'm not sure what your schedule looks like."

"I'm always free, well sort of. I work at home and can do what I do at any time of the day or night. I have an idea, why don't you come to my house and I'll make coffee here. It's more private, so we can talk without interruptions or snoopy people listening in."

"Sure, that sounds much better. I can be there in about an hour." I'm trying not to sound nervous. The idea of her and I being alone together is rather worrisome, but yet exciting. I'm sure one day her and I will have sex. Today is not likely going to be that day. That'll happen when Coach – or Demon – insists upon it. I'm way too shy to come onto her. Besides, it would be my first time and definitely not hers. It's a test my confidence will likely fail.

"Would you like me to bring snacks?"

"No Kat, I'll whip something up here."

"I don't want you to go through any trouble."

"It's no trouble! I love cooking. Besides, I could use a snack or two," she giggles.

I write down her address before we end the call. I immediately text Coach to let him know I won't be home.

Me: I'm going to Sara's after work. Kids have archery and astronomy after school. Don't worry, I'll pick them up on my way home.

Coach: You're going to Sara's?

Me: Yes. Are you okay with that?

Coach: Of course. I can't help that I'll be picturing the two of you in a heated tryst.

Me: I don't think that's going to happen, but I can't stop you from imagining it.

Coach: I give you permission to play with Sara

Me: Oh, gee, thanks

Coach: What does that mean?

Me: I'm not going to have sex with her, whether you give me permission or not

Coach: If I don't give you permission first, you'd better never have sex with anyone. That's cheating.

Me: But if you give me permission, it isn't cheating? That makes no sense. I'd still be having sex with someone without you there - cheating

Coach: But if I give my permission, it's allowed.

Me: Hmm, if you say so.

Coach: If I tell you to have sex with someone when I'm not around, and I know you really do want that person, it's not cheating. It's an order that you will need to follow, unless you use your safeword, of course.

Me: Are you saying you're ordering me to have sex with Sara?

Coach: I'm saying you can, if you want to. It's allowed, but not demanded.

Me: It doesn't matter, either way. I doubt that will happen without you there. I'd be too intimidated by her.

Coach: Don't deny yourself the experience if it comes about.

Me: Okay, I have to go. I have a patient waiting.

Coach: I love you! Have fun and don't worry about the kids. I'll pick them up at five.

Me: Okay, see you later.

I slide my phone into my shirt pocket as I'm walking into the reception area.

"Hello, Mrs. Baker. Do you want to come with me?" The woman slowly stands on her well-seasoned legs and shuffles her flat, pink slip-on shoes across the tiled floor. She pushes her walker at a snail's pace. It might take longer than a half hour just to get her into the room.

"I'm sorry, dear," she says with a tender, shaky voice.

"You just take your time. I am in no hurry," I fib to her, as convincingly as I can manage.

I don't want her to rush, possibly falling and hurting herself. First of all, she'll get injured and she really is a sweet woman, so I don't want to see her in pain. Secondly, and selfishly, if she falls and does get injured, I'll be here for at least another hour. We'll need to get her shipped off in an ambulance and then I'll have to fill out a mountain of paperwork. So, no, I don't want her to rush.

* * * * *

I'm standing in the well-lit hallway on the gold and blue carpeting, unsure of whether I want to have sex with her if she asks me to, or tell her I'm on my period, or some other tale that will likely postpone that activity. I keep staring at the golden numbers - twelvesixteen - affixed to the door, rereading them about eight times, just to make sure I have the right apartment. The building is newer than the one next to it and it's much classier.

I purposely shake my hands to ease their nervous vibration. I take a deep breath and whisper to myself, "It's okay Rayna, she's a nice woman. She isn't going to want to have sex with you today. Just lift your fist and knock on the damn door."

I rap and wait, but not for too long. She opens the door, greeting me with a huge smile. "Hi, come on in! I'm glad you came."

"Thank you. I'm happy to be here. I love your apartment!"

The brightness of the afternoon sun shining through the glass wall casts a romantic easiness about the room. The softly painted walls are decorated with beautiful pictures of the wilderness and running streams. The place seems much larger than it probably is because of the open-concept kitchen and living room. As I pass the short hallway, I can see three open doors. I can see the glass surround to a shower unit through one of those rooms making me assume that would be the bathroom.

"It's technically a condo, but thank you. I love this building much more than the place I was at before."

"Did you just move in?" I ask while breathing in the gentle scent of vanilla, realizing it's coming from a lit candle on the kitchen island. The scent adds to the calmness of the atmosphere.

"No, not really. I've been here for about two years now. It's really quiet, so I can get a lot of work done without interruptions, unlike my last place. It was way too noisy there."

"It's beautifully decorated. Did you do it yourself?" It does look professionally done.

"Yeah, I like decorating, and thank you," she says while glancing around the room, proudly admiring her efforts. "Make yourself at home. What do you take in your coffee?"

"Just a little milk, black is fine too," I tell her while sitting on a stool on the front side of the island.

A very fat, fluffy white cat comes waddling into the kitchen silently, as cats typically are. It jumps onto the counter and flops over with its tail flipping in the air. The loud purr coming from this cat has me giggling. I've never heard one this loud. I reach out and pet it. It rolls from side to side as I stroke its fine, thick coat.

"Sorry about that. Katie, off you go!" she says, shooing her away. "She thinks she owns the place."

"Cats are like that. I don't mind if she's on the counter."

"I don't like her doing that when company is over. Some people don't like cats."

"The way I see it, this home is yours and you can let your cat do whatever you want. If a guest has an issue with it, they can leave."

She looks at me and smiles. "I knew I was going to like you."

I smile as she hands me a big mug which reads, *happier with coffee*. It suits me well.

"So, now that it's just the two of us and nobody can listen in, is there anything in particular you want to talk about?" she asks while waving me to follow her to the puffy black sofa.

"Well, yes actually, but I'm not sure you'll want to talk about it."

"Try me," she suggests as she sits facing me with one leg folded beneath her. "Think of this as a safe place where you can ask anything without judgement. Whatever we talk about here is between you and I, only.

Nobody will ever hear about our conversation, not even Coach."

"You know his real name?"

"Of course! He was my Master, and friend, so we would go out to dinner once in a while, or other places where referring to him as

Demon, would not go over very well."

"What's your real name, if I can ask that."

"Sara. I didn't change my name and I never had a Master who chose one for me. They just called me Sara. Well, there was bitch, whore, slut, cunt, pig, et cetera. What's yours? I know Kat isn't your real name."

"I'm Rayna. Coach and I had a conversation about me being older than him and the whole cougar thing. I didn't want to be called C.A.T. because cougar is just too degrading, so I asked to be called K.A.T. Nobody is the wiser of the spelling, but I know and that's all that matters."

"I like it! Can I ask you what the age difference is between you and Coach?"

"I'm ten years older."

"Tell me about yourself."

"I have two kids with my useless ex-husband who has basically abandoned them when he recently moved across the country with the tart of the month. I'm happier now that he's not around and the kids are better off too. Coach moved in and he's been more of a dad than their biological sperm donor ever was. He's a good man."

"I know he is. He was always very good to me. He never emotionally hurt me, and he respected me... outside of the playroom, of course. He was very dominant when I needed him to be and I really liked that."

"Do you miss him?" I ask, hoping I don't sound jealous.

"Miss him?" she repeats and then sips her coffee. She is taking a moment, as if to think of what an acceptable response would be. "To be honest with you, I do. I miss him a lot. I'm not saying that I am in love with him, please believe that. I cared a lot for him, as my friend with benefits. When we split up, I didn't think I'd miss him this much, but I do."

"Would you get together with him again if given the chance?"

She sips her coffee again and then sets it on the table, folding her hands in her lap. "He's with you now."

"He is, but would you?"

Her eyebrows furrow, "Rayna, let's not beat around the bush, okay? What are you wanting to ask me?"

I look at her and set my cup down. "I've never seen Demon in action, not really. He won't let him out, with me. He says I'm not ready. I'll admit that when he says that, it intimidates me. The thing is, I don't know how bad he can get, so my imagination takes over and I picture him slapping me around and really hurting me. I just wonder if he'll be able to keep his Demon at bay for the rest of our lives or not. If he's right, and Demon is too much for me, he'll never be the man he needs to be. How miserable will he become over time?"

She nods, understanding my concerns. "So, are you asking if I'll let Demon play with me like he used to, like physically? Do you want to see how he is with me?"

I flash a smile and nod shyly. "Are you opposed to that?"

She picks up her cup and takes a large gulp, hugging her cup with both hands afterward. "I'm not opposed to it. My concern is, well, there's history between us. If he's all right with it…" She sips her coffee again, looking into her mug afterward. "Well, he already knows how I like to play, so I suppose that would benefit the situation. So, just so you are aware - watching your fiancée fuck me might put a strain on your relationship. Have you thought about that? I've seen it happen too many times. People think they can handle swapping with extra partners, but they quickly find out that the big green monster takes over and the jealousy ruins their marriage. I'm not saying it will happen to you two. I know he's good with sharing, as long as permission is granted. It's you I'm worried about. I'm guessing your ex cheated on you."

"How would you know that?"

"It's just a guess. I'm intuitive," she jokes. "Plus, you said he left with the *tart of the month*. That's a dead giveaway."

"Yeah, he fucked my sister. It happened years ago, and I guessed it had happened, but didn't really want to know for certain. It wasn't all that long ago that she confirmed it; last year, actually. I had already dealt with it years ago, therefore, it didn't affect my relationship with my sister. I think her and I are stronger now than ever, now that everything is out on the table. She hit on Coach once but that was before we were actually together, so I let that go."

"Do you trust her?"

"With Coach?" I ask, she nods. "Not in so many words. I really don't think she would, and I know Coach won't entertain her, but there's a little piece of me that has doubts about her self-control."

"I want you to close your eyes right now and picture me bound to a wooden horse while he pulls my hair and fucks me very hard." I do what she suggests.

"Now, I want you to picture me coming hard on his cock. Remember, we'll move well together because of our history. He'll know exactly when to fuck me harder or softer, slap me or caress me. Picture him caressing me, kissing my lips, us reaching orgasm together. If he sticks his tongue in my ass, will you want to kiss him after that?"

"Right after? I don't know," I snicker.

She giggles, "Okay, maybe not right after if that's not something you're okay with."

"I honestly don't know. I haven't even been down on a woman. I'm not sure if I would be okay with him having another woman's scent on his face. I enjoy my own scent and taste on his lips, so I suppose I'd be okay with someone else's."

"But what about watching him fuck me or me pleasuring him with my mouth? What if I make him cum? Will you be okay with that?"

"Like I said, I don't know, but I want to find out. How else will I find out if I don't actually see it happen. When I imagine him fucking you and dominating you…" my words fall away, but my eyes stay locked on hers.

"It turns you on," she says, finishing my sentence for me.

"Yes," I reply, feeling ashamed.

"Have you thought about you and I having sex?"

My breath catches in my chest. My whole body seems to ignite from a flickering flame to a raging inferno. Is my face on fire? I'm sure I'm redder than a firetruck! I can feel my hands starting to shake.

"Would you like to have sex with me?"

The sudden dryness in my throat has me swallowing hard. I gulp my coffee, but it doesn't help wash down the nervousness. My stomach squeezes when a stomach full of flapping butterflies threatens to make me vomit.

In barely a whisper, I boldly reply, "Maybe, I don't know." "Do you have his permission?" she asks.

That's a question that has me wondering its origin. "Um, strangely enough, when I told him I was coming here, he gave me his permission. Did you two plan this behind my back?"

"No! The last time I talked to him was at Fallen when you were there. I promise!" she vows with her hand in the air. "I just know he's really opposed to playing without permission. That's what split our union. I started dating someone who wasn't involved in this lifestyle. I told Coach that we were intimate, and he broke it off."

I'm relieved that he hasn't been flirting. But I wonder why I'm so concerned about it. If he starts fucking her, maybe I will be nervous. My hands are shaking again and it's not from the coffee.

"I, um… I'm really nervous."

"That's okay, Rayna. I understand. We can take it very slowly." I nod and smile at her, but have a hard time holding her gaze. "I'd appreciate that."

She takes my mug and sets it on the table. "Come with me. We can take a shower together."

She puts her hand out to me as she stands up. I take a big breath and then take her hand. What's the worse that will happen? If I don't like it, I never have to do it again. At least I won't be wondering *what if* for the rest of my life. By the end of this hour I will know if I like vagina as much as cock. This will be a learning experience, if nothing else.

She brings me into her bedroom and begins by undressing herself. I watch her while I slowly follow her lead. She stands before me completely naked. I've seen her at this level of undress, so it doesn't bother me at all. I already know she has an amazing figure.

"You are so perfect," I whisper.

"Sweetie, in no way, shape or form am I perfect."

"I don't look as good as you. I've had two children and I'm older than you." In a way, I'm confessing my insecurities.

"Rayna, I tried to have children with my ex-husband, but after four miscarriages, I decided to have some testing done. They proved I cannot carry a fetus. I left him, so he could move on and have children with someone else. Being a father to half a dozen kids was his lifelong dream. He's now remarried with eight kids--two sets of twins! It was a good thing… me leaving him. I wish I had stretchmarks and loose skin because it would be totally worth it."

"I'm so sorry," I whisper. I can see past her phony smile at how much she's hurting.

"It's in the past. If I dwelled on everything shitty that ever happened to me, I'd never get out of bed. Happiness is a choice and I choose it over sadness and regret." I'm beginning to like Sara very much.

As soon as I've removed my panties and set them on top of my shirt, bra and pants, she takes my hand and guides me into the bathroom.

After setting the water to the perfect temperature, she steps into the glass shower. I follow her in. Despite the heat of the cascading water, I'm shaking as if it were nearly freezing cold.

She begins soaping my fingers, working her way up my arms to my shoulders, neck and finally my chest. She doesn't use a loofa or a cloth, just her hands. Her tender touch feels different on my skin than a man's. Maybe the delicacy of her small hands is what makes her touch feel so faint. I don't know, but I do like it.

I take the soap and lather it up in my palms and then start at her shoulders and work my way down her arms, back up and then move down the center of her chest. I watch the bubbles lazily trail over the slopes of her breasts. I reach for the perky mounds, cupping them in my hands. I fondle them tenderly, amazed at how soft and warm they feel. Mine don't seem to feel as soft or as warm. My thumbs brush over her nipples. She takes in a quick breath and they stiffen without hesitation.

Curious to explore her, I trail my fingertips down her belly and slip my hand between her legs. It doesn't feel much different than mine. The fact that I'm touching a clitoris, but don't feel the sensations of my touch, seems odd. I'm very pleased that I'm enjoying her body. My fear has ceased, shifting more toward curiosity. I'm not even shaking anymore.

My fingers explore her labia and clitoris. My own pussy is twitching, knowing exactly how marvellous it feels to have my clit touched a certain way; a way I truly enjoy in these first stages of arousal. Is she enjoying my touch the way I imagine she is?

"Can I kiss you?" she asks.

I don't answer her, I move toward her and press my lips to hers while placing my arm around her shoulder so my hand can hold the back of her neck. Her body feels so small in comparison to Coach.

Our mouths softly kiss, our tongues dancing tenderly. Her face is so soft and tiny. Everything about her is familiar and yet a complete mystery. This is no longer an experiment, I actually want her. I want to feel her tender weight on me, or her small frame beneath me, or beside me. I just need to feel her. I can't wait to trace her sexy curves with the tips of my fingers. I yearn to taste her intimacy.

Her lips scarcely part from mine. "Let's rinse off and go to my bed."

"Yes, I want that," I whisper in response.

We quickly rinse ourselves and dry off while watching each other. Her skin has a pale creaminess about it that has me imagining her flesh donning the morning's purple bruises from a night of rope play. Her light brown hair is shoulder length and holds a soft wave even when it's damp. Her eyes are so blue that the freckles on her skin make for a huge contrast.

She takes my hand and leads me to the bed. Before we lie down, we have already started kissing. The second her body presses against mine my mind slips far away from my fears. The silkiness of her skin pressing onto mine makes our flesh mold into one. Her hair tickles my cheeks and neck.

My hands cup her face, pulling her hair from her face. She rolls onto me and straddles my hips. Her breasts are so soft that my hands want to grip them tighter than I likely should. I know how to tease her fat nipples, because I have fat nipples too. I'll just do what I want done to me.

She slowly glides down my body. She tenderly kisses my breasts, circling my nipples with her tongue. The way she does it has my pussy twitching and me moaning. She could just stay doing what she's doing, and I'd still call it a wonderful lesbian experience. But I hope she continues downward to my pussy. I want to feel that soft mouth.

I lift my head to see how it looks to have a beautiful woman eager to pleasure me. I've had dreams about this, but never imagined I'd ever go through with it. I'm pleased I allowed myself the thrill of this taboo.

Sara looks up at me just as her lips gingerly kiss the tip of my clitoral hood. Her hot breath flows down my air-chilled folds, easing a moan from my depths. I tilt my pelvis, eager for more. I want her mouth to touch me. I need it!

"Please," I beg.

Watching Sara smile just before her lips surround my swelling nub has my mind whirling from excitement. Her pouty lips form a seal and gently suck, release my clit in a steady rhythm as her tongue agilely, and with great skill, molests it.

She slips two of her fingers inside of me and immediately begins rubbing toward the front. A sudden sensation of pressure from inside of me forces outward into my clit, swelling it like a tiny balloon. It doesn't hurt, it's glorious. This internal massage is better than anything Coach has done, and he's great with his hands.

Another finger enters me, and it isn't enough. I want more. The harsh stretch doesn't hurt, it feels amazing. My pussy is full, but she's still able to fuck me at a slow and steady pace. Her whole hand pushes, hoping to enter me. I cry out when my mind swims from the sudden superb invasion. Her hand is smaller than Coaches, much smaller, and I'm able to compensate for it easily. Her hand is so much more enjoyable than his; it's less pain.

She slowly fucks me with her fingers straight, sliding in and gliding out, then pushing back in, her knuckles held out only by my tightness. Her mouth works my clit until I'm humping her hand and tongue, as she eases me closer and closer to the point of no return.

I open my eyes when I feel her hot lips on my left nipple, circling it while nipping at its tip. I reach down and cup her face with both hands, leaning up to her while she rises up to meet me. Our mouths press together with a heated passion that has me moaning for more. The familiar taste of my pussy on her unfamiliar lips is proof that her beautiful pouty lips engulfed me, tasted me.

Sara's fingers continue to fuck me while my hips hump up to meet her arm, hoping to take every inch of her inside of me. My clit burns with a need for her touch, but I'll be patient and enjoy every second she's with me.

Suddenly, a fullness has me flopping my head back onto the bed and crying out, begging her for something, anything, more maybe. I don't know; my mind is drifting further away as my body begins to float off the mattress. Her fist is spinning inside of me, pushing in, as it does. Lightly punching and spinning, punching and spinning.

Her lips suck my clit, rubbing and flipping it back and forth, up and down. Her left-hand presses down on my pelvic bone while her forefinger and thumb squeeze the lips together from either side of my clit, projecting the little button outward and into her awaiting mouth. She inhales it, taking it as a hostage between her teeth with a light nip. Her tongue continues its assault, ravishing my swollen clitoris more fantastically than I have ever felt.

My hands grip the comforter to keep from floating too far away from her. She has me so close to orgasm but has yet to take me over the top. She's holding me at the peak. My body and mind belong to her. She has me – all of me.

Her fist rotates quicker, seeming to vibrate inside of me. My clit is quivering, twitching, pulsing in her teeth. I don't exactly know what happens next because I'm lost, out of my body and gone. This all-encompassing glory has taken me away to nowhere. Nothing exists except pure, unrelenting euphoria.

My soul slowly re-enters my body, gently sinking its weight back on the bed, as it does. My lungs and throat are burning. I was screaming. I could hear myself, but I was so far away that quieting myself became an impossibility.

My eyes open to see Sara looking down at me with a sedate expression. Her lips press tenderly to mine as my breath rushes through my nostrils until I need to open my lips for more air. Our tongues dance tenderly, lovingly.

My hands explore the thighs that are spread over either side of my hips. They are so smooth and soft that my fingertips feel as rough as sandpaper in comparison.

Sara pulls away, leaning toward one of her nightstands. She opens the top drawer and pulls out a long, double-ended dildo. She lifts off me just enough so that I can open my legs, accepting one end of it inside of me. She bends it up while pushing my legs together. It's coolness rests along my hot, twitching clit. It feels so good, almost calming.

She lifts up and presses the other end inside of herself. She slowly sinks down until she rests on my pelvis. Her body has completely engulfed her half of the dildo.

I cup her breasts and tilt my pelvis. She holds my hands onto her globes. I watch as her hips sensually begin to rock up and down, forward and back. Each time she fills herself, my end presses deeper into me. As she lifts, it pulls. I squeeze my stretched pussy muscles to help hold it inside of me.

Her beauty is awe inspiring. The way the light from the window surrounds her curves, shadowing the concaves of her small muscles, as she fucks me while fucking herself.

I tilt my pelvis just a little bit more, enough so that another inch of dildo is freed for her to sink her body onto. With my hands still grasping her breast, she pulls my fingers to her nipples and pinches them so hard that my fingers ache under her grip.

Sara's head drops back as she rides harder and faster, fucking the dildo as if it were my own real cock. The friction against my sensitive clit is enough to wake it from its sedated trance. The way the dick feels inside me, rubbing on my clit while she rides it, tricks me into believing my actual cock is ramming into her. I let my mind slip into that thought, as if I am Coach and this dick is his. She is riding him, not me. It's thrilling, especially when she cums and her pussy grips and spasms, moving the dildo inside of me in unusual ways.

"Yes, cum for me," I whisper just as my own orgasm explodes through me like a tidal wave. My hips are bouncing up at her, as hers slam down. I'm fucking her. She's fucking me. We're both coming hard on the shared cock. Our bodies fight to keep moving, keep fucking, keep pleasuring the other, but it's useless. My arms and hips drop to the bed. Sara falls forward, her face buried in my neck. Both of us are panting, like dogs on a hot summer day.

She lifts herself just enough to kiss me. Our lips hold lazily together, breathing in one another's spent air. My fingers weave into her silky hair, brushing the sweaty tresses off her cheek and tucking it behind her ear.

I roll her onto her back, resting my hips between her thighs. The dildo has popped out of me, but remains inside of her, my end resting on the bed, wet and slick with my cum.

Feeling brave, I slide down her body, kissing and licking her glistening, salty skin. Between her thighs I can smell her sex. My mouth waters, something I wasn't expecting. This is the first time I've been this close to another woman's vagina. My lips press just above her clit, kissing her tenderly. I lower my mouth and press my tongue between her silky folds. I'm shocked to feel their incredible softness, as if it were pudding on my lips.

I lap at her saltiness, exploring each fold and tasting her tangy sweetness. Her scent fills my nostrils, igniting a fire between my thighs. I open my lips wide and press my mouth around her entire clitoris. Gently at first, I suck, lifting her clit against my tongue. I stroke under the hood with the tip of my tongue. Her moan is my reward.

I tenderly adore her clit and feel it swell the more I fondle it. My pussy is tingling, and I can feel the wetness of my arousal when I shift to a more comfortable position. Flat on my belly, with my hands reach under her hips, holding her thighs apart.

I try to remember what she did to me and do my best to copy. Her chest rises and falls, her breath quickening. I slip two fingers between her labia and wiggle until they are inside of her. The heat of her depth stuns me. I hadn't realized just how smoldering it is inside a woman's cavern.

My fingers wiggle and play, exploring how easily it is to push deeply into her until my knuckles press against my chin. I pull my face back so I can watch my fingers disappear into her. I add another and push.

"More," she instructs.

With her nudging, I add a forth. Her lips part and I know just how she feels. My pussy twitches, imagining my hand is inside of me, doing exactly this to my body. I do what I would want done to me. I add my thumb and gently twist, using her natural wetness to lubricate my knuckles.

Her eyes keep her mind connected to me, as I cautiously push forward. I don't want to hurt her. Sara seems to understand my hesitation and reaches down to grasp my wrist. Her hips lift off the bed as she pulls on my arm, forcing it into her. I feel her pussy let go and in a flash I'm in. What a sight this is!

My entire hand has been engulfed inside of her. The tightness that holds me in prevents me from fucking her with ease. I pull out slightly and twist, as she had done to me.

"Make a fist," she whispers through a heaving breath.

"You're so tight," I whisper in reply. "I don't know if I can."

It takes a bit of effort, but I manage to fold my fingers over my thumb and into my palm. I feel like I am in control of her body, as if I own her completely. My fist is locked inside of her, as if she were my puppet. If I pull back, she comes with me. I try again just to see if it's possible, but her outer rim is too tight. I push forward, deeper into her and slowly try to nod by wrist, like a puppet in agreeance.

Sara arches her back, releasing my wrist and reaching high above her head to clutch the rails on her headboard. Her moans ride loudly on the long, purposeful breaths that escape her. For a few moments, I'm lost in the vision of this beautiful woman skewered on my arm, writhing against it, her pleasure comes at my will. I feel powerful. I can make her cum, or not cum. It's up to me--my desire, my compassion.

I reach for the dildo as I lift onto my knees. I push it into my dripping wet cunt and start to fuck myself with the same tempo as my hand is fucking her. The only difference is my hand is waving, and the dildo unfortunately cannot. I want to feel what she feels, to know if I'm doing it right.

I lean forward and bury my mouth against her clit, sucking and flicking like a starving woman trying to drain syrup from a tree. Her thighs pull together, holding my head and deafening my ears to her pleasured cries.

My hands fuck her faster, building my own orgasm as I'm sure hers is escalating. My tongue whirls as my mouth sucks and my fist reams. The woman's strong thighs clenching over my ears are no match for her passionate wails. I can hear her song and it's revving me up. She sings for me because of what I am doing to her. If I stop, she won't cum.

I am not that cruel, but it would be ultimate torture at this stage of our arousal.

Sara screams, "I'm coming! I'm coming!"

I open my eyes to watch her erupt. This is the first time I will make a woman lose her mind at my will, but it is not going to be the last. She releases the rails and grabs her breasts, squeezing them so tightly that I'm sure they'll burst. She pinches her nipples, pulling up so viciously that I'm sure she's going to tear them off. Her flesh is changing colour under her grip, darkening to a deep red.

Sara screams. Her thighs part wide as her ass tenses, lifting her crotch against my mouth. I watch her lips part as she sucks in a long, deep breath. Her cunt is twitching, pulsing around my hand making it more difficult to keep nodding it. I try to pull and push, nod and twist, to give her the most pleasure I possibly can.

Her entire body is vibrating. I own her mind, body and soul at this very moment. Everything about her belongs to me. I am giving her this gift of euphoria. Me. I am.

Her clit is swelling and stiffening, making it easier to violate it. I suck even harder while continuing to flick and stroke with earnest.

Sara's pussy grips my fist like a vice, pinning it in place. I cannot move it. The spasms are crushing my hand, but I love it. Heat surges through her cunt like a volcanic eruption. Her muscles push, giving birth to my hand. A flood of her cum washes over my hand and chin, startling me.

I don't stop lapping and sucking on her bloated clit. Maybe she'll cum again.

Her entire body is jerking each time my tongue flicks. The control I have over her is intoxicating. She weaves her fingers in my hair, holding my head in place. I watch as she continues to flinch and contort her face in a pained expression. I am familiar with this hypersensitivity after a clitoral orgasm. She seems to want it. I know she enjoys pain and punishment, but this is something I do not like.

She finally pulls my hair to lift my mouth away from her pussy. My lips cool in the air now that they're away from the fiery heat of her womanhood.

I climb up her body, leaving the dildo inside of me. Her hands tenderly glide down my ribs and around my back. Her legs wrap around my waist and hold me against her. I wish I had a cock so I could sink into her and lose myself inside her. I want to feel her heat, her passion, her lust.

Our mouths press together in a romantic embrace. Her lips separate as her tongue slips between mine. Together they dance passionately, allowing her to sample the flavour of her own orgasm.

Her mouth feels rough in comparison to the softness of her pussy. Sara whispers, "Sit on my face."

I kiss her once more and then slowly make my way up her body, noticing how much tinier her frame is than Coach's. The cock slips from my pussy, landing on her belly. I feel her jerk to grab it. My pussy hovers over her puffy lips. I hold her gaze until she lifts her head to taste me and my lids become heavy.

Her arms wrap around my thighs, pulling me down onto her face. Her tongue tickles my aroused clit, now and then dipping down along my inner labia awakening those sensitive nerves. She kisses and licks me, savouring my flesh.

I look down and watch her enjoying me. Her eyes are closed, allowing her mind to relish in the moment, without distraction. She's tender and loving at first. Her intensity gradually escalating the more aroused I become, or am I becoming more aroused from her intensity? I can't decide.

My breaths are short and quick, laced with moans. She's building me up to a harsh climax. I can feel the urgency tightening in my belly. Fuck! She's exceptional at this!

Sara is searching for the opening of my pussy with the dildo, but she can't maneuver it to get it inside me. I lean forward just slightly, and it slips into me. She immediately begins to fuck me with long, deep strokes. My thoughts are swirling, but are quick to focus solely on my impending orgasm.

I reach out and grab hold of her headboard for stability. My thighs are beginning to quiver, and I don't want to slip down onto her face. I hold tightly as if determined to bend the wrought iron bars. It's impossible, but my grip is so intense that my hands are aching.

Sara fucks me faster, continuing with the lengthy strokes, pounding my g-spot relentlessly. Her lips wrap around my clit while her tongue continues its assault.

Within seconds, my mind is slipping away, drowning in my body's pleasure. I give myself up to her, completely. I sit up taller, shifting my hips slightly. The pounding from the head of the dildo is now striking my g-spot at the perfect angle.

Oh god! That's it! Oh yes! A rippling seizure of lust releases, shredding through me. My mind is lost in the nothingness of sexual euphoria. With my eyes shut, mouth open, head tilted back, I am locked in this position by muscles that have a mind of their own.

A loud wail rips from my burning lungs as my muscles unlock and I fall forward, pressing my face against the cool metal bar. My body jerks above her mouth, refusing to accept the end of the incredible elation known to be an orgasm.

With every ounce of strength I can muster, I lift myself from my position and slowly topple to my left, coming to rest on my back, my limbs flopping carelessly.

"Oh, fuck! That was... holy shit!" is all I can whisper.

I hear her giggle and feel her soft hand slide along my belly. She presses her body against mine, resting her head on my bicep. Her fingertips lightly tickle my left nipple, but not in an arousing way.

She's simply touching me, exploring the stiff, little nub.

"So, what do you think about having sex with a woman?"

I smile and whisper, "I am all for it."

"It's different than having sex with a man, isn't it?" Her fingers draw tiny circles on my breast causing my nipple to stiffen even more.

"Yeah, it is. You are soft and delicate. With Coach I can be rougher, I guess. I mean, I feel a need to be gentler with you because of your size and the softness of your skin. I didn't want to grab and squeeze you because I was afraid to bruise you. But, holy shit woman! You really know your way around a woman's body!"

She giggles, "I've been with a woman or two, in my days."

"More than that, I'm guessing. You are really good."

"Thank you," she says as she leans up on her elbow so we can talk while looking at each other. "Did you enjoy tasting me?"

I smile and nod, "I did! I was so worried I wouldn't. I feared I would attempt it and hate it the whole time, but feel committed once I got down there. It was quite the opposite. You're so soft on my lips. Your taste is sweet, but tangy and your scent is intoxicating.

The more aroused you became, the more I felt in control." "Did you feel powerful?"

I shrug, "Maybe a little. I had no desire to hurt you or punish you. In fact, I remember thinking about how cruel it would be for me to stop when you were almost there, like

Coach has done to me many times. I didn't want to stop you from coming. It's kind of a power-trip, knowing I had that much control over you."

"Demon… Coach, does enjoy delayed gratification. He does it to himself as well. He will not allow himself to cum until he feels he's earned the right. Well, that's not always the case. Sometimes, if he thought I didn't deserve to orgasm, he would take his pleasure from me and leave me without. I deserved it at times, but it wasn't what I would have chosen."

"Do you miss him? Or, should I ask, did you love him?"

She looks at me and smiles while shaking her head, "Sweetie, I love him but I'm not in love with him. He is a dear friend who helped me work through many of my own demons, after I came back from my tour. I was lost, hopeless and seeking punishment."

"What happened over there to cause you to feel that way?"

"Nothing good. I don't often talk about it, but since you asked and we just did what we did, I'll tell you. We were on a routine surveillance mission. There were two cars in the convoy. I was in the first vehicle. We drove straight into an IED that tossed our vehicle, killing the driver. We took on fire from the fucking mercenaries who were waiting to ambush any Americans who passed through. We were hurting, but we managed to take them out. While making our way back to the second car, another swarm came at us. It was a nightmare scenario."

Sara's words stop. She clears her throat and swallows hard. "I lost three friends on that afternoon. I welcomed the bullet hole in my foot because it pulled me away from the pain in my heart. So, when I got back home, I needed to suffer physically to overrule the mental anguish. I tried several dominants, but none stuck. I welcomed the pain Coach seemed to be able to grant me which helped free my mind. On other days, when I felt pitiful for my own sorrows, I craved his punishment. Somehow, he seemed to know what I needed, when I needed it. Because of him, I can now function well. I sleep without having nightmares every night and I don't wallow in the memory of that day. I can appreciate the fun memories I had with the guys we lost."

Sara smiles, as if remembering something funny. She shakes her head and looks up at me with a shrug.

"I'm sorry you went through that."

"Me too. So, back to you and your first sexual experience with a female." She grins and winks. "Did you enjoy being in control of my pleasure?"

"I really did! I can better understand the benefits of being a dominant. I felt powerful and in control of you. There was a strength of mind in knowing I had that much control. It's sort of the ultimate stroke to my ego. I'm beginning to understand why dominants enjoy it."

"Most are all about their ego and I do like stroking it for them."

"Have you ever dominated anyone?"

"No, I'm a submissive with no desire to be anything different. I would never grant anyone pain, but I really love it when someone hurts me. I'm a masochist, through and through. Pain takes my mind away from reality and I will always be grateful to my Masters who've allowed it."

"I haven't dominated anyone either. This whole submissive thing is still new to me, so being the aggressor hasn't even crossed my mind. I'm not a person who likes to be in control, sexually. I mean, I have two kids and a shitty ex-husband who didn't do squat to help me support and raise them, so I've always had to be the strong one. When it comes to sex, I don't want to have to make any decisions. I'm tired, if that makes any sense."

"I totally get what you're saying."

"Can I ask you something?" She nods. "After you came, you held my head so that I would continue to lick your clit. For me, it's an intensely painful tickle that I can't stand. Why did you want me to continue?"

She grins, "Well, after an orgasm, I have a strange need to be punished for taking my pleasure. If I'm not punished for coming, it doesn't feel complete, as if I'm left with the guilt. It's weird, I know."

"Yeah, that feeling of the horrible sensitive painfulness... I hate it! Coach tortures me with that sometimes and I always beg him to stop. I haven't used the safeword to get him to, but I've come very close."

Sara sits up and runs her fingers through her hair to smooth out the knots. When the light from the window surrounds her shape, I'm reminded of how beautiful she looked when she was riding my fake cock.

"Can I ask you something else?"

She smiles and says, "Sweetie, you can ask me anything you want."

"I want to watch you with Demon."

She smiles and whispers, "That isn't really a question."

I smile and nod shyly. "Will you be with him... for me?"

"I would love to. Tomorrow night at Fallen?" She stands up and takes my hand to help me up.

"Tomorrow? I'll see if I can have my sister available for the kids.

We've just started leaving them alone."

"How's that going?"

"Well, so far so good."

Sara and I get dressed and then sit back on her sofa to drink a fresh coffee. We chat about everything from family to some of the worst BDSM experiences she's been through, as well as some of her best ones.

About an hour later, I kiss and hug her before leaving. As I'm walking to my car, I feel light on my feet and thrilled that I enjoy women. This opens up a whole new world for me.

Chapter Twenty-One

Coach

I hardly slept all night. The idea of playing with Sara has my Demon rattling the bars of his cage. It never crossed my mind that I would ever have the chance to be with her again. Tossing her aside was a huge mistake that I regretted for a long time, maybe still do in some small way. I know I wouldn't be as happy if I were with her, instead of Rayna. Rayna is the best thing that ever happened to me and I would fall apart if I couldn't have her. However, I do miss Sara's eagerness to please me and her need for harsh punishments. Actually, my Demon misses her most.

I remember how she loved to be punished and would do things to piss me off, just so I'd punish her, putting her back under my control. She wanted it, of course. But, when she went with another Master to piss me off and earn a harsh punishment, she took it too far. I remember how she smiled while she told me about it. She cheated on me, as far as I was concerned. I know we weren't dating, but she belonged to me, and she allowed someone else to touch what was mine without asking if I'd allow it. That was forbidden, and she knew.

Sara repeatedly apologized to me, telling me she did it strictly for the punishment I would inflict, for such an offense. I couldn't understand how she thought I'd be all right with the betrayal. Well, she got the ultimate punishment--banishment from my attention. She didn't see that coming.

When my alarm screams, I'm jolted from my deep thoughts. I hit the button and roll over, pulling a squirming

Rayna up against my chest. Her silky nightie is the only thing separating us.

My cock is so fucking hard! I need to fuck. After licking my fingertips to moisten them, I reach under the blankets and pull up on her nightie. I slip my fingers between the fold of her pussy. I grasp her hips and pull her ass into position. I line up my stiff cock and gently push it deep into her.

"I don't want to. It's too early," Rayna groans.

"Oh, come on, Love," I beg. "My cock is rock hard."

"Can I just wake up first?" she hisses, pulling my hands from her hips and sliding out of bed.

I roll onto my back and grunt. My cock is tenting the covers and I can't help but be angry. It's not aimed at her, she's allowed to say no. My cock is not going to go down on its own, not with my mind so focussed on letting Demon out to play after such a long captivity. I wonder how far Sara wants to take it tonight.

Rayna comes out of the washroom with her housecoat on and a grimacing expression. She's in a bad mood. I wonder why. Best to not poke that bear this morning... well, poke her again, I mean.

Knowing better than to push myself on her, I jerk off in the shower. I do my best not to picture the hot image of Sara at my mercy with tears streaming down her face, but the image won't leave me. I cum so fucking hard, my knees nearly give out on me. Rayna might be grouchy, but I certainly am not. I sure hope her mood changes. If she stays miserable, she likely won't want to go to Fallen tonight. I'll keep my distance from her to give her time to work out whatever issue she's having. Women are so fucking hard to figure out.

At the breakfast table, Rayna doesn't say a lot of anything to anyone. She's pleasant to all of us, but she seems distant. I wonder what's going on in that beautiful mind of hers. I don't dare ask though. She'll likely tell me nothing is wrong. In my experience, women rarely admit to what is actually pissing them off until they are damn good and ready. Men are easy; they just say what's on their mind and get it over with.

When she came home last night, after being with Sara, she was beaming. She couldn't wait to tell me everything about her visit, and I sat quietly, listening to every word. I'll admit that I was a bit jealous, not that she was with Sara, but that I wasn't there to watch it. I did vividly imagine each position she described. In my mind, I could see every expression these women wore when they looked at each other or orgasmed. It was hot enough to have me wanting to fuck Rayna with everything I had last night.

She insisted I wait. She wants me to think of it as a reward after delaying my gratification. It's fair play because I did the same thing to her last time. She also asked me not to orgasm until later when I'm with Sara, but there's no way I could have made it through a day at the gym with a fucking rock-hard cock. I'm sure someone would have complained that they were offended at my bulge, especially if they thought they were the cause of it. A gym slut would follow me around like a lost puppy if she thought I was hard for her. I did confess to Rayna that I went against her wishes by jerking off in the shower. I could tell it frustrated her, but I couldn't simply break her rule and then lie to her about it.

After we finish eating, and the kids have gone back to their bedrooms, I start taking the dishes off the table, as is our usual morning routine. From a dead silence, she blurts, "I asked you to wait."

I stop cleaning so I can look at her. I can't read her expression to know if she's furious with me or just slightly disappointed. I sit back in my seat and lean in toward her, tucking an errant lock of hair behind her ear.

"I'm sorry if I hurt your feelings. As you know from how I woke you up, my cock was raging. I couldn't go to the gym with an erect penis."

"It would have gone away if you'd thought of something other than Sara," she hisses.

I sit back, suddenly understanding. "Wait a fucking minute! Are you jealous of our plan for Sara being with me later?"

She rolls her eyes. "No, I'm not jealous of you being with her tonight." She clears her throat and then sighs. "You dreamed of her. You kept saying her name over and over until I bumped you to get you to shut up. After that, you tossed and turned, waking me up more than once. I'm just tired. I'm not jealous. I don't like that you dreamed of her though. You sounded like you cared for her more than you say you do."

"I'm sorry I kept you up and that I was saying her name." "It's okay. You can't control your subconscious, I know that. How could you not dream of her? Tonight, you'll be with her for the first time in quite a while, so she was likely riding on your thoughts when you fell asleep and that's the reason for the dreams."

"And because you had sex with her yesterday and told me all the lovely details. I remember how she tastes and what she looks like when she cums. Your vividly detailed description was a bold reminder."

"So, you do miss her?" she asks.

"I love you, only you. She was a play toy that I enjoyed having conversations with. She's a lovely woman, intelligent and funny."

"But, do you love her?"

What is she getting at? "I care a great deal for Sara but it's not like the love I have for you. What's with you today? Do you not want me to be with her tonight?"

"I do, wholeheartedly." She takes a deep breath and sighs heavily. "What if you enjoy being with her sexually, more than you do with me? It's a ridiculous concern and I know you're going to tell me exactly that. It's just that your Demon is going to be set free with her and you're going to realize that's what you've been missing this whole time. I don't know if you'll ever be able to be like that with me. I'm scared."

"It is a legitimate concern and I'm happy that you're bringing it to my attention. I don't know how it's going to go tonight, but you are always going to be my woman. I am capable of controlling my darkest desires, as you're well aware. My concern is that you are going to fear me, after you watch me with her."

"I could never fear you," she promises. "I might like Demon more than I like you. You don't know!" she smirks. "We won't know until I see him in action."

I kiss her forehead before continuing to tidy up the kitchen. My excitement about Sara has dwindled some, now that Rayna told me her fear. How can I truly let myself enjoy Sara when I know Rayna might be over-analyzing everything I'm doing with her? What if Rayna is so jealous to see me fucking another woman that she kicks me out? That thought will haunt me all day.

* * * * *

On my way home, I pick up the pizza and wings I ordered from the restaurant down the street from the gym.

When I get home, Rayna is in a much better mood than she was this morning. I'm taking my sweaty clothes from my gym bag and tossing them into the hamper in the laundry room, when someone sneaks up behind me. I feel a tap on my right shoulder. I turn to see who tapped me, but quickly realize it was Rayna when she hops up on the washing machine with her thighs spread. She has a glint in her eye and a deviant expression. This is the Rayna I thoroughly enjoy.

I drop my bag, immediately and rush to be between those beautiful thick thighs of hers. My mouth meets hers just as my big hands scoop her ass and pull her toward me. I kick my leg back to find the door and push it closed. Our tongues entwine, as I lift her shirt and yank her bra, bouncing her tits out the bottom of it.

I suck one nipple into my mouth and bite it while pinching the other between my fingers. Rayna squeaks like a little mouse and then bites her lips closed, as she often does to remain quiet for the sake of the kids. I bite down harder. I want to hear her cry out loud, enough to satisfy my need to hear her pain. I release it as soon as she does.

I unbutton her pants and then she lifts her ass, allowing me the freedom to yank them down her legs. I leave them clinging around her ankles and lift her legs up and over my head while I pull her knees open forcefully. I dive my mouth onto her pussy and lap at her like a dog, stroking her whole slit with my fat tongue. She pulls me in closer by using her pants as a means to hold me hostage.

I look up to see her biting her lips closed and know this is something she's been planning all day. Her arousal is proof of her anticipation.

I eat her pussy until she's panting and dripping wet but don't allow her to cum. Hey, she did say not to cum before tonight. I'm not going to break that rule twice. Yeah, I know, it's cruel.

I pull her off the machine and set her on her feet, spinning her to face away from me. I free my cock from my sweat pants and grab a wad of her hair, forcibly pressing her chest over the machine. I slide my cock into her pussy and grab her shoulder with my free hand, but don't release her hair. I start fucking her with purpose, ramming her so hard, the front of the machine is lifting off the floor and slamming back down, making quite a racket.

"Quieter!" she begs.

I release her hair and grab her hips, lifting her feet off the floor and stepping back until just her hands rest on the machine. Using her weight to benefit me, I lift and drop her on my cock, rapidly bouncing her ass on my pelvis.

"Don't cum," I whisper through my teeth.

"What?" she asks while panting with each thrust.

"No coming!"

"I can't," her words fall away.

I feel her body tightening. She's going to cum. I pull my cock from her and set her back onto her feet. With a wicked sneer, I step back and pull up my pants.

She spins around with a furious expression, hitting my chest with her little fist. It didn't even make me waver. "What the fuck?"

"You didn't want us to cum before tonight."

"But you jacked off in the shower this morning, so how fair is it that I don't get to cum once too?"

"Sucks for you," I tease, opening the door and stepping through it, leaving her flushed and angry.

She yanks up her pants, as she calls out to me, "That's not fair!" "I never said I'd play fair." I can't help but laugh.

"You're an asshole," she says under her breath, but I heard her. "You're just figuring that out now?" I laugh even harder.

Chapter Twenty-Two

Rayna

For some reason, walking into Fallen tonight has me feeling powerful and confident. Why the change? I've only been here twice before, and I was curious, but fearful both times. I know he's going to be with Sara and not touching me, so maybe that has me less afraid. Worrying that others are going to see me in a compromising position always makes my insides twitchy. I'm still leery about being the center of attention with onlookers ogling me.

Demon is walking down a dimly lit hallway, towing me behind him with my hand clutched tightly in his. We stop at a doorway while he peers inside the room. With a curious grunt, he turns and pulls me as he makes his way through the crowd of gawkers who are hovering outside the open door to another room. As we pass, I try to catch a glimpse of the happenings, but can't see anything beyond all the onlookers. All I hear are pleasure moans from both men and women, lots of them. Perhaps an orgy.

He pulls me into the room we've been in before. This is where he confronted that man he so obviously hates. Gear is relaxing on a beige, leather sofa. Glitter is curled into a fetal position on the floor, with her head resting on his left foot. Her eyes are closed and she appears to be asleep.

"Glad to see you back again, my friend," Gear says with a very slight smile.

Demon grunts and nods. "Always a pleasure to be here. Good to see you buddy."

Two others are sitting at the heavy wooden table, whispering while they keep their eyes focussed on Demon and myself. I feel a bit awkward. What are they saying? It's obvious they are both submissives, judging by the collars they are wearing. Both have lettering--one says slave, the other slut. They are dressed in matching red corsets, with frilly black skirts.

Demon walks over to the fridge, without acknowledging their presence. He opens the door and takes out a bottle of water. He cracks the lid and takes a long drink before handing it to me. He grasps my other hand and walks me back to the sofa where Gear and Glitter remain, unmoved.

As he sits at the other end, he shakes Gear's hand. Glitter lifts her head and smiles at me, but doesn't move to greet me. I smile and casually wave at her. She puts her head back down and closes her eyes.

When I attempt to sit beside Demon, he stops me. "I want you on the floor."

Is he serious? Should I comply or just sit beside him, refusing to be treated no better than a household dog? I shake my head and cross my arms, not following his order.

"What did I tell you?" Demon asks in a calm, stern voice.

I look at Gear and then Glitter, who remains in her position, eyes still closed. "Why do you want me on the floor?"

"Are you too good to sit on the floor?"

"No, I'm not too good to sit on the floor. I just don't really want to."

"I gave you an order. Should I punish you for not following it?" he asks, giving me the choice--do it or get punished. I'll admit, it has my pussy heating up.

I smirk and shake my head, very unlike a submissive. Gear clears his throat while cracking his knuckles by pulling each one with his thumb. I drop my arms to my sides and look back at Demon.

I remain unmoved.

"Sit on the fucking floor, now!" he growls.

I look over at the two women sitting at the table. Both have wide eyes as they watch this confrontation.

"Do not disobey me, Kat," he hisses.

I decide to do as he tells me and sit cross-legged on the floor, facing him. He points to the floor beside his feet. I slide myself toward him and turn my back, resting my head on his right knee.

I'm humiliated when he begins stroking my head and whispers, "Good girl."

The two of them start talking about someone new who has joined the club, which doesn't interest me at all. What pulls my thoughts back to them is when they start talking about someone named Valentine. Demon says he sees him often at the gym and that he's dating Kat's sister.

Valentine? Tim is a member here? Since when? Why didn't I know about this and does my sister know? Do they come here? Why the name Valentine?

Valentine was a priest who secretly wed people when it was forbidden. When jailed, awaiting his death, he fell in love with the jailer's daughter. He wrote a beautiful note to his love using violets. He was later killed by means of a club bashing. Horrible way to die, if you ask me. I wonder how he got that nickname.

"I'll tell him you asked about him. Don't expect him to come for a visit any time soon. I don't think his lady knows about this place and I doubt he'll ever tell her." Demon's hand continually strokes my head. "Kat isn't going to say anything to her sister, is she?"

I shake my head, not verbalizing my response. I am a submissive after all. Besides, I'm a bit miffed about being squatted on the floor like a damn dog. Glitter might welcome this treatment, but I certainly don't care for it.

Demon stands and puts his hand out for me. I take it and rise to my feet, glaring at him in the process. He flashes me a wicked smile before gripping my wrist and leading me out of the room. His grip is tight, and it rather hurts. My hand is going numb by the time he gets me to a dimmer section of the hallway, where nobody is within view.

He shoves me face first toward the wall, holding me against it with his hand on my upper back. I put my hands up on either side of my face as if holding up the wall. With his free hand, he yanks my skirt up to my waist, revealing my purple thong. He reaches around my waist, pushing his hand under my panties.

His finger quickly discovers my clit and begins stroking it. He presses his chest against my back, further pinning me. He grasps my hair and turns my face toward his. His breath is hot and sweet against my neck.

"When I give you an order, you are to follow it, unobjectively. You will not defy me in front of people, ever again. Do you understand?"

"Yes, Sir. I didn't want to sit on the floor," I explain.

"I don't give a shit what you want. If you're my submissive, you'll do as I ask. What you want is irrelevant. The next time you do something like that, I'll punish you in front of everyone. I know how much you hate people seeing you in the nude."

"Please don't do that," I whisper, panting from the wonderful teasing. Two of his fingers rest on either side of my clit, alternating their massage, tormenting my little nub in a glorious way. I won't cum from this, but it sure is fuck arousing.

Demon slips his fingers inside of me. Oh, yes! He starts fucking me, slowly and deeply, while rubbing the butt of his palm against my swollen clit. I try to tilt my hips, but he has me pinned. Even breathing is more difficult with his body mass holding me firmly to the wall.

"Open your mouth," he demands. I do as he says. Suddenly, he pulls his hand from my panties and up to my face, shoving three fingers into my mouth. "Suck them clean."

I lick and suck them seductively, hoping to turn him on so much that he'll want to fuck me, finally allowing me a much-needed orgasm. Unfortunately, he doesn't. I make a mental note never to insist we practice delayed-gratification again. He owes me an orgasm. I'm not worried, I know he'll satisfy me with many before the night is over. Soon though, Sara will get her pleasure.

Demon pulls away from me and yanks my skirt even higher. He slides my panties down my legs. As he lifts each foot, my panties are stripped from my ankles. He tucks them into my mouth and then takes my hand.

He steps back and whispers, "Punishment for not following my orders. Now, bend over and grab your ankles."

I do as he says, knowing he's going to spank me until my skin is a volcanic red. He does exactly that, repeatedly slapping my ass with the palm of his hand until it's gleaming and I'm on the verge of tears. It's a strange sensation - getting spanked. It hurts, but the act of being scolded, as if I'm not his equal is comforting, like he's superior to me, even though I know he's not. He will take care of me, no matter what, like a parent who scolds a child, but will always love them even if they misbehave.

When he allows me to stand, he wraps his arms around my shoulders, pulling me into a comforting hug. "You know I love you, right?"

"Yes, I do," I try to speak even though I have my panties stuffed in my mouth.

"Now, be a good girl and obey me," he instructs before pressing a tender kiss on my lips. He looks into my eyes with a friendly grin and adds, "I will never again hide you away when punishing you. The next time you disobey, without using your safeword and giving me an acceptable excuse, I will spank you in front of whomever is there. Don't push me too far, Kat."

With one final kiss, he pulls me back down the hallway to the original room he had taken me to when we first arrived. When I am led through the doorway, I notice a heavy chain hanging from the ceiling, with a metal loop at its end. Against the wall rests a highback chair, that looks like it was handcrafted by a lumberjack in the deep forest and carried here by very strong men.

Demon walks me toward it and has me sit on the solid work of art. I hadn't noticed the wrist cuffs and ankle cuffs attached to the chair, before I sat. He proceeds to bind my wrists and ankles to the chair. He stands up and reaches over the back of it pulling two wide leather straps over my shoulders, crosses them between my breasts and hangs them down at my waist. He walks behind the chair and pulls on each strap, fastening it so that my torso is held firmly to the backrest. I am bound.

He stands in front of me. With a husky voice, he gives me his rules.

1) *Do not speak unless you are experiencing unbearable discomfort. In that case, you will use your safeword.*
2) *Do not scream.*
3) *Do not spit those panties out of your mouth.*
4) *Do not fight to get free.*
5) *Do not try to get my attention, unless you are using the safeword.*
6) *Do not be afraid of me. I will not touch you.*
7) *Remember that Sara enjoys this, otherwise she would use her safeword.*
8) *Remember that I love you, but Demon is itching to have you in his clutches, so remain quiet.*

I nod, letting him know that I will follow the rules. He smiles and then takes a deep breath, letting it out slowly. He turns away and that's when I notice Sara kneeling in the corner with her back to us.

She's so quiet and looks so small.

Demon walks over to her and stands behind her. He asks, "Is there anything you don't want me to do that you didn't tell me about, yesterday?"

"No, Sir," she replies.

"On a scale of one to five, how heavy do you want me to be with you?" His voice seems deeper and more intense.

"Four, Sir," she says.

"Only four?"

"Yes, Sir. I don't want to scare Kat."

He turns to look at me. His facial expression is harsher than it was a moment ago. "Understandable. Get up and follow me."

She stands and walks behind him. Her eyes catch mine, so I wink. She winks back, her lips rising into a smile, but it's quick to fade.

Demon ties her hands into two very thick and strong looking leather mitten-style handcuffs. He lifts her up while she raises her arms above her head. He clips the hook on the loop attached to the cuffs and lets her hang. Her feet don't touch the ground.

He swings her, allowing her sundress to flow freely in the air. Her demeaner is stoical, unfazed. Demon circles her, admiring her as she swings gently, slowly spinning.

Suddenly, he rushes her, grabbing at her dress and ripping it free from her flesh, while her body jerks from the material not wanting to give way. He yanks harder and it gives, ripping down the back seam, exposing her back.

His hand spreads wide and glides its way over her exposed back, as his eyes admire her tanned skin. He grabs her ass cheek and squeezes, firmly. She remains quiet. I would have, at the very least, winced.

He cracks her ass with his palm, making her swing just slightly. I notice that her butt has a pink handprint when he walks away, giving me a chance to admire her stretched body. He takes something from a drawer and walks back to her. He has scissors in his hand that he uses to cut off the remainder of her dress, freeing her full length. Sara is only wearing thigh-high white stockings.

"White? You know I don't like white stockings," he calmly reminds her. "Did you forget?"

"No, Demon. I did not forget."

He stands before her, staring eye to eye. His lips press to hers and I gasp, nearly choking on my panties. A flutter of jealousy tickles my tummy. I wasn't expecting that. I thought I had my emotions in check. But, this... the way he's kissing her, romantically, has me on the verge of tears. His eyes quickly open and gaze over at me, as if to suggest that he's purposely trying to make me jealous. Was that a test?

He walks back to the drawer and takes out a few items before returning to her. With a quick gesture, he spins her body to face me. He stands just to the side, allowing me to witness, without interruption. He wraps elastic bands around her tits so tightly that the globes begin to change colour, almost immediately. She's remaining quiet, as she stares forward while breathing in her nose and releasing it from her mouth.

He clips a metal thing on her nipple and her face is riddled with pain. The second nipple clamp has her panting. His body reveals his excitement with a huge bulge in his leather pants.

I watch as he attaches cuffs to her ankles with an attached spreader bar to hold her legs apart. He walks back to the drawer and collects a few more things, including two thick-stranded leather floggers that he flops over his shoulders.

He fiddles with her pussy, but I can't see what he's doing. She grimaces, gritting her teeth to prevent herself from protesting. When he stands, he gives her body a shove, making her swing. I notice two identical torturous clamps to the ones that are pinching her nipples, on her pussy lips, but these have long chains with weights that dangle to her mid-calf. The weights stretch and pull at her labia each time the direction of her swing changes, as they try to catch up, making the pull even more intense.

Demon stands off to the side with his hands on his waist, watching her intently. She cries out after nearly thirty seconds of the room falling in silence. Perhaps she couldn't hold off any longer. He doesn't stop her from swinging despite her pathetic sobs. Instead, he cracks her ass with one of the floggers as she swings nearer to him. He seems to be at peace, as if he's in his happy place. She is no longer crying out, having accepted the pain for what it is, a reminder that she's alive – as she explained to me on the day we met.

He suddenly grabs her purple breasts, to stop her swing. Her whimpering is loud and has me wanting to make him stop. I can imagine how much pain that must be causing her. I likely would have screamed out my safeword. He slowly, tenderly strokes and caresses her blood-filled tits, while pulling at the clamps to contradict the loving touches. Pain and pleasure.

Demon looks at me and flashes a wink and a crooked smile. He grabs her hair and pulls her head back before planting his mouth on hers. His kiss is passionate, hard and with purpose. His other hand slaps at her left tit and then pulls at the clamp on her nipple until she screams in his mouth.

He steps back, and in a fluid motion, crosses his arms over his chest to grab the handles of the floggers, swinging them through the air, gracefully. They whip and whirl. He's precise in his movements, never letting them pause or droop. The tips of the leather strands slap at her breast – left, right, left, right – over and over until her cries fill the room. The clamps on her nipples bob and bounce, painfully. I know that pain, it's too much for me. Those particular clamps are vicious and feel like they're biting into my skin. I don't like them, so Demon rarely uses them on me.

Gear and Glitter seem to have glided into the room unnoticed and stand quietly against the closed door. How did I not see them enter? They are silently watching while he holds his submissive's hand. Are they here to observe or join in? Did Demon invite them?

The sound of the leather strands slapping at her legs and stomach is turning me on. I love the sensation a flogger grants. When only the tips make contact, it stings the flesh sharply, but the bite doesn't linger. When most of the leather strands make contact, it's more pleasurable and the ends don't seem to sting, as much. I'm becoming very aroused, watching the flogger lap at her flesh.

Sara seems to be enjoying it as well, except when it flicks the clamps on her nipples. To me, her tits look painfully sore. I wouldn't want that, I don't think. He's never wrapped my breasts before. Maybe I'll ask him to do it one day, just to see if I like it or hate it. Judging by the deep purple tone of her breasts, I don't think I'll like it.

Demon slowly walks around her, lost in thought while admiring her flesh. He swings the floggers with a rhythmic smoothness that only develops from experience. It's obvious he's used floggers many, many times. The accuracy of his aim is perfect, a well-trained movement that comes from muscle memory. I watch his eyes and the stoical expression on his face. If you couldn't see the whole picture, you would think he was decorating a cake or gracefully painting a masterpiece on a canvas, by the concentration of his motions. Her skin is flushing hot pink as he creates his work of art, perceiving her body's marks as being more precious to him than the Mona Lisa.

He stops to slap her ass cheeks with his left hand, reddening them even more. Her body jerks as he claps against her tender buttocks. She grunts but doesn't cry out. Her eyes remain closed, but her lips are parted to aide in the rapid breaths that have her body quaking.

Still standing behind her, he reaches between her legs and runs his fingers along her stretched labia. She whimpers, but it's not just from the pain of him touching her aching lips, she's enjoying the pleasure his fingers are granting her swollen clit, as they glide along it.

"You're such a whore. Your cunt is dripping wet. You want more pain, bitch?"

"Yes, Sir," she whispers.

"I didn't hear you," he utters.

Louder, she repeats, "Yes, Sir."

"That's better. Whisper again and I'll slap your face."

He shoves two fingers into her pussy forcefully. She gasps and groans as he fucks her hotness, waving and ramming deep inside of her. Her body jerks under his pounding.

"No coming until I tell you to. Do you understand?"

"Yes, Sir," she says too quietly.

His voice is deep and calm, "I said not to whisper."

He walks around the front of her, as she watches his expression with wide eyes. Demon grabs her face in his hand and squeezes her cheeks until her lips pucker, like a fish.

"Do you want me to slap you? You must because I just explained that you can't do that anymore. Did you not hear me?" "I did, Sir," she says, louder this time.

"What's my name?"

"Demon," she replies.

"Hmm, not quite yet, but soon. Keep pushing my buttons, bitch and you'll be sorry."

He releases her face and slaps her cheek, hard. She gasps, but doesn't cry out. I think I would have freaked out and started screaming at him. I really don't know what I would have done. I know I wouldn't have whispered, that's for sure.

She must be doing it on purpose, to irritate him. Maybe she's taunting his Demon.

Demon walks over to a cabinet and opens the door, choosing a white cane. As he approaches, he swings it, making it whistle through the air. He cracks her across both ass cheeks with one swing. She squeals, but doesn't protest. Her eyes are closed, mouth open with a glint of a smile at the edges of her lips. She is enjoying the pain.

He turns her, so her back is to me. I notice a red welted line across her cheeks. His fingers caress it as though he's pleased with the way it feels. He steps to the side and cracks her ass several times with the cane.

By the fourth time, she finally protests. "No! Aaaah, Fuck!" He smirks but doesn't stop, giving her three more swats.

Her once beautiful, round ass is marked in red stripes by the time he's satisfied and spins her back around. He taps the cane up between her pussy lips and side to side against her stretched flaps. Her expression is taught, while breathing through clenched teeth. The muscles in her abdomen are flexing and relaxing with each heaving breath.

He shifts his position and taps at her clit firmly, several times. Sara is jolting with each twap, yelping as she does. He slides the cane along her clit and then taps at the little nub again, harder now. Her stomach muscles flex as she fights to flee from the rod. He taps at her left tit gently, while pinching the clip on her right nipple, slowly easing it off. Now she's yelping painful cries, especially when he grabs her nipple and rolls it between his thumb and forefinger.

He repeats the process as he removes the other clamp. Again, she screams. He presses the end of the cane against her nipple, pushing it inward. Her cries stop, but her eyes pinch shut and her jaw locks, holding the pain inside. She exhales, loudly as the cane is lifted from her nipple.

Demon pulls lube out of his back pocket and dribbles it all over his right hand, putting the small bottle back in his pocket. He squats down behind her, immediately seeking her asshole with his fingers. He pushes one, maybe two fingers into her. I can't be sure how many. She moans, tilting her ass toward him as best she can. He slips them into her ass without difficulty. She must do anal often, if she's this comfortable with the invasion.

His fingers ream and stretch her hole until more fingers are inside. He reaches around her with his other hand and tenderly rubs her clit. She's moaning softly under his touch.

I look at his face which is resting against her left hip. He's lost in his own thoughts, with his eyes aimed at the floor, but likely not seeing it. He wears this exact expression often, usually while he's deep-thinking. When his face stills like this, I can rarely draw his attention, despite calling his name several times. Was he recalling situations just like this one, and so deep in the scenario that he was oblivious to his surroundings?

She wails, almost growling, waking me from my thoughts. I look at his hand and see the weighted clamp in it. He tosses it to the side, away from them. She's breathing quickly, moaning with each breath as his fingers explore her asshole. He removes the second clamp with his other hand. He tosses that one too, and then grabs at her bruised pussy lips, viciously pinching and pulling at them. Her mouth is open, but she isn't making a sound. Her chest expands and contracts, inconsistently.

He slips two of his fingers into her pussy and begins fucking her with the same tempo as he fucks her backside. His eyes are now closed, his mind pulling him even further away from reality.

"Sir, please," she begs.

He says nothing, still lost in his thoughts. His hands pound into her, filling her, pleasuring her.

"Sir," she pleads.

"Do not cum," he replies, too late. She's already coming. Her body is tense, eyes closed. Her pussy drips her pleasure from around his fingers. I watch as the clear liquid leaks down his forearm. Before she's finished coming, he pulls his hands from her body and stands.

He grabs her throat and holds her. She can't breathe. Her eyes are focused on his, but they aren't filled with fear. He slaps her cunt with his free hand, his palm landing on her clit. Judging by how she jerks her body, that must have really stung. He slaps again and again, as her eyes and lips begin to swell, as blood pools in her face. Finally, he releases her, leaving her to gasp for air as he pulls some type of apparatus behind her. It's only now that I realize it must be a fucking machine. A fat dildo protrudes from the end of a long metal arm that attaches to the box. The long cord stretches from the back of it and remains plugged into the wall, where it has been all night.

He dumps some lubricating liquid into his palm, stroking the dildo to coat it. He arranges the machine until the dildo lines up with her asshole. He twists a knob, and then inserts the dick into her butt, twisting the knob again, to lock it in place.

The room fills with the sounds of it quickly revving up. The arm pushes forward and pulls back, speeding up to a pace he seems pleased with. Sara is moaning through parted lips while her eyes remain closed. Her body shifts and jerks, as the machine fucks her.

Demon stands in front of her and reaches for her clit, grabbing and pinching it between his knuckles. He's pulling it and twisting it, painfully yanking on it. Sara protests with each loud groan. He slaps her clit and then pinches and pulls it harshly, over and over until it's swollen and fat.

He reaches in his pocket, pulling out a pair of medical scissors. He slips the edge under the elastic holding her tit hostage and begins cutting it apart, freeing her dark purple breast. She's growling, canine-like, when he frees the second dark globe. Once they're unbound, he grabs and squeezes them as she shakes her head rapidly, still growling as if a merciful screech is holding in her throat.

Demon walks back to the drawers, picking up the weighed clamps along the way. He disposes of them and the elastics in a bucket and then pulls a vibrating wand from the drawer and a leather strap with buckles on it.

He returns to her and places the vibrator on the floor while he secures the leather strap around her thigh. He affixes the wand to the strap, pressing the bulb against her swollen clitoris. Once in place, he turns it on. She immediately jolts and moans differently than she has been. Her eyes remain closed.

He slips two of his fingers back into her pussy and fucks her slowly, while the fucking machine continues its long, deep strokes, filling her ass. He adds another finger and then another. He has four inside of her and most of his palm. The muscles in his forearm flex and roll, rippling as his hand waves inside her.

She's hanging as motionless as she can manage, but her muscles are so taught that she's almost vibrating. The sounds she's making are familiar to me. I believe I make those same noises when I want to cum, but he won't allow it.

"Cum, whore! Cum, you dirty fucking slut!" he demands, while grabbing her tit and squeezing.

Every inch of her locks tight, as a long, deep moan is squeezed from her body. Clear cum pours down Demon's arm, dripping from his elbow. He continues to violate her as her suspended body jerks wildly, from the hanging chain. He slaps her tummy with an open hand, and she grunts. He places his hand just above her pelvic bone and pushes her back against the automated, fucking dick, burying it into her at a different angle and slightly deeper.

Her face jerks up and that's when I notice her eyelids are partially open, but she's staring at nothing, lost in her own existence. She cums again. He slowly lowers her, so she's hanging on her own, the dick still ramming her ass and the vibrator torturing her clit.

Demon gets up and walks to the drawer, removing a somewhat stiff leather strap that's about three inches wide and a foot long. He slaps his palm several times at different velocities, to test its level of punishment.

He slaps the inside of his forearm and then slaps her ass with the same level of harshness. She doesn't make a sound. He continues to slap at her ass and the backs of her thighs up by the crease of her ass cheek. That is a sensitive spot to begin with. He slowly rounds her until he's standing before her. He's watching her face, as he slaps at her nipples. She seems unfazed by this new pain.

He tucks the paddle under his armpit and grasps both of her nipples, pulling her forward using just them. Now I can see the artificial dick penetrating her ass, but only half of it is inside of her, as he slowly pulls her body away from it.

As he gradually lets up on her nipples, the dildo pushes deeper into her once more. She shifts her leg just slightly to move the vibrator away from her clit, and he notices her do it. He pulls at the vibrator, rearranging it so it'll press against her clit again, and this time she won't be able to move away from it.

He stops the machine to add another attachment arm to ride alongside the first one. He pushes another dildo to the end of it and then slips it into her pussy, tightening the screw to hold the arm at that length. He turns the machine back on. Now she's being fucked in both holes at once with the vibrator still torturing her burning clit.

Her body waves from the pounding, as she hangs limply. Her muscles start to tense and that's when Demon slips his hand around her throat and applies pressure.

"Open your eyes, whore," he tells her. When she doesn't, he slaps her cheek. "Open your fucking eyes."

She slowly pulls open her lids. Her blue eyes stare blankly, into his. He holds her gaze as she moves closer and closer to yet another climax. The nearer she gets, the tighter he grips her throat. Her muscles lock as her body quivers and her face reddens. I watch her face and I know exactly when she is at the peak of her pleasure. Her eyes glaze over and lose focus.

Demon releases her throat, but she's still holding her breath. Her body is taught and unmoving. Drool seeps from her bottom lips as cum floods from her depths, spurting with every thrust from the dildos. Demon watches as her face slowly drops.

He grasps her hair and lifts her face. She is totally lost in a world of euphoria. She looks horrible and yet so incredibly at peace. Now I understand why he loves taking me to the edge, like he's doing to her.

I find myself shifting in my chair. My pussy aches with a need so powerful, it has me whimpering around my panties. When I glance toward the two onlookers, I see them watching me, not the incredible scene playing out before them. I suddenly feel selfconscious about gyrating on my seat. Gear taps Glitter's shoulder and she looks at him and nods.

Chapter Twenty-Three

Coach

Sara is coming so hard on the two cocks fucking her. If only they were real men taking her body and using it for their own benefit, that would make this even hotter than it is. I get off on watching women get used up like pieces of meat, by big, strong men, especially if I'm one of those men.

My cock has been so cramped inside my pants that I can barely keep myself composed. I want to fuck this bitch! I want to cum down her fucking throat. She's hot! Fuck, I forgot how easily she drives me mad! I knew I missed playing with Sara, I just didn't realize how much. I've let Demon out of his cage, but I won't set him completely free. This is the first time Rayna has seen me with another woman and I don't want her to regret allowing it to happen. Each time I glance at her, I can't read her expression. I can't gauge whether she's enjoying this or if she's doubting her decision to ask us to play. Her thoughts are deep, so much so that they aren't showing on her face. What is happening in her mind? I wish she would smile or grimace, do something to tip the scale either way, to let me know if she is pleased, or furious.

I have to stop worrying about Rayna and do what I set out to do – show her some of my wickedness. I let go of Sara's throat, but she continues to hold her breath. I have her lost inside herself. She's checked out and lost deep in subspace. This is where Sara is happiest.

When I used to play with her regularly, she told me that when punishment and pleasure take her into subspace, she is unreachable by the nightmares of war that haunt her through her conscious thoughts and nighttime dreams alike. Her memories can't touch her right now. The ghosts of those she's killed, and those she failed to protect, can no longer haunt her. I cherish being able to give her these moments of peace and I am honoured she would allow me this opportunity.

I slap Sara's face to snap her back to reality, for just a moment. She's too close to blacking out. She needs to breathe. The shock of the slap pulls her back to me, long enough that she starts breathing, again. Her eyes are still glazed over, but at least she's taking in air.

My fucking cock is starting to throb. I have to free it. I need to be inside her, in any hole, maybe every hole. I turn off the machine and slide it back until the dildos have slipped from her body.

She's whimpering, begging for me to put them back. "More, more, more…"

"Patience, whore!" I scold. She quiets down after I turn off the vibrator, but I don't remove the wand from her leg. Instead, I unclip the spreader bar from the ankle cuffs and leave it on the floor. After standing back up, I wrap my arm around her firm ass and lift her, while detaching her wrist cuffs from the hanging loop. As her arms fall limply onto my head, the blood begins to flow back into her limbs. She moans from the painful shift of position.

With an exhausted Sara now draped over my shoulder, I carry her over to the horse. The horse is basically a bench covered in leather, but it is only about two feet long and just high enough for most Masters, and Mistresses, to be able to fuck their bound subs without straining themselves. It is adjustable for height, for those much shorter or taller. Gear had set it at the perfect height for me, before I arrived.

I lie Sara facedown onto the horse and clip her wrist cuffs to the sides while her head limply hangs off one end. I secure her ankles to the base at the other end, which leaves her pussy partially sticking off the edge. I will rearrange the vibrator so that it's pressing onto her incredibly red, swollen clitoris, before I begin to take what I've earned. I will have her body and I will use it, however I please.

I glance toward the door. This is when I notice Gear and Glitter standing on either side of my Rayna. They are looking at me for approval to touch her. I'm sure they were watching to see if she was enjoying the show. She must have been, otherwise Gear wouldn't be asking permission to touch her. If Rayna had been showing signs that she is angry or hurt, he would have noticed and would have left her to work through her emotions. He is very good at reading people, better than I am, actually.

This is when I notice Rayna shifting her ass on the seat. Yes, she's sexually wound up and needs to release her frustration. I nod at Gear and he nods back. Glitter reveals a vibrating wand she had been hiding behind her back and presses it against Rayna's clitoris. I hear her muffled moan and watch her eyelids slowly close, but they open after only a few seconds. She locks her sexy gaze on mine.

After securing Sara on the horse, I leave her, to collect the fucking machine. As quickly as I can, I remove the added bar with the second dildo. I pull off the remaining dildo, switching it for a very long, fat one. I lubricate it, not that Sara isn't wet enough to handle it. Very carefully, I work it into her cunt. She is nice and loose, able to take it quite easily. I knew she would be. I turn on the machine and let it fuck her at a medium pace using long, deep strokes. Sara is moaning with each lazy thrust. To add to her pleasure, I turn on the vibrator, also at a medium speed. I'm sure her clit is numb, yet sore, so the less intense vibration will help it to awaken.

I remove my pants and toss them aside, and then stand before Sara's mouth, throbbing cock in hand. I reach for her and fist a wad of her hair and pull up to reveal her opening mouth. She is well trained, knowing what I expect of her. I shove my fingers deep inside to explore where my cock will soon be. I want to feel it first before I sink between those puffy, red lips.

"Suck my fingers," I tell her.

She does as I ask, sucking and lapping at them, as if they were a melting popsicle. Her grunts make it even more arousing. The air is pushed from her tiny body by the massive size of the dildo which fills her. I look over at Rayna and see her blinking often. Each time she opens them, she looks at Sara's mouth, watching her lap at my fingers. I watch Rayna's chest quickly expand and contract, just as she always does when her climax nears its peak. Glitter removes the vibrator and Rayna protests by gyrating her hips and whispering what I can only assume are pleading words.

Gear is standing behind her chair. He weaves his fingers in her hair and pulls her face upward, forcing her to look at me, not the wand near her clit. As Glitter places the vibrator back in its place, Rayna sucks in a big breath. That's when I aim my cock and slowly bury it all the way down Sara's throat.

I take my eyes off Rayna because I have a fierce need to watch my cock disappear into this woman's face. I pull back to allow her a breath. I shove forward and hold her firmly, so her nose is pressing against my belly. She can't breathe anyway, not with my cock blocking her windpipe.

I look up at Rayna to see her panting with an enraged expression. I don't think she's upset with what I'm doing. Glitter simply won't let her cum. She's getting her close and then moving the vibrator, to forbid Rayna's release. She's edging her and it's arousing me even more, to see her struggle against her bindings.

Gear has his hand around her throat, holding her head to the backrest, while his fingers roll her right nipple. He's crouched down, whispering in her ear. I'm curious as to what he's saying. Whatever it is seems to be stirring something inside of her because she's suddenly pulling at her restraints. Glitter replaces the vibrator and Rayna moans, loudly. Almost immediately, Glitter removes it again.

I pinch Sara's nose with my fingers and begin fucking her with long, deep strokes, making sure I bottom out each time. The nasal pinching adds an extra level of breath control that makes the submissive feel like they're smothering. Some begin to panic, but Sara lavishes in the anxiety. She's a pro.

Glitter slips two of her long, slim fingers deep into Rayna's pussy. Rayna groans and tries to hump the woman's fingers, but her movements are quite limited by the bindings that have her secured to the chair. Glitter taps her clit with the vibrator, repeatedly, only leaving in place for a few seconds at a time. It's enough to force Rayna close to orgasm, but not enough to allow her the pleasures of a much-desired release.

I pull my cock back to let Sara take two quick breaths. Her whole body is quivering as her muscles tense, desperate to free themselves. An orgasm tears through her. When she gasps in a breath, I push forward, blocking her windpipe again. This time, I fuck her face quicker. No more Mr. Nice-guy.

Sara has never been quick to gag. I recall thoroughly enjoying that about her. I fuck her face with long and deep penetrating strokes, poking twice when I'm buried deeply, before retracting. Fuck this feels good! I fuck her mouth with a dozen fast thrusts, while she gasps and makes sloppy, spitting sounds.

I step back and make my way behind her. Fuck, that ass is fine! The dildo fucking her pussy is stretching her wide. What an amazing sight to see. As the dildo pulls out, her labia glides along it's circumference like tiny blankets being pulled along a floor. As it pushes in, the labia curls inward, dragging along the silicone shaft.

I straddle the machine's arm and position myself to enter her ass. Before I shove into her, I gaze over at the other luscious scene in the room, simultaneously stroking my cock.

Rayna's face is flushed, glistening with sweat, and she's breathing erratically. Her eyes are looking my way but I'm not sure she's actually seeing us or if she's completely lost in her own body's desperate desires. Glitter is still rhythmically tapping Rayna's clit with the vibrator, while fingering her. Gear remains behind her, holding her neck while fondling her breasts and whispering in her ear.

I close my eyes for a moment and give into my need to set him free. I can feel the sadistic temptations building throughout my body with a rushing wave of heat. I open my eyes, see Sara in front of me, still pinned down and taking the huge cock in her dripping cunt. The dildo is slick with cum, as it casually fucks her. I crank up the machine, and watch it ram her twice as fast as it was.

My cock is thick and pulsing in my hand, as I roll on the condom. I need to fuck her, now! I slide my meat deep into her ass, in one quick motion. She bellows, but it only turns me on. She can say the safeword if she wants it to stop.

Sara's body locks up and her asshole pinches my dick with a vice-like grip. It won't stop me. She's coming. Gushes of pussy juice splash onto my legs each time the dildo pulls back. My beast is beginning to rage.

My hips start slamming against her, keeping up to the tempo of the machine. My cock buries deep into her anus while getting stroked by the fake cock within her twitching cunt. I reach forward, grasp her hair and pull back, until her moans are strained. I slap her ass cheek again and again, until it's fiery hot and then switch hands to redden the other cheek.

I release her hair and reach for the back of her neck, pinning her throat against the edge of the bench. It's very difficult for her to breathe and that's my goal. I pound her with everything my Demon has to offer, while growls of pent up rage fill the room. I bury into her backside, destroying her and taking what I want, not caring if she is finding any pleasure in this. She's had her pleasure, now it's my turn. I will have her how I want and for as long as I want.

Sara is barely making a sound. She's lost in subspace and that thrills my beast even more. I reach down and crank up the vibration on her clit. Judging by the increased volume of her moans, it's as if Sara's engine is revving up again. I know it hurts her, but in a way she enjoys.

When I look over at Rayna, I'm instantly filled with rage because Gear is so close to my woman. Demon doesn't like to share his toys with other men. It enrages him, so I fuck Sara harder, slamming against her red ass violently, filling her with every inch of me as if taking my rage out on her.

Glitter holds the vibrator to Rayna's clit, no longer pulling it away. Gear is watching me while holding her throat tightly, choking her. Her face is flushing, and her stomach muscles are flexing, erratically. She's coming. Fuck! Yes! Come, bitch!

Sara's asshole grips my cock again, as another brain-numbing climax shreds through her. I'm using Sara, at this point. My focus is on my woman. She's peaking over there, but I can feel her on my cock. Gear releases her throat and she screams with her mouth wide, allowing me to see the soaking wet panties that muffle her cries.

"Cum, you fucking whore!" my Demon yells in a deep and husky voice.

Rayna jolts, her eyes springing open, locking on mine. The colour of her face is slowly returning to normal as her climax comes to an end. Glitter doesn't move the vibrator, refusing her clit the much-needed pause it craves. No, she keeps it there, forcing Rayna to cum again, and again. Each time she nears, Gear either covers her nose and mouth or grips her throat. Breath control can either heighten an orgasm or ruin it. He is experienced with this dangerous game and I trust him, otherwise, Demon would have ripped his throat out.

I pull out of Sara's ass and turn off the machine. After yanking the vibrator from beneath the leather strap, sure to leave a bruise in its place, I hurry to unbind her restraints. She hangs limply, so I slide my arm under her waist and lift her body off the bench. I carry her over to the thin mattress and toss her down, as if she were a sack of fuckable potatoes. She lands with a slight thud.

"Do you want more, slut?"

The corner of Sara's mouth lifts, just slightly, letting me know she's still willing. "Yes Demon! Thank you, Sir," she can barely form words.

I grab her legs and yank her left one straight down on the bed, straddling it while lifting the other, so that her thigh is pressing against her stomach. I hold it in place while I slide my rock-hard cock back into her ass.

Sara's mascara is smudged down her cheeks and she is exhausted, but I'm not finished taking what I've earned. I can hear Rayna, but it's only spiking my arousal to a boiling hot level of desire. I lean forward and press my hand over Sara's mouth, sinking two fingers inside.

"You're a fucking slut. Nothing but a useless whore for men like me to use, for our own pleasure. Open your fucking mouth wide and let me see where they've all dumped their cum. You're a dirty, cumguzzling whore," I growl.

She opens wide. I form a wad of saliva in my mouth and spit it right into the gaping hole. She whimpers her protest, but doesn't fight back. I spit again and she gags.

"Thank me, whore!"

With her mouth still held open by my fingers, she manages,

"Thank you, Master Demon!"

I pull my fingers from her mouth and tell her, "Leave your fucking mouth wide open." I cover her eyes with my spit slicked fingers, blocking her from looking at me. I don't need her judgemental eyes. She's a carcass; nothing more than a warm body to fuck.

Rayna is coming again, screaming wildly as the vibrator continues to torture her hypersensitive clit. I fuck, hard and fast, ramming my prick into this tiny little whore's ass. I release her eyes and grab her hair, lifting her head, so I can kiss that gaping mouth of hers. My lips press to hers, forcefully. I know it pains her already swollen lips. My tongue digs deep in her mouth, tasting her sweetness.

I push her back down and grab her throat, holding her against the mattress. Her hands grip my forearm and hang on. My other hand viciously grips her upper thigh, using it to lift her hips off the bed so my cock can get a better angle and really fuck her deep.

I only slam her a few more times, before I can't hold it back any longer. In one quick movement, I yank out of her ass and lift her face toward me using her hair as a means. I tear off the condom and toss it. My fist strokes and chokes my cock as thick globs of cum shoot, splattering all over her flushed face. Only one wad meets its target; her open mouth.

When I release her hair, she drops onto the mattress in a sweaty, panting mess. I remain on my knees admiring the used-up slut before me, as I try to calm my breathing. I wipe my forehead with my arm, preventing a salty bead of sweat from dripping into my eye.

I look over at Rayna and see that she is also fighting to regain her composure. Glitter and Gear are unfastening her, but she hasn't moved her freed limbs from their position, even though she can. Her slatted eyes follow my movements.

Yes, now it's obvious that she thoroughly enjoyed herself. The smile of her face is evidence enough.

I lean forward and kiss Sara's lips tenderly, letting her know that I appreciate her, but also to show Rayna that I still respect and care for Sara, no matter how I just treated her.

When I sit up, I pull her into my arms, cradling her on my lap like a child. She has her face pressed against my chest with her arms wrapped around my torso.

Before our guests depart from us, Gear helps Rayna to her feet and walks her over, to be with us. He kisses her hand before, nodding to me and taking his leave. Rayna sits beside me, looking ragged and worn out. I lean toward her and kiss her tenderly.

"I love you, lady," I whisper.

"I love you and your Demon," she replies.

I'm thrilled that she isn't afraid of that part of me or that she doesn't hate me, for fucking another woman. It's one thing to imagine how thrilling it might be, to watch your partner be intimate with someone else, but to see it happening is where the real emotions will break through. It'll either be exciting, or dreadful. The latter is something a relationship can't often recover from.

Rayna kisses Sara tenderly, and then wipes my sticky cum from the exhausted woman's cheek by using a small hand towel Glitter had given her to clean herself up with. We spend the next half hour drinking water and talking about what we enjoyed and what we didn't. There wasn't much that we didn't. Rayna said she felt jealous but was able to use the emotion to heighten her arousal.

At this very moment, I am the luckiest man on the face of the earth.

Chapter Twenty-Four

Rayna

Since watching Coach fuck Sara, I've been experiencing a wide range of emotions. This is something I hadn't expected to happen. I thought that I'd have sorted through all of my emotions while it was happening. I didn't think I'd be feeling like I'm on an emotional rollercoaster--happy and turned on one minute, the next I'm crashing into a world of sadness, or worse yet, anger.

Coach has been great about asking me how I'm feeling and if there's anything I want to talk about, but this is something I have to work out on my own. Worrying him with the lame and pathetic emotional pity-party I've been experiencing, isn't going to improve my mood any. He'll likely regret going through with it and then he'll feel guilty, which will make me feel worse. I don't want either of those things. So, for now I will keep saying that I'm fine. At least until I can figure out why I'm all fucked up.

When I think about how dark his eyes got when he was fucking her, it turns me on. But, when I remember how turned-on he was when he was fucking her, I cringe. What's wrong with me? I asked him to be with her. I told him I would be okay with it. So, why am I not? Am I not?

My work staff have been curious, wondering why I've been so unusually quiet today. I keep telling them that it's the Monday woes from lack of sleep. Most of them seem to be accepting that. The people who really know me, know there's something more going on. I can't talk it out with them. I can't tell anyone about this. Maybe that's one reason why I'm so out of sorts.

"Rayna, you have a phone call." Kelly pokes her head into the exam room.

"I can't take it right now. Can you take a message and tell them I'll call back?" I'm knuckle deep in a patient's mouth.

"Sure thing!" she replies, and then ducks out of the room, as silently as the wind on a prairie.

My patient, Mr. Ugavail, says with his mouth open and tools scraping a tooth, "You can take the call. It's okay with me."

I snicker, knowing he hates being here. "Mr. Ugavail, you can't get away from me that easily. You'll likely run away if I leave you here unattended. Whoever it is, can wait."

"What if it's important?" he says clearly, having had the instruments removed from his mouth. "It could be a life and death situation. What if you won a new car and this is the only chance to collect?"

"Nice try, but I'm not falling for it. Open wide, please," I say, leaning in as he reluctantly opens his jaw.

I finish the cleaning and check-up with no other interruptions, and then let the doctor know his patient is ready for him. I feel bad for this man because his teeth are in terrible condition and he needs extensive procedures. The man doesn't have a lot of money to spend on dental work, so his teeth are pretty much rotting and breaking into sharp shards. They need to be pulled and replaced with dentures, but he simply can't afford it.

When I make my way to the head desk, Kelly hands me a scrap piece of paper with '*call Coach immediately*' written on it. As I make my way to the lunchroom to make a cup of tea, I pull my phone from my pocket and dial Coach's cellphone. I'm surprised when it goes straight to voicemail. I click on my messages and listen to the first one.

It's the secretary at the kid's school. "Hello Ms. Baxter, this is Luanne from John Frame. It's essential that you give me a call back, as soon as you get this message. Thank you."

I immediately dial the school and nervously wait for an answer. After only two rings, I'm already getting frustrated from waiting, but then I hear a click. "John Frame Elementary."

"Hello Luanne. This is Rayna Baxter returning your call."

"Oh, yes, Rayna. I hate to have to tell you this, but Ken has fallen on the playground and was transported to the hospital in an ambulance. We believe his arm might be broken. Just know that he's okay and being taken care of. We don't want you rushing to get to his side and have a car accident on the way. We tried to call Mr. Baxter, but there was no answer. We were able to contact someone named Coach. Ken asked us to call him when we couldn't get hold of you. I hope that's okay. He seemed very concerned and said he would be at the hospital when Ken arrived."

"Shit! Shit, shit! Okay, umm… thank you, Luanne."

I hang up quickly and start opening my locker to retrieve my purse and sweater. My hands are starting to shake and I'm suddenly sweating. My heart is about to pound out of my chest and I'm becoming increasingly more lightheaded with each breath. I sit and put my head between my knees, forcing myself to breathe slower. I can't help him if I'm a basket-case!

As soon as I'm feeling stronger, I slam my locker and rush to find Dr. Kim. I'm supposed to do a cleaning on one of his patients in about ten minutes.

"Hi, sorry, but I have to go. My kid broke his arm," I say while he's knuckles deep in a woman's mouth.

He sits up and looks over at me. "You'd best go then. I'll manage without you. Take care of your boy. Let us know how he is."

"I will. Thank you," I say before rushing to the entrance. "Kelly, I have to go. Ken broke his arm at school."

"Oh my god! That sucks! Okay, go take care of the little imp." Even though she's smiling, her eyes show her concern.

* * * * *

"Hi honey. How are you feeling? Does it hurt?"

Ken's eyes are glossy and heavy-lidded. "Heck no! Not anymore, right Coach?" he's giggling from the painkiller the doctors pumped into him.

"Hi love," Coach says, as he rises to his feet and kisses my temple.

"Thank you for meeting him here."

"I'd do anything for Little-man," he assures me.

"Mom, honestly, I'm okay," he says with a very wide grin and slurred words. "Stop worrying. I'm not a little boy anymore. I'm, like, a man almost. I have man-hair on my body now." His laughter is masked only by the drug-induced calmness.

"What did they give him?" I ask, as I attempt to brush an errant lock of hair from the boy's forehead. He blocks it by pushing my hand away, and then he rolls his eyes so obnoxiously, I'd likely scold him for it, if he weren't high as a kite.

Coach is chuckling. "Something I wouldn't mind having a wee bit of. The nurse told me the name of it, but I can't remember what she said. You're feeling good, eh buddy?"

"I feel great!" he announces with a freakishly wide smile. "Mom, can we get some of this and take it home?"

"No, we can't." I finally take a deep breath, knowing he's not in dire need of help, but a little sad that he doesn't seem to be needing me, at all. What happened to the little boy who used to cry for his momma when he scraped some skin from his knee?

I sigh heavily, "What did the doctor say?"

Coach says, "Doc said he'll need to get it set before they can cast it. They want to keep him for a few more hours to see if it stops swelling. They won't cast it, until it does. Hopefully, they can cast it tonight, otherwise he'll have to come back tomorrow morning."

"How bad is the break?"

"Here," he replies, pointing to the x-ray the doctor left hanging against the darkened screen on the wall. We walk over to it and he flips the switch to turn the light on. "This is the break. It isn't all that bad. It's off kilter but he doesn't need surgery." Coach chuckles when he adds, "I've done worse."

My head suddenly whirls, and I want to vomit. Coach sees me waver and grabs my arm to steady me.

"Hey, you all right?"

"Yeah, I just got a bit woozy for a second. I'm okay now, I think.

Thank you."

"You're pale as a ghost. Maybe you should sit."

"I'm fine, really."

Ken is staring at the clock hanging on the wall in front of him. He looks lost in thought. Those drugs are really spacing him out. Coach chuckles, as he watches the kid try to refocus his eyes by squinting between repeated blinks.

"So, how did you break it?" I ask.

His smile is all contorted. "Well, I didn't do it on purpose, that's for sure!"

"No, not likely," I say, trying to hold back my laughter.

"I was running beside Kyle because Leslie was going to kick the ball into the goalie's net. When Barbie crashed into my knee, I flipped right over her, and then the red dog licked me, and he was really stinky."

"What? That doesn't make any sense," I whisper to Coach, who is still laughing while shrugging. He's obviously heard this same story and couldn't make sense of it either. "What dog?"

"The big red one that lives in the blue house beside my math class," he replies, adding another level of confusion to the mystery.

"You said a Barbie doll hit your knee?"

"What?" he asks while looking at me, as if I suddenly grew another head. I'll bet he's seeing double.

"You said it was a Barbie."

He laughs hysterically. "No, not a doll. The dog's name is

Barbie. She tripped me."

"Oh, I see. Barbie is the name of the big red dog. I get it now."

"No, Mom! I don't know the big red dog's name. He stinks a lot though. His breath smelled like he had been eating worms. Maybe he was. I don't know."

I cringe at the thought. "I'm still confused," I whisper to Coach.

"Yeah, I can't make figure it out either. We'll have to wait until the drugs wear off."

"Was he here by himself or did the principle come with him? I should have had the volume up on my phone. I'm an awful mother."

Coach hugs me against him to reassure me. "Love, you are the world's best momma. You're a better mother than the moms who own those coffee mugs that claim they're the best. They aren't, it's you."

"Thank you, but he shouldn't have been here alone."

"He wasn't alone. Mr. Kants was here when I arrived. He rode in the ambulance with him. He's Ken's homeroom teacher, or so he told me. He only told me what he knew and that was that he fell outside and landed on his arm wrong. I told him he didn't have to stay. Ken assured him that I was a trustworthy guardian."

"I'll add your name to the official list of safe people. I'm surprised they called you."

"Ken told them to."

I look down at Ken to ask him if he enjoyed the ambulance ride, but he's already passed out. He looks so grown up in this bed. His limbs are long and lean, but his face remains childlike, not yet gaining the characteristics of an adult male. One day soon, he will be taller than me and his voice will deepen. Will I still see him as my little boy? Mothers always claim they do, but how is that possible?

"He's asleep," I whisper.

"That's probably a good thing," Coach replies in the same hushed manner.

Standing behind me, he wraps his arms around my shoulders and pulls me into him. He softly kisses the top of my head. He hugs me against his chest while we stand silently, watching our young man breathe deeply.

Coach can be so rough and threatening, with very little effort, but right now, here, in this moment, he's the most tender, loving man I have ever met. I love that he can sit at either end of the spectrum, at will. I've never felt this safe and loved. I would give this man my soul, if he should ask for it.

Some time passes before I shift out of his arms. He groans, but I pay him no attention as I unfold a blanket and rest it on top of the thin sheet covering my son's body. Tears well up in my eyes and I try to blink them away, but it's no use. They flow down my cheeks in silent streams.

"Love, he's going to be okay. It's just a broken bone. He will heal." Coach sits me in a chair and squats in front of me. His thick fingers gently wipe away my sadness. "No more tears. You need to show him that it's not a big deal to break a bone. Odds are he'll break at least two more before he reaches twenty. Well, if he starts to copy me, that is."

Coach's faint chuckle has me smiling, but the idea that my baby boy might suffer through another trauma, does nothing to ease my concern.

"It's not just the broken arm." I take a deep breath and clear my throat. I look up at Ken to ensure he is still unconscious. "The school tried to call his father and he couldn't even be bothered to pick up the phone."

"Love, maybe he was at work and couldn't get to his phone, like you were."

"Maybe you're right. I hope you're right."

"I'm sure he wasn't purposely ignoring the call." I can tell Coach doesn't fully believe the lies he's trying to convince me of.

I whisper, "I'm just having a rough time with my emotions since…"

"Since Saturday," he says with a nod. He doesn't look upset, overly concerned, nor unconcerned. I figured he'd be one of those, but he seems calm and ready to hear what I have to say.

"Yeah," I confirm with my face scrunched. Is he wondering if I'm overthinking the situation that I asked him to put before me?

"Love, you have to tell me what you're feeling. I promise, whatever your emotions are, they are completely normal. Please, just talk to me. I need to know what you're thinking, so we can talk it through."

"I know, I just have to work it out on my own."

"Why? We did it together, so why can't we talk about it?"

I want to say that I feel foolish but instead, I shrug and glance at Ken. I stand up and take Coach's hand, leading him into the hallway. We can still see him sleeping soundly, through the window.

"It's hard to explain what I'm going through. I mean, I had sex with her too, so why should it bother me if you did? That's not fair, right?"

"We aren't counting fairness here. If watching me with her bothers you, it'll never happen again. It's simple."

I shake my head and cross my arms over my chest. He doesn't understand the point I'm trying to get at. How can I explain my thoughts and feelings if I'm not exactly sure of what they are?

"No! I don't want that either. I don't know what I want. I feel like my thoughts and emotions are so scattered. Like I said, let me work it out on my own. We can talk about it when I figure out why the images keep spinning around in my head. It was fun, I really got excited by it, but…"

"You enjoyed watching me fuck her, but you didn't like how much I enjoyed fucking her. Am I getting close? Maybe my Demon scared you a little bit, even though I kept him calm."

I'm surprised how accurate his guess is. "Something like that. It was so hot watching you take control and make her cum so hard. When you fucked her, you looked at me and your eyes…" I shake my head, while looking away from him.

"You didn't like how I looked. I've heard people say my eyes change when my demeanor does." He shrugs.

"They do." I slip my hands in the front pockets of my nursing shirt and turn to watch Ken through the window, partly because I don't want to look at Coach when I try to explain. Maybe it's guilt for laying it all on him, or the idea that watching him take his needs out on another woman, instead of me has me jealous, but also, grateful to her. I really need to figure out if I loved it or hated it. "You looked different--meaner and raging with dominance. You wanted to own her. Your expression proved your ravenous desire for her. I've never seen that look on you, even when we're playing hard, or what I've perceived to be hard. When I picture that moment now, I am jealous. I wasn't at the time. I was fine while it was happening. I even orgasmed a few times, myself. It was sexy and dangerous and… fuck, you looked hot! Your muscles were flexing, hard and bulging, like a gladiator. Your thighs were thunderously strong when you were pounding against her small frame. I'm getting aroused right now, just remembering how I felt while watching you, but I shouldn't be getting aroused by watching my man fuck another woman. Based on everything I've known up to this point, I should feel it's wrong! You are supposed to love me enough, not to want to fuck another woman. Yet, I asked you to, so I have no right to feel jealous. I just don't understand why I can't regulate my stupid fucking emotions. I'm all over the fucking place! I'm sorry, I shouldn't... I mean, I asked you to do it. It's not like you had an affair."

Coach caresses my arm, tenderly. He turns me so he can look at me. "You feel ashamed because your moral value was tested. It's okay to want to watch me with another woman. You don't have to feel guilty, for enjoying it. It's unfortunate that people are raised to believe that it's wrong to have sex with someone else while you're in a relationship, even if that person approves. They go so far as to say that I shouldn't want to be with anyone else, like you said. Rayna, we can set up our relationship however we want it to be. It's 'our relationship' and no one else's. Their beliefs are theirs and ours are ours. We set our own rules and we follow them, unwaveringly. We enjoy our lives how we choose to, not how society tells us we should."

"I know, but it still feels wrong, but yet, completely right." "Nobody is getting hurt by what we're doing." "That's not true," I say stoically.

He asks with concern, "Who are we hurting?"

"Well, you did make Sara scream a few times," I say, with a smirk slowly overwhelming my mouth.

"You're such a smartass!" He wraps his heavy arms around my head and holds me against his hard chest. "Love, always tell me what you're feeling, so we can work through it. Whatever you're experiencing is not abnormal. You aren't the only one to feel jealousy. I was so enraged that Gear was touching what's mine, I wanted to rip his head off. Demon doesn't like to share his toys."

"So, what kept you from decapitating him?" I ask with my face pressed against his firm chest.

He chuckles, "Gear is such a great friend that I would miss him too much. And Glitter would cry. It wouldn't be worth it. So, instead, I used that rage as a tool to fuck her harder. When you came, I nearly exploded myself. My balls were throbbing from slamming her so fucking hard. It was a hot scene--yours and mine."

I pull away from him and look down at my shifting feet. Shyly,

I say, "Yeah, it really was, but…"

"But, what?"

My nose wrinkles when I tell him, "Don't ever spit in my mouth. I guarantee I will hurl if you do."

He laughs and nods, "In that case, I definitely won't do that to you."

"Thank you. It's… gross!"

"It's a way to show that person that they are worthless, to humiliate them." Even though he's explaining the reason, not that I needed him to, I'm still shaking my head. "We can talk about it more, later, if you'd like. Should we go sit with the sleeping prince?"

"Yes, we should. Any idea when the doctor is going to set the bone?"

"Soon, I hope!"

"You don't have to stay if you have clients waiting. I'm here now."

Coach looks at me and grimaces. "You don't want me here?"

"Yes, of course I do. I'm just letting you know that you don't have to be. I mean, as you said earlier, he'll be okay. You likely have a full schedule of clients waiting for you."

"I do, but I rescheduled two appointments and April is going to take over the third."

"When did you have time to reschedule?"

"On my drive here. I called from my truck."

"If your crazy ex-girlfriend hadn't smashed up that old truck of yours, you wouldn't have had the Bluetooth handsfree calling feature. So, I suppose we could claim that her jealous rage was beneficial."

He frowns, "It took weeks for that gash to heal on my leg. She's just lucky I walked away, instead of pulling her out of her window and beating the hell out of her." I can almost see his inner Demon twitching behind those eyes.

"Coach, take a breath. It's over and she served her time. She hasn't bothered us since her sentencing. Even if I pass her in a store, she always walks the other way. I think she's sad, but moving on with her life. Enough about her, she doesn't matter to us anymore."

"I'm not leaving, Rayna. Little Man needs me to poke fun at him when he wakes up. Besides, I want him to clear up that damn story about the dog tripping him. Being drugged is not conductive to storytelling."

* * * * *

The doctor set Ken's arm and wrapped it in a flexible bandage a few hours later, and then we were sent home with a time to return tomorrow morning, to have it casted. Ken explained that there were two dogs involved. One dog tripped him, and then the other licked him and he had bad breath. His story made sense, once some of the drugs wore off.

He's passed out in his bed with his arm raised up on a pillow. I will keep pumping the Ibuprofen into him every four hours as prescribed. He doesn't need to suffer. I've never broken a bone, so I can't judge his pain level from personal experience. Coach says he's broken too many bones to bother counting, especially in his teen years, when he was fighting a lot. He had a ton of misplaced rage that he eventually learned how to channel into better vices-working out and BDSM.

Chapter Twenty-Five

Coach

It's been nearly a week since Ken broke his arm, so life has gone back to being normal. He's enjoying all the attention he's getting at school. His cast is coated with multiple coloured ink doodles and so many signatures that they're starting to blend together. Rayna takes comfort that it doesn't seem to hurt him anymore, unless he bangs it on something. Little does he realize just how itchy and smelly it's going to get.

Rayna and I have talked about the night with Sara, Glitter and Gear enough that she's comfortable with doing it again, one day. Sara, Rayna and I have reservations for dinner at Altobelli's for tonight at seven. This will be the first time the three of us will have a chance to talk about the events that had Rayna's moral values causing her great inner turmoil.

Rayna has battled with her moral code. She's made the conscious decision to enjoy her life. She wants to live in the moment, as often as possible, and enjoy wherever that moment takes her. I made sure not to influence her decision in any way, that would only come back to bite me in the ass later, if I had.

She mentioned that she'd like Gear to bind her to Sara. Since she mentioned it, every time I think about the two of them bound together, my cock swells. Rayna and I haven't had sex since Saturday and my urges are raging. She's wanted to hold off on intimacy while she sorts out her mind, and I was happy to give her the time she needed. Well, maybe not happy about it, but I never let her think she was depriving me of anything.

It has helped that I jerked off in the shower, at least once a day. It keeps my cock from announcing to the world that my hormones are like a teenage boy. I don't know what it is about the ideas of Rayna and Sara naked, bound to one another and lost in the throes of erotic pleasure, that has my body reacting so intensely. I have had two women simultaneously. Shit, I've had four at once. That was exhausting. I don't recommend it. But, those two beauties together… fuck!

My five-thirty appointment showed up late, of course. Unfortunately for him, he isn't going to get a full workout today. I usually let the workout run over to compensate for their lack of punctuality and to ensure they get the full hour, but not today. Today, I will be joining two very hot ladies for an evening of great conversation and flirting. Little do they realize, they have the power to convince me to do anything, even submit, should that be their desire. Who knows, if it goes well, they might want to share me tonight. That's not the main objective, of course, but it would top the night off, perfectly. Most would agree.

The kids are each sleeping over at a friend's house tonight. While dropping them off, Rayna brought me a change of clothes, appropriate for tonight's dinner. My anticipation is already at a boiling point, so prolonging my arrival by first needing to head home to shower and change, could easily send me more over the edge between being the calm man I usually am, to becoming a sadistic fucker, with a desire for release.

She's going to be picking Sara up on her way to the restaurant. Their time alone together will give them the opportunity to talk about their *girlie* emotions, something I try to understand, but for obvious reasons, can't. I'm not so sure I want to go there anyway, I might lose my man-card, if I do.

Those two women mean a lot to me. You could say I love them both, but in different ways. Sara is my friend, a great one. I enjoy her body and the trust that she grants me. For that, I am under her spell. She owns my gratitude for all the times she allowed me to be the Demon that I crave to be, and for never condemning me for it. She has her own mental demons that need to be tamed and I am happy to help her scratch off the scabs. Even though she betrayed my trust, she can still cast a spell on me with a simple glance and hint of a grin.

Rayna, of course, owns my heart, mind and body. She can love and support me or choose to crush and destroy. She is the only woman I have ever known, including my mother, who could completely destroy me. I have given myself to her, whether she realizes it or not. She holds my life in her hands, and should she choose to drop me, I will shatter into a billion pieces. I love her and her kids, eternally. I swore I would never allow a woman to have so much power over me, but I want and need her to own me as her lover, friend, Master and soulmate.

Just as I'm unlocking my locker in the changing room, my phone starts vibrating. I hurry to finish spinning the dial, effectively opening to the lock and dig through my gym bag in search of my phone.

"Hello," I say while fighting to keep my towel around my waist. "Hey man, how's it going?"

"Oh, hey Tim. Not bad. Ah, I'm in a bit of a rush though. I have to meet Rayna and Sara for dinner and I'm running late. So, what's up?"

"Rayna and Sara? Sara... the Sara? Your Sara?"

An exasperated breath leaves me when I give up my battle to preserve my dignity, letting the towel hit the floor. "Yeah, that
Sara."

"No shit? I thought you two were finished."

"Rayna asked me to," I pause to look for eavesdroppers. "I was with Sara on Saturday. Well, Rayna was there too. She wanted to see my Demon in action, but I didn't completely take off his reigns. This dinner will be the first time the three of us will have a chance to get together. It'll be good to talk about it." He's silent. "Rayna needed a minute to toss her morals out the window and accept the idea of living her life how she chooses, and not to have regrets about it."

While I'm waiting for a response, I bend down and collect my towel, holding it up against my cock to keep it PG, not that anyone is even in the locker area.

"Hey, you still there?" I ask.

"Ah, yeah! I'm just wondering why those two gorgeous women would bother with an asshole like you. They should find someone more handsome and a better lay, like me, for instance."

"Fuck off, asshole!" I hiss with a hint of laughter in my voice. "But seriously, I have to let you go. Can I call you tomorrow?"

"Call me any time after eleven. Actually, you know what, maybe I can make it to the gym around four-thirty. We can hang out and talk more about this Rayna/Sara situation."

"No can do! I have a session at four and another right after. Can you come around two?"

"Nah, I'll be at work. All right, I'll let you go. I'll try calling you tomorrow. Have fun fucker!" His jealousy is radiating through the phone. I take pleasure in that, for some warped, testosterone driven reason.

"You have yourself a great night thinking about me ravishing my two beauties," I say, teasingly.

"I'm not going to picture you, just the ladies. Chow!" he says before hanging up.

I toss my phone in my bag and rush to get dressed. She packed me a pair of black denim pants, a turquoise dress shirt and a dinner jacket. She has great taste in clothing. I wonder what she's going to wear. I guarantee she'll dress sexy, but elegant, just to keep Sara and I enticed.

When I arrive, the ladies are already seated at a table near the back of the restaurant. They are leaning toward each other and talking rather secretively. I'd bet anything that their conversation, if overheard by fellow diners, would peak a keen interest. They each have a glass of burgundy wine in front of them, Sara's is mostly gone.

As I approach the table, I go to Rayna first and look her up and down. "You look beautiful, my love."

She intentionally wore a dress that would bring back a hot memory, that would ensure my cock would swell. The black spaghetti strapped dress she's wearing is one I am very fond of. The last time she wore it, I bent her over the hood of the car in the restaurant parking lot. I slid the short skirt up to bare her ass and ate her pussy and asshole until her knees were shaking. And then I fucked her dripping cunt until the car was rocking so hard the alarm started screaming. Did I mention it wasn't our car?

I give her a look as if to say I know what you're doing. She smirks smugly. She will pay for the attitude later when I spank her ass red hot. She's likely doing it on purpose, to fire me up. It's working.

Sara has a generous amount of make-up on, and she looks like a goddess. She rarely wears make-up, doesn't need to. Her skin is like silk and she's absolutely gorgeous, even without all the gunk on her face. But tonight, I appreciate the effort she put into looking even more striking than I've ever seen her look. Perhaps later, I will gag her with my cock until her eyes water leaving trails of mascara down her cheeks.

"You are stunning!" I whisper before taking her hand and kissing the back of it, my eyes never veering from hers. I hear her breath catch. Yeah, I still affect her in a way that pleases my dominant nature.

"Are your panties damp?"

"They would be if I were wearing any," she replies.

My cock twitches. I turn to look at Rayna. She shrugs to confirm that she is panty-less as well. My jeans are feeling a bit tighter in the crotch area and the girls know they got the better of me.

After taking my seat and ordering a glass of wine, I ask, "So, what were you two talking about when I arrived?"

They both look at each other and smile, giggling like high school girls. It's annoying, but hot, nonetheless. All I can picture is the two of them kissing, caressing each other's breasts and moaning into each other's mouths. I can visualize the shimmer of their skin as the soft light illuminates their perspiration. I can almost smell the sex in the air.

Sara speaks first, "We'll see how the dinner goes before we decide whether to tell you, or not."

"Mhmm, you'll have to wait," Rayna confirms.

My curiosity is spiking, and I don't like it. I find it irritating when I ask a question and expect an answer, but don't receive it. My jaw tightens. For some reason, the sexy expressions the women have are easing my need to spank the answer out of them.

"What are you two planning?" I ask, knowing I won't get an answer. They shrug. I glower at Rayna to let her know that she's going to regret teasing me.

"Don't worry, you'll like it," she confesses.

"Have you decided?" the waiter asks.

I quickly scan the menu while the ladies place their orders. By the time he asks me, I know what I want; stuffed mushrooms, baked lasagna and a salad with Balsamic Vinegar. My stomach is growling, and my mouth keeps filling with saliva. It might not be my need for food that's causing this reaction, but rather my desire to taste both women.

"I would love to bend each of you over the table and fuck you into a puddle." I'm not whispering. My voice hasn't altered in pitch from when I placed my order.

The waiter hears what I said, but doesn't react, other than clearing his throat. He quickly gathers the menus and walks away.

Rayna is covering her mouth, embarrassed that I said, what I said in earshot of the waiter. Sara's eyes haven't veered from my face. She's smirking like a cat who just nabbed the squirrel who's been taunting him for months. She's used to my crassness.

"I can't believe you said that!" Rayna hisses.

Sara says, "What's he going to do? The worst thing he can do is stare at us, with jealousy in his eyes."

"He might give us free dessert," I add, looking at Sara. I start snickering. "Do you remember that quaint little restaurant on the east side?"

She suddenly remembers, a smile lighting up her face. "That was thrilling!"

"What happened?" Rayna asks.

Sara tells the story, "It was a long time ago, but we were sitting at a table with a long table cloth. He slid closer to me and fished his hand down my pants. Needless to say, I was just starting to cum when the waiter came to the table to ask if we wanted dessert. He said, 'Oh, I see you're already enjoying dessert.'" She starts laughing too hard to finish telling the story.

I add, "He stood there calmly watching her ride out her orgasm. When she was finished, he walked away, but came back with two lava cakes. He didn't charge us for the desserts. I'd bet that guy jerked his cock for months, recalling how you locked eyes with him when you orgasmed."

I can tell Rayna feels like she's an outsider at the moment. She doesn't look upset, just not included in the memory.

Sara whispers, "If your skirt were a little shorter, I'd tickle your clit right here, right now."

Rayna shakes her head, "I don't think so. My luck, I'd run into one of my kid's teachers. That would be humiliating."

"You worry too much," I tell her. "It's a fantasy many people have, but never act upon. They would likely be envious."

"Maybe, but I can guarantee they'd tell everyone that I was a sex-craved hussy who loves public sexual encounters. I don't need that type of controversy."

"I promise," Sara tells her with a seductive undertone. "We are going to make many memories together that we can look back upon one day and thank our lucky stars for."

Rayna takes her hand and gives it a squeeze. Fuck! I want them both naked and on their knees in front of me, ready to comply to my demands. I can picture them open-mouthed, begging for me to let them pleasure me. To alternate mouths, feeling each woman swallow my cock with their individual talents. It will happen, one day.

"Okay, so, about last Saturday," I poke the elephant in the room. "Sara, what's your take on how it went?"

"I thoroughly enjoyed it. You weren't as rough as I know you can be. I was wondering if you had lost your touch, or if you were taking it even easier on me than I had requested, for Rayna's benefit."

Rayna mutters, "That was taking it easy?"

I smile at Rayna and reply, "I did take it a bit easier on her than I used to. It's been a long time since we've played, and I didn't want to jump right back into it with the same intensity. We'll have to work up to it, with Rayna's approval, of course. And, I also didn't want to shock you, Rayna. I can be very cruel to women, and have on occasion, at their request. I didn't want you to see that intensity just yet, maybe never."

Sara is pouting, "I like it when you're cruel to me. The pain takes me away. You're the only person who has taken me completely out of myself. I miss that. Maybe after Rayna is more comfortable, things will progress. If not, I'm okay with that, too. I really like you two and would be honoured to be a part of your relationship. I know I can't move in with you two, but I'd like to eventually enjoy you both, freely. Can we leave that as a possible option for the future? After I earn your trust, of course." She looks at me and gives me an apologetic grin.

She looks at Rayna while still holding her hand. Rayna nods, but looks a bit reserved at the notion. That is something Rayna and I will have to talk about when we are alone.

"Trust needs to be earned for you to become a third in our relationship. I am perfectly fine with the two of you spending as much time together as you'd like. If Rayna is nervous about me being alone with you, Sara, then that's off the table."

"I'm okay with that. Never would I do anything to disrupt your relationship. Your love for one another is beautiful. Attention to me is a bonus and never expected."

"I really like you Sara, but we'll have to take it slowly," Rayna explains. "I'm just getting to know you, so you'll have to give me time to catch up to the two of you. I'm trying not to feel like a third wheel here."

"A third wheel? Why would you feel like a third wheel?" I ask her.

Sara tells Rayna, "I'm the third wheel here. I'm the addition, not you."

"But you two already know each other, very well and have all these memories together."

With a loving kindness, Sara replies, "But you and Simon have something so much stronger than what we ever had. I really respect the love you two share. One day, I hope to have that for myself. It's not looking like I will, but you never know."

Rayna leans toward Sara and kisses her softly on the lips, stunning me. I can't believe Rayna would do something so bold in a crowded restaurant. Like she said earlier, *what if one of her kid's teachers are here*? I'm happy that she's opening up. She'll enjoy life more if she's not always so worried about what other people think.

Rayna whispers, "Let's just enjoy what we've started and see where it takes us."

The women are looking into one another's eyes, lustfully. My cock twitches, shifting my attention from their obvious flirting. What have I started? I think I've awoken the sexual deviant in Rayna. Sara has always been wild. The union of these two women is a good thing, I hope.

We've filled our bellies and swallowed down more wine. I've only had one, but the girls have each drank three glasses. They're getting to be a bit too obvious with their flirting, that could get us kicked out of this posh restaurant, by these stick-up-their-ass (not in a good way) people. I pay the bill and usher the women to Rayna's car. Compared to my truck, hers is far more comfortable for three adults.

Instead of one of them sitting in the front, they both get in the backseat, giggling and whispering, the entire time. I shut their door, making sure it's closed. By the time I'm sitting behind the wheel, the two of them are already kissing, passionately. At first, I watch them in the rear-view mirror, but that only lasts for a few minutes. I turn around when Rayna moans.

Sara's hand is between Rayna's spread thighs. She wasn't lying when she said she wasn't wearing any panties. The car quickly fills with the heavy breathing and scent of sex. My cock is squeezed in my pants, bent at a weird angle, and the erotic scene before me is making it that much worse. I lift up and shove my hand under my waistband to shift it to a more comfortable position.

Sara's legs part and the silky hem of her skirt climbs her creamy white thighs. Her left leg drapes over Rayna's right thigh. Their pussies are bare, clits swollen and their inner labia glisten with their arousal. They each have a hand between the other's legs, rubbing tiny circles over each other's clits. This is a beautiful moment. Each woman is masturbating the other and it is so fucking erotic. I would love to help them out, but being in the front seat would make for a very difficult task.

"Seatbelts are on?" I ask, hating to interrupt them.

"Yes," they moan.

I start the car and drive as cautiously as possible, while the women wind each other up. It's hard to keep my focus on the road and not on the sensuous scene playing out behind me. I can't lose myself in the seductive, rhythmic moans coming from the back seat, no matter how much I want to.

"Ladies, I hate to have to interrupt you again, but where are we going?"

Chapter Twenty-Six

Coach

Sara parts her lips from Rayna's. She replies, "Take us to Fallen."

When our eyes meet in the mirror, it's the deliberate wink following her words that tells me to drive and not to ask any more questions. It's obvious the two of them are cohorts in the planning of this night. What are their intentions?

I feel uneasy, probably because I'm the one who always plans how we spend our time at Fallen. When we arrive, I won't know what to expect and I don't care for it. Is this how my submissives have always felt, like they were walking in blindly? I had never really thought about it. They're submissive. They do what I say, without asking why. That's what is expected of them. However, I'm not submissive.

My stomach is feeling a bit tight. As much as I hate to admit it to myself, I don't want to go, if I'm not in control. It's selfish, I know, but I'm not the sort of person who follows along. I always know what comes next because I plan it. I'm an asshole, a control freak.

Besides, I didn't bring my leathers to wear, not that I need them. I like to dress the part. I'll be going into the house in jeans and a dress shirt – turquoise, not even black. I do look good, just not as intimidating as I prefer.

The scent of sex waves through my nostrils, drowning my brain in a sea of possibilities. Their moans and the sound of their breath catching in their throats has my cock desperate to penetrate something. I'd love to have them side by side on their knees with their mouths wide open for me to fuck one, then the other, and repeat.

The drive seems to take an hour, but still doesn't feel long enough. I was enjoying the two of them and hoping one or both of them, would orgasm, but neither did. Maybe they are saving their pleasure for me. That is an honour I will never take for granted.

"Ladies, we're here," I say after the car is in park and shut off, but neither seemed to notice. "Girls?"

They both look out the windshield, realizing that we're no longer moving. They smile at each other before undoing their seatbelts. I step out and open the passenger door. Sara takes my hand and steps out of the car, brushing her hand over the swollen bulge in my pants. Rayna slides across the seat, taking my hand and stepping out. She's grinning like she has a secret she wants to tell me, but is forbidden to.

She kisses me quickly and smiles. "Are you all right with being here?"

"I would have liked a little warning, so I could have planned something for you two and brought something else to wear."

Rayna tells me, "Open the trunk." When my eyebrows bridge, she repeats with a smile, "Just open the trunk."

I do as she instructed and find a black box. When I look up at the two of them, they have their arms around each other's back, and they're giddy. I flip off the lid and pull back the red tissue paper.

The scent of new leather fills my nostrils.

"Sara bought you a new harness," Rayna says.

"Try it on. Try it on," Sara begs.

When I take it out of the box, the girls rush over, taking it out of my hand. Rayna starts undoing the buttons on my shirt while Sara fiddles with the buckles on the harness. I brush a stray tress of hair off Rayna's forehead and follow along her hairline until I can tuck it behind her ear. Her eyes look up into mine. She looks mischievous.

"What are you planning?"

"Trust me?" she asks. Of course, I nod. "You don't have to do anything. We brought you here so we can do something that she and I both want. I hope it'll be all right with you if we don't tell you right away. Can you be patient until we're ready for you?"

She knows she's asking a lot of me. I'm not all that patient, and I don't like the idea of being separated from her in the house. It's not that I don't trust the people there. I do. I just want to be there, to witness her expressions when she sees something new. And I prefer to ease her fears when she is afraid. Rayna isn't as fragile as she once was, and I know I don't have to worry about her, but I do.

"I will try," is all I can say with positivity.

"That's all I can ask of you," she replies.

My shirt comes off and is folded and set neatly in the trunk. The women fit me into the harness and buckle me in. This one isn't broken-in so it's stiffer than my favourite one. Time will work the leather, so it moves better with my body. All-in-all, it fits pretty damn good.

"Well, Demon, what do you think?" Sara asks.

I lean down and plant a soft kiss on her lips. "I love it. Thank you, Sara."

"You're welcome. It's my way of thanking you for reconnecting with me. Even if we never play again, after tonight, I want you to keep it. It looks good on you. You look dangerous, as always."

They each put their hands out for me to take. I am a lucky man indeed, to have these two beautiful goddesses on my arms. How did I get so lucky? I cherish them, both of them.

As soon as we step out of the elevator, Sara lets go of my hand and takes Rayna's. She says to me, "Can you wait in the kitchen until someone comes to collect you? Kat and I have some setting up to do."

I don't like it, but I promised Rayna, A.K.A. Kat, I would try. "I can do that. "Nobody fucks either one of you, but me."

Both ladies nod enthusiastically. I watch them walk away, hand in hand, in the opposite direction from where I have been asked to wait. The house isn't nearly as busy as it usually is, but that's not uncommon during NFL playoffs.

"Hey Demon! How the hell are you?"

I turn to see Sprat. "Oh, hi. How are you?"

"I'm doing well. Did you come alone? Don't tell me that gorgeous woman of yours finally wised up and left your ass."

I scoff, "Pfft, no way! That woman wouldn't dare. Now that she's used to having all of this," I point to my body, "she knows she can't live without it." Yeah, I'm talking shit, but that's what guys do.

He teases, "You ain't nothing special. So, if she isn't sick and tired of your bullshit, where is she?"

"Her and Sara have something planned that I'm not supposed to be a part of, until someone comes to get me."

His face contorts. "I thought you were the dominant and they were the submissives?"

I scratch my head and grunt. "I know, I know. But when you have two hot women moaning in the back seat of the car you're

chauffeuring, you'll agree to do just about anything." Sprat widens his eyes and nods, "Been there!" "You want to join me for a coffee?" I ask.

"No, I offered to help Kristi with something. Trix and Liv are in there. At least, they were a few minutes ago." He pats my shoulder before wandering off in the direction I just came from. "Hey, you let me know when

Kat does kick you to the curb. I'll show her what it's like to be with a real man."

I shoot him my middle finger and smile with a hint of sarcasm behind it. He just laughs and continues walking. I get along great with that guy. We met here at Fallen about five years ago. The first time I was introduced to him, we hit it off.

Trix is sitting at the table sipping on a bottle of water. Her corset is pushing her round breasts up and together, forming a great cleavage that could swallow my cock, if she were into me, or men in general. Her three-inch high, stiletto boots are resting on the small of Liv's back as if she were an ottoman.

Liv, being on her hands and knees in front of her Mistress's chair, hangs her head, but tilts her face up to catch a glimpse of me. She doesn't smile, she simply casts her eyes back at the floor, staring blankly. Her red corset doesn't cover her breasts, allowing them to hang, gravity pulling hard on the weights dangling from her nipple clamps.

"Hey Trix, how's it going?" I ask as I make my way over to shake her hand.

"Oh, you know me, always excellent! How is life treating you these days? Where's Kat? Did she get tired of your shit already? Tell me where to find her so I can comfort her in her sadness." She leans forward and pats Liv on her bare ass cheek. Liv smiles at the floor. "You can get up now."

Liv stands with the aid of Trix's hand. She continues to hold the skinny woman's hand until she's seated on her lap. She kisses her shoulder tenderly as she slowly unclamps her left nipple. Liv buries the pain deep inside of her, not crying out when Trix pinches that nipple between her thumb and forefinger. She's rolling it slowly, her attention still focused on me. Liv doesn't react to her nipple being manipulated but I'm sure it hurts like hell.

"She's with Sara." I pour myself a mug full of coffee and take it to the other side of the table. After sliding a heavy wooden chair out, I sit and pull at the front right strap that extends from the middle of my back up and over my shoulder. "I think Ra... um, Kat buckled this wrong."

"Go help him," Trix whispers to her submissive, who stands up immediately, and tends to my harness. She quickly readjusts the buckle.

"That's good. Thank you, Liv. So, Trix, what have you been up to?"

"I got the promotion I've been working tirelessly at getting for the past three years. The guy who held that job, dropped dead last week." She waves for Liv to sit back on her lap.

Trix is a lawyer with very rich, well-known clientele. She is on retainer by a politician, an actor whom we regularly see in movies, and a doctor who was acquitted of murder last year, when he performed emergency surgery after he had a dinner engagement that included drinking several glasses of wine. He was on call that night and shouldn't have been drinking in the first place. I might not approve of some of her clients, but everyone who needs a lawyer, is entitled to have one, even if they're guilty as fuck!

"I'm sorry to hear he died."

"Don't be! I think he died from boredom. Either that or he needed to get away from *Mrs. Poppins*, and death was the only way to do that. Fuck! The first time I met that women, she was so damn cheerful, I wondered if she was too stupid to realize the world sucks, or if she's a drunk. Hey, maybe she had a butt plug jammed in her ass and was riding high on the naughty little secret. Either way, he's probably better off. Even at his funeral she was smiling. She's such a fake woman. Nobody is that happy, all the time." "Maybe she killed him," I post the thought.

"Nah, he was hit by a fully loaded cement mixer on his way home from work. In my opinion, I think he crossed that center line because he knew it would be a relief not to have to see that fucking smile of hers even one more time," she shrugs, letting out a hearty laugh.

"Some people can walk through life without a care in the world.

Maybe she is one of those people."

She shrugs again and then drops her hand onto Liv's thigh and lovingly strokes it with her hand. "So, how's Kat doing with her submissiveness?"

"She's doing well. She's a stubborn woman, but who knew I'd enjoy the challenge. I can never say she's boring, that's for sure. Her and Sara have hit it off nicely."

She scratches her head, "Yeah, what's with that? I mean, with the history between you and Sara, are you sure it's such a great idea to hook up with her again? What if she's still in love with you?

What's going to happen when Rayna realizes that?"

I swallow hard and then clear my throat. "Yeah, I've thought about that."

"And?" she asks.

I shake my head, "Hopefully, history doesn't repeat itself. Sara seems like she's in a good place and her mind is strong, from what I can tell. I think it'll be all right. I'm paying attention."

With concern in her voice, she asks, "Does Kat know everything?"

My eyes meet hers, but I say nothing.

"You know you have to tell her. A secret that big… You're playing with fire," Trix warns me.

She's right, I should tell Rayna the entire story, all of it. She needs to hear it from me, not someone else. I should have talked to her before she went over to Sara's place and they ended up in bed together. If she finds out, she's going to be furious that I didn't tell her. This is big and she won't like it. Maybe that's why I didn't tell her right after she met her. Fuck! I'm an asshole!

"Do you think Sara will tell her?"

"No, I don't think so," I reply with a head shake.

"Not many people know the story, so Kat might not find out, but if she means a lot to you, you might want to tell her just in case."

I nod and sip my coffee while I mull over what she suggested. She's right, I do have to tell her. Let her make an informed opinion of Sara, and whether she likes her for who she is now, or doesn't want her around because of who she was, that would be up to her. She's going to be furious that I kept it from her for this long.

"I'll tell her," I say under my breath, knowing that if I speak it, I'll have to go through with it.

"So," I change the subject. "So, tell me about this new position at work."

"Do you really want to talk shop?" she asks with a questioning quirk in her voice.

I chuckle, "No, but I'm trying to change the subject."

She laughs, but her expression quickly sours. "Ah, Ranger was here the other day. He has a new submissive. She looks young, no older than eighteen. I know Glitter checked her identification to make sure she was twenty-one, but I didn't ask how old she is. I wouldn't put it past him to date a high school girl with a fake ID."

"If he hurts her, I'll kill that motherfucker!" My mood has instantly shifted to pissed off. "I still can't believe they let that fucking asshole in here."

"Nothing was proven, no criminal charges were laid, and the women refused to file a complaint. There's nothing Gear and Glitter can do about it. They don't particularly care for the guy's style of dominance, if you want to call it that. As long as he isn't hurting anyone here at Fallen, they don't think it's right to kick him out with simple third-hand accusations and no solid proof."

I stress my point, "He is not a dominant! He is an abuser of women! A proper dominant will treasure his submissive and allow them a safeword. He does neither.

That is not dominant, that is abusive. Did anyone warn the poor girl? Did they tell her what he's going to do to her?"

"Glitter suggested she find another Master, but she said she really likes Ranger. I think he hasn't actually hurt her yet, so she doesn't know what he's capable of." Trix shakes her head sadly.

"If he hurts her…" I stop talking. My mind drifts off, creating scenarios where I am wrapping an elastic around his balls, so tight that the blood supply is cut off. I'll tie him to a tree in the forest where nobody will hear him screaming, and I'll wait until his nuts rot and fall off. All the while, I'll nick tiny cuts in his flesh, not enough where he'll bleed out, but the pain will be immense. I will do so much more to that asshole. His death will be a happy release for him.

"Don't worry, by the time you hear about it, he'll have disappeared."

I ask, "Why hasn't someone done that already?"

"Because he's connected. His brother is a detective and his sister-in-law is a high-end attorney. If he disappears, he can never come back, if you know what I mean. And nobody is willing to go that far without solid evidence. Don't worry, it'll happen soon enough. He can't contain his warped desires forever."

"He's under the misguided notion that he's untouchable. Good, he won't see it coming."

A beautiful, dark-skinned redhead comes skipping into the room. She's wearing a very short plaid skirt that doesn't hide her rounded hips, a snug white t-shirt that barely covers her full breasts, and high-heeled running shoes with thigh-high white socks. She pops the cherry-red lollipop from between her bubble gum-pink lips. I'd love to throw that little hottie over my knee and have her count the spankings I give her before shoving my fingers into her tight asshole.

"Are you Demon?" She stands in the doorway swinging her hips back and forth. I nod. "They're ready for you. Do you want to follow me?" she asks with a high school girl head tilt that has her two ponytails swinging.

My inner Demon is twitching from the irritating memories her appearance brings forth. I couldn't stand those pretty little bitches that thought they were fucking perfect in high school. Those little cunts didn't turn me on at all. My friends would go on and on about how they'd love to fuck them if they ever got the chance. When I showed no interest in them, the bitches made up rumors that I was gay.

I took the head cheerleader out one night and fucked her hard on the bench seat of my truck in her parent's driveway, at her request, of course. I held her hands over her head and let her have it. Afterward, I told her that I'm not gay, I just don't like stuck-up little twats, like her. I made her get out of my truck. Her legs were still shaking when I drove away without saying another word to her. The harassment stopped after that.

"Sure, why not?" I stand up and watch the little tease bite her puffy bottom lip and scan my body, as I set my cup in the sink. I look over at Trix and say, "Maybe I'll see you two later." "Have fun!" Trix replies.

Chapter Twenty-Seven

Rayna

Gear and Glitter began wrapping and knotting ropes around Sara first. They finished Sara's elaborate chest and pelvic harness before beginning with mine. Our bindings closely resemble one another with only slight differences. Our breasts protrude from between twelve lines of soft black rope. The decoratively weaved pattern over our abdomens and lower backs function as a safe and strong harness to elevate our lower torsos with minimal stress to our skin, or so I'm told.

The excess of rope left hanging from the back of Sara's chest harness is fed through a seven-inch metal ring that hangs from a thick chain leading to the high ceiling. Sara is asked to step onto a wooden crate that Glitter positions below the chain. The rope is then meticulously weaved into the front waffle-like knot of her pelvic harness, back up and through the loop once more. The rope is pulled until it is taut before being tied to Sara's pelvic harness with a strong knot.

She is told to clasp her hands together behind her back. They are carefully wrapped before the rope is pulled up through the metal ring. Gear pulls it until her arms are stretched high behind her back. He then secures it back at her wrists. They wrap separate ropes around her knees, in triplicate, before pulling her legs up to her chest harness and weaving the rope through it.

Sara is suspended with her arms straight up behind her back and her thighs pulled up on either side of her chest. He gives her a swing and she begins to laugh. He stops her before putting a black leather collar on her neck.

Gear asks, "Kat, are you ready?"

I take a deep breath. "I am so very ready!" My elation is obvious by the way I nearly run to him with a smile so wide that all of my teeth might be visible.

He smiles, "You look like you're ready."

"I can't wait! Where do you want me?"

"Stand on the box," he instructs as he pushes the crate with his foot to reposition it.

I step up, so that I'm standing behind Sara, who is still giggling. My mind is whirling from excitement. How is he going to bind us? When I raise my hands, at Gear's request, my adrenaline rush has my hands shaking so much that he tenderly clasps them between his hands.

"Take a deep breath and try to calm yourself. I don't want you to burn out too quickly."

I do as he says, closing my eyes for a moment while I breathe deeply. It helps calm the shaking, but I'm still grinning like a fool. That, I can't stop.

Glitter stands behind me, ready to assist Gear. He binds my hands behind my back, but doesn't affix them to my pelvic harness. He feeds the rope dangling from the front of my chest binding alongside Sara's hips and up through the metal ring. After weaving it through my harness, he pulls the rope slowly, guiding my chest under Sara's lower torso.

Glitter puts her hands under my shoulders to give me a little more support, and a sense of security, in case I fear falling. Gear ties the black rope through my harness before tying it off.

The rope hanging from my pelvic harness is guided around Sara's shoulders, through the ring and back through my harness and tied off. My legs still dangle uncomfortably. I hope he fixes that otherwise my back is going to be sore later.

Glitter kisses my forehead before taking the rope Gear is offering her. They each bind an ankle and lift my legs up, tying the ankle bindings to one of the other ropes. When I wiggle my feet, I can feel the heat from Sara's arm so they must be very close.

A black leather collar is buckled around my neck and it's snug fitting. Sara rests her cheek against my vagina, and I fear she'll find my aroused wetness disturbing, but she hasn't lifted her head or commented so it can't be all that bad. My wrists are tied to the back of my pelvic harness, no longer left to dangle.

A rope runs around the back of my head and is pulled until my mouth is pressing firmly against Sara's hot, wet pussy. She is just as wet as I am. I'm no longer as self-conscious about my arousal.

Sara's mouth presses against my pussy and doesn't pull away. She must be tied the same as me. Her breath is hot and has me moaning. I desperately want her to lick me, just as I'm doing to her, but she isn't.

Glitter taps my cheek. "Not yet. Wait for our guest of honour's arrival." She smiles lovingly, kissing my forehead once more.

The ropes dig into my skin, but I like it. The sensation of floating outweighs the discomfort. Sara's scent fills my nostrils, exciting me further. Each time Glitter and Gear's warm hands touch my skin, my pussy tightens. I know they're only checking the bindings but it's setting my skin on fire. I'm already breathing heavily. If she flicks my clit, I might cum immediately.

Gear whispers in my ear, "Does anything pinch too much?"

All I can do is open my eyes slightly and mumble into Sara's pussy, "No, just some tingling." Everything pulls, pinches and digs in, but nothing hurts enough to complain, not yet anyway. I knew there would be discomfort, so I had no expectations of feeling like I was resting in a recliner.

Quite the opposite actually. I feel less pain than I had expected.

Glitter opens the door and steps out, whispering something to someone. I strain my eyes to see who it is. I catch a glimpse of a cute woman dressed to look like a sexy high school cheerleader. I wonder if Coach would like her. He might want to smack her ass a dozen times, but I doubt he'll be sexually attracted to her. During one of our lengthy talks, he told me that high school was a difficult time for him.

Gear smiles and brushes a tickling strand of hair from my cheek, drawing my attention back to him. The way he's looking into my eyes fills me with warmth. I instantly feel loved, adored, treasured. His eyes are kind and I can see the depth of his appreciation for letting him rope my body. To him, this is his art. All I know is that it's beautiful, sensual, and so fucking arousing. I don't know how to thank him enough for allowing me to play a role in his creation.

Gear walks around us, taking multiple pictures. I must remember to ask him to email those to me. It's thrilling to be one of the subjects of his admiration, but to view his creation would really be something wonderful. The lights dim slightly, and I know that Demon is on his way.

I don't know how long we hang here, but the painful tingles in my hands and feet became almost overwhelming and nearly broke me. Now, however, they have fallen numb. Strangely enough, I am totally comfortable at this moment. Sara's calm, rhythmic breathing was the only thing that kept me together. I focussed on the expansion of her belly as it pressed into mine with every breath. And still, the light warmth of her expelled air continues to soothe my overheated sex. I am connected to Sara in more ways than just physical. We are one in the same.

The door opens slowly, and two people walk in. I can hear the scuffing of their shoes on the painted cement floor. My eyes have been closed, allowing my other senses to sharpen. A warm hand brushes down my shoulder to my elbow as someone walks lazily around us, shoes thumping with each step. I know that stride, it's Coach, or should I call him Demon, since we're at Fallen?

Sara moans softly, vibrating my clit with her voice, causing me to moan as well. She whimpers in response. I feel cool dribbles glide along my asshole. It takes me needing to swallow the wad of saliva that's formed at the back of my mouth for me to come to the realization that the drips gliding down my asshole are of Sara's saliva. It's arousing me even more, which I didn't think was possible.

"Pleasure each other," Demon instructs, his voice is deep, but spoken quietly and with firm instruction.

Sara and I begin sucking and licking each other's clitoris with great urgency. I'm on the verge of orgasm within a matter of a few seconds. Sara's clit swells in my mouth almost immediately. She cries out and stops licking just long enough that my orgasm ebbs, disappointing me. I lick and suck her mercilessly, hoping she'll return the favour and grant me an orgasm as well. Her body jerks involuntarily as she rides through her climax. I don't let up, nibbling on her sensitive clit to torture her deliciously.

She cries out again, but this time a hint of pain rides her scream. It wasn't an orgasm that caused that outcry. What is he doing to her? I wish I could see.

She sucks my clit hard, gently biting it between her teeth while her tongue whips wildly back and forth. My mind and body are swept into a mighty orgasm. I am floating--literally and figuratively. My thoughts have disappeared into a fog of nonexistence. My clitoris is the only thing I know to exist. Her tongue is my tongue, doing exactly what needs to be done to drag my climax on as long as possible.

In a snap, the intensely gratifying slurps she was granting me have flipped and are now the exact opposite – sweet torture. My body jerks, desperate to pull away from her mouth but the ropes prevent me from doing anything other than twitching, which has us both moving together.

Two thick fingers slip into my pussy until the hard knuckles are pressing against my opening. My clit twitches beneath the tip of Sara's tongue. The digits fuck me slowly at first, dipping into me and twisting, waving now and then, to add more fuel to my inner blaze.

My moans muffle into her pussy. The closer I get to orgasm, the more intensely I lap at Sara's sex. Her belly puffs with each quick lungful of air, forcing my breath from me. A finger slips into my asshole and I'm drifting away, lost in the fog again. I can hear my muffled screams, but they sound far away, as if someone else is riding through a bone-melting orgasm, and not me. But I know it's me.

His fingers slip from my sloppy wet pussy and ass, leaving me craving their return. Something cold, possibly metal, is worked into my asshole. I don't know why, but it feels like it's on the verge of popping out, but it keeps moving, as if the exposed end is swaying somehow--pulling back and forth. It remains in place, but I can feel the bulbous orb inside me pressing toward the back, as if it's touching my spine. When it moves, my clit twitches as if it were being lightly electrified.

We're given a push and we begin swinging, not much, but enough where the thing in my ass is pulling here and there, igniting my inner inferno.

Something touches my nose. My eyes open in mere slits, it's all I can manage. Two of Demon's black latex laden fat fingers are buried inside of Sara's pussy. The view is incredible. He pulls them out only to allow for a third finger to join the other two. He uses his digits to fuck Sara, effectively maintaining our swing.

I'm so intrigued with what Demon is doing to Sara that I'm able to hold back my third climax. If I cum right now, my eyes will close, and I'd rather watch him finger her. He pulls out and slips in a fourth finger with almost no difficulty. Sara is moaning like a wild animal about to ravish the carcass it just slaughtered.

He buries his fingers up to his palm inside of Sara, using it to swing us. Each time we swing toward him, his fingers bury deeper, pulling halfway out when we swing away from him. She isn't licking me anymore, only breathing quickly, and purring. She is lost in her body.

Her secretions are running over my lips and into my mouth. Her taste is tangy, but pleasant. I can't believe I'm doing what I'm doing. A year ago, I would have never dreamed of a situation such as this. *Porn does these things, not real people.* I was so naïve!

Demon folds his thumb against his palm and begins working at getting his whole hand into her. It takes a few minutes for her pussy to compensate his fist, but when it slips inside of her, she defies the ropes by curling her body. Just as quickly, she falls limp, giving in to the invasion and the rope's restrictions. He pauses before slowly twisting his hand until his inner wrist rests against my nose. He begins pushing carefully into her and pulling back, causing us to softly swing again.

Sara is screaming like a cat in heat. I know she loves fisting, loves the sensation of complete fullness. Her tongue resumes its rapid assault on my clitoris. She sucks, screams, moans and licks. Between her expert tongue and the heavy tugging by whatever is swaying in my ass, I'm so close to coming again.

I suck and lap at her clit, mirroring her mouth's actions. Both of us are breathing heavily and moaning wildly. My mind begins to slip away, but I do my best to keep working her clit. I feel light, but safely molded onto Sara, as if my featherlight weight is powerful enough to float her up to the sky with me.

Demon pinches my nostrils closed, preventing me from breathing. I try to pull my lips from her cunt, but I can't. My orgasm shreds through me, exploding the world around me. Every muscle in my body is locked in a struggle to test my strength against the ropes. My scream is imprisoned in my throat, as is Sara's. We both hold perfectly still, while our minds fade into a euphoric existence that has us wishing we could remain frozen in this moment for all of eternity.

I need to breathe. My lungs are burning. My chest is squeezing, aching to expel its last breath. I'm yanked back to the reality by a hot flood of Sara's cum pouring from her roughly fisted cunt. My nose, cheeks and lips are drenched. Streams of hot liquid soak my hair, and drip into my ears.

His fist is yanked from her throbbing pussy. It's as if it just left both of our bodies, leaving us feeling vacant and alone, together. My nose is released, and I suck in air as quickly as I can, but it takes a moment until the fresh air clears the clouds in my consciousness.

The weighted bulb is carefully extracted from my ass and then cold lube is smeared around my stretched opening. Demon's thick, hard cock slides into me, painfully spreading my asshole wider. I don't like the tension, but I do my best to relax and allow my butt to accept his size. I welcome the invasion and he knows it.

Slowly, he begins humping into my backside. My thoughts focus back on her tongue and how it's working over my clit. My pussy twitches. Sara is sucking and flicking my little button tenderly. It's so fucking good, even though the painful sensitivity of it is nearly overwhelming.

His hot, latex laden hand glides down the underside of my thigh and around to my hip, enabling him to hold us against his body. He steps into us and uses our weight as a counterbalance. He humps and we push away only to return with a thud. His muscular figure is like hitting a brick wall. He's powerful enough to prevent us from swinging in a direction he doesn't wish us to go.

Sara hasn't let up, she's licking and sucking tenderly, but intentionally focusing her attention on the underside of my clitoral hood. The sensation her gliding tongue rewards me with is purely angelic. I copy her talent as best I can, giving her the same glorious pleasure.

Demon's hand drops away from my hip. I immediately hear Sara cry out. She stops breathing for a moment, but then quickly screams. Her clit is stiffening against my tongue as if begging me to mutilate it. I bite my teeth into her, pressing my upper teeth just beneath her clit while my lower teeth press just above it. She wails until it fades into her throat, sounding more like a growling dog than a woman filled with pleasure. The vibration against my clit is sending me into another muscle clenching climax.

My tongue works her clit as our bodies clench. Our muscles pull at our bindings, adding an element of pain to go with the tenuous lack of freedom. We are coming, drifting together in a smoke-filled nothingness. We have molded into one body, one existence--it's beautiful.

I gasp in a quick breath and open my eyes. Did I pass out? Demon is looking down at my face, my hair is wadded in his fist. He's smirking. He's so strikingly handsome; his vicious looking eyes are dark and scary, but his features are sharp and perfect, like that of a magazine model.

"No sleeping!" he instructs. Maybe I did pass out.

He rolls on a condom and rams his prick deep into Sara's pussy. He fucks her hard, his balls slapping at my nose. When he holds himself inside of her, they rest on my eyes.

The ropes holding my face to Sara's pussy are released. My head is slowly allowed to hang. I'm grateful that he didn't just let it drop. I'm not sure I have the wherewithal to have stopped it from dropping hard enough to pull a muscle or tendon.

Demon pulls his thick, hard prick from Sara. His fingers reach around to the back of my neck to give it support. He pokes his prick against my lips, and I open wide. Slowly at first, he pushes his prick into my throat, nearly making me gag. He pulls out and then fucks into Sara's cunt. He leaves her and pushes into my throat. Over and over, he repeats this action, until I'm sure I'm gasping between throat penetrations.

My eyes are watering so much, I can't see anything other than blurs. Sara isn't moving anymore, but she's still lapping at my pussy, just not as intensely. She moans each time he fills her, licking my pussy as he exits.

When the light fills my eyelids, I know he's walked away. The ropes around me are being altered and my body is being manipulated by several people. It's a good thing they all have a good hold on me because I have no strength in my limbs. I'm surprised when they don't set me down. They spin me so that I am face to face with an exhausted looking Sara.

My ropes are refastened so that my legs are spread and wrapped over Sara's, my ropes bound to her ropes. My waist is cinched to hers once again and not left to droop. My chest harness is fastened to the ropes suspending her chest.

My lips find hers. They are soft and warm. She smells of my pussy and I, of hers. Together, our musk is seductive and stimulating.

The hands leave us suddenly and we are left to dangle, suspended above the floor in a sensual pose, kissing one another as if we are deeply in love. Our lust for the situation has both of us lost in a euphoric mindset brought on by relentless orgasms. Our kisses are loving and tender. Our tired tongues beg to explore one another's flavour but fail due to utter exhaustion.

His prick enters my pussy, fucking me hard. He doesn't let up even for a second. The rhythmic pounding against my cervix thrusts me into a screaming orgasm. As soon as it eases, he pulls out, shoving his prick into Sara and fucking her just as thunderously.

He repeatedly pleasures both of us until I can't remember how many times we've each cum. Sara's cheek is resting against my throat as my head hangs back. Our bodies hold still. I hear his boots on the floor, approaching our heads. My hair is wound into his grip, lifting my head until my mouth is once again, level with Sara's.

"Open your mouths!" he hisses.

Hot jizz splashes around our mouths, some finding it's mark and landing on my tongue. I hold my lips open wide, begging for more of the reward of his orgasm. He moans, groans and whimpers before it all comes to an end. He slowly backs away, huffing and puffing.

Sara and I lick Demon's cum from each other's mouths while the three of them unbind us.

I am set free first and carried by Demon and sat on a large pillow that's resting on the floor against the wall. He crouches down and smiles at me. This isn't Demon, this is Coach... Simon. My Simon.

"I love you, so much!" he whispers as his fingers brush a sweaty lock of hair from my face, tucking it behind my ear. His eyes are peaceful and affectionate, as if I am the only person in the world that means anything to him. He leans in, pressing his lips to mine and holding them there until he finishes taking a long, deep breath, and letting it out slowly.

He stands up quickly and returns to aid Gear and Glitter in unbinding a very exhausted Sara. Her hands and legs have a purple hue. When the ropes are removed, her limbs hang loosely. Coach scoops her up and carries her over to me, placing her beside me on the same big pillow. She is waving her hands and shaking out her legs awkwardly, as if they have fallen asleep. It's obvious how heavy they feel, by the effort she has to put in, to get them to move.

Our eyes meet and we burst into laughter. It's an exhausted laughter, but one I will never forget. We are joined now, closer than most women ever get to be. I care for her and want her in our lives for as long as she would care to be. I want us to become best friends and share in the good and not so good times our futures hold. Maybe I'm feeling all warm and loving after such an incredible experience. Am I looking through rose-coloured glasses, as the saying goes? I don't know, but I love how I feel.

After our harnesses are painstakingly removed, we dress and then walk arm in arm behind Gear, Glitter and Demon, as we make our way to the kitchen for something to drink and a snack.

We talk about what we loved and what we didn't love while we laugh through the more serious moments. No matter what we say, it isn't frowned upon and we aren't made to feel foolish. The way we are respected, is not what I had expected. Sure, I knew they would be honoured that we allowed them to use our bodies, but my heart feels as if it's filling with love. Maybe it's not true love in the romantic sense, but I feel bonded to these people.

More than an hour later, we say our good-byes with hugs and kisses. We drive Sara home before Coach takes us back to the restaurant. He follows behind me, as we each drive our own cars home. We make love so romantically that I start to cry. My heart is so full of love that I swear I can't bear it. Please, oh please, never let this end.

We sleep, still wrapped in each other's arms. Our bond is forever secured. He is mine and I am his, first and foremost. If ever we want to stop, for whatever reason, I know we will remain happy together, as two people who can't tell where one stops and the other begins. He owns me and I own him. We are the same, yet different. I would die for him and he would for me. I trust him with my life and for that, he gives me his undying gratitude.

Epilogue

Rayna

Renee and Tim are still together, but haven't married yet. He finally broke down and told her about his dominant side. She was excited to learn more about it. Even though he has told her about Fallen, he hasn't brought her there and I don't know if he ever will. They have a lot of issues to work through that have nothing to do with sex.

For a dominant, he's very passive, but only to a certain point. She's a bit of a hot-head who throws a fit if she doesn't get her way. He's a sweet guy and she's going to lose him if she keeps this up. I love my sister, but I feel bad for Tim.

Ken recently started his second year of high school and he's been considering joining the football team. Coach and Tim have been teaching him how to throw the ball, and I'll admit that he has a hell of an arm. The guys think he has a chance at being a star quarterback, one day.

Kim is doing very well with the brainier aspects in life. She's a heavy reader now and loves joining the science fairs and math competitions. Her best friend is a boy named Curtis. I can tell that she has a crush on him, but she swears they are just friends. I believe her because I'm pretty sure he's not into girls, but rather boys. When Coach walked out of the bathroom wearing only a towel, his eyes nearly popped out of his head. He sat down right away and kept his hand in his lap to hide the bulge he was sporting. I don't blame him, Coach looks damn good in a towel.

As for Rick, my ex-husband, he's still living across the country, but he has been single for nearly six months. He's been going to therapy because he says he's a sex addict, but

I'm not so sure. I think he's just an asshole who needs to be with young women to feel young and important. He has been calling the kids once a week, which is a huge improvement. I give credit to his therapist for convincing him to not throw his relationship with his kids away, just so he can get a piece of ass.

Coach and I got married about six months ago. So far, I don't regret it and doubt I ever will. He treasures me more than anyone ever has, and I try to take care of him as best I can. We make sure to have date night with just the two of us, at least once a month.

Aside from our sexual intimacy, Sara and I have become very close. She's like a second sister to me. One might even say she's a better sister than the one who shares my DNA. This sister hasn't gone behind my back to try to fuck my man. Then again, I allow her to, so I don't think it's a relevant comparison. It's a trust thing and I don't trust Renee like I do Sara because Sara is always open and honest with me.

She has become an acting second-aunt to my kids, as well. They both adore her and see her as being fun and bigger than life. I can see the love she holds for my kids when she's laughing with them or having a one on one conversation with them. Her eyes beam, right along with her smile, when she's with them. Of course, they don't know her true role in our lives and I hope they never do. We told them that she is Coach's friend from many years ago. They need never know anything else.

Even though I allow it any time they want, Sara and Coach still ask permission to play, every time. I tell them they don't have to, but by them asking shows me respect, and I appreciate it very much.

I love them both. Coach holds my heart, obviously, but Sara runs a close second. I love her, but I love her differently than I do Coach. It's hard to explain the difference, but I'll try.

He owns me. I own him. We rent Sara, in a way. He and I are married now. Sara doesn't live with us and likely never will. She wants her freedom to hide out in her own place when she needs time away to sort through her emotional demons. If ever it stops feeling right between the three of us, she will be asked to leave our bed and that will be that. If that happens, we hope to remain friends with her because we do love her. If she prefers to part ways, our hearts will break, but Coach and I will recover, because we have each other, always.

Coach told me the whole story about what happened between him and her. Now I know everything about why they stopped playing together. She explained that she thought going with the other dom would only earn her a harsh punishment. She didn't think he would ever cast her away because they cared for one another. Maybe they didn't say it out loud, but the feelings were there. As far as he was concerned, she cheated on him.

Sara fell into a severe depression after that. She tried to get his forgiveness, but he ignored her completely. She spiraled and ended up in the hospital after trying to take her life. Her demons got the best of her one night and without him to take her mind off of it, she lost herself. He was told by Glitter what happened, and he rushed to be by her side, but she refused to see him. She was embarrassed and ashamed, also very angry at him at that point in time. She sought counsel and found her strength. She's been doing very well, ever since.

I now know they were emotionally connected, even though there was a time when they denied that they ever felt love for one another. What happened years ago can't be changed. We learn from our mistakes and move forward, never looking back. We accept each other's flaws and don't harp on the past.

Now, nothing is hidden, and nothing held back. If something needs to be said, it is said. We immediately work through whatever comes up so that nothing lingers to fester, creating wounds that will surely scar our relationship.

Our individual lives have brought us together, in one way or another. I hate so much of what has happened to me; the shitty marriage, the awful divorce, the backstabbing sister, the kidnapping and near rape – but all of these things have made me into the strong and independent woman I am today.

I am powerful now. I claim the power I never thought I had. I own it. It's mine, and I won't let anyone take it from me. Coach taught me that. He taught me many things, but my unending power was the very best lesson I will ever learn.

To say that I am happy is an understatement. My elation each time I open my eyes in the wee hours of the morning, makes my heart flutter. My kids have me laughing every day, loving how they are growing and testing my patience, as they try to figure out what type of adult they are going to become. I am so proud of them! They are my best achievement, by far. How could I be so lucky to have everything I could ever have hoped for?

When I hear our lawnmower fire up, my heart still skips a beat.

- The End -

If you enjoyed
THE COACHING RAYNA TWO-BOOK SERIES
please take a moment to leave a review on the site you bought
your book.
Great reviews and ratings help to earn the author
promotions and awards.

More Books by Pebbles Lacasse

To read teasers and see book cover photoshoot photos by
Pebbles, visit https://www.PebblesLacasse.com

About the Author

Pebbles Lacasse is a contemporary romance and erotica author. She leans toward writing bad boys desiring women who didn't know they have a kinky side. However, she's also known for her women with a dominant nature, and a secret yearning to be loved. Her books and short stories often take her readers into the BDSM lifestyle while revolving around real-life issues, and there's always a happy ending. The captivating stories of romance, love, and tender moments keep her readers coming back for more.

As someone living with Porphyria, Pebbles stays indoors to avoid UV light which gives her plenty of time to write. That's not to say she doesn't love "glamping," fishing, kayaking, and swimming, she just has to do it with protective clothing. If there's something she wants to do, she'll find a way to make it happen.

Pebbles is very family oriented. She and her husband of 30+ years raised their children in southern Ontario where she was born, and remains to this day. A 150+ lbs Mastiff takes up a lot of room in their home and in their hearts. His best friends are the two rescue cats that think they rule the home. The chickens couldn't care less about the dog until he chases them when they come too close to his outdoor toys.

Discover more about Pebbles on her website
https://www.pebbleslacasse.com

Free short story with newsletter subscription:
https://bookhip.com/VVNPMJP

Connect with Pebbles

Facebook
https://www.facebook.com/PebblesLacasseEroticRomanceWriter/

Facebook Group
www.facebook.com/groups/pebbleslacasseandfriendsgroup/

Newsletter sign-up
https://BookHip.com/BQLKDCM

Website
https://www.pebbleslacasse.com

Instagram
https://www.instagram.com/pebbleslacasse/

Twitter
https://twitter.com/pebbleslacasse

Goodreads
http://bit.ly/Goodreads_2y5xJji

Bookbub
https://www.bookbub.com/profile/pebbles-lacasse

Amazon
https://www.amazon.com/author/pebbleslacasse

Youtube
https://www.youtube.com/channel/UC3Jb8ofSw0m3TFn4cMWu5
dw

Subscribe to Pebbles' Newsletter

Sign up to receive Pebbles Lacasse's newsletter and receive a free short story to welcome you. Be among the first to:

- Read teasers from the books she's writing.
- Learn what Pebbles does to keep herself busy when she isn't writing.
- Discover the captivating authors she's reading.
- Be led to books with similar genres grouped together just for readers like you.
- Plus other crazy antics.

https://bookhip.com/VVNPMJP

Join Pebbles' Team

Would you like to be a valued member of my ARC team? Advanced Readers receive copies of my soon-to-be published novels to read with the promise to leave reviews by the date set by Pebbles.

You'll get my books for FREE forever as long as you leave reviews!

Sound like a good deal?

https://forms.gle/gseo39XRubENVWjA9

www.PebblesLacasse.com

Erotic Romance Writer